VOLUNTEERS
for glory

DR. A. D. THORP

American Literary Press, Inc.
Five Star Special Edition
Baltimore, Maryland

VOLUNTEERS *for glory*

Library of Congress
Cataloging in Publication Data
ISBN 1-56167-477-X

Library of Congress Card Catalog Number:
98-88885

Cover Design by Cameron Thorp

Published by

American Literary Press, Inc.
Five Star Special Edition
8019 Belair Road, Suite 10
Baltimore, Maryland 21236

Manufactured in the United States of America

Dedicated To Frankford, Pennsylvania

Those who do not look upon themselves as a link connecting the past with the future do not perform their duty to the world.
—Daniel Webster

CHAPTER 1

Padreig Mulcahy, just turned sixteen and of medium height and build, sat upon the ground beneath a low-limbed chestnut tree. Azure blue eyes with prominent black pupils were concentrated on a jack-knife which he flipped end over end in a game of mumblety-peg. The various tosses scored points according to the way they stuck into the dirt. His mind was troubled by the widespread talk of southern secession and war. He had played soldier games as a boy but facing the actual experience was sobering. *War,* he thought. *Such a simple three-letter word.* How would it involve him? He was not a fighter. Would he be called upon to fight? He gave the knife a high toss in the air. To preserve the Union, yes, he would have to fight for his country. That was expected.

It was a day of blossoming spring, radiant with the vibrant fullness of an awakening earth. The bare land was being fitted with its annual raiment of luxuriant foliage, an exhilarating season of fresh scents and signs of rejuvenated life.

Along the upper reaches of Main Street in the small town of Frankford, Pennsylvania, harmonious sounds could be heard. There was a buzzing of insects joyfully escaping the chrysalis stage, the soft warbling of song birds in budding trees, and the industrious sounds of a man busy at work.

Joseph Mulcahy, a barrel of a man, swarthy, muscular and naked to the waist, wielded a hammer in his powerful grip as he beat a bar of red hot iron, forging it into a shoe for a horse standing cross-tied. The ringing clang of metal striking metal echoed on the warm spring air and sang out a rhythm for dancing sparks that darted and ricocheted from the reverberating anvil.

The perspiring smith turned from his work and looked about. "Where in Sam Hill's that son of mine? Should have been back ten minutes ago with coal for the forge. Paddy," he called. "Where are ye? The fire needs feeding."

He listened for a reply. Hearing none, he wiped his gnarled, beefsteak hands on a grimy leather apron and strode to the rear of the smithy. "Paddy, what in the devil's name are ye up to now?"

The blacksmith glared at a bucket which sat empty beside a pile of coal. Ever since the boy's mother died nine years ago, he had felt compelled to deal gently with the lad, but lately he had found it increasingly difficult to practice restraint.

The boy had developed a wanderlust and taken to fanciful fits of daydreaming. Fishing and hunting preoccupied him, together with lone ventures up the Delaware Valley to seek out buried Indian villages.

Mulcahy swore silently. He could break old Jim Ryen's neck for stuffing Paddy's head with the wild exploits of Colonel Allen McClane, Frankford's famed partisan scout in the Revolutionary War. Only last week, in a fit of fancy, the boy had whisked Doctor Leake's prized thoroughbred mare from the smithy and gone charging through town, driving "redcoats" before him and intercepting food for Washington's hard-pressed forces at nearby Valley Forge.

Only the memory of his beloved wife's last words tempered his anger. "Be gentle and patient with the boy," she had said. "He's as sensitive and scholarly as the 'little men' of the old sod."

Joseph Mulcahy gave a snort. "A leprechaun, indeed." He approached his son. "Paddy, what're ye doin'? I sent ye for coal twenty minutes ago."

The boy jumped to his feet. "Sorry, Father. Be after bringing it right away."

"See that ye do."

Joseph Mulcahy had to smile inwardly despite himself. Deep within was a hidden harbor of love for his son and his carefree traits. After all, he was not above pulling his own pranks.

He chuckled as he returned to his anvil. He recalled the day he poured brass filings down a new well hole being dug across the road at the Jolly Post Inn. To his delight, the glittering metal chips had caused a frenzied outbreak of "gold rush" fever among the townspeople when they were discovered the next day.

He moved to reheat a shoe and picked up a front foot of a horse which stood half asleep. A pungent scent of seared horn tissue filled the air as he burned an imprint on the bearing surface of the hoof wall.

"Good morning to you, Mulcahy," a rich, cultured voice greeted him. "How is that 'partisan' son of yours behaving these days? Understand the villagers are expecting to be roused from their beds next time by the reenactment of Paul Revere's ride."

The speaker laughed heartily.

Mulcahy winced and raised himself from a stooped position.

"Good morning, Colonel Burns. I'll be after havin' yer horse finished in a minute, sir."

"No hurry, Joseph. It's a beautiful morning. Makes one feel good to be alive."

"Yes, 'tis a grand mornin' indeed, Colonel." He thrust a fistful of nails into his mouth and prepared to set another shoe.

Colonel Burns, spry and energetic despite his eighty years, was a pillar of the community. Born in Ireland, he amassed a small fortune as a young man, but had been on the losing side of the Spanish Civil War and fled to England, leaving most of his possessions in Spain. Seeking a new life in America, he had settled in South Carolina and lived grandly as a planter and slaveholder. In 1842, he served his adopted country in the war with Mexico and came out of the army with the rank of colonel. In 1846, after freeing his slaves and selling his plantation, he settled down to live a life of country squire in Frankford.

Paddy, making a delayed appearance, walked slowly toward the furnace and dumped a bucketful of coal onto the forge. With the aid of large bellows, he soon had the fire burning at white heat.

"Morning, Colonel," he called over his shoulder.

"Good morning, lad. I was just inquiring about you. How have you been keeping?"

"Just fine, sir. How was your trip to South Carolina?"

"Very interesting, young man. Very interesting, indeed." He ran one hand through a cap of snow white hair. "I hear you conducted quite an exciting 'raid' on the town while I was away." A smile crinkled his leathery countenance. "Hadn't been home more than two hours when I heard the account from several sources." He slapped a boot with his riding crop and laughed. "By George, I would give ten years of my life to have seen Doc Leake's face when he spotted you whooping and hollering his prize mare down Main Street."

The color rose in Paddy's neck. He poked at the fire in silence.

The Colonel slipped both hands into the side pockets of his tweed riding coat. "Don't fret. The good doctor now enjoys the humor of the incident as much a the rest of us. Besides," a note of seriousness crept into his voice, "it appears as if you will soon be getting the opportunity to do some real soldiering."

The elder Mulcahy looked up sharply. "How's that?"

"The young bloods of our Southern aristocracy are beginning to crow in the fashion of their old cocks, Joseph. This nation is in deep trouble," the Colonel replied. "We can't hide our heads in the sand any longer. This matter of secession has to be nipped in the bud."

Joseph Mulcahy clinched a final nail in the horse's hoof and stood erect. "Don't tell me a sensible man like yerself puts any stock in this loose-tongued war talk that's been passing around?"

"I've just returned from my old home in the South, Joseph, and from what I've seen and heard, I'd say war is an inevitable as rain. Didn't you read the speech Senator Wigfall made on the senate floor last week? His state of Texas has already seceded."

"No, can't say that I did, Colonel. Been too busy for such prattlings.'

Colonel Burns reached into a vest pocket and drew out a newspaper clipping and a pair of eyeglasses. "Then I'll just read you a portion of the taunting remarks Wigfall flung at the North from the floor of the senate." Carefully adjusting his spectacles, he read aloud, "'Your flag has been insulted. Redress, if you dare. You have submitted to it for two months and you will submit forever.' Now then, doesn't that sound like war talk?"

"All depends on how you look at it."

"How you look...now see here, Joseph, the sectional differences between North and South have been papered over far too long. We will reap a sad harvest for our compromising ways." He returned the reading glasses and clipping to his vest pocket. "Just last week in Charleston," he said, "I saw the motto, 'One voice and millions of strong arms to uphold the honor of South Carolina,' flung brazenly from the windows of the *Mercury*, that able, but wicked advocate of secession. I tell you South Carolina is the Mephistopheles of the South, the seducer of states. Her leaders give no thought to the honor of the Nation, or to the honor of the people, but only to South Carolina. With honeyed words and well-timed flattery, she is detaching one state after another from the Union."

The smith picked up a set of tongs, lifted a glowing shoe from its fiery bed of coals in the forge and thrust it fiercely into a tub of cool water. The hissing steam expressed his feelings.

"And I say this to ye, Colonel. If it should come to war, I won't stand by and see any boy o' mine marched off to pull chestnuts out o' the fire for the demagogues who started it. The press, pulpit and busybody women are stirring up all this hate." He extracted the cooled shoe from its bath and slammed it onto an anvil.

Colonel Burns sat down on a nail keg, his snowy brow wrinkled. "I know the pulpit has been desecrated by seditious exhortations," he said. "I've heard it preached that theft of slaves is meritorious, murder excusable and treason a virtue, but who are those women to whom you refer? It seems an unchivalrous accusation."

Paddy seated himself on a log bench, brushed a forelock of dark hair from his eye and took in the smell of hot iron, coal fire and horseflesh.

"I'm referring to that Beecher Stowe woman and her like," his father retorted. "Writes a book, she does, that inflames the minds of unsuspectin' folks like myself who've never been to the South. Aye, and where does she write it? In the kitchen of her comfortable Ohio home between meals. She even admitted to the newspaper that the material came from abolition tracts published by that devil, Garrison. So, this woman writes a touchin' book about slavery, yet she's never been in the South, has no firsthand knowledge of slavery and is completely ignorant of slave mentality."

The angered smith bent a horseshoe nail between his fingers. "Then she has the gall to pawn off *Uncle Tom's Cabin* as truth and reality. Tell me, ye should know," he leveled a thick-knuckled finger at the Colonel, "why do Southern plantation owners on the coast hire thousands of poor Irishmen to dig ditches and drain the swamps? Ye know the answer as well as I. The Negro's too valuable. When malaria hits a slave, it's the loss of a thousand-dollar investment. A hired Irishman can be paid off, no loss to the planter a'tall. Am I right?"

"Yes, in some respects..."

"Sure'n did ye hear her response when she heard she was a distinguished author? 'God wrote it,' she said. Such blasphemy."

"How can you be so sure, Mulcahy?" The colonel's voice rose.

"Sure about what?"

"Your charge of blasphemy. How do you know He didn't inspire the work?"

The blacksmith's face went slack for a moment and his voice dropped. "Faith'n I tell ye, Colonel Burns, she didn't have to seek Topsy among the blacks. In the fair city of New York are hundred o' wee girls six to ten years of age sweepin' the crossin's of the main streets. Ye've seen them, I've seen them. Poor little creatures with ragged dresses and pinched faces. Brooms in hand, chance'n for coins from those whose boots they've swept clean. I've heard tell there be ten thousand such abandoned children in New York City alone. Slave children have a paradise compared to the dry goods box and abandoned cellar homes of their northern counterparts. I say this to ye that the North's low wage slavery's as much an evil, if not more, than the bondage of Southern blacks."

He bent over to fit the last shoe and began setting the nails. "And who will do the fightin' in this war the demagogues seem so anxious to start?" he continued.. "Ye know as well as I, it will fall eventually upon the poor dregs o' northern cities and the poor whites o' the South." He spat on the ground. "And just because fat-cat industrial barons in the North demand high protective tariffs to get richer while plantation owners in the South scream for low tariffs to gain more wealth. A rich man's war and a poor man's fight.'

He placed the horses's foot on the ground and nodded toward his son. "There's one boy who won't ever shoulder a gun. Not so long as I'm livin'."

"Have you finished your say, Joseph?"

"Aye, I've said my piece." He wiped a hairy arm across his forehead.

"Well, then, pay heed to me. There's too much of this conciliationist spirit among you'Silver Grays', not only in this town, but in the city of Philadelphia, as well. When you 'dough faces' finally discover the evils of secession, it may be too late to combat it. Is my animal ready?"

"It is that, sir."

"Then I shall be taking my leave of you."

Paddy sprang to his feet, and with cupped hands, helped the aging Colonel mount his freshly-shod gelding. As the gentry man leaned over to adjust a stirrup strap, the trace of a smile creased the tightly stretched skin over his high cheekbones. "I dare say, my boy, when the test of courage and loyalty is applied we'll see the 'dough faces' changing attitudes in answer to their country's call." He gathered the reins in his hands and, raising his riding crop in salute, cantered off.

His eyes reflecting curiosity. Paddy turned to his father. "Pa...."

"What?" came the curt reply.

"Do you think there will really be a war?"

"If the rich southern planters and abolitionists have their way, yes."

A moment of awkward silence followed. "Pa?"

"What?"

"It's Saturday. Can I have the day off like you promised?"

"When did I make that promise?"

Paddy looked surprised. "Why, yesterday. You said I could go fishing."

"Well, go along with ye. I can manage alone. Have been for too many years."

Insensitive to the hidden touch of pathos in his father's voice, Paddy darted off like an animal released from a trap and sprinted barefoot toward the center of town.

"Paddy," an aged voice called from across the way. "Come over, I want a word with ye. What did Colonel Burns have to say?"

Jim Ryen, a wrinkled relic from the Revolutionary War, beckoned from his honored place in a rocking chair on the front porch of the Jolly Post Inn.

"Can't stop now, Jim. Something I've got to tend to. See you later."

For once in his life, Paddy did not want to hear about local heroes of the revolution—not Captain Worrell or Colonel McClane, not even the surrender at Yorktown. There was new and more exciting talk to think about. With a wave of a hand, he hurried toward the center of Frankford, an industrious town located on the site of a former Indian village that once nestled on the banks of the Quessionomiink, or Eel Skin River, as the Indians called it. The stream eventually became known as Frankford Creek. Two miles to the east, the broad Delaware River flowed placidly between green shores toward Philadelphia six miles to the south.

In 1681, the region was surveyed by Thomas Holmes at the direction of William Penn and, shortly thereafter, was settled by English Quakers and Swedes, who were followed by an influx of Swiss and Palatinate Germans. The last full-scale immigration took place just prior to the Revolution when the Scotch-Irish came from Northern Ireland to seek refuge.

What was now Main Street had once been nothing more than a forest trail, a post road linking Philadelphia to New York. As Conestoga wagons and stage coaches began making the trip more frequently, the post road broadened and became known as King's Highway. Paddy had often dug his toes into the dust of the old highway, his active mind reaching out to hear the sound of hoofbeats, rumbling wheels and marching feet from the past. William Penn, George Washington, the Continental Army, the British Army—all had traveled the road in bygone days.

Over the course of years Frankford had grown. Now it was a thriving county seat of nearly eight thousand inhabitant, but close attachment to the historical past had not dimmed. Proud of their illustrious heritage, many townspeople could still recall the reception at the Allen House in 1824 for General Lafayette. The boast, "Yes, sir. I shook the hand that shook George Washington's," could still be heard.

Paddy's springtime reverie was suddenly interrupted by the staccato clatter of hoofbeats. He swerved to one side and turned quickly to see a four-in-hand bearing down upon him. The driver reined in his team and brought the stagecoach to a halt.

"Top of the morning to ye, Paddy Mulcahy, " he said with a Scottish burr.

"And the rest of the day to yourself, Duncan Gilmour," Paddy replied in brogue.

The middle-aged Scot pushed a peaked hat to the back of his head. An unruly mop of reddish hair tumbled over one eye. Mutton-chop whiskers and a wind-burned face gave him the appearance of a seafaring man.

"What had ye in mind for this morning, lad?" he inquired. "Yer father said I might find ye on the road."

"Nothing special. Thought I'd stop by and fetch John Castor. Maybe do a little fishing. Billy Batt claims the perch are biting real good at Commodore Steven Decatur's powder mill."

"Commodore Stev..." the Scotsman laughed. "The local naval hero has been dead forty years. Let him rest in peace."

A thick-jowled passenger thrust his bald head through an open window of the coach. "Hurry along driver," he growled in a German accent. "I have to connect with the horse car in Frankford this morning yet."

Gilmour bristled. "Keep yer bonnie shirt on, Dutchman. Can ye see I'm talkin' with a friend?"

The passenger mumbled a few imprecations and withdrew his head. Paddy climbed onto a single tree and shot a glance at Gilmour. "How come you always talk so rough to Germans?" he asked in a whisper.

"Can't stomach their arrogance. All business and no sense of politeness." He splattered the roadway with a squirt of tobacco juice. "Besides, they stole the throne of England from the bonnie Stuarts. The House of Hanover, German blackguards. But say, I have been asked to give ye a message when I saw ye." He picked up the reins. "Care to ride into town with me?"

Paddy leaped from the singletree onto the driver's seat. A smile wreathed his face. "Thought you would never ask," he said.

Gilmour passed over the reins. "Here, you drive the team the rest of the way."

"You trust me? I'm hell on leather, or haven't you heard?"

"I heard. Let yerself go. That square-headed passenger ain't done nothin' but complain since he got on at Trenton. Could use a wee shaking up."

Paddy gave the bull whip a loud crack and sent the team racing along the upper reaches of Main Street. Thick-trunked trees lining both sides of the road flicked past in rapid secession as the coach streaked into the village proper. Aside from the din and clatter made by the noisy intruder, a quiet and serene atmosphere hung over the town of stone houses with sloping dormered roofs, splayed windows and arched doorways. The comfortable dwellings hugged uneven sidewalks of red bricks mellowed and shaded by old trees. Ivy clung to the walls of homes where the descendants of Frankford's earliest settlers lived in staid solidarity.

Atop the careening stage, Gilmour grasped an iron rail at one end of the driver's seat. He leaned over and shouted in Paddy's ear, "Ye had better slow down, lad. Ye'll be dumping us bag'n baggage into Frankford Creek."

Paddy's nose rippled with mirth. The tendons in his strong wrists corded as he pulled on the reins with one hand and pumped the brake with the other. The four-in-hand slackened its pace and the coach entered that part of town where life revolved around well-kept stores and grist mills.

While still principally rural and agrarian, the industrial age had begun to encroach on the shores of Frankford Creek. William Whittaker's cotton goods mill, John Sidebottom's tape manufacturing plant and Jeremiah Horrock's dying and bleaching plant used the flowing water as a dump site for their waste at the same time giving employment to many of the men and boys of the town. Paddy had apprenticed in William and Harvey Rowland's iron works, but after a month had called it quits when he found the job too confining and totally unsuitable to his aesthetic nature.

Paddy slowed the lumbering stage coach to a halt in front of the Eagle Hotel and leaped nimbly to the ground. Passengers, gesticulating and making dire threats, bounded from the coach and milled about angrily in the street.

"Ye had better run for cover, lad," Gilmour said with a chuckle.

"I didn't do anything," Paddy replied. He climbed nonchalantly to the top of the coach and began unloading luggage that smelled of old leather and musty carpet.

"When yer finished," the teamster called, "wait for me here on the porch of the hotel. I have to sign some bills o' lading."

"Will do, Dunk."

The task of unloading completed, Paddy jumped to the ground and mounted the creaking wooden steps of the hotel. He located a wicker chair on the shaded piazza and sat down.

Brushing a fly from his face, he looked across the street at the resplendent Womrath mansion with its spacious, manicured grounds, a mecca for the town's social set. In a far corner of the lawn, close to where Frankford Creek flowed quietly beneath a covered bridge, some children in straw hats were romping in the latticework of a gazebo. Ned, the Negro caretaker, moved lazily beneath a stand of elm trees as he loosened the soil around boxwood hedges. The air was filled with the scent of freshly-cut grass.

Gilmour, stuffing papers into his pockets, appeared on the porch.

Paddy looked up. "Say, what about the message you have for me?"

"Hoot, mon, I near forgot. Snapped a surcingle this morning near the Walton farm and stopped there to fix it. Lad about your age came up and asked me to tell you he'd be staying at the farm this summer. Said ye was to come by whenever ye could get away from the smithy."

"John Walton."

"Aye, that's the name he gi' me. Nice chap, but kind o' quiet."

"Yes, he's Quaker." Paddy's thoughts flashed back to the previous summer and the good times enjoyed with the soft-spoken Friend from Philadelphia. "When did he come out from the city? Why didn't he stop at the smithy?"

"Well, noo, that's more'n I can say. Why not ask for yerself?" The Scotsman pulled his dog-eared hat into place. "I'll be off on a freight run to Bristol soon's I load. Why dynna ye come wi' me? We'll stop at the farm. Maybe this friend o' yours would like to ride along."

"That sounds bully. Where do we load?"

"Orchard and Tacony Street. Got to pick up hides a Hilles' tannery."

Within an hour the loaded stage was moving slowly north on Orchard Street, its wheels groaning and creaking beneath the weight of bundled hides and barrels of sundry supplies. As the four feather-footed Clydesdales leaned their massive chests into the harness, Paddy marveled at the driving power in their long, sloping croups and powerful hocks.

At the intersection of Orchard and Ruan, the team hawed westward toward Main Street. Up ahead on the left was Borough Hall, a three-story brick building that roosted over civic affairs like an officious hen. A noisy gathering in the cobblestone courtyard caught Paddy's eye. He turned toward Gilmour. "Say, Dunk, that's not a peaceable crowd. They're het up over something. Let's stop and see what it is."

"Aye, yer right, lad. Somethin's amiss."

He pulled the stage off to one side of the road. Both jumped to the ground and walked across the street. Paddy recognized a guard from the Frankford arsenal. "Mornin', Pat. What's all the ruckus about?"

"You don't know? I thought you knew everything that went on in town," Pat Burgin replied.

"Know what? What's happened?"

"The Rebs have cleaned out the arsenal lock, stock, and barrel." The guard spit on the ground as if to rid a bad taste.

Gilmour's gray eyes pierced him through. "How's that agin, mon? Ye must be daft. There ain't no rebs in this part o' the country."

"Not Rebs, maybe, but plenty of secesh agents." The guard pointed to a distinguished looking officer who was addressing the crowd. "That's General Small, Commander of the Washington Brigade from Philadelphia. Why don't you go over and listen to him. He's the one who discovered the treachery.

"I want it from yer own lips," Gilmour snapped.

"Don't have to get rough about it. I'll give you the details, if that's what you want. Do you know Cap'n Gorgas? Commandant at the arsenal?" Burgin asked.

"Josiah Gorgas. Aye, a no-good Lancaster County Dutchman."

The guard hitched at his belt. "Little over a month ago he received an order from Secretary of War Floyd. Soon after that he shipped twenty carloads of rifles from the arsenal to Washington. Just been discovered the rifles never reached the Capitol."

"Twenty carloads," Paddy blurted. Where'd they go?"

"Stored safely beyond our reach in southern arsenals waiting to be turned against us," Burgin answered.

Paddy's sloe-eyed pupils opened wide. "Judas priest!"

"Too right," Burgin replied. "Just before Floyd resigned to become a Reb, he transferred a hundred'n nineteen thousand muskets and rifles from North to South. Last official act was to telegraph the Commandant at the Baton Rouge arsenal, directing him to deliver five thousand rifles to the Governor of Louisiana." The guard scowled and scratched the seat of his pants. "We've been picked clean. We don't have muskets to arm our militia."

A facial tic made Gilmour's mutton chop whiskers twitch. "The blackguards! Heard rumors the Secretary of War was sellin' rifles to the Reb government at two'n and a half dollars apiece. How's Gorgas fit into the scheme?"

"Seems like he was in on the conspiracy," Burgin said, "his wife being a Southerner and all, daughter of 'Governor Gayle of Alabama. Through her, Gorgas got real chummy with Floyd.They must've worked hard hand-in-glove on this."

"How could a native of Pennsylvania turn on his own state like that?" Paddy asked in open-mouthed disbelief.

Gilmour jutted his chin. "Where's Cap Gorgas now?"

"Left Frankford ten days ago, the third of April," Burgin replied. "Just been reported he's turned up in Montgomery, Alabama."

"Alabama!" Paddy blurted.

"Yep, and no longer a captain. He's now a full-fledged general. Chief of Ordnance for the whole Confederate Army. Quite a fancy bit of footwork, eh?"

"Hoot, mon," Gilmour exploded. "The conniving Dutchman. Ye can't trust a one o' them. Come, let's hear what the general's got to say."

The two pushed their way into the muttering throng. "This latest plot on the part of the South," the general was saying, "is as full of criminal intent as a tenant who sneaks from a house in the dead of night and takes his landlord's property with him. This is one of many reasons why no state can ever be allowed to secede from the Union. It's high time the Silver Grays shake off their sympathy for the Southern rebels and take a firm stand behind President Lincoln and the preservation of the Union."

A majority of the crowd responded with clamorous cheers as the tall general concluded his remarks and mounted a horse, but Paddy noticed that many who were professed "dough faces" among the group quickly gathered into tight little groups. In the midst of one of these, he spied a close friend, John Castor.

One of the oldest families in town, the Castors had migrated from Switzerland, the wellspring of Presbyterianism. Because of that early influence, they were the chief instruments in establishing the First Presbyterian Church of Frankford in 1770, and served as pillars of the church.

Short and stocky with a moon face capped with sandy hair, the sixteen year old on whom Paddy's eyes were fastened had been given the nickname "Chirp" because of a bird-like trill to his voice that surfaced when he was excited. Paddy cupped hands to his mouth and called,"Hey, Chirp. Can I see you a minute?"

Castor turned at the sound of his name, and spotting his favorite fishing partner, broke away from the group with whom he had been talking.

"Hi, Paddy, what do you think about this rifle business? Hard to believe?"

"Smells pretty rotten, if you ask me." He inclined his head toward the circle Castor had just left. "What do the 'Silver Grays' think of it?"

"You know our feelings. Southern states have the same right to pull out of the Union as the colonies had when they separated from the mother country eighty-five years ago. If they want to secede peacefully, all's well and good." He glanced down at his shoes. "But this business of cornering all our guns..."

"Come along wi' ye, Mulcahy," Gilmour called from a distance. "Kynna be spendin' all me time discussin' skullduggery. I ha' freight to deliver."

Castor's pink, cherubic cheeks puffed and collapsed. "You making a trip with the Scotsman?"

"Yep, taking a run to Bristol. Want to come along?"

"Sure. Think you can swing it?"

"Hey, Dunk, can Chirp come along?"

"Aye, bring him along if ye ha'a mind to."

"Good boy, Mulcahy. Wait till I tell my brother where I'm going. Hey, Henry! Tell Mother not to hold supper. I'm heading up the valley with Paddy and Gilmour."

"Jolly good," his older brother responded. "We'll look for you when you get back."

Henry Castor, a tall, muscular stonemason, brushed mortar dust from his checkered blouse and returned to his animated discussion. His features were as strongly chiseled as the granite with which he worked

Spinning on their heels, both boys raced toward the stage and scrambled aboard.

Gilmour's whip cracked loudly as the four-in-hand moved slowly forward, turning right onto Main Street and headed north. Soon the gravel road of Bristol pike grated under the wheels of the heavily-laden coach as the village of Frankford slipped from view behind rolling hills. The sun shone brilliantly overhead., warming the spring air. From freshly plowed farmland came an occasional aroma of recently broadcast fertilizer—putrid, pungent, but honest. Songbirds frolicked in the lacy foliage of blossoming orchards by the side of the road.

Gilmour chewed contentedly on a cut plug of tobacco. He leaned over and nudged Paddy in the ribs. "We're approachin' the Walton farm. Want to invite your Quaker friend along for the ride?"

"If you don't mind. His uncle might let him come with us. It is Saturday."

"Good as done."

The Scotsman wheeled the stage down a tree-sheltered lane and halted in front of a rambling stone farmhouse. A lanky, youth, dressed in suspendered black trousers and gray cotton shirt open at the collar, rushed from the house and leaped onto the tongue of the coach. He took Paddy by the hand. "Thee wasted little time in responding to my invitation, Friend Mulcahy. What brings thee here so soon?" There was warmth in his engaging smile. Prominent eyebrows shadowed his deep blue eyes.

"Gilmour's driving us to Bristol. Can you take the afternoon off and come along?"

"Turn the stage around in front of the barn. It will only take a minute to find out. I'll be right back." The Quaker leaped to the ground and dashed into the house. He returned wearing a black, broad-brimmed Quaker hat. "Uncle William gave his consent, but art thou certain thee has room for me? It seems crowded up there on the driver's seat."

"We have lots of room," Castor replied. "I'll climb up and sit on the baggage rack. You can sit next to Paddy."

"You remember Chirp Castor from last summer, don't you, John?"

"Yes, of course. It's good to see thee again, Chirp. Thank thee for thy seat."

Gilmour looked at his timepiece and shook his head. "Should've been in Holmesburg by this time. You lads all settled?"

"Drive on, MacDuff," Castor shouted, as he moved baggage to one side and made himself comfortable on the roof of the coach: "Hey, Paddy, tell the Quaker about what happened in town this morning."

Paddy ran a hand through a shock of windblown hair and started to give an account of the situation at the Frankford arsenal.

The freight coach entered Holmesburg at mid-afternoon and was brought to a halt in front of Dr. Enoch Arthur's apothecary shop.

Gilmour dismounted from the driver's seat and stretched his weary arms. "I ha' important business to transact wi' Joe Hellings at the Washington House," he said. "Ye lads can water the horses at the trough, then unload Doc's supplies and carry them inside."

"Will do," Paddy replied.

Chores completed, Castor stopped at one end of the long apothecary counter and thrust his hand into a bell jar in search of sweets. Sam Cartledge entered the shop from a back room.

"Get your paw out of the jar, Castor, unless you have money," he called out.

The aproned clerk burst out laughing. "Go ahead. Help yourself. Doc's out for the day."

"Thanks, Sam." Castor pushed two sour balls into his puckered mouth. "Haven't seen you since our sleigh ride last Christmas. You've grown."

"Only an inch. What brings you fellas up this way? Going to fish the Pennypack?"

"Not today," Paddy replied. "We have a ride to Bristol with Gilmour."

"You fellas should join up with our Holmesburg Grays while you're here. There's a drill scheduled this evening."

Paddy placed a stick of licorice root in his mouth. "I thought your militia was called the De Silver Grays."

"We were," Cartledge responded. "So as not to be confused with the damn conciliationist 'Silver Grays' movement, we changed our name to Holmesburg Grays."

The whinnying of horses, punctuated by loud Scottish oaths, made it known that Gilmour was impatient to leave.

"We have to go, Sam." Paddy made a break for the door. "We'll stop on our way back. So long."

The sleepy hamlet of Holmesburg's elm-shaded streets, rambling iron fences and stone homes covered with sand-colored stucco were left behind as the cumbersome stage rumbled northward across a stone bridge that spanned the Pennypack Creek.

The stage rolled through Torresdale and crossed into Bucks County. At the sign of the Red Lion Inn, Gilmour spit out a quid of tobacco and reined in the team. "Bib and tucker time, lads. Everybody down."

A famous stopping-off place since early in the reign of King George III, the Red Lion Inn represented all the traditional architecture peculiar to that colonial region. Splayed windows with heavy, rustic frames were set in deep stone embrasures embellished by solid wooden shutters. A sloping water table above the porch blended softly with the triangular door cap, arched below, from which an oil lantern was suspended.

The wrought iron thumb latch, set in a heavy door, yielded to Gilmour's hand and the hungry crew followed the teamster inside. A spice-scented hallway was decorated with stuffed animal heads and old prints, the well-oiled maple flooring doweled with oaken pegs.

The four trooped into a low-ceilinged room filled with colonial fixtures and seated themselves in plank-bottom chairs around a circular table.

A bald-pated innkeeper approached to take their order. "What'll it be, men?"

he asked in a whiskey-scorched voice. An oversized belly bulged beneath his red apron like a sack of concealed potatoes.

"Make it four beef platters, mon, and one draught ale—large."

"Coming right up."

Paddy fingered the scars and indentations imprinted on the rough tabletop—marks from long time usage. "Be interesting to know," he said, "how many of these scratches and initials were made by Washington and his men, or the King's Dragoons who once ate here."

"Bother wi' ye, lad," Gilmour exclaimed. "The past ha' been properly buried. Do no' trouble yerself to exhume it. Live for today and create yer own history."

As if to lend credence to Gilmour's statement, the attention of all four was drawn to a loud conversation at a nearby table where three country gentlemen were vigorously discussing Mr. Lincoln, the new President.

A plump, middle-aged man whose bloated face bespoke a life accustomed to rich meats and fine liquors was pressing the charge. He pounded the table with a pudgy fist. "If we Democrats had stood united during the election," he stormed, "we wouldn't have to worry about this abandoned son of a bastard who sits on our Capitol doorstep today. This Lincoln, I tell you, is a mole-eyed monster. Mind you," he sputtered, "this usurper who occupies the highest seat in our government is nothing more than a slang-whanging stump speaker who enjoys his present position of power solely because of John Breckenridge."

The plump speaker held up a pink finger and waggled it for emphasis. "Do you realize this ape of Illinois sits as President having received only two million votes as against a combined total vote of three million Democrats? In ten southern states, Lincoln failed to receive a single solitary ballot. I say again, if Breckenridge and his southern friends had kept out of the race, Steven Douglas would be our President today and the present state of affairs would never have happened."

"Hard losers, these Democrats, eh?" the innkeeper twitted softly as he passed four platters around. "Anything else, gentlemen? Speak up if there is." He turned and waddled away.

"What do you think about it, Gilmour?" Castor whispered. "I mean, would things be any different between North and South if Douglas had won?"

"Nay, lad. Let two mad dogs snarl at each other over a period of time, bound to end in a fight eventually. If there be a war ye can put the blame where it belongs, on the rich southern planters and their craving for slaves."

One of the three sitting at the table where the denunciation of Lincoln was taking place rose slowly from his chair and placed a green beaver hat on his head. He had the look of an aristocrat about him. "I have met the man of whom you speak so disparagingly," he said in a level tone of voice, "and I caution you, do not be deceived by his appearance. He is extremely humble and sensitive and gives the hasty observer a wrong impression. My feeling is that he does it on purpose because of his innate shrewdness. The creating of a false impression enables him to attain his goals more easily."

He paused to smooth the velvet lapels of his coat. "You may think his speeches awkward and somewhat vague, but that is because deep down he's reluctant to impress opinionated men like yourselves with his true grasp of the situation. Good day, gentlemen." He picked up a riding crop and stalked from the room.

The Quaker bent over the table and whispered, "Do thee know who that was?"

"Seems like I've seen him before," Paddy responded, "but I just can't place him."

"That was Chapman Biddle, the lawyer."

"One of the Philadelphia Biddles?" Gilmour asked, one eyebrow raised.

"Yes. His grandfather was Clement Biddle, the famous Quaker soldier during the Revolution."

"I remember hearing about his grandfather," Paddy cut in. "He led a company of Quakers to put down the Paxton boys who were murdering harmless Indians around Lancaster."

Castor pushed an empty dish to one side and stared at the Quaker. "Where do you people stand on southern states' rights?" he asked.

Gilmour and Mulcahy shot glances of reproof in Castor's direction. It was well-established that the Quakers of Philadelphia and vicinity were held in disfavor by many because of their prominent activity in helping slaves escape via the underground railway. Since a slave was personal property, Southerners and a great many Northerners looked upon the operators of the underground railway as people engaged in trafficking stolen goods.

While Lucretia Mott and other members of the Society of Friends assisted the runaway slaves for purely humanitarian reasons, the more rabid abolitionists from the New England states saw the railway as a means of fighting undeclared war with the Southern slaveholders. The Quakers were thus placed in an odd position; their religious principles forbade the bearing of arms in conflict, yet their activity seemed to incite what they opposed—war.

Castor pressed for an answer to his question.

"Are we one nation, Friend John, or a loose association of states?" the Quaker inquired.

"It's gettin' late," Gilmour cut in sharply. He wiped his mouth with his shirt sleeve. "If we're to make Bristol with time enough to unload, we'd best be on our way."

The boys pushed their chairs away from the table, stood up and followed the teamster from the inn.

With the four-in-hand straining at the bit, the stage rolled toward the terminal at Bristol. Shades of twilight cast uneven shadows across the fertile fields and meadows and stabbed the deep recesses of bordering forests with darkness.

Paddy looked out at the rolling countryside. The region through which the coach now passed had been a hunting ground for the Unami Indians of the Leni-Lenape Tribe, part of the Delaware Nation. Later, the region played host to the embattled Colonial and British armies.

He allowed his mind to play fanciful tricks. He envisioned himself a scout for Washington's army. In his pocket were vital dispatches for the Continental Congress. He conjured a hostile band of British redcoats through whom he charged with sword flashing, tri-cornered hat flying, dashing off unscathed over the King's Highway.

"Hey, come out of it," Castor yelled a second time as he struck Paddy a playful blow on the back of the head. "I said, we're almost there."

They crossed the moonlit Neshaminy Creek to the echoing sound of bridge timbers. The lights of Bristol loomed ahead. A noisy intruder, the stage coach rattled over the cobblestoned streets of the old river town and came to a halt in front of the Delaware House.

The time-honored hostelry on the corner of Mill and Radcliffe streets was built originally in 1730 by Patrick O'Hanlin, who gave it the name of Ferry House. The present structure was altered in 1765 by Charles Bessonet. A sign, with the likeness of George III emblazoned upon it, had been hung from the front of the building. During the Revolution, a regiment of colonial troops passing through Bristol paused long enough to salute His Majesty of England with volley after volley until the riddled sign fell out of its frame. After the war, the guest log of the Delaware House boasted numerous prominent patrons who stopped often in their travels to New York, notably Presidents Madison, Tyler and Fillmore. Joseph Bonaparte, bother of Napoleon, lived on an estate across the river at Bordentown and was a constant frequenter to the friendly tavern.

Gilmour knotted the rein and sprang to the ground.

"Hope ye lads ha' money enough for a night's lodgin'." He spat a stream of tobacco juice. "Too late to head home at this hour.

Paddy turned his pockets inside out. "I haven't any money. Heck, who needs it. I'll sleep in the stable with the horses."

"How 'boot you other lads?"

"We'll bed down with Paddy," Castor said between yawns.

A boisterous crowd of river men stumbled through the swinging doors of the ground-floor tavern. Pounding and slapping each other on the back, they staggered drunkenly down the dimly lit street.

Castor screwed up his face and leered. "Boy, they're really carrying bricks home in their hats. Think you'll be able to sleep above that grog shop, Gilmour? Maybe you should consider coming out in the stable with us."

"I'll get along very well without any interference from ye, Castor. Now be off, all of ye. Paddy, see that the horses are well-fed and watered and keep a weather eye on me freight. D'ya ken?"

Paddy nodded and moved quickly to the teamster's bidding. Gilmour stalked into the Delaware House.

With the horses stabled and the freight safely stored in a padlocked barn, Castor began squirming restlessly. "What say we nose around a bit? I don't feel much like sleeping."

"Where do you want to go at this hour?" Paddy responded wearily.

"Let's look in at the tavern. Maybe somethin' interesting will pop up."

Paddy turned to the Quaker. "John? Want to mosey around a bit?"

"Not particularly. I'm bone tired, but I'll go along if thee want to."

"Well, let's go," Castor chirped impatiently.

The three boys brushed particles of straw from their clothing and strolled slowly toward the hotel. Suddenly, Paddy stopped "Hey, look, isn't that Gilmour coming out the side door?"

"It sure is," Castor chuckled. "And I'll wager I know what he's going after. Let's trail him."

"We will not." Paddy cupped his hands to his mouth and called, "Hey, Duncan, wait up."

The Scotsman turned around sharply and glowered as the three approached. "Why aren't ye wi' the horses?"

"There's a stableman keeping watch," Paddy replied. "Where're you going at his hour?"

"Hoot, mon. Can't a grown mon what ain't even father to ye go anywhere without havin' to explain his moves? I'm going to the telegraph office if ye must know."

"Telegraph office, " Castor guffawed. "Mind if we tag along?"

"Alright, ye night owls, join me if ye like, but if you've got it fixed in your salty little heads it's a fleshpot I'm seekin', ye're sadly mistaken."

With sheepish grins the three walked briskly after the teamster as he strode down Mill Street toward the railroad depot. A darkened telegraph office, shabby and coated with soot, lay at the far end of the station. Inside, a small light burned dimly above an idle keyboard.

"Doesn't appear as if anyone's on duty," Castor said.

Gilmour tried the door and found it open. He thrust his head inside and shouted. "Mackey, are ye aboot, mon?"

The sleepy telegrapher roused himself from a couch and stretched his arms. "Who be it that's disturbin' me this late at night?"

"It's me, Gilmour. I ha' to send message to the Trenton terminal."

The gray-haired dispatcher rubbed tired eyes and adjusted a pair of rimless spectacles to the bridge of his nose. "Kinda late for that sorta thing, ain't it, Gilmour? Seems to me the message, whatever it might be, could've waited till morning."

"Maybe," Gilmour responded dryly, "but since they'll be expectin' me in Trenton first thing in the mornin', I ha' thought I best to let 'em know I'm layin' over in Bristol tomorra. After all, mon, tomorra' is Sunday and I deserve a wee bit of rest, ya ken?"

"How 'bout us dispatchers?"the old man grumbled. "Ever think of us?" He shook his head. "Well, since you've put your mind to it, I'll send your message." He paused before a large wall calendar. "Saturday, the thirteenth of April, sixty-one. That's another day for the can." Tearing the page from the calendar, he wrinkled it in his hand and flung it into a wastebasket. "Be a good lad there, son," he addressed Paddy. "Strike a match to that lamp hanging above you."

"Yes, sir." Paddy climbed onto a stool and struck a match to the oil wick. The dingy, cluttered telegraph office took on a warm glow. The dispatcher glanced at Paddy's bare feet.

"Don't you find it a little early in the season to be running around with no shoes? Still plenty of dampness. You're inviting chilblains at an early age."

"Don't mind it none, makes my feet good and tough for summer."

At that moment a small metal key on the telegraph began clacking at a rapid rate, as water snapping on a hot hearth. The dispatcher quickly slipped a green isinglass eyeshade over his head and slid sideways his swivel chair.

"You'll have to hold a minute, Gilmour, something's coming over the wire."

The teamster and three boys listened silently as a message rattled off the active key. Suddenly, the telegrapher's pock-marked face changed expression. He bent forward and listened intently. The metal key ceased it staccato clacking as abruptly as it had begun. An ominous stillness settled over the musty room.

Paddy stepped closer to the board. "Something wrong, sir?"

The dispatcher slowly removed his eyeshade and sat transfixed in his chair. He gripped the soiled leather armrests with liver-spotted hands. Clearing his throat, his voice barely audible, he said, "The Rebels have seized Fort Sumter. The flag is down in Charleston Harbor."

CHAPTER 2

A bright, warm Sabbath greeted the three companions the following morning. Somewhat weary from a late night discussion on the meaning and message of Sumter, they were refreshed by a hearty breakfast that Gilmour provided for them. A decision was made. Rather than walk back to Frankford, they would hike further up the Delaware Valley and return the next day by steamboat. They thanked the Scotsman for his kindness and bade him farewell.

A narrow footpath, which closely followed the Delaware Canal, led them to the hamlet of Yardley. The rustic beauty of the old canal reflected itself in moss-covered locks, splashing spillways and miniature bridges. The occasional appearance of blunt-end canal boats, towed by spans of mules and driven by youngsters in straw hats, worked a drowsy effect on the wayfarers. Cozy little mills, lichen and vine-covered cottages and comfortable inns, mellowed and softened by the years, caught and held the eye along the way.

Upon reaching the spot where Washington had crossed his army in the winter of 1776, they ferried themselves across the Delaware and landed on the Jersey shore. Pretending to be Washington's Continentals, they marched toward Trenton. It was nearly dark when they finally reached the New Jersey state capital.

Castor stopped to remove a pebble from the heel of his shoe and spoke to Paddy. "Are you sure the *River Queen's* sailing from here and not from Philadelphia tomorrow? I hate to think of walking all the way home. Besides, where will we sleep tonight?"

Paddy rubbed swollen feet. "Stop your worrying. Captain Hinkle always sails from Trenton on Monday mornings. I should know. I've made the trip often enough."

"You will carry me piggyback, if you're wrong," Castor replied. "I'm beat."

The Quaker buttoned his shirt collar to ward off a chilly breeze that was rising from the river. "How much farther is it to the wharf, Paddy?"

"About three blocks. Let's get a move on. I need sleep."

The bulky outline of a side-wheel steamboat came into view through the enveloping darkness. The twin-stacked steamer proved to be the *River Queen*, a friendly haven for boys who found themselves penniless and stranded along its route.

"Amen," Castor shouted with arms upraised. "There it is." He executed a hornpipe dance step. "Now, for some food and sleep. We can work off passage tomorrow.

The weary trio scrambled up a freshly creosoted gangplank and headed for the galley quarters.

Early next morning they were awakened by the drumming and pounding of the steam-driven pistons flexing their iron muscles in the bowels of the boat in preparation for a hard day's work. It was Monday, the fifteenth of April.

The full light of day had not yet penetrated the warm, steamy mist that blanketed the river and docks in a hazy white shroud. The moist scent of dew-laden marsh grass permeated the atmosphere. Aboard ship, the freight-laden deck came alive with shuffling boat hands hard at work with their chores. Overhead, a strong beam of iron grillwork oscillated merrily in the manner of a child's seesaw.

Paddy stretched his arms and lifted his aching body from a bed of coiled rope on the foredeck. "Well, another day, another dollar," he mused.. "Shall we seek out the good captain? Looks like time to go to work."

"There'll be no need for work on this trip," spoke a salty voice from behind them.

Paddy turned his head as Castor and the Quaker, who were still lying wrapped in a tarpaulin on the deck, rolled over on their sides to get a better glimpse of the figure.

Captain Hinkle, a tall, gray-haired man with a weather-beaten face that resembled worn corduroy, removed a seaman's cap and scratched his head. "Morning, boys. Seeing as how I already have a full complement of deck hands this trip, thought maybe you'd rather join me on the bridge. What do you say, Mulcahy?"

"That'd be just bully, sir."

"Good. Come on up whenever you're ready. I have some coffee and hot mush ready for you."

Castor sprang to his feet. "Well, what're we waiting for, men? Let's go."

The three quickly followed the benevolent captain. From the wheelhouse perched high on the bridge came the inviting aroma of hot breakfast.

"You lads just help yourselves," Captain Hinkle said over his shoulder as his guests entered. "Everything's on the table. I've got work to do."

He grabbed a brass megaphone, thrust it through an open window and bellowed loudly. "All hands stand by to cast off." He scanned the port side of the boat fore and aft. "Alright, Mr. Murphy, up the gangplank and cast off."

Within a few minutes the ponderous side-wheeler slipped slowly into the Delaware channel, her mammoth wooden paddle wheels churning a frothy wake. Billowing clouds of black smoke trailed from her twin stacks. At regular intervals the steam whistle cut loose with a series of sharp blasts mixed with guttural grunts. The river fog, which up til now had cut off the view, began lifting rapidly as the morning sun broke through the swirling mists.

The whistle tooting stopped, and from their vantage point on the bridge, the boys were soon able to pick our familiar landmarks on the Pennsylvania shore. The first to fall under their searching gaze was Pennsbury Manor, one-time country seat of William Penn. Seen from midstream, the imposing English-style house of the Gerogian period displayed four prominent cathedral chimneys with pointed Gothic arches over each chimney flue.

The time-mellowed bricks from which the mansion was constructed had been brought from England as ship ballast. Perfectly planted with great trees, boxwood and numerous gardens, the magnificent home was symbolic of the many traditions inculcated on newcomers to the Delaware Valley by descendants of the original Quaker settlers. Foremost among those traditions was that of planting extensive gardens, no matter how fine or humble the home. In that particular area, it was said family instinct was even more strongly marked than that found among the Chinese. The first settlers, the Pembertons, Tullys, Landreths, Dungans and Palethorps, built solidly for coming generations.

Bolton Farm, ancestral home of the Pembertons, slid by on the west bank of the Delaware as the *River Queen* neared Bristol. Captain Hinkle struck a match to a well-caked pipe and rested his elbows on the windowsill of the wheelhouse. A soft breeze blowing through the open window tossed a loose, gray curl hanging below the visor of his cap. He studied the extensive Balton Farm with deep curiosity, then nodded in that direction. "Any of you lads know old Phineas Pemberton who lives over there? " he asked.

The Quaker, holding the helm in a firm grip, spoke up. "Would he be any kin to John C. Pemberton of Philadelphia?"

"That was going to be my next question. At the State of Schuylkill Fishing Club several years ago I had the pleasure of meeting the Pemberton to whom you just referred. Never did get around to finding out just what his relationship might be to old man Phineas."

"What's so all-fired important about it?" Castor inquired.

The river captain pushed his cap to the back of his head and tucked the wayward curl into place, a deep frown crossing his brow. "Nothing much," he replied softly. "Matter of fact, I'd almost completely forgotten about Captain John C. Pemberton until I picked up the paper the other day. Read where he had gone south to join the Confederates."

"The hell you say," Paddy blurted. "A native Philadelphian fighting on the side of the Reb? That's unbelievable."

"That was my reaction. Beats the life out of me why he did it. He comes from one of the oldest, most distinguished families in this part of the state. If war should come, he will be fighting against his own kin." The steam boat captain shook his head in bewilderment. "I've seen a lot of whangbang crazy family arguments in my time, but if this country embarks on a civil war, it will be the saddest, most nonsensical exhibition I ever witnessed."

He struck a match to the bowl of his pipe and drew in deeply. He exhaled a wreath of smoke.

"There was another army officer from Philadelphia at our fish fry that night. He and Pemberton were raised together in the same neighborhood. Seemed to be close friends. Matter of fact, they came to the club together. Let me think, what was that other officer's name? Oh, yes, I remember, it was Meade, Captain George Meade. Rather stern sort, if I remember correctly. We had quite a talk concerning the 'Savior of the Sea'."

Paddy arched an eyebrow, "Savior of the Sea'?"

"Aye, the Barnegat Lighthouse over on the Jersey coast. A most remarkable, scientific structure. Meade and Pemberton were in charge of construction. That was back in fifty-eight. They showed a lot of enthusiasm as they discussed the engineering details. Pity they now face the possibility of meeting each other on a battlefield."

Captain Hinkle leaned his head out of the wheelhouse window and shouted toward the fore deck, "Ho there, Mister Murphy, what's our mark?"

A deck hand studied a colored leather marker attached to a sounding line that bobbed on the surface of the water. "Mark twain, sir."

"Very good, Murphy. Steady as she goes."

The *River Queen,* riding a strong current, continued making good time on her trip downstream toward Philadelphia. One village after another slipped swiftly by on the Pennsylvania shore, Bristol, Croydon, Andalusia, Torresdale, Holmesburg, and, at last, the bustling wharf at Tacony hove into sight.

"Looks like the end of the line for us, Cap'n," Castor quipped gaily. "Thanks for the lift. Anytime you're short of deckhands just look us up."

Captain Hinkle gave Castor a playful slap between the shoulder blades. "Don't worry, son, I've got it down in the log that you each owe for one passage." Megaphone in hand, he lashed out orders sending all hands scurrying to their stations. The river men quickly and skillfully berthed the bulky side-wheeler at the wharf near Buttermilk Tavern.

The three young men paused momentarily on the lowered gangplank to wave farewell to the captain, then bounded onto the dock. Tripping over a loose hawser, Paddy quickly regained his feet and gave chase to Castor and the Quaker who were leapfrogging over bales and barrels blocking their path. Together, they threaded their way around carts and carriages, then struck inland toward the Bristol Pike a mile away.

The exhilaration of spring lightened their hearts. Flaming scarlet tanagers with ebony wings and red-crested cardinals flittered from tree to bush, their merry chirps heralding warmer weather and the joys of summer which lay in the offing.

Castor stooped and picked up a loose stone which he fired at a rabbit that darted across the pathway. The missile missed its target by several feet.

Paddy wrinkled his nose and laughed, "Piss poor aim, Chirp. You couldn't hit a bull in the ass with a banjo."

The Quaker flicked a branch as if fly-casting. "I hear the Delaware is jumping with shad," he said. "Let's arrange to meet and try our hand."

"Anytime you say," the others replied. "When do you suggest?"

The Quaker's face clouded. "I don't know. Something just dawned on me. I'm afraid I'll catch it from my uncle for missing Meeting yesterday. Sunday is strictly church and family day."

"How long you figure it will take him to get over it?" Paddy asked.

"A week...maybe two.. Let's set the date at two weeks from today. He will have forgotten the matter by then, especially if I ask for time off to go fishing." He rolled up the sleeves of his shirt. "Only three things Uncle William puts stock in. The Inner Light, making things grow and fishing."

"Good. Two weeks from today, and may your uncle see the Light," Castor said.

The sound of clattering hoofbeats from the direction of Holmesburg caught their attention.

"Somebody's in a hurry," Castor exclaimed. "Can you fellas make out who it is?"

Paddy shaded his eyes against the slanting rays of the sun. "Looks like Ab Howarth from over near Bustleton. Hells bells, he's too good a horseman to be driving an animal like that. Either he's fetching a doctor or running from the Devil."

The young rider, his face flushed and beaded with perspiration, reined in a lathered black stallion. The horse came to a rearing, whinnying halt.

"What're you trying to do, Ab, kill that stud?" Paddy called.

"Kill him, hell," the broad-shouldered horseman cried, "ain't you fellas heard the news? It's war! Word just came over the wire a short spell ago. Lincoln's called seventy-five thousand volunteers to put down the rebellion." Howarth mopped dust-stained perspiration from his brow with a hairy arm. "Been ordered to join our cavalry troop in Frankford immediately. See you in uniform." He dug spurs into the stallion's ribs and galloped off.

"War," the Quaker muttered low. "What will it mean? What will it prove?"

Castor emitted a sharp whistle. "This sure changes the color of things. I held for the South while there was still hope for peace, but now that the old flag is calling..."

The three fell silent. At the entrance to his uncle's farm, the Quaker stopped to shake hands and say goodbye. Paddy and Castor proceeded toward Frankford. They arrived at the Mulcahy blacksmith shop and found it deserted.

Paddy looked all around. "Something must be in the wind, even Jim Ryen is missing from the front porch of the Jolly Post."

Castor ran a hand through his reddish hair. "That's sure enough odd. Wonder where everybody went?"

"Have you fellas heard the news," asked a dark-haired teenager as he appeared around the far corner of the smithy. His face shone with choir boy innocence.

"Hello, Billy," Castor called in reply. "Where did everybody go?"

"In town. War's been declared. Haven't you heard?"

"Yes, about an hour ago," Paddy answered. "Ab Howarth told us. How come you aren't in town with everyone else?"

"Your father asked me to stay here and watch for you. Told him I would. Now you're back, we can go into town together."

"Well, then, come on," Castor started running. "We don't want to miss anything."

In company with Billy Batt, youngest son of Frankford's horse doctor, Paddy and Castor continued toward the town proper. As they approached Borough Hall, they were struck by an electrifying change of atmosphere.

"Great guns, look at that crowd, will you!" Castor bellowed. "Whoopee! The whole town has turned out!"

He started running faster.

Two days before, Main Street had been an ordinary apathetic thoroughfare. Now it blazed with color and patriotism. The Stars and Stripes rippled in the breeze from every available staff and halyard. The colors of the Union could be seen on most breasts and burning patriotism had swept nearly everyone to the support of the flag.

In front of Frankford's Borough Hall, a large, noisy throng had gathered— millers in flour-dusted caps and powdered aprons, pasty-faced clerks in striped trousers, machinists in coveralls and well-dressed gentlemen. In response to the occasion, the Decatur Fire Company Band burst forth with the stirring strains of *Yankee Doodle*. Men and boys began to snake-dance and shriek merrily above the sound of music. Exploding fireworks sent stray dogs yipping for cover. Puffs of powder smoke rose over the heads of milling crowd.

At the sight of their younger brothers, Henry Castor and Joe Batt cupped hands to their mouths and shouted, "Come over and join the fun, fellas!"

Joe Batt, a strapping six-footer with broad shoulders, picked up Billy by the armpits and swung him around in the air. "Too bad you're so young, baby face. You'll miss out on all the glory of soldiering."

Willie McCool, a village cutup never at a loss for pranks, grabbed Paddy by the arm and screamed in his ear. "This sure enough beats any circus parade of Porgy O'Brien's, hey, Mulcahy?"

Paddy's reply was cut short, Caught between two surging waves, he was bowled over as a mock charge led by Owen McCool and his clan swept forward to tussle with the equally large family of Williamses.

"Down with the Rebs!" Barney Williams bellowed, as he helped Paddy to his feet.

Paddy glared into Williams' animated face. "Have you all gone berserk?" he snapped as he dusted himself off.

Williams responded by covering the tip of his nose with his tongue and cocking one eye.

A wide circle of hoop-skirted girls who were watching the proceedings from a safe distance, laughed and pointed at the cavorting antics performed by newly discovered heroes.

Paddy disengaged himself from the jostling free-for-all when he heard a clarion call for Jim Ryen. In a burst of enthusiasm the crowd took up the chant. "We want Jim! We want Jim!" The Decatur brass band, sunlight reflecting off their polished instruments, began playing the old veteran's favorite tune. *Doodle Town Fifers*.

Through a pathway which opened in the throng, Paddy could see the Revolutionary War hero approaching. Bill Horrocks and Noble McClintock carried the old man by the elbows so that his feet scarcely touched the ground. A faded military coat of buff and blue sagged about his shoulders.

A cry of "Speech! Speech!" rose from the crowd as the venerable patriarch mounted the steps of Borough Hall with a glow of triumph on his creased,milk-white features. Gray hair cascaded from beneath an old tri-cornered campaign hat. In one hand he carried a rusted bayonet which he waved in the face of the throng. The shouting abated as he began speaking.

"All of ye recognize this old bayonet of mine, " he shouted, his voice crackling. "The same one I carried at Yorktown…"

Paddy's sixth sense turned his attention to a general exodus taking place by the town's distinguished elders, many were leaving in carriages or on horseback and heading north. The general movement, he surmised, meant that a more serious meeting dealing with the situation would take place at the Jolly Post. Anxious to hear what might transpire, he tore himself away from the patriotic demonstration and raced after the carriages. When he reached the Jolly Post, he stopped to ascertain whether or not his father was at the smithy. The blacksmith shop was still deserted.

A large group of men conversing in low, serious tones mounted the steps of the old inn and passed through its portals. Paddy skirted the front of the spacious hostelry and approached it from the rear. He made his way through a garden of sweet smelling boxwood and opened a kitchen door as unobtrusively as possible.

The Jolly Post, formerly a scene of skirmishes between American and British soldiers, had been given its name by General Washington after the American Army had rested there on the march to capture Cornwallis at Yorktown in 1781. Built in 1694 by Henry Waddy, the present ownership rested in the able hands of Jacob Coats and his genial wife, Mary. A meeting place for patriots during the Revolution, the well-preserved inn now hosted the descendants of those who had cherished and fought for freedom.

Paddy located a favorable spot and squeezed himself onto a spice-scented pantry shelf where he could see and hear without being detected.

Among the assembled, he noticed Sollys, Overingtons, Leipers, Duffields, Buckiuses, Pauls, Shallcrosses, Worrellses, Garseds, and many other respected villagers whose grandfathers had met in the same room years ago on equally important business. Many of those present were quaffing ale from copper mugs, other puffed on briar pipes and leaned forward in conversation. Colonel Burns sat erect at a table placed in front of a walk-in stone fireplace. Above his head, a large oil painting of Penn's Treaty with the Indians looked down serenely from the paneled wall. Colonel Burns unfolded a newspaper and called for attention. The gathering fell silent.

"Gentlemen," he said in a loud, clear voice, "I have in my hand a telegraph report from the *Charleston Mercury*. For those who may doubt what course the North should take, I would like to read Governor Picken's address to the mob in Charleston following the fall of Sumter."

A hush of anticipation fell over the audience as the Colonel carefully adjusted his pince-nez spectacles. Picking up the telegraph report, he began reading the governor's proclamation:

"It is a glorious and exultant occasion, fellow citizens. I clearly saw that the day was coming when we would triumph beyond the power of man to put us down. Thank God the day has come, thank God the war is open, and we will conquer or perish. We have defeated their twenty millions and the proud flag of the Stars and Stripes that was never lowered before any nation on earth, we have lowered in humility before the glorious little State of South Carolina!"

Governor Picken's speech was greeted by angry shouts which shook the old inn's timbers and rattled the crockery on the corniced cupboards. Cries of "Arrogance!" "Insolence!" and "Traitors!" swept through the smoke-filled room.

The Honorable Richardson Wright, a tight-lipped Quaker who had served as Speaker in the State House of Representatives, attempted to restore order. He held up both arms for attention. "Gentlemen, gentlemen, let us conduct ourselves with decorum."

The meeting quieted down and the legislator cleared his throat. "Thank thee, gentlemen. Until recent events, there have been many of us here who've found ourselves in sympathy with our Southern friends when they told us that dissolution of the Union was not what they had in mind, nor was the establishment of a confederacy a goal they specifically sought. They would have us believe that both the one and the other were secondary to the preservation of the sacred right of self-government." His voice rose, "I venture to say, there's not one descendant of a revolutionary sitting among us who does not agree with them as far as that scared right is concerned, but what right of self-government has been denied the South in our republican form of government?"

"None! None!" came of reply.

The legislator jammed this thumbs into his vest pockets. "This nation is a republic," he continued, "and a republic is a state in which the sovereign power resides in a body of people, namely, the electorate. Sovereign power is exercised by representatives elected by the people, who are responsible to the people. The South has not been denied representation in our republic. Accordingly, no right of self-government has been taken away from them. This war will be one to determine whether or not the South, or any group of people, shall abide by the rule of majority."

"Rule of majority, indeed!" a voice from the audience snapped. "And what if a disproportion exists in voting strength and representation which makes it impossible for the South to receive a fair shake in the affairs of the republic? Is that not reason enough for those aggrieved states to band together and form a new governing body more suitable to themselves? Is that not the course which the colonies took against England when they rebelled against the monarch and established this republic?"

Paddy craned his neck to get a better view of the speaker. His eyes fell on an old man who had belonged to the Whig Party under Henry Clay. Many of the old-line Whigs, after the breakup of the party, refused to affiliate with either the Republican or the Democrat party and voted in large numbers for the Know-Nothing, or Native American ticket in 1856. They were chiefly opposed to the exercise of so large an influence in American affairs by foreign-born persons and

Roman Catholics.

"Bull!" a fiery coercionist shouted in reply to the former Whig. "The colonies never had representation nor the right of self-government. The South has constitutional guarantees of both." His thick jowls waggled in the manner of an angry turkey gobbler. "The South won't tolerate non-slave states entering the Union in fear they might send representatives to Washington who will not see eye-to-eye with them on the slavery issue. That is why they want to pick up their cotton and walk away."

"There you go again with that abstract talk about slavery," a conciliatory Unionist challenged from the floor. "Poppycock!" Both climate and soil have closed the Western territories to slavery. The most rabid pro-slavery men admit the economic basis for slavery is completely lacking in the new territories. The territorial question has settled itself. The entire issue, which to you Republicans is the cause of sectional agitation and bitterness, is a mere abstraction, the South has told you that repeatedly."

"If that is so," the coercionist retorted, "why did the Rebs level Sumter? For target practice? What are they rebelling against? Are they attempting to establish the Mexican custom in the United States? Shall we resort to rebellion and Civil War every time we're beaten in an election?"

"I won't argue against you on that last point," the conciliatory Unionist responded, "but can't you Republicans see that it is you who have brought on the conflict?" The speaker rose to his feet. "Jeremiah Black of the Supreme Court gave Lincoln and the Republican party authoritative assurance that if the Lincoln administration would pledge itself, without equivocation, to uphold the Constitution of the United States as interpreted by the Supreme Court, the Southern States would annual their ordinance of secession immediately. Lincoln flatly refused to make that declaration."

A few among the audience shouted. "Hear! Hear!"

Encouraged by support, the speaker continued. "Don't forget that an overwhelming majority voted against Lincoln.. The majority of this nation want compromise. Lincoln, representing the minority, has refused to accede to the wishes of the majority. You know full well that the majority of Southern people voted for Douglas and Bell in the recent presidential election. That heavy nationalistic vote in the South indicates one thing, the South is not bent on spreading slavery into the territories, much less into the free states. It shows the South preferred the Union without slavery to slavery without the Union, because neither Douglas nor Bell held out any hope for another slave state. Looking at their vote, it is folly to assert that Southern people are aggressively pro-slavery and bent on maintaining slavery at any cost."

"Where's the rub, then?" the coercionist challenged mockingly.

"The South doesn't want you Republicans interfering with the labor system and the civilization of their section," snapped the conciliationist. "If your Mister Lincoln had heeded the prophetic warning of George Washington against forming sectional or geographical parties, we wouldn't be in this mess. Furthermore, you Republicans have acted in bad faith from the day Lincoln was inaugurated.

"Who killed the Virginia Peace Conference? Mister Lincoln. When it became evident the compromise would be carried by a fifty thousand majority in Indiana, a two hundred thousand majority in Pennsylvania, and almost three-fourths of New York was in favor of it, your wily Republican politicians preferred the reinforcing of Sumter to the promise of peace contained in the National Convention. Why? I'll tell you why." He leveled an angry finger at his adversary. "To preserve the Republican party rather than the Union. An appeal to the brain of the Nation meant your party's annihilation, while an appeal to the brawn of the North meant your party's salvation."

His voice fell. "Your party's dodge has worked. You now have political supremacy and full control of the national government, or what's left of it, and our sons will die in a bloody war as the result."

The coercionist jumped to his feet, angered and demonstrative. "You say we Republicans are sectional. We deny it. The mere fact our party failed to receive a single vote in ten Southern states is proof enough where true sectionalism lies—in the South. Let them heed the warning of George Washington with regard to geographical sectionalism."

A roar of approval greeted his fiery retort.

"I say let the erring sisters go," an advocate of peaceful dissolution shouted from the far side of the room. "It's spelled out for you in the Declaration of Independence. This government derives its just powers from the consent of the governed. The south no longer consents to be governed by you Black Republicans."

"We're dealing with open rebellion!" a coercionist fired back. "I say let the irrepressible conflict become bloody reality."

"Aye," another shouted, "secession's a dangerous philosophy we cannot, we must not, tolerate. The precedent would be a death knell, I dare say that, sooner or later, the South will be discover this truth for itself. Remember the disastrous state of affairs when the Union was governed under the Articles of Confederation?"

"Ben's right," John Solly broke in, his jaws set. "This selfish, self-centered secession act, if permitted, could snowball, counties seceding from states, townships from counties, and so on. Why, I could even wake up some morning to find my wife had seceded because I broke wind in bed." His eyes sparkled with merriment. "Some things in life you've just got to learn to live with."

A burst of hearty laughter and numerous side remarks helped ease the tension which had been building. Paddy, to relieve a cramped position, took a deep breath and shifted his weight. His head struck the shelf above. A stack of dislodged pots and pans clattered to the floor.

"Good Lord, what was that?" someone cried.

Every eye in the room trained itself on the pantry as Paddy untangled himself and crawled out.

Doctor, Leake, a graying man in his mid-fifties, stood partially erect. "Well, I'll be...if it isn't that tomfool, Mulcahy. What in the world's he up to now?"

Colonel Burns motioned with one arm. "You there, Paddy. Come here."

Paddy's face flushed beet red as he shuffled toward Colonel Burns.

"Don't fret about it, my boy." The Colonel wrapped a kindly arm around

Paddy's shoulders as he faced the chuckling crowd. "Don't suppose there's a man among us who isn't familiar with young Mulcahy. Speaking for myself, on many occasions, I've wished secretly I could trade places with the lad. I envy him,"

"Why's that, Colonel? You got some crockery you want busted up?" someone piped.

Doctor Leake broke into a smile. "I'll let you play partisan scout with my mare, Colonel."

Paddy squirmed, beads of cold sweat forming on his forehead, perspiration dripping from his armpits.

"Stop, you're upsetting the boy," the Colonel rejoined. "Sure, we say he's a fanciful daydreamer, an idealist, maybe, but despite his seemingly irresponsible, reckless ways, I say bully for him. I admire his search for harmony in life." He gave Paddy's shoulder a gentle squeeze and then a nudge as if letting a small fish off the hook. "Go out the side door, lad, or stay if you like."

With hands thrust deep in his pockets, Paddy darted for the exit.

Colonel Burns spoke after a moment's pause. "Gentlemen, it is the search for a more harmonious way of life that lies at the crux of our present situation. The people of this fair land must grow up and learn to live as a nation instead of drifting into autonomous governments for vain and personal reasons. I am convinced our new President sees this more clearly than any of us. The time for compromise has passed. I have lived in the South and owned slaves. I still have many friends in South Carolina, and I tell you this in all candor, the South is run by a feudal aristocracy which prides itself on name and blood."

He placed worn knuckles on the lectern and leaned forward. "This aristocracy prides itself on the fact that it can trace its lineage back to the Jacobites and Cavaliers of England and the Huguenots of France. They look down with haughty contempt on the man who earns bread by the sweat of his brow. It is these power-seeking barons who've taken their states out of the Union, not the people. Let me ready you another editorial."

The meeting remained silent as the Colonel with drew a folded newspaper article from a side pocket. He cleared his throat and adjusted his spectacles. "This is by DeBow from the *Charleston Mercury*," he informed them.

"'The Cavaliers, Jacobites, and Hugenots who settled in the South naturally hate, hold in contempt, and despise the Puritans who settled the North, The former are master races, the latter a slave race, descendants of Anglo-Saxon serfs…'"

With obvious distaste he thrust the clipping back into his pocket. "There, you have it, Master race, indeed. It would be wise for DeBow to recall that in contests between Cavaliers and Puritans, it was the Cavaliers who were defeated. The Jacobites went down before the party which placed William of Orange on the throne."

Scottish Presbyterians in the audience shouted their approval.

Colonel Burns held up a hand. "If you please, gentlemen." They fell silent before his austere gaze. "Thank you. Now, as you know, I have just recently returned from South Carolina. She is proud in spirit. Her cotton crop last year was abundant, her planters are plethoric with money. Charleston banks and insurance offices are as stable as any on Wall Street. Next to New Orleans she is the most populous city in the South and the wealthiest. Mark my words, Charleston aspires to be the commercial emporium of the South.

"Her newspapers have taught the people to believe that secession and non-intercourse with the North will make their city rival New York. She has adopted the vagaries of Calhoun on states' rights and proclaimed herself Cotton King, not of America, but of the world. In her false pride she believes that all nations can be brought to do her homage. I have said many times, it is my old state of South Carolina which is the Mephistopheles of the Confederacy. She has been the seducer of states. With honeyed words and well-timed flattery, she has managed to detach state after state from the Union. Her churches, merchants and planters believe their influence is worldwide through King Cotton and his prime minister, African slavery. Her arrogance, fierce intolerance and mad hatred have their prototypes in the rebellion of the devil and his angels. Selfish traits of vanity and pride and a lust for power by the barons of a feudal aristocracy have brought our country into this civil war." He paused to moisten his dry lips. "national sovereignty is paramount," he said. "If the Southern people support secession, it is because they have been deceived. Their reason has been muddled by intellectual demagogues who have injected emotional and controversial issues into the debate on states rights. The South must hold John C. Calhoun, Barnwell Rhett, the Right Reverend Bishop Elliott, Reverend Doctor Thornwell and other members of the slave-holding bar, pulpit and forum accountable for the suffering and bloodshed which will surely come upon our land."

His voice rose. "And now, gentlemen, I propose we get about the business for which we are assembled. President Lincoln has called for volunteers. As leaders of this community, it is our duty to raise a fair quota of troops and provide for them." He bowed his head. "And may God in his infinite mercy preserve the United States of America."

CHAPTER 3

On the nineteenth of April, the first company of troops recruited in Frankford prepared to leave for a camp of instructions. With George Ritman serving as captain, the company was in full field pack and ready to become part of General Small's Washington Brigade. The sidewalks were clogged with townspeople locked shoulder to shoulder, necks craning as far as they could stretch for a better view of the ceremony.

Formed into an impressive blue line in front of Doctor Deacon's residence, one hundred young men and boys stood confidently erect with eyes focused straight ahead. Self-conscious at being the center of attention, Linneus Jennings, the company color-bearer, stepped forward and held out his hands to receive a shining new flag from Mary and Emma Gibson and the attractive Mary Allen. Then, with a band blaring and flag snapping crisply in the breeze, the company wheeled and marched off in the direction of Philadelphia. Shouts, cheering and loud hurrahs bombarded them from all sides as they marched out of sight.

Not to be denied, a group of younger boys, frolicking and kicking up their heels in the fashion of young colts turned out to pasture, bounded after the marching column as far as Chalkley Hall, where, covered with dust, short of breath and perspiring, they gave up the chase and turned back home.

More determined than the others, Castor, Batt and Paddy continued matching steps with a swinging gait until they reached Broad and Prime Street Railroad Station in Philadelphia. A waiting troop train, already crowded with men from the 6th Massachusetts Regiment, was discharging steam and ready to depart. Choking on hot tears of disappointment, Billy and Chirp embraced their older brothers as they boarded.

Weeks passed quickly, and the fires of patriotic ardor lessened as the home folk waited for news. Paddy had just left the smithy for a noon hour break when he spied Chirp and Billy running toward him at breakneck speed. He maneuvered to meet them out of earshot of his father.

"What's up?" he asked, as they stopped beside him.

"Can you come into town with us?" Castor asked, panting breathlessly. "They're recruiting everybody who will come at the Eagle Hotel and over at the Odd Fellows Hall."

Paddy looked dubious. "You mean our age won't be against us?"

"Heck no, just don't give your right age. Tell them you're nineteen."

Batt ran thin, delicate fingers over the soft skin of his unblemished face. "Folks say I don't even look fifteen, but I'm willing to take a stab at it if you're game."

Paddy glanced over his shoulder. "I'm game, let's go."

Dan Thorton, the portly proprietor of the Eagle Hotel, hailed the three as they approached. "You lads coming to join the colors?" he called in a thick, rasping voice. Thin purplish veins resembling blue cheese streaked his puffy face.

The three exchanged furtive glances. "That's right, Dan," Castor replied, throwing out his chest and flexing the muscles in his arms.

"Bully for you, lads." The boniface pointed to a pair of swinging barroom doors through which drifted the stale odor of sour mash, malts and hops. "Go in and help yourself to the best. Drinks are on me for everyone who volunteers."

A land-office business appeared to be taking place on the inside. Bill Batt eyed the situation uneasily. "I don't think we ought to go in, do you?" he whispered in Paddy's ear. "If my mother found out, she'd skin me alive."

Paddy nodded assurance. "Thanks just the same, Dan, We'll take you up on the offer some other time."

"Any time, boys, the offer stands. You just belly up and treat yourselves. I'll remember."

Paddy turned to cross the street.

"Look out!" Castor shrieked. He grabbed Paddy's arm and jerked him backward from the path of an onrushing brewery wagon that came careening around the corner.

"What the...!" Paddy spluttered as a four-horse hitch flashed by with Adam and Charley Hafer whooping it up at the reins. Isaac Tibben stood on the flat bed of the wagon. In desperation, he tried to prevent beer barrels from bouncing out onto the street.

Spurred by the shouts from enthusiastic bystanders, the Hafers struck a pose of charioteers racing a Roman quadriga. The beer, requisitioned from Fritsch's Brewery to stimulate enlistments, was hauled down Main Street as far as Frankford Creek. Adam Hafer negotiated the wagon into an abrupt U-turn and brought it thundering back again. He applied brakes and halted the wagon in front of the recruiting station at the Odd Fellows Hall.

Eager hands unloaded the beer kegs from the brewery wagon amidst a melee of shouting. Uniformed men wearing blue kepis and single-breasted blue coats, some wearing shell jackets embellished with gold braid and chevrons, led volunteers indoors to sign up.

Paddy paused to study a large handbill printed in heavy black type that was pasted to the exterior of the building. In glowing phrases, the poster urged a wholehearted response to the call of colors.

"How 'bout it, lads?" barked a thick Irish voice. "Come to join Colonel Owen's fightin' Twenty-fourth, did ye?"

The trio spun around to face a burly sergeant, a veteran of regular army service. "We don't care what regiment we're in," Castor blurted, "just so long as we got in."

"That's the ticket. You fellas follow after me. I'll take ye inside and ink yer names on the roster of the Twenty-fourth. It's the best dang regiment what's been formed."

Paddy broke out in a rash of goose bumps. He followed the recruiting officer and entered a crowded room. An air of martial severity permeated the atmosphere.

"This is it," Bill Batt said nervously.

Dr. Leake moved across the room. "What is this?" He placed himself before the three with arms folded across his chest. "Well now, this is a surprise, Mulcahy, I was under the impression you would be turning up at the Seven Stars Hotel where they are recruiting the Washington Cavalry Troop." He stroked his nose. "It was for that reason I went to the extra precaution of putting my prize mare under close guard this morning. You know the one I mean?"

Paddy blushed fiery red. "I believe I do, sir."

"Thought maybe you would. Tell me, what are you doing here?"

"We've come to join the army," Paddy replied.

"The infantry? A horseman of your caliber joining the infantry? I can't believe it. Why have you turned your back on the cavalry?"

"I want to be with Billy and Chirp."

"You do, do you? Well, so you shall." He frowned. "I brought all of you into this world and I'm going to see that you remain in it. Now go on home. Come back when you are dry behind the ears."

"Hold on a minute, Doc," the recruiting sergeant cut in abruptly, "I know them as will make good soldiers. These lads here are cut of the right cloth." He nodded favorably toward the three. "Besides," his voice fell, "you know how it is with this recruiting business. After some Seidlitz powders and a good night's rest half those we signed up will have thought better of it by mornin' and turn up deserters. What say, Doc? Let me put these fine lads on the muster roll."

"When they become of age and not before," Dr. Leake replied sternly. "Look, boys, just because these volunteer regiments are being recruited for a three-month term doesn't necessarily mean the war will be over in that length of time. The day will come when the North and the South look with horror upon this fratricidal war they've conceived." He thrust a stethoscope in Paddy's face. "Now, scat!"

Crestfallen, the three turned and left the room. After the few meaningless expressions of consolation they separated, each going his own way.

Paddy walked back toward the smithy, his head down, eyes focused on the ground. He was crossing Foulkrod Street when a southern drawl fell upon his ears. "My, my, Virginia, see how downcast our little president 'pears this afternoon."

Gathering his senses, Paddy raised his head to view the benign ebony countenances of Peter Marks and his wife, Virginia, who were smiling at him from the front porch of their tidy home. Paddy saluted the aged couple with a half-hearted wave of his hand and strolled over toward the porch railing.

The old Negress, rocking contentedly, had taken care of Sharon Mulcahy in her last hours. When the angels of death finally claimed his mother's soul, it was Virginia who stepped in to help Paddy through that difficult time in the typical way of a Negro "mammy."

Virginia was born on the estate of Thomas Jefferson at Monticello in Albemarle County, Virginia. As a young woman she was the personal attendant of Thomas Jefferson's daughter. During his tenure of office as President, Aunt Virginia lived at the White House and, at the completion of his term, returned to Monticello with the Jefferson family. She was present at Jefferson's bedside at the time of his death on July 4, 1826, and helped prepare his body for burial. Shortly thereafter, she was granted her freedom by Jefferson's daughters. At the time of her marriage to Peter Marks, the President's daughters outfitted her and the ceremony was performed in the parlor of the Jefferson home.

Her husband, Peter Marks, was born in Westmoreland County, Virginia, on the plantation of James Monroe, the fifth President of the United States. Peter attended Monroe in the capacity of body servant and lived at the White House during Mr. Monroe's tenure of office. One of Monroe's final acts before his death on July 4, 1831, was to make Peter Marks a free man.

Aunt Virginia stopped her rocking and leaned forward inquisitively. "What's ailin' you, chile? I declare, you don't look like yoreself, wearin' a pore frown like that."

Paddy painfully related his rejection at the recruiting station at the hands of Dr. Leake.

"Well, good for him," the Negress retorted when he finished. "Pains me to see all those fine young boys of town marchin' off to war. No 'mount o' shootin' and killin' is gwine to help a field Nigra one jot or tittle. No, suh. De Lawd will bring judgment on Pharaoh when and how He sees fit."

Paddy elevated one of his dusty shoes onto a warped porch step and leaned over to tie a shoelace. "I don't think you understand, Aunty. This war's to preserve the Union. No state or group of states can use interposition and nullification against a national law."

He plucked a honeysuckle blossom from an overhanging vine and sucked on the sweet nectar. Licking the stickiness from his lips, he said, "That point was settled when the Articles of Confederation were rubbished seventy-five years ago."

Uncle Peter stifled a toothy grin as he stroked his gray woolly beard with dry, brown, bony hands and turned to his wife. "'Pears lak our little president has a mind and doctrine all his own. Jist lak old Massa Monroe."

"Don't you be teasin' mah boy," his wife scolded. "Cain't you see his pore heart is near broken? Sides, does a body good to hear young folk agrowin' up with nobility sproutin' on their tongue." She lifted herself from the rocker. "Come in the house, chile, whilst I fix you some jelly cake."

"Not today, Aunty. Thank you just the same. I just feel like walking."

"Well, I do declare. Ain't never seen you so het up a piece of mah jelly cake couldn't wring a smile from your face." She looked perplexed. "Calcalate you menfolk are all about the same," she drawled. "Member Massa Jefferson ridin' off cross-country all by hisself when things warn't goin' jist right." Her dark eyes flashed. "You be sure to come by tomorrow when you feel more like talkin', you heah?"

"I hear."

Paddy snapped off another blossom from the honeysuckle vine and, placing it in the gap between his upper front teeth, continued on his way.

Other citizens were also experiencing depressing gloom. In the spacious Ring Barn at Darrah and Fillmore streets, Porgy O' Brien sat hunched and silent on the top seat of a gaily-painted circus wagon. A short, plump, bald-headed Irishman, he was owner and ringmaster of the famous circus which bore his name. Over the years he had made Frankford a winter training center for his new acts. Every year when spring arrived there were always a few young boys who disappeared from town only to reappear in late fall when the circus returned to winter quarters.

Paddy was tempted to follow the sawdust trail as a bareback rider, but that dream collapsed after his father's threats to do bodily harm to O'Brien should his son vanish from the village at the same time as the circus.

During the long winter months the Ring Barn was an ideal loafing place for men and boys alike; a place where they could sit for hours and watch rehearsals-the Lervanda family troupe from Cuba; Mollie Brown, the first woman rider to turn somersaults on horseback and countless others. George Adams, a world-acclaimed clown, was the favorite. He took a shine to Barney Williams at their first meeting because of Barney's gift to amuse and his rare sense of humor. Adams worked hard with Barney to develop his talent and "Rubber-face" Williams became an apt pupil.

Paddy walked slowly toward the colored carts and gilded wagons circling the Ring Barn. The acidic odor of manure and sawdust hung heavily in the hot, humid air. A lion paced restlessly back and forth in its cage and roared in short bursts at Paddy's approach. The rumbling roars shook the bulb-shaped owner out of his stupor and he looked down from his perch atop the wagon.

Oh, so it's you, Mulcahy," O'Brien said dejectedly. "Sure'n I thought ye'd been ridin' off with the cavalry."

"So did I."

"Yer father."

"No, Doc Leake. Castor, Batt, and I-"

"Porgy, you should have seen it," George Adams chortled as he rounded the wagon from the other side. "The three of them sneaking into the recruiting hall and trying to volunteer, and with no whiskey to give them 'Dutch courage', either. Pink-cheeked boys in the tow of a sergeant from the cruddy regulars. What a background for a comedy routine."

"You saw us? Where were you?" Paddy asked.

"'Cross the street in Dan Thornton's tavern. Told the old skinflint I was going to enlist. After I had my fill of free drinks, I told him I'd changed my mind." The loose jointed clown doubled up with laughter and slapped his knees. "You should've seen the expression on Dan's face. What an act it'll make."

Still despondent, O'Brien said, "I'm afraid there'll be no more comedy routines for quite a spell." Placing his head in his hands, he continued. "I bring the LaRue family acrobats all the way over here from the Continent and one week before we take to the road, some knuckle-headed Southerner decides to shoot the flag off a dirty old fort I've never heard of. Now, poof, nobody's interested in circuses anymore. The financial loss'll ruin me."

"Cheer up," Adams boomed. "We'll be filling dates inside a month. Way things are shapin' up, from what I hear, our boys'll whip them Rebs within the next sixty days. Don't worry, we'll be back in business by June."

"Sure'n I wish I could believe it," O'Brien wailed. Easing himself down from the wagon seat, he placed a hand on Paddy's shoulder. "How 'bout doing a favor for an old friend?"

"Sure, Porgy. What is it?"

"Exercise them Percherons over there in the ring for me. Would ye do that?"

"Be glad to. It'll take my mind off things."

* * * * * * *

The months passed slowly. April had scented the air with hyacinths, daffodils and tulips. Apple blossoms, lilacs and the delicate sweetness of peonies embellished May. May gave way to delightful June and hollyhocks flowered at every picket fence. The warm weather nurtured beds of pansies and geraniums at every stoop. A jolt to the tranquillity, Ab Howarth's body was returned from Virginia and buried in North Cedar Hill Cemetery.

Silent witnesses to peace, the gray-garbed Quakers moved quietly along the streets, or stopped to chat now and then with neighbors. Other than the occasional passing of a wagon or carriage, the only sounds to be heard were the humming of bees, the drumming of locusts and the twitter of birds. The entire village took on the summer look of a picturesque print by Currier and Ives. When night descended, wrought iron street lamps cast pale yellow rays from the glass boxes suspended by goosenecks, a lonely vigil for the young men who had marched away. It was at night, more than any other time, that Paddy's thoughts drifted to his friends enjoying camp life along the Potomac.

There had been no major engagement between the gathering forces of the North and South; only talk and more talk. Many in the North were beginning to denounce Lincoln for the way he was conducting the affairs of state. He had not reconvened the Congress, being content to direct the war himself without the aid of the legislative branch of the government. The size of the army and navy were increased without legislative approval. In Frankford, angry voices rose in opposition to the way he was increasing the national debt and spending huge sums of money without congressional authority. "Unconstitutional," they cried. Talk of impeachment hung in the air.

From his enemies in the South came a never-ending stream of abuse. Also coming in for a share of the Southern abuse was General Winfield Scott, hero of the war with Mexico. A Virginian by birth, the old man had remained loyal to the Union, serving as General-in-Chief of the Northern troops.

Paddy picked up a copy of the Richmond Examiner which Colonel Burns left earlier in the day for Joseph Mulcahy to read. His eyes drifted once more over the glaring editorial on the front page:

"The capture of Washington is perfectly within the power of Virginia and Maryland, if Virginia will make the effort by her constituted authority. Nor is there a moment to lose. The entire population pants for the onset...From the mountain tops and valleys to the shores of the sea, there is one wild shout of fierce resolve to capture Washington City, no matter what the hazard. That filthy cage of unclean birds will most assuredly be purified by fire.

"It is not to be endured that this flight of abolition harpies shall come down from the black North for their roots in the heart of the South, to defile and brutalize the land. Our people can take it, they will take it, and Scott, the arch traitor, and Lincoln combined, cannot prevent it. The just indignation of an outraged and deeply injured people will teach the Illinois Ape to repeat his race and retrace his journey across the borders of the free Negro states more rapidly than he came; at the same time, traitor Scott will be given the opportunity to try the difference between his tactics, the shanghai drill for quick movements, and Lincoln's.

"Cleansing and purification are needed and will be given to that festering sink of iniquity—-that wallow of Lincoln and Scott-the desecrated city of Washington; and many indeed will be the carcasses of dogs and caitiffs that will blacken the air on the gallows before the work is accomplished. Let it be."

Paddy folded the newspaper and laid it aside. In the distance he could hear the sound of trumpets. He stood up quickly and rushed into the street where a regiment of cavalry, moving from Trenton to Philadelphia, appeared over the crest of the hill at Harrison Street.

He shaded his eyes for a better view. Mounted on spirited horses were fine-looking young men wearing light blue capes and hoods lined with bright yellow silk, the yellow part thrown back over the shoulder.

Paddy raised a hand in salute as the proud troopers swept by. Several of the horsemen, their faces radiant, acknowledged the recognition with a brisk salute. When the men disappeared from sight, Paddy turned and shuffled slowly back into the hot blacksmith shop. Feeling his father's gaze upon him, he forced a half smile.

"The yellow capes kinda made those fellas look like butterflies, didn't you think?"

Joseph Mulcahy dealt his anvil a smashing blow with the hammer to hide the anguish he felt over what he knew to be his son's deepest desire.

Across the street on the front porch of the Jolly Post, Jim Ryen was experiencing another form of personal misery. The fast-flowing tide of time and events had left him wallowing in its wake. His tales of the Revolution and the "old days" went begging; he could no longer command an audience. People were just not interested anymore. The younger boys of the village turned to the fresh, new heroes of the day. As a result, the aged veteran of the Battle of Yorktown had been seen more and more in the company of Peter Craig, Frankford's oldest resident.

At the remarkable age of 103, the former slave was still able to maneuver around town with amazing vigor and vitality. His accomplished gifts of easy conversation and amazing memory made him a favorite of old and young alike.

In mid-June, the two old cronies were seated as usual in the cool shade provided for them by the vine-covered porch of the Jolly Post. Ryen fanned himself with one hand and beat off a troublesome fly with the other as he nodded drowsily. "Here come more soldiers, Peter. Wonder what those fellas want?"

"Calculate we'll soon find out," the tall Negro said, leaning forward. He squinted from under white, arched eyebrows. "'Pears as if they're going to stop."

Two uniformed horsemen, both carrying rolled posters under their arms, dismounted at the hitching rail.

"Howdy, neighbors," Ryen croaked cheerfully. "What can we do for ye?"

"You the owner here?" a soldier asked gruffly.

Ryen rolled his eyes. "Could be. What's on yer mind?"

"We'd like to post some recruitment bills if you don't object," the other man said pleasantly.

"Don't mind at all, sonny. Ye go right ahead. Always willin' to help the army." He laid his fan to one side. "I'm an old army man myself, you know. Fought at Yorktown-"

"Slap one on each side of the doorway, Rufe," the first soldier barked. "The senator'll want them bills where everyone can see them."

Stung by the abrupt rebuff, but undaunted, Ryen rose from his rocker and shuffled forward to examine one of the posters. "Say, ain't you fellas making some kind of mistake? Those posters call for men to enlist in a Californy regiment. This here's the state of Pennsylvany."

"There ain't no mistake. This here's Senator Baker's way of doing things. If he wants to recruit a California regiment in Pennsylvania, that's what he'll do." He turned swiftly on his heel. "Come on, Rufe, shake a leg. We gotta get all these up before his honor arrives in town."

"Ye mean a real, genwine, bona-fidy United States Senator is comin' here?" Ryen asked, startled.

"That's right," the second soldier replied. "Stick around, you'll enjoy meeting the matchless orator from Oregon."

Ryen screwed up his face. "Oregon? Jist a minute ago ye said he was from Californy."

The young soldier smiled as he remounted his horse. "Said no such thing. All we said was that Senator Baker was comin' here to raise California troops. If you get to meet his honor you 'll soon discover what we mean."

The two couriers rode off at a gallop, leaving Jim and Peter scratching their heads.

It was late that afternoon when two impressive- looking officers arrived at the Jolly Post and passed inside.

Across the street, Joseph Mulcahy prepared to close for the day. He removed his leather apron and hung it on a peg. "You might as well go on over and order dinner, son," he said wearily. "I'll be along shortly."

Paddy unbent himself and stretched his aching back muscles. Washing his hands and wiping the grime from his face, he slipped on a clean shirt, kicked off his work shoes, and strolled leisurely across Main Street to the Jolly Post, pausing momentarily to study the recently posted handbills on each side of the doorway before entering the building.

"Evenin', Paddy," Mary Coates called pleasantly from the far end of the hallway. She was a portly woman with a sunny disposition.

"Evenin', Mary. What's good for supper?"

"Roast lamb, boiled potatoes and peas," the proprietor's wife replied excitedly. She came closer. "Do you know who we have with us this evening?"

"No, who?"

"Senator Baker of Oregon. I understand he's Lincoln's closest friend."

"Jeepers. I've read about him in the papers. Senator Baker, huh?" He peeked into the oak-paneled dining room, his inquisitive eyes falling upon two officers who were sitting together at a table. "Is that him, the gray-haired one?"

"Yes. Certainly is a distinguished-looking gentleman, isn't he? Why don't you sit at a table nearby. Maybe you will get a chance to meet him."

"That would be bully. Never met a senator before." He lowered his voice. "Seat me up close, will you."

Moving with self-conscious awkwardness and stumbling over a chair at one point, Paddy sat down at a table facing the two men. His attention was immediately drawn to the young officer sitting with the Senator. There was something extremely fascinating in the makeup of the man who appeared to be in his early thirties. His hawk-eyed, keen, perceptive face bore a warlike drooping mustache and a spade beard at the chin. The most prominent feature of his handsome face was a straight, powerful-looking nose, as finely chiseled as the prow of a clipper ship. His hair and beard were raven black. Sensing Paddy's level gaze, the officer nodded in the boy's direction. At that moment, two men in civilian dress entered the dining hall and looked for a place to sit. Paddy noticed one of them stiffen.

"By all that's holy," he exclaimed as he walked toward the table where the two officers were conversing. "I say, aren't thee Isaac Wistar? Haverford College? Class of forty-three?"

The officer rose from his chair, his tall, lean frame lithe and wiry. There was a look of recognition in his deep-set, dark eyes.

"Yes, I'm Wistar. And you're Jim Levick. Did you think I may have forgotten? How are you, Jim?"

"Just fine, thank thee, Isaac."

They shook hands.

"Isn't that Bill Stroud with you?" Wistar inquired genially.

"Certainly is. Bill, it's Isaac Wistar."

The other civilian made a move from the doorway and, again, there was a moment of reunion between old acquaintances.

"Bill, Jim," Wistar interjected, "I'd like you to meet my good friend, Senator Edward Baker of Oregon."

The Senator fairly sprang from his chair, the epitome of duty consciousness.

He was a robust individual possessing the well-fed look of a successful politician. A close friend of Abraham Lincoln, he had been given the honor of introducing the new President to the crowd at the inauguration. Later, as Lincoln's chosen companion, he had ridden in the President's carriage at the head of the inaugural parade.

The Senator cleared his throat. "My pleasure, gentlemen, I assure you."

"Thy pleasure, indeed," Levick retorted. "Rather, our pleasure, Senator. I have read with abiding interest thy speeches delivered on the Senate floor. I was particularly attracted to the oration in which thee stated, 'I want sudden, bold, forward, determined war!'"

The Senator beamed with gratification. "Ah, yes. That was one of my most important speeches, the one in which I also said I do not think anybody can conduct war of that kind as successfully as a dictator. Won't you gentlemen join us?"

"We'd deem it a privilege, sir."

There was a scraping of chairs as the four men seated themselves.

Mary Coates placed Paddy's supper before him and gave his forearm a gentle squeeze. "This should give you something to talk about," she whispered. "Imagine, Senator Baker here, of all places."

"Tell me, gentlemen," Senator Baker spoke, "why it is you're not in uniform? The country is in dire need of every able-bodied man, you know. We have a big job to do. Isn't that so, Isaac?"

Colonel Wistar nodded with a touch of mock deference.

"We are members of the Society of Friends, sir," Levick replied. "Our faith forbids us to bear arms against our fellow man. But rest assured, we'll serve our country in the way we know best, as physicians."

"Wistar and I are both birthright Quakers, but that hasn't..."

"So, it's Doctor Levick and Doctor Stroud is it?" Wistar interceded adroitly. "Do you practice in these parts?"

"No, Friend Isaac. Our offices are located in the city."

"What brings you this way?"

"We're en route to Stroudsburg," Dr. Levick replied.

"Bill 's mother has been quite sick of late; thought we'd take a look at her case."

"Yes, would that thee could travel with us, Friend Isaac," Doctor Stroud broke in. "It's our plan to spend the night with another old friend from school, William Hilles."

"Hilles? Where's he living?"

"Attleboro. In case thee hadn't heard, he and Sarah Allen were married several years ago." The doctor paused significantly. "Thee remember her, of course?"

There was a decided trace of innuendo in the doctor's last question, causing Senator Baker to arch his eyebrows. "So that's it, eh, Wistar? A woman. I've often wondered what drove an aristocratic Easterner like yourself to come West as an Indian fighter and trapper for seven years."

The Colonel's face colored, and he remained uncomfortably silent.

"Indian fighter!" the Quaker physicians exclaimed in unison. "Thee, Isaac?"

"Yes, gentlemen," Senator Baker replied swiftly. From a vest pocket he withdrew an elk's tooth which was fastened to one end of a gold chain and began twirling it about his forefinger. "Isaac here was one of the most noted prospectors, trappers and Indian fighters known throughout the mid and far West."

"All right, Senator. That will be enough," Wistar cautioned.

"Enough, indeed." Senator Baker thrust the elk's tooth into the faces of the astounded physicians. "Why, this man's story is a saga that should be put down for everyone to read. When he first started reading law under me in San Francisco, after having knocked about in the wilderness for seven years, he was more like a wild animal than a man. Do you remember the San Francisco insurrection which took place in fifty-six? Well, it was Wistar here who quelled that insurrection almost single-handedly."

"Senator..."

With a grandiloquent wave of his hand, Baker brushed aside Wistar's protest and continued speaking. "With only six armed deputies to back him up, Isaac faced the entire armed mob which came to storm the arsenal on the Bay. Yes, gentlemen, the store of arms and ammunition at Benicia was saved from the hands of the San Francisco mob that day because of Wistar's courage and method of handling the situation."

The Senator paused. "If Major General William T. Sherman, who was supposed to be in command of the 'Frisco militia, hadn't been so indecisively weak and vacillating, the insurrection never would have gained such dangerous proportions. Sherman's hesitation and inactivity in the matter were understandable, it stemmed from one important thing." Baker snorted disdainfully. "For a while, it looked as if the insurrectionists would win. Sherman, a prominent bank president, was just plain scared his business would suffer as the result of any action on his part to put the insurrectionists down. Well, he lost our account, anyway. We withdrew our money from the Lucas and Turner bank after that mess, didn't we, Wistar?"

"Yes, Senator, we did."

"Thee are now of the legal profession, Friend Isaac?" Dr. Levick inquired.

"Yes, I'm..."

His reply was cut off as Senator Baker continued. "After Wistar passed his bar, we formed a partnership. I dare say ours was the foremost legal firm in San Francisco." He raised a hand for emphasis. "While it may have been my influence which held California against secession, it was Wistar and his six deputies who courageously stood off the insurrectionist's bold attempts to capture the state that fateful day."

"To answer your question, Jim," Colonel Wistar broke in firmly, "Yes, I'm practicing law. I returned to Philadelphia in fifty-eight and opened my own office."

"Thee have been back here three years? A wonder we haven't met sooner."

"With all this history of violence," Doctor Stroud rejoined, "it sounds as if thee have relinquished thy Quaker faith. What has thy conscience said to thee about the matter?"

Colonel Wistar bristled. "You should remember my thoughts on that subject from our days at Westtown and Haverford. I've never sanctioned the negative virtues of sinless prigs who've no higher ideals than the mere prattling of pious platitudes, probably the main reason I left home and went West."

Senator Baker's eyes began twitching. "Come now, Isaac I didn't mean to..."

"Let me finish," Wistar commanded. "Virtue's good, but like other good things, is better conquered than inherited. When it proceeds without effort from mere vacuity of mind, it possesses less moral and intellectual value than a smaller measure conquered by the efforts of more generous, but erring souls."

Doctor Stroud's delicate features turned crimson. "I had no idea thee felt so strongly..."

"Come now, gentlemen," Baker interrupted. "Let's not get ourselves entangled in any theological discussions. As a matter of interest, though, I might say my parents were also Quakers who migrated to this country from England. Father took up teaching in Philadelphia." He stroked his chin reflectively. "Let's see now, Wistar, where was that weaving mill in which I worked as a young man? Oh, yes, I remember, Eleventh and Christian streets. Yes indeed, that's where it was, Eleventh and Christian. When I was nineteen we moved to Illinois where, if you will permit me to say so, my career ran parallel to that of my close friend, yet often times opponent, Abraham Lincoln."

"Excuse me for interrupting, Senator," Doctor Levick broke in, "but wasn't Lincoln's firstborn son named after thee? I've heard it said so."

"That's correct. Because of our close friendship, he named his first son Edward Baker Lincoln. Everyone called the boy, 'Ned.' It was a terrible blow that he died so young. Shortly thereafter, I moved to California. I was about Wistar's age at that time."

"How is it that thee have come to represent the state of Oregon in the senate and not California?" Doctor Stroud asked.

"Harrumph." Baker shoved the elk's tooth into his vest pocket and set his jaw. "It was an unpopular position we took, Wistar and I, against the insurrectionists who were predominant in San Francisco at that time. Because of our opposition, our law practice suffered after the insurrection was put down. Wistar decided to return home to Philadelphia, and not long after that a golden opportunity presented itself in Oregon, an opportunity to run for senator of that state. I decided to make the move which has proven to be providential, not only for me, but for my old friend, Lincoln, as well."

"What are thy plans now, Senator?" Doctor Stroud inquired. "I see thee are in uniform."

Baker preened the ornate epaulets, signifying the rank of colonel, which hung from his shoulders. "A number of citizens from the Pacific coast, now living in Washington, have recently urged me to form a regiment here in the East which will be accredited to the distant state of California. I'm resigning my position in the senate to recruit and lead this California regiment into the field." He paused to stroke his chin. "Wistar has taken leave of his law practice to assist me. I might say that, altogether, we hope to raise more than just one California regiment right here in Philadelphia and surrounding towns."

The two physicians exchanged glances.

"Thee mean to say," Doctor Levick replied, "that thee are confident of enlisting several thousand men from this vicinity to fight under the banner of California?"

"Precisely . This area is stocked with descendants of Cromwell's Roundheads. The finest material available anywhere from which courageous and intelligent soldiers can be molded, a proven fact during the revolution. I say they will fight for the nation regardless of the state emblem under which they enlist."

The Senator's gaze fell on Paddy whose rapt attention was hanging on every word. "To prove my point, I venture to say the lad sitting over there would make a likely volunteer for the first California regiment. What do you say, young man?" he called in a strong voice. "Would you be willing to fight in a California regiment under Colonel Wistar and me?"

"I'll be doin' all the talking that's required of the lad," an angry voice spoke from the doorway.

Unaware of his father's arrival, Paddy stiffened and turned his head sideways as Joseph Mulcahy approached the table.

The blacksmith leveled a leathery finger at Senator Baker. "I'm going to tell ye just like I've told everybody else. No son o' mine's going to get himself killed pulling chestnuts out o' the fire for you loud-mouthed politicians who seek political capital for yerselves. Let them who brought on this war by gratifying sectional fanaticism and class jealousies, let them do the fightin' . They're the men you want, Senator, not my boy."

Paddy shifted uncomfortably in his seat. From the corner of one eye he saw the tall ex-Indian fighter rise slowly and advance toward Joseph Mulcahy. Wistar extended a hand. "Allow me to introduce myself, sir. I'm Colonel Isaac Wistar."

The blacksmith took the outstretched hand and was pleased with the firm grip. "Good day, Colonel. My name's Mulcahy. That's my son, Paddy."

Officer and boy exchanged nods. The Colonel focused his attention on the elder. "My compliments on your positive and forthright expression of conscience, Mulcahy." He paused and cast a sidelong glance at his circle of friends. "Although Senator Baker and I are good friends," he continued, "we are at opposite poles in our thinking. The Senator believes, or thinks he believes, in all the American theories dealing with the infinite wisdom of ignorant individuals, however mercenary and degraded, provided that they're collected in noisy masses to vote. Perhaps that explains why he has drifted from the Whigs to the Republicans." A wry smile crossed his face. "I do not believe the mathematical absurdity that a thousand fools collected in a mob are capable of emitting wisdom, learning and judgment."

Stroking an earlobe between his thumb and forefinger, he continued. "Let me say, Mulcahy, there are those who, never having had a difficult or complicated decision to make, expect all men to be forever cocked, primed and ready for mental emergencies. Recently I've been accused by newspaper patriots, ignorant of all issues but their own, of being in doubt as to which side to take in this fight."

Focusing his gaze through slit eyes, the Colonel continued. "My state was about to take one side, Mulcahy, my personal friends, or most of them, the other. My oldest and best friends are Southerners. They counted me as one of themselves, sure that I would be in service on their side. They'd even gone so far as to provide me with a place of rank in their army. Yet, when my native state called for defense, I found I could not and ought not evade the struggle. The days of recrimination and discussion are over, and this useless war was commenced. In the prime of youth and vigor I owed a duty somewhere. To whom? Not to the federal government whose partisan usurpations and sectional mismanagement have goaded resistance, still less to the South where my only tie is sympathy and friendship for individuals, which does not justify taking up arms against my native state to whose allegiance I was born and reared." The Colonel folded lean, muscular arms across his chest. "There was but one answer. I must align myself on the side of Pennsylvania against all her enemies wherever the march leads."

Joseph Mulcahy stared directly into Wistar's eyes and let them drop. "The boy's all I have left," he murmured. "Carefree lad, not yet seventeen."

"By your leave then, sir." Wistar turned and strode back to his table.

Like a raging bull suddenly tamed, the blacksmith heaved a deep sigh. After a moment of silence, he surveyed his son and finally spoke with a catch in his voice. "I leave it with ye, Paddy. If it be yer wish to serve with this Wistar fellow, I'll no longer be standin' in the way." His eyes misted with tears.

Rising slowly from his chair, Paddy walked to his father, touched his gnarled hands lightly, then turned to the two officers. "When and where do I sign up, sirs?"

Senator Baker leaped to his feet. "Bully for you, my boy. Your fellow townsman, Joe Williams, will begin recruiting at the Odd Fellows Hall first thing in the morning. By the way, Wistar, where are those authorization papers I had? Wilkins will be needing them tomorrow."

"His name is Williams, Senator."

"Oh, yes, to be sure...Williams." Baker fumbled among a mass of papers, some of which were stored in his hat, others about his person. "That's odd, should have them here someplace." He shot a wary glance at Joseph Mulcahy. "Received authority from Abe Lincoln personally, you know. Fine man, our President."

"Come along, son. The Senator'll find what he's looking for in the morning."

Paddy followed his father outside. "Sure like the cut of that Colonel Wistar's jib, don't you, Pa?"

"Aye, son, he's the only reason I'm letting ye go. As for that other buffoon, I hope the powers that be will keep him cooped up in Washington. He'll do less harm as a senator." The blacksmith shook his head. "A strong, generous person he might be, but an erratic character if I ever saw one."

Early the next morning, Paddy roused his two close companions, Batt and Castor, and gave them a recount of his meeting with Colonel Wistar and Senator Baker. Finishing a hasty breakfast in the Castor family kitchen, the three started for the recruiting station at a dogtrot. A barrage of questions fell on Paddy's ear as he led the way into the center of town.

"You really got 'heft' with this Senator?" Billy Batt asked.

"Said so, didn't I?"

"Well, for our sake I sure hope so," Castor said with excitement. "You say Joe Williams is in charge?"

Paddy nodded and cocked his head. The sound of martial music from a fife and drum corps, services which had been paid for by Colonel Wistar, could be heard in the distance. At the recruiting hall, boys were milling around in boisterous groups with grim-faced elders watching.

"Look," Castor said, pointing. "Joe Williams is taking no chances on making a poor showing in his recruiting effort. He has three brothers in line and three cousins."

"Yes, and wouldn't you know," Bill Batt said with a snicker, "there's 'Rubber-Face' Barney at the very head."

Paddy scanned the faces of others in the queue and recognized several who had been turned away from earlier enlistment in the 'three-months' regiments because they had been either too young or too late applying.

"Look at all the other brothers waiting in line," Castor rejoined. "There's the Stotts, the Hafers and the Smith twins with their oldest brother, Dick."

Paddy waved a greeting to Isaac Tibben who was standing with George Hart and Tom Pilling.

"Come on," Castor said impatiently, "let's latch onto the end of the line before it's too late."

The three fell quickly into place behind John Lightfoot, Sam Barwis and Dave Chipman. Within four hours, under the efficient procedure of Joe Williams and the close supervision of Colonel Wistar, one hundred forty-seven recruits had enlisted in the First California Regiment for a three-year term of service in the Union Army.

Events moved swiftly. Late that same afternoon the company marched from Frankford to the Broad and Prime Street Station where a train was waiting to take them to Suffolk Park on the Darby Road between Philadelphia and Wilmington. At Suffolk Park they were quickly integrated with five other companies already in training. Following a paltry supper, each man was issued one blanket and a ground cloth on which to sleep. That night the sound of the bugle worked its effect on the raw recruits for the first time. Night descended and the young initiates fell asleep beneath the watchful eyes of a thousand stars shining in the firmament.

Early the next day the camp was aroused and the routine of army life began. The most promising individuals among the group were hastily selected as non-commissioned officers and training began in earnest. For one week the volunteers practiced marching army style, twenty-eight inches to the step. Since uniforms were not available, the recruits dressed in civilian clothes of every kind and color. Fence posts split and cut into short pieces were substituted for muskets.

A few condemned muskets were utilized by alternating squads of non-commissioned officers who practiced the manual of arms in preparation for instructing the men in their use when muskets became available.

Toward the end of the second week an announcement was made which caused excitement to run through the camp. Billy Batt and Chirp Castor had just finished their noon day meal and were cleaning their utensils when Paddy rushed over to them. He grabbed them by the arms. "Boy, is there a big surprise in store for you fellows. Come with me."

"Come where? What's up?"

"A company of Zouaves are being added to the regiment. They're supposed to arrive any minute."

"So what," Castor retorted. "I have to clean my shingle."

"Wait a minute, did you say Zouaves?" Batt dropped his tin plate. "It wouldn't be my brother's outfit by any chance, would it?"

"How would I know?" Paddy replied with a twinkle in his eyes.

From a distance they heard the sound of approaching drums.

"Here they come, better tag along." Paddy turned and raced toward the parade ground. Castor and Batt dropped their dinnerware and followed.

A company of Zouaves, made up of members from the various fire companies around Philadelphia, marched onto the field. They were dressed nattily in light blue, wide-cut pants with red stripes running down the sides. White leggings confined the lower part of the pants, creating a pantaloon effect. Red cutaway jackets displayed rows of bright bell buttons with only the one at the top buttoned. The shirts were a pale yellow with the name of their fire company embroidered on the bosom. Set squarely on their heads, regulation kepis of dark blue gave them the appearance of professional soldiers as they swung by in review before the awed recruits. Drummers sounded a lively cadence. Flaring their sticks rhythmically on rosewood drums, the strength of their strokes alternated between loud and soft to the snappy beat of *Daddy-Mammy, Daddy-Mammy*.

Short and peppery Lieutenant Frank Hibbs barked commands. "Company halt. One. Two."

The first company of troops to leave Frankford as three month volunteers stopped in their tracks.

"Right face. Present arms." The bell-like commands rang out loud and clear on the warm summer air.

Chirp and Billy watched mesmerized as their older brothers executed the drill with the military precision of a cadet. An accompanying fife and drum corps brought the review to a close with the toe-tapping strains of *The Girl I Left Behind Me*. With the breaking of ranks, brothers and friends rushed madly toward each other.

"Hey, Joe! Henry! Over here!" Chirp yelled.

Henry Castor shoved a kepi to the back of his head and exclaimed, "Saints preserve us! What are you pups doing here?"

"Paddy has 'heft' with Senator Baker," Billy explained. "That's how come."

"Baker?" Henry Castor looked at Joe. "Isn't he the 'heavy' who had us shipped here?"

"Yes, he's the one who's 'big military' in Lincoln's eye, or so he says." Joe Batt studied the surrounding troops. "This sure is a ragtag-looking bunch. I thought we were being sent to join something special."

"Maybe that's why you older fellas were sent here," Bill Batt injected plaintively, "to make us into something special."

Joe Batt ruffled his brother's hair. "Sorry, kid, I didn't mean anything by that. Of course we're going to make you something special."

During the ensuing days, the tempo of elementary drill picked up considerably under the guidance and direction of the older and more experienced Zouaves. There was additional cause for celebration when, on the Fourth of July, the long-awaited uniforms were finally issued to the new recruits.

With loud whooping and yelling the overjoyed volunteers discarded civilian clothes for the regulation blue flannel blouse, light sky-blue kersey trousers and straight cut, single-breasted, dark blue coat of the regular service. Glistening black waist belts and shoulder straps were slipped into place with pride. Brass buttons embellished with miniature eagles and a large oval belt buckle boldly inscribed with the impressive letters, U.S., were unmistakable signs of authority which left a sobering imprint on the mind of each proud owner. The crowning moment of glory came with the placement of dish-topped kepis with black leather visors upon the head.

Filled with genuine admiration at the change which had been wrought in his appearance and that of his friends, Chirp Castor shouted gleefully, "By jingo, we're honest-to-goodness soldiers now, no mistake about it."

"'Cept for one thing," Paddy replied. He turned to Lieutenant Williams. "Hey, Joe, when do we get the guns that go with these outfits?"

Batt looked askance at Paddy's brazen disregard for rank.

Joe Williams, tall and patrician, approached Paddy. "From now on it will be Lieutenant Williams," he admonished gently. "You'll make things a lot easier for me if you'll just remember that." He turned to include the group standing nearby. "All of us here have come from the same small town," he added, "but for operational and organizational purposes it will be necessary that intimacies be disregarded for a while."

Stretching his rubbery face into an apish contortion, Barney Williams mimicked his brother's last remark, to the amusement of those around him.

"I don't cotton to going 'heavy military' on you," Lieutenant Williams continued apologetically, "but I think you understand the circumstances."

Paddy's hand flew to the visor of his kepi in an open-palmed salute. "Yes, sir, Lieutenant."

A smile crossed the officer's sunburned face, creasing the crow's-foot wrinkles at the corners of his eyes. "As to those muskets you were asking about, we will be leaving for Fortress Monroe any day and you will be issued arms there."

"How soon did you say we were leaving, Lieutenant?" Chirp inquired.

"As soon as the ten companies arrive from Fort Schuyler, New York."

"New York!" Dave Chipman blurted. "I thought this was to be a regiment made up of Philadelphians only."

"It will be. The men who are joining us were recruited in and around Philadelphia, but were sent to New York for muster."

"Sure sounds like a roundabout way of doing things." Tom Pilling muttered. "Philadelphia to New York to Philadelphia."

"Like looking up your butt to see if your hat is on straight," Barney Williams cut in with a smirk.

Lieutenant Williams flashed his brother a look of reproof. "The Senator can be erratic at times," he said in a monotone.

Three days later, on a Sunday, Baker's 1st California Regiment was visited by Reverend Murphy, Father McGovern and other dignitaries from Frankford.

The ten companies from Fort Schuyler arrived in camp late that afternoon. Dressed in Confederate uniforms, they caused quite a stir until it was learned that Senator Baker had confiscated the gray uniforms in New York, where they had been awaiting shipment to a Confederate artillery regiment. En route, the ten companies had marched through Philadelphia. Because they carried the flag, 1st California Regiment, the unsuspecting populace of their native city welcomed them with wild acclaim, supposing them to be actual volunteers from the far-off state of California. The case of mistaken identity brought about rumblings of discontent from the troops involved.

Within twenty-four hours, the fully assembled regiment was ready for movement. The sixteen companies were organized into two battalions of eight hundred men each, Majors R. A. Parrish and Charles W. Smith each commanding a battalion. At noon, on the ninth of July, the regiment boarded the train for Fortress Monroe.

The troop train, yellow passenger cars trimmed in dark red, was soon loaded to the brim with the pushing, shoving crowd of excited soldiers. Those who could, thrust their heads through open windows for a breath of fresh air. When everything was ready, Colonel Wistar signaled the engineer and the train began moving slowly, then more rapidly as it attained the maximum speed of fifteen miles per hour.

Arriving at Fortress Monroe on July tenth, each man was issued a musket upon disembarking and the regiment was marched into bivouac. After several days of instruction in the use of firearms, the regiment was marched a few miles beyond Fortress Monroe to Hampton where it was assigned a position to picket an extended front.

Senator Baker, whose duties in the Senate had hitherto occupied most of his attention, now camped with his regiment in the field as their commander for the first time. A daily routine of constant drill, marching, guard and picket duty, and such other instruction as was necessary for actual field work, occupied the soldier's time twenty-four hours a day.

Whether by accident or design, the post of orderly to Colonel Wistar fell to Paddy Mulcahy, although there were some disconsolates who claimed it was more "heft" than accident. If there was any basis for that charge of favoritism, it did not evidence itself to Paddy. In addition to his consuming chores as Wistar's orderly, he was given notice to engage in bayonet practice and all the drills and devices required of the others. Late in the evening of July thirty-first, Paddy slowly dragged his weary body from the drill ground toward the regimental headquarters. Shrill notes of a bugle and shouts of soldiers cleaning up for mess floated on the hot, humid night air. Drawing near to the command tent, he caught sight of a dispatch carrier dashing away on horseback. He hastened to the tent flap, and could hear Colonel Wistar muttering inside.

"The panic is subsiding, indeed. I'll wager the politicians who expected to follow McDowell's improvised rabble into Richmond are still trying to recover their breath."

Wondering what it meant, Paddy entered the Sibley tent with a degree of apprehension.

Colonel Baker, appearing pale and limp, sat sprawled in a canvas camp chair, his arms dangling loosely over the sides, his eyes staring blankly at the roof of the tent.

Wistar, his fists clenched tightly, was standing tall and erect beside a camp table. His face wore the fiercest expression Paddy had ever seen.

"Private Mulcahy," Wistar barked savagely.

"Yes, sir?"

"You will inform the bugler I want 'general' sounded immediately."

"Yes, sir. Anything else, sir?"

"There is. We've just taken one helluva licking at a place called Bull Run. This regiment will move within one hour to the defense of Washington."

"Yes, sir!" Paddy saluted and bolted from the tent. The thrill of excitement surged through his body.

CHAPTER 4

The disastrous results of the battle of Bull Run, fought late in July, stuck as bitter gall in the craw of the North. Some measure of consolation was derived, however, from the fact that Washington had been saved as a result of Beauregard's failure to follow up his success at Manassas. Summer passed with no further major encounters between the opposing armies. Fall arrived. A delightful early autumn enveloped the Potomac The beautiful wooded heights were crowned with camps, the plains and fields with snow-white tents. Dust hung in lazy clouds over numerous drill grounds and winding roadways.

A change in command of the Potomac army had taken place. General McDowell, who had been defeated at Bull Run, was replaced by General George B. McClellan. Dubbed "Little Mac" by the rank and file, McClellan was a dapper young man who was rapidly becoming a storm center of controversy in his own right and as a commander. At the age of thirty-five, he was called upon by President Lincoln to undertake the tremendous task of building a volunteer army the like of which had never been seen on the American continent.

Under his watchful eye the First California Regiment from Philadelphia was strenuously drilled and disciplined in the martial art. They had also been called upon to construct Fort Ethan Allen on the western bank of the Potomac near the Chain Bridge.

Following a hard day's work on the fort, the Frankford volunteers of Company D were busily engaged with menial duties around their encampment. Chirp Castor squatted in front of his tent and worked laboriously to polish his smooth bore musket with wet wood ashes.

Perspiration dripped from his pink cheeks and trickled down his bare, hairless chest. He spoke in a low growl. "By jimmy, if I had known army life was anything like this, they would never had gotten me to sign up for three years. There's no sense to it. Get things clean just so you can dirty them up again." He gave his musket barrel a vigorous brush. "Make you hurry up with one job, just so they can make you stand around and wait for another. Getting so a fella doesn't have to worry about being killed in this war, exceptin' maybe by the food and boredom."

Bill Batt grinned. "We should have thought of that when we saw the flags flying and heard the bands playing back in June." He put down the bacon grease he had been using to polish his shoes. "It's too bad we're not older like Joe and Henry. Maybe we could have wrangled some of those two-day passes for a trip into Washington from time to time."

"And if we had Mulcahy's gift of malarkey we could sit around headquarters all day on our hunkers and boil coffee. What a snap." Castor held his musket up to the sunlight and gazed down the barrel. "And take them Quakers like John Walton, hiding at home behind their religion so they won't have to join the army. Pretty soft, I'd say."

Billy looked down at his shoes and resumed polishing. "Maybe if more people had the courage of their conviction like the Quakers, we wouldn't have wars. Besides, I'll wager John's wishing he could be with us."

"In a pig's eye, he is," Castor retorted.

"What are you fellas grousing about?" came a voice from behind.

Castor and Batt looked up sharply. "Hi, Paddy." Billy put his shoes in the tent, stood up, and stretched. "We were just talking. Anything of interest happening at headquarters?"

"What's it worth to you?" Paddy rubbed a thumb and index finger together.

"What's it...?" Castor sprang to his feet. "You're not going to hold back information on us for a price, are you? We're your friends, remember? Come on, what did you hear?"

"Well, for one thing, there's going to be a treat on the shingle tonight."

"What's it going to be? Pork and hardtack instead of hardtack and pork?"

"Nope, tonight we get beef and potatoes with white bread. And get a load of this--butter!"

"Butter!" Castor exploded. "You're kidding."

The Smith twins and George Hart bounded from their tents. "Did we hear somebody mention butter?"

"That's right," Batt responded. "Paddy here says-"

George Hart set his jaw. "I'll be obliged to cotton you, Mulcahy, if you're pulling our leg. We've been goin' at it hard today while you've been playing nursemaid at headquarters. There'd just better be butter on that shingle tonight. I'm in no mood to be made sport of."

"Paddy hasn't steered us wrong yet," Bob Smith put in, smiling at his friend.

Tom Pilling joined the group. "Well, I'm a gone sucker. Couldn't help but over hear the conversation, Paddy. What's up? Why the feast? The 'big military' getting ready to fatten us up for the kill?"

"That's it!" Castor shouted. He studied the expression on Paddy's face. "That's it, isn't it? We're going into battle."

"Didn't say so, did I? I can't be giving-"

"Who says we're going into battle?" Isaac Tibben called from across the company street. He leaped to his feet and ran toward the crowd gathering around Colonel Wistar's orderly. John Lightfoot, the Hafer brothers and 'Rubber-face' Williams crowded into the expanding circle.

"Come on, Mulcahy, spill it," Barney Williams clamored. "We won't let on to the Colonel that we know anything, honest."

The high-pitched voice of Dave Chipman rose above the hubbub "Squash it, here comes the lieutenant."

Joe Williams, lean and bronzed by the sun, shouldered his way through the crowd of fellow townsmen. "One of these days you're going to get shot for divulging military information, Mulcahy. Tell me, what choice morsel did you lift from the griddle this time?"

"I only told 'em what we're having for supper, Lieutenant. That's all."

Second Lieutenant Frank Hibbs, short and officious, moved into position beside Joe Williams. "Then where did that talk originate about us moving out?"

"Listen to that sawed-off shavetail," Barney Williams muttered. "He's nothing but a puppet who dances every time my brother pulls the string."

"I asked you a question, Private Mulcahy," Hibbs snapped. "Answer me."

"I don't know what you're talking about, sir. I never said anything about us packing up."

"Never mind, Frank," Lieutenant Williams interceded. "If Paddy says he knows nothing about it, then believe me, nobody does."

"Well, since that's the case," a mature voice broke in, "perhaps I may have the distinction of supplying you men with information for a change."

The men turned around as one at the sound of Captain Ritman's stern voice. The heavily-bearded veteran of the Mexican War advanced to within a few paces of where Paddy was standing and fixed a jaundiced eye upon him. He turned and addressed the men. "There will be a dress parade at four-thirty. General McClellan has come to review the regiment. You lads get busy with spit and polish. Hop to it."

He turned toward Paddy. "Have I overlooked anything, Private Mulcahy?" Old enough to have been Paddy's father, he winked good naturedly and walked off before Paddy could respond.

When the appointed hour rolled around, every bayonet and gun barrel in the regiment gleamed. The rays of the setting sun reflected brightly on polished brass buttons and buckles. Black leather belts and cartridge boxes were greased to a sheen. In response to the assembly call, the soldiers placed jaunty forage caps on their heads and formed quickly on the color line to the strains of *Hail Columbia* from the regimental band.

Field officers, their uniforms bedecked in gold braid, rode onto the parade ground, many of them swaying uncertainly, as if riding for the first time. Colonel Baker and his seconds sallied forth on horseback and took their position in front of the regiment. Filled with admiration, every eye in the ranks focused upon Lieutenant Colonel Wistar. The hawk-eyed warrior was arrayed in a new uniform. Gold braid and buttons sparkled on his short blue shell jacket. Girt with sash and sword, white-gloved and precise, he sat his mount grandly, his shining jackboots set firmly in the stirrups.

The sound of music stopped, whereupon Colonel Baker signaled the order to "present arms." In a thrilling display, McClellan, riding at the head of the largest staff and escort the young soldiers had ever seen, came cantering along the lines.

He wheeled his mount, returned, and posted himself in the center of the greensward.

As a salute to the General, the regiment executed the manual of arms, which it did with snap and precision while McClellan watched approvingly beneath his cap visor.

The drill completed, Colonel Baker rose in his stirrups and addressed the troops in a loud voice befitting one of his orations from the senate floor.

"Men, it is my privilege, and honor to introduce to you our gallant and courageous commander, General George B. McClellan."

An outburst of cheering and the tossing of caps in the air made McClellan beam with pleasure. He spurred his horse closer to the regimental line. Paddy scrutinized the General carefully as though sizing up a new boy in the neighborhood.

McClellan was a short man with a wiry, athletic physique. His handsome features were classically Scotch-Irish. His French style mustache and goatee gave him a dashing look. Well groomed black hair extended below his kepi in abundance.

He looked up and down the lines for several moments, then spoke in a clear, resonant voice. "It gives me particular pleasure," he said, "to greet you men from my native city of Philadelphia."

Loud cheering interrupted him. McClellan held up a hand. "I was thrilled," he continued, "when my good friend, Colonel Baker, informed me of the eager, totally unselfish manner in which you men sought enlistment in his command. We Philadelphians have been noted for our city of brotherly love, a distinction we are proud of and make every effort to live up to, but these are not peaceful days. We spring from the cradle of liberty, and, because of that fact, we should fight with all our might to preserve the Union which had its inception in our Independence Hall."

Loud huzza caused the General's high-spirited horse to rear skittishly. McClellan reined his mount and asked for silence. 'This is a splendid regiment," he continued, "as are your sister regiments from Philadelphia, the Sixty-ninth, Seventy-second, and the Hundred and Sixth of the Pennsylvania line."

He paused. "Through some misfortune you have been designated as a California regiment. That is a mistake. I like to see credit given where credit is due. Therefore," and he drew himself to full height, "from this moment on you shall be designated the Seventy-first Pennsylvania, brigaded with your three sister regiments from Philadelphia in what shall be known, henceforth, as the Philadelphia Brigade."

"Three cheers for Little Mac!" The call echoed down the regimental line. Caps were tossed into the air to the accompanying cheer, "Hip, hip, hurrah! Hip, hip...."

Paddy noticed Colonel Baker was livid and quivering with outrage, a man who had just been denied custody of his only child. The wild demonstration gradually subsided and McClellan held up his hand once more for silence.

A soft breeze rising from the Potomac fluttered the company guidons. Orange rays from the setting sun spotlighted foliage on the trees that cast uneven shadows. The long line of blue coated soldiers appeared as palings of a fence silhouetted upon the ground.

With order restored, McClellan raised his voice for a final remark. "Men, we've had our last defeat, and we have made our last retreat. I am confident when I say to you, the war will be short, sharp, and decisive." He saluted smartly, wheeled his horse and rode off with the accolades of the troops ringing in his ears.

The regiment was dismissed and the soldiers quickly moved into tight little groups to discuss the hidden meaning, if there was any, in the General's closing remark. As Paddy stood listening to the speculative conjecture, word came that he was wanted at regimental headquarters immediately.

Shouldering his musket, he crossed the parade grounds which now lay steeped in the shadows of enveloping darkness. Angry words from inside the headquarters tent caused him to halt outside. Colonel Baker was raging at the order which removed his First California Regiment from its anomalous position under direct control of the War Department and placed it on the roster of the State of Pennsylvania.

"McClellan won't get away with this!" Baker shouted. "It's a grave injustice to California. I'll lay this matter before the President. He gave me authority to form this regiment."

"Is it really worth all that trouble?" Paddy heard Wistar reply. "I see nothing wrong with the order. It's just a shame we've been given such a high number on the state roster, though it's unavoidable under the circumstances. Ours was the first three year regiment mustered in Pennsylvania. If it had not been for the absurd error in the original presidential order authorizing our formation, we would have received the first number following those of the disbanded militia regiments of three-month's service. We're entitled to that."

"You're upset because of the high number," Baker said bitterly. "Then you also repudiate my original intention of having California represented in the field." He stormed from the tent.

Paddy made certain that his expression betrayed nothing. He entered the tent and snapped to attention. Colonel Wistar sat erect at the table and removed his white gauntlets. "At ease, Mulcahy." He handed him an oilskin packet. "You will deliver these dispatches to Colonel Baxter at headquarters of the Seventy-second. You are to deliver them personally. Give them to no one else." He handed Paddy a second packet. "Deliver these orders to Colonel Owens at headquarters of the Sixty-ninth. Have I made myself clear?"

"Yes, sir. Will that be all, sir?"

"No, one more thing. We have a long day ahead of us tomorrow. I would suggest you return here as quickly as possible and get as much rest as you can. Don't spend the night gossiping with your Irish friends in the Sixty-ninth."

"I won't sir." He saluted, left the tent and headed for the camp of Baxter's Fire Zouaves about a mile down river. The 72nd Regiment, recruited in July, was composed solely of volunteer Fireman from Philadelphia and surrounding communities. Six members of the Decatur Fire Company of Frankford had joined the 72nd. among whom was Albert Dungan, the grandson of veteran who had served with Washington's Army at Valley Forge.

The firemen were just finishing their evening meal as Paddy entered the encampment. He delivered the dispatches to Colonel Baxter who, seeing hunger in Paddy's expression, invited him to stay for supper.

It was close to eight o'clock when Paddy finally arrived at Colonel Owen's camp. The Irishmen had already retired for the night and the camp was in total darkness, except for a light in the headquarters tent and a few dying campfires. Sleeping somewhere in the dark tents surrounding him was Danny Williams who had enlisted in the 71st Regiment with his older brothers, Joe, Andy and Barney. When Timothy Carr, his closest friend and companion, joined the all-Irish regiment, Danny jumped from the 71st to the 69th Regiment. He was officially listed as a deserter on the records of the 71st, although still serving the army and his country.

"No wonder Danny wanted to be with Tim," Paddy mused as he hurried toward Colonel Owen's tent. While ice skating on Frankford Creek two years before, Tim had saved Danny from drowning. The two had been inseparable ever since.

His mission accomplished, Paddy returned to the camp of the 71st and crawled wearily into his tent.

Billy Batt stirred in the blankets. "That you, Paddy?"

"Yep."

"We really moving out tomorrow like everybody says?"

"That's my guess," Paddy replied sleepily. "They're sure burning midnight oil at regimental headquarters."

The next morning reveille sounded earlier than usual. A light frost covered the ground. The roll call was taken and at seven-thirty the assembled regiment was given orders to break camp and be ready to leave with full marching equipment.

Lieutenant Williams summoned the men of Company D. He gazed for a moment at the eager faces of those he had known from boyhood. He called for attention. "Fellows, report to the supply wagons to exchange weapons. McClellan is sending us upriver to cover the Reb's northern flank."

"Hot damn!" Castor exploded. He danced a little jig step. "Once there, we can roll the Rebs right down the alley into Richmond."

"Just like that," George Hart remarked, sarcastically.

The company fell into an orderly line to exchange smooth bores for rifles. When it came his turn, Castor tossed his musket onto the wagon, grabbed a greasy new Enfield, and started to run.

"Hey, you dumb jack ass," the supply sergeant bellowed, "come back here and collect your forty rounds! That ain't no pea shooter you got. It uses bullets, or didn't you know?" Castor drew himself up short. "Don't holler at me in that tone of voice, you turd-bird. I'll whip the blue farts out of you."

"You'll do what? Why, you...."

The inflamed supply sergeant made a vicious lunge at Castor with a raised musket stock. He never reached his adversary. Before he had time to know what hit him, he was pinned to the ground beneath a blanket of Castor's friends.

"Break it up! Break it up!" cried Lieutenant Hibbs.

The soldiers unscrambled themselves. Hibbs grabbed Castor by the shoulder. "I should set you on a barrel for those remarks. That man has stripes, or didn't you notice? Lucky for you we're breaking camp."

Castor shot a scornful glance at the rough, bearded sergeant. "Stripes. Does this army think it can polish a turd with stripes? I don't cotton rudeness from nobody."

"Come on, Chirp, cool off," Paddy said taking his friend firmly by the arm and leading him away.

Billy followed on the run. "Hey, Chirp, you forgot your ammo." He handed his companion forty rounds of fifty-eight caliber ammunition. He pointed to the conical, counter-sunk bullets encased in paper cartridges and winced. "Wonder what it feels like to have one of these lead slugs hit you?"

"I'm aiming to let the other fellow find that out," Castor replied.

The men returned to their camping ground just as the long drum roll sounded.

"Fall in!" Captain Ritman barked tersely.

In brisk response to the captain's command the young volunteers from Frankford fell quickly into line with full field packs. The exciting prospect of facing combat for the first time quickened the heartbeat and pulse of every man.

"Right shoulder, shift!" came the order.

Enfield rifles, glistening bayonets affixed, were thrust into position.

"Company, right face! Forward, march!"

"Here we go. We're off," Batt said, his voice wavering. Paddy gave him a soft pat on the head.

In ranks off four abreast, D Company quickly moved out and into the regimental line.

The sun was just rising in the east, and had not yet dispersed the swirling mists that shrouded the Potomac camps in a wispy veil of dampness. The long blue column of soldiers marching steadily through the cool haze which blanketed the Virginia countryside was suddenly treated to a stirring sight. As footlights suddenly illuminate a darkened stage, the first rays of daylight broke through the lifting mist to reveal the Stars and Stripes flying in splendor at the head of the moving column. It was a breathtaking moment. Adding to the excitement, the regimental band struck up a lively march tune of Philadelphia origin.

Several years before the war, a company of visiting firemen from Charleston, South Carolina, approached William Steffe in Philadelphia asking him to compose an air for some words which began, "Say, Bummers, will you meet us...." Steffe, living at 36th and Chestnut streets near the University of Pennsylvania campus, responded to the request and wrote the music which the firemen wanted. Later, the Southern Methodists adopted the catchy tune, changing the words to, "Say, Brothers, won't you meet us, on the other side...." and furnishing a chorus: "Glory, glory, hallelujah."

Hearing the Methodist version, several members of the 12th Massachusetts Regimental Band became so intrigued by the tune they decided to add it to the repertoire of songs which they sang as a quartet. One member of the quartet, John Brown, was the continuous butt of wit because of the similarity of his name to that of the famous abolitionist, and his name was injected into the song to tease him. From that chain of circumstances evolved the words fitted to Steffe's music, written for Southern firemen, using Massachusetts lyrics and incorporating the Southern Methodist chorus of "Glory, glory, hallelujah."

The marching column took up the popular strain and started to sing in lusty fashion.

"John Brown's body lies a-molderin' in the grave,
John Brown's body lies a-molderin' in the grave,
John Brown's body lies a-molderin' in the grave,
And we go marching on."

Chirp Castor's voice came in loud and strong on the chorus. "Glory, glory, hallelujah. Glory, glory, hallelujah...."

The jaunty song was repeated over and over until, tiring at last, the band put away their instruments and only the monotonous sounds of route march could be heard: the steady tack-tack of a drum beat, the jingle of tin canteens and the sliding sound of striding feet. The regiment crossed the Potomac into Maryland and at a hand signal from Lieutenant Williams, the men fanned out into the fields to act as flankers.

"Hey, Mulcahy," John Lightfoot called, "How far we going today?"

Paddy gave the shoulder straps of his knapsack a hitch. "Far's I know, the Colonel figures on doing sixteen miles. Twenty tomorrow."

John Stott noticed Paddy's labored breathing. "What's the matter, Mulcahy? Soft life as a headquarters orderly beginning to tucker you?"

"Go fly a kite."

Laughter greeted Paddy's discomfiture.

A mounted staff officer stopped to confer with Captain Ritman for a moment, then galloped off to the main column.

The countryside was ablaze with autumn colors. Corn shocks resembling Indian tepees dotted the fields, and ripening pumpkins lay scattered among the leafy shocks. Everywhere blue uniforms contrasted with the maize and orange colors of the landscape.

"Sorta wish I was back home helping Dad husk corn," Billy blurted wistfully.

"Well, I know I could sure go for some of your dad's apple cider right now," Castor responded, placing parched lips to the nipple of his canteen.

Henry Castor and Joe Batt. assigned the job of bringing up the rear and prodding stragglers, approached their younger brothers. "Want me to carry your pack awhile?" Joe inquired of Billy.

"Naw, it ain't heavy. Straps are beginnin' to cut a little, but it ain't heavy," Billy replied with a show of independence.

Secretly he marveled at the ease and bearing with which his older brother shouldered the baggage of war.

Chirp stopped and pointed at his shoes. "Look at ' em, Henry. Just look at 'em. What do they make them from, worn out dollar bills?"

"Wouldn't be a bit surprised. Heard the other day not one out of four pair can bear the test of a ten-mile tramp. Seems to be holding true for this company. Look at mine and Joe's. They're breaking apart at the seams."

"Yeah, sure wish the scalawag patriot who filched the government was walking in them right now."

Joe glanced over his shoulder. "More foot trouble," he commented flatly. "There's that poor McErlain fella straggling again. Guess we'd better fall back, Henry, and help him along."

"Be right with you, Joe. You kids be sure to sing out if you need help," Henry admonished. "You understand? Don't be bullheaded about asking."

"All right, grandma," Chirp retorted. "We'll remember."

The flankers continued to move steadily forward through the fields in relative silence, a situation which began to wear on the ebullient nature of Barney Williams. Strutting ahead of the company, he began reciting poetry in a loud voice:

"The boy stood on the burning deck,
His feet were full of blisters,
He climbed aloft, when his pants fell off,
And he had to wear his sister's."

Hoots and catcalls greeted his attempt at levity.

"I don't care if he is the lieutenant's brother," Dave Chipman raged, "and I don't care if he does come from the most prominent family in Frankford. So help me, if he recites any more of that damned idiotic poetry, I'll-"

His threat was drowned by an outburst of loud guffaws.

"The way Dave loves peace and quiet," Paddy observed wryly, "it's a wonder he ever joined this man's army."

"I'll say," Castor replied. "Remember that first Sunday in camp when he hid all the bugles so they couldn't play reveille? He did us a favor that morning."

"Hey, Captain," Bill Bromley shouted, "we've been picking them up and putting them down for two straight hours. How about a halt?"

Captain Ritman surveyed the main column of troops through his field glasses, then raised his sword in the air. "All right men, we have time for a fifteen minute rest. Make the most of it."

Paddy dropped to the ground. He turned toward Castor. "Hey, don't drink so much water. You'll founder yourself and we'll end up carrying you the rest of the way."

"That's the best offer I've had all day," Chirp replied. He put the canteen back to his lips and drank deeply.

Bill Batt cocked his head. "Hey fellas, listen. Can you hear that?"

The shrill sound of fifes accompanied by the deep, resonant rattle of drums could be heard in the distance above the sound of tramping feet emanating from a far-off column.

"Sure is exciting to listen to, don't you think?"

Paddy gave a weary nod.

Castor dropped to his knees. "Look over there, quick. This ought to be good."

His friends turned their heads sharply. A short distance away, Barney Williams was sneaking up on the prostrate form of Dave Chipman, who lay half asleep on the ground, his head propped on a knapsack, his kepi pulled over his eyes to shut out the sun's glare. There was a malicious look on Williams' face as he crept stealthily forward.

Billy shaded his eyes. "Oh, oh, sleeping beauty is going to have something pulled on him."

"Quiet, let's see what 'Rubber-face' will do," Castor cautioned.

Williams hovered over Chipman's body like a bird of prey then, placing a foot on Dave's chest, spread his arms and began orating in a loud voice. "Friends, Romans, and countrymen, lend me your ears. I have come to bury Caesar, not to praise...."

Chipman sat upright, grabbed his rifle and flailed at Williams' retreating figure. "Come back here, you bloody itch! Come back here where I can get my hands on you !" he shouted.

Williams scurried to safety, laughing as he ran.

"One of these fine days," Paddy murmured, "that practical joker is going to get his due."

"And Dave's just the one who can do it," Castor replied. "Look, he's lighting out after him."

The sharp command, "Fall in," from Captain Ritman brought the episode to an abrupt end. The flankers rose from the ground, dusted themselves and resumed marching. As the day wore on, fatigue reduced questions and responses to simple phrases and eliminated all joking and badinage. Toward evening, the flank companies were called in and the regiment went into bivouac for the night. Campfires, lighted for cooking purposes, helped to ward off the penetrating autumn chill that came with the dark. Following a supper of pork, hardtack and coffee, the weary volunteers crawled into their blanket rolls while overhead a bright harvest moon rose slowly in the cloudless sky, its silvery beams shining peacefully on the still forms asleep on Maryland soil.

In keeping with typical fall weather, the next day dawned cool and brisk. Long before the sun rose, the march was resumed. Late that afternoon the head of the column entered Poolesville, a small Maryland town situated in one of the richest agricultural districts of the state. Gentle swells of land, wooded vales, verdant slopes and broad fields surrounded it.

Two miles to the west lay the sweeping Potomac, beyond which was the far-off shadow of South Mountain. There was a combination about the setting to delight the soul of any painter who appreciated rural scenery. The modest village which the troops were entering consisted of a few rundown frame houses and weather-beaten out-buildings huddled together as if there were but one corner lot and they were all trying to get as close to it as possible. Clinging to the ends of the houses, as though placed there as an afterthought, were brick chimneys, many of them crumbling. Rickety wagons and carriages occupied skeleton sheds. The inquisitive soldiers from Pennsylvania looked searchingly, but in vain, for a substantial dwelling with the tidy, well kept grounds to which they were accustomed. There was absolutely no freshness about the place, no signs of life.

"By, jimmy," Bill Batt exclaimed, "it looks as if time has sucked the juice out of everything around here."

"You can say that again," Paddy retorted. He recalled Colonel Burn's pet expression about the South—*Too poor to paint and too proud to whitewash.*

The regimental column came to a halt on a dirt roadway and the tired troops were ordered to stand at ease. Loitering on the front porch of a shabby hotel, a group of bucolic villagers canvassed the soldiers, their scornful eyes surveying the weary troops.

"When're you Yanks figgerin' on crossin' the Potomac to take another whuppin' from the Johnnies?" one bearded villager jeered.

"Just as soon as I teach you some manners," Chirp shot back.

Lieutenant Williams strode forward. "That will be enough, Castor."

The seedy-looking villager spit a quid of tobacco and pointed at Castor. "Fer a little pup he sure makes a big bark, don't he?"

His friends responded with derisive laughter.

Lieutenant Williams watched the color rise on Castor's neck. The tight rein of authority made the tormentor more audacious. "Ever seen any Virginians, sonny? One of 'em would make three the likes of you. Why, boy, they're taller'n Blue Ridge pines and tougher'n Allegheny nails."

"And in between meals they eat little critters like you," one of the others cut in boldly, causing more raucous laughter.

"How is it you're not fighting on their side?" challenged someone nearby. "Or did the best part of you get clipped off with the cord?"

The startled soldiers turned to see a dark-haired, solidly-built sergeant advancing toward the brash villagers.

"Go ahead, mister," he said, glowering at Castor's antagonist. "Say something smart to me." A demure dimple located in the center of his chin seemed strangely out of character with his pugnacious jaw.

The sergeant's menacing manner caused the tobacco-chewing villager to move closer to his companions.

Captain Markoe of "A" Company rushed forward and grabbed his subaltern by the arm. "All right, Donaldson, save your fighting for those Southerners who've got the courage to put on a uniform. Those borderline bullyrags aren't worth a tinker's damn. Come along."

The sergeant, in his early twenties, withdrew reluctantly and walked away as the column began moving upon command of Major Parrish. They marched out of the village to a spot a half mile from Poolesville where the regiment was directed to pitch camp. The encircling camps of other regiments lay all around.

Paddy had finished helping Chirp and Billy set up their tent and was sitting down to rest when he was approached by Bill Bromley, Colonel Baker's orderly. "Colonel Wistar wants you to report to him on the double, Paddy. His tent's pitched over by the orchard." He pointed.

"Thanks, Bill." Paddy rose to leave.

"Let us know what's going on as soon as you can, will you?" Billy inquired.

"Yes, and see if you can finagle a soft snap like an aide-de-camp or something for me," Castor said.

"I'll see what I can do," Paddy replied. He grinned and dashed off in the direction of the regimental command post.

Colonel Wistar greeted him with gusto. "How'd the march go for you and the boys?"

"Just capital, sir. We didn't mind the twenty miles."

"Bully, glad to hear it." He girded a sword belt around his waist. "See that my quarters are put into shape. After you've had supper, report to me at division headquarters."

"Division headquarters, sir?"

"That's correct. It's located in a large brick farmhouse at the far end of a lane on the other side of this orchard. You'll have no trouble finding the place." The Colonel put on his coat. "Baker and I are riding over there now to pay our respects to General Stone. Charley was a client of ours during the old days in San Francisco. You can tell your friends they're fortunate to have General Stone as Division Commander. We could use more regular army men of his caliber."

Paddy carried a roll of blankets and placed them on a folded cot. "Is the general a West Point graduate, sir?"

"Yes, and with honors. But like Bill Sherman, he retired from the army to enter the banking business in San Francisco. Unlike Sherman, he has more of the banker look and banker ways. He's truly a gentleman."

Paddy struck a match to the wick of an oil lantern. "So you think the boys'll take to him? Is that it, sir?"

Wistar laughed heartily. "Haven't I given you enough assurance and information to relay to your comrades, you Irish pixie?"

"I didn't..."

The amused colonel cut off his attempt at an explanation with a chuckle. "All right, you can tell your friends that Charley Stone is a top-grade soldier, honest and brave. Occasionally he's carried away by chivalrous notions, but considering everything, he's a fine man to serve under. The finest, most capable field leader we have today."

"Thank you, sir," Paddy responded with a sheepish grin. "The boys'll be glad to hear that."

Wistar strode to the entrance of the tent, stopped and looked at Paddy with a flicker of amusement in his eyes. "You know, sometimes I have the feeling that leaving you alone with all those maps and orders is like leaving a Trojan horse behind."

"Aw, Colonel," Paddy protested with a wounded expression, "you know I'd never..."

All right, my faithful servant, just see that you report to me at headquarters as soon as you've finished here."

"Yes, sir."

The Colonel put on his hat and departed. Going quickly to work, Paddy finished his assignment in the tent and checked with Corporal Clausen who was standing guard. He headed for the officer's mess, bolted a warmed-over meal, and started toward division headquarters. It was pitch black. He found the lane Wistar described and in a short time arrived at the rambling brick farmhouse. Lights burned brightly at the windows. Those shining from upstairs spread a shadowy glimmer across a second story balcony.

"Halt! Who goes there?" came a gruff challenge.

"Private Mulcahy. Orderly to Colonel Wistar," Paddy responded matter-of-factly.

"Proceed."

When he reached the house, he found Bill Bromley sprawled half-asleep on a stuffed sofa in a narrow hallway. He roused himself and rubbed bleary eyes as Paddy entered.

"Hi. Pull up a chair and make yourself comfortable. The big military are upstairs talking."

"Wonder how long they're gonna be? I'm beat."

"That goes double for me," Bromley said, yawning. "Those flatfoots in the regiment who think being an orderly is all peaches and cream can have my job anytime they want it. At least they can sleep at the end of the day."

Paddy stretched his arms. "Think I'll go outside and sit on the upstairs porch. The air'll do me good."

Bromley looked up with surprise. "Upstairs porch? How did you know there was one?"

"Noticed it when I came in. A good orderly has to be observant."

"Cripes! Stay inside and catch some shut-eye instead of snooping around, will you?"

"Who's snooping? Just want to get some air."

"Don't kid me. If the sentries find you eavesdropping you'll be jugged for keeps, if not shot."

"You're a worrywart. I won't be getting into any trouble just sitting on a porch." He fitted a forage cap to his head and left by the front door. He exchanged a few idle words with the sentry, then strolled around to the side of the building. To his dismay there were no steps leading up to the balcony. Glancing first in one direction and then another, he proceeded to shinny up a post and climbed over the porch railing. Purple clouds were drifting lazily across the face of an orange moon.

Dropping softly on his knees, he crept slowly to a position beneath an open window through which the sound of voices could be heard. He raised his head cautiously and peeked into the room. Colonel Baker was sitting with his back to the window. Wistar was seated on Baker's left, and facing both across a circular table was a handsome officer with a well-groomed spike beard. Paddy surmised the third person to be General Stone, a much younger man than he expected.

He crouched low. The General was speaking.

"...and I know I can trust Wistar's men anywhere. To serve under that young taskmaster they'd have to be good." There was a moment of silence. "As for your sister regiments, the Sixty-ninth, Seventy-second, and Hundred and Sixth, I firmly believe they should undergo additional training before they're entrusted with active brigade status. I've been thinking it over, and if it meets with your approval, I would like to brigade the Seventy-first, temporarily, mind you-with Colonel Deven's Fifteenth, Colonel Lee's Twentieth Massachusetts and Colonel Cogswell's Forty-second New York."

Colonel Wistar tossed a leg over one arm of his chair and tilted backward. "It's all right with me, Charley. How does it strike you, Ed?"

Colonel Baker drew heavily on his cigar and exhaled a puff of smoke. "Well now, I don't know," he replied with senatorial turgidity. "We're friends of long standing, Charley, and I respect your judgment as a trained army officer, but this shuffling which my California regiment has been through lately doesn't please me in the least. Also, it's my understanding that since most of the troops gathered here are inexperienced, the order has been given to exercise caution and discretion. Is that correct?"

"That's correct," General Stone replied.

"It is also my understanding that there is no preparation being made higher up for any general advance in this area."

General Stone steepled his hands, fingertips touching his nose. "That's correct. We're here solely to observe the ferries and fords of the Potomac in front of Poolesville."

Baker spoke in a lofty manner. "That being the case, how can you account for this request to separate my regiment from those of Owen, Baxter and Morehead?"

"Charley just finished telling you, Senator," Wistar responded. "While it's true that we plan no movement, we don't know that the Confederates aren't harboring an idea to sweep through here to strike Washington from the north. In such an event, Charley would feel more secure if he were able to throw in a brigade that was fully trained and led by officers in whom he has confidence. It's natural that his first choice of troops and officers would be those from his native state of Massachusetts. He's selected our regiment to augment them until our sister regiments from Philadelphia are fully trained and ready."

The general's face clouded. "I'll not be coy with you. I do have an ulterior motive." He directed his words toward Senator Baker. "You've heard the stories the abolitionists are circulating about me in Washington?"

Colonel Baker nodded soberly. "Yes, Charley, I have. As a matter of fact, just before I left Washington two days ago, I saw a copy of a letter which Colonel Lee of the Twentieth Massachusetts sent to your Governor Andrew."

"With regard to what?" Wistar asked.

"It stated, among other things, that General Stone, whatever his defects might be on the slavery issue, had promised the Twentieth Massachusetts would not be deprived of its due share of active service."

"What kind of insubordinate talk is that?"

General Stone appeared tired. "Now we're getting to the real reason why I want you and your regiment brigaded with Devens and Lee for a while, Isaac. I can trust you, and Ed. Devens and Lee are courageous men and well-trained officers, but they possess that unhappy New England trait of working behind your back. Their laxness has led to a complete breakdown of discipline among the men. Allow me to explain."

Paddy looked over the windowsill and saw Colonel Wistar's tightly drawn lips. His prominent cheekbones jutted like granite abutments.

"Lately, we've been confronted with an increasing amount of provoking incidents that are far from trivial. Colonel Lee's Twentieth regiment, for instance, is composed mainly of city bred Harvard boys who've apparently moved a long way from the old tradition of the Minuteman with his ever-ready rifle. At target practice, most of the boys simply pointed their rifles in the general direction of the target, shut both eyes, and pulled the trigger. It has taken more than the necessary amount of time to correct the situation."

The general paused to sip some ale from a bottle sitting before him on the table. "One Massachusetts battery," he continued, "gleefully reported to me that it had bombarded and routed a whole regiment of Confederate cavalry on the Virginia shore. Cavalry indeed! We found out later that it was a colored funeral procession which they shot up!"

The mental picture of the scene caused Wistar to laugh.

"You may laugh, Isaac. I agree there is an element of humor in both incidents, but serious consequences arise from that pattern of undisciplined behavior in raw recruits. Two weeks ago, the bandsmen of Deven's Fifteenth Massachusetts staged a little revolt on him. When they discovered they had to put in an hour every day learning to be ambulance men, carry stretchers and provide a wounded man care and comfort, they objected. They actually refused to turn out for drill and announced that they would die before they would do such duty."

Wistar said crisply, "I'd have accommodated them in that."

"I trust those men were properly disciplined," Baker broke in.

"They were." Stone reached into his pocket and drew out a cigar which he lighted. "But the most flagrant breach of discipline occurred just recently. The one, incidentally, which led to all the trouble. You know the President is trying desperately to keep Maryland in the Union. About a month ago a delicate situation arose when the Twentieth Massachusetts, abolitionist to the core, helped a runaway slave escape to the North. The slave was owned by the Governor of Maryland, no less."

Wistar emitted a low whistle.

Stone nodded. "Needless to say, there were repercussions from official sources in Washington. I felt it necessary to issue general orders advising the men not to incite or encourage insubordination among the colored servants in the neighborhood of our camps. Shortly after I issued that warning, two slaves sought refuge within the lines of Lee's Twentieth. Obedient to orders, a young officer returned them to their owners. As a result, the entire regiment became upset and some of the men wrote home about it.

"Shortly thereafter, Colonel Lee received a stern letter from John Andrew, our governor, officially reprimanding the young officer for returning the slaves and rebuking Colonel Lee for countenancing it. Lee passed the letter on to me."

The general paused to take another drink. "I sent a heated reply advising the governor that he had no business meddling with army discipline. I told him that the young lieutenant and Colonel Lee had done what they were told and were not subject to reprimand from him. I also advised Andrew that in the future I would thank him to keep his hands off. A little over two weeks ago I received a slanderous reply to my letter. I replied in kind, telling Andrew where he could go. The letter to which Ed just referred is one that Lee wrote to Andrew assuring him that I would not vent my feelings on his pet regiment."

Wistar sat dumbstruck. "By God, trained or untrained, in case of emergency you'd be better served by the Philadelphia brigade than by these Massachusetts misfits. We do not tolerate insubordination."

"That's precisely why I asked McClellan to send you to me. I want to integrate your exemplary regiment with Deven's and Lee's for a while. Perhaps their men will pick up that certain something which your boys possess."

"You' ll find they ' re the best," Colonel Baker agreed proudly. "They exhibit a strong feeling of devotion for their country that's devoid of petty selfishness and sectionalism."

General Stone smiled. "I'm looking forward to a closer acquaintance with them."

"You'll not find them wanting, Charley," Wistar assured him. "But tell me, what about those attacks on your loyalty which you mentioned? I don't tolerate gossip and I don't listen to it, so I'm completely uninformed."

The general rose slowly from his chair and walked toward the open window. His approach caused Paddy to squirm as he hugged the wall beneath the sill to escape detection and he waited breathlessly. Above the beating of his heart, he heard the sound of heavy boots stop and retrace their steps back to the table. Breathing more easily, he strained to hear the general's reply.

"Yes, Isaac, I should have reasoned as much where you were concerned. I just took it for granted that Ed kept you better informed."

Paddy heard the senator clear his throat.

"Despite my shortcomings as a politician, Charley," he said, "I, too, abhor gossip. I also know how touchy this ex-Indian fighter can be about character assassination. Therefore, I said nothing to Isaac about the matter until I could hear the whole story from you."

"Thanks, Ed," Stone murmured.

Wistar sounded irritated. "Will somebody please tell me what this undercurrent is all about?

"Let me straighten it out for you," Senator Baker responded. "Charley, you will be interested in this. Just before I left Washington I had a final chat with Abe Lincoln. While I was with the President, Senator Sumner dropped by to put his oar in the water. As usual it didn't take him long to get around to damning the anti-abolitionist officers, as he calls them, whom he feels are running the army."

"Sumner spoke that way in Lincoln's presence?" Stone exclaimed, amazed. "Why, just last month on the floor of the Senate he accused the President of being a dictator and imperator. What else was it he said of Lincoln? 'How vain to have the power of a god and not use it like a god.'" Stone shook his head. "How does the President tolerate that?"

"Lincoln is a patient man," Baker answered. "Besides, he likes to draw out his antagonist's views. He feels it enables him to cope with them more effectively. It might please you to know that when Sumner finished castigating you, the President turned to him with a smile and said, 'Oh, I could never believe General Stone would be disloyal."'

Annoyed, Wistar twirled the ends of his moustache. "Who besides Sumner is tied up with these disloyalty charges?"

"Senator Ben Wade of Ohio. In the House, Thaddeus Stevens of Pennsylvania and a few others. By the way, Charley, I think you should know that Governor Andrew has turned all of your correspondence over to Sumner."

Visibly disturbed, General Stone rose from his chair. The sound of his pacing boots made a hollow echo on the bare floor. "The jackal! What does he hope to gain? Definition of policy was clearly set forth in the President's inaugural address."

The irate general returned to the table and sat down. "Lincoln dealt specifically with the problem when he stated, 'I have no purpose, directly or indirectly, to interfere with the institution of slavery in the states where it exists. I believe I have no lawful right to do so. and I have no inclination to do so.' Could any presidential directive or statement of policy be clearer? I have followed presidential policy to the letter, and I stand accused of being disloyal."

"On what grounds?" Wistar pressed.

"My defamers," Stone answered deliberately, "accuse me of protecting rebel property, permitting flags of truce with the rebels, consorting with mysterious messengers and allowing Southern sympathizers to pass through my lines on their way home. I freely admit that I have done some of these things. For performing such acts of courtesy and military acumen, I stand accused by the abolitionist politicians of being in league with rebellion "

Wistar removed his leg from the arm of the chair "You, in league with rebellion? Preposterous!" He glared at his former law partner "Ed, what goes on here? Why should a commander of Stone's integrity and loyalty be slandered by venal officials?"

Colonel Baker fingered his rimless spectacles. "Calm yourself, Isaac, I will explain."

"I'm listening."

"Good.. Let me caution both of you, civil authority in Washington is going to ride herd on the generals in this war. Military leaders will have to show their heart is in the cause and the definition of 'the cause' is going to be in the hands of men who have ideas that were not taught at West Point."

"God help the country," Stone exclaimed.

"Not necessarily," Baker replied "Already there have been two incidents where generals have failed to please the men in government. Remember McClellan's proclamation issued in Western Virginia in which he said his army would not interfere with slavery and would repress any attempted servile insurrection? Fortunately for him, his policy reflected that of Lincoln, gradual emancipation and opposition to any wartime destruction of slavery. For that reason he was spared the axe, but what the representatives of the people saw was a general going beyond his function of framing military strategy.

"On the other hand, you have Fremont's tactless declaration. His proclamation freeing the slaves in Missouri was contradictory to government policy. Lincoln had no other choice but to relieve him of command. "

"That still doesn't explain the spurious charge that Stone is in league with the rebellion," Wistar countered.

Baker fidgeted. "Charley has dared to talk back to civilian authority. That's where he's made a fatal mistake. "

"Civilian authority! Since when has a handful of abolitionists constituted civilian authority?" Wistar stormed. "They're a rabid, volatile minority who in no way represent the overall feeling of the North. Have they forgotten that Stone was the first man mustered into service to defend the country against the rebellion? What of his record as Inspector General in Washington when it became his responsibility to maintain order and prevent a secessionist coup during the inauguration? Lincoln's safety was placed in Charley's hands during those hazardous days. Has the President forgotten?"

"No, the President hasn't forgotten, but you must understand that the abolitionists, even though a minority, are bent on shaping the course of this war. They are a power to be reckoned with."

General's Stone's fist came down hard on the table top. "I have never trespassed into the field of policy at any time. I have followed and administered presidential policy to the letter. Why then must these abolitionists invade the military field, disrupting discipline and dictating strategy?"

Outside, a rising wind caused the shutters to creak on rusty hinges. Paddy attempted to change his crouched position. The porch flooring groaned beneath his weight. He huddled closer to the dark wall and held his breath in fear of being discovered.

"It's only the wind, Isaac. Come, sit down," he heard Baker say.

When the sounds of conversation resumed, Paddy garnered enough courage to peek into the room again. Colonel Baker was removing a folded newspaper from his tunic.

"Now that we've exposed the political situation as it stands," Baker said, "I am confident that what I have to show you will be passed off with no recrimination. There is no doubt in my mind that you have acted with proper discretion, and have performed your military duties exactly as Lincoln would wish. Such will be my report. Now for the unpleasant part."

He unfolded the paper. "I want you to know the President sent this to me by special courier, with a note telling me to show it to you personally. He does not want you to be disturbed by what it says. You have his backing."

General Stone looked puzzled. He reached over, picked up the newspaper and read the banner headline. His face turned livid.

"What is it?" Wistar asked, alarmed.

Stone read with uncontrolled rage. "General C. R. Stone accused of treason on Senate floor by Senator Sumner." His voice fell to a rasp. "Denounced and accused of treason in the Senate."

Wistar sprang erect, his voice cold and menacing. "Allow me the honor of calling the Senator out."

"Isaac!" Baker cried. "Haven't the things we've just discussed meant anything to you? We must keep clear heads for the sake of the country. That is precisely why the President went to the special pains of having me break the news to

Charley, to prevent this sort of thing."

Stone hunched forward. "Wistar is right. For the good of the country it's time these Jacobins were brought to book. I have no recourse but to challenge. It is time the sacred cows find out they're not exempt from slaughter."

"I beg of you, Charley," Baker pleaded, "sleep on it. A move of this sort will cause all the sacred cows in Washington to turn against you, if only to preserve their congressional immunity."

"My mind is set."

"Don't do it. Even political enemies become thicker than thieves when one of their number is attacked in Congress. I know how they operate. I was one of them. Give it up."

"The die is cast." Stone wrote something on a paper with a flourish.

Colonel Baker rose hastily from his chair and circled the table. "Be sensible. You know as well as I that Sumner is slippery in these matters. He's notoriously evaded several duels at the expense of a caning or two. This will come to no avail."

"Precisely why I shall send my adjutant to deliver the challenge personally." The general folded the note. "Captain Stewart!" he called in a loud voice.

A tall, agile officer entered the room through a side door. A crisp, warlike moustache graced his handsome Hibernian countenance. General Stone rose from his seat. "Gentlemen, may I present my adjutant, Lord Ernest Vane Tempest, youngest son of the Marquis of Londonderry. A captain in the British army, he's on a leave of absence serving as an observer in our army under his family name of Stewart. Stewart, may I present Senator Baker."

The young aristocrat nodded his head and extended a hand. He cut a dashing figure. "The name and fame of the eloquent Senator are well known to me. It's an honor to make your acquaintance, sir."

"And that is Colonel Isaac Wistar, Stewart."

"Colonel, my pleasure, sir."

A look of mutual admiration was exchanged by both men as they shook hands.

Wistar grinned. "I've heard tall tales about this wild Irishman's exploits. For the short time you've spent in Washington, Stewart, I must say you've garnered quite a reputation among the ladies, the brawlers and the drinking crowd."

"Since the Colonel shows a particular interest and affinity for such affairs, perhaps he will join me on my next escapade?"

"Ho, Wistar. Perhaps that will teach you not to tangle with Irish wit," Baker exclaimed.

"Enough jesting. We've serious business at hand," General Stone interrupted. He proceeded to give Stewart his instructions. The adjutant seemed happy to oblige.

"I shall leave for Senator Sumner's residence immediately, sir, present him with your challenge to a duel, and insist on an immediate reply. If he attempts to put me off, I shall handle it myself."

"Please, Charley," Baker cajoled, "for the sake of an old friend, I implore you to postpone the matter."

"I'm sorry, Ed, but Sumner must answer for his lies and slander," Stone replied with an air of finality.

Wistar turned to Stewart. "If you'd like company on your night ride, I've a young Irish orderly who would fill the bill. You're welcome to borrow him."

"Thank you, Wistar. You're most gracious. Where is the chap? I should like to leave as soon as possible."

"Unless my senses fail me," Wistar answered, "he's outside that window on the balcony."

Paddy froze.

"Private Mulcahy," Wistar ordered in a stern voice, "come in here."

Paddy blessed himself hurriedly and tried to regain his composure. He stood up shamefacedly and entered the room by way of a door at the far end of the porch.

General Stone scowled. "What's that? An eavesdropper?"

"How long have you been out on the balcony, Private Mulcahy?" Wistar asked.

"From the moment I reported here, sir, just like you told me."

"How dare this insubordinate scamp pry at my window?" Stone glowered at him. "He's overheard everything."

"Explain yourself," Wistar interceded. "Why were you listening to a conversation of superiors that was no concern of yours?"

"Saints preserve me, sir, I had no thought of prying into matters that were none of my concern." A look of guileful innocence spread over his face. "You see, sir, when I got here, I saw the sentry posts at the front of the building were well-manned, but no one seemed to care about this balcony or the other three sides of the building. After scouting around a bit, I noticed this room could be easily reached by a Rebel who might be lurking under the cover of darkness. Seeing how things were, I thought it best to station myself on the porch out there and watch."

He coughed and blew his nose. "Excuse me, sir. Must have caught cold. Awful raw and damp standing guard in the night air." He wrinkled his forehead quizzically. "Did I do something wrong, sir?"

"By Jove," Stewart said with a laugh, "this chap is priceless. He's either the most astute foot soldier in your army or its most crafty liar. Such devotion above and beyond the call of duly could only be found in an Irishman."

"I'm an American," Paddy snapped.

"Oh, I say, he's a gem, Wistar. Must have kissed the Blarney Stone. Come along with you, Chappy. We have a long ride ahead of us."

Paddy cast an approving eye toward the energetic nobleman as he started fastening the top button of his tunic in preparation for leaving.

"Now just hold on there a minute, soldier," General Stone commanded sharply. "Come here and face me."

"Yes, sir."

The General's eyes glowed with warmth and paternal kindness. "There's a heavy frost tonight, soldier. Take this requisition to the quartermaster and draw an overcoat for yourself. It will be a long, cold ride to Washington."

"Thank you, sir."

Colonel Wistar walked to a far corner of the room. "Private Mulcahy, I want a word with you before you leave."

Paddy hastened to the Colonel's side. "Yes, sir?"

Wistar spoke in a whisper. "If you ever repeat a word of what you heard this evening, you will answer to me. Understand?"

"Yes, sir."

"One more thing. I want no lapse of memory on your part as regards Sumner's reaction when Stewart presents him with the challenge. Is that understood?"

"Nothing will escape me, sir." He saluted and left the room at Stewart's heels.

Mounting a chestnut gelding at the regimental corral, Paddy felt a buzz of excitement course through his body. He checked the girth, ran one hand down the animal's neck and gave it a gentle pat.

Stewart, in high spirits, sprang into his saddle and pointed toward Washington. "Tallyho!" he cried. "Let us go beard the lion in his den." The pair took off at a trot, then forged into a gallop.

A cold, gray dawn was breaking as they entered the sleeping city, their mounts beating a loud tattoo on the deserted streets.

Paddy warmed his ears with his hands. His teeth chattered from the cold. "What will Sumner's wife think, us barging in at this early hour?" he asked.

"The stuffed shirt is a bachelor, Chappy." Stewart wheeled his mount. "Here we are. This is the house number."

He dismounted quickly and strode toward a brick dwelling. Paddy hurriedly fastened the horses to a hitching post at the curb and followed. Stewart grasped a heavy brass knocker and pounded it forcefully on the paneled door.

"I'll wager this is the earliest the good Senator's been roused from bed in a long while." He grinned.

Presently they heard the sound of heavy feet echoing down the hallway and a light turned on. The door was opened by a powerfully built body servant of middle-age.

"Yes? What is it you want?"

Stewart bowed with a flourish. "I bear a note from General Stone which is to be delivered to the Senator personally."

"Stone? The traitor? Be off with you. The Senator desires no personal communication from that Rebel consort."

"Of that I haven't the slightest doubt, my good fellow. Now will you be good enough to announce me to your master?"

The man started to close the door, but Stewart quickly thrust a boot inside. "I said announce me!"

"You braying jack ass, I'll announce you sure 'nough."

The man made a sudden lunge at Stewart, which the Irish nobleman countered by grabbing the man's right arm at the wrist and elbow. Using the arm as a lever, he spun his own body in such a sharp pivot that he sent the ponderous Negro sprawling on the sidewalk. The freedman was off his back in an instant, charging wildly at his adversary. Paddy caught a fleeting glimpse of shining steel as Stewart's sword flashed in the air. The flat of the blade struck the servant squarely alongside the ear and he slumped into a silent heap on the brick sidewalk.

"Step over the bounder and follow me, Chappy," Stewart called as he sheathed his sword and darted into the house.

Paddy responded quickly, his relatively short legs trying desperately to match the long strides of the tall nobleman who was ascending a flight of velvet-carpeted stairs two at a time.

"What the devil goes on down there, Robert?" a gruff voice boomed from an upstairs room. "Robert, answer me."

"Ah, the lion's den," Stewart exclaimed happily.

The nerve-tingling prospect of what lay in store caused Paddy's heart to beat erratically. He was anxious to see the man who stood for something the South wanted exterminated from the Union, a man who had become what the South wanted to secede from. No other figure in the federal government so cleverly exposed the sin and guilt of the South while evading the same issues in the North. A one-idea man, he was elected to fill the Senate scat of Daniel Webster, the preeminent statesman of Massachusetts for many years. Unlike Webster, he carried the reputation of being exceedingly pompous and vain about his scholarship and given to name-calling.

Paddy recalled that several years ago Sumner had been caned into unconsciousness on the Senate floor by Representative Brooks in retaliation for a vicious verbal castigation which Sumner delivered against the aged Senator Butler of South Carolina, Brook's uncle. Following the beating Sumner absented himself from the Senate for the next few years, claiming he had been made an invalid by the incident, despite the fact that a prominent Washington physician declared he had suffered only surface wounds. The assumed martyrdom helped him to get reelected, after which he went abroad to indulge in a continuous round of social engagements, obviously enjoying good health.

Stewart burst into the room where the senator was lying in bed.

"Who are you?" thundered Sumner. "How dare you break into my house. Where's Robert?"

"Resting peacefully on the sidewalk, your lordship."

Paddy cast a furtive glance over Stewart's shoulder for a glimpse of the notorious abolitionist. Sumner's massive head with cold, granite-like features, lay propped on several pillows. His wealth of gray, curled locks looked as if they had been marcelled. The senator glared at Stewart with piercing eyes. "What's the meaning of this?"

Stewart advanced to the foot of the bed. "Calm yourself, Senator. I bring you a message of importance from General Stone. I'm sure you will find it stimulating."

"Stone? I hold no truck with the likes of Stone. Get out of here immediately."

"Not so fast, Senator, not so fast." Stewart drew Stone's letter from his tunic and tossed it on the bed. "You will read that letter this instant, and when you've finished, you will provide me with a prompt, suitable reply. Do you understand?"

Sumner raised himself on one elbow. "I'll do no such..."

"I said read that letter." Stewart moved closer.

"Very well, since you leave me no choice."

The senator placed his spectacles on the bridge of his nose, tore open the sealed envelope and began reading. His pale face suddenly became apoplectic. His heavy breathing made the bedcovers heave. "This is an outrage." He threw the letter to the floor. "So, Stone thinks he can challenge me to a duel, does he? Well, he'll not get away with that. I shall report this matter to the President."

"Not until you've given me your answer with respect to a time and place for meeting General Stone on the field of honor," Stewart shot back.

"How dare you address me in that manner, you insolent pup. I'll have you court-martialed for your part in this cabal against a duly-elected representative of the people. Who are you? What's your name?"

"Pip, pip, Senator. No speeches, please. I am Lord Ernest Vane Tempest on detached service from Her Majesty's army, serving as an observer with the army of the United States."

"Eh? What's that? You're British?"

"Irish, to be more specific, Senator, but British, nonetheless." A provocative smile crossed Stewart's lean face. "In case you've forgotten," he purred, "may I remind you of the delicate situation which presently exists between our two countries? You should be aware, Senator, that at this moment there's good reason to believe that Her Majesty's government will extend recognition and aid to the Confederacy. As members of the ruling class, my father and his associates will have a great deal to say regarding this matter. Now, do you still wish to threaten my post?"

Sumner's puffy face turned livid. He appeared visibly upset and unnerved. "This...this affair must be kept within the family," he spluttered. "I...I wouldn't want a purely personal matter to assume broad proportions that would cause international repercussions."

"Then you will be good enough to give me a reply that I can carry to General Stone."

"That's impossible. I shall need a day or so to choose my seconds and develop a suitable time and place."

"Let's have an understanding right now, Senator." Stewart's expression was deadly serious. "I will not be deceived, cajoled or put off. I want a definite written reply this instant. If you continue to refuse, I shall be obliged to call you out myself."

Paddy squirmed uneasily in the doorway. Stewart reminded him of a coiled snake with its head raised, bobbing and weaving and ready to strike.

Sumner heaved a sigh of resignation and reached for pen and paper at the side of his bed. With an unsteady hand he proceeded to write according to Stewart's directions. "Does that meet with your satisfaction?" he grumbled as he handed the note over.

Stewart glanced at the note and beamed. "This fills the bill nicely, thank you. I shall look forward to the pleasure of seeing you on the field of honor at the appointed date. Good day, Senator."

A shrill cry of warning filled the bedroom as Paddy screamed. "Look out behind you! The servant! He's got a gun!"

Stewart whirled, at the same time drawing a pistol.

"No, Robert, for God's sake, no!" Sumner shrieked.

The sullen freedman lowered his weapon and snarled through curled lips.

Stewart bowed again with a polished flourish. "A wise choice, Senator. Come, Chappy, let us depart."

The two left the house and a wave of relief swept over Paddy as he climbed into the saddle.

Stewart had already mounted his horse and was chuckling at the disturbed expression wrinkling Paddy's features. "What's troubling you, laddy-buck? Your sense of propriety been rudely jolted?"

"I don't follow you," Paddy replied as he bent low to adjust a girth strap.

"You look like a lost little boy. Are you disillusioned by what you've seen and heard the past few hours?"

"Not 'specially." He straightened and looked directly into Stewart's eyes. "It just puzzles me to see grown men in high places behaving like school kids."

Stewart gave his thick mustache a thoughtful tug. "Perhaps you're right. Maybe men never really grow up. Then again, it's an exciting way to live. Come, you need sleep. We'll put up at the Willard and return to Poolesville after we've rested."

CHAPTER 5

The camp of the 71st Pennsylvania appeared to be deserted, lying calm and serene in the late October haze of russet hues. Paddy stood in the company street and placed his hands on his hips. He surveyed the line of empty tents.

Strange. Wonder where everybody went? he pondered.

The stillness was suddenly broken by the sound of someone calling his name. He turned and strolled toward the tent of Tony McErlain from where the call had come.

"Where you been?" McErlain inquired in a weak voice. "And where'd you get that coat? Like as not I'd be with the others if I had a topcoat like that to keep out the chill."

Paddy flopped wearily onto a blanket. "Been to Washington on an errand for General Stone. He got me the coat. Where's the rest of the fellas?"

"Gone over to the Potomac on picket duty. Left early this morning."

Paddy noticed that the thin, dark-haired soldier appeared paler and more frail than usual. "You sick?" he asked.

Tony nodded. "It's my lungs again. Been spitting blood since yesterday. I reckon this sleeping out in the dew and dampness ain't helping things much."

Paddy was alarmed. "Have you seen the surgeon about it?"

"No, and I'm not going to. They'd send me home."

"How about Lieutenant Williams? You talked with him?"

"I told him I didn't feel well. He said to stay in my tent."

Paddy shook his head. "You look like walking death. Why don't you let me fix it with the Colonel so you can go home for a while. With colder weather coming–"

"Don't you even so much as say one word." The wan soldier gripped Paddy's shoulder with bony fingers. "I'll be getting over this spell. If you only knew how much I wanted to march over to the river this morning with the boys, you'd understand. Watching them go off without me was like...well, it reminded me of those hot days in summer when I used to watch you and Billy Batt splashing as free as you please in Frankford Creek, and me...I was cooped up in that stinking hot mill, working a loom."

"I know how you must feel about it, Tony, but you should think of your mother, too. You're all she's got. Please let me talk to the Colonel."

"No."

"Have it your way, then." Paddy struggled to keep his eyelids open. "You'll have to excuse me, I'm beat and need sleep. Here, you can have the coat if you'd like. It will keep you good and warm."

"Could I? Gee, I'd sure appreciate it."

Paddy took off the coat and handed it to his friend.

"Thanks. Thanks a heap, Paddy." The sickly volunteer spread the topcoat over his blanket and fitted the collar beneath his chin. "I'll see you get this back soon as they make issue to us," he added wearily.

"No hurry. Take care of yourself."

He walked slowly to the far end of the company street, crawled into his tent, lay down and was soon fast asleep.

It was well past midnight when he was suddenly aroused by loud singing and the trampling of feet. Someone gave the soles of his shoes a jarring kick.

"Where have you been hiding, Mulcahy? We just about gave you up as a deserter."

Paddy recognized Castor's shrill voice. "I've been off playing hopscotch with cannon balls," he replied.

"Very funny. Well, you sure missed it. We saw our first Johnnies today, didn't we, Billy? They were across the river from us." Castor stacked his musket and crept into the tent. Billy Batt crawled in behind him.

Paddy yawned. "So you had a picnic, did you?" Billy Batt unfastened a cartridge belt. "I wouldn't exactly call it a picnic. Captain Ritman gave us strict orders that there would be no horsing around."

"That's right," Castor cut in. "The orders were, 'shoot to kill.' Seems like the Massachusetts boys have been getting too friendly with the Rebs, exchanging coffee for tobacco and the like. But not anymore, we changed those arrangements today."

"Yep, Chirp took himself five potshots at the Rebs," Billy injected.

"Did you hit any?" Paddy asked.

"Couldn't tell, it was too far off. I know this much, a man with a good eye and a steady hand still has to have plenty of luck to hit a barn door at fifty paces with the smooth bores they have handed us. When it comes down to a fight with the Rebs, we're going to be up salt river. They have Springfields. All day long they were out-shooting us at greater range and with greater accuracy."

"You know who they've got to thank for that advantage," Paddy retorted.

"Yes, Floyd and Gorgas. They sure did a slick job of cleaning us out."

Bill Batt covered his body with a blanket and rested his head on a knapsack. "Wait till you see how swell the Potomac looks up this way, Paddy. It will remind you a lot of the Neshaminy and Pennypack. A little wider, but lined with thick woods and, well, just wait till you see it. The whole time I was on picket I couldn't help thinking how much fun it would be if we could take time out, make a raft and explore its source like we used to do on the Neshaminy back home."

"We've got a war to finish before we can do those kinds of things again," Castor said ruefully.

"Right now I'm willing to settle for a good night's sleep," Paddy said with a yawn. "How about you fellas turning in."

"Fine by me," Castor replied. "Wait'll I kick my shoes off. What's left of them, that is."

The camp of weary soldiers fell silent.

For the next three weeks the labors of the 71st Pennsylvania were directed toward integration drills and maneuvers with the 15th and 20th Massachusetts regiments, and the 42nd New York. Picket duty and the pleasantries of camp life occupied the balance of their time.

It was on Sunday, the twentieth of October, that Paddy awoke earlier than usual. The day had dawned clear against the cool sky of an autumn morning. Billy and Chirp were still sleeping soundly on either side of him. He lay quietly. A light breeze rustled the dry corn tassels which hung from shocks behind the tent. He was reminded of the pleasant peal of church bells that sounded across Frankford on still Sunday mornings.

The rhythm and harmony of fall filled him with a longing to be back in the Delaware Valley. Bronze and scarlet leaves swirled in a tight little circle in front of his tent. A lone cricket chirped somewhere in the grass. Overhead, migratory birds were winging southward and the fresh air bore the scent of purple clustered grapes and the tangy odor of wood smoke. The tranquil scene made him wish that he could capture it and preserve it from the cold clutch of approaching winter. There was beauty in the gorgeous raiment of the earth in the fall, like a rich robe for the last long dreaming.

He reached into his haversack and drew out a piece of hardtack. He took a jaw-cracking bite of the army's staple and crawled carefully from the tent so as not to disturb his sleeping comrades.

In front of an adjacent tent, the Smith twins were working around a small cook fire. Dave Smith used the handle of his bayonet to crush coffee beans on a rock. Bob was frying bacon.

"Good morning," they called. "Join us in breakfast?"

"No thanks," Paddy replied. "Think I'll walk around first and work up an appetite." He noticed a semi-circle of soldiers gathered at the far end of the company street.

"What's going on down there?"

"Don't know. Bob and I just got up."

Paddy stretched his arms. "I'll stroll down and find out."

As he approached the strangely silent group, he saw Frank Lightfoot break away and run to meet him.

"What's up?" Paddy inquired.

"It's Skinny McErlain. He's dead."

"Dead!" Paddy gasped. "When?"

"Sometime during the night. Must have known it was coming, too. Last evening he told Chipman if anything ever happened he wanted to be buried out here in the open. We're gonna put him over in the orchard. The Captain's got a detail working on the hole now."

"I can't believe it," Paddy responded. He walked slowly toward the spot where McErlain's body lay stretched out on a blanket and gazed down at the lifeless form. Gripped by a strange sensation, he wondered just how a mother would feel when told that her only son had died. Tony's lips, which once made his widowed mother's sacrifices seem worthwhile, were drawn tight. His hands, which in childhood tugged at her skirts and reached for a cup of milk, were cold and still. His staring eyes, once boyishly alive and sparkling, stood out in bold relief against a pale face like blue lakes in a snowy landscape.

With trembling hands, Dave Chipman and John Heap covered McErlain's body with a gum blanket. Paddy shook his head and clenched his fists. He wished to God that those responsible for this conflict could witness some of the results.

He had turned to leave the scene when Colonel Wistar suddenly appeared on horseback. The regimental commander dismounted quickly and went into conference with Captain Ritman and Lieutenant Williams, while the soldiers of D Company milled around within earshot.

"You are two of my finest officers," Wistar was saying, "but in the future, please bear in mind that a good officer should investigate and care for the health of his men. Providing instruction and good leadership is not enough. It's a damn shame that so many young lads like McErlain lie about their health in order to join their friends in the service. If I'd known he'd had consumption as a child, he would have never signed on. That's all the more reason why we should keep a weather eye out for those who don't belong in the field for physical reasons. In the future, I want every case of illness sent to the surgeon for examination. That's what he's paid for."

Both officers nodded solemnly.

Wistar patted each of them on the shoulder. "Don't take that as a rebuke, gentlemen, but heed the lesson you've learned today." He paused. "I presume, Captain, that you will express our sympathies to the lad's mother?"

"That good woman was my housekeeper, sir. I shall write to her with dispatch."

Wistar cleared his throat. "Then let us be about our business, gentlemen. You may form the company, Captain."

"Yes, sir."

In response to a terse command from Captain Ritman, the volunteers from Frankford lined up in formation with heavy hearts to pay final respects to their first casualty. Marching slowly, they followed as McErlain's body was carried to the freshly-dug grave in the orchard. With heads bowed, they listened to Colonel Wistar say a few words over the lifeless form, then give the signal for the body to be lowered into the grave. Heavy breathing mingled with the sound of falling pebbles and loose dirt as Tony's body disappeared into the ground.

In response to a signal from Captain Ritman, the soldiers from Tony's Sunday School class moved forward to the edge of the grave. Standing shoulder to shoulder, wearing sorrowful expressions, they raised their voices in a hymn.

Paddy listened to the words and studied the faces of his blue-capped comrades. Why did religion play such a big part in their lives, he wondered. A shiver went down his spine as John Stott's bass voice came in strong on the final verse.

"Till my ransomed soul shall find,

rest beyond the River."

Again, Paddy shivered. The words almost sounded like prophesy.

It was over. Tony McErlain's grave was closed until the judgment call.

At Colonel Wistar's direction, Paddy followed his commanding officer to regimental headquarters where they were met by Colonel Baker who was in obvious good spirits.

"Isaac, by God man, where have you been? Never mind, listen to this. Stone has ordered a battalion of the Fifteenth Massachusetts across the river to scout and demonstrate against the enemy north of Leesburg."

"He has?"

"We're to test their mettle. Drive them, if necessary."

"Test whose mettle and drive whom?" Wistar asked.

"The Rebels, of course." Baker twirled a cigar between thumb and forefinger. "Last night a colored teamster, a deserter from the Thirteenth Mississippi at Leesburg, was brought into headquarters. He told us the Confederates at Leesburg are sending their baggage to Joe Johnston's lines at Manassas and expect to retreat soon."

"Don't tell me Stone is putting stock in the tale of a deserter."

"What if I tell you that McClellan has ordered the move?" Baker retorted. "It was Mac who decided to investigate immediately upon receiving the report from Stone."

"Is that so?" Wistar said in a monotone.

"First, let me give you an overall picture of the operation," Baker replied. "McClellan has sent McCall's division upriver on the Virginia side with orders to halt at Dranesville, which is ten miles southeast of Leesburg. In the meantime, Stone is to effect a demonstration northeast of Leesburg to prod the Confederates out of that town. We expect to squeeze them like one would pinch a bug between the fingers."

"I don't like the sound of it," Wistar commented dryly. "The Confederates are operating on a short interior line. They are in position to move their entire force to destroy each of our expeditions piecemeal, one at a time. I'm afraid your bug will chew off both fingers before the pinch can be made."

"You're impossible, Isaac. We've got them where we want them and we're going to make the most of it. We can drive them right down on McCall's bayonets."

"And I say we are liable to get our wings clipped."

"Bosh." Colonel Baker thrust the cigar in his mouth. "By the way, Isaac, I would like you to meet my new adjutant. I have requisitioned a British observer. Same as that Irishman of Stone's." He rose from his camp stool and strode to the front of the tent. "Fred, would you come in here, please?"

A short, wiry officer, graying slightly at the temples, entered the tent with a springy step. Baker took him by the arm. "Fred, this is my former law partner,

Colonel Isaac Wistar. Isaac, this is Fred Harvey, a captain in Her Majesty's Coldstream Guard."

Wistar extended a hand. "Glad to have you with us, Harvey."

"It's a pleasure to be here, Colonel."

Baker broke in. "Speaking of Stone, Fred has just hand-delivered me a note from the President. It seems Sumner lost little time in laying his duel in Lincoln's lap. Have you that note, Fred?"

"No, I haven't, Colonel. I gave it to you."

"Oh, yes, so you did." Baker fumbled in his pockets. "Hmm, yes, here it is." He pulled out a letter. "The President has upheld Charley's action with these words, 'I don't know that I should have written such a letter, but if I had wanted to, I think, under the circumstances—under the circumstances, mind you—I would have had a right to do so.'"

Baker folded the paper and stuffed it back into a coat pocket. "That, gentlemen, is an example of how truly magnanimous and deft Abe Lincoln can be in a ticklish situation. Now, if Charley Stone can only fashion himself a victory in the field, God willing, perhaps it will soothe his ruffled feelings to the extent he'll forget his bitter animosity toward Sumner and drop the entire matter."

"The able senator has already broken the engagement twice," Wistar retorted. "I doubt whether Charley will ever get an opportunity to defend his honor against the scoundrel."

"Well and good. It would be better for the country and all concerned if the whole affair were forgotten. As a matter of fact, I'm riding over to speak with Charley at General Headquarters as soon as I leave here. I'm in hopes this note from the President will serve to placate him." Baker turned to leave. "And Isaac, I'd advise you to have your men ready to move at a moment's notice. I'll keep you posted as to developments. Come along, Fred."

Wistar watched with raised eyebrows as Baker departed. Rubbing fingertips over his lips, he sat down in a camp chair. "Paddy!"

"Yes, sir?"

"Run over to the Sutler's wagon and get me a half dozen good cigars. Make it a dozen. and no tobies. That inferior Pennsylvania tobacco gives me the dry heaves."

Paddy left and returned shortly with a box full of prime Havanas. "Shall I put these in your moisture packet, sir?"

"If you will, please. And Paddy, one thing more."

"Yes, sir."

"Stop imitating Colonel Baker's mannerisms every time you pass the sergeant of the guard. I was watching you. It's not funny."

"But, Colonel, I wasn't..."

"I said no more of it. Do you understand? Despite his eccentricities, Colonel Baker is still a fine, able gentleman."

"I'll remember, sir."

"Good. Now gather your things together and bring them here. I want you close at hand tonight in case I have need of your services. Remember, while you're cleaning out your pup tent, don't breathe a word to anyone about what you've just heard regarding a possible general movement."

"I won't, sir."

That night Paddy experienced the pleasant luxury of sleeping on a cot at the entrance of Colonel Wistar's tent. He had been slumbering peacefully for approximately five hours when he suddenly became conscious of someone shaking him by the shoulder.

"Mulcahy, wake up," a sentry said softly.

"Huh? What's the matter? What do you want?"

"Get the Colonel up. There's a courier out here with orders from General Headquarters."

Paddy sprang from his bed and struck a match to a lantern wick. "Send him in. I'll wake the Colonel. Hey, is it raining?"

"Like cats and dogs." The sentry left the tent and in a few moments a soldier appeared whose wet poncho glistened like a seal skin in the pale lantern light. He saluted and handed a packet to Colonel Wistar.

"Are you to wait for a reply?" Wistar asked drowsily.

"No, sir."

"Very well, you are dismissed." Wistar unfolded the dispatch, held it close to the lantern, and began to read.

Hdqrs. Baker's Brigade
1 A. M. 21 October 1861
Special Order
The right wing California Regiment (less camp guards) under command of Lieutenant Colonel Wistar, will proceed to Conrad's Ferry, to arrive at sunrise and await order. The men will take blankets, overcoats, and forty rounds in their cartridge boxes, and will be followed by one days' rations in wagons.
By Command of Colonel Baker
Commanding Fred Harvey
A.A.G.

Colonel Wistar folded the order and placed it in an oilcloth packet. He glanced at his watch. "Hmm, two-thirty." He pulled at an earlobe with long bony fingers and frowned. "Paddy."

"Yes, sir.

"You will advise Major Smith that I want the first battalion ready to move out in one half hour. Take this packet with you so that Smith can read the contents and return it to me. Get a move on."

Paddy dressed hurriedly, draped a gum blanket around his shoulders and disappeared into the stormy darkness.

Promptly at 3:00 a.m., the long drumroll sounded and the First battalion of 570 cold, wet, shivering soldiers marched away from the shelter of their camp through a drenching rain toward Conrad's Ferry on the Potomac. Paddy trudged through the mud in company with his friends.

"This stuff is for the birds," Chirp grumbled. "What's the Colonel trying to prove pulling us out on a night like this?"

"Maybe he wants to find out if we can swim," Isaac Tibben retorted. He pulled the visor of his kepi over his eyes to shelter them against the driving downpour.

"I could've shown him that back in my tent," John Stott growled. "The canvas leaks so bad I had to tread water while I slept."

"Did you fellas ever stop to think this might be leading up to the real thing?" Billy Batt ventured hesitantly, looking around him for confirmation.

"What? On a night like this?" Dave Smith responded. "Don't talk crazy. Not even dogs would fight in this weather."

John Ferkler shifted his musket uneasily. "What about it, Paddy? Is this march leading up to the real thing?"

Paddy wiped away a stream of water that was trickling down his neck. "How would I know?"

"How would he know, he says. I'll lay anybody five to one Mulcahy knows more about what's going on than the senator from Oregon," Adam Hafer jibed

At that moment Barney Williams' shrill voice rose loud and piercing from the end of the column. "Hey, where's Chipman?" he yelled. "We got a rocking chair on wheels for him back here."

Laughter ran the length of the column, following which the march continued in relative silence.

Toward morning the rain stopped and the weather began clearing. The battalion passed through Conrad's Ferry at sunrise and was brought to a halt just beyond the tiny village where the men rested in ranks on the towpath of a canal.

Colonel Wistar scanned the opposite shore of the Potomac through field glasses. "Paddy!" he called.

"Yes, sir."

"Who is the closest mounted officer in the vicinity?"

"The chaplain, sir. Shall I fetch him?"

"Yes, right away. I want him to deliver a report to General Stone."

In response to Colonel Wistar's bidding, Chaplain Kellen rode with haste toward General Stone, located five miles down river at Edwards Ferry. He returned two hours later. Wistar strode forward to meet him.

"Glad you're back safely, Robert. Anything new from headquarters?"

The Chaplain mopped his brow. "Yes. General Stone says to remain where you are until further orders." He paused to catch his breath. "If you hear firing that might indicate heavy pressure on the scouting party of the Fifteenth Massachusetts which has been across all night, cross a sufficient strength to assist and extricate them, but use great caution."

"Thank you, Robert. Have Major Smith tell the men to break ranks and rest."

The chaplain saluted and rode off. The presence of a large body of troops on the tow path brought forth a steady stream of river men from the houses on Conrad's Ferry. Milling about in groups and filled with curiosity, they busied themselves asking and answering questions. The fact that a Yankee scouting party had evidently run afoul of trouble on the Virginia shore seemed to be especially gratifying to them. Rumors of an impending battle began to develop and spread swiftly.

Dave Chipman, with a show of disgust, surveyed Barney Williams' active participation in the rumor market. "Look at that prattling gossip monger, running all over the place like a sandpiper scurrying on the beach in search of food."

Sitting nearby, Crosby Slocum nodded, smiled affably and resumed cleaning his rifle.

Orderly duties being temporarily suspended, Paddy took leave of Colonel Wistar and strolled to where Billy Batt sat high on the canal bank by himself. He was staring at the river with a fixed, blank expression, his arms wrapped around his upright musket as though he were hugging it.

"What's troubling you?" Paddy inquired. "Those wild rumors got you worried?"

"Not exactly. I just got a funny feeling, that's all."

"Funny feeling? Like what?"

Batt cleared his throat. "Remember 'bout a year ago when us boys broke into Fritsch's brewery just for the thrill of it and swiped some beer?"

Paddy chuckled. "Sure do. That was the night old man McCool almost loaded our pants with rock salt."

"That's right. And we were scared stiff, remember? Scared because we knew we were breaking into a place where we didn't belong."

Paddy sat down. "I remember all right. If it hadn't of been for the excitement of adventure driving us on, we'd never of been able to make it in there that night."

"That's what I mean about now," Batt murmured. "I have the same scared-stiff feeling, but no excitement driving me on. Once we cross the river we'll be trespassing into somebody's home. Like with the brewery, we'll be breaking into someplace where we don't belong."

"Of course we belong over there. It's a part of the country we have to bring back into the Union."

Batt shook his head. "Turn it around and look at it the other way. Suppose this was Frankford and it was the Rebs who were getting ready to attack us from across the Pennypack. You would fight like all get-out, wouldn't you?"

"Yes. I'd be defending our home."

"There, you see? This isn't like being on our home ground where we have something to fight for." He chewed on one of his fingernails. "When McCool's old man chased us out of the brewery that night, we knew down deep he wouldn't really harm us because, well, because he just couldn't. He knew our folks, and knew we meant no harm. This is different. The people across that river won't be scaring us off with rock salt fired from a shotgun. They're going to be shooting live bullets. To kill."

Paddy's face registered misgiving. "I see what you mean. Guess maybe all of us are whistling past the graveyard at this point. Come on, let's go down and join the others."

The two stood up and scrambled down the steep bank. It was eight-thirty when Colonel Baker and his staff finally rode into Conrad's Ferry. The battalion formed on the color line and came to attention.

"The senator looks pleased as a pup with a choice bone," Barney Williams chortled.

"Silence in the ranks," Sergeant Wilson barked.

Baker rose in his stirrups and addressed the troops. "Before this day is over, men, you shall be veterans, victorious veterans of your first battle. The General has placed utmost confidence in your ability to fulfill your duty. I wish you the very best of luck and leave you with this charge. Press forward where you see my white plume shining amidst the ranks of war!"

"Oh, brother," Chirp blurted as the ranks were dismissed. "He's some character, ain't he?"

"I'll say," Tom Pilling replied. "Where'd he ever get the training to lead a brigade?"

"In Mexico, that's where," came a quick reply. The men turned their heads at the sound of Captain Ritman's voice.

"Did you know him during the Mexican War, Cap'n?" Frank Lightfoot asked.

"I did. I served under him at Cerro Gordo. Because of his bold leadership in that battle, Baker was given command of a brigade which he led during the rest of the war with distinguished credit."

"How old a buck is he, Cap'n?" John Heap cut in.

"The Senator will be sixty-two next month."

Adam Hafer scratched at his nose. "That's a little old to still be playing games in the saddle, don't you think?"

"If you young whippersnappers can keep pace with him, you'll be putting in a good day's work," Captain Ritman retorted.

Nearby, Colonel Wistar rode his horse in a tight circle, appearing visibly disturbed by Baker's remarks. He advanced his steed to the side of his superior officer and spoke in a low tone. "I don't want to seem critical, Ed, but why all this undue emphasis on a battle? According to the orders I received from Stone, we're to assist and extricate the scouting party which is across the river only if the need arises. And even then with considerable caution."

Baker's benign, fatherly countenance turned pugnacious. "Caution? Enough of caution. I see an opportunity to strike a blow of sufficient importance here to justify the risk incurred. I've ordered up the Philadelphia brigade on my own responsibility."

Wistar's jaw dropped. "You did what?"

"You heard me. I've sent word for them to report here immediately. We have soldiers who can accomplish this deed." He studied his former law partner with narrowed eyes. "However, since you appear at odds with me over the matter, I shall return to divisional headquarters for clarification." Wheeling his horse sharply, he galloped off in the direction of Edwards Ferry, leaving Colonel Wistar dumbfounded.

Befitting the acumen of a former commander of Indian rangers, Wistar finally managed to recover himself and he spent the interlude inspecting terrain and gathering fragmentary reports as to exactly what was transpiring over on the Virginia side of the river. It was past the noon hour when Colonel Baker returned to Conrad's Ferry. He dismounted quickly and hastened toward Colonel Wistar, his face radiant.

"Perhaps these orders will set your mind at ease," he said briskly. "Here, read them for yourself."

Wistar took the paper which Baker handed him and began reading.

Headquarters Corps of Observation,
Edwards Ferry, 21 October 11:50 a.m.
Colonel E. D. Baker, Commanding Brigade
Colonel: I am informed that the force of the enemy is about 4,000, all told. If you can push them, you may do so as far as possible in order to have a strong position near Leesburg, if you can keep them before you, avoiding their batteries. If they pass Leesburg and take the Gun Spring Road, you will not follow, but seize the first good position to cover that road. Their design is to draw us on, if they are obliged to retreat, as far as Goose Creek, where they can be reinforced from Manassas and have a strong position. Report frequently, so that when they are pushed, Gorman (at Edwards Ferry) can move on their flank.
Respectfully yours,
Chas. P. Stone,
Brigadier-General, Commanding

Wistar handed the orders back to Baker and shook his head. "Someone's been feeding Stone misleading information. That small scouting party we've got across the river isn't large or strong enough for an offensive maneuver. They're only over there to see if a Negro teamster's tale of Confederate withdrawal is true or not. From the reports I've received it also appears the Confederates might be wise to your little game of trying to squeeze them and are doing just what I predicted. Concealed by the terrain, they're withdrawing their troops from Gorman's front at Edwards Ferry and concentrating them against us across the river. There's a neat little ambush developing if I ever saw one."

The conversation was interrupted by the approach of Fred Harvey on horseback. Sitting his mount as if born in the saddle, the British observer dismounted and handed a note to Colonel Baker. "Additional orders, sir."

"Thank you, Fred." Colonel Baker opened the folded note and read it aloud.

Headquarters Corps of Observation:
Edwards Ferry, 21 October, 1861.
Colonel E. D. Baker, Commanding Brigade
Colonel: In case of heavy firing in front of Harrison's Island, you will advance the California Regiment of your brigade, or retire the regiments under Colonels Lee and Devens on the Virginia side of the river, at your discretion, assuming command on arrival.

Very respectfully, Colonel,
your most obedient servant,
Chas. P. Stone,
Brigadier-General, Commanding

Baker folded the note. "There, you have it in writing again, Isaac. I'm in full command with permission to advance the California Regiment, if I so desire."

Wistar grabbed the hilt of his sword in exasperation. "What the devil goes on here? Those are the same as our original instructions, and they certainly don't complement those orders you just showed me." He paused and glared from overhanging eyebrows. "Just what did you tell Charley when you saw him at headquarters? Whatever it was, I'd say from this dispatch he's thought it over and gone back to his original plan. And where'd he get the notion that Devens and Lee have full regiments across?"

Baker removed his spectacles and started wiping moisture from them. "Oh? How many of them are across?"

"Devens has crossed six hundred and twenty-five men and Lee has taken over three hundred. I'd like to point out it took Lee four solid hours to cross over just three hundred men. There are five hundred and seventy men in my battalion. Figure it out."

"Tut, tut, Isaac. Don't tell me you, of all people, are afraid to tackle a hazardous situation?"

"Don't tut, tut me. I have a battalion of men for whose safety I'm directly responsible." He turned and gazed at the rushing river. "To cross a force of over five hundred men with a boat capacity inadequate for advance and absurdly insufficient for retreat is sheer folly, especially on a permissive and discretionary order wrung from a superior five miles away."

"I didn't wring a permissive and discretionary order from anyone. By God, Wistar, if I didn't know you, I'd say you were a coward. You must have left your fighting pluck out West with the last Indian you killed. The country needs a victory over those damned Rebels. The President wants a victory, and I shall see to it that both country and President have their victory. Captain Harvey, I want the second battalion of my California regiment ordered to this spot immediately. And tell Colonel Cogswell to hurry up his Forty-second New York."

Having thus shed his ire, Baker turned back to his former law partner. "Just what is the available boat capacity?"

Through clenched teeth, Wistar replied, "Operating between the Maryland shore and the island, there are..."

"Island! What Island?"

"Harrison's Island, the one Stone mentioned in his dispatch where Devens and Lee made their crossing about a mile downstream. The island is two miles long and several hundred yards wide."

"Oh? Go on."

"As I started to say, there are two flatboats operating between the Maryland shore and the island. Each boat is capable of carrying thirty to forty men each.

Transportation from the island to the Virginia shore consists of exactly one flatboat capable of carrying fifty men. Oh, yes, there's also one skiff on that side which can handle three or four men."

Baker's countenance softened. He placed his hands affectionately on Wistar's broad shoulders. "Forgive my rash outburst, Isaac. We shouldn't be acting like this toward each other. We've been close friends for too many years. Tell me, what is your opinion of the situation?"

"Exactly as stated before. There's an absence of cooperation in all the other quarters. This lack of preparation for a general advance is conclusive evidence that Stone's sole purpose in sending us here is to, as he so clearly put it, extricate the scouting party across the river. What other reason is conceivable in light of the fact that Stone ordered down but a single battalion and a few guns? The details for the extrication he's left to your discretion as brigadier, commanding on the spot."

Colonel Baker stared across the river. "What would you suggest we do?"

"The obvious thing would be to place a small infantry detachment on the island. It offers a defensible position from which moderate musketry fire could easily keep the top of the bluff on the Virginia shore clear. It's only from that bluff that the enemy's fire could reach our troops retiring across the river. A few guns placed in position on the Maryland side would not only aid the operation, but effectually protect the return of the covering force from the island "

"You're still worried about being trapped and beaten, aren't you, Isaac?"

"Precisely. That's exactly what the Confederates are planning. I've seen Indians pull that trick too many times not to be able to recognize it."

"Bosh, Isaac, you're seeing ghosts. Encirclement, that's the ticket. If we can put your men across the river and join them with those of Lee and Devens, we'll have a force strong enough to roll the Confederates right down on the points of Gorman's bayonets at Edwards Ferry."

"If you think you can pull off such a neat trick with a combined force of only fifteen hundred men," Wistar said resignedly, "you go ahead. I rest my case."

"That's the spirit. Are your men ready to cross?"

"They've been waiting on the bank of this canal for the past eight hours. If they're not ready now they never will be."

"Bully, start them moving."

Weary from long hours of idle waiting, the troops greeted Colonel Wistar's order to advance with a wild outburst of cheering following which Captain Ritman hurried his company of Frankford volunteers downstream to the water's edge opposite Harrison's Island.

"All right, lads. Step lively. Keep your powder dry, and don't rock the boats. The river is swollen and the current is swift. If you capsize these scows, it'll be a wet walk back."

Paddy pushed and shoved his way into a crowd scrambling for the honor of being in the first boat. Using elbows and shoulders to good advantage, he managed to get aboard at the very last minute.

Captain Ritman cupped hands to his mouth. "All right, shove off."

Loaded to the brim with standing soldiers, the barge had begun to move slowly out from shore when an officer appeared charging down the riverbank and with a tremendous leap landed safely on the stern of the departing boat.

Paddy looked up with surprise. "Captain Stewart, sir!"

"Ho there, Chappy. Good to see you again. How's it feel to be facing battle for the first time?"

"Don't know as I can put it in words, sir. How's come you're here?"

Stewart removed his cap and ran a hand through his thick crop of black hair. "I sat in on a conversation between Slone and Baker this morning. Very interesting. You might say the Senator's line of appeal and reasoning struck me as being a bit strange and erratic. So much so that as an observer for Her Majesty's government, I thought it wise to take leave of headquarters and come up here. I'd like to see how your political generals conduct themselves in the field."

"You think something might go wrong?"

"Love a duck, Chappy, I talk too much. Don't let it upset you. Introduce me to your friends."

"Sure, be glad to."

Stewart's admirable traits captivated Paddy's comrades, who received the British captain warmly.

In the face of a chill wind sweeping down the river, the crossing continued beneath a gray overcast sky. Reaching Harrison's Island, the first boat load of soldiers from the 71st Regiment disembarked on a miry bank that sucked their feet to ankle depth in mud, causing them to flounder until they reached solid ground. Not long after, the second load of troops arrived and the shuttling flatboats returned to the Maryland shore for more cargo.

Before long there was confusion on the island. No one seemed to be in charge, nor was anyone superintending the passage of the troops, and no order was maintained in their crossing. Acting on their own initiative, the men began to straggle toward the western side of the island where a single barge waited for those who wished to ferry themselves across to the Virginia shore.

Staring down at the intruders from the opposite bank was an imposing wooded, rock-studded bluff, named Balls Bluff, that wore a foreboding frown on its face. It was covered by a thick stand of trees, fern and skunk cabbage. With misgivings, Stewart surveyed the formidable land barrier.

"Bloody Mary, don't tell me your Colonel plans to fight raw troops up that cliff?"

The young soldiers surrounding him also looked with awe at the precipitous height confronting them. A low whistle escaped Chirp's lips. "Man, that must be over two hundred feet straight up."

Isaac Tibben shouldered his way to the barge. "Only one way to find out," he shouted. "Let's cross over. Maybe there's a bypath we can use to get to the top. Come on."

There was a general rush for the barge which, when loaded to capacity, was poled slowly across the water. This time, the men disembarked on a caked mud bank at a spot where a secluded sanctuary had been created at the water's edge by leafy boughs sweeping low from mammoth sycamores. The mixed scent of muddy river water and decaying leaf mold filled the air.

Joe Batt and Henry Castor reached out and took their younger brothers by the arm. "You kids stick close to us, do you understand?" Joe ordered. "I don't like the smell of this clambake one damn bit. Give me your musket, Billy. I'll carry it for you so's you can climb easier."

"Ah, cut it out, Joe. You're always treatin' me like I was still a baby or somethin'. I'll shoulder my own load."

"Hey fellas," Chirp broke in with unrestrained laughter. "Take a gander out there at Rubber-face, would you?" He pointed toward a skiff being rowed in midstream by two soldiers. Standing in the prow of the small boat, Barney Williams struck a pose similar to that of Washington crossing the Delaware and was reciting at the top of his voice,

"Listen my children and you shall hear,

of the midnight...."

"That tom fool idiot will be swimming ashore if he don't watch his step," Henry Castor said disgustedly.

After exploring the shoreline, Isaac Tibben waved his arms and called to the others. "Here's a path to the top. Let's move on up."

Those who were already scaling the bluff continued their upward climb; the rest proceeded to use the more circuitous route by way of a dry gully which Tibben had discovered. They arrived at the summit and, panting heavily, flung their sweating bodies to the ground. The grassy field where they stood covered about two acres and was surrounded on three sides by a dense growth of trees; the river and bluff were at their back.

The succoring force could distinguish the forms of Colonel Deven's command crouching in battle position in the woods, off to the right. Behind them, at the far end of the glade, was a reserve detachment of soldiers under Colonel Lee.

Earlier, the scouting party, made up of troops from the 15th and 20th Massachusetts, had advanced to the outskirts of Leesburg. Attacked by a large force of Rebels, they had retreated to their present position in the timber that bordered the Potomac. The sporadic sound of firing served notice that the enemy was advancing from the direction of Leesburg. Apprehensive, the green Massachusetts soldiers watched the battalion from the 71 st Regiment clamber over the bluff and fall into position. Colonel Wistar arrived on the scene and quickly surveyed the precarious situation. He began posting the battalion to cover the center of the line and the left flank. Bob Smith, bearing the flag, was ordered into the center of the battle line. A gentle breeze from the front was stiff enough to flutter the colors at right angles with the staff.

Colonel Devens, a Boston Lawyer, hurried to where Wistar was directing the activities of his men. "I say, Wistar, where the devil is Colonel Baker? We've been waiting three hours for orders."

Wistar replied in a voice full of disgust. "He has spent the last hour superintending the lifting of an additional barge from the canal."

Devens frowned. "You mean to say he's neglected to give orders to an advanced force in the face of the enemy while he performs a job that should be left to a subordinate?"

"That's it."

"Oh my God."

A sudden crashing commotion in the rear caused both officers to turn around quickly. A squad of artillery under the command of Lieutenant French appeared through the trees. Swearing at the top of their lungs, they labored and strained in an attempt to hoist two mountain howitzers over the crest of the bluff. Directing the back-breaking ordeal was Colonel Baker. As soon as the two cannons had been pulled clear of obstacles, Baker ordered them into the center of the line and placed between the 15th Massachusetts on the right and the 71st on the left. The two howitzers were soon joined by a twelve-pounder from a Rhode Island battery under the command of Lieutenant Bramhall.

With the artillery posted to his satisfaction, Colonel Baker strode toward Colonel Lee and shook him by the hand. "I congratulate you, sir, on the prospect of a battle."

The gray-haired commander of the 20th Massachusetts forced a wry smile.

Turning to the Massachusetts soldiers, Colonel Baker sang out, "Boys, you want to fight, don't you?"

They responded with a ringing cheer.

"Listen to them damn Harvard boys," Chirp Castor growled. "I'd yell like hell, too, if I knew I was gonna be in reserve."

Those in the scouting party from the 20th Massachusetts began peeling off their overcoats, fancy gray coats with brilliant red silk linings, and hung them on trees in preparation for the fight. The coats were quickly peppered by a volley from enemy skirmishers who mistook them for soldiers.

Unnerved by the attack, Lieutenant Hibbs jumped to his feet and brandished a sword. "Load in nine times!" he cried.

Lying prone on the ground, the soldiers of D Company responded by thrusting their muskets forward perpendicular to their bodies. Lieutenant Hibbs started counting.

"One!"

Each volunteer extracted a cartridge from the leather box attached to his belt.

"Two!"

They tore off the ends of paper cartridges containing black gunpowder with their teeth.

"Three!"

They poured gunpowder into musket barrels.

"Four!"

They withdrew long, slender ramrods from beneath musket barrels.

"Five!"

Buck and ball cartridges were rammed.

"Six!"

Ramrods were replaced on the underside of musket barrels.

"Seven!"

Percussion caps were placed on firing nipples.

"Eight!"

Every musket was raised and primed.

"Hold your fire, men," Wistar countermanded.

He stepped to the fore of the battle line, his hands on his hips. "Any of you ever hunted grizzly bear?" he inquired.

No one answered, they just stared.

"Let me tell you, it takes cool nerve. You have to get in close. When a bear rises on its haunches to strike, you shoot for the throat." He paused and looked up and down the line. "I want you men to exhibit the same cool nerves and steady hands required of a bear hunter. Now relax."

As soon as the Colonel had departed, Dave Chipman rolled over on his side and berated the soldier lying next to him. "Blast your short body, Lesher, if you stick that ramrod up my ass one more time while I'm loading, I'll blow your damn brains out."

"Chipman!" Lieutenant Hibbs screamed, "how many times do you have to be told that profanity is forbidden under army regulation Number Fifty-two! If I hear you one more time, you'll ride the saw-buck with a kerosene gag-rag in your mouth." He turned to Lesher. "And I have told you, when loading by file in prone position, be careful how you handle the ramrod."

Barney Williams tucked his head in an armpit and sheltered it with a hand. He called out in a loud falsetto, "Hooray for me, the hell with you, general orders fifty-two!"

Lieutenant Hibbs spun on his heel. Who said that?" he screeched.

Barney's puckish face reappeared, innocent eyes opened wide. "It was a Johnny Reb over there in them woods, Lieutenant. I saw him giving you the sass with my own eyes. Honest."

Hibbs slapped his thighs in exasperation and stormed to the end of the line.

The desultory exchange of musket fire which had taken place in front of the position held by the contingent from the 15th Massachusetts slackened until there was silence.

"Them Johnnies shooting at us from the woods," Billy Batt whispered, "I wonder what they look like."

"Why they look just like us," his older brother replied. "They're Americans, same as we are. What did you expect?"

The youngest Batt moistened dry lips. "Sure is strange why we should be out here trying to kill each other. Ain't it, Joe?"

"Hush, Billy, and keep your eyes peeled."

More Union troops appeared over the crest of the bluff. A company of men from the 42nd New York, the Tammany regiment, filed into position under the leadership of their regimental commander, Colonel Milton Cogswell, a graduate of West Point.

Spotting the newly-arrived troops, Colonel Baker broke off his conversation with Wistar and shouted a cheery greeting. "Cogswell, welcome to the fray!

"One blast upon your bugle horn is worth a thousand men!"

The poetic lines from Scott's *"Lady of the Lake"* caused startled men to turn around and stare.

Henry Castor scowled. "We are in a pickle and he's reciting poetry? He's off his nut."

"Amen to that," Joe Batt retorted.

The New Yorker approached with a steady stride. Baker placed a hand on Cogswell's shoulder and addressed him in a condescending manner. "Milton, as a professional soldier, will you do me the honor of examining my battle line?"

"Yes, I would like to inspect the field," Cogswell replied gruffly.

"Excellent. Come along, I'll point out the features to you. Are you coming, Wistar?"

"No, I'll wait here."

At Baker's request, Colonel Cogswell began the tour of inspection. Nearly fifteen minutes elapsed before the two officers returned. Cogswell appeared visibly upset.

"The troop of cavalry which General Stone sent to you," he inquired of Baker, "have you thrown them in advance of the infantry over on the right?"

"No. Since I foresee no need of horses in this engagement, I've ordered the cavalry to return downstream to Edwards Ferry."

Cogswell was dumbstruck. Tugging idly at an earlobe, Wistar arched his eyebrows and focused his gaze on the ground.

Oblivious of the unspoken censure, Baker squared his shoulders. "Tell me, Cogswell, what do you think of my disposition of the troops?"

"Do you really want me to tell you?"

"Yes, of course."

"Well then, speaking frankly, you have placed the troops in an untenable position. Your disposition of the entire force is defective."

His unexpected reply caused Baker's jaw to sag as if unhinged.

Cogswell pointed toward a steep wooded hill that rose sharply beyond a deep ravine off to the left. "If the enemy should suddenly occupy that hill," he said grimly, "your left flank and the entire line can be enfiladed and destroyed."

Frankford volunteers lying nearby glanced up at the dominant wooded slope which menaced their exposed flank across a dry gully.

"Our whole action must be concentrated on the left, not on the right as you have it," Cogswell concluded. "We must occupy that hill before the enemy does."

Baker's lower lip trembled pettishly. "Thank you. That will be all. You will take charge of the artillery."

"Any instructions as to its use, sir?" Cogswell asked coldly.

"Yes, Colonel. You will fire cannon balls from them."

"Very good, sir." The regimental commander of the 42d New York saluted and strode off.

Giving the senator wide berth, Wistar strolled toward his men under the pretense of examining their line.

Colonel Baker paced back and forth alone for several minutes. "Isaac!" he called in a loud voice. "Come here!"

"Yes, Ed. What is it?"

"I want you to throw out two companies as skirmishers. Check the woods and crest of that hill across the gully for the precise location of the enemy's right. Have the men carry the colors. Break out the flag if the hill is clear and I will advance the main body. If attacked by a superior force, fall back fighting." Baker drew out a watch. "It is now three o'clock. It will be getting dark in two hours. Have your men move now, and I want you to pick your two best companies for the job."

Wistar nodded. "That will call for the Frankford boys under Ritman and A Company under Markoe. On further thought, I'll leave the rest of the battalion under the command of Major Smith and accompany the movement myself."

"Now that sounds more like the Isaac Wistar of old," Baker exclaimed happily. "Go ahead and good luck."

Skirmishers, who are to the main body what antennae are to insects, moved forward at Wistar's command. They crossed the deep, dry gully which lay thirty yards in front of their battle line and deployed in the woods on the other side. Advancing quietly and cautiously, muskets held at alert, the blue-clad defenders of the Union snaked their way from tree to tree as they ascended the steep wooded slope. A long, tapered bayonet fixed to the muzzle of Paddy's musket seemed to be guiding him forward like the needle on a compass. He breathed heavily and was perspiring from anxiety.

They finally reached the top of the hill and quickly dropped in their tracks in response to a hand signal from Colonel Wistar. Confronting them was a triangular-shaped field covered with tall broomgrass. Motioning for those near him to remain where they were, flat on their bellies, Wistar began crawling forward stealthily. Paddy, because of his obscure position, did not catch the signal as it was passed along the line.

He started to inch his way carefully into the dense cover and had traveled several yards when a sudden disturbance made him stop short. Almost as frightening as if a gun had been discharged at his ear came the sound of a dislodged panic-stricken rabbit flying in terror toward the safety of its warren. Concealed in the grass a short distance from where he lay, someone else noticed the speed and direction which the rabbit was taking and was impressed by the animal's prudence.

"Go it, Molly Cottontail. Wish I could go with y'all."

The exclamation caused Paddy to freeze. The dialect he just heard was definitely Dixie.

"Yes, and 'y gollies, Jim, I'd go with Molly, too, if it warn't for my character," another voice responded.

Paddy's temples pounded. Somewhere in front of him lay two Confederate soldiers, maybe more, who were totally unaware of his presence. The proximity of the skirmish line had evidently escaped their notice. While trying to decide on a course of action, he heard the metallic click of a musket lock from the direction where he knew Chirp was posted about five yards away. He parted the grass and saw his friend stand upright, take aim and fire.

The sharp report from Castor's musket was followed by a scream of anguish from the field. A sight of frightening magnitude bulged Paddy's eyes. An entire

Confederate regiment, the 8th Virginia, rose en masse from its concealment in the tall grass. Leveling a thousand rifles at the Federal skirmish line which lay cringing on the edge of the woods, the Virginians fired as a unit. Pausing to reload, they charged through the heavy pall of powder smoke with fixed bayonets. Mouths wide open, the grayclad enemy split the air with a blood-curdling yell that telegraphed fear into the uninitiated ears of the thin blue line.

At the center of the Union skirmish line, Bob Smith broke out the colors in response to an order from Colonel Wistar. The Colonel brandished a sword and shouted.

"Rally on the color line and fall back!" The command was repeated along the line. Sight of the Stars and Stripes floating calmly above the battle smoke helped restore courage to faint hearts and with a retaliatory shout of their own, the Frankford volunteers, many of them descendants of men who had fought at Trenton, Germantown and Valley Forge, returned the Confederate volley with telling effect. The advancing enemy faltered momentarily, recovered, and charged at close quarters.

Paddy noticed a tall figure emerge from behind a tree and spring at Chirp, who was caught unaware. He screamed a warning at the sight of a bayonet flashing at the end of the Rebel's rifle, but was too late. Castor clutched painfully at his stomach and doubled up as if stricken with green apple colic.

In horror, he saw the enemy soldier shake his rifle in violent desperation to dislodge the murderous blade from Chirp's midriff.

Castor's head flopped weakly from side to side. The Confederate looked into his victim's pleading eyes and discharged his gun. Castor's body recoiled backward into a bloody heap.

Hot tears poured down Paddy's cheeks. In a fit of crying rage, he raised his musket, aimed it at Chirp's slayer and fired. The man's hands flew into the air as he pitched forward, his face a bloody pulp.

The terrible grief which Paddy felt completely overshadowed the horrible fact that he had just killed some mother's son.

The rest of the skirmish line began retreating slowly down the wooded slope under overwhelming pressure from the enemy. The Union soldiers hugged trees for protection as they descended, managing to slow down the charge of yelling Confederates with an effective fire of two volleys per minute.

Dave Chipman moved into position on Paddy's right. In his anxiety to stop an onrushing Confederate, he forgot to remove the ramrod from his musket barrel before firing. Paddy saw the rammer explode from the muzzle of Dave's gun and sail harmlessly into a nearby tree. Infuriated by the mistake, Chipman tore at his quarry with his bayonet leveled to kill. As he closed in on his adversary, his foot tripped on an exposed tree root and he toppled forward helplessly.

The intended victim lunged swiftly, impaling Chipman's head on a bayonet. The steel entered Dave's gaping mouth and protruded from the back of his skull with brains dripping from the bloody point.

Concerned only with his own safety, Paddy continued to load and fire as he retreated further down the hillside.

The right wing of the skirmishing force was nearly destroyed. Taking cognizance of the situation, Wistar ordered the left wing to fall back rapidly to escape a like fate. The Colonel's appearance and manner were ferocious..

Earlier in the action he had been struck in the jaw by a bullet and a profuse flow of blood from the wound became matted in his beard. Blood bubbled at the corners of his mouth when he spoke and dripped down his front.

Acting in response to the Colonel's orders, remnants of the skirmish line began drawing in hastily from all sides to form a cordon around the flag. Fighting desperately and contesting every foot of ground, they made a determined effort to stave off the Confederates who were bent on capturing the Federal colors before they could be carried to safety.

"Rally 'round the flag, boys!" Lieutenant Williams shouted hoarsely. "Don't let them..." His words were choked off abruptly as he lurched forward with an ugly red stain soaking the front of his tunic.

"Andy!" Barney Williams screamed above the rattle of musketry. "Help me with Joe! He's been tumbled!"

Andy Williams rushed to the side of his stricken brother and felt his chest. "He's dead, Barney. Oh, my God, what will Mother..."

"Both of you take his body from the field and be quick about it," Wistar bellowed.

Shouldering the lifeless form of their oldest brother, Barney and Andy quickly dragged him across the gully and into the main line which was a few yards away.

"We're almost home!" Wistar shouted to the other men. "The rest of the battalion will cover you. Run for it!"

He had cast a fleeting glance around to make certain that no one capable of being saved would be left behind when he suddenly buckled and Paddy flew to his side.

"What is it, sir?"

"A mini ball in my thigh. Same damn spot I took an arrow in the upper Klamath country."

The Colonel's boot began filling with blood. "Hand me your knife."

"There's no time, sir. The Rebs are almost on us. Let me..."

Wistar grabbed the knife which Paddy handed to him and with one bold slash cut a slit in the bottom of his boot. Blood rushed in a stream from the opening. "I can make it now. Give me your hand. And run."

The first battalion from the 71st Regiment, seeing that their Colonel faced imminent capture, waited until both he and Paddy disappeared from view in the deep gully, then delivered a withering volley which stopped the onrushing Confederates in their tracks. Taking advantage of the covering support, Wistar and Paddy scrambled to safety.

At a signal from Colonel Cogswell, the brass twelve-pounder and two mountain howitzers roared with a vengeance, their sights trained on the charging foe. A Confederate officer caught in the shell burst of a canister, stood still, apparently uninjured, but a second glance by those watching showed that his head was gone and in its place projected the long white bone of his neck, hot and smoking.

Sour-tasting vomit bubbled in Paddy's throat and flowed from his mouth as he watched the headless body pitch forward.

Undaunted, the enemy continued to press forward despite the devastating hail of lead. Lieutenant Hibbs, sole surviving of officer in Company D, shouted the order, "Load and fire at will!" His command was followed immediately by the ringing of hammers in barrels and the clicking of gunlocks, a metallic snapping that ran along the line. Volley after volley, searing sheets of flame, finally drove the Confederates from the gully and forced them to retire up the hill. Rebel sharpshooters continued to peck away at the Union line.

"Cease firing!" Wistar shouted. "Dress on the colors and keep low."

The 1st Battalion of the 71st Regiment realigned themselves quickly and fell exhausted by their arms. They appeared to be coal miners after a hard day in the pits. Faces that had been boyishly pink were blackened beyond recognition. Lips were caked with black grime from biting the twist off cartridges. After firing several rounds, their hands had become blackened and smeared from handling the rammer. Sweat, streaming from their foreheads, had been wiped from their eyes, enabling them to sight their muskets. In the process, the grime was transferred from hands to face, transforming the latter into a black mask.

The late October sun was sinking rapidly in the west, and the chill air of an autumn evening bathed their necks and faces with a dampness that penetrated their flimsy blue uniforms and chilled them to the bone.

Crawling warily along the line, Chaplain Kellen stopped and tapped Paddy on the shoulder. "Mulcahy."

Paddy looked up with bloodshot eyes. "Yes, sir?"

The chaplain spoke low. "Will you come with me. Someone wants to see you."

"Who...?" Paddy cut off his own question, picked up his musket, and with one eye peeled on the hill, followed silently after the chaplain. In the rear, near the crest of the bluff, he saw Joe Batt rocking and sobbing with his brother's head softly cradled in his lap. Paddy dropped his musket with a wail and rushed to the spot.

"Oh God, no," he cried.

Billy Batt's blue tunic was slashed from throat to belt buckle, a mass of pulsating lung tissue protruding from an ugly tear in his chest wall. His breath came in short, sonorous death rattles.

Joe wept softly. "Billy? Billy boy, Paddy's here."

The dying volunteer's eyelids fluttered faintly, but there was no sign of recognition. He gasped in delirium. "Your father told me.. .Wait for you here at the smithy, now...now you've come. We can...can go into town together."

The white of his eyes rolled back as a gush of foamy blood boiled from his mouth.

Paddy drew back, clapping his hands over his eyes. "He's dead! Billy's dead! Oh, dear God!"

Joe Batt jumped to his feet and with tears streaming down his blackened cheeks, took up a musket. "I'll make 'em pay for this! Every bloody one of ' em!"

He started to run wildly toward the front line.

"No, Joe!" Henry Castor cried out. He grabbed his companion by the legs and brought him to the ground. "We've both got a score to settle, but we can't do it alone. Wait'll we get the order to counterattack."

Rolling over on his face, Joe covered his head with his arms and sobbed. In the shelter of some nearby trees, Colonel Wistar was tending to his wounds with Colonel Baker looking on helplessly. A dispatch courier, who had just arrived on the field, handed Baker a note. "Message from General Stone, sir."

"Thank you, my boy. Wait over there."

"What's it say?" Wistar asked weakly.

Colonel Baker glanced over the message and read in a whisper. "Four regiments have been seen by our scouts crossing an open place and marching toward you." He let the paper fall to the ground. "This dispatch has traveled five miles and crossed the river twice," he said, crestfallen. "We should soon be feeling the effects of their arrival at the front." The deep lines at the corners of his mouth were drawn. "I've been a fool, Isaac, a bullheaded old fool. Our situation is developing along the same lines you so wisely predicted. How can you ever...."

Wistar stood up feebly. "Let's not look over our shoulder. We've got to get these men out of here."

"The officer who dies with his men will never be judged harshly," Baker muttered.

His words were drowned by a thunderous crashing roar. Both officers turned in time to see the twelve-pounder recoil over the edge of the bluff and hurtle downward. A deep groan escaped Baker's lips. Adding to the distress of the moment, he saw that an effective fire from Confederate sharpshooters had killed or dispersed all of the artillery men so that the two howitzers stood idle.

Stewart and Harvey also noticed the critical situation from a vantage point some yards away and made a bold dash for the inactive cannon. They began working on them without awaiting orders. The two Englishmen were joined quickly by Colonel Cogswell and the aged Colonel Lee. With the renewed assistance of artillery fire, the beleaguered Federal force managed to turn back the Confederate's fifth attack on the hard-pressed line, but at great cost. The scanty ammunition in the limbers had been exhausted. To make certain that the Federal field pieces would fire no more, Confederate sharpshooters further disabled the howitzers by shooting the spokes out of the wheels.

Seeing that the cannons had been put out of action, John Stott slowly drew a deck of cards from his coat pocket.

"What are you preparing to do?" George Hart blurted. "Ask the Johnnies over for a friendly game of whist?"

Stott shook his head. "I don't know as they would bring me any bad luck," he answered simply, "but I don't want to be killed and have my mother learn they were found on my body." He gave the deck of cards a pitch.

Lying close by, Paddy turned his tear-burned eyes toward the heavens to observe large banks of purple clouds drifting across a grayish black sky where a patchy orange, red and lavender sunset resembled the glow cast by a distant fire.

He lowered his gaze. In the surrounding woods, night shadows were turning the trees into weird silhouettes. Ignited by the heavy musket fire, small fires of burning leaves sent up screens of curling smoke. His nostrils picked up the dank odor arising from the darkened gully that reeked of a spice-scented smell that he had always associated with the shroud and grave.

"It's going to be a cold night" Joe Heap said offhandedly.

"For some, it's permanently cold," Frank Lightfoot responded glumly. He stared at the dead bodies littering the field.

The stress of fearful sights, sounds and smells was beginning to take its toll.

"When does a battle end?" Ferkler whined. "We can't keep fighting until no one's left. We'll all be killed, like Castor lying up there in the woods, cold and still forever."

"Not a pleasant thought, is it?" Adam Hafer retorted dolefully.

"Well, I'm for getting out, now! Hand me the white feather, anything you like, but I'm for quitting." He cupped his face in his hands and began crying. "It's milking time back home," he sobbed. "I want to live to milk cows again. Wash up with Pa after work, sit down to eat with my folks. Have a family of my own. I don't want to be killed!" He removed his hands from his face. "Why don't you say something? I'm a crazy coward, that's what you're thinking, right?"

Lieutenant Hibbs crawled forward to investigate the commotion. He placed a hand on Ferkler's shoulder. "Take it easy, Ferky. We'll get out of this mess safely. Wait and see."

"I don't want to wait and see. I've done my share of fighting, now I want to pull out. I'm scared. Do you understand? Scared! Scared! Scared!"

"We all are, Ferky," Hibbs replied softly. He turned toward the men nearby. "You, Tibben, Heap, Hafer, talk to him. Take his mind off things."

"We'll do our best, Lieutenant." There was a new-found respect in their voices.

"If you need me for anything, just call, I'll be posted by the flag."

Joe Heap stared after the departing officer.

"It's amazing," he murmured.

"What's amazing?" Tibben asked.

"How a taste of combat has made a man out of Hibbs. I would never have believed it could happen. Him of all people, running this company all by himself. Amazing."

Several yards behind the battle line the principal officers were engaged in a serious council of war.

"It seems to me," Colonel Lee said, shaking his head, "that a quick, easy death is the most providential thing that could happen to us."

Baker wiped beads of perspiration from his face. "In that case, the bullets are looking for you," he said, "but avoid me." He paused. "Cogswell, how would you handle the present situation.

Cogswell studied the terrain. "With our left enfiladed and overpowering frontal fire facing us, it's dangerous either to maneuver or withdraw," he replied. "I'm still of the opinion that our sole course of action lies here on the left. About fourteen hundred men remain in the command and though pinned fast, they are firm. Engaging the entire command, we should drive the enemy's flanking force from the gully and hill beyond, and, cutting our way through the woods, make an attempt to join forces with Stone down river at Edwards Ferry."

"I will follow your recommendation," Baker responded firmly. "We shall fight our way out. Gentlemen, return to your commands and order them to change front immediately. We will prepare a column of attack." He looked about. "The darkness will make an excellent shield for our movements."

Colonel Wistar had started toward his battalion when, suddenly, he spun around like a top and fell to the ground. Confused and unable to see for a moment, he groped for his sword which had dropped from his grasp. A stream of blood flowing down his arm soaked his hand and rendered the search impossible.

Colonel Baker quickly put an arm around his waist and helped him rise to his feet. "What is it, Wistar? Hit again?"

Wistar's sleeve had a jagged tear at the right elbow and the arm swung crazily. "I've taken a ball in the elbow joint," he said, wincing with pain.

"Here, my man," Baker shouted at Paddy. "Catch hold of your Colonel and get him down to the river."

Paddy sprang to his feet and rushed to Wistar's assistance.

Seeing their indomitable commander being led from the field sent a wave of consternation sweeping through the battalion of soldiers from the 71st Regiment as they prepared for a last-ditch effort to break out of the trap.

Struggling beneath the heavy burden of Wistar's crippled body, Paddy guided him safely down the steep slope to the water's edge and placed him on a barge.

"Will it be all right if I leave you here, sir? Those boat men can ferry you to safety across the river. I'd like to go back to my friends."

"You don't have to, you know," Wistar whispered.

"I want to."

Weakened by the loss of blood, Wistar made a feeble gesture with his hand. "Go back then, son," he murmured, "and may God go with you."

Arriving on the scene and spoiling for a fight, two fresh companies of the 42nd New York, under Captains Gerety and O'Meara, clawed their way to the top of the Bluff. Paddy, his uniform stained with blood, followed in their wake.

Regaining the summit, he noticed with alarm that wild confusion reigned in the eerie, smoke-filled dusk. Shouting furiously, Fred Harvey ordered troops to reform on the colors in preparation for a counterattack.

Paddy grabbed George Hart. "What's happened?"

"Our position was overrun just after you left. Baker's been killed. We're going to try to recover his body."

The beleaguered blue line, shot-torn flags waving defiantly in front, surged forward at the signal from Harvey. The Confederates, breaking before the onslaught, retreated across the gully in disorder and retired up the wooded slope. At the place where he had last seen Baker alive, Paddy recoiled upon seeing his still form lying face up. Blood trickled from a hole in the senator's forehead. His face was as white as marble.

Senator Edward D. Baker

Colonel Issac Wistar

Death of Colonel Baker at Balls Bluff
Loudon Museum/Leesburg, VA

"Can't say he didn't go down with the ship," Tom Pilling said sorrowfully, as several men picked up the Colonel's body and carried it to the rear.

George Hart grimaced. "Yes, and he took Stott along with him. Look."

He pointed to a place where John Stott lay on his back, arms out flung, palms turned up, his eyes staring blankly at the rising moon. Strewn about his lifeless body was a blood-soaked deck of cards.

Pilling wiped gunpowder from parched lips with a tattered sleeve crusted with cockleburs. "That's a bust hand, if I ever saw one," he said.

The besieged Federals flung their taxed bodies on the ground to await the next development. Soldiers who had run out of ammunition crawled around in the dark. Resembling ghouls, they gathered cartridges from the leather boxes on the hips of the dead. Hanging over the field was the acrid stench of flesh and blood commingled with the woodsy odor of decayed organic matter.

Paddy glanced at the night sky. The stars which were appearing reminded him of tiny shore lights seen from the deck of a ship. He rubbed his tired eyes and buried his head in the crook of his arm.

Captain Harvey, having successfully recovered the body of Colonel Baker, reported to Colonel Cogswell.

"My compliments, sir," the British observer said formally. "You are to assume command of the field. Colonel Baker so advised me a few moments before he met his untimely death."

'Thank you, Captain. We'll make another attempt to fight our way out. Form your men into a column of attack while I look for Devens and Lee."

Both regimental commanders from Massachusetts were engaged in an animated conversation on the edge of the bluff. Colonel Devens gazed down at the moonlit Potomac and waved his arms. He broke off the conversation abruptly as Cogswell approached.

"Glad you're here, Milton," he said brusquely. "Now that Baker's dead, we've decided to make a run for it across the river."

Cogswell bristled angrily. "As the duly appointed successor to Baker, I am obliged to countermand your plan. A retreat across the river is impossible. The only movement that can be made is to cut our way through to Edwards Ferry. Gentlemen, you will assemble your troops for the attack." He turned on his heel and strode rapidly toward the left flank, ready for action.

Posting himself at the head of the column composed of troops from New York and Philadelphia, he raised his sword to signal the charge. Suddenly from the rear came a discordant cry, "Retreat to the river! Retreat to the river!"

The entire right flank was hastily evacuated by troops from the 15th and 20th Massachusetts regiments. Reacting to the unauthorized order triggered by mob impulse, they scrambled wildly to the river. Some ran stolidly, mechanically, fearfully; others plunged, while others simply ran-shoulders forward, elbows stiff, their ghastly faces turned toward the darkened sky, their mouths gaping like banked fish sucking at air.

"Look at them yellow-belly abolitionists skedaddle," a New York volunteer shouted derisively. "All they do is talk a good fight."

"Go, you Molly cottontails!" Paddy shouted. The expression which he had borrowed from the Confederates was taken up by others.

"Go it, Molly cottontails!" they hollered.

"Hey, Lieutenant!" John Heap screamed above the clamor. "Ferkler and Evans are deserting!"

The two soldiers had thrown away their muskets and were running panic-stricken toward a path that led to the river.

There was a loud blast from a bugle. "Forget them!" Cogswell bellowed. "We're charging down river!"

With a deep-throated cheer, detachments from the 42nd New York and 71st Pennsylvania rushed forward and pitched into the enemy, the darkened woods illuminated by an orange glare from a barrage of muzzle fire. Paddy saw Captain Harvey reel backward as if kicked by a mule. The left side of the Britisher's head was blown away revealing brains and an eye socket. Bloody hand-to-hand combat became fierce as the Confederates, in overwhelming numbers, poured in from front and flank. All semblance of organization disappeared in the ensuing melee.

A grim-visaged Confederate drove at Paddy through the hazy glow of battle fire. Setting his feet firmly, Paddy successfully parried the enemy's stroke and with a sharp counter thrust jabbed his own bayonet into the groin of his off-balanced adversary. The crippled enemy dropped his hands to his pierced testicles and fell to the ground in agony.

Before he could recover himself, Paddy was beset by two more Confederates charging abreast of each other. Quaking with fear, he struggled to brace himself for their attack when someone suddenly swept by him on the dead run, his musket held horizontally across his chest. Feinting adroitly, the stocky soldier brushed aside the two bayonets leveled at Paddy, stepped in close and, employing his musket with swift leverage, clubbed one of the Confederates on the jaw with the stock and in a synchronized movement, sent his bayonet through the throat of the other.

Like wild-eyed colts exchanging glances, Paddy recognized his benefactor as the sergeant named Donaldson who had stepped out of line in Poolesville to challenge the roughnecks bully ragging Chirp.

The hatless non-commissioned officer brushed a lock of black hair into place and dashed off toward the spot where the flag was in imminent danger of being captured. Paddy followed in close pursuit.

A volley of Confederate bullets cut the flag staff in two and Paddy saw the riddled body of Bob Smith sink slowly to the woodland floor, his hands clutching the broken staff in a viselike death grip. In a wild melee of swinging fists and thrashing muskets, Sergeant Donaldson wrenched the tattered colors from the hands of their captors and stoutly defended them as the order was given, "Fall back!"

Paddy grabbed Dave Smith by the collar and pulled him away from the trampled body of his twin brother. "You've got to save yourself!" he shouted. "Come on, we're falling back."

Retiring with disciplined order, the Philadelphia and Tammany troops were pushed back and driven over the bluff. Paddy recoiled, sickened at the shocking scene. The rocky face of the bluff was littered with the mangled forms of Union soldiers. The broken bodies of those who had plunged headlong over the cliff were draped in the branches of trees at the bottom where they dangled grotesquely in the moonlight. Screams of anguish from the wounded mingled with the terrorized shouts of those seeking a way to escape. Following the example set by Colonel Devens, many of the demoralized men had shed their clothes and plunged into the cold water in a desperate attempt to swim to safety. The murky water of the Potomac was churned into a muddy froth by their thrashing, a helpless school of fish swimming frantically to escape a predator. Blue-coated bodies of the drowned were swept downstream by the swift current.

The flatboat, which had operated between the Virginia shore and Harrison's Island, was no longer in service. Overloaded by retreating Massachusetts troops who could not swim, the bottom of the barge had fallen out in midstream and it had sunk with all on board. Enemy rifle fire from the crest of the bluff had capsized two small skiffs that had been put into service.

Paddy, contemplating a course of action, was suddenly bowled off his feet by someone running through the dark.

"I say, Yank, terribly sorr...Chappy!" Captain Stewart jerked Paddy to his feet. "Sticky wicket, this. You all right?"

"Short-winded, that's all."

"Good. The jig's up, lad. Better have a go at the river with me." Stewart kicked off his boots and unfastened a belt buckle.

Paddy started to follow suit when his attention was caught by Colonel Cogswell's voice rising above the tumult.

"Volunteer riflemen over here!" Cogswell shouted.

"Volunteers to keep the summit clear while the main body escapes!"

Paddy glanced up at the sheets of galling red fire pounding down from the crest of the bluff by a wildly cheering foe.

Stewart took off his pants. "Come along with you, Chappy. All that matters in this world is you. Save yourself!"

Paddy bit his lower lip. "That's not what I was taught." He saw Barney and Andy Williams rush forward to answer the call for volunteers. Joe Batt, Henry Castor and Dave Smith followed close behind. Paddy reached for his musket and fastened a cartridge box to his waist.

"Don't be a bloody fool, Chappy! He who fights and runs away, lives to fight another day."

"Not tonight, Captain. My place is here. You run along with the 'Self' people. We'll cover you."

He turned and ran quickly to the spot where volunteer riflemen were forming around Cogswell. The doughty West Pointer addressed a begrimed soldier.

"The recovery of your regimental colors from the enemy was beyond the call of duty. What's your name?"

"Frank Donaldson, sir. Sergeant, 'A' Company, Seventy-first Pennsylvania."

Cogswell wrote hurriedly on a slip of paper and handed it to the soldier whose adroit maneuver had saved Paddy from almost certain death. "Donaldson, you are now a first lieutenant, battlefield commission."

"Thank you, sir."

Cogswell circled his arm. "Take this half of the group and move them up the gully. Try to clear the crest of the bluff with cross fire."

"We'll do our best, sir." The newly commissioned officer raced his men toward the dry gully.

Colonel Lee, humiliated by the conduct of his troops, appeared out of the darkness. His voice was weak. "Milton. I've come to offer my services if you will be kind enough to accept them."

Colonel Cogswell scowled.

"I'm an old man, Milton, but like you, a graduate of the Academy. I'd like to redeem myself if I can," Lee said.

Cogswell's expression softened. "Of course. I welcome your help."

"Thank you." Hatless, the gray-haired Lee turned toward two officers who were standing beside him. "These gentlemen also join me to help restore some honor to the Twentieth Massachusetts. Major Paul Revere." He inclined his head toward one. "Lieutenant Oliver Wendell Holmes." He nodded toward the other.

"Paul Revere?" Cogswell inquired.

"My grandfather, sir." The reply came from a short, compact major who stood veiled in the shadows and pall of gun smoke.

"Colonel Lee, you and your junior officers organize the rest of the men into a skirmish line," Cogswell barked. "String them out along the riverbank so that the fire will strike the summit of the bluff with frontal force. Have the men discard their smooth bores for those stacked rifles."

Colonel Lee cupped his hands to his mouth and began issuing orders. Paddy grabbed a rifle and dashed toward a position pointed out by Lieutenant Holmes. He had almost reached the protected spot when a fusillade of Confederate fire struck him full force. A searing-hot lead ingot burned into the pit of his abdomen. His body crumpled and he sank into a whirling black cavern of unconsciousness.

CHAPTER 6

In the nearby town of Leesburg, an anxious citizenry listened for hours to the roar of battle coming from the direction of Balls Bluff. Well into the dank October night they waited and prayed and listened. Finally news came of the Southern victory. A bell tolled the glad tidings from a cupola on top of the colonial brick courthouse. The staid structure located in the heart of the small village became the center of attention. Built of brick that had mellowed to a soft, reddish bronze over the years, its dignified facade was distinguished by four massive white pillars that supported a dormered roof above a wide piazza. Lights shone brightly at all the windows.

Villagers, shadowy figures milling about in eerie torchlight, became boisterous as they congregated around the courthouse grounds. Cheering and shouting accolades to their Confederate heroes, they finally turned their attention upon the captured Federal troops herded beneath the trees on the courthouse lawn. Unloosing venom, they began jeering unmercifully and casting aspersion at the enemy.

Two shawled women smiled contemptuously as they gazed at a group of wounded prisoners warming themselves around a small fire.

"My, how dirty and nasty these Yankees look," one exclaimed. "I declare they're worse than vermin."

In another quarter, some of the town's patricians began discussing the political causes of the war with a group of captured officers. Conversing with the effervescent temperament so peculiar to the Southern-born, their manner became so disagreeable and quarrelsome that the Federal officers found it necessary to abstain from conversation.

A crowd of youngsters, waving torches, stood in the main thoroughfare and started to sing:

"Yankee Doodle fare you well,
Rice and Cotton float you;
Once we liked you very well,
But now we'll do without you."

In happy response to a roar of laughter from their elders, the boys launched into a second verse:

"Yankee Doodle had the luck,
To get a new religion;
A sort of holy zeal to pluck,
At everybody's pigeon."

A lanky Confederate soldier with recessed eyes and prominent cheekbones clapped his ribs with mirth and waggled a rock size chin. "Ah killed me a chance o' Yankees today, that's for sartin' sure," he chortled. "Give us another chorus, boys." A thin stream of tobacco juice drooled from one corner of his mouth.

The youngsters sang loudly:
"Yankee Doodle strove with pains,
And Puritanic vigor;
To loose the only friendly chains,
That ever bound a nigger."

Faint at first, as a breeze stirring in the tops of trees, came a deep humming response from the captive Northern volunteers. The sound swelled and burst into song.

"The Union forever! Hurrah boys, hurrah!
Down with the traitor, up with the star;
While we rally 'round the flag boys,
We'll rally once again,
Shouting the battle cry of freedom."

Catcalls greeted the outburst. "Shut yore mouths, you damned Yankees."

A Confederate officer strode hurriedly toward the disturbance. The black facings on his coat collar and cuffs and the black stripes down the sides of his trousers distinguished him as a surgeon of rank. He shouted sternly at the townspeople. "Clear out of here, all of you. There are men dying on these grounds. Your behavior shows exceeding bad taste."

The gang of boys moved off slowly, singing as they departed:
"Yankee Doodle knows as well as I,
That when his zeal has freed 'em;
He'd see a million niggers die,
Before he'd help to feed 'em."

The surgeon clenched his fists and returned to the courthouse porch.

Semi-comatose, Paddy lay nearby on a bed of straw. Excruciating pain shot through his body with every breath. He rolled his head. Objects began to appear out of focus and spin dizzily in a nightmarish fashion. Confederate corpsmen, holding lanterns which shone like fireflies in the dark, passed among the wounded and rendered what aid they could.

One corpsman, older and more grizzled than the rest, stopped and looked scornfully at a young soldier who was lying face down with a gaping wound in his back. "Shore is a mahty pore place to be hit, Yank. In the back."

Grimacing, the young prisoner twisted painfully and pointed to a large hole in his breast. Tears swelled in his eyes. "Here's where the ball went in, sir."

Faces, once tanned, now appeared ghostly in the pale lantern light as the stretcher-bearers carried the critically wounded into the courthouse and placed them on improvised operating tables. A ringing sensation developed in Paddy's ears as his faculties gradually returned. He heard the indistinct sound of voices which seemed to be coming from across a wide chasm. A field officer was conversing with the surgeon on the steps of the courthouse.

"I tell you, Doctor Chenewith, when it came time to fire on the old flag this afternoon, I felt absolutely sick." There was a pause. "The stubborn resistance of those outnumbered Federal boys on the left flank was admirable."

"It's not pleasant to see their shattered bodies being brought to me," the surgeon said as he slipped into a gown handed him by an aide.

The field officer stroked his chin. "At one point," he mused, "I could have sworn I saw an old friend of mine on their side." He turned to his orderly. "Rufe, didn' t you meet Attorney Wistar when you were with me in California?"

"Yes, sir, I did. A man don't soon forget a firebrand like that Wistar feller."

"That Northern Colonel who rallied his men in the woods when we first struck. Did you get a close look at him?"

"Yes, sir, and like I tole you, if that warn't Wistar, he sure 'nough swore and fought like him."

"I remember you mentioning the fact. I had forgotten."

Sitting with his back propped against a Doric column, Lieutenant Donaldson glanced up at the Confederate field officer. "If you're referring to the Colonel who led a skirmish line to the top of the hill shortly after three o'clock, it was Colonel Wistar you saw."

The officer stepped forward and looked down. "Isaac Wistar?"

"Yes, sir."

"Tell me, how did he fare?"

"Very badly, sorry to say. Wounded severely in three places, but still living from last account. That's his orderly lying over there." Donaldson nodded his head in Paddy's direction.

The Confederate glanced at the blood-soaked cloth covering Paddy's abdomen and beckoned for the surgeon. "How bad off is that boy, Doctor?" he asked gravely.

The surgeon shook his head sadly. "There's nothing we can do. A bullet has penetrated his left umbilical region. I examined him as soon as he arrived." He bent low and felt Paddy's pulse. "That's odd, he's still living. However, he must be removed immediately to death row."

He signaled to the hospital steward. "Sergeant, send a litter detail."

"Yes, sir."

From the captured soldiers lying on the dark ground in front of the courthouse there suddenly arose a buzz of excitement which sounded like the hum of bees around a hive. Those who could, raised themselves on elbows as the figure of a dark-haired girl swept by in a hurry. A rotund little man in civilian dress ran after her.

Straightening at the sound, the surgeon fixed his eye on the girl as she mounted the steps to the porch.

"Rebecca! What is the meaning of this? Why aren't you at home with your mother?"

The slender, dark-haired girl stood defiant and silent as the panting civilian ascended the steps behind her.

"Good evening, Doctor. I'm terribly sorry about this interruption. We found your daughter giving refreshments to the wounded Yankees. I told her she must go home, but she wouldn't listen. She insisted on running to you instead."

"Becky, I'm surprised at you," her father admonished. "This is not the proper place for a sixteen-year-old girl. Now you go home with Mayor Orr and let the medical department care for the wounded."

The girl gazed compassionately at the disheveled, dirty Union soldiers lying near her. "The medical department seems to be doing precious little for those poor boys," she replied in a soft, yet willful voice.

"They're Yankees, child," the mayor rejoined tartly. "They came here uninvited, and they'll be better off forgotten until we've cared for our own."

"I declare, that's the most unchristian statement I've ever heard. Father, I will not leave here until I've at least washed their faces and given them something warm to drink."

The surgeon's daughter knelt by Paddy before anyone could restrain her. The sight of blood oozing from his untreated wound caused her to reel in horror. "Father, how can you stand there while this boy lies here slowly dying? Do something for him."

The surgeon raised his daughter to her feet. "I can only dance at one wedding at a time, Becky. I've been operating continuously for three solid hours. This is the first rest..."

"Stretcher, sir," a litter bearer cut in. "Who's it to be?"

The surgeon pointed to Paddy. "Carry him to the death ward," he murmured.

"The death...Father, you can't! Suppose he were Jed?"

"Even if he were my own son, I could do nothing for him. That boy has an abdominal wound for which there is no hope. We must spend our time and effort on those who have a chance of surviving."

Paddy's lips moved as the medical corpsmen placed his body on the stretcher. "Pocket," he gasped faintly, trying to reach a pocket. "Letter to...fa...father. Please mail letter...father."

What's he sayin' ?" the first corpsman drawled.

"Somethin' about a letter to his fathah," the second answered. He reached in Paddy's coat pocket and pulled out a blood-soaked envelope. "No use mailin' this. Can't read the address for gore."

Joe Batt, watching and listening to the proceedings, jumped to his feet. "Get another envelope. I'll tell you how to address it, you murderin' butchers."

Becky buried her head on her father's chest. "Save him," she pleaded, tears running down her cheeks. "Try to save him, for my sake. Don't let his friends go away saying my father is a murderer."

The surgeon gave his daughter a gentle pat. "All right, I'll operate, knowing that it's futile, but I want you to return home this instant with John Orr. Do you hear?"

The girl threw her arms about her father's neck and kissed him on the cheek. "All right, I'll go," she consented.

Draping a crocheted shawl over her head and pushing a loose curl into place, she descended the courthouse steps with the Mayor of Leesburg. Doctor Chenewith turned to the corpsman.

"Bring the lad inside," he ordered.

The swaying motion of the stretcher made Paddy's senses swirl as they carried him indoors. The interior of the brick building reminded him vaguely of a picture he had once seen depicting Dante's "Inferno." The air reeked with a nauseating mixture of coagulated blood, cauterized flesh and chloroform. Working by the light of smoking kerosene lamps, perspiring surgeons with pinched faces labored perseveringly over still forms lying on crudely constructed operating tables. The litter bearers lifted Paddy onto a table that was still wet and sticky with blood from the last occupant. On the table next to him lay a young Confederate cavalry man with a chloroform mask over his face. A thigh bone resembling a jagged icicle jutted through a tear in the man's pant leg. The attending surgeon, his blood-stained gown more like a butcher's apron, cut the cloth away from the leg, cleansed an area above the wound and placed a tourniquet close to the groin.

Using a knife that had not been cleaned for many hours, he cut vigorously through skin and muscles, the severed muscle bundles reacting violently with clonic contractions similar to the throes of a decapitated snake. Paddy turned his head away as the surgeon began sawing through the femur as if it were a piece of cord wood. He held his breath as he heard the amputated limb plop on the floor in a pool of blood.

A corpsman stepped up to the table on which Paddy was lying and tapped him on the shoulder. "Raise your hips, Yank, I gotta take your drawers off."

A stabbing pain shot through Paddy's abdomen and chest as he complied. A steward handed a can of chloroform to Doctor Chenewith.

"Y'all have to hurry along with this operation, sir. We're runnin' out of anesthetics."

"We'll be running out of everything, including lives, before this senseless war is over," the surgeon countered.

"Are you ready, sir?" the two corpsmen asked.

"Yes, I'm ready."

The men pinned Paddy's arms to the table. Doctor Chenewith moved toward his head and spoke in a fatherly tone. "Try to relax, son. Pray to our Savior who died for us. I'll pray with you."

He placed a cloth saturated with chloroform over Paddy's face. Almost instantly Paddy struggled violently in a vain effort to free himself from the suffocating fumes which choked his breathing. Seized by a terrifying sensation of drowning, he experienced the helpless feeling of being sucked steadily down into a dark ocean which finally closed over him and blotted out the light. His mind swam in a whirlpool of blackness.

It was some time later that he returned to consciousness as through a fog and heard the voice of the doctor.

"Wrap him up good and warm, Corporal. I don't want him to take cold."

"Yes, sir," the corpsman replied. He tucked a blanket around Paddy's body, which had been moved onto a stretcher.

The young cavalryman who had recently undergone amputation was sitting with a drawn, dazed expression on his face on a stretcher several feel away, his hands groping at the place where his limb had been.

"Mah leg!" he screamed, "Whar's mah leg? What have y' all done with mah leg?"

He suddenly spotted the severed part of his anatomy still lying on the floor where it had fallen. The mute, shocking answer to his query sent him into hysterics.

"Steward," the surgeon shouted, "give that man an eighth grain of morphine and be quick about it. Can't you see I'm busy?"

A haggard-looking hospital steward responded quickly to the sharp command and administered the sedative as directed. When he had finished, he motioned for two corpsmen. "All right," he ordered tersely, "Carry him outside and load him into an ambulance."

"Steward, will you come here, please?" Doctor Chenewith called.

"Yes, sir. Is your patient ready to be moved?"

"He is, but I don't want him put in the ambulance. I want him taken directly to my home which is only a block from here. If you will send Corporal Jackson with the litter, he can point out the house to your stretcher bearers."

"Beggin' your pardon, sir, but you ain't figurin' on harborin' a Yankee in..."

"You heard my orders, Sergeant. This lad has been extremely fortunate. With proper care, and barring the development of lockjaw, gangrene or blood poisoning, he should survive. If left unattended and subjected to the exposure of a cross-country ride in an ambulance, he would surely die."

"But, sir, orders state clearly that all the captured must be moved to Manassas immediately, irrespective of their condition. Stone is threatening to cut us off. Most of our troops have already evacuated Leesburg..."

"All the more reason for haste, Sergeant. This patient is my responsibility. When he is fit I shall see to it that he is placed in the hands of the proper prison authorities. Now, have him taken to my home as I have ordered."

"Yes, sir." The steward cupped his hands and called for the litter bearers. "If I ever get caught in the same fix as you," he muttered loud enough for Paddy to hear, "I just hope some Yank treats me half as good as you're gettin' it."

"Steward," Doctor Chenewith called again as he prepared another patient for surgery, "better cover the boy's face with a light cloth. I don't want him developing pneumonia from the night air."

"Yes, sir."

A cloth was placed over Paddy's face. The stretcher upon which he was lying was lifted from the floor by strong arms and he was carried from the building.

"Hey, you," someone on the porch hollered at the passing litter bearers. "How's our friend, Mulcahy, comin' along?"

Recognizing Henry Castor's voice, Paddy managed to brush aside the cloth from his face and spoke through cotton-dry lips. "They're puttin' me up at the surgeon's house."

"Shut up, Yank, and get that cloth ovah yer face," one of the corpsmen growled.

"What luck," Paddy heard Barney Williams exclaim in the distance. "I swear that Mulcahy could fall through a backhouse and come up with gold bricks in each hand."

Arriving at the home of Doctor Chenewith, the corpsmen set their litter on a porch considerably different from the courthouse porch. The atmosphere, instead of reeking with the stench of the wounded, was filled with the cool fresh scent of boxwood and ivy. One of the men lifted a brass knocker and pounded on the front door which was quickly opened. Paddy heard a woman's voice inquire mildly, "Yes, gentlemen, what can I do for you?"

"Evenin', ma' am. The Colonel sent this heah wounded Yank over for a spell of lodgin'. 'Pears like he ain't in a fit 'nough condition to move with the other prisoners."

There was silence. "My husband always knows what's best," the woman responded softly. "Bring the poor boy inside."

Paddy removed the cloth from his face as the stretcher was lifted and carried into the house.

"Lay him there on the sofa," Mrs. Chenewith directed calmly. "Careful now. That's fine. I'll wait until the doctor comes home before deciding which room to put him in."

The corpsmen rolled the stretcher into a compact bundle. "Will that be all, ma'am?"

"Yes, thank you. I can manage. I've been helping with surgery patients for many years."

"Good night then, ma'am. He won't be givin' you any trouble. The dose of morphine we uns gave him at the hospital should be takin' ' fect any minute."

"That's fine. Good night, boys. I'll see you to the door."

As soon as the three had left the room, Paddy began looking about at his surroundings. A log fire burned brightly in a brick fireplace to ward off the fall cold. Light from a brass student lamp, together with a rosy glow from the fire, enriched a cozy living room furnished comfortably with chairs and tables of colonial design. Hooked rugs covered the floors; samplers and old prints hung on the walls. A grandfather clock chiming the hour of eleven stood in a far corner of the room. Paddy heard the front door close and then a girl's voice called from upstairs.

"Is that you, Daddy?"

"No, dear, your father's hasn't come home yet," Mrs. Chenewith replied from the hallway. She reentered the living room and, drawing up a rocking chair, seated herself by the sofa on which Paddy was lying.

She was an attractive woman with a well-preserved figure and dark hair graying at the temples. Her gentle manner and pleasant face, devoid of lines, bespoke good background and a gracious life well-spent. Her soft, brown eyes were both sympathetic and kind as she reached for Paddy's pulse.

"Tell me, son, where were you..."

"Mother!" The girl who had been at the courthouse earlier in the evening rushed into the room and stared at Paddy. "What is he..."

"Please dear, be more quiet," Mrs. Chenewith interjected. "This is a patient of your father's. He's been brought here to recover from surgery. Abdominal, I would say from all appearances."

"Abdominal? Why I declare that must be the same boy who was being carried off to the...." She bore a striking resemblance to her mother. She dropped to her knees and smiled into Paddy's face. "Then Father was successful, after all. Are you feeling better, Yank?"

The morphine which Paddy had received before leaving the hospital was beginning to take effect and he nodded weakly in response to her question.

She placed a warm, satin hand on top of his. "What's your name?"

He made an attempt to moisten his lips. "Mul...Mulcahy," he murmured.

"Mine's Rebecca, but most folks call me Becky."

Her mother tapped her lightly on the shoulder. "You run along now, Becky, and get to bed. This boy needs rest, not idle chatter with a sixteen-year-old child."

"Mother, how many times do I have to tell you that I am not a child. I'm a young woman."

"Very well then, young lady, off to bed."

"I want to wait up for Father."

"Becky!"

"Oh, all right." The tall, slender girl tossed her head and started to leave the room.

"Aren't you going to kiss me good night?" her mother called after her.

Becky stopped and turned slowly. "Of course, Mother. I'm sorry."

Paddy slept peacefully through the night. Early the next morning, he was still lying on a sofa in the living room. The homey aroma of wood smoke, boiled coffee and freshly cooked sausage permeated the atmosphere. He heard Doctor Chenewith speaking softly from an adjoining room.

"Yes, I must admit, Sarah, my initial examination was not too thorough as a result of being conducted hastily. That boy in there owes his life to Becky and a belt buckle, not to me. I was going to set him aside to die."

"Now, now, dear. You mustn't blame yourself that way," his wife chided. "With hundreds of wounded soldiers to examine in so short a time, and in the dark, it's understandable one case might have been misjudged. Besides, everything has turned out all right."

"That's true, dear, but the question now is how many other poor souls might have been saved if given closer attention?"

Neither said anything for a minute.

"Last night," he continued slowly, "I had a most peculiar dream about the shepherd who, leaving his flock of ninety-nine sheep, went off in search of a stray...."

"You found the stray," his wife told him. "Do not torment yourself with the thought any further." She cleared her throat. "You say the bullet did not penetrate the peritoneum nor injure the viscera in any way?"

"No, the bullet ricocheted off his belt buckle upward, tore through his abdominal tunic, and lodged in a costal cartilage. Here's the piece of lead I removed."

His voice rose angrily. "Those hollow-core bullets should be outlawed. As soon as they strike...well, you can see what happens. A flat, jagged piece of metal the size of a half-dollar shatters and rips all the way through. Abdominal and chest wounds are usually hopeless cases. Most bone cases require amputation."

"War in its entirety should be outlawed," Mrs. Chenewith retorted, "not just the style of bullets."

Becky entered the dining room from the kitchen followed closely by a thirteen-year-old boy with dark curly hair similar to his sister's.

"I have the cambric tea and oatmeal ready, Father. Shall we see if our patient will take nourishment?"

"Yes, dear. Bring in the tray." Doctor Chenewith rose from the table.

The young boy wandered into the living room by himself and was gazing at Paddy studiously.

"I declare, Jed, stop starin' like that," Becky exclaimed as she entered the parlor with a steaming tray. "Where are your manners?"

"I ain't starin', Sis. I was just lookin' to see if he had horns."

"Horns? Of course Yankees don't have horns. Must you take for gospel truth every foolish remark our politicians make?"

"I was just checkin', that's all." The boy concentrated his attention on Paddy. "How's it feel gettin' shot in the belly, Yank?"

"Jed! Keep a civil tongue in your head or leave the room," his father broke in. "Put the tray on a table, Becky." He took Paddy by the wrist and smiled. "How do you feel this mornin, son?"

"Pretty good, sir. It hurts though when I breathe."

"Hmm. Let me have a look at your wound." The surgeon raised the bandage covering Paddy's waist. "Laudable pus, erythema, some fever," he mused. "Does this rib hurt when I press on it here?"

"Ouch!" Paddy cried out.

The doctor shook his head.

"I don't know," he murmured. "I had hopes that possibly you could be moved to Richmond in a day or so, but with that cartilage apparently beginning to sequester.."

"Can't the boy stay here until he's out of danger?" Mrs. Chenewith asked, interceding on Paddy's behalf. "You know full well, David, that he won't receive proper care and attention if he's sent to that Libby Prison. Let me put him in the front room upstairs. I'll tend him till he's strong enough to travel."

"I don't believe it...."

"You said this morning our army has changed its mind about evacuating Leesburg now that Federal forces have been withdrawn across the Potomac. You'll be on hand for a spell to look after him."

"All right, Sarah. I see no harm in it. The boy can stay here if you want. We're overcrowded at the hospital."

"Thank you, dear."

Mrs. Chenewith sat down on the edge of the sofa and stroked Paddy's head. "What is your full name, Mulcahy?" she asked in a soothing tone of voice. "You haven't told us."

"It's Paddy Mulcahy, ma'am."

"My, that's a delightful name. And where is your home?"

"Frankford, ma'am. A small village just north of Philadelphia."

"Quaker city boy, eh?" Doctor Chenewith rejoined with interest. "I know the town very well. Took my medical training at the University of Pennsylvania. Matter of fact," his expression changed, "there was a classmate of mine who came from Frankford. His name was Joe Leake. Are you acquainted with him?"

"Yes, sir. We shoe his horses at our smithy."

"You do. Then you are a blacksmith by trade."

"I'd be obliged, Paddy," Mrs. Chenewith interjected, "if you would let me write a letter to your mother telling her that you are in good hands. I know she must be worrying about you."

"My mother died when I was eight," Paddy replied somewhat abashed.

The woman withdrew her hand and searched her husband's face. "David, I declare, you can't let them send this young man to prison when he's better. Isn't there something you can do to have him exchanged?"

"That's a mighty tall order, Sarah, but I can inquire into the possibilities." The surgeon turned to his son. "Jed, fetch my coat from the hallway, please. I must be getting over to the hospital." He smiled at his wife. "I have a great number of other patients who also have a call on my services in the event you have forgotten."

The surgeon placed a fatherly hand on Paddy's shoulder. "You lie there quietly, son, until I can send over some corpsmen to carry you upstairs."

He kissed each member of his family on the cheek and departed.

Two litter bearers, dispatched from the hospital, arrived at the house toward noon. Under the watchful eye of Mrs. Chenewith, they removed Paddy to a bright, cheery upstairs room, undressed him and placed him carefully in a spacious four-poster bed. Warm rays of sunlight slanted through the lace curtains at the windows and fell in golden pools on the white chenille bedspread that covered him. The aching muscles in his body relaxed almost instantly and he was soon lulled to sleep by the downy softness of clean bedding and the peaceful charm of quiet surroundings. But all was not well. At night, demon dreams haunted him with frightening recollections of the battle. He grieved over the deaths of Chirp and Billy. Of some solace, the grandfather clock in the downstairs living room chimed the hours with methodical regularity.

Near the end of the first week, his recovery was set back by the development of necrosis in the injured costal cartilage and the fetid discharge which resulted filled his room with an unbearable stench. In an effort to alter the pathological process, Doctor Chenewith packed the fistulous tract with caustic soda. The burning action of the treatment resulted in sleepless nights and days of painful exhaustion which caused Paddy to lose weight. Dark circles formed beneath his sunken eyes.

When the necrosis had been fully checked. lint bandages soaked in a chloride of lime solution were substituted as treatment and it was shortly thereafter that Doctor Chenewith left for Manassas along with the balance of Confederate forces still remaining in Leesburg.

Daily visits by Becky became more frequent as the attractive girl sought to relieve his boredom. She engaged him in games of checkers and whist, drew him into conversation and brought him books to read. With every accidental touch of hands, there was an exchange of lingering eye contact.

Paddy closely observed the protocol handed him by his father. "Never move fast around a strange horse, or woman. Let them scent you first. If they want to establish friendly relations, they'll let you know in good time."

The third week of November was coming to an end. Color had been restored to his face and his strength had returned. He was now permitted to get out of bed and walk around the room.

It was a Saturday afternoon and he stood alone by a front bedroom window. He watched the first snowfall of winter blanket a tranquil landscape beneath a mantle of white. He saw two horsemen suddenly appear at the far end of a side street. Riding through the snow at a trot, they reigned in their horses in front of the house and dismounted.

"Take the horses around back to the barn, Jackson, and cover them well," one of the riders exclaimed.

Paddy recognized the tall, well-proportioned form of Doctor Chenewith. Snorting and blowing snow flurries from their nostrils, the horses were led away by the surgeon's orderly.

Paddy heard the front door open and close. He moved quickly across the room and concealed himself at the head of the staircase and watched Mrs. Chenewith embrace her husband.

"David, it's so good to have you home again," she cried happily. "Let me take your overcoat."

"It's good to be home, Sarah, if only for a short while," he replied huskily. "Army life isn't the life for me."

His wife's face registered deep concern. "I declare to goodness David Chenewith, you're chilled to the bone. You march yourself in the living room and sit down by the fire. I'll fix you a hot brandy."

"Thank you, my dear. It has been a long, cold ride."

Becky rushed into the hallway at the sound of her father's voice, threw her arms about his neck and kissed him joyfully. The doctor beamed delightedly.

"I declare," he chortled. "I do believe the only reason we men go off to war is so we can be properly pampered and fawned over when we return home. Where's Jed?"

"Playing outside somewhere in the snow, I reckon," Becky replied. She gave her parents a gentle push toward the living room. "You both go in there and sit down, do you hear? I'll prepare the hot brandy."

The doctor put an arm around his wife's waist and led her slowly into the parlor as Becky disappeared into the kitchen. "How is my patient progressing,

Sarah?"

"I would say he's almost well again, David. The wound has healed nicely and both his strength and color have returned."

There was a pause. Paddy crept silently down three steps so that he could overhear what was being said.

"Have you been successful in your efforts to get him exchanged?" Mrs. Chenewith asked.

The doctor cleared his throat. "No," he answered abruptly. "As a matter of fact, the purpose for my being here deals directly with the boy. I've been censured quite severely for harboring a wounded prisoner in my home. The orders I carry in my pocket say I must see that he's delivered to Libby Prison immediately."

"Oh, David, no."

"Those are my orders."

"When will this senseless war cease?"

"Not for some time, I'm afraid."

"Will there be more fighting soon?"

"I hardly think so, not until spring. Neither side is capable of maneuvering large bodies of inexperienced soldiers into battle during winter weather." The doctor coughed softly. "There's been a great deal of talk circulating among our troops lately that the North is about ready to give up."

"We've heard the same kind of talk here in town," Mrs. Chenewith replied slowly. "There are those who say the disorderly rout at Bull Run and the recent disaster at Balls Bluff have so mortified and disheartened the North that they're willing to sue for peace."

"Poppycock," the doctor retorted "They may be holding their breath in dread anticipation of the next encounter, but they will not sue for peace. I read something in a Washington paper the other day that impressed me deeply with respect to the present feeling above the Mason and Dixon Line."

"What was that, dear?"

"It was an article telling how vast crowds turned out to view the body of Senator Baker lying in state in city after city as it was carried across the continent to be buried in Oregon. The cortege was accompanied by continuous strains of funeral music every foot of the way "

"What special significance do you attach to that, David?"

"Only this. His heroic death on a field lost, but not dishonored, has thrilled the North, not yet accustomed to such spectacles. The so-called disaster at Balls Bluff has now been tempered with a certain proud response of feeling hitherto unknown in the North since the intense mortification in July."

"You just referred to Balls Bluff as a field not dishonored," Mrs Chenewith inquired curiously. "We here in town have been told it was another cowardly retreat by the Yankees."

"Exaggerated hogwash for home front con- sumption. Colonel Hunton of the Eighth Virginia told me there had been no Yankee disorder on the whole, no panic, and no flight such as occurred at Bull Run. He stated flatly that the Union force was gallantly led, but had been, by someone's error, surrounded by a superior force, in fact, ambushed in an untenable position. Though ultimately cut to pieces and destroyed, they defended themselves with perfect order and unflinching courage, inflicting damage not inferior to their own."

"The truth will out," Mrs Chenewith murmured.

"Yes, and from what I can gather, our young patient and his comrades from Philadelphia fought like hellcats to the bitter end. For nearly two hours a battalion of them, along with several companies from the Forty-second New York, stood off the entire Seventeenth and Eighteenth Mississippi regiments, a portion of the Thirteenth Mississippi, the whole Eighth Virginia and three companies of Colonel Jenifer's Virginia cavalry. Four thousand against eight hundred!"

"Dear Savior, they must have suffered dreadfully."

"They did. Reports published in a Philadelphia paper which fell into our hands recently, placed the casualties at three hundred and five out of a total of five hundred and seventy engaged. That's a fifty-four percent casualty rating." The doctor paused. "I would say they gave no quarter nor sought any."

"David?"

"Yes?"

"I detect a touch of admiration in your voice when you mention the deeds of those Philadelphia soldiers. I know you're loathe to discuss politics, but is your sympathy wholly with the Southern cause?"

After a moment of silence, he said, "I don't know, Sarah. I don't rightfully know."

Silence again.

"As far as Philadelphia is concerned," the surgeon continued, "you must remember that I lived there for three years and was treated kindly. Living among people with different customs and traditions and making an honest effort to fit in with them breaks down the invisible barriers that surround unfamiliar ways. It creates understanding and develops a mutual respect. If that were not true, why did John Pemberton, a Philadelphia Quaker and acquaintance of mine, break with his native state, and his family, and his close friend, Meade, and come South to direct one of our armies? That mutual respect and sympathy for the other side undoubtedly works both ways."

Another period of silence and Paddy heard a chair scrape on the floor as the doctor arose.

"Quite frankly, Sarah," he said in clipped tones, "I'm against the entire policy and philosophy of secession. And this war...it's like a mountebank's prescription...cures no ills and does more harm than good. An intelligent person knows better than to take the advice of medical quacks when his life is in danger. What beats me is why they've allowed cheap political quacks and the like to prescribe war in the first place."

"A plague on both their houses," Becky's voice broke in from the dining room. "Here's your hot brandy. Sit yourself down and enjoy it, and no more talk of this disgraceful war."

"Thank you, sweetheart," her father replied.

The sound of someone at the front door made Paddy dart for cover. Jed

Chenewith, covered from head to toe with snow, burst into the hallway, crying.

"Jed, boy, what's ailing you?" his father exclaimed anxiously.

"David, look at his face," Mrs. Chenewith cried with alarm. "It's cut and bleeding." She rushed to her son and clasped his head to her bosom.

"Here, let me have a look at you, son," the doctor said crisply. "What happened? Fall off the sleigh?"

"T'warn't no sleigh," the boy sobbed. "T'was the fellers down at the livery stable."

"What about them? What did they do?" his father probed.

"They said we were Yankee lovers. Said since I liked 'Blue Bellies,' they'd give me one."

Mrs. Chenewith opened her son's coat hurriedly and raised his blouse. "David," she screamed, "the child's abdomen is black and blue."

"They punched it and rubbed snow on it," Jed whimpered. "Did the same thing to my face."

"The monsters," Becky blurted angrily. "I'm going right down there and give them a..."

"You'll do nothing of the kind," her father ordered sternly. "Jed, lie on the sofa where I can examine you."

Becky clenched her fists. "It isn't fair, Father. You're a doctor. Why I declare, you brought most of those idiots into the world. They should know you're honor bound to save a life by whatever means, regardless of the patient's birthplace. Why, you had no more right to forsake Pad...I mean the boy upstairs, than a minister has the right to turn someone away from church because of his color or pocketbook."

Doctor Chenewith looked up from the sofa. "Nobly spoken, my dear, but you must remember one thing. Many of our friends and neighbors have already lost someone dear to them in this war. It is neither prudent nor gracious on our part to provoke and antagonize them."

The surgeon stroked his son's head, then turned and addressed his wife reassuringly. "The boy has suffered only minor lacerations and bruises, my dear. They look worse than they are."

His wife heaved a sigh of relief. "Thank heavens," she murmured. She took her son by the hand. "Come along with me, Jed. I'll dress those cuts and bruises."

"Oh, I almost forgot, Sarah," the doctor said hastily, "we're having a guest for supper this evening."

"A guest? Who?"

"Lamaar Fontaine. He rode up from Manassas with Jackson and me. He's been ordered to..."

"Father," Becky protested, "did you have to invite him here tonight of all nights? I overheard your conversation with Mother. Since you'll be taking Paddy away tomorrow I wanted to have him down for dinner."

"Paddy may sit with us, my dear," Mrs. Chenewith assured her.

"Eh? What's this I detect?" the surgeon asked inquisitively. "I was under the impression that you and Lamar were quite sweet on each other. When he was stationed here in town you fretted something fearful if he didn't come to call on you every evening." He shot a quizzical glance toward the staircase. "Don't tell me our vanquished foeman has conquered?"

"Father!"

"David, stop teasing the child," Mrs. Chenewith interjected. "Where is Lamar now?"

"He stopped to pay his respects to the Hempstones. He should be along shortly."

Jed brightened. "Oh, boy. Maybe he'll ride me past the livery stable on his horse. That'd sure show those fellers."

"You'll do nothing of the sort," Becky replied sharply.

"Gee whillikers, Dad, tell her..."

"We'll talk about it later, son, right now I want you to go with your mother and get cleaned up. I'd better go upstairs and have a talk...have a look at my patient."

"Becky, I'll be needing your help in the kitchen." Mrs. Chenewith seemed preoccupied as she spoke. "Come along."

"Yes, Mother."

Doctor Chenewith finished the hot brandy which his daughter had prepared for him then, striding across the room, he ascended the stairs and entered Paddy's room, greeting the lad with a pleasant smile and a friendly wave of the hand.

"Well, young man, it's good to see you on your feet. My wife tells me you've made a remarkable recovery during my absence."

"Yes, sir," Paddy responded. "I'm feeling pretty fit again, thanks to you and your family."

The surgeon sat down in a chair and eyed his patient curiously. His piercing eyes began to sparkle and the trace of a smile curled the corners of his mouth. "Hmm, you're a fine-looking chap, now that the bloom of health has been restored to your cheeks." He laughed lightly. "The reason for my daughter's apparent change in affection becomes more understandable. Would you say that she's found a diamond in the rough?"

Paddy blushed. "I beg your pardon, sir?"

"Never mind, son. I'm a poor one for making jokes. Lift your shirt and come here. I want to give your wound a final examination ."

The surgeon ran skilled fingers over Paddy's bared midriff and nodded with satisfaction. "Very good. Very good, indeed." His voice fell. "You know, of course, what this means?"

"Yes, sir," Paddy murmured. "Prison. Which one will I be sent to, sir?"

"Lieutenant Fontaine is under orders to escort you to Libby Prison. You will leave with him for Richmond first thing in the morning."

"Is that where my friends were taken?"

"Yes." Doctor Chenewith stood up and placed both hands on Paddy's shoulders. "I'm sorry it has to turn out this way, son. I tried to arrange..."

"Don't worry about it, sir. I already owe my life to you. That's more' n anybody could ask."

"You're a courageous lad. Will you have dinner with us tonight? I'd like you to meet Lieutenant Fontaine. He's a fine young officer from Mississippi. He rides with the Second Virginia cavalry."

"I. . .that is. . .well, thanks just the same, sir, but I' d rather not. I'm afraid I've caused you and your family enough trouble and embarrassment."

"You've done nothing of the sort. We'll be expecting you downstairs in an hour."

Paddy turned his head and stared at the floor. "Not tonight. Maybe some other time...when things have changed."

Doctor Chenewith shrugged his shoulders. "All right, son. I understand." He walked slowly from the room.

Paddy flung himself face down on the bed and fell into a troubled sleep. It was almost an hour later when he became conscious of a soft hand shaking him. He opened his eyes and looked into Mrs.Chenewith's face.

"May I speak with you a moment, Paddy?" she asked.

"Yes, ma'am."

"My husband tells me you will not honor us with your presence at the supper table. Won't you change your mind?"

"I don't think it best, ma'am. You saw what happened to Jed on my account." He rubbed his fingers across his lips and looked at the floor. "Besides, it wouldn't be right for me to impose on the officer who is here to visit your daughter." He paused. "We are enemies, you know. Could be uncomfortable for everyone."

A door slammed downstairs. There was a shrill cry of excitement from Jed. "Lamar! Oh boy ! Hey, Becky, Lamar's here!"

Jed's outburst was followed by the hearty sound of deep masculine laughter mixed with the jingle of spurs and heavily booted footsteps. There was a tangled rush of conversation.

Mrs. Chenewith squeezed Paddy's hand and smiled. "The conquering hero has arrived," she said. "They say Lamar is valiant on the field of battle, a glorious sight, but when he's in Becky's presence...well, the way that daughter of mine wraps him around her little finger is a pity."

She wrinkled her nose. "I think it's unbecoming for a man to show such subservience to a woman. It makes him appear kind of foppish, don't you think?"

"I wouldn't know, ma'am. I've never been around women much, except Aunt Virginia."

"Aunt Virginia?"

"Yes'm. A colored woman that helped raise me after my mother died. She once took care of Thomas Jefferson's daughters. After the President died, she was freed and moved to Frankford."

Mrs. Chenewith arched her eyebrows. "That is amazing."

"It's true enough. Her husband, Uncle Peter, was personal body servant to President Monroe."

"And both are still living? My, what a remarkable association with the past you must have through them. I should like to meet your Aunt Virginia and Uncle Peter some time."

"You'd be welcome anytime."

"I know," Mrs. Chenewith replied. "Why don't you come downstairs and tell us more about Frankford?"

Paddy shook his head. "I don't mean to be ungrateful, but it's best I stay up here until it's time for me to leave. The lieutenant, the doctor, Jed, they're all on a different side from me."

Mrs. Chenewith scaled his lips with her fingertips. "Are you familiar with the Twenty-third Psalm?" she asked.

"I can't rightly say. I never had much religion."

"Doesn't your father take you to church?"

"No, ma'am. Pa hasn't been to church since Mother died. Besides," he continued slowly, "we're Roman Catholic. We're not allowed to read the Bible. Only scripture I ever learned was taught to me by Aunt Virginia. She lives by the Bible."

Mrs. Chenewith smoothed her dress and curled a loose lock of hair with a finger. "I would say that the Twenty-third Psalm should be doubly important to you," she said. "See if you can recall it. ' The Lord is my Shepherd, I shall not want. He maketh me to lie down in green pastures, he leadeth me beside the still waters....' "

A smile crossed Paddy's face. "I remember that. Aunt Virginia used to say it was written especially for me, the part about lying down in green pastures and following still waters."

The woman's eyes were searching. "Do you recall what comes next?"

Paddy shook his head. "No, ma' am."

The woman clasped his hands. "Thou preparest a table before me in the presence of mine enemies, thou anointest my head with oil, my cup runneth over....' "

Paddy's gaze was fixed on the snow-etched window panes, his emotions taut as an overdrawn bow string. He gave the woman's hand a gentle squeeze and kissed her lightly on the cheek. "I will escort you downstairs," he said in a firm voice.

Mrs. Chenewith stepped back to survey him. "You make me very happy." Arm in arm they descended the stairway. Conversation at the dinner table was kept within the realm of propriety by the deft maneuvering of Doctor and Mrs. Chenewith who faced each other from opposite ends of the table.

Paddy sat beside Jed who was dressed in a Kate Greenaway suit, his Sunday best. Seated directly across the table, Lieutenant Fontaine fawned over Becky who was seated next to him. There was a cocksureness about the tall young officer that radiated from rugged, bony features too prominent to be called handsome. Reaching into a pocket, he extracted a folded slip of paper and handed it to Becky.

"Now that we've all finished eating," he drawled, "I'd like to present you with this poem, sugar. I wrote it especially for you."

"For me?" Becky cooed. "How terribly sweet of you." She took the paper from the officer's hand. "Why I declare you must have worked hours composing this. What have you called it?"

"'Picket Guard,' or 'All Quiet on the Potomac.' Why don't you read it to the others?"

Emitting a low cough, Doctor Chenewith reached for his brandy. Becky puckered her face. "I'll do no such thing," she replied with a coquettish smile. "I just couldn't bear to share this with anyone. Not until I've had an opportunity to read it by myself first, in the secret recess of my own room."

Lieutenant Fontaine gave her shoulder a soft pat. "Of course, sparrow," he rejoined glowingly. "You are perfectly right, as usual. It was plum foolish of me to suggest you share it. The poem is to be your own personal remembrance of me."

The covetous look which the dashing officer bestowed on Becky made Paddy seethe with agitation. Her virginal beauty, revealed and outlined by flickering candlelight reflecting from silver and glassware, had entranced and captivated him so much that all during the meal he had cast sidelong glances in her direction.

Clothed in a low-cut dress of blue organdy, her shapely figure made her appear more mature than she realized. Her face reminded him of a cameo he had once seen. Her brown eyes sparkled with animation beneath long, dark lashes when she smiled, her pink lips curled like the petals of a rose when she spoke. Soft tresses clung about her slender white neck, coming to rest lightly on her bare shoulders.

On one occasion he chanced a stolen glance at this girl who had helped nurse him back to health, and instantly her eyes met his with a warm, searching smile. Deep inside at that moment he began to feel a strange emotion taking hold of him for the first time in his life.

Jed was squirming restlessly in his chair. "Hey, Lamar," he blurted, "tell me more 'bout that cavalry fight you all were in last week."

"There'll be no talk of fighting at this table," Doctor Chenewith cut in sternly. "Mind you now, Jed."

"Aw, gee whillikers, Pa."

"You listen to your father, son," his mother insisted.

Lieutenant Fontaine colored and shot a reproachful glance in Paddy's direction.

"You haven't said two words, Yank," he spoke airily. "Why don't you speak up? Tell us something about where you all come from."

Becky stretched out a hand. "Yes, would you please? We'd like so much to hear about your home."

Paddy thought her voice held a different tone, one more inviting than she used when addressing the officer at her side.

He rubbed the tip of his nose with the back of his hand. "Really not much to tell about," he responded. "Frankford's just a small industrial town out in the country. Lot of history about the place and interesting people."

"Like who, for instance?" Lieutenant Fontaine asked in a haughty manner.

Paddy turned the spoon slowly in his hand. "Stephen Decatur, the naval hero, for one," he replied. "Also, Peter and Virginia Marks who were personal servants to Presidents Jefferson and Monroe. They helped raise me."

Fontaine leaned forward. "You mean nigger slaves?"

Paddy fixed him with an icy stare. "Neither," he said sharply. There was an uncomfortable silence. The Chenewith's colored maid, standing in the background, gave him a broad smile. "Porgy O'Brien quarters his famous circus in town," Paddy continued, "and the Griscoms have an interesting family tree. They are directly related to Betsy Griscom. You would know her by her married name. Betsy Ross."

The Confederate officer flushed a deep red. "Oh, yes. She put together a flag of some sort, didn't she?"

"Lieutenant!" There was fury in Doctor Chenewith's voice.

Lieutenant Fontaine leaned back in his chair and lit a cigar. "Tell us, Yank, do you ride with the hounds and hunt on horseback up your way?"

"And do you have cotillions?" Becky asked with a soft purr.

"The aristocrats engage in such pastimes," Paddy responded evenly. "I'm just the son of a blacksmith. Most of my spare time is spent fishing and riding steamboats on the Delaware."

Lamar exhaled a wreath of smoke. "Now that's downright amazin'. I thought all you Yanks did was grow pale and puny in your factories and clerical offices."

Paddy bristled. "There are quite a few who are so occupied."

"I declare, I wish you two would stop the badgering," Mrs. Chenewith interceded. "I would like to hear more about the colonial history surrounding Frankford. I think it's perfectly marvelous that a boy of Paddy's age should possess such a keen interest and knowledge of genealogy and historical lore."

Paddy shifted uneasily as the attention of both Jed and Becky focused on him intently. The flustered Confederate cavalryman flicked his eyes in the manner of a high-spirited race horse suddenly finding itself being crowded to the rail.

"Go ahead, son," Mrs. Chenewith urged. "Tell us about some of the interesting incidents you can call to mind."

"Well, there's the story of Lydia Darragh," he replied hesitantly. "She was a Quaker maiden, about Becky's age, who lived in Philadelphia during the British occupancy. Overhearing a plan of the British army to attack the American army at Valley Forge, she stole from the city at night and in a snowstorm walked the entire distance to Frankford where she warned General Washington's scouts about the attack."

"And was the British attack a success or failure?" Mrs. Chenewith inquired.

"It was a failure, ma'am. When the British moved...." Paddy launched into a detailed account of the whole incident involving Lydia Darragh and passed on to others. His affluent outpouring of fascinating history held all but the Lieutenant captive for nearly an hour.

Finally, Doctor Chenewith pulled out a watch. "My gracious," he exclaimed, "it's nine-thirty. I don't know when I've enjoyed a dinner conversation as interesting and pleasant as this one has been, but the hour is getting late and our two guests have a long journey tomorrow."

"Shucks, Pa," Jed protested, "let Paddy talk a little while longer. I want to hear more about the Doan's Caves on the Delaware, home of the highway robbers."

"Not tonight, son. It's bedtime."

Lieutenant Fontaine butted his cigar in a tray and stood up quickly with an odd smirk on his face. "Your father's right, Jed boy. Besides, you wouldn't want to deprive Becky and me of a few moments alone, would you?"

"Is that the only reason you come here? For some sparkin' ?" the boy retorted.

"Jed, where are your manners?" Mrs. Chenewith scolded lightly.

Becky smiled sweetly at the officer standing awkwardly beside her. "I must confess, I'm dreadfully tired tonight, Lamar. You do understand, don't you?" She smiled.

She circled the table and lingered at Paddy's side. "May I help you upstairs, Paddy?" Her soft voice was inviting and warm.

"I...I can make it all right," he stammered. "Thanks just the same."He turned and said good-night to those about him and retired upstairs to his room. Shortly thereafter, he heard the others retire for the night, and the house became dark and quiet.

Plagued with turbulent thoughts that raced through his mind, he wracked his brain and pitched and tossed and turned restlessly for several hours as sleep evaded him. Finally, overcome by fatigue and mental exhaustion, he fell into a troubled slumber.

When he awoke his room radiated with sunlight ricocheting brightly from snow-encrusted window encasements. A sound of footsteps approaching in the hall caught his attention, followed by a gentle knock on his bedroom door.

"Paddy, are you awake?" Becky called softly.

"Yes."

"May I come in?"

"I'm in bed, but you can come in if you want to."

The door opened and Becky entered the room. She walked toward the window and drew the blinds shut. "Did you sleep well last night?" she asked over her shoulder.

"Yep, guess so."

The girl turned, walked quickly to the bedside and sat down. Her long, delicate fingers sought his shoulders then traveled down his arm and lingered by his hands, clasping them tightly.

"What do you mean, you guess so? Did you, or didn't you?"

She bent over him suddenly, her soft fragrant hair brushing against his cheeks. "Oh, Paddy," she cried "I couldn't sleep a wink last night. My heart and mind were so full of you."

Paddy squirmed uneasily. "What did you think of the poem?" he blurted.

"The poem?" Becky sat bolt upright, her symmetrical breasts distending her tight-fitting calico blouse. "Paddy Mulcahy, you are impossible. How can you speak of something else when...when I'm here trying to tell you I love you. That...that poem," she stammered angrily, "it was just something a soldier would write to another soldier. I'm not a trooper, Paddy, I'm a girl, and I'm in love with you. Can't you tell?"

The impact of her tender, meaningful words set his body trembling with throbbing emotion, a feeling completely new, strange and wonderful.

He let his arms circle her neck and gazed into her eyes. "Becky, I never had anyone love me in my whole life. Pa and me, well…"

His words were cut off by warm, full lips pulsating on his own. In rhythmic unison, their quivering breasts heaved against each other as they clung in a close embrace.

"I love you, Becky," he managed to whisper. She drew back and caressed his face, the palms of her satin-smooth hands, hot and moist. She breathed heavily. "How long have you loved me?"

"I guess it's what I been feelin' for some time, 'specially last night. Couldn't sleep a wink, neither. My chest burned and my stomach, I even cried, thinking of you."

"Oh, Paddy, my darling. So did I."

She kissed him again eagerly and pressed her nose and checks against him. "They can't send you to that horrible Libby Prison, my darling. I know a way. I'll help you escape."

"No, Becky. I couldn't do that to your father, not after what he's done for me."

"Please, Paddy, for my sake."

"No . I'd never be able to look you or your family in the eye again."

"But Christmas will soon be here. I'll die knowing that you are in prison."

"I'll be exchanged in due time. I'll come back."

"Will you? Will you come back to me?"

"There's not a man in Jeff Davis' army that could stop me."

She squeezed both his hands until her knuckles were white. Tears streaked her cheeks. "I'll be waiting for you," she cried softly. She dried her tears on his cheek and reached for an envelope which she pressed into his hand.

"This is a lock of my hair," she said quietly. "Carry it with you until we meet again."

CHAPTER 7

Libby Prison, located along the waterfront of the James River at Twentieth and Carey streets in Richmond, Virginia, loomed dark and foreboding in the frosty twilight as Paddy approached under custody of Lieutenant Fontaine. The converted four-story ship chandler's warehouse possessed a dirty brick exterior blocked with barred windows which covered its ugly face like pockmarks.

Guarding the main entrance, a lone sentry shivered in the cold wind sweeping across the river in raw blasts. He stamped his feet vigorously in the deep slush made sooty by coal dust. He presented arms stiffly as Lieutenant Fontaine dismounted.

"At ease, Corporal," Fontaine snapped briskly. "I've brought Major Turner another pigeon for his coop." The officer turned toward Paddy.

"All right, off your horse. This is as far as you go."

Paddy swung his aching body from the saddle and landed rubber-legged on his feet.

"Don't just stand there. Get inside with you." The short tempered cavalryman gave Paddy a rude shove toward the doorway and followed him into the building.

Inside, a portly, gray-haired major of pleasant mien looked up from behind a littered desk as they entered his office. He extended his hand to Lieutenant Fontaine.

"Good evening, Lieutenant. What have you brought us? Another houseguest?"

"Yes, sir. Here are his papers."

The major studied Paddy's identification form. "From the Seventy-first Pennsylvania, eh?" He shot Paddy an inquisitive glance. "You should feel right at home here, boy. We have quite a few of your comrades billeted on the second floor."

Another Confederate officer sitting next to a pot-bellied stove eyed Paddy narrowly. His pointed features indicated cruelty and sadism. He snarled at Paddy. "You captured at the Bluff, boy?"

"Yes, sir."

"How come you so long gettin' heah?"

"I..."

Paddy's response was cut off by Lieutenant Fontaine. "He's been hospitalized in Leesburg. Had a penetrating abdomen wound."

"Belly wound, eh? He's lucky to be alive." The pinch-faced officer laughed coarsely. "Or, mebbe he ain't."

Placing a bottle of whiskey to his mouth, he drank heavily, then smacked his lips and wiped his chin. "We don't cater to damn Yankees around heah, wounded or otherwise," he growled contemptuously. "If you still need attention, boy, y'all have to shift for yourself as best you know how." He stood up and staggered drunkenly toward Lieutenant Fontaine. "I didn't get your name, trooper. Who are you?"

"My apologies," Major Turner broke in hurriedly. "This is Lieutenant Fontaine, Second Virginia cavalry."

"Fontaine, glad to make your acquaintance, suh. I'm Lieutenant Todd." The drunken officer spun on his heel and faced Paddy. "That name mean anything to you, boy?" he asked in a rasping voice.

"No, sir, it doesn't." Paddy stepped out of range of the officer's foul breath.

"It don't, eh? Well it will. I run things for the major around heah. Nice and orderly like. That's the way I like things. Show your face at a window and I'll have your goddamned head blown off. Break any the otha rules around heah and I bayonet you personally."

He took another drink of whiskey from the bottle clutched loosely in one hand then swayed unsteadily. "So, you don't know who I am, eh? The name Mary Todd sound familiar to you, boy?"

"Yes, she's the wife of President Lincoln."

"Now you're catchin' on, Yank. I'm brother-in-law to that bastardly Illinois ape who fancies himself President. Mary Todd's mah goddamned sistah. What dya think o' that?"

Paddy gritted his teeth and turned fiercely on Major Turner. "I don't have to listen to that kinda talk. Take me upstairs to my comrades. I want to be among gentlemen."

"Gentlemen!" Lieutenant Todd reached for his sword. "By God, Yank, I'll cut your tongue out for that insult."

Major Turner rose from his chair. "Now hold on, Lieutenant, control yourself. The boy meant no harm. I'll have Keeler take him out of here right away. Keeler!"

A guard appeared at the doorway. "Yes sir?"

"Take this prisoner to the second floor."

"Yes, sir."

Lieutenant Todd downed another swig of whiskey. "Yeah, put this cotton-picker up with the rest of his filthy breed." He spat on the floor. "Tell the dirty rats upstairs you're bringin' 'em a clean one to contaminate."

The guard led Paddy from the room and headed him toward a flight of rickety stairs. "That Lieutenant Todd air quite a piss cutter, ain't he, Yank?" the Southerner whispered. "It's a mite hard tellin' who hates him most, you uns or we uns."

Paddy cast a glance over his shoulder. "Is he really Mary Todd's brother?"

"Yep. We uns 'round here often wonder if she takes after him. We shor pity poor Mister Lincoln if she does."

"Is his bite as bad as his bark?"

"It's worse, Billy, worse. Jist yesterday I seen him bayonet a prisoner in the laig, but don't worry none, us boys'll treat you right when he ain't around." The guard shook his head, perplexed. "I declare, I cain't see why young fellers like us is out tryin' to kill each otha nohow."

They continued up the stairs in silence.

The unheated interior of Libby Prison was cold and damp, causing Paddy to shiver perceptibly. Dank brick walls threw off a fetid odor that reeked of human excreta, a sickening stench which turned his stomach.

Arriving at a landing on the second floor, the guard drew the bolt of a heavy planked door that squeaked on rusted hinges as it swung open.

"I sure 'nough hate to do this, Yank, but heah's whar I gotta leave y'all."

"It's all right, Johnny. I understand."

Paddy stepped through the doorway and the door closed solidly behind him. A gasp of horror escaped his lips as he viewed the scene before him. The converted storage room in which he found himself was packed with shabby, blue-clad prisoners, some of whom were lying on beds of dirty straw, others sat dejectedly with knees drawn beneath their chins. A few leaned idly against the walls. The atmosphere of the crowded room was stifling, a putrid scent arising from foul-smelling uniforms and neglected wounds. Gasping for a breath of fresh air, Paddy began searching the gloom for sight of an acquaintance among the sea of expressionless faces staring back at him. From the far end of the room came a feeble shout.

"Hey, fellas! Look what the wind blew in. Mulcahy has come to deliver us."

Paddy recognized the voice of Barney Williams, but not the cadaverous face. He picked his way carefully so as not to step on anyone and came upon the Frankford volunteers who were huddled together.

Barney advanced to greet him. "What brings you to this rat hole? We were all praying that you had escaped. What happened? Did you try?"

"No, I didn't try. I could not break faith with the doctor."

Bromley, Lightfoot, Pilling and Heap raised their eyes from a game of cards, called a greeting, and returned to their game.

Isaac Tibben, one leg swathed in dirty bandages, was lying on a pile of straw. He raised himself on an elbow and waved with a free hand.

Joe Batt and Henry Castor gathered Paddy in a warm embrace. "You look like you've been eating high off the hog," Joe Batt said appraisingly. "How are you feeling?"

"Pretty good, until I got a whiff of this hole."

"You'll get used to it," Castor grimaced. "It grows on you like a beard. By the way, what do you think of our heavy 'brushes'?"

Paddy grinned. "You resemble a couple of dirty old billy goats."

"Here now, that's no way to talk," Batt retorted. "We're right proud of this face lace."

Paddy screwed up his nose. "Not only do you look like billy goats, you smell like 'em. When did you fellas wash last?"

Castor folded both arms across his chest. "Remember the rain we marched through on our way to the Bluff?"

"Yep."

"Our bodies and uniforms haven't been touched by water since."

A firm hand on his shoulder caused Paddy to turn around sharply. He stood facing Lieutenant Donaldson.

"Excuse me for breaking in like this, Mulcahy," the officer said by way of apology. "Just wanted to come over and say it's good to see you well and sound again, despite the circumstances."

"Thank you, sir. If you hadn't saved my life at the Bluff, doubt if I'd be here."

The officer ran a hand through his shock of thick, black hair. "The name's Frank, Mulcahy. We don't stand on ceremony in here."

Paddy moved to one side. "Lieu...I mean Frank, I'd like you to meet the older brothers of my two closest friends."

"We've already met," Joe Batt countered as he exchanged a friendly glance with the officer. "We've become one big happy family in this cubbyhole. After a few days in here you get to know everybody and his brother like a book."

"That's right," Castor rejoined. "This is a real fraternal order we have here. Some stinkin' bums think we oughta call ourselves the Order of the Bath, but that would be stretching a point."

Paddy wrinkled his nose. "I know what you mean."

Lieutenant Donaldson squatted on the floor, his square-rigged jawbone jutting upward. "What say, Mulcahy, how's about giving us an account of your experience in Leesburg? We're dying for news."

"There's not much to tell. I was in bed most of the time."

"Anything at all will do," Castor begged through his scrubby beard. "Tell us about the family that took you in. What were they like?"

"Yes," Joe Batt prodded, as he flung his large frame on a bed of straw. "How do they feel about the war up that way? Are they red-hot secesh, or merely going along for the ride?"

Paddy eased himself onto the floor and in a slow, halting manner began relating everything that transpired during the time in which he had been separated from his buddies. Later that night, he bedded down with the others and, supported by a feeling of buoyancy wrought by the reunion with old friends, fell into a sound sleep despite the depressing circumstances.

In the long, cold days that followed, he slowly familiarized himself with the monotonous routine and stifling ways of prison life, the experience becoming indelibly seared on his mind like a recurring nightmare.

Prison life, he decided, was the common denominator which brought out unexpected capabilities and deficiencies. Many soldiers who, in the ordinary routine of life and even in the new environment of the ranks, had been respected failed when subjected to the severe strain of imprisonment. Surprisingly enough, many of the eccentrics and misfits showed themselves able to cope with situations to which their superiors surrendered.

As a whole, the strong and energetic preserved those characteristics, while most of the weak became helpless. The veneer of a man's conventions was peeled away, showing the real man beneath. The confined man was stripped naked before his fellows.

Among the prisoners were traders, speculators and businessmen, as well as those who were thriftless and improvident. A few always seemed to have money with which to buy the belongings of the others. Throughout the prison there were marketplaces and so-called restaurants, places to barter where vendors sat with their legs under them like tailors, loudly proclaiming the quality of the beans or mush they sold for a stipulated price.

The greatest difficulty was getting through twenty-four hours a day with a healthy mental outlook. With nothing to do, the hours dragged by monotonously. In an effort to combat the boredom some of the men slept fifteen or more hours a day, but the majority found that impossible and were forced to seek other methods of passing the time. Some of the men devised games, laying out checker and chessboards on pieces of plank. It was not uncommon for them to get so intensely interested in chess that they would faint from excitement because of their weakened condition.

Playing cards were used long after the corners disappeared and the number and shape of the spots on their faces became uncertain.

The more industrious labored for hours with a pocket knife as a tool making jewelry from gutta-percha buttons or carving on beef bones when they had them, just like Eskimos in the Arctic carving walrus teeth and tusks.

The most popular pastime was the forensic discussion of the probability of being exchanged and there were those who discussed the question from morning till night. The optimists believed that exchange was a matter of only a few weeks away, while the pessimists were sure that the incompetence of the government prevented their immediate release. They were so strongly convinced that they did not expect release under any circumstances.

A strong passion for gambling prevailed, and the men readily staked food, clothing, blankets and other precious belongings which had escaped the notice of prison guards.

Those men with a limited outlook on life needed excitement as a necessary stimulus and this was easily obtained by a game of chance, or if facilities for a game were lacking, they made wagers on every conceivable event.

A determination to escape lay uppermost in the minds of a few who were constantly devoted to working out some fantastic plan which would give them their liberty. Some plotted rebellion against authority, which was seldom carried out.

Some became expert psychologists, able to calculate just how much impertinence any particular officer would endure. Others played with fire by devoting themselves to the task of irritating the guards, yet affording them no pretext for punishment. The most flagrant of that sort were the 'roughs' from New York City.

Most pathetic of all were recruits from the country who found no pleasure in any of the amusements offered by their city-bred comrades. Most of the fellows raised on farms found prison life a major disaster, an appalling, overwhelming catastrophe. They lapsed into a helpless, hopeless state of despondency, caring for nothing, thinking of nothing, engaging in nothing. Huddled in dark corners like captured beasts, many of them died from home-sickness.

The educated men possessed strong reserves and struggled bravely to keep up their courage, knowing that their chances of survival depended on it. Because of their greater intellect, they generally endured the hardship and privation more successfully than the ignorant man. They organized debating societies, language classes, and even formed a miniature government where questions were raised and debated in a House of Representatives.

In the evenings the prison room resounded with songs of sentiment, patriotism and humor. Wild cheers greeted college and bivouac songs, "Benny Havens 0" being the favorite, causing West Pointers to reminisce. At the close of each evening, they settled down with the plaintive notes of "Home, Sweet Home."

The officer of the day looked in at nine o'clock punctually every evening to give the order, "Lights out!" Nighttime passed unvaried except for the rough tramp, or hoarse challenge, of a sentinel at the outer door.

The food served at Libby Prison was the worst sort, consisting mainly of cornbread in which portions of the cob and husk were often found ground with the meal. Because the crust was so hard, the prisoners referred to it as "iron clad" and in an attempt to make it more edible, managed to make mush of it. At infrequent intervals each man was doled out two or three ounces of meat. The scant bill of fare was usually rounded out by a pint of black-eyed peas soaked in vinegar, the peas full of worms and maggots that floated on the surface.

The greatest concern arose from the lack of medical attention and the total absence of medical supplies. Joe Batt, oldest son of Frankford's foremost veterinarian, stepped into the breach, and took it upon himself to act in the unofficial capacity of surgeon.

In response to his requests, the prisoners quartered on the second floor of the prison regularly drained the vinegar from their pea soup so that he had an ample supply of that supernatant fluid.

Employing a knowledge and technique gleaned from watching his father treat animals, he prepared wet vinegar compresses which he applied to wounds requiring attention. In nearly every instance, the dressing was successful in promoting healing. One exception was the suppurating wound on Barney Williams' arm which continued to get worse. Tortured by pain and fever, the puckish smile faded from his face and his feeble attempts at pleasantries became noticeably forced.

On the twenty-third of December, Joe approached Paddy and said in a worried voice. "If Williams is to survive, that arm of his will have to be amputated immediately."

Paddy's face clouded. "Can you do it?" he asked.

"Don't talk nonsense. Even with the proper instruments, I wouldn't hazard such an operation. I'm not a qualified surgeon."

"What are we going to do? We can't let him die."

Joe pulled thoughtfully at his lower lip. "You and Donaldson gather snow from the window sills," he said slowly. "Pack it around Barney's shoulder above the wound. I've got an idea."

"Like what?"

"I'm going to try to get him moved out of here and taken to the hospital."

"How?"

"Never mind, just pack his shoulder like I told you."

Paddy moved away. "Frank and I'll get started on it right away."

He went in search of Donaldson while Joe made his way toward a group of high-ranking officers conversing in a far corner of the large room. He addressed himself to Colonel Lee.

"Begging your pardon, sir. Could I speak with you a moment?"

The gray-haired commander, who was beginning to show the effects of prolonged imprisonment, spoke feebly. "Why, of course, Sergeant. What is it?"

"It's about Barney Williams, sir. The boy is going to die unless his arm is taken off real soon."

The Colonel's weary expression caused his jowls to sag. "He's the young brother of Lieutenant Williams who was killed at the Bluff, isn't he?"

"Yes, sir. They come from one of Frankford's oldest and most respected families. You've got to help save him, sir."

Running a hand through powder-gray hair, Lee frowned. "I wish there was some way that I could, Sergeant, but for the life of me, I don't see how."

"Beggin' your pardon again, sir, but there is a way," Joe Batt rejoined. He seemed to tower over the small man beside him.

"How's that, Sergeant?"

"You and Jeff Davis were classmates at West Point, I understand."

"Yes, we were. As a matter of fact we were close friends in those days, but..."

"Then surely he would intervene on Barney's behalf if you asked him," Joe Batt blurted. "Send him a personal note. Tell him the boy's life hangs in the balance."

Colonel Lee placed liver-spotted hands on Batt's arms. "All right. I'll send Jeff a note immediately. If the bonds of friendship have not been overly strained, it might do the trick."

"Thank you, sir." Batt turned to leave.

"Oh, Sergeant, one thing before you go."

"Yes, sir?"

"I've been meaning to tell you, in all my days of soldiering I've never seen wounds heal as well as most of those you've been treating with vinegar packs. The common belief of our surgeons that wound repair must necessarily be a slow, painful process does not strike me as being very sound now that I've seen how well the wounds you treat heal with a minimum of inflammation. Keep up the good work, Sergeant."

"I'll do what I can, sir. Meanwhile, the sooner young Williams is taken out of here, the better I'll feel."

"Be assured, I'll have a note off to Jeff Davis shortly."

Having packed Barney's shoulder to Joe Batt's satisfaction, Paddy and Lieutenant Donaldson placed three more chamber pots full of snow where he could reach them when needed. At that moment the door to the prison room swung open to admit a woman whose appearance caused a stir of excitement among the prisoners.

"Hey, look who's here," someone jeered derisively. "It's 'Crazy Bet' again."

"Crazy or not, I love her," another voice barked. "Long as she brings food and goodies, that is."

"Did you bring mincemeat this trip like you promised?" another called out.

A short, sharp-featured, middle-aged woman nodded pleasantly in response to the last question. Humming to herself she began passing out toiletries, books and food items from two large market baskets which she carried on each arm.

Paddy stared at the small, commanding figure. Dressed in a heavy cloak with a shawl drawn tightly over her bonnet to keep out the cold, she resembled a dutiful housewife on a shopping trip. He turned toward Lieutenant Donaldson. "Hey, Frank, who's she?"

"Miss Elizabeth Van Lew. Come, I'll introduce her to you."

"Why do the boys call her 'Crazy Bet' ? Is she really off her nut?"

The husky officer who stood almost a head taller than Paddy lowered his voice. "No, far from it, although she does put on a good act."

"An act?"

"Yes, she's a Federal spy."

"Her! A spy!"

"Keep it down, not so loud."

Paddy's voice fell to a whisper. "I'm sorry." He cast a furtive glance at the matronly woman as she drew closer. "You said you'd introduce me to her. Do you know her that well?"

"Yes. She and my mother attended the Friends School together in Philadelphia."

"She's a Philadelphia Quaker?"

"A Quaker, yes, but not from Philadelphia. Her home is here in Richmond. The Van Lews are an old aristocratic family of great wealth and prominence in this city."

"If she's that well-known and not really crazy, how can she pull off this act?"

"Remarkably easily. Because of her abolition sentiments, that is, her love and labors for the Negro race, she'd been marked by the people of Richmond as an eccentric or queer for a long time. Since war's broken out, she has fostered the belief that she's harmlessly insane so that she can carry out her activities as a spy. She's done it unflinchingly and with cunning. Her last visit was just before you arrived from Leesburg. I guess she was forced to 'cut stick' for a while. She usually comes several times a week."

"You think the Rebs might be on to her?"

"Hardly. They let her wander around in the prisons almost at will. It amuses the guards to see her pass, as you see her doing now, singing softly to herself and muttering meaningless words."

"Doesn't she need a permit?"

"Oh, yes. That's where the rub comes in. Now and then, her permit is revoked, but that doesn't stop her. She goes blithely to General Winder, the provost marshal of Richmond, or to the secretary of war, and gets another one. Both men know her well and treat her kindly."

Paddy turned his gaze on the slightly built woman. "For a little old lady with a market basket, she sure swings a lot of weight."

"Yes, fortunately." The officer pointed through the bars of a window next to which he was standing. "That's the Van Lew mansion over there on top of Church Hill. In the last letter I received from home, Mother told me that before Miss Van Lew's father died, the house was a constant center for balls and receptions given in honor of great men like Bishop Moore, Chief Justice Marshall and such distinguished families as the Lees, Wickhams, Adams, Cabels and Carringtons. Mother attended one affair at which Jenny Lind sang. Edgar Allen Poe, invited down from Philadelphia, was called upon to read his poem, *'Raven',* to the guests on one occasion."

Paddy stared at the imposing mansion through the window bars and gave a low whistle. "Quite a place," he murmured. "Although I can't fancy myself hob-nobbing with that kind of people."

"I wasn't trying to impress you, Mulcahy. Merely giving you some of the color and background that surrounds the place."

"You don't have to apologize, sir. I like to hear about famous places and people." He looked again through the barred window. "Is your family...?"

"Forget my family for a moment," Donaldson interrupted. "Seems like you've suddenly become a luminary in your own right."

Paddy turned around, hands thrust into his pockets. "What do you mean?"

"Over there. Both Colonel Cogswell and Miss Van Lew are motioning for you to join them."

Paddy shot an inquisitive glance in the direction in which Donaldson pointed. "It's not me they're signaling. It's you they want."

"Wrong, Mulcahy. Seems they want us both. Come along. We'll see what's up."

Colonel Cogswell and Miss Van Lew were joined by Colonel Lee and Major Revere. The woman removed her shawl and bonnet, exposing a spinsterish face framed by faded blonde curls that fell to her neck in tightly twisted rope-like strands. Paddy thought her curls resembled twisted wood shavings cast off by a hand plane.

The woman embraced Lieutenant Donaldson and withdrew a letter from a concealed slit in her woolen cape. "It's from your mother, Frank," she said in a low voice. She started to say more but, biting her lower lip, checked herself as if deeply distressed by something.

"You are Private Mulcahy?" she asked, fixing her attention on Paddy.

He shifted uncomfortably under her penetrating gaze. "Yes, ma'am."

"Colonel Cogswell informs me that you have come recently from Colonel

Chenewith's home in Leesburg. Is that correct?"

"Yes, ma'am, I have."

"Tell us, what did you overhear from Doctor Chenewith regarding Confederate troop movements? Were there many troops stationed in Leesburg the day you left?" The woman's eyes were searching slits.

Paddy was struck by her needle-sharp nose and pinched, ribbon thin lips. While she seemed to be exuding infinite charm, her manner was at the same time piercing and abrasive-a resolute personality.

"A woman with a cause," he remembered his father saying, "is worse than screamin' banshees."

"I can't say, ma'am," he replied carefully. "I didn't listen at any keyholes and I didn't stop to count soldiers the day I left."

"Private Mulcahy," Cogswell said, bristling, his rock-ribbed military countenance glowering. "Dispense with that glib talk and answer Miss Van Lew."

Paddy recoiled at his intensity. "Yes, sir."

"Frank, can you vouch for this boy's loyalty?" the woman asked Lieutenant Donaldson point-blank.

A disarming smile crossed the officer's face. "Yes, Bet. He not only conducted himself favorably in battle but was also Colonel Wistar's trusted orderly."

"In that case, I should think he'd be more willing to cooperate with me." She turned on Paddy and demanded officiously. "The War Department is extremely anxious to find out all it can about the winter plans of the Rebel forces in Virginia. You certainly must have heard some military discussion while lodged in the home of a Confederate surgeon, now didn't you?"

Irritated by her brassy manner, Paddy stood motionless and silent, lowering his eyes before Colonel Cogswell's penetrating stare. "No, ma'am, I didn't," he muttered.

"Oh, come now."

"Please, Bet, you're rubbing his fur the wrong way," Lieutenant Donaldson interceded. He addressed Paddy. "Miss Van Lew doesn't want to make you turn informer on your friends, Mulcahy, she..."

"Friends!" the woman exclaimed.

"Of course. What else could you expect? They saved his life and housed him for almost a month despite public censure from their neighbors." Donaldson changed tactics. "The cavalry officer who escorted you to Richmond, Paddy, did he mention anything that might be of interest to our side?"

Paddy shifted his feet and raised his head. "Yes, he said he'd have plenty of time to enjoy himself in Richmond because a good many of the Second Virginia cavalry had gone home for the winter. He talked like there'd be no more fighting till spring."

Miss Van Lew brightened. "That's what we want to hear."

"Hold on, madam," Cogswell cautioned. "Let the boy tell it his way."

Donaldson stood with arms folded across his chest. "Without betraying any confidences, Paddy, did Doctor Chenewith, at any time, mention a change of camp?"

Paddy paused a moment before replying. "The morning I left Leesburg," he answered slowly, "I heard the Doctor tell his wife it would take him much longer to get home in the future because the Confederate Army was moving south across the Rapahannock River."

"That will be welcome news in Washington," Colonel Lee observed.

"On your way to Richmond," Miss Van Lew inquired, "did you pass through Manassas?"

"No, ma'am. We traveled by way of Warrenton."

"Didn't that strike you as being strange? Warrenton is almost thirty miles west of Manassas and a more indirect route into Richmond. Altogether you must have gone fifty miles out of your way."

Paddy stared at the woman blankly. "You can't prove it by me, ma'am. I don't know anything about the roads in Virginia. Besides, maybe it wasn't safe for a Reb like Lieutenant Fontaine to be travelin' the shorter route, which you say goes through Bull Run."

"It would have been a safe enough route if the Confederates occupied their lines at Manassas in force as we've been led to believe. Wouldn't it?"

"I guess so."

"What are you driving at, Miss Van Lew?" Major Revere asked.

"Just this. Your soldiers should be better trained to observe and report what they see and hear-anything irregular. Piecing together the kind of information this boy has just given me would have enabled us to know how weak the Confederate lines at Manassas are. Unfortunately, we've been getting information too late to take advantage of it. For instance, we know now that instead of ninety thousand troops supposedly manning the Confederate lines at Manassas, there were scarcely forty thousand. As a result of that misinformation, General McClellan let a whole summer go by without attacking for fear of being soundly beaten by overwhelming forces which didn't exist."

"A point that's puzzled and annoyed me," Colonel Cogswell cut in, "if the Confederates possessed the great superiority which McClellan attributed to them, why didn't they walk right in and pick up Washington? They could have easily done so with the army Little Mac conjured up in his dreams."

"Well, I can tell you this," Miss Van Lew answered, "McClellan's been roundly criticized lately for his timidity, especially since circumstances involving the Quaker guns have been brought to light."

Colonel Lee arched bushy eyebrows and looked over the tops of his glasses. "What's a Quaker gun?" he inquired curiously. "I've never heard of such a thing."

Miss Van Lew compressed her lips. "The seemingly heavy placement of artillery which served to deter General McClellan's attack upon Beauregard's fortification at Manassas has since proven to be nothing more than logs cut and fashioned to resemble cannons and placed on wheels. Because such a cannon wouldn't harm a soul, they've been dubbed Quaker guns. The subject has become quite embarrassing to General McClellan and a choice topic of ridicule in Washington."

Colonel Cogswell was brusque. "I'll hand the Rebs this much, they're masters at deceit when it comes to covering up shortage of ordnance."

Miss Van Lew nodded agreement, her twisted curls dancing like loose ends of rope. Her face suddenly took on a gossipy expression. "There's also another major officer who's been drawing heavy fire in Washington." Her voice rose slightly. "You all know him."

Colonel Cogswell placed his hands on his hips. "To whom are you referring?"

"Why, General Stone, of course," the woman replied. "Did you know his misbehavior at Balls Bluff resulted in nine hundred casualties?" She glanced about the room. "You can see some of the results here."

"You are in grave error, madam," Colonel Cogswell retorted. "General Stone was nowhere near the Bluff, that battle was Senator Baker's stillborn baby."

"God rest his soul," Colonel Lee muttered sorrowfully. He looked at the floor. "If there's any blame to be placed, I too must share it."

"There's no sense crying over spilt milk," Cogswell rejoined. "Besides, no one's blaming anybody for what happened."

"You are wrong there, Colonel," Miss Van Lew corrected. "Just recently Senator Sumner rose in the Senate and labeled the disaster at Balls Bluff. 'The most atrocious military murder in history.' He's called for General Stone to be court-martialed."

Paddy sucked in his breath. *So*, he thought to himself, *that's how Sumner was going to worm his way out of the duel with Stone, have him arrested.*

"Sumner has been directing such extensive political and newspaper condemnation against Stone," the woman continued, "that Congress has now called on President Lincoln for full information and investigation."

"I trust the President has turned a deaf ear to the political jackals?" Cogswell growled.

"Yes, the President has said he feels the matter is contrary to public interest at this time."

"Good for him," Cogswell retorted. "He's using his head."

Colonel Lee's eyes wandered about the room for a moment, then focused themselves on the woman. "When you first came in," he said, "you mentioned that you had something of vital importance to tell me regarding my welfare. I can't forget the ill-concealed expression of dread on your face when you said it. What other news do you bring us?"

Miss Van Lew's face clouded. "I've come to warn you...." Her voice faltered and she appeared deeply upset.

"Warn us? About what?" Cogswell prompted.

"This morning," she replied, "word came to me of a dreadful action which the Confederate government is contemplating against Colonel Lee."

"What sort of action?" Colonel Lee asked quizzically.

She stood mute, eyes downcast. She spoke in an ominous whisper. "There is a move afoot to have you hanged."

Colonel Lee gasped.

"Hanged!" Colonel Cogswell roared. "What the devil for? Why should they want to hang Lee?"

Every eye in the prison compound looked up sharply at Cogswell's outburst. Miss Van Lew clasped her hands to her mouth. "Colonel! Please! The boys...."

"We have no secrets, madam," the officer thundered. "What reason does the Rebel government advance for proposing such a dastardly act?"

Appearing visibly shaken, Miss Van Lew continued. "It's a result of the Mason-Slidell affair," she responded weakly.

"Mason? Slidell? Who are they?" asked Colonel Lee.

"Agents of the Confederacy who were on their way to curry England's favor...."

Muttering in low overtones, the Federal prisoners crowded toward that end of the room to listen.

"...they were seized three weeks ago on the high seas off Cuba by Captain Wilkes of the Navy. Finding it necessary, the Captain had to use force in removing them from the steamer, *Trent,* an English vessel." She paused to clear her throat. "The English are furious over interference with their ships on the high seas. Because of the incident, England is threatening immediate war against the North."

"Very interesting," Cogswell said, "but how does the Trent affair involve the neck of Colonel Lee?"

The woman gave the Colonel of the Tammany Regiment an uneasy glance. "Since the Confederacy is an unrecognized government," she replied, "Secretary of State Seward has decreed that Mason and Slidell shall hang along with some captured privateers whom the Secretary has classified as pirates."

"In which case," Colonel Lee broke in stiffly, "the Rebels intend to forfeit my life by way of reprisal, is that it?"

Miss Van Lew nodded affirmatively.

Lee's eyes closed. "It shocks me that Jeff Davis, my closest friend at the Academy, could be party to such infamy."

Hands clasped lightly behind his back, Colonel Cogswell walked toward a window and stood staring out. "By damn, they're bluffing," he ejaculated. "I can see it now. They plan to intimidate the North the same way they did with those Quaker guns at Manassas. When the intended fate of Colonel Lee is announced to the North, the Rebs expect a public furor that will force Seward to lift the sentence of death he's passed on the Southerners."

"Colonel, your reasoning may be fairly close to the truth," Miss Van Lew responded. "I will contact my associates. Perhaps we can determine just how far the Confederate government is prepared to go in this diabolical scheme."

Preparing to leave, she put on her bonnet then covered her head carefully with a shawl. "Good-day, gentlemen. I shall report to you as soon as I've uncovered more information."

Reassuming the guise of someone slightly demented, she picked up her empty market baskets and, mumbling to herself incoherently, left the prison.

The next day, Major Turner, accompanied by a squad of guards with fixed bayonets, entered the second floor compound of Libby Prison.

"What is the meaning of this?" Colonel Cogswell stormed, feigning ignorance.

Major Turner glanced apprehensively at the menacing faces of the prisoners who were beginning to crowd around him.

"I have orders to remove Colonel Lee from these quarters, Colonel. That's all I can tell you," he replied.

Lieutenant Todd, his courage bolstered by whiskey, swaggered brazenly toward Cogswell. "Y' all really want to know what we're fixin' to do with this bird?" he sneered in Cogswell's face. "We're gonna take him out and teach him how to fly. With a rope around his neck!"

Colonel Cogswell doubled massive fists and cocked an arm to deliver a heavy blow at President Lincoln's brother-in-law.

"Please, Milton, all of you, listen to me," Colonel Lee pleaded. "Resistance here will only result in further reprisals and unnecessary bloodshed. Let them take me peacefully."

A thick-bearded sergeant from the 20th Massachusetts Regiment shoved Lieutenant Todd roughly aside and approached his regimental commander. "Have you any message for the regiment, sir?" he asked, almost childlike.

"Yes, Patrick. Tell the men...." Colonel Lee cleared his throat. "Excuse me," he stopped to cough, then continued in a husky voice, "when emotion takes an old soldier like me, it usually takes him hard. Tell the men their Colonel died like a brave man, Patrick."

"Yes, sir." The sergeant drew back and saluted. "God be with you, sir."

"I'm sure he will be, Patrick. Thank you."

The hostage was led away.

Joe Batt cupped his head in his hands. "Well, there goes the last hope we had for saving Barney's life. If Jeff Davis stoops so low as to condemn a friend as close as Colonel Lee, what chance has Barney got?"

Henry Castor stood next to Joe Batt. "Is young Williams' condition that serious?" he inquired.

"If that arm isn't amputated soon, he hasn't got a chance. Gangrene has set in." Batt gritted his teeth and shook his head. "Remember how we older fellas use to think of him as a spoiled rich kid? Crazy and irresponsible."

"Too right," Castor replied. "The capers he's cut since joining this regiment would fill a book."

"True, but lately I've been able to see the stuff he's really made of. Driven to distraction by pain, he never whimpers or complains. Still tries to think up them damn silly poems to make others laugh. And you know something? I think he knows he's going to die."

Castor chewed on a hangnail. "Must have been kind of rough on Barney. I mean, having to grow up in the shadow of an older brother like Joe, who was just about the most personable figure around town."

"Yes, guess it's pretty tough being a younger brother. Take my Billy for instance...." His voice trailed off into silence.

The evening meal was passed into the compound at the regularly appointed hour, but unlike other evenings, the prisoners ate the paltry offering in relative silence. Dispensing with their usual after-dinner activities, they retired early with their thoughts.

They had been asleep several hours when the dark room was suddenly rent by a shrill, piercing cry that awoke every man in the compound. Reverberating from the brick walls, the outbursts varied from guttural to high-pitched screams. In the eerie darkness, Paddy saw Barney Williams groping and stumbling blindly. His gangrenous arm swung in a grotesque manner. Howls of anguish came from his drawn mouth that resembled dried prune skin. Friends reached out quickly with helping hands to restrain their delirious comrade.

Joe Batt clapped his hands over his ears to drown out Barney's pitiful cries. "I can't take anymore of this!" he screamed. "It's murder! Seeing a boy die helpless...."

Henry Castor rushed to his side. "Easy, Joe, you did all you could to help."

"It's still murder!" Batt wrenched his arm loose from Castor's grip. "This does it! I'll sign any damn paper the Rebs give me to get out of here!"

"Joe, you're talking crazy. You can't do that. You can't break faith with your brother like that. He gave his life, remember?"

"I remember too well. That's why I'm gonna sign a parole, but the minute I'm free, I'm gonna break it."

"You'd break a parole?"

"Wait and see if I don't! I'll come back and kill every bloody Reb I can lay my hands on. If they can conduct themselves without honor, so can I."

"If you feel the same way by morning, I'll sign parole with you," Castor rejoined sharply. "We'll break it together, but for now, let's go over and see what we can do to ease young Williams' torment."

The first gray light of morning was just beginning to appear at the barred windows of the prison when the angels of mercy finally gathered up the soul of Barney Williams in comforting arms, carrying it aloft to rest with his brother's.

In answer to a request from Colonel Cogswell, a Confederate burial detail made its appearance about an hour later under the beady, calloused eyes of Lieutenant Todd.. Devoid of any outward sign of feeling, they covered the corpse with a blanket and prepared to remove it while grief-stricken volunteers from Frankford looked on silently.

The shrouded form was lifted from the floor and carried to the door. Suddenly, Joe Batt rushed forward and towered menacingly over Lieutenant Todd's smaller figure. "You sawed-off son-of-a-bitch!" he shouted. "Don't you want this boy's home address? How will you know where to send his body?"

"Have you got the money to pay for ice embalming and shipping costs?" the officer retorted. "You money grabbin' Yanks don't send your dead home for decent burial unless a family can foot the bill. Why should we be any different?"

"The Williams family will send you the money."

"And what are we to do with the stinkin' corpse until they do?" Todd suddenly flashed a sword. "If you haven't got the money, Yank, step aside. We'll see that his body gets sent straight to hell in the fertile soil of Virginia."

Enraged beyond self-control, Joe sprang forward like a cat, kicking the sword from Todd's grasp and throttling the officer by the throat with his massive hands. Not a single guard moved to his defense.

"Sergeant Batt!" Cogswell's deep bass roared. "Unhand that officer this instant. Do you hear me?"

Breathing heavily, Batt slowly withdrew his hands from the officer's throat. "First chance I get," he hissed in Todd's face, "I'm going to kill you for those last remarks."

Shaken and unnerved, Lieutenant Todd quickly ordered his men to form around him and directed them to leave the room with their burden.

A prisoner from Cogswell's New York Regiment reached over approvingly and slapped Batt on the back. "Nice goin', Sarg. I've been living for the day I'd see that arrogant tyrant forced to 'cut stick' by one of us."

"Yeah, bully for you, Sarg," another man chimed in. "We were all ready to jump in if you needed us."

The gratifying exhibition of Lieutenant Todd's downfall served as the chief topic of conversation for the balance of the day, but as night drew near the prison compound became strangely quiet with an all-encompassing corporal feeling that carried a distinct holy tenor. As stillness settled over the crowded prison, the prevailing spirit was reflected in the far-off expression that appeared in the eyes of the men.

Despondent and introverted, each man seemed to be seeking seclusion as the room grew darker. Throughout the Christian world this night, a singular event was being celebrated. Elsewhere, people were commemorating the ancient birth of a babe in swaddling clothes and they would be singing, "*Peace on earth, good will toward men.*" It was Christmas Eve.

Paddy lay on a bed of straw, hands clasped behind his head. He stared at the bleak ceiling. His thoughts traveled homeward, visualizing Frankford as he remembered it at Christmas time, inviting houses pleasantly decorated with evergreens and bright ornaments that shimmered as stars in the glow of candlelight.

Experiencing a twinge of homesickness, he recalled one particular Christmas Eve almost two years ago. As a Christmas present for their father, the Williams brothers asked Joseph Mulcahy to make them a pair of wrought iron mud scrapers fashioned in the form of horses. Delivering the gift through the snow that Christmas Eve, Paddy had stopped outside the bay window of the Williams' house to steal a wistful glance at the gay festivities taking place within the luxurious dining room, the wondrous scene holding him spellbound for several minutes.

Shivering in the cold, he watched in awe as Negro butlers moved unobtrusively around a stately dining table where the entire Williams family was seated at a holiday reunion meal. His eyes, accustomed to the plain settings of tin and ironstone on a bare table, watched with fascination the glittering silver and crystal spread on white linen. Everything in the room shone and sparkled with brilliance and splendor. Uncle Peter Marks, who in his time had waited upon President Monroe, was employed yearly for one specific purpose, the honor of serving the plum pudding. Dressed in a red coat, he ceremoniously brought forth the delicate, traditional dessert bedecked with sprigs of holly and illuminated by flames of burning brandy poured on a silver platter around the base. The sound of *Ohs* and *Ahs* and squeals of delight from the children were clearly audible through the frosted windowpane against which Paddy's pug nose was pressed.

On that Christmas Eve, it was Barney Williams who first discovered Paddy standing in the snow outside the window. He insisted that he come inside for some hot chocolate and a piece of plum pudding, then in a good-hearted gesture, he gave him one of his own presents-a pair of warm mittens. "I already have two pairs," he said. Now, Barney was dead. His oldest brother, Joe, was dead-Joe Williams, tall, dignified, and aristocratic, from whom the townspeople of Frankford had expected great things some day.

Paddy swallowed hard and rolled over on one side, staring into space. The scene at the Williams' house would be changed this night. The silver and crystal would be less radiant, the hot buttered rum would not taste as sweet, the flames around the plum pudding would burn lower. His thoughts turned to his father. Joseph Mulcahy would be drinking lonely wine tonight, as always, while he sat in their darkened house on Orchard Street. It had always been that way, ever since Sharron Mulcahy had passed away. The church bells of Frankford would be pealing on the frosty air about now and many families would be loading themselves into sleighs to attend special vespers services. He wondered, since most of the young men were in the army, if there would be the usual caroling in the streets.

He thought about Becky Chenewith. Why hadn't she written to him? Perhaps it was just girlish pity she had felt for him, which his absence had corrected. Suddenly he felt warm and glowing inside. There would be genuine family happiness in the Chenewith house tonight. They were that kind of people. Oh, if he could only be with them.

Coming out of his reverie, he gazed around at the bleak dismal room. The place was still crowded with a huddled mass of miserable, emaciated men, the chamber pots, the stench, the....

Startled by something awe-inspiring which his roving eye chanced to fall upon, he sat upright. Were his eyes deceiving him, or could it be that the moonlight streaming through the barred windows was playing tricks this night?

He strained his eyes for a closer look. Moonbeams striking frozen droplets of water clustered on a far wall of the prison room turned the mysterious stalactite formation into a sparkling ornament of beauty that closely resembled a shimmering star in the darkness. He fell to his knees and crossed himself.

"Blessed Mary, Mother of Jesus," he murmured. The others saw it too and marveled at the strange illumination never witnessed before. Was it an omen? Was God trying to brighten their ordeal on this holy night? Was this to be their Star of Bethlehem?

In a corner, John Heap and Tom Pilling began singing softly, *"Oh come all ye faithful, joyful and triumphant...."*

They were joined by others from St. Mark's Sunday School class: *"Oh come ye; oh come ye, to Bethlehem; come and adore him, born the King of Angels...."* The lyrical tenor voice of John Stott was noticeably absent, having been stilled forever at Balls Bluff.

Following the lead of John Lightfoot's resonant bass voice, the prisoners picked up another tune and filled the gloomy compound with, *"Hark the herald angels sing, glory to the new born King."*

Long before the song ended, many of the prisoners had buried their faces in the straw bedding and begun sobbing. The rest continued to sing unabashed while the tears flowed. Then silence again, broken only by the choking sound of men crying and the occasional audible whimper of the one word representing universal love and affection-"Mother."

Sometime later, the faint sound of other voices, Southern voices, could be heard singing beneath the barred windows of Libby Prison.

"*Silent night, holy night....*" Crowding to the windows of their cell block, the prisoners looked down upon a group of Confederate soldiers standing in the snow and singing by lantern light.

One of the bearded prisoners pressed his face against the bars and bared his teeth. "Go on, ya dirty...."

Another grabbed him by the arm. "Cut that out. Those Johnnies aren't our enemy, it's the ones who rule over them." He pushed the bearded man to one side and shouted through the bars. "Merry Christmas, Johnny Reb! Merry Christmas!"

Immediately the cry was taken up by others among the prisoners in response to which the Southerners doffed their floppy campaign hats and shouted in reply, "Merry Christmas, Yanks, God Bless y'all!"

The moon rose to its zenith and the strange light on the prison wall disappeared as mysteriously as it had come and it was dark and silent once more.

On Christmas Day, Paddy, to his utter surprise, was called to the door of the prison compound by a strange new guard who abruptly thrust an envelope and large cardboard carton into his hands.

"It's from Leesburg," the guard said tersely, then closed the door and left hurriedly.

Turning aside a volume of inquiries from curious onlookers, Paddy sought seclusion. He tore open the scented envelope with uncontrollable excitement and quickly extracted several sheets of stationery. His eyes darted hungrily as he began reading:

Dear Paddy,

Merry Christmas! I do hope the guard, whom Father has paid well, will follow my instructions and deliver this letter and package to you the first thing Christmas morning. That way you can pretend you are descending the stairway in our home. Make believe the package is waiting for you beneath a tree we trimmed together last night. Pretend, my darling, that my written words are those of love and affection which I hope someday to be able to speak face to face on a Christmas morning.

Darling, I miss you so much. Has your wound given you any further trouble? Oh my dear, I hope not. At night I lie awake and...

He continued to read and reread the long letter, not only on that day, but on subsequent days, reading it early in the morning when he awoke and just before he went to sleep at night. The gift package contained mincemeat, preserves, soap, hand-knitted socks and several other items which helped to brighten his prison life somewhat.

The year 1862 was ushered in by a joyful party to celebrate not only the New Year, but also the release of Colonel Lee as a hostage. The North's capitulation to the South's threat of retaliation put an end to the hanging. The Trent affair was closed.

Throughout the month of January, there was increased talk among the prisoners of a sweeping parole soon to be granted to all the inmates of Libby. The rumor caused hopes to soar and restored a trace of vitality among the men, but the rumor proved unfounded.

On the twenty-fifth of February, Miss Van Lew paid another of her visits to the prison compound. Without pausing to exchange greetings with the enlisted men, she hurried directly to Colonel Lee and excitedly handed him a Washington newspaper with bold black headlines.

Colonel Lee scanned the paper. His face turned white. He called for silence and the room was immediately hushed as he began reading aloud: "Brigadier-General Charles P. Stone was arrested in Washington this morning at two o'clock by a posse from the Provost Marshall's office, and sent to Fort Lafayette, New York Harbor...."

Bulling his way forward, Colonel Cogswell grabbed the paper from Colonel Lee's trembling hands. "Let me see that," he demanded.

Prisoners jostled each other and crowded close to hear every word the Colonel spoke as he began reading from the article. His words pierced them as if shot from a cannon.

"The charges against General Stone were: first, for misbehavior at the battle of Balls Bluff; second, for holding correspondence with the enemy before and since the battle of Balls Bluff, and receiving visits from Rebel officers in his camp; third, for treacherously suffering the enemy to build a fort or strong work, since the battle of Balls Bluff, under his guns without molestation: fourth, for a treacherous design to expose his force to capture and destruction by the enemy under pretense of orders for a movement from the commanding general, which had not been given."

"What's the story, Colonel?" a voice called out. "I thought Baker was responsible for that disaster?"

"Not according to the court-martial findings," another shouted. "It must have been Stone's doing all along."

"Right!" came another cry. "Working for the Rebs the whole time."

"Prison's too good for the traitor," several said angrily.

"Shoot him!"

"No! Hang him! "

"That's the ticket, hang him! My best friend was slaughtered in cold blood at the Bluff," a corporal said.

Paddy blurted in anger, "Those are lies! All lies!"

"What's that you say, Private Mulcahy?" Colonel Cogswell's eyes pierced him like darts as he handed the paper back to Colonel Lee. "What makes you so positive those are lies?"

With every eye focused upon him, Paddy suddenly felt like crawling into a hole. There was a moment of silence. Cheeks flushed and eyes resolute, he replied, "As Colonel Wistar's orderly, I—well, that is, I often heard the Colonel and Senator Baker discussing orders that came from General Stone. One night in particular I heard the General talking politics and military matters with—"

"Pipe the Irish blarney!" a crude voice shouted derisively. "Little Paddy 'Mulkayhee' sittin' in on a discussion of orders, strategy and politics with a general, a senator and a colonel. You've gone 'Libby-loony,' Mulcahy."

"I didn't say I was in the room. I was standing guard on a porch outside an open window."

A roar of laughter greeted his explanation.

The trace of a smile appeared on Colonel Cogswell's broad face, then vanished as quickly as it came. He stepped forward.

"Men, what Private Mulcahy has just said is true. The charges you've read against General Stone are a pack of filthy lies. What say you, Colonel Lee?"

"Absolutely. Those charges are the boldest perversion and misstatement of truth I've ever heard."

Cogswell eyed Paddy narrowly. "Have you any knowledge as to who's behind this attack on the General's good name?"

Paddy shifted awkwardly.

"Come now, Mulcahy," he prodded. "You seem to have overheard a lot of things you shouldn't have. Speak up."

Paddy bit his lower lip. "Yes, sir, I'd say this was Senator Sumner's work."

Colonel Lee knit bushy eyebrows. "Sumner. Oh come now, lad, you're taking things too far. The Senator's name doesn't even appear in print." He opened the paper. "Here, let me read what it says. 'The joint committee on the conduct of the war, recently appointed by Congress, is composed of Senators Wade of Ohio, Chandler of Michigan, and Johnson of Tennessee, together with Representatives Goode of Massachusetts, Covode of Pennsylvania, Julian of Indiana and Odell of New York.'"

He folded the paper. "There, you see, Sumner's not mentioned at all. I'm afraid you've made a serious miscalculation, son."

Miss Van Lew spoke from the background. "On the contrary, Colonel, the boy is right. The hand behind this whole investigation has been Senator Sumner. If you remember, in December I told you how public indignation was being stirred up, even at that time, against Stone by Sumner's disparaging speeches dealing with General Stone's purported misconduct."

"But why?"

The woman hesitated for a moment, and cast an anxious eye at the sea of faces surrounding her. The news-hungry prisoners crowded closer, staring intently.

"Yesterday I returned from Washington through the lines," she continued. "While still in the Capitol, I heard and saw much of what was going on." She paused. "There's a young Irish nobleman on duty as a British observer with our army. He has been spreading word that Sumner wanted Stone imprisoned to escape fighting a duel which the General challenged him to...."

Stewart, Paddy thought to himself.

"It's interesting to note that when the country was sufficiently aroused, it was Sumner who was the driving force which moved Congress to appoint a committee to investigate the conduct of war. It was this committee which proceeded into the inquiry using methods common to nearly all similar bodies."

"If what you say is true," Colonel Lee asked, puzzled, "why didn't Sumner get himself appointed to the committee? I should think..."

"The Senator's purpose was accomplished, Colonel. With cunning and guile, he preferred to remain in the background and had his close friend, Ben Wade, appointed as chairman of the committee instead."

Colonel Cogswell curled thick lips. "The able Senator from Massachusetts couldn't have picked a better hatchet man. How did the actual inquiry go?"

"I'll wager it was like a pack of hound dogs tasting blood for the first time," Major Revere broke in.

"Yes," the woman responded grimly, "so much so that some of the committee members publicly hailed the arrest of Stone with open demonstrations of delight."

Colonel Lee's mouth flew open. "No!"

"Yes, as a matter of fact, it's been this unfair treatment accorded to the General which has placed my feelings on his side. The investigation was a farce. Witnesses were summoned and examined without order. There was no cross-examination. The accused was not confronted with the witnesses nor told their names, nor the charges upon which he had been already tried, condemned, and sentenced before he was even allowed to appear, and no record was kept of the details."

"Good God, woman. This can't be true," Colonel Lee blurted, shocked and amazed.

"It's as true as I'm standing here."

"Didn't Wistar come to Stone's defense?" Colonel Cogswell snapped. "Certainly he and Baker knew more of the real situation than anyone. They were with Stone almost constantly."

Miss Van Lew cleared her throat. "Colonel Wistar was silenced officially. He was not permitted to appear at the trial, and I've heard that in the hospital where he's recuperating he goes almost apoplectic with rage whenever the subject is mentioned."

Paddy touched Lieutenant Donaldson on the arm. "Sure must've taken a powerful lot of heavy military to gag the Colonel," he whispered. "I'll bet he's really hot."

Colonel Lee was solemn. "Didn't McClellan intervene on Stone's behalf?"

"Yes, he did. He said that he did not see how any charges could be framed on that testimony. It's McClellan's statement which has made the committee's charges against Stone so ridiculous. Why, even Secretary of War Stanton, when ordering the arrest, said he did so only at the solicitation of the committee. And Stanton is a Democrat."

"Who did you say was Secretary of War?" Cogswell interjected.

"Edwin Stanton."

"Stanton? What became of Simon Cameron?"

"Poor man, he was ousted by the committee on the conduct of war in one of its first official acts. To soothe Cameron's wounded pride, Lincoln just recently appointed him ambassador to Russia."

Colonel Lee shook his head. "A sorry spectacle. How can the government ask these boys to die for their country when grown men who direct our fortunes behave that way?" His attitude stiffened. "Listen to me, gentlemen. This grave injustice against General Stone will not go unrectified for long, you may be assured. Our President will see to that." He turned quickly to Miss Van Lew. "Am I not right, madam?"

"I...I wish to heaven you were, Colonel, but...." Her voice faded. "The President has already refused to intervene."

"What? Refused to intervene?" Colonel Cogswell's eyes bulged beneath his shaggy eyebrows. "Preposterous! Is the president's memory so short that he's forgotten it was Stone who first came out of retirement to organize the defense of Washington during those perilous days before the inauguration? Lincoln's life was dependent on his loyalty and courage in those treacherous days. What kind of an ingrate have we elected as Chief Executive?"

Ruffled by Cogswell's outburst, Miss Van Lew made a determined effort to answer his stinging criticism. "As I told you in December," she replied firmly, "the President made every effort to stave off the investigation on three separate occasions. Since Congress overruled his objections and proceeded with the investigations anyhow, he has remained aloof from their findings because he feels they are detrimental to the best interests of the country. I think he's wise."

"The false charges against Stone seem to be broadcast well enough in this newspaper," Cogswell retorted. "Does the President take the public to be deaf, dumb, and blind? Or does he expect them to stick their heads in the sand like ostriches? Best interests, indeed. I say he should defend Stone."

"Colonel, you're not being fair. The President did all in his power to suppress the derogatory abuse levied upon the General. He did all he could to keep it from becoming public."

"Then how in the hell did it get into the papers?"

"I don't know. It's strange. The secrets of the investigating committee were not even divulged to the authority from which it derived. The Senate had to pass a resolution calling upon the President to produce evidence taken before its own committee, its own committee, mind you. Like a wily fox, Sumner supported the Senate resolution knowing full well the President would never comply."

"Sumner, the great public-spirited defender," Cogswell growled. "I'd like to lay hands on him."

"Well, he played it safe enough. As expected, the President declined to lay the evidence before the Senate in a message which, as Mister Blair pointed out, bore marks of having been written in the war office. The fact remains, however, that the information withheld from the senate by the President consisted strangely enough of evidence taken by one of its own committees whose membership would not reveal their findings to the main body."

Cogswell stroked his chin. "Perhaps I've been unduly harsh on the President, but I still think he should exert some effort to have Stone released from prison."

'The President is undergoing trying times...."

"So's Stone. So are we."

"You don't understand," the woman said slowly. "Haven't you heard?"

"Heard what?"

"His son, Willie, died of typhoid last week."

A stillness hushed the room.

"How old was the boy?" Colonel Lee asked at last.

"Eleven."

"The poor father. What anguish he must be suffering. My heart goes out to him."

"This makes the second boy the Lincolns have lost, doesn't it?" Colonel Cogswell asked softly.

"Yes, Ned died in Springfield several years ago."

"That leaves just Tad and Robert."

Colonel Lee stared at the floor. "How is the First Lady taking it?" he inquired in a hollow voice.

Miss Van Lew frowned. "Badly, very badly. She has closed the White House to all visitors and keeps herself locked up in a dark room." Miss Van Lew studied her fingernails for a moment. "There is something else," she stammered. "I know it must be terribly distressing to President Lincoln."

"What is that?" Cogswell asked.

"From the moment Willie passed away, she has been trying to communicate with the boy."

"Communicate?"

"Yes. In the dark room in which she has closeted herself, she has been holding spiritualist seances almost constantly."

A ripple of murmuring arose from the prisoners as they glanced at each other askance.

Miss Van Lew looked at a watch pinned inside her coat and placed a shawl over her head. "It's late. I must be returning home. I will try to bring you more cheerful news next time."

Cogswell and Lee escorted the woman to the barred doorway and bade her farewell.

The days passed slowly. The whistling winds of March caused the old tobacco warehouse to creak and groan in an eerie manner, but like the old adage, it is an ill wind that blows no good, something good happened. On the fifteenth of March, machinery was put in motion to prepare the prisoners for exchange. Forms were brought for them to sign and the necessary steps for freedom were laid. Dazed by their good fortune, the prisoners shook their heads in disbelief, fearing everything was too good to be true. On the twenty-fifth of March, the day arrived for which they had been waiting and praying.

With heads erect, eyes staring straight ahead, some blinking like moles, the ragged and emaciated body of men marched out from the fetid confines of Libby Prison into the world of sunlight and fresh air.

At a signal from Major Paul Revere, the released Federal soldiers started to sing the national anthem as they quick-stepped toward a river boat berthed at a nearby wharf. Attracted by the startling sound of the *Star Spangled Banner* being sung in their streets, a crowd of curious onlookers gathered and glared with indignation. Some, hearing the national anthem for the first time in over a year, turned away and hung their heads.

The steamer that was to take the prisoners to City Point, Virginia, for exchange was rapidly loaded, lines were cast off and the long anticipated trip down the James River began.

From his place at the stern of the vessel, Paddy caught a fleeting glimpse of "Crazy Bet" standing among the crowd on the wharf. Waving a lacy handkerchief, she appeared to be dabbing at her cheeks as the boat sailed out of sight. At that distance, though, he might have been mistaken.

Arriving at City Point late in the afternoon, the men lifted tired eyes to view the comfortable-looking brick dwelling of A. M. Aiken which rested on a gentle slope of ground rising above the river. The sight of women and children standing on a wide, pillared porch aroused pangs of homesickness. The rude plank wharf at Aiken's Landing groaned and creaked beneath the weight of disembarking soldiers who climbed wearily to the brow of the hill overlooking the barren, windswept river. Weak and exhausted by the unaccustomed exertion, the men flung themselves to the ground without bothering to remove knapsacks.

Rolling over on his stomach, one of the men studied a large, three-decked bird box set upon a high pole. "Damned if that ain't the biggest birdhouse I ever seen," he exclaimed with interest. "Looks like a New York City apartment house."

A small pig-tailed girl dressed in a voluminous hoop skirt wandered from the house and stood nearby gaping at the bearded fierce-looking Yankee parolees.

"That's a martin box" she ventured timidly. "In another four weeks the martins will be returning to drive the hawks away from our chicken yard."

"You don't say," a soldier much older than the rest replied. He held out his hands toward the little girl. His voice was gentle and kind. "I've three the likes of you at home, miss. How old are you?"

"Five."

"Live here, do you?"

"Yes all my life. I like it along the river 'specially when the boats come in. Do you live 'side a river?"

"No, I live in upper New York State in the country."

The wisp of a girl took the older man's hands. "Did you really come from a bury hole?" she blurted wide-eyed.

"Bury hole? What's that sweetheart?"

A soft voice laughed in the background. The men turned around and saw the girl's mother. She smiled pleasantly. "Ann must have heard me say y'all looked like you'd just returned from the grave. Bury hole is her expression for grave."

The woman took her daughter by the hand. "Come along, Ann."

"Please Mama, let me stay and talk to this nice man."

"I said come along, Ann."

The Union soldier from upper New York State returned the little girl's goodbye wave then gazed up at the birdhouse. "I'll tell you this frankly boys " he said soberly, "when those birds and McClellan resume their hawk driving come spring, I'm gonna be settin' at home peaceable like enjoyin' the chatter of my own little girls. Yes siree bob. No more fightin' for me."

From a group standing on the slope came a sharp cry of excitement. "Here she comes boys! Here she comes!"

They pointed toward midstream where the flag-of-truce boat *New York*, her massive side-wheels thrashing muddy water was pushing steadily toward the Virginia shore. Instantly there was a general rush for the waterfront. The long denied sight of Old Glory flying proudly at the boat's stern mast proved too much for many of the overwrought, weakened men, causing several to faint. Breaking under the emotional strain, tears of joy rolled down their cheeks while others stared at the approaching vessel like youngsters lapping taffy sticks.

As soon as the side-wheeler docked, the seamen quickly went to work helping the derelict human cargo board ship. When they were all loaded, the side-wheels reversed directions and the puffing steamboat moved slowly away from Aiken's landing and headed across the choppy James River to Fortress Monroe.

Next morning the prisoners were transported further north to Camp Parole at Annapolis, Maryland, where the sick could be nursed back to health. Those in fair physical condition were permitted to proceed home, and they departed daily from the camp in small groups.

The majority spared no time in their haste to return home to loved ones. The impulse for others was to stop over in Washington where they could satisfy long dormant desires in the flourishing fleshpots.

Following the former course, Paddy, along with Lieutenant Donaldson, Joe Batt, Henry Castor and a sprinkling of other fellows, entrained directly for Philadelphia by way of Baltimore. Silent, each with his own thoughts, the small group sat composed, their faces reflecting dreams of home as the train carried them to their destination.

Passengers proved to be disconcerting and annoying as they stopped in the aisle with monotonous frequency to study the mens' badges and caps. The intruders nodded, fawned and beamed, but every attempt to strike up conversation was turned aside by the soldiers preoccupied with thoughts of home.

Not until the familiar landmarks of Philadelphia came into view did their tongues loosen. In a pent-up torrent, they began to shout with joy as they peered and pointed through the car windows.

Moving toward his haversack as the train began to reduce speed, Lieutenant Donaldson placed a hand on Paddy's shoulder. "How about stopping at my house for dinner, Mulcahy? I'd like my family to meet you. You would still have plenty of time to make Frankford before dark."

Paddy hesitated. "It...it isn't that I wouldn't like to Frank, but I'd like to hurry on home and see Pa. It's been eight long months."

"I understand, old friend. Promise me you will come to the city for a visit when you can. General Meade is my neighbor. Never know when you'll need a favor."

"I promise."

The train ground to a halt.

"All off for Philadelphia!" George Hart chortled.

"Garden City of the World!" others chorused with happy excitement.

"Hey, Paddy," Joe Batt called over his shoulder, "you coming with us?"

"Just a minute."

"Well, hurry it up. If the schedules haven't been changed, we've only got fifteen minutes to catch the dummy to Frankford."

"Be right with you."

Paddy grasped Lieutenant Donaldson by the hand.

"So, long, Frank and...thanks for everything."

"So long, Paddy. Be seeing you."

Seated at last in a horse-drawn, open-sided dummy car that rattled, creaked, and swayed as it moved, the Frankford volunteers poured over the many things they were going to do when they got home. For Joe Batt and Henry Castor, it was going to be a painful ordeal and the reopening of old wounds, facing grieved parents who would be asking all sorts of questions regarding the deaths of their younger brothers. For those more fortunate, there would be happy reunions with families, but the sobering prospect of uncomfortable inquiries from parents of dead comrades lingered tormentingly in the back of their minds. *How does one go about answering such questions?* they wondered. The answer would have to be met soon, for the precious, long-awaited moment had arrived.

Rolling into a car barn bordering Frankford Creek, the dummy came to a stop. The soldiers, vibrating with anticipation, clambered from the car. Familiar old places came into sight bringing back a myriad of childhood memories. Millers were busy at work in the grist mills along the creek banks, and jets of steam poured from flues in Sidebottom's tape factory. Industrial smoke trailed skyward from the chimneys of Horrock's bleaching and dying plant. With a momentary touch of sadness, Paddy gazed toward the open windows of the latter establishment and recalled the death of Tony McErlain, who had worked behind those walls.

Adam Hafer spread his arms and crowed, "Even from this side of the creek, the town looks good. Come on, let's make our grand entrance."

Picking up their haversacks, the prisoners of war quickly crossed the covered bridge spanning Frankford Creek and with happy hearts advanced up lower Main Street.

Old Ned, hard at work pruning trees on the lawn in front of the Womrath mansion, looked around curiously at the sound of footsteps and happy voices. Seeing the men in blue uniforms, he stood up straight as an arrow and dropped his pruning shears. "Glory be to Moses!" he cried.

Jubilantly, he rushed toward the soldiers whom he had known as boys and grinned open mouthed, his mahogany face rimming a set of pearl white teeth. "Mistah Castor, suh, Mistah Batt, suh, and I 'clar to goodness, heah's Mistah

Mulcahy and Mistah Lightfoot and...." Tears began to flow down his gray stubbled cheeks as he wrung each one by the hand. Then breaking away and dashing madly across the street toward the Eagle Hotel, he screamed at the top of his lungs. "Glory Hallelujah! Evahbody harken to Old Ned. The boys has come back! The boys is back!"

The commotion brought excited men running into the street from all directions. Women with market baskets slung on their arms scurried hurriedly out of store fronts. Inquiring faces looking out of shop windows, disappeared quickly, and reappeared in the street. Squealing youngsters rushed forward eagerly. In a moment's time lower Main Street was swarming with a cheering throng of people who pressed in from all sides shouting all sorts of questions and completely surrounding the somewhat embarrassed returnees. Dan Thorton, proprietor of the Eagle Hotel, bounded down the hotel steps and bulled his way to the fore.

"You boys can all have a drink on me," he bellowed. "Don't none of you dare to refuse, or I'll be obliged to knock your heads together." He laughed loudly. "Course, I don't really think I'm capable of that anymore. Look at the size of you."

The crowd roared approval. Suddenly spotting his mother standing in the background, John Heap called out in a loud voice. "Ma! Ma! It's me!" and shouldered his way to her side.

"Son! Oh, my son," she cried. "Thank God." Her sunbonnet and market basket went flying as they embraced.

Despite the fact that his return was unexpected and knowing full well the smithy was located almost a mile from the center of town, Paddy nevertheless scanned the happy, demonstrative throng for some sight of his father's face, but Joseph Mulcahy was nowhere to be found. He did notice, however, that not all were joining in on the joyous occasion taking place in the street. His eyes came to rest on Dave Chipman's mother and widow McErlain, both of whom were holding onto a porch railing for support as they forced back the tears and watched from a distance.

Paddy started to elbow his way slowly through the crowd. Once free, he walked hesitantly toward the two women and removed his kepi, his fingers perspiring as he gripped his leather cap visor nervously. He greeted both women with an uneasy nod. "I...I just came over to say that I'm sorry, and if there's ever anything I can do...that is, if there's anything you'd want to talk about...."

Mrs. McErlain, looking pale and worn, clasped his hand tightly. "You dear, sweet boy. You thoughtful child. Yes, I want you to come and see me as soon as you can. There's a lot I'd like to talk about."

Dave Chipman's mother clutched his other wrist. "Yes," she said in a broken voice, "we need someone to talk to about our sons."

Both women suddenly drew back their hands as if alarmed by something they just remembered and turned their faces away.

He stood awkwardly for a moment, completely puzzled, then pivoted and walked slowly away. Odd, he thought to himself. There were others, now that he thought about it, who behaved in the same strange way. Several old acquaintances had looked at him, started to speak, then dropped their gaze as if something was the matter. Oh well, he thought, shrugging his shoulders. He lowered his head and started running in the direction of the smithy.

He dashed across Orthodox Street and without looking where he was going, nearly bowled an elderly couple off their feet. He stopped short, recovered himself and looked up to apologize. "Aunt Virginia! Uncle Peter!" he shouted. He threw his arms around the aged couple. "This is home. Now I'm really home," he said.

"Chile! Chile!" the Negress responded, sobbing as she pressed him close to her bosom.

Uncle Peter moved slowly to one side and hung his head. Virginia Marks released her embrace and looked deep into Paddy's eyes.

"Tell me, Chile, is you all right?"

"I'm fine. Jim-dandy fine. How's Pa? I want to hurry and surprise him."

Uncle Peter's lips were trembling and tears flowed from his wife's eyes.

"Chile, I guess it's de Lord's will you hear it from me," she cried softly.

"Hear what? What are you crying about?"

"It's about your pa, Chile. Last week he was kicked by a horse. Oh, Chile, we didn't know you was evah comin' back. Your pa is dead. We buried him three days ago."

Color drained from Paddy's face. He felt weak. The world seemed to collapse around him.

"What will you do, Chile?"

Paddy shifted the weight of his knapsack. "I'll go home and re-open the smithy. Pa would want that." He moistened lips that were dry as flannel. His voice was harsh. "And I'll study war no more."

CHAPTER 8

It was one of those beastly hot late afternoons in August that so often enveloped the Delaware Valley in stifling humidity. Paddy sat in the smithy at his father's roll-top desk. Around his neck was a towel soaked in cold water to ward off the head-splitting temperature. Grief over the loss of loved ones showed on his face. Dark circles shadowed his eyes. A feeling of loneliness gnawed at him. He fingered the lock of hair that Becky had given him and stroked it gently. Headlines from an outdated newspaper stared at him from its place on the desk: "Seventy-first Pennsylvania Saves The Day For McClellan at Glendale on the Peninsula." He took a soiled invitation from a cubbyhole in the desk and read again:

You are cordially invited to attend the
wedding of Isaac Jones Wistar to Sarah Toland,
Saturday, June 5th, 1862

He cursed himself for not attending, not even giving the courtesy of a reply. He thrust the invitation back into its slot, rose from his chair and prepared to close the smithy for the day. Making certain that the fire in the forge was extinguished, he strode outside, closed the large double doors behind him and bolted them.

He stood for a moment and listened to the soothing chimes of twilight vespers that came from the belfry at St. Mark's Church. The metallic hymn was floating melodiously on the evening breeze when the sound of an approaching horseman caused him to turn his head and shade his eyes against the setting sun. Was a heat mirage playing tricks with his vision?

Running toward horse and rider, he let out a wild whoop. "Frank! Is that really you?"

Donaldson sprang from the saddle and gathered Paddy in a bear hug. "You old son of a gun, Mulcahy. Good to see you."

Paddy stepped back a pace to survey his former comrade-in-arms. "What is this? Jackboots, sword, and captain's epaulets? And that regimental number on your hat?" He leaned forward and squinted. "One Hundred and Eighteenth?"

Donaldson removed the gauntlets from his sweaty hands. "You've about summed it up, Mulcahy. What say we go into the Jolly Post and have a yarn over a cool drink."

Paddy slapped his friend on the arm. "Bully idea. We've got a lot to catch up on."

Seated at a table, both men were approached by Mary Coates. "It's a blister today, Paddy. Will you have your usual, fresh lemonade ice cold?"

Paddy ran his tongue over parched lips. 'The usual," he replied. "And Mary, I'd like you to meet Captain Frank Donaldson. Frank, this is Mary Coates."

The portly innkeeper's wife beamed. "Indeed a pleasure, Captain. Paddy has spoken highly of you on many occasions. What may I bring you?"

Donaldson opened the collar of his uniform. "The lemonade sounds great to me."

Paddy placed his elbows on the table and cupped his chin in his hands. "Now, how's the regiment and what went wrong on the peninsula?"

Donaldson's expression turned serious. "The regiment suffered some heavy casualties, but fortunately they included none of your Frankford comrades. I presume you read in the papers that we saved McClellan's ass at Glendale."

Paddy nodded his head.

"You have most of your answers in McClellan," Donaldson continued. "He had his usual 'slows' from the start. Why he split the army into two wings, one on each side of the Chickahominy, is hard to fathom, almost led to a complete disaster. We hear Lincoln is quite put out with him. Have you heard about the exchange of telegrams between the President and Little Mac?"

"No."

"From the beginning, Lincoln sent telegrams asking McClellan for daily, detailed progress reports, all of which were completely ignored. Finally in desperation, Lincoln sent a telegram demanding that McClellan send him information regarding what he had accomplished that particular day. Little Mac fired a telegram back saying, 'Today we captured two cows. What shall I do with them?'" Donaldson found it difficult to keep a straight face. "Do you know the president's reply? He wired, 'Milk 'em, George!'"

Paddy's reply sounded harsh. "Be funny if it wasn't so bloody tragic."

"True, old friend, but these days a touch of humor alleviates a multitude of sins. Fortunately for him, our good president has a sense of humor, without which I would fear for his sanity." Donaldson took a long drink of lemonade. "Have you ever read Bunyan?"

"Last year of school we had to read Pilgrim's Progress," Paddy replied.

"The Peninsular campaign was Pilgrim's Progress personified, Mulcahy. The army was Mr. Standfast. We started up Assault Lane toward the Celestial City under the command, we thought, of Mr. Greatheart. Unfortunately, Greatheart hesitated in the face of the Lions and the army got bogged down in the Slough of Despond, was taken by the Giant of Despair and cast into Doubting Castle. As a result, we never made it to Beulah Land."

A smile crossed Paddy's lips. "Very well put, Captain. Now explain yourself and the new regimental number you're wearing."

Donaldson tilted his chair back and pointed to one leg. "I was wounded at Fair Oaks. While recovering in Philadelphia, I was approached by some gentlemen from the Corn Exchange Bank. They offered me a captaincy if I would help them recruit a regiment that will bear their name, Corn Exchange. On the state roster it will be known as the One Hundred and Eighteenth Pennsylvania. The bank is offering five hundred dollars to everyone who will enlist for three years in the Corn Exchange Regiment."

Paddy's mouth flew open. "Bounty soldiers? What kind of men are you trying to recruit?"

"Only the best. That's why I am here, I want Frankford men in my company." The cleft in Donaldson's chin was more noticeable than ever. "I have been authorized to offer you a lieutenant's commission if you will assist me."

"Me? An officer? Forget it. I'm a follower, not a leader." Paddy measured his words. "Besides, I'm not so sure my heart is in the war anymore. Look what they did to General Stone, cashiered him out of the army and placed him in jail. There's too much dirty, underhanded business going on. I think I want no part of it."

Donaldson's dark eyes flashed as Paddy had seen them do on several occasions. He spoke quietly. "I've misjudged you, Mulcahy, also Frankford. I was under the impression this town provided the best citizen soldiers available anywhere. Let me ask you something. Do you believe in the law?"

"Of course I do."

"Do you think it's always perfect?"

"Well, no, not always."

"That being the case, would you like to live where there was no law?"

Paddy felt defenseless as he recalled his father's experience in that same room a year ago before Colonel Wistar. With a dry throat, he replied, "No."

The officer reached for his hat. "And there you have it, Mulcahy. Nothing and no one is completely perfect in this world." He paused and stood erect. "Well, there's a war to be won and a Constitution to be upheld. I might as well head back to the city."

"Don't bullyrag me, Captain. Sit down." Paddy flashed him a disarming smile. "Let's talk about it."

He scratched the back of his neck with two fingers. "Frankford's been picked like a Christmas turkey. Colonel Chapman Biddle has been in town two days recruiting for his One Hundred and Twenty-first Regiment, got a slew of mountain men from Venango County. Now he wants some Frankford stock to round out his regiment."

Donaldson eased himself back into a chair and picked up his drink. A half-smile showed on his dimpled cheeks. "Tell me more."

"Well, he's gone about it in the right way. Picked Jim Ashworth as captain, and Garsed as lieutenant, both old-line Frankford. Between them they've picked up one hundred and fifteen volunteers at last count. Got an entire Sunday school class out of Saint Mark's Episcopal Church, Aaron and John Settle, Ed Tibben...."

"Any relation to our Sergeant Tibben?"

"Brother." Paddy paused to finish his drink. "There's supposed to be a muster roll call under the trees in front of Saint Mark's in about an hour." He wiped his mouth with the back of his hand. "Want to ride down and see how much five hundred dollars will buy?"

Donaldson let out a hearty laugh. "You haven't changed a bit, Mulcahy."

Together they left the hostelry and after procuring Paddy's horse, proceeded to ride down Main Street until they reached a large gathering in front of the church. A slight evening breeze was cooling the temperature somewhat.

Captain Donaldson rested both hands on his saddle horn as he surveyed the scene. "Tell you what, Mulcahy. I'll ride up and introduce myself to your Captain Ashworth. Meanwhile, you circulate among the recruits and salt the mine with our bounty offer." He put his hand to his mouth to cover a slight cough.

"Don't like it, but I'll give it a try," Paddy replied. He dismounted and walked to where old acquaintances were waiting to be sworn into the 121st Pennsylvania Volunteer Regiment. In whispered tones he spread the word of five hundred dollars to be paid to anyone enlisting in the Corn Exchange Regiment. Completing his task, he was startled to hear Captain Ashworth's voice above the hubbub. Turning, he observed Ashworth rising in his stirrups and speaking. his voice loud and strong.

"Men, we have another regiment recruiting here this evening. Captain Donaldson is willing to pay five hundred dollars to anyone wishing to enlist in the Corn Exchange Regiment from Philadelphia."

Even at a distance, Paddy could see the color rise on Donaldson's cheeks.

"Any man who wishes to avail himself of this offer," Ashworth continued, "may feel free to withdraw from our ranks at this time."

A rush of not too friendly murmuring rose from the assembled families and curious onlookers. After a long pause, Captain Ashworth reseated himself in the saddle, not one of his recruits having withdrawn from the ranks. He turned toward Donaldson. "Satisfied, Captain?"

Donaldson blushed and forced a smile. "As I said, sir, all's fair in love and war. You've got loyal men. I wish you the best." With a crisp salute he wheeled his mount and cantered off a short distance to wait for Paddy.

"Well, there you have it, Captain," Paddy observed as he led his horse within earshot. ''Difficult to buy Frankford loyalty." He mounted and adjusted his feet to the stirrups. "It's lonely at the house without Pa. Will you be my guest for the night?"

Glancing sidelong at Paddy, the officer noticed the pathos in his voice.

"Accept with pleasure, old friend," he replied. The two trotted off in the direction of Mulberry Street.

Later that night while aglow with the spirit of renewed comradeship, Paddy signed papers that would bind his life to the Com Exchange Regiment for three years. During the ensuing days, both men scoured the town and countryside for likely recruits and managed to find a few. Jake Hallowell and George Kimball, both in their early forties, agreed to close their store for the duration and enlist; they reasoned that the sooner the war was over the sooner things would return to normal.

Bob Dyer and his younger brother were enticed from their father's farm on the Bristol Pike by the lure of five hundred dollars, more money than they had seen in their lives. The restless energy of two teenagers was harnessed in Joe Tibben, youngest of the Tibben family, and his counterpart, Willie McCool, youngest of the McCool clan. Dick Allen, the doctor's son, considered the five hundred dollars as a means to further his education. Luke Jobson was encouraged to leave his apprenticeship at Horrocks' Mill. At final count, twenty recruits had been added to the ranks of Company H of the Corn Exchange Regiment.

Cheered by salutations from their fellow townspeople, on Wednesday, August 20, the levies marched to rendezvous with the 118th Pennsylvania Regiment at Camp Union near the Falls of Schuylkill.

Leg weary and exhausted by the long hike in searing August heat, the small body arrived at the camp late in the afternoon. Located at an attractive spot on the west side of Indian Queen Lane near the Falls Station on the Norristown branch of the Philadelphia, Germantown and Norristown Railroad, the camp was beautifully arranged in a large field surrounded on three sides by forest. Nearly the full complement of one thousand uniformed soldiers were already gathered, many of whom were business and professional men from Philadelphia. Under the watchful eye of Major Herring there had been constant attention given to minute details so that no fault passed without notice. Duty, obedience and discipline were instilled, and on that elementary training was grafted the grave responsibilities of soldier life.

Captain Donaldson led the way as the recruits from Frankford marched into the tented arena. They were bedraggled and disheveled from the day's trek, an odd lot of older men with beards marching beside young, pink- skinned boys, all exhibiting discomfiture as they passed before the curious gaze of uniformed comrades-to-be.

Company H soldiers were in their tents cleaning up in preparation for the evening meal. Captain Donaldson gave a hand signal for his men to halt in the company street, and dismounted. The Frankford volunteers shifted awkwardly in their tracks and glanced around self-consciously.

"Sergeant Cassidy," Donaldson called out. "Front and center."

"Yes, sir, Captain. Fine it is to have you back, sir. And I see ye've had good pickins, sir."

"I think so, Sergeant. How did things go in my absence? Any problems?"

"Jolly good, sir. Lieutenant Batchelder kept things running smoothly, sir."

Donaldson removed his hat and mopped his brow. "It's getting late, Sergeant. I want you to take these men over to the quartermasters, have them outfitted with uniforms and accouterments then bring them back here and assign them tents. We'll withhold introductions until roll call in the morning. We're exhausted."

"Aye, Captain. It's as good as done, sir." After an exchange of salutes, both men parted.

"All right buckaroos," the sergeant bawled in a voice completely different than when he addressed his superior, "follow me and be lively about it."

To all but Paddy, the experience at the quarter- masters was the first of rude awakenings. The garments, which were handed out somewhat indiscriminately, were not made by fashionable tailors, and the effect in most cases was humorous. Tall, slender Jake Hallowell returned to the quartermaster and requested a size adapted to his shape, but they had nothing to accommodate him; the bottoms of his pantaloons were three inches above his ankles with a corresponding declension at the top, and from his waist down there was room to spare. Bob Dyer, a stout chap, appeared in a pair of pants that came to his armpits and his toes could not be seen. Each countenance registered disbelief as the men stared at the shapeless mass of cloth hanging to their frames; their was no room for pride or satisfaction. The insult was compounded when the footwear was issued; they were all too large.

Willie McCool's forage cap covered his ears, but he was assured it would shrink to proper size in the first rainstorm. Joe Tibben's cap sat nattily on the crown of his head, after the manner of British soldiers.

Later, as the sun sank in the west, the company cooks offered the men coffee, bacon and soft tack. The coffee came in quart-size tin mugs, the bacon on tin plates and the bread was placed in outstretched hands. A study of the men's expressions as they sat on the grass partaking of their evening meal revealed the whole gamut of content, discontent, near anger and indifference. Some blessed or cursed the short rations with the famed appetite of the ostrich or the robust health of the anaconda and ate with a relish that exhibited the peaceful complacency of easy digestion.

That night with tattoo and lights out, the Frankford volunteers fell into fitful sleep on their beds of straw wondering if it was worth five hundred dollars, preservation of the Constitution notwithstanding.

Bright and early the next morning the full impact of camp life unfolded. There was a hasty breakfast, and then with the sun rising higher in the sky, the bright-eyed master of the day gazed on the raw recruits at company drill. Squads of men were evolving the mysteries of "Shoulder arms. Present arms. Carry arms. Right shoulder shift," and loading and firing. Others, perspiring freely, marched by the flank, wheeling, fronting, and facing.

The Frankford recruits were taken out to the parade ground under the watchful eye of Captain Donaldson. Under scrutiny from sergeant Cassidy they were informed that a soldier's position should be one of "grace and ease". That information had an opposite effect. All felt completely ungraceful and stiff. Combined with inquisitiveness on the part of each to see whether the others were "graceful and at ease", made them behave like clowns. Many otherwise intelligent men were not certain which was their right hand or their left. When the order came to "Right face," face met face in inquiring astonishment, and frantic attempts to obey the order properly caused still greater confusion. The marching and wheeling resulted in tortuous, uncertain lines and semicircular formations that were ludicrous caricatures of the command given.

Compliance with the commands came easy to Paddy who had been through the course. He had time to carefully study Sergeant Cassidy; a man not to be trifled with, he thought to himself. The man's bearing and manner bespoke of a hard life on the wharfs of the Delaware. He had a heavy shock of red hair and thick lips which, when parted, exposed prominent teeth with a gap between the front ones. A muscular chest and arms bristled with red hair and freckles. His voice was harsh.

"You, there!" Cassidy screamed at Luke Jobson, "kape your heels together and don't be standin' with one foot in Bull Run and the other in the 'Third Ward.'" He surveyed the company front with piercing green eyes and barked his next command.

"About face! To the rear, march!" His eyes bulged as he witnessed Joe Tibben marching in the opposite direction, away from the squad. "You there, sprocket ass!" he screamed, "where in thunder do ye think yer goin'?"

An adolescent whose voice was changing, Tibben had a squeak in his voice. "I thought I was right and they was wrong," he replied.

Sergeant Cassidy's bulbous jaw jutted as he spoke. "Army ain't no place for thinkin'. Ye'll git yerself killed if you don't follow orders exactly. That understood?"

"Yes, sir," Tibben replied meekly as he hurried back into formation.

Captain Donaldson moved several paces forward. "Sergeant, have the men stand at ease for a moment. I want you to meet a friend of mine, we fought at Balls Bluff together. He won't accept a commission, but I believe he can be of assistance to us in the drill."

"All right ye buckos, stand at ease," Cassidy shouted.

Donaldson's voice rang sharp and clear. "Private Mulcahy, front and center."

Paddy stepped forward and saluted. "Sir."

The officer stood with arms akimbo. "Sergeant, I'd like you to meet Private Mulcahy."

"Mulkayhee, is it now," Cassidy replied with a broad grin. "I've been sayin' to meself, that man has the look of a soldier about him. And Irish to boot."

He extended a vicelike handclasp. "Glad it is to have you with us 'Mulkayhee. ' Any suggestion ye might have how to teach these dumb johns their right foot from their left?"

Paddy cast a puzzled glance at Captain Donaldson.

"It's all right, Mulcahy," Donaldson said with a nod. "If you have any suggestions we'd like to hear them."

"Well, you might try the old 'hay foot, straw foot.'"

"Anything's worth a try," Cassidy replied. "I'll send one o' the boys out for the necessary material." He brushed a fly from his nose. "Shall we continue squad drill, sir?"

"Yes, Sergeant. I want these men ready for company drill in two days. Battalion drill is scheduled in five days."

There was an exchange of hand salutes and Paddy returned to the ranks.

At noon there was a break for soup, boiled beef and vegetables. Paddy seated himself on the ground beneath a large oak tree, and while he ate, proceeded to study the men who comprised H Company. His eyes kept returning to one fellow whose back was turned; there was something familiar about the well-proportioned ears, black hair and slender neck. When he had finished his meal, Paddy stood up, stretched and strolled casually to where the soldier was sitting by himself. As he came abreast he looked down into the eyes of his Quaker friend.

"My God, John!" he gasped, "what are you doing here? And in uniform!"

The Quaker dropped his plate and sprang to his feet. "Friend, Mulcahy! Are thee of this company?"

They embraced warmly and began an immediate rush of questions as they held each other at arm's length. When Paddy had at last completed his explanations, he searched deep into the Quaker's eyes. "Why?" he asked. "Why?"

"A test of conscientious objection," Walton replied, as he brushed crumbs from his coat. "Heard about Chirp and Billy and it weighed heavily on me. Should others freely give up their lives so we Quakers can live at peace. I've come to render unto Caesar that which is Caesar's."

"Och! Lizzen to der tight-fisted Quaker. Not vun mention of der five hundred dollars." A nearby group of three burly soldiers started to laugh.

"Who are those mugs, John? You know them?"

"They're in my squad, Germans from York. Been on me from the day I arrived. Their ringleader is the one with glasses."

Paddy fastened his attention on the one indicated. The man had a large nose, which he used frequently in a nervous twitch to push his glasses back onto the bridge of his nose; they seemed to be constantly slipping.

"What's your name, Dutchman?" Paddy asked tartly.

"Schneider," came the reply.

"Well, Schneider, it seems like you've got a big nose to smell five hundred dollars Corn Exchange money as far west as York."

A drum roll calling them back to the drill field cut off any further conversation.

On Sunday, August 31, before a crowd of five thousand assembled friends, families and other onlookers, the Corn Exchange Regiment, numbering one thousand, passed in review for the first time to the accompaniment of music from Beck's Band. Following the review, the men stood in rapt attention on the parade ground as Parson Brownlow, the renowned Union clergyman, statesman and soldier from East Tennessee, preached a memorable patriotic sermon that thrilled the audience. To close the ceremonies, Reverend John W. Jackson presented each soldier, on behalf of the members of the Corn Exchange Association, a Bible, a hymn book and a blanket.

As they were being handed out by Reverend Charles E. Hill, chaplain of the regiment, a mounted courier came dashing in. He dismounted quickly and ran onto the flag-draped reviewing stand where he quickly found Colonel Prevost.

When the man left, the Colonel rose slowly and in the silence, with every eye focused on him, he spoke loud and strong and without emotion.

"Ladies and gentlemen, men of the Corn Exchange Regiment, this has been a disastrous day for the Union in another battle at Bull Run." A gasp of horror rose up from the crowd. "General Pope is in full retreat. Due to the gravity of the situation, all regiments organizing in Philadelphia are to move to the front immediately. I will meet with company commanders in my tent immediately."

Paddy grabbed Captain Donaldson by the sleeve. "Frank, this is madness. Our men have had only ten days of instruction. To send them up against seasoned Johnnies will be murder."

Donaldson pulled free of Paddy's grip and started to leave. "We've chosen the best, Mulcahy. Pray to God they are, and can meet the challenge." He disappeared in the milling throng.

By ten o'clock that evening Camp Union was abandoned, and at midnight the 118th was at the Broad and Prime street depot waiting its turn for transportation to Washington. In the arch-domed station, pandemonium reigned. Steam from fired-up locomotives rose like tiny cloud puffs until they were lost among the echoing girders. For the first time the men fully understood the importance of the step they had taken. The hour had come for them to leave home associations. As departure time drew nearer, the laughing and jesting ceased.

Familiar with the military's penchant for hurry-up-and-wait, Paddy placed his knapsack against a station pillar, sat down and leaned back to observe the emotional scenes taking place around him. Two redheaded youngsters clung to Sergeant Cassidy's pant legs as a sobbing wife wrapped her arms around his shoulders. Luke Jobson was standing solemnly with his arm around his widowed mother. Captain Donaldson's parents wore anxious expressions as they huddled in serious conversation with their son.

Paddy's gaze suddenly riveted on a beautiful girl who appeared lost. She looked bewildered and completely out of character with the surroundings. A gray Quaker bonnet held back a wealth of chestnut hair and her lithe figure was sheathed in Quaker gray. Tears filled her eyes as she frantically searched the crowd until they finally rested on John Walton standing stoically by himself.

She let out a muffled cry of, "John," and rushed into his arms. They embraced and kissed warmly, then stepped back to survey one another.

"Dear sister, Hannah. How good of thee to come." He brushed a stray curl away from her eyes. "Have Mother and Father come with thee?"

She stifled a sob. "No, they would not be seen among the military. Oh, dear brother, please give this up for our sweet Jesus' sake. Thee cannot and must not kill."

"There's a time for peace and a time for war," he replied softly. "I must see it through." He clasped her pale white hands in his. "Tell me, have I been 'read out' of meeting?"

A flood of pent-up tears gave him his answer as she placed her head on his shoulder. "Yes," she cried, "you and Major Perot."

"So be it," he murmured.

The long, tedious wait for transportation finally terminated at five o'clock on the morning of September 1, as the men of the 118th were packed inside cattle cars. Some crowded onto the roofs of overloaded boxcars.

Captain Donaldson took Paddy to one side. "Keep an eye on those two young cut-ups, McCool and Tibben," he cautioned. "They seem to think this is some kind of picnic."

Before Paddy could reply, his prophesy was fulfilled. The two were already perched on top of one of the boxcars. Standing as a choirmaster, arms outstretched, fingers spread wide, McCool called in a loud voice, "Let's hear it, men. 'Hold on Abraham.'"

There was an immediate, enthusiastic outburst of the popular tune from the men seated on top of the cars.

"We're going down to Dixie, to Dixie, to Dixie,
We're going down to Dixie
To fight for the dear old Flag;
And should we fall in Dixie, in Dixie, in Dixie,
And should we fall in Dixie,
We'll die for the dear old Flag."

From inside the cars came the echoing chorus:

"Hold on, Abraham,
Never say die to your Uncle Sam,
Uncle Sam's boys are coming right along,
Six hundred thousand strong."

A sudden lurch of the train as it started to move nearly pitched McCool overboard. Tibben grabbed his friend's legs and held fast as he squeaked, "Better settle back, Willie, here comes Paddy."

It was two o'clock in the afternoon when the regiment debarked at President Station in Baltimore and was promptly marched to the Washington depot on Camden Street. Another long delay was announced, no rail cars would be available until late that night. Angry and impatient, the enlisted men tried to make themselves comfortable. Paddy noticed that a number of the officers were slipping away and heading for the Eutaw House for a substantial meal and luxurious rest. Not to be outdone, he waited for an opportune moment and followed them.

The chandeliered dining room of the Eutaw House was packed with a noisy assortment of officers and civilians eating and drinking. Carefully picking his way so as to be inconspicuous. Paddy selected a place at the end of a long bar and proceeded to order some Baltimore seafood and a drink. The boisterous conduct of soldiers from another regiment was drawing frowns and disapproving glances from an old general seated with his family at a nearby table.

Paddy turned to the bartender. "Who's the heavy military over there?"

"General Wool from the Mexican War," came the reply. "He commands our city. If those loudmouths don't quiet down soon they'll receive a 'wooling' for sure."

By ten o'clock the noise had risen to a din and the hotel corridors resounded with the carousing.

Not wishing to be involved, Paddy sought a sofa in the lobby and curled up to get some rest.

About midnight the frolic was suddenly interrupted by the summons to hurry to the depot. The regiment was ready to move out.

Caught in a wild scramble for the doorway, Paddy was suddenly accosted by

Captain Donaldson. "What are you doing here, Mulcahy?"

"Resting."

"Have you seen the lieutenant?"

Before Paddy could reply, Captain Crocker of C Company came running up to them all out of breath. "That son of a bitch is upstairs in bed with a wench!"

He paused to get his breath. "Room a hundred and two. Give me a hand, Frank."

Both officers raced for the stairs and bounded them two steps at a time. Receiving no orders to the contrary, Paddy followed at their heels.

Captain Crocker, a bull of a man with a full beard, tried to turn the door knob. "It's locked. Back off, Frank." He hurled his massive frame against the door which flew off its hinges and landed with a bang on the floor.

Lieutenant Batchelder sat bolt upright in bed as a blonde head ducked beneath the covers. "What in the hell!" he exclaimed.

His words were cut short by Captain Donaldson who lifted him upright by the armpits. "Lem, help him into his clothes."

Bellowing with laughter, Captain Crocker proceeded to dress the inebriated, struggling young lieutenant. He was led downstairs, fully clothed, ushered through the doorway, and partially carried to the rail depot. To their surprise, instead of finding active preparations going on for departure when they reached the station, they found the men sound asleep.

It was later learned that General Wool had used that method to rid the hostelry of its noisy guests; the ruse was successful. Chagrined and disappointed, the men found poor consolation in fretting away the balance of the night chaffing over a lost opportunity. The train did not move out until ten o'clock the next morning. It was a slow run to Washington, and they did not reach their destination until four in the afternoon.

The regiment was marched to the Soldier's Retreat to be fed. The title proved a distinguished misnomer, if by the term retreat was meant ease, repose and comfort, and it proved a travesty on subsistence if it was intended to imply a nourishing meal. Sour bread, coffee-colored water, decomposed potatoes and decayed beef were in stark contrast with the comforting, well-served supplies furnished by the Volunteer and Cooper-Shop Refreshment saloons in Philadelphia. The soldiers howled their dissatisfaction.

The night was spent in the government corral where famished mules brayed discordantly and teamsters yelled their imprecations as wagons came and departed. There were few periods of quiet, and little rest.

On the morning of September 3, the 118th crossed the Long Bridge and bivouacked on Arlington Heights at Fort Albany. The journey which began on the 31st at midnight was at last concluded.

In the field for the first time, the men soon discovered that any discomforts were insignificant contrasted with the sorry plight of the shattered battalions of the Potomac Army encamped in the vicinity and recuperating from the Bull Run disaster. The Corn Exchange Regiment was about to join that army.

Split in two, for political purposes, just before the second battle of Bull Run, the Potomac Army, half under the command of McClellan on the peninsula and half under Pope's jurisdiction in northern Virginia, was again reunited under one leader. McClellan, whose popularity among the soldiers had never wavered, was reinstated as supreme commander in a desperate move by President Lincoln, and General Pope was sent packing.

Pope's vanity and bluster continued to be a constant target for ridicule, especially when soldiers recalled the pompous speech he made to the Potomac Army when he assumed command a few weeks before his disastrous defeat. Hooting openly, they retold how Pope suffered under a delusion that the Confederates were retreating westward at Bull Run when actually they were attacking him in the rear, taking away vast storehouses of his supplies and capturing rail lines and wagons, while he busily attacked a small Confederate force to his front. His departure from the eastern theater of war was greeted with unconcealed joy by the men.

To overcome the tribulations of inexperience which come to soldiers the same as to a collegian, the men of the new regiment were apt to gibe and twit in the manner of youths at an academy.

It was during one of those infrequent periods which a soldier can call his own that Willie McCool, a kepi placed sideways on his head in Napoleonic fashion, jumped onto a cracker barrel in full view of the company and called for attention. He started reading from a copy of General Pope's notorious speech. In a mocking voice bursting with eloquence, he shouted, "Men, I have come to you from the West where we have always seen the back of the enemy, from an army whose business it has been to seek the adversary and to beat him when he is found." Puckering thin Irish lips, he paused and bowed to the cheers of his amused comrades, then raised his hand for silence. "Whose policy has been attack and not defense...."

"Even when the Rebs are on your rear stealing railroads and ammunition wagons?" squeaky Tibben interrupted gleefully.

McCool fixed his eyes on the text before him. "I desire you to dismiss from your minds certain phrases which I am sorry to find so much in vogue amongst you. I hear constantly of taking strong positions and holding them against the enemy, of lines of retreat, and of losses of supplies. Let us discard such ideas."

"What with Rebs up your ass hole like picnic ants?" Joe Bryam jeered.

Drawing himself up like a Prussian martinet, McCool tossed his heckler a comical look and continued reading from Pope's speech. "Let us study the probable lines of retreat of our opponents," he thundered, "and let our own take care of themselves."

His audience whooped and hollered. "Bully for General McCool!"

Led by Joe Tibben, eager hands lifted the freckle-faced comedian from the cracker barrel, hoisted him onto willing shoulders and paraded him down the company street.

Paddy surveyed the rowdy sport from a distance, his face clouded with censure. "McCool and Tibben," he muttered. "What a pair."

Together, they had gone beyond the bounds and limitations of regimental discipline. Colonel Wistar's iron hand would have squashed them in an instant. It disturbed him the more he thought about it. Under Colonel Prevost there was a certain laxity in the regiment that Wistar would never have tolerated in the Seventy-first.

The matter of the pup tents for instance, Paddy thought to himself. All over camp the canvas shelters were decked out with signs of an objectionable nature, proclaiming, "Shelter halves ain't fit fer dogs," "Sons of bitches live here," "Mongrel dog fer sale...three cents," and so on. The flagrant breech of proper military conduct which rankled him most was when the new men, seeing an officer approach, popped their heads out from under the tents and started to bark like dogs, never so much as receiving the slightest reprimand unless it happened to be Captain Crocker or Donaldson. His angry thoughts and the wild demonstration of "McCool for Commander" were brought to an abrupt end by the sound of bugles and the long drum roll calling the regiment to the color line with a hint of urgency.

Mounted on a gray roan, surrounded by his subaltern, Colonel Prevost sat ready and waiting as the troops fell hurriedly into position. He was a spare man of middle age, tall and lean, with soft Huguenot features. His grandfather, General Augustin Prevost, had commanded the American forces at Savannah during the Revolutionary War, the Colonel having inherited a touch of military bearing from his illustrious grandfather.

Now his steel grey eyes passed up and down the regimental line like a speculator counting profit and loss. He spoke in a rich, full voice filled with foreboding.

"Men, one week ago today our regiment was dispatched from Philadelphia to help stem impending disaster to our nation's Capitol. Through God's will that disaster was averted, but we have another critical situation facing us."

A ripple of murmuring ran through the ranks.

The Colonel set his horse forward a pace. "I am a lawyer by profession, schooled in the belief that a brief should be well-prepared before a joust in the courts is attempted. By the same token, I believe a soldier should be well-schooled before he's thrown into the cauldron of battle against veteran troops."

Paddy saw an involuntary quiver pass through Captain Donaldson.

Prevost continued in a voice more becoming to a schoolmaster than an army colonel. "The majority of you have had only two weeks training, the rest, four weeks at the most." He paused to check a break in his voice caused by the sight of the eager young faces staring back at him. "Boys, the time has come. General Lee has lost no time in following up his advantage at Bull Run. His army is now at Frederick, Maryland, threatening an invasion of the North."

A gasp went up from the assembled troops and they began murmuring.

"In his present position," Prevost continued, "Lee can forge through Pennsylvania to Lake Erie and split the Union, or swing east and capture Baltimore or Philadelphia. There's no use telling you what that would mean, the end. Right now, there is nothing to stop him."

"God preserve us," John Walton muttered through blanched lips.

Standing next to the Quaker, Paddy had terrible visions of the rebels sacking Philadelphia. His right hand gripped his musket stock firmly until the sweat made it slippery.

"You men," Colonel Prevost continued, "will move north within the hour. As a singular honor paid out of respect to the fighting ability demonstrated by your fellow comrades from Philadelphia, you will be incorporated into the First Brigade, First Division of Major General Fitz John Porter's Fifth Corps. You will be fighting with veteran troops, the Twenty-second and Eighteenth Massachusetts, the Thirteenth and also the Twenty-fifth New York, the First Michigan, and the Second Maine. Good luck, and may God be with us all."

Striking the regiment head-on like a cue ball plowing into the center of a rack, the announcement of a northern invasion by the Confederates set off an interaction of conjecture as the Corn Exchange prepared to break camp.

"Mulkayhee," Cassidy bawled. "Detail yerself as one to help see each man carries no more than is necessary. And you there, Dutchman. This ain't no time to be conductin' a rattle band. Stop yer jawin' and git packed."

"Ve vas chust thinkin,' Sergeant, py golly. Don't you zupose someone ought to vatch that lieutenant in Company G?"

Cassidy thrust his ruddy face forward. "What's your beef, Schneider?"

"Lieutenant White, zir. Ve chust found out he's a Reb." Schneider sniffed and wrinkled his nose. "He's liable to chump camp and giff infermashun to der enemy."

"Faith'n we know all about Lieutenant White, ye pretzel bender. Sure'n he's from rich, aristocratic folks in Warrenton, Virginia, served with the Middleburg Black Dragoon cavalry he did, and he don't like divorce, or dissolved unions. That's why he's with us."

"So, he's vun perfect spy."

"Do ye mind leavin' that up to the Colonel? Come on now, ye lard ass, ye and yer friends get about mindin' yer own business."

Amidst the radiant splendor and beauty of early September, the 118th moved out from Fort Cochran promptly at noon, crossing over the Potomac by way of the aqueduct bridge and marched into the city of Washington where for one solid hour the men wandered up and down broad, dusty highways, apparently without aim or purpose. Citizens were conspicuously absent from the Capitol's thoroughfares; the dwellings and mansions wore the forsaken, deserted look of a ghost town. While the bustle and disorder attending the Second Bull Run disaster had subsided, evidence was still lacking to assure them that everything was all right. Growing restless and weary of the aimless tramp, the troops turned onto Seventh Street and gradually left the hot, dusty city behind.

"Looks like the military finally figured out which way was north," Dick Allen said tersely as he shifted the weight of his pack.

"I won't complain until somebody pulls a boner like Baker did at the Bluff," Paddy retorted.

"That must've been..."

Allen's remarks were cut short by the snorting of Captain Donaldson's horse as it pulled alongside the Frankford volunteers.

"Hey, Cap'n!" McCool shouted. "How about horses for us?"

"If you wanted to fight sitting down, you should have joined the cavalry,"

Donaldson replied with a grin. "Too late now, you're up Salt River." He leaned forward in the saddle. "How's it going, Mulcahy?"

"Not bad. Where' s our order of assignment to be executed?"

"Silver Springs, just north of Washington's outer earthworks." He surveyed the marching column with a jaundiced eye. "I'm afraid we'll have a sorry time of it for a while."

"From the veterans?"

The captain nodded. "Wouldn't be a bit surprised." He put his spurs to his horse and cantered forward.

Garrisoning Washington's outer earthworks, stone-faced artillerymen of the Second Pennsylvania stared apathetically as the Corn Exchange Regiment tramped through the fortifications and passed beyond.

The long blue column moved slowly into open country. Suddenly from its head there came the loud blare of drums and bugles and a huge band wheeled out and fell into position before them. Breaking rank and gaping, the raw recruits rubbernecked at the unexpected reception, happily commenting on the sound of a parade.

"All right you dregs, dress it up," barked Sergeant Cassidy. "We're comin' to our brigade."

Instantly, nervous hands straightened slant-topped kepis and sagging belts, weary shoulders snapped to attention. Beardless chins jutted, keen eyes staring straight ahead. Led in review before six sister regiments, the new levies marched to the pulsating strains of "*Hail Columbia*."

At roadside, long ranks of combat veterans looked on with critical appraisal. Sensing the gaze upon them the recruits swelled with self-importance as they moved rapidly along with snap and verve. Any fond hopes which they may have entertained in regard to their welcome at the hands of their new comrades were rudely crushed by degrading remarks.

"Well, derned if it ain't the five-hundred-dollar boys from Philadelphia come to our rescue," a rough voice jeered.

"Hey, Jim, how's come they march so slow?" another mocked.

"Aintcha heard? They got money bags strapped around their ass cheeks."

A storm of laughter drowned the sound of the band.

"And look at them new shoes and uniforms. They'll sure make buzzard bait when the Johnnies pick their bodies after a fight."

A bearded sergeant pointed at Schneider and hollered, "Hey, Four-eyes! Does your mother know you're out?"

Schnieder turned his head and stuck out his tongue. His childish reaction brought on a chorus of jeers.

The review finally ended and the 118th went into camp. Veterans in the surrounding camps kept alive a sporadic hooting and running cat-calls that extended into the night. Thoroughly spanked by the verbal abuse, the disillusioned recruits tossed and turned and tried to sleep.

From a nearby tent, Paddy heard Schneider and the Dutchmen engaged in a bitter denunciation of their reception.

"Seems to me we should pack up and leave. Who do zey zink zey are, anyways? By gollies, nobody's ever yelled inzults to me like zat."

"Stuff it in your canteen!" Paddy recognized the voice of Sergeant Cassidy. "You dutchmen'll be the first to throw your weight around after ye've seen the elephant. Right now ye'll lie here and take it. They may have been defeated, but those are men out there."

Cassidy's rebuke brought on a silence that continued until reveille the next morning.

The march through Maryland was taken up early the next day with the Corn Exchange placed in the van to prevent any further altercation with veteran regiments. The oppressive September heat soon became more intolerable than the blistering words sustained the day before. The air, unruffled by the slightest breeze, was stifling, and huge volumes of grinding dust was impenetrable to the eye as well as overpowering. Wholly unused to such fatigue and totally unacquainted with reducing their loads to the minimum by dispensing with useless appendages and trappings, the march toward Rockville began to tell heavily on the unschooled and unconditioned levies.

Tramping in the fashion of an experienced soldier, Paddy moved along stolidly and leisurely, unencumbered by a heavily laden knapsack. He had reduced his personal baggage to the few indispensables conveniently transported over his shoulder in a light, adjustable blanket roll which contained his house and home and what little extra apparel the day demanded.

Walton eyed Paddy with envy. "I wish I'd heeded thy advice, friend," he said, gasping. "I feel as if a knife were cutting through my chest."

"I can't go another step," McCool whimpered as he clutched at his belly.

"It's not too late to strip down. Fall out of line and pack like I told you at camp," Paddy ordered.

Necessities and comfort being cogent factors, both soldiers dropped from the marching column to remedy the situation. They were not alone. The day's march began taking a shocking toll. Worn, weary, overburdened men began dropping by the wayside. Near Rockville, sixteen miles from Washington, the color guard fell by the way in complete exhaustion. Colonel Prevost had to bear the standard to bivouac. Each company started with a hundred men. The trek ended with three men to a company present for duty as the most creditable showing at the end of the first day.

Studying the situation, Paddy decided on a course of action. With the regiment completely disunited, his presence would not be missed, and a few hours of sleep would restore his strength. With a little luck, he might be able to hitch a ride on one of the wagons moving in a never-ending stream on the dark road; that way he could steal a full day or more on the march. He decided to put his plan into effect.

Revived and invigorated by a four-hour nap in the cool shade, he stealthily made his way toward the sound of rumbling wagons. Lanterns illuminated the canvas tops in the darkness. As he stood by the roadside contemplating which wagon to hop, he heard a familiar Scottish oath.

"Git back from the road ye blue-bellied bastard!" a teamster roared. "These horses are skittish enough without ye stirrin' 'em up."

Paddy let out a joyous yell. "Gilmour! That you? This is me, Paddy. Paddy Mulcahy."

The teamster swung a lantern around to get a better look. "By Bonnie Prince Charlie's kilt," he cried, "hop aboard, lad, and be quick aboot it. What are ye doin' out here all by yerself? Never mind. It's good to see ye."

Paddy felt the glow of rekindled friendship. "I heard you'd gone driving for the army. Never thought we'd meet like this."

"Like I've always said, lad, it's a small world. But tell me, where's yer regiment?"

"Everywhere between here and Washington. It's a new regiment, I didn't rejoin the Seventy-first.''

"Aye, these new levies," Gilmour growled, "clutterin' up roads like they owned them instead a takin' to the fields where they belong. We've enough trouble as it is without havin' them hoggin' our right o' way.'

"Trouble?"

"Aye, lad, trouble indeed. Here now we've McClellan, himself a bonny Scot, tryin' to stop Lee's invasion of the North with troops still demoralized from their last whippin' at Bull Run. To make matters worse, an epidemic of sickness has hit the horses. Last count there were four thousand head unfit for service among the artillery, cavalry and wagoners." The teamster snapped his bull whip at the swaying rumps of his four-horse hitch.

"What kind of sickness is it, Dunk?"

"The veterinaries' don't rightly know what it is, laddy. Or how to treat it. All I can tell ye is it's a violent thing. Horses perfectly sound one day come up dead lame the next, slobberin' strings from the mouth like a mad dog and blisters and ulcers formin' on their nose, lips, tongue and mouth so's they can't eat. The army transport is in dire straights, lad. The Rebs run off with half of it at Bull Run, and what's left ain't no account with sick animals." He spat a quid of tobacco juice from the corner of his bearded mouth. "Can't see how Little Mac 'spects to mount any offensive of sorts. Say, talkin' about veterinaries, understand Doc Batt's youngest bairn was killed."

Paddy stared into the starlit night. "Yes. I was with him at the end."

"Aye, dirty business this. Been half a mind of late to quit waggonin' and jump into a fightin' regiment, one like the Seventy-first. Them boys is real stoppers. Twice they've put their fingers in the dike for Father Abe's army, Glendale, now again after the Second Bull Run. Aye, it's been Billy Penn's boys what's slammed the door on any chances the Rebs might've had at clinchin' final victory so far." He cocked his head inquisitively. "How come you ain't with 'em anymore?"

"Some of my friends from the Seventy-first helped organize this new regiment from Philadelphia, the Hundred and Eighteenth. They wanted experienced help so I joined them."

"Aye, we can use more good regiments." He paused to wipe tobacco juice from the corners of his mouth with a grimy sleeve. "A dirty, sour-tastin' sight last week," he muttered, "seein' them thousands o' disorganized troops, fragments of commands tramplin' over each other tryin' to get away from the Rebs. Disorderly wagon trains, or what was left of 'em. Guns without officers. Caissons without guns, aye, a hopeless, fleeing mob."

A lantern swinging from the top of the canvas- covered wagon laced Gilmour's bearded, grizzled countenance with flickering highlights and shadows. His deep-set burning eyes resembled some wild beast of the forest peering into the black night. "I ha' to admit I was one o' them caught up in the tidal wave o' despair," he continued, "that is until a wild-ridin' colonel came dashin' through the rain and darkness. He was dealin' blows with the flat of his sword and swearin' at the top o' his voice. I'll ne'er forget his expression, or the words. 'Clear the way, you rabble, ' he shouted. ' How dare you mingle and hang about fighting troops. Clear the road for the Seventy-first.'"

"Wistar!"

"Aye, I met your Colonel Wistar that night. Even grabbed a gun and joined his men in the rear guard fightin'. As for Wistar, he gave imperative orders respectin' teamsters and stragglers as might not've found favor with the oratorical patriots at home, but he got the job done." The teamster paused trying to bring the scene back to life. "Sully's First Minnesota would take a position and deploy for resistance while the Seventy-first gained distance and repeated the process to cover Sully's men withdrawin', drivin' the rout before 'em all the while like shepherd dogs biting at the heels of a flock." Gilmour lit a cigar and offered one to his traveling companion.

"No, thanks, Dunk."

The Scotsman exhaled a wreath of smoke. "As a military operation by the rear guard, all this would've been a damn sight easier if it hadn't been for a worthless mass of panic-stricken stragglers crowdin' between us and the rest of the division. With them blockin' us off from the main body, quick support from that direction was impossible. And them square-head Germans, thousands of 'em from Siegel's routed division, abandoned their colors, threw away their guns and deliberately went to sleep around fires kindled in the woods. Just waitin' to be taken prisoner after the passage of the rear guard."

"Our soldiers did that?" Paddy asked incredulously.

"Our *soldiers*, hell!" The Scot flailed his whip. "Throne robbers. They ain't our kind o' people. Wistar's boys begged to be let loose on the dirty coffee-boilers, promisin' there'd be none left for the enemy. But the integrity of the rear guard was too important to permit riskin' it even for vengeance." He removed the cigar from his mouth and gave a coarse laugh. "Some of 'em didn't get away unwhipped of justice. Ye should've seen Colonel Wistar chargin' his horse into the sleepin' squad of loafers. Many a square-head ended up a squashed melon to the great delight o' the gallant lads in the hard-worked rear guard. After the pursuit ceased, the Seventy-first put into camp at Langley on the Potomac. Here I be back with the wagons."

"The Seventy-first, where is it now?" Paddy asked, trying to disguise his interest.

"Well, noo, lad, I'd say if ye crept back and slept on those flour bags a wee bit, ye'd wake up to hear yer friends singin' in the mornin' . They're a lively steppin' crew, but I figure this train'll catch up with 'em around Hyattstown."

"Hyattstown? That's halfway to Frederick. What're they doing way..."

"Hoot mon, lad, Bobby Lee's got real bloodhounds tailin' him in the Philadelphia Brigade."

CHAPTER 9

The next morning Paddy awoke refreshed and tingling with eagerness to reestablish connections with his former regiment. He heard sounds of a route march that came floating back on an early morning breeze, the distant sound of drums rising above the steady squeak of the wagon wheels. Intermingled with the staccato drum beat, he could hear spirited singing to the tune of *"The Girl I Left Behind Me."*

Wiping sleepy dust from half-open eyes, he scrambled onto the driver's seat. "That the Brigade?" he asked breathlessly.

"Soon's I can make out the words they're usin', I can tell ye, lad."

Gilmour hunched forward and bent an ear. Words of the song could be heard faintly above the clatter of horses and wagons.

"Last night I slept in a hollow log
With the bed bugs all around me.
But tonight I'll sleep in a feather bed,
With the girl I left behind me...."

The teamster nodded and grinned. "Aye, that's them, all right. Nobody else in the army would dare to use them words. Listen."

"She jumped in bed and covered up her head,
And swore I couldn't find her.
But I knew damn well she lied like hell,
So I jumped right in beside her...."

Paddy felt a surge of excitement. Colonel Wistar and his men were marching just ahead. Joe Batt, Henry Castor and others from home would be a welcome sight. The singing grew progressively closer and louder.

"I plunked her once, I plunked her twice,
I plunked her once too often.
I broke the main spring of her harp,
And sent her to her coffin.''

Color rose in Paddy's face as Gilmour gave him a playful slap across the shoulder blades. "Aye! That's real soldiers singin' fer ye, lad. Real soldier-singin.'''

"Kind of bawdy I would say." Paddy's reply was interrupted by a mounted officer who came galloping alongside the wagon train. With one arm upraised, he signaled a halt.

"We wait here till Hyattstown's been cleared," he shouted and clattered past.

"Say, Dunk, would you mind if I jump off and run ahead?"

"Go right ahead, laddy. The boys'll be glad to see ye."

Paddy sprang from the wagon and started to run past veterans troops who were standing at arms in the dusty fields. A short distance beyond he caught sight of the Seventy-first, the men leaning on their rifles. Some of them began singing *"Wait for the Wagons."*

Joe Batt spied him first. "Jumpin' Jericho! Look who's here!"

In an instant Paddy was surrounded by all his old friends from Company D.

"Hey, Paddy," Isaac Tibben bellowed, "where's my baby brother? Mother wrote that both you and he had joined the One Hundred and Eighteenth."

Making a futile effort to answer all their questions at once, Paddy started to recount the sad plight of the new regiment on its initial march, then joyfully explained the reason for his presence so far ahead of the Fifth Corps.

"Gee, pipe the new uniform," Joe Heap exclaimed when Paddy had finished talking. Dirty fingers reached out to touch the slightly worn material.

"Yeah, and look, shoes," someone said.

Sobered, Paddy glanced down and saw that half the men were without shoes. The other half did not even wear a reasonable facsimile.

Lightfoot noticed Paddy's discomfiture. Always ready to put another at ease, he laughed lightheartedly. "We ran out of them back at Alexandria trying to keep up with the Johnnies "

Charley Layton, who by his antics seemed to have taken over Barney Williams' post as regimental clown, stepped forward to shake Paddy's hand. His uniform was full of holes, grease and dirt, and not content with the allotment, all three were evidently contending which should have the whole suit. It seemed to Paddy that dirt was the winning thief.

"Hey, Charley," several chorused, "tell Mulcahy what you told General Howard when he ordered you to wash your uniform."

Layton looked around and blew his nose on a shirt sleeve "'Wash 'em?' says I to the general when he ups and has the impudence to refer to the sacred soil on my clothes. 'Wash 'em, General? I'm bound to say you're a darn fool, sir. The mud's what holds 'em together, stick 'em fast, like. If I was to put these clothes in water, General, they'd dissolve like salt.'"

A roar of laughter rent the air at the twice-told tale.

"Bully for Charley Layton, son of the heaviest fingered butcher in Frankford," someone shouted .

The happy banter was suddenly stilled by a voice from behind "At ease, men. Who do we have here?"

Paddy turned around and, galvanized, snapped a mechanical salute. Before him stood Colonel Wistar. Silent for a moment, the Colonel studied the regimental number 118 set in the hunting horn insignia on Paddy's forage cap.

"Something about your old regiment you didn't like?" he asked.

The question and withering stare made Paddy squirm. "No, sir," he replied. "I can explain if I could speak with you alone."

"All right, join me under that tree."

Henry Caster took Paddy's arm. "You'll need all the glibness your Irish tongue possesses to pull out of this one. But before you go, tell me, how's my mother? I understand she's taken Chirp's death very hard."

"Can you wait till I come back, Hen? Don't want to cause the Colonel to fidget."

"Sure, see me when you're finished."

Colonel Wistar sat with his long legs straddling a log. He looked up as Paddy approached and scratched his nose with his fingernails. "Well, Mulcahy, what might I understand?"

"Sir," Paddy began uneasily, "after I got out of Libby, the war seemed different to me, lots different. Crooked politics, stupid blunders, a senseless slaughter of brothers."

A sympathetic warmth telegraphed itself in the Colonel's dark eyes.

"Guess I rebelled much like you did when you were my age, when you left your home and family and gave up your Quaker religion to go out West."

Wistar's eyes opened wide. "How did you know that?"

"I overheard your conversation in the Jolly Post that day you came to town looking for volunteers."

"By George, aren't you the observing one." He slapped his knee. "So I did discuss my youth with old friends from Haverford that day." His piercing eyes took on the expression of a badgering lawyer pressing for a point. "Didn't your father help you during this troubled state of mind?"

Paddy studied the Colonel's hawkish features and secretly wished that he were his father. "My father was killed by a horse shortly before I arrived home," he said.

Wistar rubbed a hand across his spike beard. The softness in his eyes deepened. "I'm sorry to hear that. A good father can be a real source of help in time of trouble. No one should be without family and roots. But I see you are back in uniform. Who, and what, changed your mind?" There was a curious ring in his last words.

"A comrade of mine from the Seventy-first is responsible. Captain Donaldson. He came to Frankford about three weeks ago to seek me out for this new regiment."

Wistar rose from his seat and put an arm around Paddy's shoulders and flashed a broad smile. "I know. I sent him."

"You? You sent him?"

"Yes, son. When you didn't show up for my wedding, I knew something must be wrong. So I had a talk with a friend or yours, Joe Batt. He told me of your torment, after which I sent Frank Donaldson to talk you into joining the Corn Exchange Regiment. But, as a matter of curiosity, I see you're still in a private's uniform. My idea was to have you take a lieutenancy, you're top-drawer officer material."

A mounted dispatch rider interrupted their conversation. "Begging you pardon, sir, message from General Sumner."

"Yes? What is it, Captain?"

"By way of a compliment to the Seventy-first for its recent service, the General wishes you to push your regiment forward to explore and clear the ravine up ahead. He wants the army's rear guard driven before involving the mass of the column."

"Convey my respects to the General, Captain. Tell him we will move at once."

The courier wheeled his horse and disappeared across the fields.

Wistar paused to tighten his sword belt. "It may be a day or so before the Fifth Corps reaches us here. Care to fill in as my orderly?"

"With pleasure, sir." The prospect of fighting at the side of old comrades once again was a happy one.

"Good. Come along," Wistar replied crisply.

The quiet village of Hyattstown, Maryland, lay at the bottom of a wide, deep gorge of the Monocacy Valley where the main road of the advance was intersected by that of a crossroad following the line of the river. Neglected stone arches of an old turnpike bridge loomed gray and solitary in the foreground, their picturesque setting closely resembling the ancient ruins of a long forgotten Roman aqueduct.

Moving forward at double quick, their rifles held at "right shoulder shift," the men of the Seventy-first halted just long enough on the brink of the ravine to look down on the empty town, its houses closed and shuttered, the inhabitants holed up in the cellars. Grim-lipped and determined, they proceeded to descend the steep decline.

From the deep, echoing gorge came the ceaseless, drowsy, splashing sound of falling water, the wooded ravine a peaceful scene of singing eddies and mossy bridges. Laurel and green hemlock bent low over the cool stream like Narcissus in love with his shadow. Heedless of the tranquil, placid surroundings, the dirty destruction-bent blue-clad infantrymen stumbled and splashed as they forded the slippery shallow depths.

Suddenly, over the heads of the attacking force, screaming shells began whizzing and whirring as Union batteries posted on a dominant crest commenced to bombard the town. Progress became more difficult as the enemy's retiring skirmishers were met in force.

Studying the situation through field glasses, Colonel Wistar called Paddy to his side. "We're going to charge up that hill, Mulcahy. Go back across the river and have the reserve advance half of its force in support."

"Yes, sir." He turned and ran toward the rear.

The leading companies pushed on through a field of deployment.

Wistar watched their preparations with uneasiness.

"Captain Ritman."

"Yes, Colonel?"

"We've two choices facing us and not much time to choose. We can form a square and await their attack or, taking advantage of their condition, go right for them. What do you say?"

"Sir, all the field glasses of the Second Corps are no doubt leveled at us from the high ground across the river. I propose we give them a show."

"Brash way to exercise judgment, Captain. Especially since textbooks do not recommend infantry charges against mounted cavalry. But it does denote what we need, offensive pluck. Sound the attack."

The vibrant notes of a bugle call echoed up the Monocacy Valley and a headlong charge of infantry on cavalry was executed without a moment's loss.

Paddy, musket held at trail arms, ran forward with the reserve companies. The enemy horsemen fell at once into a disorder which they found impossible to remedy under the pressure and were forced to make a rapid retreat to restore their line.

The Seventy-first reserve companies arrived on the scene and formed a long, thin line with wide intervals, refusing wing with the main body of troops.

Colonel Wistar clapped Paddy on the back with exuberance. "Good work, Mulcahy. Any orders from the other side of the river?"

"Yes, sir. You're ordered to hold ground, but make no aggressive movement as might bring on an engagement too big for you to manage. Colonel Sully and his First Minnesota are moving up to support you."

"Hold, eh? That might be a bit difficult. Baker's entire brigade of Confederate cavalry is in front of us. The rear of Longstreet's Corps, we've learned from prisoners, is not far off." He tugged at an earlobe. "Since we're now three miles in advance of the main column, we present a remarkably fine chance for an enterprising enemy to surround and capture our isolated position. It would be quite a feather in the cap of the Reb commander who captured the Seventy-first Pennsylvania. But we'll take our chances."

Toward sundown, a sudden clap of thunder and a pelting downpour of cold rain served to strengthen Wistar's conviction that his men could hold their present position throughout the stormy night. To that end, pickets were sent out while the rest of the regiment prepared to spend a miserable time of it on the soggy ground beneath dripping trees.

A group of men, seeking warmth and protection against the driving rain, piled themselves around Empire, the Colonel's three-quarter bred horse, a familiarity to which the horse had become accustomed. The phlegmatic regimental pet had learned to fear none of war's alarms, and was cheerfully stimulated by the heaviest firing and most unexpected events happening around him. Wistar glanced at the soldiers nestled around his prized mount. He withdrew a flask of whiskey from one of his holsters and passed it to Paddy.

"Better sup on this, Mulcahy. We've no rations with us. This'll help ward off infection and lung fever."

Just before dawn a Negro body servant belonging to the Confederate Colonel Baker was roughly hustled into camp. Looking for his master's horse in the darkness, he had gotten himself entangled inside the Union lines and fallen captive to alert pickets. To all questions regarding Confederate numbers, placement and intentions, he steadfastly refused an answer. Hungry, wet and irritable, the officers and men of the Seventy-first were in no mood to trifle as they swiftly lifted the uncooperative slave onto a horse, angrily put a noose around his neck and ran the other over a low limb where they secured it. All was readied to start the horse with a blow from a saber and launch the Negro into space. The darkey's face expressed fear and he cried forlornly that he would give them the information they wanted. Scowling, the soldiers listened in silence as the man revealed that General Lee had been reported on the Pennsylvania border at Hagerstown. Maryland, and General Longstreet's rear guard had moved north toward Sharpsburg.

General Sumner's long blue column, the Federal 2nd Corps, was put in pursuit of Lee's forces at daybreak.

Paddy approached Colonel Wistar, who stood engaged in conversation with his staff in the shelter of a pine thicket. Having dispatched a detail to bring up rations from the wagon train, Wistar turned toward his orderly. "Well, Paddy, I guess this is goodbye for a while."

"Please, sir, grant me one request?"

"If I can. What is it?"

"Let me travel to Frederick with the regiment. I can wait for the Hundred 'n Eighteenth there."

The Colonel wore a worried frown. "You've already missed one day's roll call with your company. I'll write an excuse. Come along."

Two days later the Second Corps approached the outskirts of Frederick. Spires in the distance rose above the town like miniature needles. The Seventy-first was halted in a broad fertile field from which picket fences had been removed to facilitate easier passage. The men had just flung themselves to the ground for a brief respite from the grueling march when an aide-de-camp to General Howard, a new brigade commander replacing the wounded General Burns, rode up to Colonel Wistar and dismounted.

"General Howard's compliments, sir. He wishes to consolidate your drum corps with that of the Eighty- second New York. He thinks it will create a better effect on the doubtful loyalty of the populace of Frederick when we move in. My orders are to take your men back with me, sir."

Paddy saw the color rise on Wistar's neck.

"The Eighty-second be damned," the Colonel replied. "That pipsqueak regiment hasn't even seen enemy powder smoke while we've lost over four hundred men in action. You tell General Howard he can consolidate my drum corps with his darlings in the Eighty-second when pigs whistle Dixie."

"That is your reply, sir?"

"That's the sum of it, Captain. Good day."

Wistar slapped his thigh. "That pumped-up prig. Effacing the music of his oldest and best regiment in favor of the youngest. It should be the converse, as decency requires."

"Who's this General Howard, sir?" Paddy inquired cautiously.

"He's an ostentatious, aggressively pious New Englander. We've had run-ins before. His dislike of me, I suppose, is purely theological, since I stiffly declined to encourage or take part in the public wrestlings in prayer with which he bedevils his staff and edifies admiring young newspaper reporters."

Twenty minutes later the embarrassed ADC to General Howard returned, this time with a mounted provost guard at his back. He saluted half-heartedly.

"Begging your pardon, sir. General Howard's orders, sir. Either you give up your drum corps or consider yourself under arrest."

Before the disbelieving faces of his ragged, barefoot veterans, Colonel Wistar slowly drew his saber. "My sword, Captain."

The ADC was evidently not prepared for this turn of events. "I cannot accept your sword, sir," he stammered clumsily. He cast a wary glance at the threatening eyes of Wistar's rugged soldiers. "Can't you recant, sir? It's just musicians the General wants."

"My drum corps is part and parcel of the regiment, Captain. A source of enjoyment on the march, fighters in battle, not litter bearers like most, mind you, but gun fighters."

The men shouted approval.

Scowling, Sergeant Knorr advanced with his cap visor pulled well down on the bridge of his nose. "Give 'em what for, Colonel."

Wistar glared at the provost guard. "No field officers being present, Captain, I shall surrender my command to Ritman here and retire duty bound to the rear."

The ADC dismounted. "Sir, I don't like this a bit. You're the best field officer we have in the entire corps. Perhaps if you go see General Howard, or at least put your objections in writing, things can be smoothed over."

"Yes, I'll send Howard my written objections," Wistar replied through drawn lips. "Jenkins, bring me your drum. I'll use it for a table."

The Colonel withdrew a soiled envelope from his tunic and proceeded to write freely with a pencil stub:

September 13, 1862
General: I have no explanation to offer, either written or verbal. If I or my regiment deserve censure, which has never been the opinion of more experienced brigade commanders, a better mode of administering it might have been selected than the insidious insult of breaking it up into detachments to swell the pageant of another. I have the honor to be, sir, with respect,
Isaac J. Wistar
Colonel, California Regiment
(In arrest)
P.S. I have no stationery but this envelope.

"There," he said with satisfaction as he handed over the letter. "There's my reply to General Howard."

Howard's aide folded the envelope without reading it and saluted. "I'm sure this will patch things up, sir."

"I'm sure it will," Wistar said with a wry smile.

Toward sunset, Howard's aide-de-camp returned again, this time more embarrassed than ever.

"Well, what is it this time?" Wistar demanded.

"The general has told me to bring you in, sir."

"And if I refuse?"

"Well, sir, we...we...didn't discuss that possibility. After all, sir, you are an officer and a gentleman."

"Indeed. Then I'm entitled to have my orderly accompany me. Come along, Mulcahy."

"You lucky beggar," Tibben hissed in Paddy's ear. "I'd give two year's pay to see this."

At headquarters, Colonel Wistar and his orderly were ushered into the presence of General Howard, who squirmed uneasily on a camp chair beneath a tent fly. Around him were assembled his staff, presumably to be taught a lesson in the niceties of personal and official dignity.

Paddy took an immediate dislike to the beetle-browed brigade commander. There seemed to be a "Holier than thou" attitude hovering over him, the type to pray openly in market places. The general rose awkwardly and tugged at his overly long coattails.

Looks like a professional pallbearer, Paddy thought to himself.

Howard spoke in a less than assured manner. "Good evening, Colonel Wistar. Major, get our good Colonel a cracker box that he may sit down."

"I prefer standing, thank you."

Howard, losing control of himself at the rebuff, thundered, "Sir, I consider your communication insulting and manifestly intended to be so."

Paddy stole a sidelong glance at Wistar, who stood silent and defiant.

"When you receive an official order," Howard sputtered, "it should be obeyed at once. Explanations asked afterward."

Wistar stared through his superior without answering.

"Will you obey the order now?" Howard shrieked.

"No, sir. Never."

"What is your objection?"

"I decline to discuss it. You have preferred charges against me for disobedience of orders. I will defend myself only before a court of your superiors."

Howard shifted uneasily, his manner becoming more supplicant. "Well, I must admit General Sedgewick discourages the charges, thinking you must be under some misapprehension."

"No misapprehension whatsoever, sir."

"But the order was General Sedgewick's," Howard replied with exasperation, "and merely transmitted through me."

"Then, sir, why did you not so specify, as per usual with a transmitted order? It would have been instantly obeyed."

Howard fairly bristled with indignation. "Do you mean to say you regard General Sedgewick's orders as more obligatory than mine?"

"No, sir. Not with regard to military orders." A half smile peeked from the corners of Wistar's mouth. "But this is not a military order. It refers simply to regimental pageantry. General Sedgewick knows me and my regiment well, and we know him. We would obey without question any order whatever from him, knowing he had some good reason."

The general chewed at a fingernail then, spitting it out, exclaimed bitterly, "All right, Wistar, I release you from arrest and abandon the charges."

Wistar made a slight deferential bow. "Thank you, sir."

Outside, as if sensing his master's successful joust with the general, Empire's welcoming whinny sounded a triumphant blast on the night air.

"You had better report back to the regiment, Mulcahy," Wistar said wearily. "I'm going back to spend the night with my wife."

"Your wife?"

Wistar chuckled. "Why, of course, you puritan. She's traveling with the rest of the ladies in the wagon train. A woman is as essential to a warrior as his shield. Do you disapprove?"

"Never gave it any thought. If you get wounded, I guess it's nice to have them around." Paddy turned to leave. "Good night, sir."

Returning to his regimental bivouac, Paddy experienced the heart-burning thought of the girl who had nursed him back to health and who, at that moment, was probably sleeping soundly in her comfortable room only twenty miles to the southwest. He wondered if she still remembered, still cared. Maybe someday he would see her again. He crawled into his tent and went to sleep with an aching heart.

The following morning, Saturday, the thirteenth of September, the Seventy-first readied itself for a parade through the town of Frederick, the prospect of pomp and circumstance reverting battle-tested veterans to boys again. Envisioning triumphant passages through Southern towns had been part of the tempting bait which had lured many an adventurous youth into the army. Now, even though trailing a victorious invader, the soldiers prepared to feast as best they could on the stuff that romantic dreams are made of.

The fife and drum corps, recently the storm center of controversy, set the pace with *"John's Brown's Body."* Fatigue was forgotten and the regiment moved with a lively step to the popular strain. Spirits were enlivened despite the sultry heat and the cloud of choking dust kicked up by the marching columns.

Henry Castor looked down at the roadway unfolding beneath his long strides. "Hardly seems possible," he mused aloud.

"What's that?" Joe Batt asked.

"To know that eighty years ago my grandfather marched his same route with Mad Anthony Wayne's forces on their way to Yorktown. I hope we have the same good fortune."

With flags unfurled, the Seventy-first entered Frederick toward evening. All doubts as to the town's loyalty were quickly dispelled by the wild cheering which greeted the Federal troops and open display of the Stars and Stripes. An excited throng crowded the sidewalks. With bayonets fixed to rifles, the long columns appeared to be a bed of spikes as they moved through the town.

"This town sort of reminds me of Frankford on market day," Charley Layton said aloud. He screwed up his impish face as if sniffing for something.

"What are you hinting at my good fellow?" Tom Pilling inquired. "What's on your mind?"

Layton kept his eyes peeled on the passing houses. "Like I've always said, let the rest of the regiment feast on glory, my hunger is for a good dinner. Observe the matron in Quaker garb gazing from yonder window. Methinks she's just busting to feed some of us as would ask for it. Where's Knorr?"

"The sarg is busy impressing the womenfolk on the other side of the street. Git up and git."

Assured of reasonable safety from Sergeant Knorr's direction, Layton broke ranks and with high expectations approached the Quaker lady at the window. He lifted his cap and inquired politely but anxiously. "Madam, what is there in the village?"

"A college of some reputation, sir," came the pleasant reply.

"Great heavens, madam, I can't eat a college," Layton replied, looking wounded. "I meant food."

"Layton! Get back in the ranks!"

The stern command from Lieutenant Hibbs sent the butcher's son scurrying back into line, cutting short his personal investigation of the local food situation.

At the center square of Frederick, the column was turned unexpectedly toward the west, its course changed from the northerly direction they had been following.

"Wonder what's up?" Castor inquired of no one in particular. "Going west isn't going to keep us between the Rebs and Baltimore or Philadelphia."

The approach of Colonel Wistar, riding along the line astride Empire, silenced conversation.

"Private Mulcahy," he called, "fall out."

"Yes, sir."

The Colonel paused a moment until the men of Company D passed out of earshot. He gazed down from his position in the saddle. "Paddy, I'd like to carry you with us, for the sake of my morale if nothing else, but your rightful place is in the Hundred and Eighteenth. It's a new regiment and they will need your experience. I'm left with no alternative, I must order you to bivouac in the field up ahead until your regiment arrives."

"But, sir, couldn't I...?"

"No. You wouldn't want me to have another run-in with Howard, would you? Good luck, son, and God bless you."

Paddy raised his arm in salute. "Good-bye, sir."

He watched forlornly as Wistar wheeled his horse, waved, and cantered after his regiment.

Trailing his rifle, Paddy started to trudge over a road that led to the field designated by the Colonel. The sun was hotter than ever, and the dust thicker. For days the roadway had carried heavy columns of marching men, mostly the Confederate Army, and now the Corps of Federals pursuing them. Lumbering artillery and wagon trains ground the stones into pulverized gravel. On each side of the road the fields were well tramped by the infantry. Broken fences lay amidst a debris of wrecked wagons and telegraph poles. Everywhere abandoned property was strewn about as though a violent windstorm had cleaned out someone's attic.

Off to the west, the low-lying Catoctin mountain range served as foothills running parallel to the more prominent South Mountain belt that rose dim and majestic beyond them. Clothed in a grandeur of patriarchal forests, their foliage slightly brushed and tinged by autumn's colorful pigments, the South Mountains stretched from north to south as far as the eye could see in the hazy distance.

Dejected, Paddy turned into a large field occupied by troops with a strange sounding western twang to their speech. Paying little heed, he sought shelter in the shade of a tree, flung his body to the ground and covered his eyes with one arm. He had just started to doze off when a voice inquired, "You a straggler, bub?"

Paddy uncovered his face and saw two soldiers standing over him, one a sergeant, the other a corporal. Both resembled tassel-topped farm boys curious at the presence of someone on their land.

"I'm waiting for my regiment to catch up with me," he replied.

"Now ain't that one fer the jayhawks?" the corporal retorted. "What outfit you with, bub?"

"Hundred and Eighteenth Pennsylvania Fifth Corps."

The corporal scratched his head. "Never heard of them. Where you hail from?"

"Philadelphia."

"Philadelphia, huh? Then you should be with the Philadelphia Brigade. By gum, they are real soldiers. Just passed by here a mite before you came." The bucolic corporal held out his hand. "Name's Baron Mitchel. Twenty-seventh Indiana. Folks call me Bart. This here's Sergeant John Bloss."

Paddy rose to his feet. "Glad to meet you. You're the first Westerners I ever ran across. My name's Mulcahy."

"Howdy, Mulcahy. The sarg and me's been scrounging around for interesting knickknacks. The Rebs camped here last night and left a lot of gimcracks around worth picking up. Sarg just found a wallet with twenty Confederate dollar bills in it." The corporal laughed. "John says he'll use 'em in place of leaves and corn cobs when nature calls. Cain't wait to wipe his ass on Jeff Davis's face. How about it, Sarg?"

"That's right," the Sergeant responded dryly. He looked up from a kneeling position near a clump of bushes. "You interested in seegars, Bart? There's three of them here in an envelope."

"If it's Southern tobacco leaf, I reckon I could be. Cain't stand them tobies made from Pennsylvania leaf."

"Don't be so damn particular. Here. Catch."

The corporal caught the envelope thrown to him and withdrew two cigars. "Have one, Mulcahy?"

"No, thanks. Tobacco smoke cuts my wind. Figger I'll need all I can get if we're going to cross those mountains up ahead."

A sheet of paper which had been wrapped around the cigars fell at his feet. He picked it up. "Since I haven't got any Confederate bills, reckon I'll use this," he said with a half-smirk. "Been marching all morning. My bowels are in an uproar. Excuse me."

He loosened his belt, dropped his pants and squatted in the field. His eyes drifted haphazardly over some writing on the paper which he held in his hand. Idle curiosity suddenly gave way to intense study; the crinkled paper was studded with names familiar to every enlisted man in the Union Army: Generals Jackson, Longstreet, McLaws. At the bottom was a signature, R.D. Chilton, Assistant Adjutant General to Major General D. H. Hill, Commanding Division.

"Holy Mary!" Paddy exploded.

The sergeant chortled. "What's the trouble, got one caught crossways?"

"Crossways, hell. Take a look at what those cigars were wrapped in."

Sergeant Bloss took the paper from Paddy's hand and started reading aloud. "Headquarters, Army of Northern Virginia. Special Orders number one ninety-one." He fell silent, his eyes bulging as they raced over the document.

"What's it say?" Corporal Mitchel asked.

"Balls of fire! Do you know what I have here in my hands?"

"A piece of toilet paper."

"Toilet paper, hell. This here's General Lee's whole northern plan of invasion. Must've dropped out of General Hill's pocket when he left in a hurry last night."

"Good Lord! What'll we do with it?"

"Do with it, we gotta get it to McClellan on the double. According to this, Cousin Bobby's got his army split up three ways. Longstreet's ahead of us in the mountains, Jackson's at Harpers Ferry and Lee's on the Pennsylvania border."

"What's the date on it?" Paddy cut in.

"September ninth. That's four days ago. Still time for Little Mac to capitalize on it. By jingo, this means we've caught Lee in the same predicament you're in, with his pants down."

Aware of his forgetfulness, Paddy hiked his trousers. "There's one rub," he replied. "By the time it goes through channels, it will be too late."

"You don't know our Colonel Colgrove," Bloss retorted. "I'll get this over to regimental headquarters right quick. Like as not, Mac'll have it by tonight. Bart, you take Mulcahy over to have 'shadow' soup with the boys if I'm not back in time."

Sergeant Bloss stuffed the Confederate campaign plan into a pocket and started running across the field.

"Sure hope he gets it through in time," Paddy said. "By the way, what's this 'shadow' soup he was referring to? Something new? I never heard of it before."

The corporal grinned. "You'll find it real appetizing, Mulcahy. Our cooks make it from the chicken which us boys forage."

"Chicken? You fellas really eat high."

"You won't think so after you've heard how it's made. The cooks put a large kettle of water on to boil, then hang a chicken so's its shadow falls in the water. After boiling the shadow for a half hour, they add salt and pepper and serve."

"Humph. Thought it'd be something like that. Seems as if those who can't learn the drill and those too dirty to stand inspection are sent to the cook house to get them out of the ranks." He frowned. "And me with a stomach that feels like a shriveled prune."

That evening, as the shadows began to lengthen, he sat down to eat as a guest of the Western troops, exchanging comments and experiences with them and making comparative notes of home. Prepared by regimental cooks, a luxury for troops in the field, the supper rations consisted of coffee, salt pork and "skilly galley," hardtack soaked in water, drained and fried in pork fat.

It was an hour or so later when, like the end of a beautiful dream, the pleasant fervors of bivouac life were abruptly terminated by a sharp call to arms. The camp of the Twenty-seventh Indiana sprang to life with active preparations to move on. The night had become cool. Wrapping himself in a blanket, Paddy stared after the departing regiment until the last man disappeared down the darkened turnpike which led to the South Mountains. In the stillness, amid dying campfires, he settled back in lonely vigil.

The next morning was growing old when finally, to his great relief, the Fifth Corps began to pass by on the road. The Corn Exchange Regiment, drooping with fatigue, came into view. The wilted men marched four abreast in route step, their presence voiced only by the shuffling sound of tired feet, the rubbing and straining of innumerable straps and the flop of full canteens. Through the canopy of dust, Paddy could see that somehow the regiment had managed to get itself back together as a unit. With a quick break he darted from the field and made a furtive attempt to conceal himself in the ranks, but not quick enough to escape detection by Sergeant Cassidy, who sidled up to him.

"Holy Mother, Mulkayhee, where ye been?"

"I might ask you the same question. I've been waiting here since yesterday afternoon. Glad you and the boys finally caught up."

"Hope ye can make the captain see it that way. He was countin' on ye to help round up these stumble-bums when they fell by the way."

Paddy frowned. "Never thought of it that way. The cap'n really mad?"

"He ain't happy. Thinks maybe you deserted."

Paddy pondered his predicament for a moment. "Best defense is a good offense," he replied. "Guess I'd better report to the Captain right away."

He strode forward and reached the side of Captain Donaldson. His colorful story of a chance meeting with the 71st and Colonel Wistar let him escape without rebuke or censure.

The long winding column continued its slow march across the floor of a fertile valley. The sound of heavy gunfire could be heard up ahead in the mountains. Toward evening the sounds of battle diminished and died away. Electrifying news came back through the column. Longstreet and Hill had been decisively beaten and the mountain passes at Turner's and Crampton's Gap had been forced.

For the 118th, the steep ascent up the South Mountain through Turner's Cap was begun the next morning as anxious troops followed the old national road. Evidence of recent fighting was seen everywhere in the freshly-dug graves beside the road and in the piles of unburied dead gathered in heaps or stacked like cordwood.

Willie McCool, ignoring the fact that he got sick and vomited each time, stopped and stared at the mangled bodies of human forms and bloated horses, their bellies swollen up like a drum.

"Want me to carry your pack?" Paddy asked, feeling concerned.

"'Preciate it, if you don't mind." McCool let out a gasp. "Say look at that one, he's cold and yellow-white as beef tallow." Clapping his hands over his mouth, he turned away. His Adam's apple began to pump convulsively.

"Why don't you stop looking?" Paddy growled impatiently.

McCool shook his head. "I got to. I'll never get used to..." His words were choked off by a stream of sour hardtack pouring from his mouth.

On reaching the summit of South Mountain, the column was halted to catch its breath and the exhausted but inquisitive troops broke up into small groups. Before their eyes lay a scene broad in the scope of its grandeur, a rare landscape of mountain and valley, hill and dale, streams and villages, and upon which was spread a breathtaking martial display, a concentration of masses of soldiery in full view.

From the mountains to the Antietam, a small winding stream flowing to the south on a course parallel to the mountains, was a distance of approximately five miles. Appearing in miniature, almost toylike beyond the Antietam, lay the tiny town of Sharpsburg, Maryland. Within that area, deployed over plain and valley, massed in column and by the flank, some moving and others at rest, was nearly the entire Army of the Potomac, its infantry, cavalry, artillery and trains.

The day was perfect, the air clear and still. A brilliant sun overhead caused dazzling reflections from flashing points of bayonets and the bright barrels of muskets stacked in "lines of masses." Kindled for a noonday bite, hundreds upon hundreds of pin-point campfires sent wispy shreds of smoke curling skyward from the valley below.

Stretching out to the right and front, climbing the hills and sinking over them out of view, were columns upon columns of infantry attenuated by distance to widths so narrow as to be dwarfed and scarcely distinguishable. Canvas-topped wagon trains, appearing as mobile white beads on a string, moved over the ribbon-thin roads. Others were being gathered to park. Quarter-masters, wagon-masters and teamsters were detaching ordnance. Surgeons, arnbulances and stretcher-bearers were detaching from the combatants. The entire country, roads, fields and timber, swarmed with maneuvering soldiery.

From a grandstand seat high on top of South Mountain, the uninitiated men of the Corn Exchange looked down spellbound and speechless as the stupendous panorama unfolded before their eyes; the magnitude of the sight far exceeded the scope and wildest stretch of imagination. Here at last was the realization of dreams come true, a patriotic spectacle that blew a reviving breath of fresh air into sagging spirits, restoring enthusiasm and making worthwhile all that which had preceded.

Seated on the ground at an open place in the mountain forest, Paddy shaded his eyes for a clearer view.

"Glory be, what a sight!" he exclaimed.

"Yes, indeed," Bob Dyer replied. "That sure is a mass of men down there. They look invincible. Glad they're on our side."

An officer from Company G approached the small group. Of medium height and build and in his early twenties, his strong, inquisitive features closely resembled those of a cavalier. He knelt down on one knee.

"'Scuse me, men. Can y'all tell me where I can find Cap'n Donaldson?"

The sound of his thick Southern drawl caused others to look around sharply.

"He's gone forward with Colonel Prevost, Lieutenant," Sergeant Cassidy answered. "Be back shortly. Anythin' I can do for ye?"

"Reckon not, Sergeant. I'll just wait heah until he returns, if y'all don't mind."

"Make yerself right at home, sir." Cassidy hesitated a moment, studying his fingernails. "Ye're Lieutenant White of G Company, aren't ye?"

"That's right, Sergeant."

A silence fell over the group. Cassidy stared at the valley then spoke as if to break the spell. "Quite a sight, ain't it, Lieutenant?"

" ' Deed it is, Sergeant. We'll probably nevah see the likes of it again."

Several of the men made awkward movements. "Doesn't it bother you?" McCool blurted. "I mean, knowing your kin and neighbors are down there coming up on the other side of the Antietam?"

Every eye focused itself on the Southerner as he knit his brow. His high cheekbones were impressive. He spoke through thin, resolute lips.

"What y'all meant to say is, if you were me, native of Warrenton, Virginia, and a former lieutenant in the Black Horse Cavalry, y'all can't see yourselves fighting turncoat for the North. Is that it?"

"Not unless you vas up to some tricks," Schneider called out.

The officer turned his eyes upon Schneider. "Y'all must be the one whose been circulating stories about me," he said in a menacing voice. "You had better copy the good manners set by your Philadelphia comrades before I'm forced to call you out. When the South fired on the flag at Sumter, it was as if they had taken a shot at my father. Filial obedience dictated my choice to stand by the Union."

"Don't pay any attention to that square-headed Dutchman, Lieutenant," Dick Allen said with a scowl. "You're more of a man than any of us here."

"Sir, here comes the Cap'n now," Sergeant Cassidy cut in.

Regaining his feet, the Southerner called out, "Captain, can I see y'all a moment?"

"Sure thing, Lieutenant. What can I do for you?"

"Just ran into some prisoners from around home. Boasting in anger, they let slip some information I think ought to be passed on to headquarters right away. Captain Saunders keeps putting me off. Thought maybe you could help."

"I'll try. Come, I'll take you to Prevost." The two officers walked hurriedly away. That a great battle was imminent was plain to see. Much to their chagrin, the men of the Corn Exchange regiment could not stand long and marvel at the splendid military scene passing before their eyes in the valley below as if in panoramic appointment for their special entertainment.

To the accompaniment of resonant drums and bugle blasts, the regiment passed down the mountainside and was soon swallowed up among the legions shaking off impediments in preparation for battle. With the rugged mountain region behind them, the soldiers entered on a level expanse where marching was easy and where novelty met the eye at every turn. There were gently rolling hills, streams and rocky glens. The entire countryside held the quiet reserved look of uneventful propriety. Waving cornfields, lush pastures and pleasing gardens surrounded vine-trellised farmhouses. The landscape was a quilted patchwork bordered by weathered rail and whitewashed picket fences.

Through the small towns of Boonsboro and Keedyville, the bayonet-tipped ranks of blue pressed steadily onward, pouring through the tiny villages as venous blood coursing through a distended vein. Tin-roofed red brick houses nested in rural contentment along the main thoroughfare. Villagers gazed at the passing pageantry with wonder, their faces expressing the fact that nothing had ever happened here except the quiet, undramatic, unrecorded round of births, deaths, christenings and weddings. For them, excitement had limited itself to corn-husking, barn-raisings, plowing ground in the spring and harvesting crops in the fall.

All of life in the particular region seemed to move like the tide of the Potomac, which flowed several miles to the west, slowly, steadily, without fuss or furor, patiently molding the land to its own liking.

Hoop-skirted maidens leaned over picket fences and hovered near moss-covered spring houses and wells. Seductive sirens, they gaily offered cool relief to the perspiring columns of marching men. Here was the romance and glamour of campaigning in strange, new territory, but the susceptible troops discovered that urgent need elsewhere prohibited them from stopping to enjoy the hospitality.

A damp, smoky mid-September dusk began cloaking field and forest in a hazy shroud as the Corn Exchange moved into bivouac. The regiment came to rest on a high ridge that overlooked the sluggish, copper-colored waters of the Antietam. From that eminent position, they also had a commanding view of the open rolling fields and countryside which lay on the opposite side of the stream.

Of more pressing and immediate interest were the bright red pennants flying from the spear-tipped lances of the Sixth Pennsylvania Cavalry grouped in an adjoining field. Dropping camp chores, McCool, Tibben and several others raced off in high excitement to ferret news and exchange greetings with Frank Dorsey, Harrison Shallcross, John Sidebotham and about thirty others from Frankford who were known to be riding with that particular body.

Those remaining in camp went about the business of tenting up for the night, building tiny campfires over which to boil pots of coffee using makeshift kettles from empty cans with bailing wire for handles. The stimulating odor of coffee, together with bits of bacon and pork crackling on forked sticks, soon filled the evening air with a tangy aroma that put life back into tired bodies.

His supper disposed of, Paddy stabbed a knife into the ground to clean it and started to munch on a hardtack biscuit. He glanced up as Captain Donaldson, who was smoking a laurel root pipe, came by. "How do things look?" he inquired.

The officer sat down. "When did you and those Indiana boys find Lee's general orders?" he asked.

"Last Saturday afternoon."

"Three and a half days ago," Donaldson mused.

"Something wrong? As if I didn't know."

The captain winced. "McClellan has the 'slows' again. He's imagining great hordes of gray ghosts facing us, as always." He gave the tobacco in his pipe bowl a strong tap. "Those captured friends of Rudy White's couldn't understand why we haven't finished off Longstreet and D. H. Hill. At last report Lee's men are still some twenty miles north of here, close to Hagerstown. Jackson's men haven't arrived, and A.P. Hill is still at Harpers Ferry. Like those Reb prisoners said, we should be destroying Lee's army piecemeal right now, not sitting around on our broad asses. It'll soon be too late. By the time Mac's ready to fight, the whole Confederate Army will be united in front of us, although the prisoners did say it's dwindled in size. Thousands of Johnnies took advantage of an order excusing barefoot men from marching into Maryland."

Paddy ground his teeth into the hardtack. "Maybe the sickness in our horses is slowing up Mac's plans."

"There's not much you miss, is there? How did you find out about the epidemic?"

"A teamster friend of mine told me about it."

"The one you hitched a ride with?"

"I didn't say I hitched any rides."

"That's right, so you didn't." A bemused smile crossed the officer's face. "But I've still got my own ideas as to how you covered the ground so well." He paused and gazed toward the southwest. "They say Franklin is dragging his heels since his victory at Crampton's Gap yesterday."

"His corps supposed to join us here?"

"I don't know. His original orders were to relieve General Miles' beleaguered command at Harpers Ferry and chew up A. P. Hill's Corps before they could join forces with Lee in front of us. Since he didn't follow Mac's orders, our chances of cutting the Confederate Army in two and beating it in detail are gone. At last report, Franklin's still sitting on his hunkers at Crampton's Gap."

Paddy scowled. "Here we go again."

The officer exhaled a series of smoke rings. "Should have kept my mouth shut. Didn't mean to upset you."

"You haven't. Not exactly. This war's become a comedy of errors, but I'll stick around for the laughs."

"Since that's the way you feel, here's another rib tickler for you. Colonel Prevost just informed us that our Corps Commander, General Porter, is under suspended court martial charges brought against him by Pope after the Second Bull Run."

"Generals," Paddy replied. "Peevish little pricks." He gave an obscene gesture with one his fingers. "What are the charges? Trumped up, like they pulled on Stone?"

"In some ways, yes. Men like Pope always look for a whipping boy when their own plans go bust. Porter, Franklin and Griffin, all three have been cited for disobedience of orders and misbehavior in the presence of the enemy. Officers of the line at Second Bull Run claim that Porter actually saved our army from greater disaster by pulling out when he did. Seems as if Pope, with his delusions of grandeur, thought he was attacking a small retreating rebel rear guard at Manassas when in reality, Longstreet was entrenched and ready to attack with thirty thousand men. When Porter contacted the enemy, he had only nine thousand troops. The consensus of opinion is that by falling back to the main body, Porter took the only logical action any intelligent officer would have taken under the circumstances."

"I'll be damned." Paddy snapped a twig between his fingers. "Guess it would be too much to expect everything to be sweetness and light between Mac and his corps commanders, wouldn't it?"

Donaldson rose from a squat position and stretched his legs. "Just like believing in the tooth fairy. General Burnside's miffed because Joe Hooker openly solicited an independent command, which Mac granted him on the right wing. Burnside's crying because a subordinate has been given command of two corps."

"What bone did Mac throw Burnside?"

"Reno's Ninth Corps, over on the left. General Reno was killed at South Mountain. There's bitter feelings on this field, make no mistake about it. Burnside has refused to take command, claiming it's a demotion. He's helping Major General Cox in an advisory capacity until the campaign is over. It's a damn shame human lives are the pawns in this game."

Sergeant Cassidy, standing within earshot, sought to relieve himself of a full bladder. He unbuttoned his fly. The stub of a cigar was clenched between his teeth. "Seems to me our generals behave like a pack o' stud dogs squirting piss on each other's legs," he said from the corner of his mouth.

Donaldson struck a match to his pipe. "Our commanders," he said, "haven't learned the secret of organization and cooperation. There's the rub. Catch up a handful of snow and throw it, it flies to fluff. Pack it, it strikes like stone." He slammed his fist into an open palm.

The sound of thunder rumbled across the sky and echoed over the encamped army.

"Sergeant Cassidy?" Captain Donaldson called.

"Yes, Cap'n."

"See that the men are under shelter halves tonight, we're in for a storm. And no campfires. That's orders."

"Yes, sir."

The officer turned to Paddy. "There's a meeting scheduled at headquarters at nine. It's almost that now. I have to run."

"Sure, Frank. See you later."

"Have thee a tent mate for tonight?" the Quaker asked, coming up from behind.

"I promised McCool he could team up with me, but it would be warmer if we slept three. Besides, we can use your shelter half to cover the front of the tent.

Let's unpack."

The weary soldiers quickly bedded down for the night. Raindrops, like little feet, started to patter on the unbleached muslin tents as an air of tension settled over the darkened camp. The men sensed something ominous, a dread as to what the next day might bring. Above the sound of rain, hushed whispers could be heard in nearby tents as the occupants discussed the muffled tramp of marching men who could not be seen, only heard as ghostly figures moving in the dark.

"I swear to God we're being surrounded and don't know it," McCool said.

"Listen, Willie," Paddy shot back, "an unguarded remark like that could set this green regiment into panic. We are not being surrounded. Shove it in your canteen."

The Quaker rolled over on his side, a touch of humor showing in his shadowy eyes. "Thee are beginning to sound like a skilled mercenary, Mulcahy. Let Willie talk if it makes him rest easier. The sound of his voice is better than the eerie silence."

"Well, go ahead and talk if you have to. Me, I'm going to sleep."

Morning was ushered in by a gray overcast. A foggy mist crept over the ground like a disembodied serpent, filling the hollow places and drenching the groves and valleys in dewy dampness. Random picket tiring could be heard, followed by advanced batteries cannonading with a deep *boom, boom.*

Joe Tibben shivered in the early morning mist. He clutched his musket in a tight grip and strained his eyes toward the west and the source of action. "Sounds like somebody's unloading boards over there," he observed.

Those close to him nodded as they peered through the haze under dripping cap brims. Suddenly a brilliant sun dispersed the fog so that blurred backgrounds and the outlines of trees and farm buildings came into focus as though spotlighted on a stage.

"Glory be, look at that!" McCool shouted. He pointed toward long stretching ranks of blue soldiers, spearheaded by battle flags and bayonets, who were advancing through a cornfield off to the right. The over-awed men of the 118th looked for the first time upon the pageantry, the splendor and the futile waste of life occasioned by war as it unfolded before their eyes. Charge and counter-charge surged back and forth through a cornfield. Uttered without concert, deep-breasted northern cheers, signaling a temporary success, were answered by the high-pitched Rebel yell of Confederates driving forward to retake lost ground. As the morning wore on, the fierce combat raged with mounting intensity. Sulfurous clouds of smoke and dust blanketed the battlefield.

"Seems to me we should be relievin' that pressure over on the right by strikin' left and center," Sergeant Cassidy grumbled. "Wonder what Mac's waitin' for?"

"How 'bout lettin' der chenerals fight der war der vay dey vant?" Schneider said over his shoulder.

"I'm aimin' to, kraut head. Suppose ye feel nice and cozy lyin' up here, jist watchin'."

Toward noon a big commotion heralded the arrival of General McClellan and his mounted staff. They proceeded to post themselves on the high rise of ground occupied by the Corn Exchange Regiment. The excited troops, crowding in as close as they dared, greeted their commander with wild cheering and enthusiastic shouts in response to which McClellan stiffly tipped his hat, then turned and went into a huddled conference with a group of subordinates.

Curious and inquisitive as small boys gathered around a surprise package, the milling foot soldiers, little men coming from average walks of life and of little consequence in world affairs, looked with awe and interest at the glittering display of aristocracy and wealth surrounding McClellan. Murmuring, whispering and pointing, they singled out prominent, fashionable figures such as a French duke and two princes who were heirs and claimants to the throne of France when the usurper Napoleon III had been relieved of his duties.

Resentful of their lower station, some of the men directed scornful glances and angry remarks at the finery of John Jacob Astor, wealthy scion of American aristocracy, as he strutted in his special accommodations and favor upon the splendid horse which he rode in a tight circle. When the conference between McClellan and his commanders of the Fifth Corps broke up, Paddy hastily sought out his close friend and confidant.

"What's going on, Frank?" he asked anxiously. "I don't like the looks of things. This battle just isn't moving right."

"It isn't," Donaldson snapped with a show of annoyance " At ten o'clock Burnside was supposed to strike a stone bridge crossing the Antietam down there on our left. He was to hit the Confederate's weakened right flank, from which they've been pulling their reinforcements. It's now one o'clock and Burnside still hasn't moved to the attack. As for the center, Colonel Webb's just been sent to order Meagher's Irish Brigade into action to be supported by Caldwell and Brooks. Here's my field glasses if you want to take a look. I've seen and heard enough."

Taking the glasses that were handed to him, Paddy put them to his face and adjusted them to fit his vision. Coming into focus were gallant ranks of Irishmen from New York moving forward into battle with snap and precision, a band playing at their rear cheering them on with the *"Garry Owen March."* Maintaining the perfect alignment of a holiday parade, the magnificent array moved to the charge, every step keeping time to the beat of a drum. Dazzling to the eye, the sun glistened on thousands of gleaming rifle barrels.

Colors floated in the breeze leading them onward, the green harp of Erin flying prominently in its place beside the national standard. As the advance progressed, scathing Rebel fire cut fearful gaps. The lines halted with deliberation and readjusted. Dead and wounded were strewn on the ground, thickening as the distance from the enemy diminished. Twice and again the green standard, more distinctly noticeable than the regimental color, fell, only to be promptly seized again and borne gallantly forward.

Vast curtains of smoke concealed the gray-clad enemy in a sunken lane, the cloud rising at intervals to disclose the Confederates unmoved and holding firm to their shallow trench. Nothing, it seemed, diminished their courage, and nothing could stay the onslaught of the determined Irishmen.

The deadly moment of impact came, and the lines impinged. The enemy, in total confusion, broke for the friendly cover of nearby timber. The Irish Brigade, still maintaining their organization with commendable exactitude, pressed them in their helpless flight until finally, with shout and cheer, friend and foe were lost to view in the same woods the enemy had sought for safety.

Standing and watching the developments from their prominent hill, the Fifth Corps Reserve, numbering close to thirteen thousand, split the air to a man with wild cheering at the victorious sight.

Sergeant Cassidy reached for his stacked rifle.

"We've split 'em. We've cut their center. Do we go in now, Cap'n? Now'd be the time."

"This should be it, Andy. Wait'll I check with Colonel Prevost." Captain Donaldson, with other company commanders, raced to the side of their regimental commander.

The men watched anxiously as another conference took place between McClellan, Porter and Morrell. McClellan peered through his glasses in momentary silence, then nodded negatively toward General Porter.

"Ye mean he's not sendin' us in?" Cassidy cried in anguish. "He's got the Rebs on the go. We've split their center."

"Hold your men steady where they are, Sergeant," Donaldson ordered disgustedly. "We're to stay put."

"What's the sergeant getting so all fired up about?" McCool asked. "I think the view's fine from right here. Don't you think so, Quaker?"

The Quaker wiped beaded drops of perspiration from his forehead. "I'm afraid I'm a coward, friend McCool. I have a physical fear of going forward, and a moral fear of turning back."

"You're just being honest out loud," Dick Allen retorted as he ran a thumb down the length of his bayonet. "You know, there is something that has always amused me. It's the way newspapers make a big to-do about how 'the army was eager to be let against the enemy'. One would think it was true," he continued satirically, "because truthful correspondents have said so, and honest editors confirmed it. Funny thing about it though, when you come right down to hunting for this particular itch, it's always the other regiment that has it." He gave his blade a final test for sharpness. "Anybody, I mean anybody, who says he wants to 'go in' is either a pathological liar or brainless fool."

Straining outwardly, but inwardly thankful for the good fortune which kept them out of the fight, the men in the reserve corps watched the fighting die out on the right, shift to the center, then pass from sight to the left, where the action centered on a picturesque stone bridge that arched over the Antietam at a cliff-sheltered defile well shaded by buttonwood trees. A vital link, needed to forge victory, the narrow bridge was the passkey that opened the door to the weakened Confederate right. Burnside's 9th Corps finally managed to storm the arched stone bridge at one o'clock where, for some unexplainable reason, they were ordered to halt. Not until three o'clock in the afternoon did they begin a victorious sweep toward Sharpsburg, only to be met head on at the climactic moment by A. P. Hill's Corps of Confederates just arrived on the field from Harpers Ferry. The opposing lines were soon stalemated and the heavy sounds of battle slackened.

"What a hodge-podge fight this has been," Cassidy growled as he kicked dirt. "The way McClellan's run the show, we'd of been better off goin' in one by one and sluggin' it out donnybrook style."

Captain Donaldson's lips had moved as if to give a silent amen to the statement when a stray cannon ball came bounding into the area, tossing earth into the air as a plow turns a furrow. McCool, seeing the missile's speed readily diminishing, dashed out to catch it as if it was a baseball.

Cassidy screamed. "Look out ye idiot! Ye want to get killed?"

Grinning foolishly, McCool spread his legs and let the cannon ball shoot harmlessly through.

Excitement for the day over, the soldiers went about preparing their evening meal with glum spirits, for it was evident that the day's battle had accomplished nothing. Campfires were aglow and the men gathered around for a closer study and reevaluation of recent events.

Paddy stirred restlessly. Gradually he edged his way to the camp boundary, stole from the bivouac area and hurried toward the right flank. Sporadic picket firing sounded along the length of the entire front. Walking, running, stumbling, he worked his way through shattered commands as he frantically looked for his friends in the 71st. Adding to the discomfort of being lost, heavy rain began falling and he cursed himself for not bringing a poncho as his soaked uniform began chafing his body like sandpaper.

A voice in the night rose to a challenge. "Halt! Who goes there?"

Paddy drew up short. "Friend. Looking for my regiment, Seventy-first Pennsylvania." He prayed the sentry would not spot the tell-tale insignia of the 118th on his cap.

"The 'stoppers,' eh? Pass, friend. You'll find them 'bout a half mile straight ahead near a place called Poffenberger Farm."

"Much obliged."

Bundling up as best he could against the cold rain, Paddy moved on. Lights from the designated farmhouse appeared dimly through the downpour as he neared the place. Above the steady sound of rain, there arose a chilling sound of agonizing screams from the wounded and dying men who were lying in the rain on the muddy ground outside the farm building. Some writhed like decapitated snakes, others lay pale and still on rows of stretchers. Inside the building and out, amputations and other surgical operations were proceeding by lantern light, and the whole area was a slippery mixture of mud and blood. Severed limbs of all shapes and sizes were heaped in grotesque piles. Piles which, in the dark, resembled diabolical centipedes from Hell.

Closing his eyes and ears to the terrible nightmare, Paddy quickly detoured the crowded field hospital, anger and bitterness welling within him as he tried to put out of his mind the barbaric results of war.

Directly across his path was a camp of soggy pup tents silhouetted in the darkness by light from brightly burning campfires. He stopped and peered cautiously into one of the tents, at the same time inquiring as to the regimental identity. Two heads rose as one from beneath a covering of blankets and stared at the intruder.

"We're the Holmesburg Grays," they said. Paddy dropped quickly to his knees and struck a match. The flickering flame illuminated drawn, tired faces familiar to him. "Solly! Tris Boileau!" he blurted.

"Well, I'll be damned, if it isn't Mulcahy. What are you doing here?"

"Just checking up on things. Have to see if the army is still in good shape. Say, is Sam Cartledge around?"

Tris Boileau threw off a blanket and sat upright.

"Next tent, matter of fact. But this isn't exactly Doc Arthur's drug store if you came looking for sweets and sours."

Bill Solly rolled over on his side and shouted under the tent. Hey, Sam, stick your head out and see what the rain's washed in."

There were several seconds of shuffling, swearing disturbance in the adjoining shelter. Cartledge, recognizing the figure kneeling before the neighboring tent, called out cordially, "Hey, Paddy, how are you? What brings you this way?"

"I'm looking for my old regiment, the Seventy-first."

The three soldiers from Holmesburg exchanged hesitant glances.

"Something wrong?" Paddy asked with a feeling of uneasiness.

Sam Cartledge, his dark, handsome features steeped in gloom, spoke. "Their camp's about a hundred yards in front of us. What's left of them."

"What's left of them. What do you mean?"

"The Seventy-first lost every field and staff officer, including their colonel. They have only one captain and three lieutenants remaining for duty and not quite two hundred and fifty men."

Paddy sprang to his feet. "I gotta go. See you later."

"Sure thing, Paddy. Take care of yourself."

With muscles taut and a feeling of trepidation gnawing inside him, Paddy snaked his way toward the camp of his old comrades. Looming out of the rain-sheeted darkness and looking almost macabre, a group of soldiers clothed in dripping ground blankets huddled over a prostrated figure lying near a large fire. Pilling turned at Paddy's approach and gave a blank nod of recognition.

'Tom. Who is it?" Paddy asked weakly.

"Charley Layton. Got one through the belly. Won't be long."

"Can I talk to him?"

"Won't do no harm. Spread, fellas, Mulcahy's here. Wants to talk to Layton."

Paddy knelt down, his soaked uniform clinging to his cold body like wet wall paper. "Hi, Charley. How's the butcher boy? Anything I can do for you?"

Too weak to speak, the movements of the muscles of Layton's mouth indicated that he was making a dying struggle to talk. In a moment, death came, calm and peaceful; a few faint breaths, a slight rattling in his throat, a short, quick convulsive shudder and the book of life was closed on another of Frankford's sons.

Lieutenant Hibbs bent over to feel Layton's pulse. He spoke in a sad voice, "It's all over. Cover him."

Paddy grasped Tom Pilling by the arm. "How bad a shape is the company in?"

"Cut to pieces. Layton, Hunt, Standing, Lieutenant Greth, Fulton, Lightfoot." He hesitated, reluctant to go on.

Paddy prodded him. "Go on."

"Hen Castor and Joe Batt went up together. Just like their younger brothers at the Bluff."

Tears poured from Paddy's eyes. "Dead! Joe! Henry!" He fell to the ground, sobbing. "Thirteen thousand of us in reserve," he cried, "and what's McClellan do? Nothing! We could've helped you. That bastard, Burnside, if he'd attacked on the left flank in the morning, it would have taken the pressure off...."

Pilling put a hand on his shoulder. "Come, on, Paddy. Let's boil you some coffee."

Paddy drew a muddy sleeve across his face. "What a stinking state of affairs. Generals fighting among themselves like school kids while we do the dyin'."

"C'mon over to the tent and rest awhile," Pilling urged again, softly.

Paddy stood up. squared his shoulders and dragged his feet slowly, then flopped grief-stricken on a damp ground cloth inside Pilling's tent.

Pilling lighted a small cook fire and placed a pot of coffee on to boil. He wiped a pair of grimy hands on his shirt. "Want to hear about it?" he asked. "This morning's battle on the right flank, I mean."

Paddy wiped his nose, sniffed and rubbed his wet eyes. "Yeah, tell me about it. What went wrong this time?"

Pilling settled back on a bedroll and locked his hands around his tucked-up knees. "It started early. Joe Hooker started the attack at daybreak, moved out through a cornfield and was badly beaten. He was severely wounded and carried off the field and his whole corps put to flight. Mansfield's men, coming to the support of Hooker's corps, took up the fighting against the Rebs and it was about that time Lee began his desperate gamble. Withdrawing unemployed troops from in front of Burnside on our left, he shifted them to reinforce the Reb lines attacking Mansfield on our right. Mansfield was killed about eight o'clock in the morning."

"His men break?"

"Had to. Lee's reinforcements were too much for them. That's when we began to cuss. We could see the battle was raging fiercely before us here on the right, but we couldn't hear anything on the left where the sound of Burnside's guns should have been heralding the attack we expected him to make on Lee's weakened wing. Staff officers, one after another, were sent off to try to get Burnside moving, but...well, you know."

"Yeah, miffed because he couldn't run the whole show, he just sat on his ass and sucked his thumb."

"So we've heard."

Pilling uncoupled his hands and stretched his legs. "Well, like I was saying, our brigade was being held in reserve at the center of the line for quite another purpose, but with the successive routs of Hooker and then Mansfield, an emergency arose which brought us the order to move off to the right to take up the attack in the quarter where Union forces had already been defeated twice."

"'Holier than thou' Howard still leadin' the brigade?" Paddy cut in.

"Yes, sorry to say. Old General Burns may have been a rough Scot and hard taskmaster, but at least he was soldier's soldier. Sure hope he recovers from those wounds he got on the peninsula and comes back soon."

"So what happened after the brigade got ordered into battle?"

"We forded the Antietam, dripping wet, and dressed lines. Since Sumner makes no bones about us being his favorite division, he accompanied us in person, but at the last minute Sedgewick appeared and took the division forward himself, not knowing that over half the men would never return. You should have seen the advance. What a sight. Not a voice and scarcely a shot disturbed the maneuver of five thousand men. Maintaining perfect order and alignment, the three long lines moved forward at the quick step with arms at right shoulder shift." Pilling winced. "The parade didn't last long. Shells flying thick as hornets started exploding over, under and around our columns as we entered the cornfield and we began to encounter the dead and wounded of the two previously beaten corps. Mutilation in shocking forms covered the ground on every side."

Pilling closed his eyes. "I'll never, as long as I live, forget the pleading look in the eyes of one wounded seventeen-year old as our advancing column marched over his helpless body with a steady tread."

"Let's leave out the gory details. What happened next?"

"Our line, which was third and last, got through the cornfield all right, passed safely through one patch of woods, and crossed the Hagerstown Pike. The front line was driving the Rebs into a second patch of woods on the other side of the Pike. It was when we crossed the road that things began to go wrong."

"What do you mean?"

"Our line and the line in front were still parallel, but the first line, in crossing a fence at the far side of the second patch of woods, made a slight change of direction to the left so that its alignment formed an angle in relation to ours. Say, how's the coffee coming?"

"Just about boiled. So then what happened?"

"The Rebs, still free from pressure on their right flank by the unaccountable inactivity of Burnside, were able to detach heavy reinforcements to our sector. They came into position in line of battle more in conformance to our line of march than to the alignment of our front. Under cover of rocks and trees, they were in an enviable position which at the moment of contact not only gave them both front and flanking fire against our columns, but also made it easier for them to change front rapidly to meet our attack, which finally developed. We were set up like ducks in a shooting gallery."

"What part of our line got hit first?"

"The extreme left of the first line. They were just about blown off their feet by frontal fire delivered at close range. The second line, seeing the first line had become roughly engaged, halted and attempted to change front."

"Where was the Seventy-first?"

"On the extreme right of the third and supporting line and furthest from the point of enemy contact. At that, we were only sixty paces back of the engaged first line until we got separated from the rest of our brigade and–"

"Separated? How come?"

"The Colonel ordered us to lay down to avoid unnecessary casualties until our service in the action might be demanded." Pilling paused to moisten his lips. "He had no sooner given the order than Empire was shot from under him, right through the neck. I mean it was God-awful watching our pet die like that."

He paused to pour two cups of coffee. "Gorman's brigade", he continued, "in an effort to change front under enfilading fire, lost cohesion and broke."

Paddy curled a lip. "Our friends from the Bluff, the Fifteenth Massachusetts."

"Yep. Running like rabbits again. The second line, ranks being partly faced to the rear for the same purpose, to get away, was not in shape to withstand the rush of fugitives and was almost instantly run over by the breaking first line. Both lines came tumbling back on our regiment like apples spilling out of a basket. You couldn't hear yourself think for the screaming. Wistar gave orders with his sword. and brought us to our feet with bayonets leveled. Knowing the integrity of the entire right wing of the army depended on the resistance we put up, we forced the routed men around our flanks and with the Rebel lines laid bare, dove into them, and managed to check them for the time being."

Paddy blew on his coffee to cool it. "Were you able to hold them off?'

"No. The line on our left flank was disjointed, as I said, General Richardson, commanding at that spot, was killed and his division roughly handled. Large Rebel forces, striking from that direction, soon enveloped our entire left flank and Johnnies were pouring at us from front, left and rear."

Paddy ran a hand through his matted hair. "You poor bastards. How did the Colonel meet the situation?"

"We were isolated. Capture or retreat stared us in the face. Wistar, seeing that we had successfully covered the retreat of the division, ordered us to retire. That's when we got pummeled. It was God-awful seeing fellows you grew up with dropping like wheat before a scythe." Pilling shook his head. "Hen Castor and Joe Batt, both killed within three feet of each other. And young Layton, I can still see him watching his father slaughter on frosty mornings. Remember the funny woolen cap he used to wear? Always had it pulled way down over his ears, and his nose dripping like a leaky faucet?" He studied an empty coffee tin. "Can't believe Joe and Hen won't be standing next to me at muster anymore. Doesn't seem real, somehow."

"The Colonel, what happened to Colonel Wistar?" Paddy cut in weakly.

"Don't know. Last I saw him he was blazing away with a pistol."

A sudden hubbub of excitement came from the direction of the campfires. Muddy trouser legs hurried past the front of the tent.

"Somebody's probably made it in from the battle field," Pilling said as he peered outside. "Better see who it is."

Together they scrambled out of the tent into a dark night that was cold and misty from the recent rain. The shadowy figure of George Hart ran past them, his black poncho flapping as he hurried in the direction of regimental headquarters.

"George," Pilling called. "What's up?"

"Joe Wilson's just made it back to camp. Claims the Colonel's still out there, alive."

A chill swept through Paddy's body. "Come on. If the Colonel's out there, I'm going after him."

"Don't be a..."

"I said I'm going after him."

"You'd better talk with Wilson first. Get some idea of where the Colonel's located."

"All right. You coming?"

"Wait'll we hear what Wilson has to say."

Bedded down beside a warm fire by sympathetic and inquisitive comrades, Joe Wilson, his face blanched by shock, made a struggling effort to look down at the wide tear in his pants leg through which jutted a leg bone, bloody and caked with mud.

Bill Bromley held out a whiskey flask. "Here, take some of this. It will help ease the pain."

Wilson raised himself feebly on one elbow and took a big swallow.

Pilling stepped into the light of the fire and knelt down. "Glad to see you back, Joe. For a while I thought we'd lost another tenor. Anything I can do to help?"

"You can fetch me a sawbones damn quick. This leg's killing me. Bromley, give me some more of that whiskey."

"Sure thing. Here."

Wilson took another deep drink and brushed his lips with a tattered sleeve. He turned his head and looked into Pilling's face. "Since my tenor singing is all that concerns you, you'll be happy to know Lightfoot was still living, last I saw him. He's blown so full of holes he'll probably sound more like a pipe organ than a bass." A shooting pain in his leg made him screw up his face. "If he can learn how to finger them holes, he might be able to pass himself off as a piccolo." A grin brought on by the effects of raw whiskey crossed his face.

"Bully for Wilson," Isaac Tibben chortled. "He's not so bad off."

Paddy, fretting with impatience, dug his fingernails into the palms of his hands and stepped forward. "Where's the Colonel? Hart said you..."

"Well, look who's back, the wandering blacksmith. How you doing, Mulcahy? Hey, Bromley, give me more of that whiskey. I'm beginning to feel good again, real good."

"Look, Joe, I want to know where..."

"Forget it, Mulcahy. You couldn't get through the Reb pickets, for one thing, and you'd never find him out there in the dark if you did get through." Wilson's manner and speech were becoming inebriated.

"All right, Joe," Lieutenant Hibbs counseled softly. "Better lay back and take it easy until our surgeon gets here."

"Lay back, nothing. The news walker wants to know about the Colonel. Right, Mulcahy? Hey, Bromley, feeling's still getting through to one little piggy."

"Here, keep the flask."

"Thanks. Like I was saying, at the bloody end of things, the Colonel wheels the column to the left using himself as the pivot point. Killed and wounded dropping around him like they were just too tired and disgusted to go anywhere. Then the Colonel went down, big hole in his shoulder. Bet you could put your fist in it. Blood gushing from it like it was an open bilge."

"Joe, please..."

"Listen to me. Sergeant Rogers, G Company, puts a tourniquet on the Colonel's shoulder. Starts to help him off the field when the Colonel shouts, 'Leave me. Save yourself and my sword.'"

"Rogers drops the Colonel, takes the sword like he was told, goes rushing after our retiring column like he was stuck in the ass with it."

"Where did Rogers leave the Colonel?"

"Out where the big rocks are."

Hunched shadows moving in the background came forward and heaped more wood on the campfire. Lieutenant Hibbs covered Wilson with another blanket.

Paddy knelt down. "Is he still inside Reb lines?"

"Told you he was."

"Why didn't he try to make it back with you?"

"Couldn't. Too weak to move. Kick in the belly's what did it."

"Kick in the belly? What...?"

Wilson nodded weakly. Secondary shock caused his voice to fall to a whisper. "Happened while Jackson's troops were charging over us. Colonel sat propped against a rock. Young lieutenant left the Reb battle line, ran over to Colonel and demanded his sword." Wilson swallowed hard and wiped his dry mouth. "When Reb learned Colonel's sword was safely out of reach, got real mad. Started kicking the Colonel in the belly, demanding his parole."

"The dirty son of a..."

"Shut up," Lieutenant Hibbs snapped at Paddy. "Go on, Wilson, what followed?"

"Colonel swore like blue blazes. Told Reb lieutenant to go to hell." Wilson coughed spasmodically and took another sip from the flask. "A courier, one of Stuart's, came over, fella named Mosby. Collars lieutenant kicking Wistar and yells for General Stuart. Stuart was standing not far off. Had a big ostrich plume stuck in his hat. He came running."

"Go on. What did Stuart do?"

"Grabbed the lieutenant and hollered, 'What's your name?' 'Lieutenant Hill, Twelfth Georgia. sir,' the Johnny answered. 'Join it immediately,' Stuart says."

"Then what happened?"

Wilson, approaching a state of stupor, rolled his head from side to side. "Courier tells us his name's John Mosby. He fixes the tourniquet on Wistar and puts him in a more comfortable position. Gave us both a drink from his canteen."

Overcome by shock and whiskey, Wilson's head sank to his chest.

"He's passed out," Dave Smith murmured.

Paddy rose from a kneeling position and turned toward Pilling. "You know where those big rocks are?"

"Yes."

"How about showing me the way?"

"In the dark? It would be like trying to find your way around on the ocean at night. Besides, the Rebs hold the ground."

Paddy spun on his heal. "All right, I'll go it alone."

"Now hold on a minute, I didn't say I wouldn't help. Come on, I'll try to show you the way."

There was a sudden movement behind them. "Pardon me, gentlemen."

Both soldiers turned startled eyes on a tall, middle-aged man dressed in civilian clothes. Dignified in appearance, there was a comfortable, homely mien about him.

"Please excuse my intrusion," he apologized, "but I couldn't help overhearing your conversation a moment ago."

"Yes, what can we do for you?" Pilling inquired.

"I, too, am searching for someone," the civilian replied. "I've been told my son lies somewhere in the vicinity of the rocks which you were just discussing with your wounded companion." He nodded toward Wilson. "I beg of you, permit me to join your company. We could search the area together."

The soldiers exchanged puzzled glances.

"What regiment is your son with?" Pilling asked.

"Twentieth Massachusetts."

"That's Colonel Lee's old regiment," Paddy said. "They were at Balls Bluff with us. What is your son's name?"

"Captain Holmes, Oliver Wendell Holmes."

"I know him. He was one of those who volunteered to help fight rear guard at the Bluff. So you're Holmes' father."

A faint smile crossed the drawn lines of anxiety which creased the corners of the world-renowned physician's mouth. "Holmes' father," he repeated with a touch of amusement. "Heretofore my son has basked in the notoriety of my name." He frowned. "Hereafter, God willing, I'll gladly be referred to as the father of Captain Holmes if I can find my boy alive."

"You come with us," Pilling replied tersely. "I'll show you where the Twentieth was positioned just before they broke. They were in the first line under Gorman."

"Thank you. You are most generous and kind."

The famed author raised his coat collar as protection against the night dampness and walked off with his two escorts. "Speaking of generosity," he injected seriously, "I heard a most ungenerous statement that doesn't tie in correctly with the description of affairs as given by your wounded friend back there."

Pilling shot the physician an inquisitive glance. "How's that, sir?"

"While talking with Colonel Palfrey, I was informed by him that when Sedgewick's attack failed, it was the Seventy-first who were the first to break"

"If you'll pardon the language, sir," Pilling retorted angrily, "the Colonel's a bloody liar. I don't know about the rest of our brigade, but we in the Seventy-first sure enough held. Who does Colonel Palfrey think it was that kept the Confederates in check while Sedgewick's first and second lines were fleeing around our flanks to the rear?"

Dr. Holmes smiled. "Forget I mentioned it, Corporal. I'm more than aware that there is a certain selfish shrewdness not absolutely unknown among my New England compatriots when it comes to covering up a defeat of their own by falsely attributing the cause to others."

The three trudged in silence toward the darkened battleground. Scattered groups of medical corpsmen were busy at work gathering the wounded. Carrying litters and dim lanterns, they appeared as flitting fireflies in the eerie darkness. The crisp night air was pungently filled with the musty odor of corn husks and the spicy scent of bruised pennyroyal vines which had been trampled underfoot.

Crumpled bodies, the angry welts of war, covered the ground in increasing numbers as the search party approached the site of the day's heaviest fighting. Now there was a heavy carrion odor of death hanging over the field, stifling and gagging. The wailing siren song of the stricken came from all directions. Screams of pain and crying, low moans and groans, feeble calls for help and the deep guttural rales of the dying. Paddy placed his hands over his ears.

"This is God-awful," he muttered.

"Like a scene from Dante's Inferno," Pilling replied.

Suddenly the high-pitched, nervous voice of a Confederate picket rang out through the black night.

"Halt! Who goes there?"

"Yanks, Johnny," Pilling called out warily. "We're looking for our colonel."

"Y'all unarmed?"

"Yes."

"Advance and be recognized."

The three moved forward cautiously and caught sight of a Confederate soldier peering at them from beneath a slouch hat, the brim of which drooped like the floppy ears of a hunting dog. The picket's musket was level and primed. "Who's that theah civilian y'all got with ya?"

"Doctor Oliver Wendell Holmes," Pilling responded. "He came with us to search for his son."

The picket stroked a pointed chin. "Oliver Wen...say, y'all ain't that feller what wrote the poem, *Old Ironsides?*"

"Yes, son. That was one of my works."

"Wal, now, I do declare." The picket lowered his musket. "Ah don't read or write none, but a preacher man done read it to us. Neavah reckoned I' d meet a famous feller like y' all out heah in this pea patch."

"How's chances of continuing our search, Johnny?" Pilling inquired.

The picket tugged at a large, bony nose. "Wal now, seein' as how it's Mistuh Holmes a lookin' for his boy, cain't 'low as I could refuse none. Y'all go on through. Ah'll fix it with the other boys. Password's 'Corn Harvest.' That'll get y'all by."

"Thanks, Johnny. Which way do we go?"

"Straight ahaid. 'Bout a hundred yards from heah ya'll bump into a Dunker church, or what's left of it. When you get theah give the password and ask fer Courtney Grimm. Tell him Clete Clatterbuck sent ya. Courtney'll see to it y'll git to whar yore goin'. And say, Mistuh Holmes, suh, I declare, do hope your boy ain't hurt none."

Tenderness showed in the doctor's cavernous eyes. "Thank you for that, soldier. And God bless you."

Passing safely through the Confederate picket line, the three searchers crossed the Hagerstown Pike and tread carefully across a road thickly strewn with the ghostly forms of crumpled dead. Upon reaching the shell-pocked ruins of a Dunker church, they were again challenged by a Southern picket. All three gave the password and hastily explained the purpose of their mission.

"Whar is it y'all wanta go?" the second picket inquired.

Pilling quickly described the area which he and his companions sought.

The picket smiled broadly. "Know exactly whar y' all mean," he chortled. "Us Johnnies sorta caught'cha by surprise theah, didn't we, Yank?"

He called over his shoulder to another soldier standing in the shadows. "Jim, mind ma post fer a spell. I'm takin' these heah Yanks on a tour of our rock garden." He took Pilling by the arm and pointed in a northwesterly direction. "Y' all got yourself a mite turned around comin' out heah in the dark, Yank. The field yer lookin' fer is up yonder through them woods. Y' all follow me." He struck a match to a lantern and, cradling a rifle in one arm, led the small search party in the direction to which he had pointed.

"There's those weird rocks," Pilling blurted as the group emerged from a patch of woods. "This is the place."

Dr. Holmes stopped short and stared down at the rigid, silent bodies lying about him in the gloom. Painfully, he scrutinized several of the pale, agony pinched death masks.

"I wish to God my rabid abolitionist and secessionist friends could witness this terrible sight," he said sadly. "Oh what a plague they've loosed upon the soul of this nation by their uncompromising attitudes." He knelt and looked closely at the twisted corpse of a Southerner. "I see no secession in this face," he murmured.

"Ain't a very purty picture at that, is it Mistuh Holmes?" the picket responded. "Just don't seem right somehow, us killin' each othah. 'Specially seein' like as how us boys all grew up in the same country together."

The noted author rose slowly to his feet, his jaw grimly set. He turned toward Tom Pilling. "Would you be kind enough to show me where my son's regiment was located?"

"Yes, sir. Right this way. Be back in a minute, Paddy." Paddy nodded and continued his search among the slain.

Something familiar about one particular corpse lying face down caused him to hasten to the spot. He paused for a second praying that it was all a bad dream. With cold sweatless hands he rolled the lifeless form over on its back and stared sickly into the shot-torn face of Joe Batt. Not more than two feet away was the body of Henry Castor, clenched teeth fixed firmly in the soil by rigor mortis. A cry escaped Paddy 's lips. Trembling with shock, he fell to his knees and covered his face with his hands. Pilling returned and gaped momentarily at the bodies over which Paddy was mourning. Gently he placed a pair of rough hands on his comrade's heaving shoulders.

"You all right?" he asked.

"Bloody hell! No, I'm not all right," Paddy hissed.

Pilling's voice was stern. "Shake it off and let's find the Colonel. Last I saw of him, he was right over there somewhere." He lifted Paddy to his feet. "By the way, Doctor Holmes found his son."

"Alive or...."

"He's alive, but stunned. Should be as good as new in a few months. Got shot in the neck."

Suddenly both men were alerted by a faint call coming from a short distance away.

Pilling stiffened. "Listen. Over there by that big boulder. That's the Colonel's voice. Come on."

Sprinting over the rough ground littered by hundreds of dead, the two soldiers circumvented a huge limestone promontory and drew up short at the presence of Colonel Wistar who faced them in the flickering light of their lantern. His back was supported by a large rock. He made a feeble attempt to rise and fell backward.

"Mulcahy," he mumbled, "thy blessed Irish face is a welcome sight." He rolled his eyes toward Pilling. "Good to see you, Corporal."

"Take it easy, sir. We'll carry you out of here," Pilling replied.

Paddy placed the Colonel's wounded arm around his shoulder. "Did I detect a Quaker expression, sir?"

A wan smile showed through Wistar's matted black beard. "There are no atheists out here, Mulcahy."

Wistar, pallid and tottering, his uniform torn and bloodstained, was gently raised to his feet and carried from the field.

CHAPTER 10

Early the next morning, Paddy retraced his steps to the encampment of the 118th only to find that it had been vacated. Artillerymen were lounging in and about a nearby battery, some engaged in cleaning their guns while others sat idly smoking pipes.

"Can you fellas tell me where the Hundred and Eighteenth went?" he inquired anxiously of one group.

A huge, broad-shouldered cannoneer, exposed to the early morning chill dressed only in pants and a red flannel undershirt, stood up and came forward.

"What's the matter, sonny? Get yourself lost when the shooting started yesterday?"

"Yeah, ramrod, I went up front where the real soldiers were."

"Why you little..."

"Easy, Jack," a companion cautioned. "The sprout meant no harm." He pointed off to the left. "You'll find your regiment over by Burnside's bridge."

"Thanks."

Paddy made his way down a sloping dirt road which led toward the stone bridge and passed over that portion of the field where the battle had been waged on the banks of the Antietam. Abandoned muskets and cartridge boxes still lay everywhere among the unburied dead. He crossed the blood-soaked, bullet-marked bridge and came upon a roadway that ran beneath a steep embankment, the narrow road leading up and downstream. Taking the left branch which wound to the top of the bluff, he came upon a regimental field kitchen where a young cook was busily engaged boiling coffee.

"Any handouts?" Paddy called.

A dark-haired, rosy-faced cook straightened and smiled. "Can't see no harm in it. Come on up. You lost?"

"Not exactly, but I would like to find the Hundred and Eighteenth Pennsylvania."

The cook doled out a canful of coffee. "Hundred and Eighteenth, let's see now, they went by here 'bout two hours ago. Probably find them in the big field just ahead. What part of Pennsylvania you from?"

"Frankford, a little town just north of Philadelphia."

"I'm from Ohio myself." He bent over and raked the fire. "Sure is pretty country around here."

"It is today. What's you name?"

"McKinley. William McKinley."

"Mine's Mulcahy. Say, this coffee's good." He smacked his lips, set the empty coffee tin on a rustic camp table and stood to leave. "Thanks a lot, McKinley. You keep giving handouts like this and they'll make you president someday."

"President? Not me. I think I'll take up cooking for a career. You know, big hotels, places like that."

"Good luck," Paddy called over his shoulder, "and thanks again."

The First Brigade, First Division, Fifth Corps lay in an open plain located on heights overlooking the village of Sharpsburg. From that point sporadic sniper fire pecked away continuously at the corps' position. To avoid stray bullets, Paddy changed his path of approach and moved through a sector occupied by the Twenty-fifth New York, soldiers who began hooting unmercifully when they saw the regimental number on his cap.

"Just get in from Washington?" a rough sergeant called in thick Irish brogue.

A pock-marked corporal lying nearby picked up a stone and hurled it in Paddy's direction. "Your bounty money ain't gonna do you no good here, fancy pants. Beat it."

The sergeant gave Paddy a jolting shove. "You heard what the corporal said. Beat it. We don't want any bounty grubbers 'round us till they've proven they can fight. Git."

Paddy fixed the New Yorkers with a silent glare and moved on down the road a short distance where Captain Donaldson sat crouched behind a stake and rider fence. his eyes glued on the village and the source of sniper fire. He turned and scowled as Paddy approached. "Where have you been, Private Mulcahy?"

"Over with our old regiment. They sure..."

"Listen, I'm sick and tired of the 'old regiment' dung. It's this regiment that demands your time and effort. Who in the hell do you think you are running off without permission? A privileged character?"

"But Frank..."

"Don't Frank me. From now on it's captain, and don't you forget it. You're under nonconfined arrest for leaving a post in the face of the enemy. Report to Sergeant Cassidy. I'll deal with you when matters have been settled."

"All right, it that's the way you want it, CAPTAIN!"

Paddy stalked off in a rage to locate Sergeant Cassidy, where he began a bitter denunciation of the captain. Cassidy listened patiently. Finally, exasperated, he broke in sharply. "Faith, lad, ye didn't leave the good captain with no other choice."

"Aw, go to hell. He's getting to be just like all the other officers, turning 'big military.'"

"That's enough. Ye've said jist enough, Mulkayhee." He grabbed Paddy by the arm. "I can't stand punks what's done wrong then ain't big enough to take their medicine. Just how long do ye think this here company would hold together if everybody and his brother was allowed to go barrel-assin' off like ye did? The captain done absolutely right, ye' ve been in need of woolin' and ye got it." He released the vice grip. "As a veteran, a battle-tested veteran and a friend o' the cap'n's, ye shoulda stuck around and helped him with these straw-feet. Ye just ain't growed up yet, Mulkayhee."

There was a moment of silence before Paddy jammed both hands in his pockets, focused his eyes on the ground and kicked a loose stone. "Yeah, guess maybe you're right at that," he grumbled. "Guess maybe I should've been more help."

Cassidy grinned. "That's the ticket. Now I'll be after seein' what I can do to patch things up with the cap'n."

Throughout the balance of that day, Thursday, the eighteenth of September, there was no action along the bloodied waters of the Antietam and around the village of Sharpsburg. A rooted belief in Lee's preponderance of numbers, a chronic complaint in the army for over a year, had discouraged McClellan and most of his subordinates from resuming the attack. As a result, Lee was permitted to retreat unmolested the night of the eighteenth and what might have been a decisive success was a drawn battle in which the North's chief claim to victory was possession of the field.

On the nineteenth, despite the comforting knowledge that Lee had withdrawn his battered army across the Potomac during the night, matters again assumed a serious aspect for the untested soldiers of the Corn Exchange.

At seven the next morning, the regiment was drawn up in parade and each man furnished with sixty rounds of ammunition and orders concerning a prospective battle. The orders were precise. Every man capable of carrying a musket was ordered to join the ranks, even the musicians, and no assistance would be given the wounded during engagement, a precaution to prevent the men from leaving the ranks until the fighting was over.

Colonel Prevost rode along the regimental line to make sure everyone understood.

The maneuvers of immense columns around them served to reassure the untried levies, who had never been incorporated in a body of troops ready for combat. They held a fixed belief that it would be impossible for an enemy to oppose such a formidable array, and their courage was strengthened. The reality of the situation came when they observed long trains of ambulances and stretcher bearers at the rear, ready for service.

Within an hour, the Corn Exchange Regiment, in company with its brigade, division and corps was marching into Sharpsburg from the east. The village was scarred and blackened from heavy shelling. Gaping holes appeared in most of the red brick buildings and tiny whitewashed clapboard houses. A hilly street, running through the center of town, was lined on both sides by brick sidewalks warped with age. Giant shade trees crowded rustic picket fences. The men turned their heads frequently to see the pathetic charm of the place.

The men in Porter's Fifth Corps, passing through the heart of town, were suddenly confronted by McClellan and his staff, who came galloping up the hilly street. Spontaneously, the soldiers swung their hats in the air and gave their young commander an enthusiastic cheer. They failed to notice a change in the rest of the army. There were few hurrahs from the other corps, and none from Hooker's men, who stood on the Hagerstown Pike and stared icily. The complacent look, which Paddy had seen on McClellan's face two days before while directing battle near the regimental position, had disappeared. Instead, there was a troubled expression, an awareness of the fact that his big opportunity had passed when he let Lee slip through his fingers.

Late that afternoon, the probing finger like columns of McClellan's pursuing forces halted for the night on the north bank of the Potomac. Campfires were lit, meals cooked, bedrolls spread on the ground and pickets staked out.

In the gathering dusk, two silhouetted figures approached the tent in which Captain Donaldson and the regimental surgeon sat conversing in low tones.

Sergeant Cassidy knocked lightly on a tent pole. "Can I see you a minute, Cap'n?"

"Of course. What is it?"

"It's about the Quaker here, sir. He wants to turn in his gun."

"Turn in his gun?" The officer rose quickly from a camp chair and faced the dark-haired private who stood framed in the receding light of the setting sun. "What is this, some kind of joke?"

"No joke, sir. Thee have been informed correctly."

"Don't you think it's a little late for such a decision? You should've thought about that before you signed up." Donaldson stepped forward, searching the unflinching eyes of the soldier who stood before him. "You realize," he said, taken aback, "that tomorrow we'll probably be engaging the rear guard of Lee's retreating army?"

"Yes, sir."

"And you know that orders state specifically that all men capable of bearing arms will do so?"

"Yes, sir, I do. I'll go forward with the regiment tomorrow, and I'll carry a gun if that's what thee want, but I won't fire it."

Dr. Joseph Thomas, a recent graduate from the University of Pennsylvania medical school, stood up and coughed quietly. He was a man in his late twenties, tall, lean as a poker, possessing a dignified. professional bearing. The lower half of his face was completely hidden by a thick bushy beard above which a pair of studious, sensitive eyes peered from deep recesses. Thrusting his thumbs into a green sash worn around his waist, a field-surgeon emblem, he looked at the Quaker. "Are you afraid?"

"No, sir, I'm not afraid. It's just that I can't forget the faces of all the dead we've seen ever since we crossed South Mountain." The Quaker shifted his body slightly. "It's beginning to dawn on me why we've been instructed to obey the commandment, 'Thou shalt not kill.'" He wet his lips. "I can see now that war solves nothing. Marching from one place to another to kill, like wild beasts on the prowl, is all it is. The procedure keeps turning in the same never-ending cycle.

How can killing solve anything?"

The surgeon stroked his beard. "Well, from a practical standpoint," he replied, with a subtle trace of humor in his voice, "it does complement old age and the ravages of disease. I'd say it helps to prevent over- population, or am I ahead of my time?"

"Of course there's killing," Captain Donaldson cut in brusquely. He stared impatiently at the Quaker. "Why did you join the army? Think it was a traveling debating society?" He groaned and shrugged his shoulders. "What's the use. Having been raised among them, I know how stubborn these Philadelphia Quakers can be when their mind's made up."

"Maybe the chaplain could be of some help," Doctor Thomas suggested.

"The chaplain? Our chaplain? You must be joking. Old 'Blue Nose' is nothing more than a self-ordained shouting evangelist who's run by rum, hypocrisy and unbridled emotion." Donaldson took a cigar out of his pocket, bit the end off and spit it on the ground. "Most of those buggers serve in the field so they can pick the pockets of the dead. Look at those three they just court marshaled ...."

Sergeant Cassidy cleared his throat for attention. "Beggin' yer pardon again, sir, but that brings up another small matter that needs discussing. The chaplain's packin' up to leave."

"Leave? Well it's about time. Why?"

"Well, sir, 'bout an hour ago, while the boys was settin' up camp, a couple of 'em cut down a tree near the chaplain's tent." He paused to rub a hand across his mouth. "It seems, sir, that when the tree fell, it crashed right through ol' Blue nose's. . .beggin' yer pardon sir, the chaplain's tent. It ruined the canvas, sir, busted all his baggage and nearly stove his head in. Last I seen of him he was runnin' off to say goodbye to the Colonel."

The officers exchanged amused glances.

"Must've been a pretty big tree," Donaldson responded.

"Yes, sir, it was all o' that, sir, a big one."

Donaldson studied his fingernails for a moment, then glanced up with a glint of encouragement in his eyes. "Would you say the incident was an accident, Sergeant?"

"Well now, it's hard for me to say, sir. I think I saw Willie McCool and Tibben give it a sorta...well, sir, a kinda push toward the chaplain's tent."

"Kind of push? Could it have been an accidental kind of push?"

"Oh, it could've been that, sir. Those sweet lads wouldn't do anything on purpose. Ye might go so far as to be callin' it an act of God, sir." A broad grin split Cassidy's face.

"Over and done with," Donaldson replied. "Now to get back to the problem at hand." He turned toward the Quaker. "The orders given to me are plain enough. Everybody goes forward with a rifle tomorrow."

"Yes, sir," the Quaker replied impassively.

Donaldson removed his cap and scratched his head. "Can't see troubling regimental headquarters over it at this late hour. They've got troubles enough of their own." He looked down at the ground for a moment then focused his attention on Thomas. "Doc, that bad hand you were telling me about, do you suppose you'll be needing assistance in case we tie into a scrap tomorrow?"

"Bad hand? Wha...oh, that one." The surgeon gazed ruefully at an apparently normal appendage. "Yes, it will handicap me. I could use someone to tie tourniquets and sutures for me."

"Good. It's settled then. Walton, you will act as Doc Thomas's assistant in the field. My orders."

"Yes, sir." The Quaker saluted and walked into the darkness with Sergeant Cassidy.

The twentieth of September dawned bright and clear. Dew, like a myriad of sparkling jewels, blanketed the ground, glistening on grass and leaf. The Federal camps bustled with activity as soldiers prepared for the day. In the bivouac of the 118th, an early breakfast was interrupted by orders to move to the riverbank at once with Barnes' brigade, and by nine o'clock the troops were crossing at Blackford's Ford.

Awaiting his company's turn to ford the river, Paddy sat down on a spongy bank of the Chesapeake and Ohio Canal, which closely followed the shoreline on the Maryland side of the Potomac. Removing shoes and stockings, he tied them securely about his neck so they would remain dry during the crossing. From midstream came the sound of shouting and lighthearted bantering as the troops splashed through knee-deep water where it spilled over the breast of an old mill dam. Roars of laughter greeted those who stumbled and fell headlong into the water.

The dam's breast, about ten feet wide, had obviously been long neglected. Many of its moss-covered planks had rotted away or been removed, and water rushed through the numerous crevices, trickling down the slippery outer face clothed in a coat of green slime. Upstream from the dam stood three desolate-looking stone piers marking the site of a bridge which had formerly spanned the Potomac at that point, the bridge having been part of a roadway leading to Shepherdstown and Martinsburg located across the river in West Virginia.

The Quaker approached Paddy from behind. "A penny for thy thoughts, friend."

"Huh? Oh hi, John. I was just daydreaming."

"About what?"

"Home, the Pennypack, the Neshaminy, Washington Crossing. Never see water or a millrace that I don't think back on the fun we used to have in Bucks county. Remember?"

"Sure do. Seems like centuries ago, doesn't it?"

"It sure does. Hey, where's your rifle?"

"I gave it back."

"Gave it back?"

"That's what I said. I've seen too much. I can't kill anybody."

A burst of jeering cropped up at their rear, causing both men to look around sharply.

"Chust lizzen to der Qvaker vunst," Schneider mocked loudly. "He's given der gun back yet." He peered through his thick glasses and sniffed nervously, twitching his nose. "So vat is your plan, Qvaker? Is you gonna blind the Rebs mit der inner light?"

"Go climb a tree, you Dutch ape," Paddy snapped.

"Ignore him, friend. Name calling's for girls. Besides, it'll only lead to trouble."

"Trouble. That's what that no-good German son of a bitch has been looking for. You Quakers need some Irish fighting blood pumped into your veins. Only way to teach a German respect and courtesy is to knock his square head in, so Gilmour says."

"I ' m sure thee would gain a lot of respect that way, or would thee? Listen, stay out of trouble. I'll see thee later. I've got to join Doc Thomas, he's about ready to cross."

The soldiers of H Company, marched four abreast, crossed over the dam and arrived as a unit on West Virginia soil, that part of the state which had separated from the seceded state to stay in the Union. Near the river's edge, a rapid current flowed through a twenty-foot space which had been left open for a fish-way.

"Man-O-Day, look at those trout," McCool sputtered. "Anybody got a fishing pole they want to lend? I'll go divies on the catch."

"Mulcahy's got hooks and a line in his knapsack," Tibben replied gaily. "I saw them when he was packing up. Ask him for a lend."

"Hey, Paddy," McCool called, "how's about..."

"Draw in yer net, Simon Peter," Cassidy cut in. "Get a move on. This ain't no time to be plannin' a fish fry."

"Aw, Sarg."

"I said move."

Up ahead, Paddy was absorbed in something far more disturbing. He stood in the dusty roadway and gazed at a precipitous, almost perpendicular bluff strewn with boulders and tangled underbrush and stunted trees.

Luke Jobson shook him by the shoulder. "Hey, Mulcahy, what's the matter? You look like you just saw a ghost."

Paddy mopped perspiration from his forehead. "Could be that I have," he mumbled. "Sure as hell hope not."

Those already across were marched to a spot about a hundred yards from the ford and brought to a halt in the road. Off to one side, the inquisitive levies could see a ravine that led to tableland above. They noticed that the pathway was obstructed and partially concealed by thick underbrush. Two tumble-down gateposts marked the entrance and indicated it to be an abandoned private lane. Built into the treacherous-looking glen were several lime kilns, long fallen into disuse. The similarity of surroundings-high bluffs in front and a wide river in the rear, caused Paddy to pale and recall with pain the disaster at Balls Bluff of nearly a year ago.

"Looks like the place where we came in, doesn' t it?" a voice said at his shoulder. He turned around and saw both Captain Donaldson and Lieutenant Batchelder staring up at the terrain with equal foreboding.

"Too much so," Paddy answered. He leaned heavily on his rifle. "Say, Captain, about what happened the other day, I'd like..."

The officer cut him off. "I haven't forgotten, Mulcahy. Don't think I have."

"Aw, Fran...I mean, Captain, I said I'm..."

A twinkle appeared in Donaldson's eyes. "Give me a good account of yourself today and I'll let you off the hook. Agreed?"

"Agreed."

"Here comes our last company across," Lieutenant Batcholder interjected. He shaded his eyes against the sun and suddenly stiffened. "Hey, do you fellas see what I see, or are my eyes deceiving me?"

His companions turned quickly. Behind a screen formed by men of Company K, who were at that moment filing from the dam breast, they caught sight of a heavy column of troops marching up the river road from the south and retreating across the Potomac into Maryland.

"What do you make of it, Frank?" Batchelder asked.

"Don't know. We'll find out soon, though. Here comes Prevost and Barnes to investigate. Let's go down and see what's up."

"Think we oughta?" Paddy retorted with a quiver in his voice. "After all, Captain, who knows, we might get court martialed for leavin' a post in the face of an enemy."

"Go to hell, Mulcahy!"

"I take it then, it's safe for me to join you?"

"Yeah, come along news-walker," Batchelder grinned.

General Barnes, the precise but personable brigade commander, was bending over his saddle horn and pointing with curiosity. "What men are these?" he called to the unexplained troops.

"Sykes's brigade of regulars, sir," a man in the column answered.

Mounted on a horse next to Barnes, Colonel Prevost showed visible signs of being upset by the retrograde movement. He turned toward the general in alarm. "If this is Sykes's brigade, then what in thunder are we doing over on this side of the river?"

"That's what's puzzling me," Barnes replied. "Movement of the brigade over here was with the understanding I was to cooperate with Sykes generally in reconnaissance."

"Then why are they returning to Maryland?"

"I won't know the answer to that until I've had a talk with Sykes. We'll wait here till he shows up."

Just then a comic-looking, oversized soldier of Company K, his pants rolled to the knees, jumped the fish-way with an awkward leap and shouted at the retreating column of troops, "Seen any Rebs?"

"Nary a one, sonny," a bearded, ratty regular responded. "They're as scarce as hen's teeth over here."

"That's right," chimed in another. "All you bounty volunteers gotta do is claim the soil of West Virginia for yourselves."

The hard-bitten regulars roared coarsely as they continued crossing the river.

Donaldson watched the antics of the oversized soldier with amusement. "Isn't he the one Lem Crocker fondly refers to as 'Bucket-head'?"

"That's the one. Name's Peter Haggarty." Lieutenant Batchelder's blue eyes sparkled. "His head's so big the quartermaster couldn't find a cap large enough to fit. You can always spot him by the way he wears the peak of his kepi on the back of his head like a dunce cap. Crocker says he's a good soldier. Doesn't know what fear is, mainly because he has no real knowledge of it."

Donaldson chuckled. "No wonder he and Crocker hit it off so well. They're both cut from the same cloth. Remember Lem at the Eutaw House in Baltimore? Blind as a bat from drinking and belligerent as a-"

"Remember? How can I ever forget?" Batchelder retorted. "Just when I had that red-headed chambermaid ready for the mattress, the drunken clod comes in and breaks down the door to my room. He must be powerful. Lifted the door right off its hinges. Then he just stood there pointing at us like a looney and laughing like hell."

"That was some night," Donaldson replied with a grin. "And to think it's been only three weeks ago. Seems more like three...." He interrupted himself to observe a mounted staff officer who came galloping up the road from the south.

The horseman reined in a lathered mount and halted beside General Barnes. "The enemy's approaching in force, sir. General Sykes wishes you to...."

The untried, untrained soldiers standing within earshot glanced up nervously at the ominous tidings. The distressing sight of retreating regulars helped increase their tension.

Having received his orders, Barnes stiffened and thrust his boots firmly forward in the stirrups. "Prevost, can you get your regiment on top of this cliff?"

"I can try."

"Good. Do so immediately."

Within a matter of seconds the air was filled with a swirling din of shouted commands, staccato bugle calls, the jingling sound of metal accouterments and the nervous comments of troops facing the prospect of battle.

Climbing and crawling, clawing and scratching, the Philadelphia Corn Exchange made its way slowly up the steep ravine to the top of the bluff, from where they had a commanding view of the country around them. A mile or so distant, the fields changed to forest where a wide belt of timber skirted open land. Several spires rising above the sleepy hamlet of Shepherdstown could be seen peeping above trees far to the left.

The report of Confederates approaching in force met with sudden confirmation as they came into sight. The musket barrels of an entire Rebel division, massed in battalion columns, gleamed in the sunlight at the fringe of distant timber. Off to the right, not a half mile away, a whole Confederate brigade came sweeping down with steady tread. Well in advance of their main line, the heads of skirmishers ducked and darted above tall grass and corn.

Colonel Prevost rose in his stirrups. "Come on, soldier," he roared at the color bearer. "Get that flag forward on the double."

Impatient at the delay, he leaned out and spanked the color bearer's backside with the flat of his sword, "I said get forward," he roared. "The rest of you. On my right by file into line. Crocker, deploy your men as skirmishers and move out."

'Bucket-head' Haggarty took a moment to give his ill-fitted kepi an angry pitch in the air and shake a fist at the regulars who were seeking haven across the river below. "C'mon back you dirty lyin' bastards," he yelled. "C'mon back and lend us a hand."

Elsewhere on the forming line, Willie McCool shuddered and huddled close to Paddy's shoulder.

"Holy Mother," he whimpered. "I'm gettin' scared, real scared. Why are we up here alone? Where's the rest of the brigade?"

"Beats me," Paddy muttered. He looked toward the soldier on the other side of him.

"How you doing, Tibben?"

Tibben made a valiant effort to reply, but words failed him.

Sergeant Cassidy, inspecting the line, stopped and bent down on one knee. He tightened a chin strap. "You there, Mulkayhee. Can I be dependin' on ye to show these youngsters how to handle the ropes?"

"Like they were my very own," Paddy replied.

"Don't worry about us Frankford boys, Sarg," Dick Allen cut in as he chewed idly on the end of a small twig. "A little action will palliate our overwrought nerves."

Cassidy spat. "Yer a cool operator, Allen. Faith'n I hope ye live long 'nough to git back to yer doctorin' studies. Ye can be workin' on me anytime." He stood erect and turned toward Hallowell and Kimball. "Sure'n how would the old folks be takin' matters? Can I be gettin' ye a rockin' chair fer more comfort?"

"Go to hell," Jake Hallowell snapped tersely as he apprehensively scanned the advancing Confederate lines.

Hallowell's sour, disgruntled expression instantly afforded a source of relief and comfort to the jittery young soldiers around him. It was a part of home, a commonplace expression reminding them of peaceful days when they had nothing more important to do than torment him in his hardware store.

"Ol' Jake looks like he'd just got rooked on a bad business deal," George Dyer murmured.

Forced laughter greeted Dyer's wry comment.

Down on the road at the base of the cliff, Lieutenant Davis, acting assistant adjutant general of the brigade, was hurrying on his way to withdraw the regiments especially assigned to him. Seeing that the 118th was making no move to withdraw, but was actually engaging the enemy, he called up the ravine to Lieutenant Kelly. "Hey, there, Kelly. Tell Colonel Prevost General Barnes directs he withdraw the Corn Exchange at once.

"You just watch my dust," Kelly's voice echoed down the ravine. He turned and ran to where Colonel Prevost was busy organizing the regimental line in front of center and repeated the order from General Barnes.

The Colonel's countenance wrinkled as if he had swallowed lemon juice. "From where did you say you heard this?" he inquired tartly.

"From Lieutenant Davis, sir, of General Barnes's staff."

"I don't receive orders that way," Prevost shot back sharply. "If General Barnes has any orders to give me, let his aide come to me in the accepted manner. Return to your post."

Kelly turned white. "Yes, sir."

The Colonel directed his attention once more to the Virginian standing next to him. "Now then, Lieutenant White, what troops are we facing and what do you make of their numbers?"

The handsome Southerner who had renounced his section's cause to stand for the Union, took another look through his field glasses and scanned the Confederate battle flags approaching. "'Pears to be A. P. Hill's division of Jackson's Corps," he drawled from the corner of his mouth. "That'd constitute 'bout six brigades totaling roughly seventy-five hundred men, suh." He lowered his glasses.

"Are you certain? Can you make out the various regimental commands by their flags?"

"Yes, suh."

'Then give them to me, Lieutenant."

The Southerner raised field glasses to his eyes once again and turned them slowly on the advancing lines. 'Theah's the Seventh, Eighteenth, Twenty-eighth… uh . . . Thirty-third. . . uh, Thirty-eighth North Carolina Regiments all manning their center, suh. South Carolina First Rifles and the Twelfth, Thirteenth and Fourteenth South Carolina moving in from the left flank."

Listening attentively to the enemy's roll call as though it were a death knell, Paddy inched forward to catch Lieutenant White's words.

"Theah's three brigades of Ewell's Division comin' in from the right flank, suh. That's the Fortieth, Forty-seventh, Fifty-fifth and…uh…the Twenty-second Virginia."

Men close enough to overhear were trying to pick up the scene through squinted eyes.

'The Fifth Alabama battalion, First, Seventh and Fourteenth Tennessee…." The engaged officer continued sounding off the Confederate's roll call as if reciting the beatitudes.

"They'll mop us up," Tibben said weakly. "Oh, my God, I've pissed my pants! Why doesn't the Colonel get us out of here like he was told?"

"Shut up," Paddy snapped.

"…and the Fourteenth, Nineteenth, Forty-fifth and Forty-ninth Georgia, suh." Lieutenant White removed the binoculars from his sunburned face. "That's it, suh. All told, twenty-five regiments and two battalions are advancing on us." He cleared his throat. "If I might be presumptuous enough to suggest, suh, we'd best get up and git."

"Not until I've been properly ordered to do so," Prevost retorted. "Are the rest of our troops still retreating across the river?"

"I'll check with Lieutenant Kelly immediately, suh."

Paddy, who had heard enough, sprang to his feet and raced to the side of Captain Donaldson. "For God's sake!" he blurted breathlessly, "you know Prevost.

Tell him we have to pull out of here. I don't want to go through another Balls Bluff."

Donaldson spat fiercely. "I can't tell him anything, you know that."

"You have to. Baker was a clag horn, but this colonel's a stubborn jack ass. The Bluff will look like a tea party compared to this."

"Ours is not to reason why," Donaldson replied.

Paddy slammed a fist on the ground. "What a mother crucifyin' army. One regiment, in the field twenty days. Never fired a gun. And Prevost wants to stack us up against what looks like the whole bloody Confederate Army. He's off his nut, I tell you."

"Take it easy, Mulcahy. At Gaines Mills, we had only forty-nine regiments against their one hundred and twenty-four and we still beat holy hell out of them."

Paddy ground his teeth and scowled. "Let's talk about the present. There's only seven hundred and fifty of us to their seven thousand six hundred. Once, just once, I'd like to meet the Rebs on even terms. Sure we've got as many troops as they do. More. But when a fight develops we're always left holding the short end of the stick. And I mean short. . .What stinking, lousy leadership."

"Cut it. Dig in. Here they come," Donaldson said abruptly.

Driving Captain's Crocker's skirmishers before them as chaff before the wind, the Confederate lines came bearing down on the lone regiment perched precariously at the top of the cliff. A shrieking wild Rebel yell split the air followed instantly by a rain of lead that zipped overhead like a swarm of angry bees. A second volley sent bullets tearing through the regimental line with appalling effect.

With vengeful irony the withering fire cut down Lieutenant Rudhall White in its scorching blast. The Southerner toppled dead beneath the flag which he had chosen to defend rather than assail. Captain Ricketts, exhibiting deep concern and grief, rushed instantly forward to his subaltern's aid. Onlooking men unused to such a sight saw the body of the captain fly suddenly in the air like a mortally wounded bird, wings outstretched, and fall lifeless.

With a grim gaze fixed on the charging foe, Paddy sighted his musket and squeezed the trigger with frightening results. Before his startled eyes the firing pin came down on the cap, but instead of exploding a charge the nipple snapped off and fell harmlessly into the dirt. The unnerving and shocking experience was repeating itself all along the embattled line in alarming proportions. One out of every two muskets in the regiment was proving to be defective.

Many of the men, failing to notice the defect in the initial excitement, kept ramming cartridge after cartridge into the barrels in the belief that each had been discharged until at last their pieces were filled to the muzzle. Cap after cap was exploded in vain attempts to fire. Seized by panic after several futile tries, instead of taking up abandoned guns from the dead, the soldiers with pieces foundered and ramrods jammed, crowded about the field officers and anxiously inquired what they should do.

Angry and disgusted, Paddy swore loudly and tossed his faulty English Enfield aside as he wrenched another from the frozen grip of a dead man.

Dick Allen, calm and business-like, sat on the ground and in the manner of a surgeon removing a splinter, picked away at the defective nipple to clear the vent.

Hallowell and Kimball gathered stones and began setting their muskets off ingeniously, pounding the hammers down with rocks. Others with faulty guns, seeing the efficiency of this action, quickly adopted the strange procedure.

On came the enemy in thousands, Confederate battle flags flapping in their faces, and everywhere roars and yells, shrieks and cheers all blended into one chaotic din. The toll of death and injury increased fearfully as the beleaguered men of the Corn Exchange received their baptism with what amounted to olive branches in their hands. Valiantly they battled against the insurmountable odds, martyrs' fingernails fighting off the claws of lions.

The Quaker, his uniform soaked with blood from the wounded, busily engaged himself tying tourniquets and removing the injured to safety.

"Qvaker, help me," Schneider called frantically. Blood gushed from gaping wounds in both of his legs. "Help me. Please, Qvaker."

The Quaker darted to the side of his stricken tormentor and knelt down on both knees. He looked compassionately into the Dutchman's pleading.face. The lenses of Schneider's spectacles were splintered, his fright-filled eyes barely visible behind the cobweb of shattered glass. "Here, friend Schneider, drink this whiskey while I try to stop thy bleeding."

Schneider, blatantly opposed to and scornful of all who imbibed the sinful brew, drank readily of the stimulant handed to him. "Get me out of here, Qvaker. Och, Gott in Himmel, get me avay at vunst."

The Quaker paused to see if the bleeding had been checked in Schneider's legs, then pulled some rope from a pocket. "Cross thy wrists friend, while I bind them." He hastily looped and tied a rope into place. "Now, slip thy arms over my head." Straddling the Dutchman's prostrate body, he raised himself on hands and knees and slowly dragged his burden from the line of fire. Reaching the sheltered ravine, he hoisted the wounded man across his shoulders and carried him down a path which led to the roadway.

Meanwhile, the charging Confederates had come to within fifty yards of the 118th's sorely pressed front, the hot fire at such close range increasing casualties on both sides with frightful fatality. Off in another direction, a calamitous development was rapidly taking shape. Confederate forces driving down from the north succeeded in crossing the ravine and were threatening to overrun the Corn Exchange's right flank, thus cutting off the path of retreat.

Under the immediate supervision of Colonel Prevost, the two right companies of the regiment promptly changed direction by the right flank and gallantly stemmed the enemy's onslaught. Of serious consequence, however, this movement on the right was mistaken by the center companies for a withdrawal, inducing them to break temporarily, and with colors to the fore, the center companies began moving in disorder to the rear.

Catching the disordered retirement in time, Colonel Prevost promptly checked it. Heroically seizing the standard from the hands of a color sergeant, he waved the flag defiantly and brought the center back into the conflict, completely restoring alignment. Still waving the flag, he was suddenly sent spinning to the ground, a musket ball in his shoulder. Disregarding standing orders to ignore the wounded, Frances Daley of E Company immediately dropped his musket and hastily bore the Colonel from the field and down to safety.

General Barnes was riding along the congested roadway. In the act of following up his orders for all troops to retire, he suddenly encountered the pair. Stunned by the sight of Prevost's gory form, the brigadier brought his horse to a rearing halt and stared.

"Good God, man, what's happened? Where is your regiment?"

"Fighting desperately on top of the hill where you placed it," Prevost answered weakly.

The general turned livid. "I sent you orders to retire
in good order."

"I never received them, sir, and I'm sorry I'm too seriously wounded to take them off, they are suffering dreadfully."

"I will do so myself," Barnes snapped. "You there, Major," he called to a nearby officer. "Clear you troops from this roadway. Get them across the river on the double and order all batteries to stand by to cover a withdrawal of the Hundred and Eighteenth."

The general quickly dismounted, unsheathed his sword and dashed up the ravine.

Corporal Daley cast an anxious, sidelong look at the Quaker who had just placed Schneider on a stretcher. "You going back up there?" he asked in a parched voice.

His face a dusty mask, the Quaker bent down and picked up a fallen rifle. With an impassive expression, he gave it a hurried examination. "Like it says, there's a time for peace and a time for war. Coming, friend?"

Daley nervously mopped his brow with a bloody sleeve and nodded. "I'm with you. Let's go."

On top of the bluff, Lieutenant Colonel Gwyn had assumed command of the regiment and in lightning response to General Barnes's frantic orders, strove to break off engagement and retire the troops to safety.

Born in Londonderry, Ireland, Gwyn was by nature impulsive and sometimes vengeful, possessing the strong, exacting likes and dislikes characteristic of his race. Young, handsome and an accomplished officer, he was also bold and aggressive as a leader. His traits had already won him many warm friends and at the same time made bitter enemies.

The Quaker and Daley scrambled over the crest of the cliff and, running a zigzag course stoop shouldered, flung themselves into the regimental battle line and opened fire on the enemy.

"Fix bayonets." Colonel Gwyn shouted.

The air rang with the clang of heavy metal knives slammed into place. The order to retire, which had been hoped for, came at last. Drowned out at first by the battle's roar, the Colonel's shrill voice rose again like a stricken child calling above the sound of pounding surf. The welcome order, passed on by Adjutant James Perot, was hurriedly repeated along the line.

Brave soldiers, who for more than half an hour had fought manfully against frightful odds, broke in wild confusion and ran for safety. Unable to keep pace with the rapidly retiring soldiers because of a crippling injury sustained early in his life, Major Perot remained on the field. True to the instincts of genuine courage, he stood erect and faced the foe with a pistol resting on his left forearm. He emptied it rapidly.

Paddy checked his flight long enough to cast a glance at this singular exhibition of raw courage. He saw a bloodstained soldier kneeling at the adjutant's side, the resolute figure calmly loading and firing at will.

Quickly reversing course, Paddy bucked the fleeing tide and raced to the spot.

"Pull boot, John! Don't try'n be a hero. Listen to me. I tried it once."

"Do as Mulkayhee says!" Cassidy screamed from nearby. One of his arms was bloody and limp. "Me and the wounded will hold 'em off. Ye youngsters run for cover. Beat it!"

Major Perot, a usually genial thirty-seven-year-old Quaker graduate of Haverford College, turned and glowered. "Thee heard the sergeant. That was an order. Both of ye, out of here!"

"Yes, sir."

The two comrades turned and darted for the ravine down which the greater part of the regiment had already dashed. Since the march up, a tree had fallen across the path and was now obstructing the retreat. Over and under it the thoroughly demoralized men jostled and pushed each other. The enemy reached the crest of the bluff and poured down sheets of fire. The slaughter was fearful. Men were shot as they climbed over the tree, their bodies, suspended from the branches, plainly visible from the other side of the river.

Others, purposely avoiding the death-trap ravine, were driven headlong over the bluff, many seriously injured or killed outright. Among those was Captain Courtney O'Callaghan, badly disabled, never again fit for active field service.

An abandoned mill standing on the ford road at the base of the cliff commanded the ford and dam breast. As soon as the last of the fugitives disappeared from the bluff, the Confederates rushed for the building and from the doors, windows and roof, poured a relentless fire on the blue-coated refugees fleeing across the river. Observing the telling effect of enemy marksmanship on those who crossed, the bulk remained huddled together, crowding each other in the bridge arches at the base of the bluff. A few, hoping to escape the fatal bullets, took to deeper water and crossed where the Potomac was of sufficient depth to cover them with only their heads exposed.

In the midst of rout and confusion, the regimental colors were borne to the water's edge near the dam breast, but at the sight of the terrible fatality attending those preceding him, the bearer paled and hesitated to cross.

Major Herring, realizing the least delay would place the national standard in hopeless jeopardy, seized the staff and put it in the hands of Bill Hummell of D Company. Ordering him into the water, the major covered Hummell's body with his own. With the flag unfurled and waving defiantly in the face of the enemy, the two men successfully made the Maryland shore.

Peter Haggarty, fully incensed by the rout, rashly leaped on a stump and shook his fist at the advancing Rebels and did about every other foolish thing he could think of.

" Bucket-head! Take cover!" Captain Crocker yelled, "This ain't no Irish wedding! Get down!"

Haggarty grinned apishly. "Sure'n there ain't a Rebel bullet what's made that'll touch me at all, Cap'n. Not at all."

A second later he emitted a howl that for volume and intensity equaled the mourning for his ancestors from the days of Brian Boroihme. The foolhardy descendant of the Haggartys bent over painfully, skipping, dancing and limping around as if he'd been kicked by a mule. Blood spurted from one thigh.

"Farewell, Haggarty," Lem Crocker commented cruelly. "Your big head'll never be seen in this regiment again."

From a cleft in the bluff, the Quaker surveyed the slippery, half-submerged dam breast now thickly covered with the dead, wounded and dying. He turned to Paddy.

"Have thee any suggestions, friend?"

"You're damned well informed I have. Into the water, quick! If we can make the first bridge pier out there, we can hedgehop from one to the other."

"Nothing ventured, nothing gained. Let's go." Both soldiers raced to the water's edge, took shallow surface dives and, swimming submerged for as long as their lungs would allow, came up and swam to safety behind the first of the stone pilings. A blanketing hail of enemy rifle fire pinned them close. The slap of lead bullets on the water's surface sounded like the bubbling of boiling sap.

The Quaker breathed heavily. "Well, so far so..."

His words were drowned by a thunderous roar from a Federal battery which opened up from the Maryland shore. With fuses cut far too short, the artillery was sending deadly missiles whistling into the disorganized masses of their own troops fleeing across the river.

Aghast, Paddy saw a soldier nearby lift the head of a friend from the water, look heartbroken at the blank staring face and let it drop back into the river.

"Dumb stupid bastards," he bellowed. "Can't they see what they're doing? They're gonna butcher us all."

The Quaker swept a mat of wet hair from his eyes. Helpless and fearful, he gaped as shell after shell came roaring and crashing into the stone arches of the old bridge piers where cringing groups of Union soldiers crowded for cover.

A cry and wail of horror, heard plainly above the din of battle, welled from those on the West Virginia shore who were still looking for a way to escape across the river. Frantically waving handkerchiefs tied to ramrods, they endeavored to signal the gunner to desist, but to no avail. The fatal error continued unrectified. Many on the crowded bank, hoping for better treatment, turned with their white insignia toward the enemy and, ascending the hill, surrendered.

The Federal artillery continued all the while to blast away. In due course of time, Captain B. F. Fisher and Lieutenant L. R. Fortescue, of the signal corps, with the aid of their telescopes finally detected the error and took immediate steps to correct it. Using longer fuses, the Union batteries brought their aim on the intended target.

Berdan's sharpshooters appeared on the Maryland shore and deployed hurriedly in the bed of the canal. They called loudly to those still exposed to seek what cover they could, then opened vigorously with unerring rifle fire. The West Virginia shore was soon cleared of Confederates.

"Now's the time," Paddy screeched. "Make a break for it."

Instantly there was a thrashing of water as those around him began to swim feverishly for shore, pulling themselves to safety beneath the blazing barrels of Berdan's sharpshooters. Flinging themselves face down on the wet bank, they lay still and panting.

A warning of caution coming from the sharpshooters caused the men to lift their heads and turn to see the reason. They could not believe what they saw.

They held their breaths as they watched "Old Man" Madison of H Company attempt to cross the dam in an upright position. Past the prime of life but still wiry and full of energy, he scoffed with reckless abandon at their entreaties to seek cover. His attitude was quickly discerned by the enemy, who proceeded to deal with him. By the time he reached shore, five balls had passed through his body.

Near the spot where Paddy and the Quaker lay, the old man had turned sideways to glance resentfully at his persecutors when a final shot entered his cheek and passed through both jaws between his tongue and the roof of his mouth. Maddened to a towering rage, he vented his anger in a frightful howl. Sputtering and spitting blood, he faced squarely about, gave his tormentors a final shot and slumped to the ground.

"Drag Madison out of here!" Paddy shouted at the Quaker. "I gotta go back."

"Go back? Have thy senses left thee?"

"No. It's Tibben." Paddy pointed toward midstream. Joe Tibbens doubled up and leaning against one of the bridge pilings, was clutching at his side and crying in anguish.

"I gotta bring him in," Paddy cried. "His brother'd never forgive me if I didn't."

Overhearing the remark, a sharpshooter called out encouragement. "Go to it boy. Try it. We'll cover you like a blanket."

Paddy dove into the water.

"No greater love hath man...." the Quaker murmured as he watched with bated breath.

Working before the anxious eyes of a gathering crowd, Paddy reached Tibben's body and lifted it on his shoulder. Bearing him to shore, he deposited him on the riverbank amid shouts of admiration. Captain Donaldson, coming up from behind, clapped him on both shoulders. "Good work, Mulcahy. I'll see you get a promotion for this."

"A promotion?" A grin cut off Paddy's response. "All I want to know is, does this get me off your black list?"

A broad smile wreathed the captain's face. "It sure does. All right, men," he ordered, "get the wounded up to the ambulances. Mulcahy, you take charge."

Peter Haggarty, who had had a musket ball removed from his leg by Doctor Thomas, looked up from a stretcher as Paddy formed the men of Company H near the ambulance train.

"Just heard what you done, Mulcahy," he called feebly. "Nice..."

He was interrupted by Doctor Thomas. "Here. Stop exerting yourself, Bucket-head. Take this quinine."

Haggarty took the pill handed to him and rolled it curiously between his fingers. "Hey, Doc, what do I do with this? Put it in the hole?"

"No...oh, go to hell."

Slowly the regiment gathered itself as remnants of companies fell in on the color line for roll call; friend sought for friend with anxious, searching glances.

Looking like miners from an underground disaster, the survivors lined themselves up. A short distance away, they could see comrades being loaded into ambulances, the floorboards leaking blood in a steady stream.

Propped up in the rear of one wagon was Willie McCool. He waved an injured arm for everyone to see.

"Hey, you fellas," he called, "want a free ride home in a meat wagon?"

Lying next to McCool, Dick Allen forced a grin and pointed to a shattered leg. "Here's my furlough," he said weakly, responding to a question from his tent mate, Joe Byram. He winced in pain as the wagon began moving.

Posted on a rise of high ground that overlooked the bloodied Potomac ford, the rest of the First Brigade fell into solid ranks and watched in silence as their baptized sister regiment organized below. Experienced soldiers, jealous of hard-earned glories, had been loathe to receive the inexperienced newcomers with any kind of hearty welcome until their mettle had been tested. Favorably impressed, the men who boasted fifteen hundred battle casualties sustained in the seven days of fighting on the Peninsula and at Bull Run were now ready to extend their plaudits and the hand of fellowship. Waiting until the begrimed Philadelphians had marched into their presence, the brigade of veterans suddenly removed their caps to a man. Placing them on the tips of their bayonets and raising their rifles high, they burst forth into wild cheering which made the welkin ring. The Corn Exchange was being heralded among the glorious army coterie known as a "fighting regiment," their recent daring exhibition having quenched any criticism or doubt.

The men of the Corn Exchange, basking in the light of this new-found favor, were interrupted in their pleasure by a short announcement from Lieutenant Colonel Gwyn.

"Men, you have performed admirably today. My good friend, Colonel Johnson, has informed me that the boys of his Twenty-fifth New York wish to extend their feeling toward you by sharing their whiskey rations."

An enthusiastic shout greeted the announcement.

"Furthermore," the Colonel continued after calling for silence, "to compensate for your suffering and hardship, General Barnes has advised me that as a personal gift from him, you are granted two extra barrels of whiskey."

"Hot damn, reverend!" Luke Jobson shouted in jubilation. "Come on Paddy, let's go drain the barrel."

"Don't know whether I want to drink with those bastards or not."

"Ah, come on. They're admitting they were wrong about us. Come on, let's join them."

"How about it, John?" Paddy asked, turning toward the Quaker. "Feel like drinking with them?"

"I'll go over with thee, but I won't drink." The Quaker smiled ruefully. "The more rules I break, the less chance I'll have of being reinstated at meeting."

"After what we've been through, you're thinking about religion?" Jobson retorted. "You've been kicked out of the church anyhow. Let the bars down."

"Like I said, I'll go with thee. As for thinking about religion..." the Quaker glanced at the lumbering ambulances, "I can't think of a better time."

"Don't throw a wet blanket on us," Jobson cut in. "Let's drink."

The troops from New York and Philadelphia gathered in a large field specially chosen for the happy occasion, a convivial celebration to strengthen the bonds of comradeship, acceptance and affection. Numerous barrels of whiskey conveniently placed for easy access turned the affair into a contest to see who could drink the most. Flowing like proverbial Irish buttermilk, the stimulating spirits loosened tongues and flamed into boisterous hilarity.

Above the sound of noise and confusion someone shouted, "Toast!"

"A toast!"

"Somebody give us a toast!"

In response, a New Yorker jumped up on a whiskey keg and, raising a brimming cup, proposed loudly, "Jeff Davis! May he be set afloat in an open boat without compass or rudder. May that boat and contents be swallowed by a shark, and the shark swallowed by a whale, the whale in the devil's belly, and the devil in hell, the door locked and the key lost. And further, may he be chained in south hell, with a northeast wind blowing ashes in his eyes for eternity!"

The final line met with a thunderous, raucous ovation.

Standing apart from the enlisted men's frolic, Colonels Gwyn and Johnson were engaged with other officers in pleasant bantering and boasting.

Colonel Johnson inquired, "What say, Gwyn? Let's liven things up with a little wagering."

Eyes red-rimmed, Gwyn spoke thickly, his words slurred. "Fine. Whad'ya suggest?"

The New Yorker winked at his junior officers. "I propose you pit the best of your pioneers against our champion in a tree-falling contest, the tree to fall in a given direction. Agreed?"

"You've just made yourself a wager, Johnson. I'll lay you an even hundred. Crocker, tell Danny Oakley to sharpen his blade and come here. While you're at it, let the men know what's takin' place. Wagerin' on their regimental champion'll boost their spirits."

Major Herring stared after the departing captain and spoke in an edgy voice. "They've a belly full of spirits as it is, Colonel. I say it's risky business, too many hotheads. The whiskey and wagering might lead..."

"Don't talk nonsense," Gwyn cut in. "Our men brawling with Johnson's fine lads? Absurd, absolutely absurd. Here, have another drink."

When all was in readiness, the two contestants faced separate trees of equal girth and height as the men crowded around, shoving and shouting, each prepared to back up his champion. At a signal, bared to the waist, Danny Oakley sent his blade biting into a designated tree, his axe hacking out a huge chip with each blow.

"Look at them muscles," Jobson hollered. "Go to it, Danny boy. This's gonna be easy money, Mulcahy."

"'Pears that way," Paddy answered tersely. "That New York fella's fallin' way behind. Oakley's tree'll be goin' down any minute...whup, there she goes."

"Tim-ber!" someone called.

In happy accord, the wild, exuberant shout of victory burst from the men of the 118th, but a lack of concurrence on the part of the defeated New Yorkers disrupted the harmony of the situation.

Seizing the victorious axe from Oakley's perspiring hands, the defeated man gave it a hasty examination then waved it aloft and shouted angrily, "This here is our axe! You bums stole my best blade! All bets is off!"

An order from the highest military authority in the land could not have been more effective in setting soldier against soldier. In one inflamed explosive moment, the entire area was filled with the challenging shouts of maddened men, fists flying ferociously. Fired by the effects of whiskey, even the reluctant were caught up in the wild free-for-all and the excitement of hand-to-hand fighting. No less immune to stimulants, the officers jumped into the fray on the side of their men. Teaming up like a two-horse hitch, Captains Crocker and Donaldson started fighting their way through the entire Twenty-fifth New York Regiment, throwing brawny fists every step of the way, belaboring and punishing their assailants severely. Turning around, they slowly fought their way back.

The enlisted men, less fierce than the two adept officers, hurried to where Crocker and Donaldson had cleared a path.

Some of the New Yorkers began running to nearby regiments, carrying word that the Philadelphia "bounty boys" had suddenly grown so big they were ready to take on the entire brigade. The response was not only galvanizing, it was a threatening situation as the full brigade sprang to their muskets.

Word of the whiskey riot reached General Barnes at headquarters. He quickly ordered a battery forward and, out of desperation, directed the guns trained on the whole brigade, but the belligerents would not be quieted. Two full regiments from the First Division were immediately called to Barnes's support, who ordered the cannon be loaded with canister. It was not until the lanyards were in the hands of the gunners that the rioters ceased and returned to their camps.

General Barnes was furious as he fumed and swore. "Where're Gwyn and Johnson?"

"Over by them woods, sir," an Irishman replied. "And ye'd better hurry, sir. They're fixin' to tear each other to pieces."

Chafing under the affront to the 118th's integrity and believing that honor demanded a hostile meeting, a challenge had passed from Colonel Gwyn to Colonel

Johnson. Presented with the formalities of the code and having been promptly accepted, the two regimental commanders, accompanied by chosen seconds, faced each other with drawn pistols.

"Good heavens," Barnes roared as he rode in on the scene, "they're going to fight a duel?" Spurring his horse, he rode straight at the combatants, reining up between them. "Drop those pistols!"

"Get outa the way," Colonel Gwyn bawled drunkenly. "Sonovabitch called me a liar. I'll settle with him right now."

With alarm, the brigade commander shifted his glance from one to the other. "No you won't, you're good friends. You've just had too much whiskey. Do as I say. Put away those pistols."

"Not until he apologizes to me and the regiment," Gwyn growled.

"If I overlook this entire outbreak, will you both shake hands and give it up?" Barnes cajoled.

"Providin' Johnson retracts what he said about my Philadelphia boys."

Other friends quickly interceded, the episode was defused and apologies accepted.

The following day was Sunday and the camps along the Potomac were warmed by a bright sun shining overhead. There was the soft breeze of an early autumn. The lingering effects of whiskey hangovers caused a quiet to settle over the camps. It was too soon for reminiscence, but thought and talk ran freely regarding the previous day's events. There was also a better realization of the loss of those who, in the service of their country, had sacrificed their lives.

Seated on the ground in front of his tent, Paddy rubbed a hand over a swollen ear and rose painfully. "Seen the Quaker anywhere this morning, Luke?" he inquired.

"Yeah," Jobson replied through bruised lips. "Said he was goin' over to the riverbank for meditation."

"Thanks." Walking stiff-legged, Paddy made his way slowly toward the Potomac and found the Quaker sitting, head bowed, in full view of the bluff and battleground on the opposite shore. The still forms of the dead remained in plain view, a sorrowful sight. The ground being within enemy lines, there had been no opportunity for a decent burial.

Rather than disturb the silent figure, Paddy circled him and made his way toward the sound of excited voices coming from the water's edge. General Barnes was waggling a stubby finger in the face of a burly, bearded captain. "I've told you, Crocker, the answer is no."

"What's the fuss about?" Paddy asked a nearby picket guard. "That damn fool captain wants to cross the river and recover the bodies of some friends of his. Listen."

"Now see here, Crocker," the brigade commander said, losing patience, "I've listened to your appeal to go care for your comrades across the river and even presented it to General Porter. His answer was a flat, emphatic refusal. There is no communication with the enemy and he doesn't propose to open any. I'm sorry, but war is war and this in neither the time nor the occasion for sentiment or sympathy."

Crocker turned his heavily bearded face toward the Virginia shore, then, before anyone could stop him, splashed doggedly across the shallow ford. "Thanks for your consideration, General," he called over his shoulder, "I'm going anyway."

"Criminy," the picket exclaimed with wide-eyed amazement. "What gives with you Philadelphia boys? Alone you take on a whole corps of Confederates, you start an open riot in the brigade, your colonel tries to blow Colonel Johnson's brains out and now that captain of yours thumbs his nose at the high command. What's in the Philadelphia scrapple you fellas eat? Gunpowder and vinegar?"

"We get our independence from Independence Hall," Paddy replied.

"Yeah, well I'll lay you ten to one that captain gets himself shot for this. If the Rebs don't get him, General Porter will."

The news of Captain's Crocker's disregard for instructions and deliberate action on an errand of mercy spread through the camps like wildfire, and soon the riverbank was crowded with soldiers. It was a novel spectacle to see an officer, fully accoutered with sword, belt and pistol, cross the river at the dam breast above which was an entire Southern army corps.

Bound on his unauthorized mission of peace and humanity, Crocker forged resolutely forward. A little experience might have taught him that his reception would have been more cordial if he had left his weapons behind.

Finding the bodies of Captain Saunders and Ricketts and Second Lieutenant Moss, and bearing them one by one on his shoulders to the Maryland shore, Crocker was about to embark on another crossing when he was suddenly interrupted by an orderly from General Porter.

"Just one moment, Captain," the orderly said sharply. "General Porter's sent me to warn you that if you should cross to the Virginia shore one more time, he'll order a battery to shell you."

Crocker scowled. "Private Mishaw's over there badly wounded, but still alive. I'm bringing him back. You tell the general to shell and be damned." So saying, he continued his operation while comrades watched with awe and admiration.

Once more on the West Virginia shore, he eased his large muscular frame into one of the lime kilns which had been blasted by erring Union artillery fire, and soon reappeared bearing the bloody and dirt-stained body of a groaning, badly-wounded private.

"Thank God you've come, sir," the youngster cried softly. "Now at least I can die beneath the flag."

"Buck up, boy, you're not going to die. Up with you.. .easy now."

A menacing, cold voice spoke from behind. "Drop that man, Yank, and put up your hands."

Turning sharply, Crocker gazed open-mouthed at a Confederate general and numerous staff, all of whom were staring at him from the river below. Just then, an aide-de-camp rode forward. "What're y'all doin' up theah, Yank? Theah's no flag of truce in effect here 'bouts."

Crocker laid Mishaw's body gently on the ground and advanced toward the Confederate group. "I'm aware of that fact," he answered boldly. "As you can see though, I'm removing the dead and wounded."

"Come down heah," the aide commanded. "General Jackson wants to have a talk with you."

The bushy-bearded general slouched forward in his saddle. Wearing a battered hat, his piercing eyes were fixed on the advancing soldier. He showed no sign of emotion. "What is your name and rank, soldier?" he asked brusquely as Crocker came within speaking range.

"Captain Lemuel Crocker, sir. Hundred and Eighteenth Pennsylvania Volunteers."

"Captain, eh? By whose authority are you here? You see, we were not informed of your coming."

Something about the rough but gentlemanly demeanor in the man known affectionately as "Old Stonewall" made Crocker feel at ease, as if he had met someone cut out of the same cloth as himself. He straightened his kepi, hitched up his sword belt and replied, "I have no authority, General. Matter of fact, my corps commander, General Porter, flatly refused me permission to cross. However, the dead and wounded of the regiment that fought on this ground yesterday came from the blood of Philadelphia's best citizens. Regardless of the laws of war and the commands of my superiors, I am of the opinion humanity and decency demand they be properly cared for. No one else attempting it, I determined to risk the consequences and discharge the duty myself."

A trace of a twinkle showed in Jackson's eyes. "How long have you been in the service, Crocker?"

"Twenty days, sir."

The swarthy general struggled to suppress a smile as he tugged at his beard. "I thought so," he replied gently.

The aide moved to Jackson's side. "Surely, General, you don't believe..."

Jackson cut off his protest. "Of course I believe the gentleman, Henry. The excellent caliber of fighting men turned out of Philadelphia is well established. Just wait till A. P. Hill hears of this." He slapped his saddle girth, amused. "One regiment of twenty-day levies standing off his whole division. It differs measurably from the report he handed to me." Jackson turned his attention to Crocker. "You have a glib tongue, Captain, but that trait alone has not saved you. Rather, it has been your honesty and courage which have impressed me. You may continue your labors until they are fully completed. Fifty yards downstream, there is a small boat which should be of help in ferrying your comrades across to the other side." He bowed his head. "And may God rest their souls."

Crocker stared respectfully at the God-fearing Confederate General. "If you'll allow me, sir," he said, "it's plain to see why your men will go through hell and back at your command. Wish to God we had a general of your caliber in our army."

"The opportunity did present itself," Jackson replied sadly. He regained his formal military bearing. "Henry, have this field surrounded with a cordon of cavalry patrols to protect the captain from further molestation or interruption."

"Yes, sir," the youthful captain answered. "May I make a request, sir?"

"Make it brief, Henry."

"With your permission, sir, I should like to seek a reciprocal exchange of courtesy with the Yankee captain." The Confederate captain glanced across the river with a plaintive expression.

"I see what you mean," Jackson replied tersely. "Perhaps you can pull it off, if you're able to muster the determination and ingenuity exhibited by our guest." Jackson swivelled in his saddle and sucked on a lemon. "Crocker, may I present Captain Henry Kyd Douglas of my staff."

Both officers saluted.

"Crocker," the Southerner drawled, "my mother and father live over yonder in that big house amidst your camps. I'd be obliged if in some way you could help me to cross the river so I could see about their health."

"So you're the one," Crocker replied. "Our regiment happens to be bivouacked on your father's estate. We heard the old gentleman on the hill had two sons in the Confederate Army, one on the general staff."

"You haven't answered my question."

"I wouldn't trust it, Henry," a nearby major cautioned. "Them Yanks get a hold of you and ya'll be finished for good."

Crocker stiffened. "If our government can be busted up by a Rebel soldier going to see his mother, why damn it, let it bust. Douglas, you be down to the river at seven o'clock tomorrow evening. I'll have everything arranged."

"Ah, thank you, Crocker. I'll be much obliged."

Again they saluted. Wheeling his horse, the Confederate captain galloped after Jackson and his staff down the river road.

Resuming his ghoulish operation, and using the small boat pointed out to him by Stonewall Jackson, Captain Crocker took the final cargo of dead and wounded to the Maryland shore. He had no sooner set foot within Union lines than he was promptly surrounded by a provost guard who placed him under immediate arrest. Maddened by what they thought to be an unjust act, a crowd of sympathetic enlisted men who had been watching the entire proceedings from a distance, closed in during the arrest. Brushing the mob aside with fixed bayonets, the guards hastily removed the prisoner and ushered him into the presence of General Porter, who, shocked at such a wholesale accumulation of improprieties and angered by such disobedience, proceeded to explain the law and regulations governing armies confronting each other.

There followed a moment of painful silence, as though in some way the general was meditating his own impending court-martial as a result of Pope's accusations after the Second Bull Run.

"Tell me, Captain," he said in a soft tone, "did you happen to see the twelve-pounder which our regulars left over on the other side during the fight yesterday? I'd like to recover it if at all possible."

"No, sir, I didn't," Crocker replied, breathing a little easier. "There's a caisson over there, but not enough left of it to retrieve."

"Humph, I see," he replied. "Let's return to the subject at hand. Considering your inexperience, unquestioned courage, and evident good intentions, together with Colonel Barnes's plea for leniency in your case, I'm releasing you from arrest and restoring you to duty. Every man's entitled to one mistake, Captain, but see that it's not repeated. That's all. You're dismissed."

In the days which followed Antietam, the Army of the Potomac settled down to refresh and retool itself. When not drilling or on picket duty, the men whiled away their time at baseball and other competitive outdoor sports, or held forensic discussions among themselves. The battle of Shepherdstown had not been much of a battle as battles go, yet the peculiar circumstances attending it gave the encounter an importance to the men of the 118th that transcended the extent of losses or numbers engaged. As a tactical movement, it had been merely a successful reconnaissance to determine the plans and movements of Lee's army after its flight across the Potomac.

The big battle of Antietam, the bloodiest and most costly single day's fight in the war, had already been fought; some claimed it a victory, others a draw. Regardless of viewpoint, the Confederate invasion had ended in disaster and the rout of Lee's army. The Army of Northern Virginia, losing more than one third of its entire strength in killed, wounded and prisoners, had crossed to the south of the Potomac with an army numbering nearly fifty-thousand men and officers.

As for the Potomac Army, the strange, crippling malady which had first shown itself among the horses of the Federal transport, artillery and cavalry commands right after the Second Bull Run had spread to epidemic proportion so as to seriously impair the army as far as any offensive operation was concerned. The exact nature of the situation seemed to be misunderstood in official circles, particularly by Lincoln, either because there had not been a clear, instructive communication regarding the disease from McClellan or because of a basic lack of medical knowledge. In any event, McClellan's continued inactivity triggered a telegram from the President.

"I have read your dispatch about sore-tongued and fatigued horses. Will you pardon me for asking what the horses of your army have done since the battle of Antietam that fatigues them?"

Of more pertinent interest to the soldiers than any political or military aspect was the fact that provisions, shelter and other comforts were slow in coming. In the absence of shelter, tents and gum blankets, and activated by the onset of invigorating fall weather, the troops constructed crude quarters from the boughs of trees and bushes, the improvised products being poor substitutes for tight, cozy 'dog houses'.

Settled in a state of domestic tranquillity, and rather enjoying it, the Army of the Potomac received information in early October that split tried and true comrades apart with angry and impassioned arguments. Lincoln had published an Emancipation Proclamation.

Huddled around a glowing campfire on a dark night, save for a new moon cradled above the stars, the volunteers from Frankford vented their feelings. Shuffling close to the roaring fire to escape a penetrating raw bite in the air, Bob Dyer said, "I've a good mind to pack up and go home. I came to save the Union, not free a bunch of black slaves."

"You go and you won't be the only one," Vandergrift replied. "Desertions are taking three out of ten over the hill already."

George Dyer looked up, his face masked in the shadows. "Can you blame them? Honest Abe told us we were fighting this war to preserve the Union. Now he deals us one off the bottom of the deck."

"It's a cheap political trick," Jobson said from the semi-darkness. "Look at how the words are put, promise much, but do nothing. Gives freedom in the South where there isn't a Fed to make it stick, and leaves slavery untouched in all the loyal states. Such hypocrisy. What's Lincoln think we are, idiots?"

"What's he think?" Joe Byram broke in. "He isn't thinking, period. Why this bloody proclamation'll cause a slave uprising that will end up with helpless women and children being slaughtered from burning and raping all over the South. They haven't anyone to protect them, their men are all in the army."

Howard Snyder spit out a piece of hardtack. "You scare too easy, Byram. There won't be any slave insurrection. The Darkies are too passive.

"I still don't like it," George Dyer rejoined. "I'm no Reb sympathizer, but it isn't fair. This proclamation strikes out property valued over a billion dollars. Four million slaves taken by force from Southern owners without compensation. It isn't right."

"Isn't right?" Snyder retorted. "This is war! Anything done to weaken the enemy helps make it that much shorter. Besides, didn't Lincoln offer to buy every slave in the South for two hundred dollars a head. Buy them and ship them off to a colony in South America, but the slave owners wouldn't listen to the offer. Too late for them to cry now."

Chewing heavily on a cud of tobacco, Jake Hallowell reached out to poke at the fire. "If you young pups are through underestimating the President, I'll tell you why he sprang this proclamation the way he did. Make no mistake about it, he's shrewd and smart." He turned his head. "Quaker, how about fetching more logs for this fire, it's getting cold. That proclamation was handed out, " he continued, " because the weak-kneed folks at home needed another crutch to lean on. After all the setbacks this army's taken, just preserving the Union isn't enough anymore. It also means that England and Europe are not going to decide how this war comes out. It's going to be fought to the finish right here at home."

"All right," Luke Jobson cut in. "Everybody's expecting England to jump in on the side of the South at any minute. How's freeing the slaves going to keep her from doing it? Course if she does, she's crazy. Without firing a shot she's already seen our merchant marine destroyed. Can't see why she'd want to join the South when spoils are being given away free."

Byram jabbed a bayonet into the ground. "England would fight for the South," he said, "because British industrialists don't like the textile and iron industries they see springing up all over the North. They don't like the protectionist Morrill Act and our high tariff war. Actually, the only thing that's held them in check this long is a debate as to which is more important, Yankee corn, or Southern cotton, and how much chance the South has of winning. Commercial competition, there's your answer."

"The bloody English also fear our experiment with democracy," Paddy blurted. "It's something new among big nations and they're afraid it might succeed and topple them from the status of privileged and power bloated aristocrats. Our South's run by the same kind of privilege and power people as you'll find in England. I'll fight 'em both."

"Hurray for the Irish," Luke retorted.

"I'm not kidding. You want to hear something? Just read this." Paddy extracted a copy of the *Richmond Examiner* from a pocket inside his tunic. "A Reb floated it 'cross river to me while I was standing picket this afternoon."

George Kimball reached for the newspaper. "Here, let me see it, Mulcahy. What's so all-fired upsetting about it?"

"Read that editorial on the front page, and remember this paper's the official mouthpiece for the whole Reb government."

Taking the newspaper, Kimball drew nearer to the fire and in a firm, steady voice began reading the article aloud:

"The establishment of the Confederacy is a distinct reaction against the whole course of the mistaken civilization of this age. That is the real reason we have been left without the sympathy of the nations, until we have conquered that sympathy with the sharp edge of the sword. For 'Liberty, Equality, and Fraternity,' we have deliberately substituted Slavery, Subordination, and Government. Those social and political problems which rack and torture modern society, we have undertaken to solve for ourselves in our own way, and on our own principles, that, among equals, equality is right; among those who are naturally unequal, equality is chaos; there are slave races born to serve, master races born to govern. Such are the fundamental principles which we inherited from the ancient world. Which we lift up in the face of a perverse generation that has forgotten the wisdom of its fathers. By those principles we live, and in their defense we have shown ourselves willing to die."

Kimball paused to clear his throat and blow on his chapped hands. He continued reading:

"Reverently, we feel that our confederacy is a God-sent missionary to the nations, with great truths to preach. Thank God the Confederates have some statesmen, and thinkers up to the mark and level of the situation. There are men in the Confederate states who have long felt and earnestly striven to express, though timidly and speculatively, on what foundation of fact, and with what cornerstone of principle our social situation was one day to be built. Now is the time. Let them speak in no apologetic tones."

Kimball lowered the paper. "I'll be go to hell. They must be outa their Goddamned minds."

Hallowell gave a sage nod of his head. "Now you see it, master race. The British people have a weakness, humanity. They freed their slaves years ago. Lincoln spotted that weakness and exploited it. With this new turn of events, the English people won't let anyone lead them into war on the side of the South and that dirty word, slavery. You can understand the shrewdness behind Lincoln's Emancipation Proclamation coming at this time. It will keep England out of the war."

"Shrewd or not," Jobson responded, "I still don't like the idea of freeing the slaves all at one time. Up till now Lincoln's always said gradual emancipation was best, and he promised no wartime emancipation."

Byram thrust out his bearded chin. "Black slaves, they don't know anything about freedom and the responsibilities involved. How can four million uneducated Africans make good citizens?"

Sitting hunched with a blanket drawn tight around his shoulders, the Quaker looked up. "Every man should have a free, unfettered choice of what he wants to do with his life. friend. No human soul should be held like cattle, born, bred, and milked dry in bondage. When God created us, He gave us all one thing in common, a free will."

All eyes turned on the impassive figure.

"Those are noble sentiments," Byram retorted, "but this isn't a noble world. Besides, a darkey isn't capable or dependable. You think they'd seek education and advancement on their own? Never. They just don't have it in them."

"Neither would thee, friend, if thee had been held in abject slavery for over a hundred years." The Quaker plucked a frosted blade of grass which he proceeded to suck between his teeth in a moment of contemplation. "I find it interesting," he said, "that the French Normans used the very same arguments against our Saxon forefathers." He stood up and started toward his tent. "Remember one thing," he said over his shoulder, "our Savior told us to love one another, or have thee become Rebels also?"

"Nigger-lovin' Quakers," someone muttered.

Paddy turned on the heckler. "What makes you think you are superior to our colored town folk? They are good human beings."

"Crissakes, not you too, Mulcahy."

"Me, too. Want to make something of it?"

At that moment Donaldson stepped out of the darkness. "You men will have to stuff this in a canteen. You're not only keeping the whole camp awake, it's also against general orders."

"Against general orders? What are you talking about, Cap'n?" a voice asked from the darkened perimeter.

"McClellan's just published General Order Number One Sixty-three. It bans all political discussion in the army, starting immediately."

"No talk of politics?" Jobson blurted. "You must be joking, Cap'n! What goes with cards, whiskey and campfires? Politics. It'd be like serving beer without pretzels!"

"Sorry, Luke, but this emancipation thing has been raising merry hell. Desertions have cut the army by nearly a third." He paused. "Mac's warned the entire army of the danger to military discipline from heated political discussions. Wants you to be reminded that the remedy for political error is to be found only in action at the polls. There is an election coming up in three weeks."

Hallowell shouldered his way forward. "What's Little Mac's personal opinion of this proclamation, Cap'n? Have you heard?"

"Yes. He doesn't like it one damn bit." The officer squatted near the fire and picked up a loose stone which he tossed lightly in one hand. "Shouldn' t be telling you this, but I feel like the rest when it comes to cutting off free speech. It's being said McClellan wrote to his wife that it's doubtful if he'll remain in service much longer. Because of Lincoln's recent change of tack, and the continuation of Stanton and Halleck in office, he's written it's almost impossible to retain his commission and self-respect at the same time."

Paddy spat. "For a general, he writes too much out loud."

Captain Donaldson looked up grim-faced. "I'll buy that, Mulcahy." He gazed into the fire. "It'll be common knowledge by tomorrow, so you might as well hear it now. Burnside, Franklin, Baldy Smith and several other generals have put in for transfers to the Western army."

"Why Baldy?" Paddy asked. "The others I can understand, but Smith, he's one of our best."

"It hinges on that old devil, politics." Donaldson let the stone fall from his hand and stood up. "Some New York democrats have just talked McClellan into running for president against Lincoln in the next election. Mac's..."

"He's got my vote," Byram broke in.

"Mine, too," chorused others.

"Go ahead, Cap'n, what else?" Paddy interjected.

"Mac's agreed to their proposition, written them a letter acceding to their terms and pledging himself to carry on the war in the sense already dedicated. I got it from a friend of mine on the staff that when Smith was shown the letter, he said it looked like treason and he put in for immediate transfer."

Paddy's eyes registered concern. "What do you mean by, 'carry on in the sense already dedicated'?"

"Conciliate and impress the South with the idea our armies are intended merely to execute the laws and protect their property," Donaldson replied.

Kimball knocked some ashes from the bowl of his pipe. "I'll be go to hell if that ain't treason talk"

"Glad someone sees it that way," the officer said.

"I agree," Hallowell snapped.

"Ah, what do you old men know about anything?" a voice challenged from the background.

"Before you younger men come to any half-cocked conclusions," Donaldson rejoined slowly and evenly, "you'll do well to consider this. When asked why the Rebel army wasn't bagged right after Antietam, a colonel on Mac's staff answered, 'That's not the game. The object's that neither army shall get the advantage of the other. Both will be kept in the field until they're exhausted, then we'll make a compromise and save slavery.'"

"The sonovabitch who said that ought to be canned from the Army," Hallowell roared.

"He was. Lincoln broke him three days ago, but others remain."

Kimball scratched the gray hair showing at his temples. "Well, one thing's plain enough, this pot's getting dirtier by the minute. Any way you look at it, the days of fighting on simple enthusiasm are gone."

"That just about sums it up," Donaldson said dryly. He turned to leave. "You men better turn in. We're being reviewed early in the morning. Dignitary from Washington wants to meet the boys who fought at Shepherdstown."

"Who's that?" Paddy inquired.

"President Lincoln, Old Honest Abe himself."

CHAPTER 11

O ne week after being reviewed by the President, the Potomac Army was served with preliminary orders to prepare three day's cooked rations, reduce officer's baggage to minimum and draw an issue of sixty rounds of ammunition per man. As examined through the eyes of veteran soldiers, the orders were too definite and specific for a reconnaissance and indicated a general advance.

On the first of November, four days before the vital off-year congressional elections were held, the Army of the Potomac shouldered its rifles, unfurled its flags and marched south in a return to active campaigning.

The first day's march continued well into the night with the Union volunteers bundled in great capes to ward off the chill November winds. At ten o'clock, the 118th went into bivouac at Bryant's Farm located on the Potomac near the base of Maryland Heights. Not far off was the deep gorge of the Potomac at Harpers Ferry. Early the next day, the morning sun burst forth in golden radiance on the grandeur of those lofty summits of Maryland, Bolivar and Loudon Heights and trickled down as gold dust on the sparkling Potomac and Shenandoah waters. In one broad sweep of visual splendor, the men beheld the startling contrast of the placid, smooth-flowing Potomac and the rushing madness of the Shenandoah as they joined together.

Immediately in front, Maryland Heights rose abruptly one thousand feet from a rock base to sparsely timbered slopes, grim, barren and formidable. On the right and over the Potomac a mile or more, stood Bolivar Heights, bold, brown and treeless. Down the river a little farther on the Virginia side, where the Shenandoah left the valley and mingled with the waters of the broad Potomac, was Loudon Heights. It rose in majesty, cozily nestled at an angle formed by the junction of the two great rivers. Precipitous, rocky and wooded, its foliage was ablaze with the golden hues of autumn.

Partly visible was Harpers Ferry with shattered brick chimneys sticking up like jutting stove pipes, the ruined walls of its arsenal still standing, silent witnesses to the preliminaries from which the war had sprung. Southward, two prominent ranges forming the boundaries of the great Shenandoah Valley dwindled in the misty distance till mountain and horizon united in a blurred, indefinable haze.

Formed in long, stretching lines, the blue-coated columns started to cross the Potomac on a pontoon bridge nearly a mile long laid above a dam opposite the lower end of Harpers Ferry.

Beneath swaying pontoons that closely resembled the giant bulbs of some unearthly plant, the quiet lapping waters of the Potomac fell over the dam breast and were quickly lost in the distance as they dashed away in a mad rush over rock and boulder.

At Harpers Ferry, the troops were routed through a narrow thoroughfare that skirted the town along the river's edge. A mystical kind of spell connected with the surroundings caused heads to turn with curiosity at the location where servile insurrection against law and order had been instigated by the bearded John Brown.

The insurrection had been fought to the finish against the entire power and jurisdiction of the United States Government. The capture of Brown by a detachment of marines under Colonel Robert E. Lee, his subsequent trial, hanging and martyrdom, were still fresh in the minds of the marching men who silently pondered and passed through the area.

The never-ending columns moved on and crossed over the Shenandoah by another pontoon bridge which held its swaying place tenaciously in spite of the rough, angry waters below. The riverbed was full of rocks, some hidden, others visible, against which the swift currents dashed and threw spray high in the air.

Finding themselves once again in Virginia, the army bent forward on its mission of coercion to enforce submission to a consolidated Union. Strangely enough, it did so on the soil of the commonwealth whose first deputies had inserted in the earliest deliberations of the Constitution that the fundamental law must express, not simply infer, that the strength and power of the nation was available to coerce refractory states.

The troops were happy to find that the region they were entering abounded with farm products such as poultry, beef, pork and mutton, fitting substitutes for their monotonous diet of salt pork and hardtack.

The rolling countryside had escaped any severe scarring from the devastating hand of war, and the granaries, barns, henneries and spring houses paid handsome tribute to the, by no means modest, demands of the soldier whose search missed nothing.

It was during the afternoon march that an unwise pig decided to run through the lines of the 118th, a breach of discipline not tolerated for an instant. Appointing himself a court martial of one, Luke Jobson immediately convened himself, passed sentence and executed, heedless of strict orders against foraging.

As his bayonet pierced its side, the pig squealed so loudly that the sound brought Captain Donaldson galloping down the line to secure the pig and arrest the offender. But before he could reach the spot, the pig had been divided and concealed, the men moving on in perfect order with expressions of Sunday school innocence on their guiltless faces.

The men engaged in personal association with some of the citizens along the way, but as they got further into the interior they sensed a bitterness and resentment towards them. The young Federal soldiers held no special love for the enemy, nor abiding affection for aiders and abettors, but those feelings had never had occasion to take shape before. Now they were crossing into a section where press, rostrum and pulpit had taught that every Northerner was to be despised and his society rejected with open manifestations of that hatred shown in a spirit of retaliation. There was little intercourse between the soldiers and the citizenry.

With pickets staked out for the night and campfires burning brightly in the darkness, the men went about their routine chores. Bob Dyer watched in idle curiosity as his brother removed a piece of tin from a cartridge box and then punched holes in the tin with a bayonet and began grating field corn from the cob with his unpatented utensil.

"You expecting to eat that horse feed?" he asked from a distance. He moved closer to let his fingers run over the brittle sun-baked dent. "Cripes, George, it's hard enough for ammunition."

George Dyer kept at his work, ignoring his younger brother's lack of confidence, and soon had tempting corn cakes frying with pieces of fresh pork from Jobson's contraband pig.

When the tasty fruits of his culinary genius had been appraised and accepted, others quickly followed his example and the camp came alive with sizzling corn fritters.

Paddy, dejected, sat alone by the side of the road. He munched on skilly galley, his charcoal blackened fingers serving as fork and spoon as he slowly transferred food from hand to mouth. A wooden road sign, weathered and warped from long exposure, creaked lonesome sounds as it swung on its chains in the rising wind. Mournfully reminiscent of Balls Bluff and Becky were the barely distinguishable words, "Leesburg Pike." Overhead, wispy white clouds drifted across the face of a pale moon. He took a final bite of food and pulled the cape of his greatcoat tightly about his head to ward off the penetrating chill. He failed to notice the approach of Captain Donaldson.

"Looks like you've lost your best friend, Mulcahy. Anything I can do to help?" the officer inquired.

"Nope. Got the aches, that's all."

"Maybe some good news will cheer you up. Cassidy and the others captured at Shepherdstown have just been exchanged. They are down at headquarters."

"Cassidy's back? Capital. How soon will he rejoin the company?"

"In a few minutes, but before you leave to chew the fat there's something else you'll want to know."

"What's that?"

"We won't be continuing south toward Warrenton tomorrow, we wheel east by way of Leesburg."

Paddy leaped to his feet. "Leesburg? Did you say Leesburg?"

"Yep. Better get spruced up for that girl of yours." Casting him a sly wink, the officer departed.

Unconsciously, Paddy wiped his dirty face with an overcoat sleeve.

Later that night, as the wind howled through the sleeping camp, his thoughts went wild, racing and beating in his brain like a caged bird. It was almost a year to the day since he had seen Becky. Would she still care? Had her mind been changed by time and events? He tossed restlessly in his blanket roll when suddenly another thought struck him. She did not know that he had changed regiments! If she should be looking for him, it would be amongst Wistar's Seventy-first. If she searched faces without inquiring, she might think him dead. The possibility of that caused him to smile.

A hero's return from the grave, he thought to himself as he fell into blissful sleep.

The next morning he awoke intoxicated with the bright prospect of marching into Leesburg before the searching eyes of Becky Chenewith. The return of Sergeant Cassidy from captivity added to the air of exhilaration and for the first time in many days, the route column was alive with noisy, good-natured bantering.

As the regiment neared Leesburg, idle chatter ceased as all eyes were peeled for snipers. The landscape had become a symbolic blend of rolling, fenced-in acres with imposing mansions ruling in stately grandeur.

Captain Donaldson, riding a slow pace alongside the marching column, made several furtive attempts to gain Paddy's attention. Successful, he bent low in the saddle and spoke in a whisper. "We'll be entering Leesburg from the west, swing south and bivouac on the Monroe plantation four miles beyond. I'll ride ahead and see if your lady friend is searching for you in the column."

Paddy's heart began to beat faster. "Appreciate it," he replied.

"Don't mention it." Donaldson let a folded fist dangle loosely by his saddle girth. "Here, take this pass. Quick."

"Wha. . . ?"

"It gives you twelve hours liberty, but for God's sake, be on time for muster in the morning." He put spurs to his horse and galloped off toward the head of the column.

Paddy unfolded the note and read its contents. An amused smile crossed his face.

To whom it may concern: The bearer of this pass is on detached service for the express purpose of requisitioning medicinal supplies in the town of Leesburg. All courtesy and considerations are to be shown this agent. By order of Lieutenant Colonel Gywn, 118th Pennsylvania Volunteers.

Paddy tucked the pass inside his tunic for safekeeping and started to fuss and fidget. He hitched the various accouterments that hung from his body and made passing attempts to smooth his hair, and dust his soiled uniform.

After what seemed an eternity, Captain Donaldson returned, his face wreathed in a big smile.

"You've spotted her!" Paddy blurted.

Donaldson nodded. "Yes, standing by a picket fence alongside the road just up ahead. Looks pretty as a picture, too."

"Can I bolt now?"

"Go for it, but don't forget, muster tomorrow morning."

"I'll be there."

Holding his rifle at trail arms, he darted from the ranks and raced beneath the naked elm trees that lined the roadway, his feet kicking up crisp, fallen leaves that snapped and crackled under his pounding feet. A delightful pain shot through his chest as he spied the girl who had nursed him back to health. Standing lonely vigil, like a sentry on duty, her slender frame bundled to ward off the chill November air, she appeared to be quivering as she silently surveyed the passing troops. Turning suddenly, as if his approach had been unconsciously telegraphed, she saw him running toward her.

Lost somewhere in a foggy dream, he heard her call his name and repeat it. A moment later her delicate arms were about his neck, drawing his head close to her breast. He entwined his arms around her slim waist and pulled her close.

"Paddy!" she cried. "Oh, darling, I thought I'd lost you."

She kissed him on both cheeks, her fingertips pressed lightly against his temples as she drew back to gaze deep into his eyes.

"When I didn't see you with the Seventy-first, I thought...oh, I thought you'd been killed at that dreadful Antietam."

He removed the soft hands from his face and gave them a tight squeeze. "Why didn't you ask some of the boys in my old regiment? They would have told you I joined a new one."

"They all looked so fierce and dirty, I couldn't find the courage to speak."

He laughed lightheartedly. "They're mostly the same ones you felt sorry for a year ago."

She dropped her head. "I wonder. Somehow they're changed, it's in their faces." Removing her hands from his, she placed them against his cheeks. "Have you seen your face recently, my darling?"

"What's the matter with it?"

"It's changed, too. I don't see the boy in it anymore."

"What did you expect? Discovering the world ain't the nice dream..."

"Isn't," she cooed softly.

"Isn't," he repeated, slightly irritated, "what you thought it was. Bound to harden you in some way. War and politics are dirty business."

"That is why it is a woman's duty to keep a cheerful home," she replied. "A pleasant place where husbands can retire from the cruel demands of a man's world. Why don't you come home with me and see for yourself?" Her voice faltered. "You can come for a little while, can't you?"

He felt for the pass in his tunic. A smile lit up his face. "I believe I can. Like you say, maybe things will look better."

"I know they will. And, sweetheart, don't fret over what I said. Remember, women want to marry men, not boys."

"Are you proposing?"

A deep blush colored her face. "Gracious no." She paused to recover herself. "But folks do say you Yankees need prodding when it comes to love, same as you do in war."

"They do, eh? They don't know us when we finally put our mind to a thing." He linked his arm with hers. "Let's go. I don't like to do my courting with the whole corps looking on."

They walked slowly toward the village. Mounting the steps to the Chenewith home, he paused momentarily to recall the painful nightmare and circumstances which had brought him to the house originally.

Becky opened the door and stepped inside. "Mother, come see who's here."

Mrs. Chenewith appeared in the hallway. "Why, I declare, if it isn't father's prize patient." She moved forward and placed an affectionate kiss on Paddy's cheek. "It's good to see you again and looking so well, Paddy. We've often wondered about you. Does your wound ever give you any trouble?"

"No, ma'am. Doesn't bother me a bit. How's the doctor?"

"Just fine, thank you. We had word from him only two days ago. His letter was smuggled through your lines."

He searched for some sign of bitterness or hatred in the woman's face, but all he could find was solicitation and charity.

"I declare, Becky, just look at this poor boy's shoes. Why, they are paper-thin and all broken out at the seams. I thought it was only our army who had to go barefoot. Fetch a pair of Father's boots and see if they will fit."

"No, please don't," he replied. "We're expecting winter supplies any day. Besides, we can march in our stockings just as well as the Johnnies."

A look of sadness crept into the woman's kindly face. "Yes, I suppose that you can. Our common forefathers did it in the Revolution. No reason why their sons cannot carry on in the same tradition, regardless of the army they are in. But let's have no more talk of war. You march yourself right upstairs young man and take a good hot bath. Becky and I will prepare dinner to do justice to a hungry soldier. Be off with you now."

Warmed by an intoxicating feeling of contentment, Paddy mounted the staircase in response to Mrs. Chenewith's bidding and was soon lost in the forgotten luxury of hot water and soap.

Dinner by candlelight was spent in a congenial exchange of pleasantries and news which only intelligent women know how to develop gaily and successfully. Both mother and daughter appeared visibly upset at Paddy's account of his father's death, but in a sympathetic manner were able to again restore happiness to the occasion.

"Say, where's Jed?" he inquired. "Here I've been so glad to see you both, I plum forgot about him."

"Father sent him to the Virginia Military Institute early in September."

"Virginia Mili. . .he's a little young to become a soldier, ain't he?"

"Isn't," Becky corrected lightly.

Paddy grinned sheepishly. "Isn't he?"

"Yes, he's too young to become a soldier," Mrs. Chenewith rejoined, "and thank goodness for that. Jed wants to become a doctor like his father. Since he'll need good background training, we decided to enter him at the institute this year, the school situation being what it is at the present. My husband tells me your

General McClellan is a University of Pennsylvania graduate."

"I believe he is, ma'am, if I remember correctly."

"That's where Jed wants to go for his medical training. Same as his father did."

"Maybe he can live with us since he'll be in the neighborhood," Paddy said inadvertently.

Mrs. Chenewith raised her eyebrows and looked questioningly, first at one and then the other. "Oh? What's this? Something I don't know about?"

"Paddy's just teasing, Mother."

Paddy noticed how radiantly beautiful and alive Becky looked when she blushed.

Observing this, Mrs. Chenewith smiled softly. "Goodness, mothers can be so blind at times. All along you've had me believing it was Lamar Fontaine who held sway."

Mention of the officer's name filled Paddy with instant jealousy.

"Mother! How can you talk like that? Just because Lamar wrote that silly old poem that's being published in every newspaper in the South doesn't mean I'm beholden to him."

Paddy sat back in his chair. "Poem? What poem?"

"The one Lamar gave to Becky that last night you were with us. The one entitled '*All Quiet Along the Potomac Tonight*.' It was written in memory of a friend." The gentle-faced woman directed her attention to a cup of tea sitting in front of her. "Somehow or other it found its way into the newspapers and has become widely read and favored in the South."

"Mother, I'm sure Paddy doesn't want to hear about Lamar's fame, and neither do I. You know I don't approve of girls playing off one beau against another as though it were an amusing game."

"I'm sorry, dear, I meant no harm. Can't a mother tease a bit? To make amends, you may both go into the other room and sit by the fire while I clear the table."

"I'd be obliged if you'd let me help you with the dishes, ma'am. Won't feel right if you don't."

"That's sweet of you, Paddy, but your toils have been far greater than mine. Please, for my sake, do sit by the fire and enjoy your leisure. Now both of you be off." She made motions as though shooing chickens from the porch.

Left to themselves, the two lovers visited until late into the night. Finally, arm-in-arm they made their way upstairs. On each face was a newfound glow of excitement, joy and rapture. Life-giving love had been offered and received.

Pausing at the door to his room, Paddy gathered Becky close in his arms, breathing heavily at her ear. "Are you all right?"

"Yes, my darling, oh, yes."

Their lips met feverishly.

"Good night, my love."

"Good night, Becky, my darling."

Morning came too soon and the comfortable confines of the bed in which he had fought for his life a year ago restrained him with its inviting softness as though disliking to part with an old friend. Employing sheer will-power, he managed to tear himself away and dress.

Breakfast was dispensed with in comparative silence, no one knowing quite what to say in view of Paddy's imminent departure and its implications. He slowly drained the last drop of coffee from his cup, wiped his mouth, rose from the table and shouldered his rifle and haversack.

"It's been good having you as our guest once more," Mrs. Chenewith said simply. "Come again whenever you can...and may God bless you and keep you safe."

"Thank you, ma'am. You've been very kind. Will you tell the doctor I asked about him?"

"I will, in my next letter."

Becky eyed his tools of war with foreboding.

"I'll hitch up the carriage and drive you part way down the Middleburg Pike," she offered.

"No, you'd better not, Becky. It'll be bad enough if your neighbors find out you lodged a Yankee last night. It'll only make it worse if they see you driving me through town in your carriage. When I come back, I want them to be my friends."

Ever discreet, Mrs. Chenewith hastened into the kitchen to see if something was burning on the stove.

Paddy gathered Becky in a warm embrace and covered her lips with his. Every sinew in her soft, lithe body seemed to tremble under his touch. "Come back to me soon," she managed to whisper. "I'll be waiting for you. Always."

In the center of Leesburg where most of the citizens still lay sound asleep in their warm beds, gluey-eyed Union soldiers began moving about. Chilled men flapped their arms energetically to stir circulation and wait for the call to move south. Paddy passed them at a quick pace and made his way toward the Middleburg Pike. On both sides of the pike the surrounding fields were covered with a crusted layer of hoarfrost, a white deposit of ice needles that formed during the night, still shimmering like sequins.

Finding the road empty of wagons and troops he traveled at a dog-trot until the flag of the 118th came into view. It was waving in a field to the left where soldiers in long johns and tilted kepis were busily dressing.

Noticing Paddy's approach, Captain Donaldson advanced from the camp to greet him. He started to sing a parody which made Paddy's neck grow red with embarrassment. "Last night I slept in a hollow log with bed-bugs all around me, but tonight I'll sleep in a feather bed...."

"Cut it out, Cap'n. You want the other fellas to find out? They'll roast my ears to kingdom come."

"Had to have my little joke before breakfast. Were you well received?"

"Was I? Just hope Lincoln and the slaves know what a sacrifice I made returning. If I hadn't promised you I'd be here for muster...."

"Yes?"

"Oh, hell, who'm I kidding? I couldn't have squatted at her house knowing the regiment was still out fighting. Sure hope this war ends quick enough. I have a hearth that needs taking care of. But say. . ." he reached inside his tunic and withdrew the pass, "how'd you get Colonel Gwyn's signature on this? Forge it?"

"No need to. Not with romantic Irish souls like Gwyn's around. He was asking Batch and me what happened at Balls Bluff. In the course of the conversation I made mention of your experience. Without batting an eyelash he picked up a pen, wrote out the pass, signed it, handed it to me and said, 'Give this to the lad and let him live a little tonight with the Colonel's compliments.'"

"Well, what do you know. The Colonel's a gentleman and a scholar from the old sod. Mighty decent of him."

Donaldson chuckled. "Yes, but I wonder how far you'd have gotten if your name had been Schneider? Look, I have to run along. Glad you had a nice furlough. See you later."

"Right, Frank. And say, thanks again."

"Don't mention it."

Sergeant Cassidy moved in from the side. "Where ye been all night, Mulkayhee? Coffee-boilin' or flesh-pottin'?"

"Better'n that, Sarg. Yes, sir, better'n that." An impish grin split his face. "What's new with the army?"

"Whiskey'n chaplains. Faith now, ain't that a fine combination for ye?"

"Whiskey and chaplains? I don't get it."

Cassidy spat a quid of stale tobacco juice at the frozen ground and wiped his mouth with a begrimed sleeve. "Seein' as how cold it's been gettin' of late, General Barnes took a change o' heart last night, reissued whiskey rations to the regiment. Said he hoped we'd learned how to the handle the stuff and not be after takin' on the whole brigade in another whiskey rebellion. Wagon train what brought in the whiskey also brought in our new chaplain, from the old sod, he is."

"A priest?"

"Faith'n who'd let a priest ride all the way from Washington with a load o' whiskey? The whole ration would've been consumed by the church before it ever came close to our hands." He stopped to light a pipe. "The new one's an Orangeman. Name's O'Neil. Starch-collared Methodist, he is."

"Any relation to our Lieutenant Colonel O'Neil?"

"They're brothers. So I've put the word out, no droppin' o' trees on his tent."

A sharp bugle blast sounded on the frosty air followed quickly by the long drum roll that broke off all conversation and sent both men scurrying for his position in line. Orders for the day were received amid loud grumbling and some swearing when it was announced that the fatiguing and laborious duty of guard to the wagon train had fallen to the lot of the Corn Exchange.

Since the trains required exclusive use of the road, the muttering troops slowly deployed on their flanks and were soon moving across dense fields, through thick brush, over fences and every conceivable obstruction as they tediously carved a way for themselves. To be expected at the start, the road was blocked for several hours, the march annoyingly slow and beset with harassing delays, then as obstructions cleared from the roadway, the speed of the wagons increased so that it soon taxed the endurance of the infantry trying to keep pace with their charge.

The next day the march was resumed at seven in the morning and the 118th was assigned to rear guard, a duty not so distasteful as the wagons, but by no means to be courted. To drive up the habitual coffee-boiler was no disagreeable duty, but to urge along the honest soldier fatigued to real exhaustion aroused a sympathy which was difficult to conquer. Because there happened to be little straggling on this occasion and the duties of the rear guard being correspondingly light, the charge of the ammunition trains was also imposed on the disgruntled men of the Corn Exchange.

Procrastinating and nerve-racking delays followed the additional detail and it was not until ten o'clock that night when, supperless and exhausted, a bivouac was made at Warrenton where a sudden and violent taste of winter blew in from the north and it commenced snowing.

The entire countryside soon became covered with a soft mantle of white, bare trees on distant wooded slopes appearing as a stubble of beard against the backdrop. Tracking the driven carpet of white with their blood, the raw, frostbitten feet of men without shoes oozed soaking crimson drops with every step that left behind a trail of stained footsteps which remained as ugly red blotches reflecting in the darkness.

Finally settling themselves for the night, the weary troops huddled as birds against the bitter wintry blasts and shivered beside inadequate campfires. In silence they munched on hardtack and salt pork or painfully tended to bleeding, frozen feet. Dr. Thomas passed among the men to render what aid he could with the medical supplies at hand. Peering beneath the hood of his great cape, he examined Sergeant Cassidy's abraded feet with disturbed speculation.

"Frankly, Sergeant, there's little known about frost-bite and its treatment. However, I don't hold to the common belief that rubbing the affected part with snow is proper treatment, seems to break down the tissues and lead to gangrene."

"What would ye be suggestin', sir?"

"I don't know for sure. At school a classmate from the north country claimed the best thing to use was kerosene."

"I'd be willin' to try the devil's own fire, sir."

"Let's give the kerosene a try. Quaker!"

"Yes, sir."

"Round up all the kerosene you can find. Ransack the wagons if you have to, but get it and bring it here. You there, Jobson, Byram, go with the Quaker and lend a hand."

"Yes, sir."

The detail disappeared into the darkness. Cassidy flashed a toothy smile. "Sure'n I kin see why they call ye practicin' physicians. But don't mind me little joke, sir. If me feet can teach ye anythin', ye go right ahead and practice on 'em."

"Your little joke strikes close to truth, Sergeant. Vivisection on a grand scale. That's war for you."

"Doctor Thomas! Doctor Thomas!" came a shrill cry, "You've got to come with me right away, sir!"

The surgeon turned to face a young private. "What is it, soldier? You sound like someone's having a baby."

"Worse than that, sir. It's our captain. Says he's going to drink himself to death, and by your leave, sir, the way he's pouring whiskey down, I believe he means it."

"You're the Reverend Doctor Henry Boardman's son, aren't you?"

"Yes. sir"

"Thought so. I've often attended your father's church when time permitted. Who is your captain?"

"Captain Scott, sir. B Company."

Cassidy let out a guffaw. "Ah, the bonnie Scot from Glasgow. Damned if I don't think he's proposin' the best treatment I've heered yet. I'll go with ye, Doc."

The pug-nosed Scotsman, idol of his men whether he be drunk or sober, was sprawled in a camp chair in front of his tent. Clutching a canteen of whiskey, he rocked back and forth and sang at the top of his voice, "Oh, ye'll take the hi' road and I'll take the low road...."

At the approach of the regimental surgeon, he stopped singing and shouted, "Bonnie nicht to ye, Doctor! Have a wee nip wi' me."

"I think you've had enough, Captain. Give me the canteen and get some sleep," Thomas replied.

"Sleep!" roared the raw-boned Scot. "Aye, mon, ye're daft. I aim to resume me glorious uninterrupted intoxication..." a loud burp punctuated his fluent use of the King's English. He brushed his lips with a sleeve, "excuse me, and keep continually and conscientiously drunk for the rest of the winter."

"Any man what can rattle off words like that ain't drunk, Doc. Let him finish. I'll stay on to be seein' he comes to no harm," Cassidy volunteered.

"You'll stay with him for sure, Sergeant, but just long enough for me to find Colonel Gwyn. Captain or not, he'll freeze to death if he passes out drunk in this weather."

Cassidy sampled the canteen's contents and was seized by a fit of choking. "A-r-r-rough! Not on this liquid fire, he won't! Wonder how this stuff would work on me feet, Doc?"

"Probably eat them right off. All right, Captain, hand it over. That's an order."

The following day word spread that for some unknown reason the army was being halted around Warrenton. Conjecture ranged from weather conditions to a supposed surrender by the Confederacy. In happy anticipation of a prolonged halt, the men began erecting shelters out of spruce boughs and logs, cozy places where they could hibernate until spring.

Busily engaged chinking cracks in his log cabin one afternoon, Paddy chanced to see Captains Donaldson and Crocker ready to mount saddled horses. Quickly wiping his hands on his pant legs, he hurried toward them.

"What's up, Captain? Anything of interest?" he inquired.

Donaldson's countenance was grave. "We're on our way to pay respects to

Lieutenant White's folks. They live a few miles from here at Sulphur Springs."

"Oh? May I ride along?"

"Welcome, of course, but I don't know where you'd find an available horse," Donaldson replied.

Crocker placed one foot in a stirrup. "Scott won't be using his for while. He's still carrying a brick in his hat."

"That's a thought." Donaldson mounted his horse. "Wait here, Paddy. Lem and I will ride over to the corral and see what we can rustle."

The two officers returned with Captain Scott's horse at the end of a lead. Donaldson pointed to a shaggy brown mare. "You're in luck, Mulcahy. Mount up."

Paddy sprang nimbly into the saddle. "You think White's folks will welcome us? After all, he fought on our side and we're damn Yankees."

"He fought for his country," Crocker replied. He urged his horse into a trot. "Rud gave me his personal effects to deliver in the event of his death, and that's what I'm going to do."

The ride continued in silence through the dense woods when, above the dry bone knock and creak of bare branches, there came a low earth-rumbling caused by a large body of horsemen. The three riders pulled up short and listened to the approaching sound. Metal accouterments could be heard jangling and clinking.

Crocker leaned forward in his saddle. "Think they might be Rebs, Frank?"

"Can't tell. Better run our horses behind that ledge of rock until we're sure."

Hiding under cover until the advancing horsemen proved to be friendly, the three emerged from their place of concealment and waited for the mounted column to pass.

Suddenly a voice rang out. "I'll be a bow-legged bastard! Frank!"

One of the troopers cut his horse out of line and raced toward Captain Donaldson, who shouted in response. "Joe!"

Riding up to each other, the two embraced warmly.

"How are things, little brother?"

"Good, Joe. And you?"

"Couldn't be better. But say, what are you doing this far from camp?"

"We're paying a social call to a comrade's family. Why is the cavalry coming in like this? Thought you fellas..."

"We don't know. Figure something big's in the wind. These friends of yours?"

"I'm sorry. Meet Lem Crocker and Paddy Mulcahy."

The cavalryman extended his hand. "Captain, glad to make your acquaintance." He turned in Paddy's direction. "So you're Mulcahy. Frank's often mentioned you in his letters. Good to meet you. Say Bruzz, have you had any word from the folks lately? One thing a trooper doesn't enjoy is regular mail."

"Yes, a letter came just before we took up the march." He reached inside a coat pocket and pulled out a folded envelope. "Here, take it. Read it when you've got some time."

"Thanks, Bruzz. By the way, our new captain is Ulrich Dahlgren. Remember him?"

"Certainly ought to. We fenced each other at the Philadelphia gymnasium. He's quite a swordsman." Feigning pain, he rubbed an arm in reminiscence.

Standing in his stirrups Joe Donaldson looked toward the column. "Here comes Ulrich now. I'll call him over. Yo, Ulrich, come see what the wind blew in."

Turning at the call was an officer about twenty years of age, tall, lean and striking, his handsome Nordic features partly effaced by a well-trimmed mustache and goatee. Sitting a spirited charger with the grace and ease of an errant knight, a flair of cocksureness about him, he cantered forward. Sighting his former fencing partner, he quickened his approach. An animated reunion ensued during the course of which Paddy backed off a few paces and listened. Then with an eye to the urgency of other business, the conversation ended and the soldiers parted with hearty handclasps.

Crocker looked back over his shoulder. "That friend of yours is quite some popinjay, Frank. Almost expect to find his kind riding with Stuart's Virginians, not among our seedy 'yellow-legs."

"Sounds as if you put little stock in our cavalry."

"I don't."

"Well, I'll have to agree they haven't shown us anything so far, but give 'em time."

"Time for what? Riding lessons?"

"Maybe. Don't forget most Southerners are practically born in the saddle, learn to ride behind hounds before they can walk. In the northeast, on the other hand, my brother, Joe, might be called an exception. He would ride cross-country on a Sunday whirl or an occasional fox hunt. Soon as they get some good leadership and experience, our boys'll match anything the Rebs have to offer."

"I won't hold my breath."

Managing the reins in one hand, Paddy let a free arm dangle loosely at his side. "Frank, how come that fella Dahlgren's not in the navy? Isn't his father an admiral?"

"Yes. And as a navel gun architect, he ranks as one of the best in the world."

"That's what I mean. You'd think Dalgren'd have sea legs, want to take after his father."

"You don't know Ulrich. Has a mind of his own. Didn't you hear the way he explained it back there? Said he wanted to 'look into the enemies' eyes.'"

Crocker snorted. "Fat chance he'll have. Our cavalry's used for nothing but a bunch of errand boys. Nobody's seen a dead trooper yet."

Putting spurs to their horses, the three took off at a gallop. On reaching the town of Sulphur Springs, a fashionable resort before the war, they stopped short and stared with misgivings at a burned-out rubble of charred boards and twisted wreckage. Crumbling brick chimneys stood forlorn and barren against a gray sky.

"What a sorry sight," Crocker muttered. "Think our army's responsible?"

Donaldson's lips drew taut. "More than likely. Guess you'll find soldiers without principal in any army, but there's no excuse for this kind of thing. What do we do? Turn back?"

"No, not yet." Crocker scanned the surrounding countryside. "Rud mentioned something about his house being a half mile from town. We'll look around. Maybe it wasn't touched."

Paddy suddenly pointed toward a large manor house located on top of a distant hill. "There's a place up there, maybe that's it."

"Could be. Let's ride over and find out."

As they drew near they could see the dwelling had been spared the ravages of war, but the spacious grounds showed evidence of neglect and hard times. Grass had grown up in a graveled driveway, broken branches and limbs from trees cluttered an unkempt lawn. Pillars that supported a wide verandah in front of the house were badly in need of paint and showed signs of rot. A few scattered chickens and a scrubby cow idled about, eking an existence from a frost-withered garden patch. Off by itself in a field was a family burial ground, a small lot enclosed by a rusted iron fence caving in at places. Varying in age and condition, the tombstones seemed an ever-present reminder to the White family of its heritage.

"I wish now we hadn't come," Crocker murmured. "In my mind I can picture Rud playing on that sun-filled porch in happier days."

Paddy glanced about. "That, or riding up this driveway with his friends in the Black Horse Cavalry. He sure must've felt strong for Union."

The three dismounted and slowly ascended the creaking porch steps. Wind in the eaves caused the old boards overhead to creak and groan. Raising his arm, Crocker knocked on a heavily paneled door that was opened by an aged Negro. Gray ringlets surrounded the servant's face, which became a stern mask.

"Go 'way, Yankees. 'Nuffin' left here to steal. Go 'way'n let Massa and Missus be."

For all the hardness and severity in Crocker's full-bearded countenance, there was soft gentleness in his voice.

"You've nothing to fear, Uncle. We come in peace. Do the Whites live here?"

"Yessuh, they do. What fo yo' want to see the folks?"

"Lieutenant White was a close friend of ours. We've brought his belongings home as he requested."

"Somethin' happened to Marsa Rud? Oh, Lawd, please say nothin' done happen to Marsa Rud. Ah been his body servant since he was a chile."

"Who's that at the door, Amos?"

"Yankees, ma'am. Somethin's happened to Marsa Rud."

A frail, gray-haired woman, shawled and bearing a striking resemblance to the deceased lieutenant, appeared in the doorway. She surveyed the soldiers icily. "Be brief about your business, Yankees. What is it you want?"

Crocker removed his hat. "I've brought you Lieutenant White's personal effects, ma'am. He was killed in the fighting at Shepherdstown. We were friends of his."

Paddy gazed down at his battered shoes rather than look at the woman's grief-stricken expression.

Bursting into tears, the Negro fled inside the house, his broken-hearted sobs falling heavily on the painful silence.

The woman moved her lips. "Won't you come in?"

"Thank you, ma'am."

They followed silently as she led them into a large parlor filled with musty dampness and remained standing at attention while she seated herself in a rocking chair. An oil painting hanging above a fireplace caught Paddy's eye. Framed by brass sconces, the dry-cracked likeness of a dignified, wing-collared family patriarch stared back at him in cold surveillance.

"Please sit down. My husband will be here presently." Mrs. White fought hard to keep back tears. "May I have my son's possessions?"

Rising, Captain Crocker handed her a package of contents wrapped in oilcloth.

Mr. White, tall, erect and distinguished-looking, appeared in the doorway. Moving to his wife's side, he placed a gentle hand on her shoulder. "Is this true, what Amos tells me?"

She nodded and wiped her eyes with a lace handkerchief. Paddy wished he had stayed in camp as he heard Captain Crocker speak.

"May we extend our deepest personal respects and sympathy, sir?"

There was silence. Mr. White kept both hands firmly at his side. Finally, he approached each man, shook hands, and received introductions.

"My son joined a Philadelphia Regiment. Are you from that city?"

"Yes, sir, we are," Donaldson answered.

"I see. Well, perhaps you're a better breed of Yankee than we've met so far." He returned to his wife's side and picked up a gold watch that lay amongst the articles spread in her lap. Opening the case with an unsteady hand, he read an inscription half aloud, "To my son, Rudhall White, on his twentieth birthday. Father." Tears welled in his eyes. "Tell me, did my boy suffer?"

Crocker and Donaldson exchanged glances. "No, sir, it came very quickly."

Anguished, Mrs. White buried her head in the things her son had carried off to war in his pockets.

Comforting his wife, Mr. White turned. "Rud was our only child. We're both very grateful for your visit. By staying and having dinner with us, you would do us an even greater kindness."

Crocker looked at the others. "We'd like to, sir, but..."

"Please, stay a while longer and dine with us. It's hard to believe we will never see our son again. You were his friends. In many ways, you probably knew and understood him better than we, his own parents."

"We accept your kind invitation," Paddy heard Crocker say.

Two hours later the visit with Lieutenant White's bereaved parents came to an end and the three men returned to camp in silence, each man riding with his own thoughts.

During the bleak days of gray overcast that followed, the Army of the Potomac remained inactive around Warrenton. The Army of the Northern Virginia, under Lee, moved eastward from the Blue Ridge Mountains and gathered in force around Culpepper between the Rapahannock and Rapidan rivers.

In the camps of the idle Federal troops, time passed with monotonous regularity. The numbing cold, boredom, sickness and disillusionment began to sap morale.

Desertions increased at an alarming rate. Among the captured waiting for exchange at Camp Parole in Maryland, and in the various hospitals where they were recuperating, many were walking away from the war.

Few returned to take up their rightful places in the ranks. Those seeking reunion and renewed service with old friends and regiments proved to be the patriotic, the adventurous and the lighthearted. Exemplifying these were Joe Tibben and Willie McCool, both of whom had been wounded at Shepherdstown.

Sneaking into camp under cover of a snow storm on the morning of December 10, the two posted themselves out of sight at the far end of their company street. Placing a smuggled bugle to his lips, the mouthpiece of which was so cold that it stuck to his flesh, McCool drew in his breath and with a loud burst signaled General Assembly in clear, resounding notes.

Instantly, the camp came alive, a hustling beehive of activity as half-clad soldiers came scurrying out of warm doghouses from all directions. The startled men grabbed stacked rifles, adjusted clothing and quickly formed ranks. Surprised at hearing a call that signified final notice for breaking camp, the assembled troops stared about looking for the meaning of it. McCool and Tibben, radiant in their moment of triumph, sauntered into view. McCool's face was a comically drawn mask. "All right, men, let's get on with the war," he shouted.

Sergeant Cassidy's mouth flew open. "Ye simple-minded, bird-brained idiots!" he roared. "It ain't just our company what heard that bugle. Look! The whole regiment's...Mither o' God, the whole brigade's turned out! Git in this tent before they find out who blew that call. Faith'n ye'll both be sent to the hospital fer good."

Making a headlong dive for the specified hiding place, the culprits quickly covered themselves with blankets and waited breathlessly as an angry uproar over the false alarm was turned aside by glib assurances from Sergeant Cassidy that no one in his company had blown the bugle. Deeming it safe at last, with sheepish expressions, they crawled from their haven.

Paddy shook hands with both. "You monkeys haven't changed a bit. But it's good having you back, eh Sarg?"

"Good? It's worse'n wakin' up to find ye've got the pox. Wait'll I lay me..."

Paddy stepped between. "Aw, lay off ' em, Andy. We haven't had a good laugh in a long time. No harm's been done." He looked around. "Where's Allen? Didn't he return with you?"

McCool stopped laughing. "No. He's got a disabled leg and been discharged. Going back to medical school with a lot of firsthand knowledge to boot."

Tibben's sparkling-eyed expression took on an anxious look. "Where'd our friend get to, Willie? Don't think he ran off with all our booty, do you?" He turned toward those gathered around. "We brought presents for all you boys."

"Booty? Presents? What are you talking about?"

"You'll see, Mulcahy. Our business partner's an old friend of yours. Used to be your personal carriage man."

"You're off your nut. I never had a...."

Careening into view at that moment, a clattering sutler's wagon bore down heavily on the milling group of soldiers, its paraphernalia, knickknacks and supply of luxuries foreign to camp life jouncing and rattling about wildly.

Paddy gaped and gasped. "Judas Priest! You fellas didn't steal a sutler's wagon, did you?"

"Course not," Tibben replied with a mock display of injured feelings. "We heard the owner also traded with the Johnnies. To make the blockade more effective, we lifted his wagon. You wouldn't want to see all that stuff traded or sold to the Rebs, would you?"

"Well, no, not exactly but..."

"Ho, there, Paddy Mulcahy," a voice called. "Would ye' 'ave a wee dock and doras wi' an auld friend?"

Spinning on his heel, Paddy faced the driver of the confiscated wagon. "Gilmour!"

"Aye, lad. Pipin' in the hagis and ramshead for your very own pleasure."

With one grand leap, Paddy sprang onto the wagon tongue. "It's good seeing you again, Dunk, but I don't understand. How's come you're here?"

"Waggonin' jolts the kidneys, lad. Gives a mon callouses in the wrong places. It's me aim to march a wee bit and sling a rifle. To boot, there's another auld friend of mine in your regiment."

"Who's that? Captain Scott?"

"Aye, how did ye know?"

Paddy pushed Gilmour's floppy hat down over his eyes. "Because you're birds of a feather, that's why."

Further attempts at conversation were drowned by a wild clamoring set up by fellow soldiers not wishing or intending to be denied a share in the tempting spoils. Jumping in the nick of time, both men on the wagon barely escaped being crushed as the surging mob tumbled the wagon over on its side, in a jubilant free-for-all scramble for the contraband. If permanent furloughs had been issued, there could have been no greater joy in the Corn Exchange regiment than at that moment.

Men grown haggard and dispirited by war romped and frolicked in the snow, laughed, traded stories and freely helped themselves to the purloined luxury items throughout the rest of the morning, but the pendulum of fate was swinging.

By noon it stopped snowing and many of the men, glutted to satisfaction, began moving to the comfort of their quarters. The company street was nearly deserted when Captain Donaldson appeared, dejected, his usual happy self somber.

"Sergeant Cassidy."

"Yes, sir."

"Have the men ready to stand inspection in one half hour."

"Inspection? In this stuff? Whatever for, sir?"

"Division call's in one half hour, Sergeant. See to it."

"Yes, sir. All right, men, everybody hop to it. Inspection in a half hour."

To the tune of perennial grumbling, shoes were polished and gun barrels, bayonets and buttons laboriously burnished with fine wet gravel.

At one o'clock the regimental bugler appeared in front of division headquarters located on a hill in full view of the troops. Planting himself conspicuously, he blew the first few notes of division call. Customarily, another call of some sort followed immediately after the last note died away, but whether trying to imitate McCool's fractiousness or peeved at the unknown prankster's infringement, the bugler would not have it so.

He stood erect with shoulders square, heels together–unusual for a mounted man–and with calm assurance of his own importance, knowing he was observed, deliberately surveyed the anxiously waiting men. Then, as if determined to continue their expectancy, he slowly wiped the mouthpiece, pressed the instrument to his lips, distended his ponderous jowls and without sounding the faintest note, removed it and doubled over with laughter. This he did all by himself; nobody laughed with him. He repeated the same operation again and again, each time laughing louder. Finally, either concluding his efforts were not appreciated or weary of the effort, he straightened himself, and the "general" rang out full and clear. A derisive yell from the troops followed the last note and the disgusted bugler sought obscurity amidst shouts of, "Shoot him!", "Stuff rags in his horn!", Put him out!" and Tramp on him!"

The levity was brought to an abrupt halt by the appearance of Colonel Gwyn and his mounted staff, all of whom were grim-visaged as they approached the regimental line.

"Look at them faces," Cassidy muttered. "Somethin's rotten in Denmark."

Colonel Gwyn halted his horse in front of the colors. Everything hushed. "Men, I'll be brief. President Lincoln has just relieved General McClellan of his command. Your new leader is General Burnside."

It was as if a bomb had been exploded. Stunned, the regiment stood in shock, unable to believe what they heard. McClellan, despite his shortcomings, had become a symbol for them. He was father, brother, teacher, pastor; he was a focal point around which everything revolved.

Over a period of time there had grown such an enthusiasm and affection for McClellan that a total severance of his authority at this point could only mean disruption and collapse. He had lifted the army by its bootstraps following Pope's disaster at Second Bull Run, and from that moment had received a devotion they gave no other man. With his own peculiar brand of magic, he had changed them from a mob of disorganized soldiers into a disciplined body, pulling them back single-handedly from the depths of demoralization and had taken them to Antietam where they fought heroically. If he had failed, and he had on several occasions, the fault lay not with him, but with Lincoln and the meddling fools in Washington. To have him summarily relieved and Burnside replace him, the one whose behavior had cost them the victory at Antietam, was too much.

"No! No!" came the angry cry from hundreds of throats. "We want Little Mac! Down with Lincoln! Down with political scoundrels!"

Gwyn brandished a sword and called for order. When a semblance of order was restored, he rose in his stirrups. "I'll be having no more outbursts like that from this regiment, understand? Despite your feelings, and mine, we must restrain ourselves by good sense, patriotism and discipline."

Subdued threats of vengeance and mutterings of insurrection wilted under the fire from Colonel Gwyn's tongue. He searched the ranks with a piercing eye.

"I'm glad we understand each other. At three o'clock, the general will review his army for the last time. I want no more such demonstrations. You are dismissed."

Gilmour growled as the men broke ranks. "His army. That's the vain kind o' talk what got Little Mac into this bloody stew. Always it's been 'his' army, nobody else's. Know what they call you lads in Washington? 'General McClellan's bodyguard.' Aye. I tell ye what happened today's for the good. A general's got to learn he ain't no god."

Joe Byram walked slack jawed and morose. "He's been a damn sight better to us than Lincoln and the filthy politicians. Always interfering and criticizing us from far off where things are safe and comfortable."

Luke Jobson spat on the ground. "Joe's right, Mac's been offered up as a sacrifice to satisfy the abolitionists. Honest Abe's done us in again, same as when he freed the slaves after telling us we were fighting to preserve the Union."

George Dyer curled his lips. "Abe Lincoln's a two-faced, conniving liar that can't be trusted, and this latest act proves it. I say we oughta change front on Washington, oust the government, and put Mac in control of all civil and military authority."

"Hoot, mon, ye sound like a pack o' small dogs yappin' at the heels of a big mon," Gilmour snarled.

"We have our reasons."

"Do ye now? By the sword o' Saint Andrew let me tell ye what I think o' generals, ward heelin' politicians, and the like. They're the same as ants on a log that's being swept along by a flood tide, and each ant thinks he's doing the steering. Now, by all that's holy, ye lads are beginning to talk and act just like one of 'em.'"

"What makes you think Abe Lincoln's any better at steering the log than us miserable ants?" Willie McCool asked defiantly.

"Because he's aware of grave responsibility, ye insolent pup. Aye, responsibility, that's the word. He's a shrewd mon. Ruthless ye say, but he's the only one what's been lookin' at this bloody war in its broadest light. Ye should be thankin' the good Lord he's got the patience, strength 'n courage to steer a course as well as he's been doin', what with all the little yappin' dogs snappin' at his heels."

"Sure'n I for one agree with the Scotsman," Cassidy responded. "Men like Abe Lincoln gotta be dead a hundred years before anybody finds out how great they really was."

"Just like with sergeants, huh?" Tibben's roguish face quickly disappeared behind Jobson's broad shoulders.

"I seen ye, ye smirkin' golliwogg. Wish the Rebs had o' blowed yer tongue out while they was at it. The rest o' ye squirrels git back to yer quarters. And soft pedal the hard talk, like the Colonel ordered."

"Aw, go steer a log for yourself," McCool said with a smirk and darted away.

Walking away slowly, the Quaker dropped back a step. "How do thee feel about matters, Friend Paddy?"

"Mac got what was coming to him. A general has no right mixing in with politics. Stirs up hard feelings and we catch the sparks."

"I agree with thee."

The army was assembled to bid farewell to its beloved commander, and a sadder gathering could not be imagined. Victims of nation-wide innocence, they were young men who had gone to fight a picture-book war. Many were teenagers filled with yearnings for impossible romance and adventure. Nothing was left of that early spirit now except their love for McClellan. He remained the justification of their early hopes, their last defense against complete disillusionment. Could the war go on if he was taken away?

With their blue uniforms standing out in bold relief against snowdrifts and a pearl gray sky, the men in the Fifth Corps assumed a place in line along one side of the Centerville Pike. Powdery snow began falling, filling the folds and creases in General Porter's new hat and neat uniform as he calmly sat his horse at the head of the corps, knowing inwardly that he, too, was being removed from command because of the vindictive charges filed by Pope. Word had already leaked to the troops that the officer who had brought down orders relieving McClellan had also brought orders that Porter was to be court-martialed and cashiered. This additional information served to increase the army's seething resentment against Washington officialdom.

General Sumner's Second Corps, of which the Philadelphia Brigade was an integral part, moved into position directly opposite the Fifth Corps and with solemn expressions, faced their comrades in arms across the muddy Pike.

Paddy searched the closed-up columns of Sumner's Corps and caught sight of the Seventy-first Pennsylvania. His former comrades looked fiercely grim and mad enough to chew nails. He saw Isaac Tibben kick at some packed snow, then raise his head, and, spying his younger brother in the ranks of the Hundred and Eighteenth, wave halfheartedly.

Batteries of field artillery, drawn up in the intervals between brigades, rumbled into place as sullen infantrymen watched with an awful, moving silence.

All was in readiness, everything quiet and still, and at last their handsome general, astride his great black horse, came riding between the lines. Thunderous cheers rolled up from column after column of men as they yelled their farewells. As he moved slowly along, tears streamed from McClellan's eyes. In his wake rang out heart-rending cries of "Send him back!" A seismic buildup of dangerous proportions was developing.

At their commander's approach, the Corn Exchange Regiment snapped to attention and presented arms in unison with the Philadelphia Brigade across the way. Chins pressed tremulously against cap straps, breathing came hard as McClellan paused, halted and nodded farewell to the troops from his native city.

Taut as finely drawn wire, pent-up emotions suddenly snapped under the stress and strain of the moment. In a fulminating stroke, whole regiments broke and rigid rows of muskets jerked askew as thousands of heartbroken men surged forward. Flocking around their broken commander, they cried and beseeched him not to leave.

A scarred and grizzled captain grabbed McClellan's reins. "Say the word,

General! Say a word and we'll settle matters in Washington for you!"

General Humphrey, his bony countenance florid from wind and whiskey, crowded his horse in close. He brushed the gesticulating captain aside and turned to McClellan. "By God, the army's yours! Take it. March on Washington and throw the scoundrels into the Potomac."

McClellan's tears stopped suddenly. His features froze. All around him the overt acts of mutiny were spreading. Meager's Irish Brigade pressed in upon the tumultuous scene and started throwing their rifles and flags into the slush on the road and begged McClellan to ride over them. "Lead us to Washington, General! Lead us to Washington!" they screamed. "We'll follow you!"

McClellan's shocked expression conveyed his disbelief at this pledge of loyalty. He called for order, but to no avail. After several futile attempts to make himself heard above the uproar, he stiffened in the saddle and stood bolt upright. "Pick up those flags," he commanded. "They are covered with too much blood and honor to be stained by Virginia mud. By such action you do me dishonor. Pick up those colors! Pick them up instantly!"

Crestfallen, the mutinous soldiers slowly picked up their flags and returned meekly to the ranks so that his cortege could pass.

The Quaker placed a hand on Paddy's shoulder. "Thee can put this down as being McClellan's finest hour, friend."

"You're dead right on that score. Never thought he'd pass it up. The boys offered it to him, but he wouldn't buy. He could have been a dictator."

Guns boomed a salute in the distance as McClellan, crushed and weeping, boarded a special train. At the last moment there was another abortive outbreak as soldiers broke ranks and in desperation swarmed about his Pullman car, uncoupling it and swearing that he would not leave.

Making an appearance on the rear platform, McClellan dried his eyes and pleaded in a pained voice. "Stand by General Burnside as you have stood by me and all will be well. Now couple the car, for I must leave."

Obeying with loyalty bordering on voluntary servitude, the men restored the car to the rest of the train and stepped back.

There was a jettison of steam. The train gave a lurch and ground slowly out of the siding. Soldiers wearing hang-dog looks, hands thrust deep in their pockets, watched silently as the train gained momentum, the cars clicking rhythmically over the iron rails and gradually disappearing from sight. In the gray, snowy distance a mournful cry from the locomotive whistle drifted back across the winter dusk.

Several days later, the Federal camps around Warrenton were aroused at six in the morning by bugle calls signaling Burnside's intention to move. Camps were broken, wagons loaded to capacity, and soon regiment after regiment swung into a column on the muddy pike. Marching proudly in the lead, the men of Burnside's former corps sported short side whiskers worn with a smooth chin as a mark of distinction for their commander whose mutton chop whiskers they copied and which they now called sideburns in his honor.

An early morning drizzle turned into a drenching downpour as the army headed east, flags cased against the angry skies. The road and fields were churned into a sea of mud by thousands of plodding feet, the deep, loamy gumbo holding footsteps fast in a tenacious sucking grip that seemed unwilling to let them go, sometimes drawing men to their knees. Scattered signposts along the bleak, desolate route pointed to an unfamiliar destination, Fredericksburg.

CHAPTER 12

On Saturday, December 13th, Burnside launched a long delayed attack on Lee's impregnable fortifications overlooking Fredericksburg, Virginia. An impenetrable fog was so dense that it, with the smoke of battle, made objects close at hand scarcely visible. Between nine and ten o'clock, the fog lifted a little and unfolded a scene thrilling in its inspiration and awful in its terror. The men of the 118th stationed on Stafford Heights, stared across the Rapahannock. The streets of Fredericksburg were clogged with soldiers. Glistening rifle-barrels and somber blue coats surged in indistinguishable columns, all pressing for the open country to seek some relief from the deadly plunge of exploding cannon shots that were ripping the town apart.

Paddy knelt on one knee and shaded his eyes for a better view of the stirring scene. Nearby, oblivious to it all, Captains Donaldson, Crocker, Bankson and Scott indulged in a game of euchre.

At one o'clock the regiment was called to attention and, with the division, began the movement to the pontoon bridges. The march was tedious, halting and hesitating. The bridges were crowded and the streets jammed from the slow deployment under the withering fire that met the fresh victims being fed piecemeal into slaughter.

Paddy studied the flame-sheeted slope of Marye's Heights. Long lines of Federal infantry formed with regularity. Moving with precision, they disappeared almost as quickly as they were seen before the furious cannonade and deadly musketry. Horror was everywhere and the 118th was about to plunge into the very jaws of the carnage.

Paddy mopped his brow and turned to the Quaker. "This is plain murder," he growled. "No way those heights can be taken except by flank attack."

The Quaker rubbed an inflamed eye with his finger. "That is for damn sure," he replied. "Burnside is a stubborn fool to keep this up."

A sign nearby that spelled out in large block letters "Van Haugens Variety Store" was suddenly torn into fragments by a shell burst. Pieces of shell and sign rained down on the ranks of Company K with chilling effect. In the rear, another shell burst over the 1st Michigan, killing sixteen of its soldiers whose startled shrieks could be heard above the din and roar of battle. A long drum roll signaled the brigade to advance. Colonel Gwyn raised his sword and bellowed, "Corn Exchange, forward!" The column of Philadelphians moved as one and waded knee deep through a mill-race under heavy Confederate fire.

The assault up the steep slope to Marye's Heights was begun and maintained with reasonable regularity toward a rubbled brickyard. Mangled, bleeding forms lay strewn everywhere around the kilns. The 118th's advance continued upward and onward toward a board fence. The fence was about five feet high, of three boards, with intervals between them. Bodies of the dead, who had tried earlier to remove the boards, were heaped one upon another.

"Tear away those blasted boards!" Major Herring shouted from his horse. A ball struck his right arm and buckshot tore through his coat.

"This is awful!" someone said.

"This is what we came here for," quietly replied the Major as he dismounted.

Strong arms frantically seized and tore all the boards away. Thinned out, exhausted, with energies taxed to their limit in the face of such fearful odds, instinctively the line halted. The stone wall, behind which belched the deadly rebel musketry, was two hundred feet away. Off to the left was an undulation broad enough to shelter the entire regimental front. The 118th was ordered into the depression.

Darkness fell and a pale winter moon bathed the blood-soaked battlefield in a ghostly light. Clothes were removed from the dead to warm the wounded. Naked corpses lay in grotesque positions. From the littered slope carpeted with blue-coated bodies came sounds terrible to hear. There were cries for help, some calling on god for pity, and delirious voices calling out the names of loved ones.

Paddy, choking on the powdered dirt in his mouth, tried to console Bob Dyer, who had covered himself with his brother's slain body as a shield against bullets and cold weather. Helpless, the Frankford volunteers looked on with anguish as Joe Byram, hemorrhaging badly, slowly froze to death before their eyes.

Paddy turned his thoughts to Becky. He wondered if he would live to see her again. Long into the night he relived every precious moment they had spent together. The thought of her sustained him.

All the next day, Sunday, the 118th remained pinned down, bodies flattened on the earth. About noon, Captain Crocker could no longer brook this forced restraint. Angered beyond endurance at foes who kept him thus confined, he rose suddenly from his place, seized the colors, advanced with them a few paces to the front and jammed the staff well into the ground. He shook his fist and shouted, "You slave-holding whore-mongering bastards, come out and fight like men!"

Verbal abuse and a volley of balls from behind the stone wall greeted his temerity as he returned to the line unscathed.

Late that night, the 118th was ordered to retreat through Fredericksburg. Once the beautiful colonial seat of gentle ways and drowsy streets, it was now blown to bits and badly ransacked. All manner of household goods and furniture littered the streets. Shutters on broken hinges, moved by the whistling winds, banged eerily against the hollow shells of houses. Kneeling figures, eyes glazed by death, still sighted their rifles.

Upon reaching the Rapahannock, the weary men noticed with alarm that all the pontoon bridges had been taken up, save one, and it was being demolished by the engineers. Colonel Gwyn dashed forward on horseback. "Hold on, you sons of bitches!" he shouted. "My men have to cross!"

"You the last?" an officer replied.

"Yes."

"Tell your men to shake a leg."

In quick-step, the Corn exchange marched across to join the rest of the demoralized army in winter quarters at Falmouth.

The temper of the army and homefront had to be assuaged, and to this end, General Burnside was summarily removed from command by President Lincoln. At the same time, a copy of a letter to General Hooker was circulated for all to read:

Executive Mansion
Washington, D.C.
January 26, 1863
Major General Hooker:

General:

I have placed you at the head of the Army of the Potomac. Of course I have done this on what appears to me to be sufficient reason, and yet I think it best for you to know that there are some things in regard to which I am not satisfied. I believe you to be a brave, skillful soldier, which of course I appreciate. I also believe you do not mix politics with your profession, and in that you are right. You have confidence in yourself, which is a valuable, if not indispensable, quality. You are ambitious which, within reasonable bounds, does good rather than harm, but I think that during General Burnside 's command of the army you have taken counsel of your ambition and thwarted him on various occasions; thus you did a great wrong to the country and to a meritorious and honorable brother-officer.

I have heard, in such a way as to believe it, of your recently saying that both the army and the government needed a dictator. Of course it was not for this, but in spite of it, that I have given you command. Only those generals who gain success can set up dictators. What I ask of you is military success, and I will risk the dictatorship.

The government will support you to the utmost of its ability, which is neither more nor less than it has done and will do for all commanders. I much fear that your spirit of criticism with which you have infused the army, will now turn upon you. I shall assist you, as far as I can, to put it down. Neither you, nor Napoleon, if he were still alive, could get cooperation from an army while such a spirit prevails.

Watch rashness; beware of it. But march forward with energy and sleepless vigilance and give us victories.

Yours truly,
A. Lincoln

Gratified and flushed with vigor, Hooker immediately set out to restore the morale and health of the fractious army. An unremitting care for their needs, combined with a new liberality that permitted occasional absences, won the soldiers to him. "Fightin' Joe, a soldier's soldier" became the byword.

One significant smoke signal, ignored by all but the pure in heart, was the addition of two new expressions among the troops. The increased number of prostitutes in the camps became known as "hookers," and a large shot of whiskey was given the same sobriquet, "hooker".

Jealousies, cabals and dissensions seemed to be a thing of the past. Intriguers and plotters were disposed of. The troops were in sympathy with their commander and chieftains, and in the camps there was a feeling of success in the temper of things as the Potomac Army eagerly girded itself for renewed campaigning.

Early on the morning of April 27, the "general" sounded across the plains of Falmouth and with eight days' rations strapped to their backs, the blue-clad forces, spruced up and in high spirits marched out of camp. Adding to the joy of the occasion were song birds warbling contentedly in the bordering woods. Lacy leaves, new and emerald green from spring budding, moved softly in the warm breezes, their lazy motions seemingly set to ballet music. Rising from every side was the refreshing, earthy fragrance of spring turned sod that made it wonderful to be alive and on the march once more. Even the rumor that Fightin' Joe Hooker had remained behind, drunk and carousing in a fleshpot at Aquia Creek, did not disturb the tranquillity of the army, who were in a gay mood as they tramped west.

The route which they took led away from Fredericksburg where Lee's forces were entrenched. The road soon became littered with abandoned clothing and other impedimenta as sage veterans stripped to the bare essentials--a rifle, food, a blanket, gum blanket and a single piece of shelter tent. Thus lightened, the columns swung along in the unseasonably warm weather that baked out the winter's aches and pains. The confident men filled the air with lusty singing:
"The Union boys are moving, on the left and the right,
The bugle call is sounding, our shelters we must strike,
Joe Hooker is our leader, he takes his whiskey strong,
So our knapsacks we will sling, and go marching along.
Joe Hooker is our leader, he takes his whiskey strong,
So our knapsacks we will sling, and go marching along,
    Marching along, marching along,
    With eight days' rations, we'll go marching along."

McCool and Tibben, tramping at the head of the regiment, led off a second verse in loud, piping voices:
"Our overcoats and dress coats are strewn along the road,
They crowded them upon us, we couldn't tote the load,
Contractors put the job up, and we must foot the bill,
But, Sam, our dear old Uncle, we know it's not your will. . ."

Others joined in:

"Contractors put the job up, and we must foot the bill,
But, Sam, our dear old Uncle, we know it's not your will."

They continued until parched throats wore out. That night bivouac was made in the pleasant outdoors for the first time in many days, and it felt good again. After a brief supper, the men prepared for bed. Deep within the forest, tree peepers began their chorus, breaking the silence of evening with their staccato notes: a half-whistle, half- buzzing sound that lulled the tired soldiers to sleep. The air was perfumed with the fresh scent of mayapple and fern, and the moist bark of trees with the sap running. The woodland floor was carpeted with shy spring beauties. Star-of-Bethlehem and jack-in-the-pulpits peeked from beneath their delicate hoods while watchdog flames from the campfires curled to sleep in glowing beds of coals.

Late in the afternoon of the next day, the lead columns suddenly changed direction and turned south. To their astonishment they were able to make an unopposed crossing at Ely's Ford on the Rapidan. Accustomed to being outmaneuvered, they could not believe this turn of events, but as time wore on with still no sight of the enemy, one thing became clear, they had made a successful encirclement of the Confederate's western flank undetected.

Catching Lee napping, General Hooker had completely stolen a march on his adversary, confirmation of which came in a general order published for the men in the field:

Headquarters Army of the Potomac
Camp near Falmouth, Virginia
April 30, 1863
General Orders No. 47

It is with heartfelt satisfaction, the commanding general announces to the army that the operations of the past three days have determined that our enemy must either ingloriously fly, or come out from behind his defenses and give us battle on our own ground, where certain destruction awaits him.

The operations of the 5th, 11th and 12th Corps have been a succession of splendid achievements.

By Command of Major General Hooker
S. Williams. Assistant Adjutant General

The pronouncement brought forth a chorus of elation, but among the vanguard there was an apprehensive shaking of heads, for all was not sweetness and light up front. Something had already occurred that smacked of the familiar standard operating procedures customarily accompanying their usual defeats.

Under personal supervision and direction of General Charles Griffin, the advance army was led on a surprising sweep around Lee's left by the 118th, together with the first brigade from the first division, Fifth Corp. On the morning of April 30, the brigade skirmishers were brought to a temporary halt in front of a line of earthworks near a pretentious mansion called the Chancellorsville House.

Since the appearance of the breastworks indicated hasty construction, the brigade was promptly deployed, skirmishers and battle line moved forward quickly and the fortifications speedily taken. A few Confederate laggards offered little resistance and indicated astonishment at the unexpected presence of the enemy.

The first portent of things to come was learned later that afternoon. The column resumed its march, doubled back toward Fredericksburg on the old turnpike road and advanced about two miles when it was again interrupted at the foot of high ground at the top of which a single enemy gun could be seen moving rapidly away. Once more deploying, the brigade set itself to charge the eminence which was apparently abandoned and only awaited occupancy. As time dragged by, even the dullest could see the necessity of seizing the place immediately, and they could not understand the failure to do so. Figuring that the ridge was apparently the key position, if a battle was to be fought in the vicinity, the soldiers waited, anxious and ready for the orders to occupy. It was cleared land and completely out of the wilderness through which they had been traveling.

Beside the incalculable advantage of controlling such a point, it was believed its crest commanded a view of most of the country beyond; but events decreed otherwise. Hooker sent orders of a far different nature than had been originally sent to the army as a whole. He gave positive, imperative directions to General Meade, ordering him to withdraw the advance troops to the Chancellorsville House immediately, and not to engage the enemy.

Incensed at the peremptory order to stop, Generals Griffin and Barnes made earnest appeals for revocation and entered objections against their enforcement, but to no avail. As a result, the forward elements of the Fifth Corps were withdrawn, and the soldiers became discontented. Enthusiasm vanished and the bright hopes of success disappeared. The conviction that the campaign would culminate in routing the enemy was replaced by sullen disappointment. The men went into bivouac firmly convinced that somebody had again blundered.

Bedding down for the night, Paddy lay with his hands folded behind his head, eyes staring fixedly at a tent pole. The Quaker next to him stirred and rolled over on his side.

"Forget about it, friend. Fretting on matters beyond thy control won't do thee any good. Try and get some sleep."

"Sleep? Who in the hell can sleep while a drunken commander lies nursing a hangover miles away from where the action is? If Hooker had been sober and where he belonged, we would be in Fredericksburg by now. In one whiskey breath he's got Rebs whipped without firing a shot, in the next he's got the shakes and pulls us back, again without a shot being fired. Right now he's probably seeing monkeys crawling all over him."

"Yes, it's a crying shame. We could have run right down their backs the way we were moving. And with Sedgewick's Corps hitting them from below, we would have had them in a nutcracker. Beautiful opportunity while it lasted."

"Yes, but it'll never be pulled off now. Lee knows now where our army is, and he'll come barrel-assing down on us, and we'll end up in the same old pickle barrel. And this tangled mess of jungle ain't no place to fight, we'll be trapped in it, you wait and see. Our generals aren't worth a tinker's damn."

"Amen to that, friend. Better roll over and say thy prayers for a better tomorrow."

Adding to the general gloom were the baleful screech of owls, the plaintive cries of whippoorwills and the buzzing of insects. Different species of the latter, not content with making night noises, investigated the change in their environment. Large black ants wandered through the hardtack in haversacks, stopping now and then to refresh themselves with a lunch. Thousand-leggers crawled over sleeping faces, necks, and hands unnoticed, but stag beetles and horn bugs nipped wherever they alighted and were quickly crushed.

Heralding the first day of May, slanting beams of early morning sunlight tinged the treetops, crowning them with a golden majesty that reflected from the peaked tin roof of the Chancellorsville House. The commodious, two-story brick building had been designed as a summer boarding house styled along the traditional lines of Southern architecture. The hostelry bordered the Fredericksburg and Orange Plank Road. Prominent pillared porches, one built on top of the other, faced toward Fredericksburg, which lay twelve miles to the east. Owned by a well-known family of the vicinity, the great house still remained occupied by some women who, as the sun rose higher, came out on the lawn. Standing alone and defiant, they glared at the intruders camped on the grounds.

A short distance away, Paddy relieved his bladder in a thicket then, scratching at his disheveled hair, yawned, dug at his eye sockets, stretched his arms and called to McCool who was kneeling by a smoking cook fire.

"Hey, Willie, you got coffee ready yet?"

"Yep, come and get it. Boy, ain't this some morning?"

Rising to his feet, he screwed up his nose and inhaled deeply.

"What's so good about it?" Paddy grumbled.

"Mmm, just smell that air. Fresh as a daisy. Sort o' purifies a man's soul."

From the direction of the Chancellorsville House came a high-pitched, scolding, female voice. A pinch-lipped, middle-aged woman, her hair tied back in a bun, shook an angry finger in Captain Donaldson's face. "And I'll have no truck with mere captains," she screeched. "I want to talk directly with your commanding officer. These . . . this damn Yankee trash must be removed from my premises immediately. Immediately, do you hear?"

"I'm sorry, ma'am, but we've strict orders to remain where we are. You've my word as a gentleman the men will not offend you in any way nor trespass on your buildings."

"That matters not in the least. I don't want you damned Yankee tramps purloining and despoiling my property. Why don't you go meet General Lee like men instead of hovering around a house full of defenseless women? You cringing cowards, I'm sure General Lee's just waitin' to extend you the hospitalities of the country."

"I'm sure he is, ma'am. I'll convey your message to Colonel Prevost." Flushed and embarrassed, Donaldson made a hasty retreat.

Coming to the aid of the spinsterish woman, a bevy of ladies in light spring costumes appeared on an upper porch and, likewise unabashed or unintimidated, began to hurl taunts and aspersions at the men of the regiment camped below. Every so often they spit on the blue-clad troops.

McCool wore a puzzled expression as he looked up at them.

"Gosh all hemlock. Would ya listen to what they're callin' us? And such screamin'. If I knew my mother ever carried on like that, I'd hide my head in shame."

"Don't mind 'em," Paddy snorted. "Their kind don't know any better. 'Bitchy mean' as Pa used to say."

Tibben approached, stopping to glance over his shoulder. "Really giving us hell, ain't they? We oughta figure out a prank to pull on 'em."

"You do, and the cap'n 'll put your ass on a sawbuck. We ain't to go near them buildings."

"What's the matter, Willie, you sick? Turning away from a little sport just because. . .but maybe you're right. Like they say, they're poor defenseless women, except for their big mouths, that is. Say, did you hear about Cap'n Crocker?"

Paddy slipped into a blouse. "No, what about him?"

Tibben tried to suppress his laughter.

"Last night he couldn't get comfortable on the ground where he was sleeping. Kept turning and rolling all night trying to remove some bumps sticking into his gum blanket. Found out this morning when it got light enough that he was sleeping over a new, shallow grave, the bumps he'd been tugging at all night trying to smooth over were the nose and fingers of the partially covered occupant."

McCool doubled over with laughter. "Boy, oh boy, would I like to have seen his face when he found out. What did he do?"

"Do? Man, he shook, spit, coughed and reached quick for a hooker of whiskey. Now he's telling everybody the soft spongy body was what made his bed so springy and comfortable."

"Too bad...too bad it didn't happen to Cassidy. You know how squeamish he is about things."

Paddy started to walk away. "This war's making you jokers morbid. I'm going to browse around a bit. Maybe learn what's up."

By accident rather than design, he came upon Colonel Prevost partaking of a morning drink with Captains Donaldson and Crocker. Donaldson lifted a glass. "Hold on, Paddy. Have an eye opener."

"Don't think I'd better, Cap'n, thanks."

Recently returned to duty, looking tired and drawn, Colonel Prevost raised his head. "Don't stand on formality, son. If you're a friend of Donaldson's, there's plenty of Drake's plantation bitters to go around. Must say though, it's a poor substitute for regular rations. Here, help yourself."

Paddy accepted a bottle from the Colonel's outstretched hand and, murmuring the customary, "Here's how," took a short swallow. "Thank you, sir."

"You're quite welcome. God only knows what today's fortunes will bring. Might as well fortify ourselves for the worst, the way matters have been handled so far."

Crocker wiped a trickle of bitters from his beard. "I just hope Fightin' Joe gets here before it's all over. A little nip never hurt anybody, fits you for a fight, but this business of getting shot in the head when you're in command of an army going into battle, well, that's something else again."

Suddenly, without warning, they heard prolonged heavy musketry coming from the front and rapidly increasing in furor.

Prevost stiffened. "See to your men. This sounds like the beginning of something."

Spinning on his heels, Paddy raced back to his tent and grabbed his musket. He checked his cartridge box and fell into line with his platoon.

Blue smoke began drifting through the thickets in a suffocating cloud. For an hour Griffin's division stood and listened to the sound of fighting being fiercely waged, then for some unknown reason, they were ordered to march in the direction of Banks Ford along the Rapidan. The route ran through desolate, uninhabited timber and continued for several miles to within sight of the ford. Nothing seemed to be happening at the river. No enemy appeared and the disgusted column retraced its steps back to the vicinity of the Chancellorsville House.

A noticeable change had taken place during their absence. Officers and staff were now gathered on the porch of the mansion, the presence of the ladies adding a sprinkling of society and domestic life to the scene.

Cassidy ground his teeth. "Saints preserve us. If that ain't a sight to frost yer eyeballs. Look at them popinjays lollygaggin' around like they was cocks in a barnyard."

Jake Hallowell wore a disgusted look. "I knew those clucks were sitting on their brains. The fighting is up front, so they march us five miles to the rear. Giving us the day off, I suppose."

"If brains were gunpowder, our generals wouldn't have enough to blow their noses," Luke Jobson grumbled.

His observation was cut short by the approach of Captain Donaldson. "Know what the fighting's been about all day?" he exploded. "That hill we could have had yesterday for free. Lee's got it now. Syke's division has been butchered trying to take it."

McCool shifted his feet. "Let's pack up and go home."

"Shet yer fat Irish face," Cassidy warned, his countenance falling. "What's orders Cap'n?"

"None, yet. Wait, here comes the Colonel. We'll soon find out."

Gathering into a group, the men of the regiment fell silent.

Prevost, looking fatigued to the point of being ill, posted his mount. "We're moving front. Company commanders form a line of battle."

Organizing quickly, the regiment moved forward into dense timber and underbrush, which obscured any vision over ten feet away.

"Which way is front in this jungle?" Tibben whispered. He was instantly quieted by a blow on the back.

After considerable distance had been covered, the weary troops were ordered to halt in an area where the wilderness seemed less thick and tangled. With darkness fast approaching, pickets were established well in advance of the line.

Nursing forty-year-old legs, Kimball crouched low and looked about. "Don't sound like any front's around here. Wonder what battle the general's got us workin' on?"

Comrades ignored his dry humor, anxious, uncertain expressions on their faces. Feeling abandoned, and with night coming on, certain that they were without support, and with no knowledge as to whether they were to make an attack or receive one, they recalled only too well the previous day's mismanagement and the attending results. The sturdiest spirits became apprehensive and gloomy. Just as twilight gave way to total darkness, General Barnes rode up to the scene and, seeking Colonel Prevost, immediately went into a conference.

Cautious of everything, the inquisitive troops strained to overhear the conversation. The brigade commander spoke with concern.

"You're all alone out here, far in advance of the army and liable to be attacked by overwhelming numbers at any moment. Orders for an advance to this position not being countermanded by that sot back at headquarters, I'm ordering you to retire on my own responsibility."

Colonel Prevost fingered the hilt of his sword. "Thanks, Jim. Don't want these boys to go through another Shepherdstown. Have you any information as to how Sykes fared?"

"Yes. After rough handling, he finally secured the ridge we could have had yesterday without cost, occupied it and discovered that it commanded all the open country beyond."

"Well, at least it is in our hands now. That's some comfort."

"Is it? Wait until you hear what has developed. Against appeals and stern protests from corps commanders, Hooker has ordered the entire line abandoned."

"Abandoned! You can't mean it."

"I do mean it. Lee is probable wondering what kind of knucklehead he is up against this time."

"Shouldn't wonder." Prevost heaved a sigh. "Shall we retire?"

"Yes. Hooker has since had a change of mind, but it's too late. His initial order has been executed and the ridge evacuated. Somehow or other he seems to have forgotten you are still out here, so the order is to fall back."

"I will start as soon as I call in my pickets."

"No, you don't have time. You will have to abandon them. Withdrawal must be made directly to the rear right now, silently and with extreme caution."

"But, Jim, some of my best men are out there."

"Sorry. Bringing them in would alert the enemy. You would be swarmed and cut to ribbons."

Standing within earshot, Captain Donaldson stepped forward, grim determination written on his face.

"Begging you pardon, sir, but the Colonel is right. Good men are out there keeping watch for us. We can't desert them."

Prevost rose in the saddle. "Captain Donaldson, you will place..."

"Hold on, Charley. Let him speak." Barnes leaned forward. "And just how do you propose saving this regiment and removing pickets at the same time, Captain? Without bringing on a general engagement, that is."

"With your permission, sir, I could crawl forward and bring them in so quietly you'd think they were snakes."

"Without being fired on? It's risky business, Captain. Besides, in this pitch-dark entanglement you could easily stumble right into the Reb lines."

"I'll take those chances, sir."

General Barnes glanced at Colonel Prevost. "All right, Captain. Go ahead, and good luck. To play safe, Charley, you start withdrawing the regiment."

Alone, Donaldson moved out into the eerie darkness while the main body prepared for retirement. As if sensing something afoot, heavy cannonading suddenly exploded from the Confederate lines, shells filling the starlit sky with red phlogistic streaks of fuse fire and flying missiles screaming overhead with hissing shrieks that thundered into the Union lines and the timber to their rear.

Lost to any idea of direction in the confusing wilderness, Donaldson moved stealthy forward, guiding himself by the sounds coming from the enemy lines. He could hear creaking gun carriage wheels as batteries were moved. Somewhere ahead, Confederate soldiers were driving stakes and cutting logs for breast works; in the background a banjo strummed as voices sang to the accompaniment.

Moving slowly and cautiously, he descended a sharp declivity. At the foot was a bog beyond which there was a corresponding rise to the descent he had been following. Everything was hidden in impenetrable blackness, he judged this rise to be the enemy's main line and concluded, but with no reason except supposition, that it was probably the eminence which Sykes had taken earlier from which he had been summarily withdrawn. Confronted by treacherous bogs so near the enemy line and with nothing to indicate that he could accomplish his mission, he called softly in guarded tones.

"Where's the picket line?"

There was a rustle in the brush ahead. "What picket line, mister? Give the password."

"Clover leaf. That you, Lem?"

"Yes. Frank?"

"Yeah." He pushed through the underbrush a few more feet and motioned for silence.

Crocker's fierce countenance was dimly outlined.

"What's the trouble?"

"Hooker has left you on a doorstep. The regiment has been pulled back. We have to rescue the pickets."

"Thanks for coming to take us off the hook. The Quaker is behind a forked tree just fifty feet to your right. He will help you bring in that side. I will see to the others. And don't get yourself tumbled over. I owe you a drink for this."

With each picket moving to the rear at two minute intervals to prevent telltale noises, the men were soon assembled at a prearranged meeting place, and after a long toilsome march, rejoined their command at four in the morning somewhere on a road leading to Banks Ford.

Throughout the next day there were occasional sounds of engagement elsewhere about the lines, but to the men of the Corn Exchange, relieved from the noise of battle and the excitement of marching, the masterly inactivity became a subject for discussion. The timid, panicky operation of the two previous days had encouraged the enemy to assume the offensive, and it was thought that their aggressive maneuvers would soon force the Federal leaders to find the surest way for a safe withdrawal if they were not already contemplating such.

Just before sunset, there was considerable firing to the extreme right of the army. At dark it culminated in a loud, continuous roar accompanied by a thunder of artillery, indicating heavy engagement. There were a few moments when a human voices could be heard above the sounds of battle, but the piercing shriek of the Confederates, with no corresponding return of Union cheers, told too plainly that the right had yielded. As the yells ceased, the firing slackened, and as night closed in, the 118th was ordered away from the position it had held all day.

Moving rapidly toward the Chancellorsville House, the men were thrown into earthworks recently vacated by the previous troops who had constructed them, and it was learned that the army was extending its right to recover lost lines. A series of unauthorized, demoralizing and dispiriting tactics began, with directions passed along the line from man to man to spread out and cover more ground.

Someone ordered them to turn their cap visors backward so the rays of the moon would not reflect off them. They were cautioned to keep perfectly still, to lie down, to stand up, to come to ready and then to sit down. Those and various other instructions, repeated frequently and communicated along the line in whispers, continued until the men were so nervous and unstrung that in order to establish confidence, many of the officers grabbed rifles and followed the movements with them.

The engagement ended about nine o'clock when General Howard appeared, followed by fragments of his shattered corps of Germans. Inquiry brought information that those were the forces which had speedily crumbled under Jackson's onslaught. The men moved silently, continuing to pass for over an hour. Their condition did not indicate any problems. They were evidently being placed, for the present, well out of reach of danger. A long silence followed.

The insect world was hushed. Night birds were voiceless and inquisitive squirrels looked down from their hiding places in the tops of the trees, chattering wildly for awhile then they too hushed. Frightened deer sought the safety of the wilderness depths, foxes sought their holes and rabbits their warrens. A broken twig sounded like a cannon, and the faintest whisper, an explosion. Gentle breezes became whistling winds, and falling boughs, an army on the march. Heedless of sentiment, the soldiers viewed the quiet as ominous, men insensible of fear considered the stillness portentous. A full moon shone brightly, glimmering through the treetops, occasionally fading as swift-moving clouds covered its brilliance. The pale, changing light and deathlike stillness made everything appear unreal and ghostly.

A slight flutter up front tensed every nerve as the men tried to ascertain the cause. The sound grew to recognition as a voice cautioned the men to hold their fire, and General Griffin, returning from an observation of the grounds, passed through the line. An officer of unquestioned skill and untiring energy, he had the unbounded respect and implicit confidence of every soldier in the division. His presence was assuring, and demonstrations were restrained only by the necessity for quiet.

The awful silence reigned until disturbed again by a sound resembling a whir and a sigh as if distant winds were increasing in velocity. It was the buzz and tramp of soldiers in motion with the accompanying rattle and jostle of arms and equipment. It grew louder as it approached until even the untutored could not mistake it; the disciplined Federal battalions were massing for assault. A voice commanded, "Battalion. Halt. Front. On center. Dress." A pause. "Battalion. Right shoulder. Shift Arms." Another pause. "Forward guide. Center march." Off to the right and front, rifles flashed and every gun roared as the Union Army became hotly engaged in the fury of a night attack.

Behind breastworks, removed from the scene of action, the men of the Corn Exchange strained their faculties in an effort to follow the course of the battle, listening, peering and squinting into the darkness.

Gilmour stared over a parapet. "Hoot, mon," he said in a low voice, "this is worse'n being cooped in a barrel with someone beatin' on the sides."

"Why don't you go to sleep like the lieutenant?" McCool twitted. "See, he's not worrying about anything. Sleeping like a baby."

Gilmour glanced at the curled-up form of Lieutenant Batchelder, whose nightmares, dreams of gaping wounds beyond the help of surgical skill, had become legendary.

"No thank'ee, lad. Rather stay awake than have his haunts."

Tibben, standing close by, turned with an evil expression on his face. "Ever seen him wake up shrieking like agony and death? Watch, I'll show you how it's done. I'll tickle his crotch."

Taking a ramrod, he wiggled one end of it in the groin of the sleeping officer. Instantly Batchelder grabbed for the pubic region and shot bolt upright, screaming.

"My balls! I've had my balls shot off! Oh, God, somebody help me!"

He began rolling and groveling in imaginary pain. Tibben stood by laughing heartily.

Gilmour's weathered countenance remained serious. "Ye're a miserable little prick, tormentin' a mon like that. Hope he finds ye out."

"He has no idea of what's going on," McCool replied, smothering a grin. "It's just a dream. See, he's back to sleep already."

"Aye, but I'm warnin' ye. Don't ever try to pull any o' yer dirty tricks on me. I'll have yer gizzards."

The moonlight battle subsided during the early morning hours and word filtered back to the reserve troops that Dan Sickles had been fighting his way home, his Third Corps badly damaged in the effort.

Sunday, the third of May, dawned in springtime splendor for the 118th who sat around suffering from gnawing hunger pangs. The officer's supplies were completely exhausted and rations for enlisted men had thinned to a few crackers and a scant allowance of coffee. Some of the men who never before used tobacco found it temporarily effective in satisfying their hunger.

Suddenly another clap of battle burst on their ears as a shirtless, sweating courier dashed into camp. They heard him shout, "Where's General Griffin?"

"Over there." Paddy pointed to a group of officers gathered in front of a Sibley tent.

The courier wheeled his horse, quickly covered the distance and dismounted. "General Griffin?" he inquired.

"Yes, Sergeant."

"General Meade's compliments, sir. We are being hard pressed near the Chancellorsville House. You are ordered to advance your division immediately and form on the lawn to the left."

"Return my compliments. We will move at once."

A short march followed as the men of the Corn Exchange moved back to the familiar grounds of the frame and brick structure that was now aflame and burning full bore.

Down toward the Orange Plank Road, other Federal troops were hotly contesting the outer works, resisting heavy Confederate assaults and getting ready to retire to the interior lines still in the process of preparation. Battle-ripped causalities streamed into a nearby general field hospital that was fast coming within range of the fighting. Indiscriminate shells began dropping into the area: explosive blasts killing surgeons and attendants and mangling and killing the wounded where they lay.

Riding amidst the perils of the moment came a mounted staff accompanied by a major general. The anxious men gazed at him, hopeful for some kind of relief. A dominating figure of a man, over six feet tall and beyond middle-age, the general was stern-looking to the point of austerity. His gaunt, bearded face was drawn and his deep-set eyes dark and piercing as a falcon's. Beneath a slouch hat, dusty and pulled down almost to the tip of his large Roman nose, he halted and swivelled in the saddle to examine closely the state of affairs.

"Who's the big military?" Gilmour muttered in Paddy's ear.

"New corps commander. Old 'Four Eyes' Meade. Crusty old goat."

"Aye, the one who took Dan Butterfield's place while I was home on furlough. First I've had a look at him. That nose o' his makes him appear like one o' them old-time knights with a helmet visor down, a real snappin' turtle, I'd say."

Meade, having sought out General Griffin, spoke in a gruff, biting tone. "Move your division into battle. You will probably be overrun, but make the semblance of a fight while you can."

Griffin nodded. "We shall do our best, sir. If you will grant me the artillery to use, we can make the Rebs think hell isn't half bad."

"Permission granted."

Compressing his lips, Meade squared his jaws, wheeled his horse and galloped off.

Griffin called to the artillery. "Double shot those pieces. Let the enemy approach to within fifty yards, then roll shot along the ground like this." He stooped, imitating a bowler. "Barnes, put your brigade in support of the batteries!" he shouted. "Adjutant, give word to move the rest forward!"

Posted in reserve, a few in the 118th availed themselves of the privilege of lying down, while the majority assumed crouched positions with heads erect, eyes strained and muskets upright, ready for instant service.

Lieutenant Batchelder, forgetting his dreams, mounted an abandoned chest and stood recklessly exposed. Heedless of danger, he proceeded to view the battle through a pair of field glasses. His figure, a conspicuous target, soon drew fire from enemy snipers, which brought him to the attention of Colonel Prevost.

"Lieutenant, get down and return to your post. Since you're so interested in seeing action, your company can move over to the Burns White House where the defense line needs additional support. Captain Donaldson, take your lieutenant and men and move out."

Among the less adventurous, there was spontaneous combustion. The men gritted their teeth and swore as they glared at the officer.

Donaldson took his subaltern by the arm. "You'd better bring up the rear. Up front your back would make a tempting target."

"What do you mean?"

"You don't know? You've just become a prize bastard."

Sergeant Cassidy came running back along the column, his face drawn and registering alarm as he bumped men aside right and left with his broad shoulders.

"Cap'n Donaldson, sir."

"Yes, Sergeant? What is it?"

"Up ahead, sir, Saints preserve us, detour the men, spare 'em the sight o' witnessin' it."

"Witnessing what?"

"The most disgraceful sight I've iver laid me eyes on, sir. I beg ye, reroute the column."

"Impossible, Sergeant. We've orders to proceed directly to the Burns White House. What's got you so worked up?"

"If ye've no mind t' turn, ye'll be after seein' it soon enough for yourself, sir. I'll be gettin' forward."

He turned and ran off toward the head of the moving column.

"What in the world was that all about?" inquired Batchelder, scratching his head.

"Beats me. Never saw Cassidy so unhooked before. Better go have a look. You come with me."

Quickening their steps, the two officers entered a wooded area where advance elements of the company were breaking ranks. Excited men crowded around to gape into a large tent with its flap open, the occupants exposed to plain view.

Batchelder drew up short. "That's general headquarters. See the flag on top?"

"Yes, and there's Mulcahy. Let's find out what going on."

Paddy raised his chin that he had rested on the muzzle of his musket.

"Come to see the inspiring sight, Cap'n? Have a look. Doesn't cost anything."

Donaldson craned to see over the heads of the soldiers standing in front of him. A loud murmuring filled the air.

There, in full view of the stunned troops, was General Hooker sprawled in a drunken stupor on a cot while staff officers lolled about, drinking expensive French wine. Littering the ground were scores of abandoned bottles, corks, and broken, empty baskets.

The men began turning away in angry disgust from the sound of popping champagne corks to the realistic sounds of battle where their sorely pressed comrades were retreating.

Amused by the scene, Tibben pressed his face over McCool's shoulder and said, "Don't nobody light a match. You'll blow 'em all to hell."

"Might not be a bad idea," one grim soldier replied.

Unable to curb his curiosity any longer, McCool slowly edged his way to the tent and peered inside at Hooker's prostrate body.

A staff officer seized him roughly by the collar. "Get a move on. This ain't no side show."

"Yes, sir. Right away, sir. May I ask what happened to the general?"

"He's been shot."

"I can see that. Shot in the head!"

Fearing the consequences of his levity, McCool darted into the crowd. He noticed restrained smiles which assured him that he had not shot too far from the mark. General Hooker was drunk.

Captain Donaldson gave a ringing command and the men continued their march.

Cannons were thundering into position and being quickly assembled. Hundreds of unorganized men were passing to the rear. Riderless horses, many of them badly wounded, wandered about helplessly. One, with blood spouting from a wound in the chest, was galloping aimlessly in all directions. A mounted officer, observing the suffering creature, fired two pistol shots and put the beast out of its misery. He turned and rode rapidly away.

Company H marched out of the woodland and arrived at an assigned angle in the defense breastworks. Active participants could see little of the battle. Those who chose to take the risk of observing from a position in front of the White House experienced a thrilling and rare sight. Open ground to the front covered about one hundred and fifty yards, dipped slightly in the center and terminated in a sparsely wooded crest.

In the timber on the crest, the Union line was firing and loading with deliberation, then slowly retiring. Confederate battle flags, butternut uniforms and gleaming muskets were gradually advancing. Thousands of men were firing as they moved forward, ramrods flashing in the sun. On they came, unerringly, into the terrible fire punishing them. The Union line stood their ground for the moment of impact, a mingling of blue and gray. Federal shouts of defiance were met with Rebel cheers and yells of victory. The shapeless mass, with shrieks and groans, finally broke for the artillery, the one for capture, the other for protection. The piercing yells of the Rebels seemed for the moment to drown out all other sounds, but before the Union line had found friendly shelter behind their cannon, the guns belched with death-dealing canister and the enemy yells of delight changed to wails of disappointment and frustration. Their advance broken, their lines confused beyond recovery, they fled the field and disappeared.

Powder-stained, smudge-faced fugitives from the retreating Federal force spilled over the breastworks as comrades in reserve took up the gauntlet, flinging death and destruction at the retreating enemy. Leaping in desperation, a tall, lanky refugee bounded into the entrenchment and lay panting heavily, his face pressed against the loose soil of the parapet at Paddy's feet. The rancid odor of sweat, smoke and congealed blood gave off a fearful odor.

Paddy put his musket to one side, opened a canteen and knelt down. He turned the huddled form over slowly.

Drawing back suddenly at sight of a familiar face, he yelled, "Willie! Somebody get McCool! It's his brother, Henry."

Volunteers from Frankford congregated hurriedly as the youngest McCool dropped to the ground. "Hen! Henry! You hurt?"

"No. Shaken up a little bit, but not hurt. Gimme water, will ya?"

"Here, let me have a look at you." Jake Hallowell ran his hands over the oldest McCool's body. "You'll be all right. Can't find a hole anywhere."

Tibben snickered from relief. "You try the seat of his pants, Jake?"

Paddy retrieved his emptied canteen. "How come the Ninety-first got mixed up in this, Hen? Thought you were in reserve on our left."

The eldest McCool raised himself on an elbow, bracing himself against the breastwork slashings. "Meade sent us up to help French's Second corps."

Gilmour spat. "Too bad Meade did no' have full command o' the whole shootin' match. Heard he was all for sendin' for'ard the entire First and Fifth. Can ye imagine it? Thirty thousand fresh men in reserve for three days and we ne' er got put closer to the Johnnies than telegraph distance. Aye, sad commentary."

Luke Jobson brushed powdered dirt from a sleeve. "Seems like our generals are afraid to end this war for fear of losing their jobs."

"Well, just wait'll Father Abraham hears about Hooker's conduct." Bob Dyer paused to wipe his nose. "I warrant he'll lower the boom on any further employment of Fightin' Joe."

Willie McCool dabbed at his brother's begrimed face with a wet handkerchief. "Have you seen Joe and Owen?"

"They're both all right last I saw. Joe was bringing off Captain Williams..."

"Ed Williams?"

"Yep. Shot up bad. Way it's going, won't be any of Frankford's aristocrats left by the time this war's over."

Paddy shook his head. "Heard the Hundred and Fourteenth was in the thick of it on Orange Plank Road. How about your brother, Owen, in the Twenty-eighth?"

"With Geary in the Twelfth Corps, somewhere in front of us. Keeping my fingers crossed. They ran out of ammunition the same time the Second Corps did."

"Ran out?"

"Sure. Haven't you heard? That rumpot who's supposed to be running the show forgot to bring his heads of ordnance along on this campaign. And not only ordnance, the commissary's also been left behind at winter camp."

"Left behind? You're joking."

"Joking, hell. You seen any grub wagons this side of the river? Nobody's eaten for twenty-four hours. And there ain't no ammunition train, either. Standing orders are to retire when you run out of ammunition. You can just bet your boots there'll be a general retreat."

"How about the thirty thousand of us in reserve?"

"Too late. Jig's up, and Hooker's running scared. Nothing left to support you. Artillery's just about shot itself out. See or hear any shells being fired?"

The anxious men listened and looked.

"By God he's right. All the limbers are empty."

"What did I tell you?" With his younger brother's aid, the eldest McCool regained his feet.

"When and where did your regiment go in, Hen?"

"By the Chancellorsville House just after the Reb shells set the place on fire, place was blazing like a paper box when we arrived. Some women trapped in a cellar were screaming like mad, pleading to be carried to safety, so a few of us dropped our muskets and pulled them out from the smoke and falling timbers. Then you know what they did? Seeing they were safe, they turned on us and gave us one helluva cussin, called us damned Yankees and everything else in the book."

"Aye, laddy, that's a woman fer ye," Gilmour said with a bearded scowl. "Flighty as a mare in heat. 'Specially with the rag on."

Surgeon Thomas, short of breath, broke in on the group. "Where's Captain Donaldson?"

"Over here, Doc."

"Can you and your men lend me a hand? The woods in front of us have caught fire. I need volunteers to help drag out the wounded before they fry."

"Done."

"Good. Have your men grab those canvas artillery buckets and fill them with water and wet rags. You'll need cloth to cover your faces."

With water-filled buckets clutched in each hand, volunteers from the Corn Exchange regiment started down the battle-scarred slope at a dogtrot. The woods, where hand-to-hand fighting had recently been waged, were a scene of hell incarnate. Roaring flames crackled and leaped through the treetops. Fiery rivulets raced over the ground, burning up leaves and twigs. Volumes of dense smoke formed a suffocating cloud.

Hovering above the pall was the acrid stench of seared and burning flesh coming from the dead and wounded. Helpless and distorted creatures cried out in agony; men and boys were screaming and gasping in an effort to escape the smoke and flames. With steel nerves, the rescuers strove to carry off friend and foe as the fighting came to an end on Sunday evening, May third.

The next day, the beleaguered Union forces received the electrifying news that Sedgewick's Sixth Corps had successfully stormed into Fredericksburg and, in a brilliant stroke, driven the enemy from Marye's Heights.

Twelve miles away, the opportunity was open for him to join his powerful corps with the rest of the Potomac Army in a huge pincer movement that would catch the whole of Lee's army in between. The opportunity went begging. Incapacitated and reluctant, Hooker was determined to retreat; Sedgewick would have to do likewise.

True to the axiom that all great battles conclude with violent storms, late on the afternoon of May fifth, the sky grew dark and menacing with the sound of thunder rolling up from the south.

Buttoning an overcoat at the collar, Colonel Prevost approached Captain Donaldson. "I'd like to see you a moment, Captain."

"Yes, sir."

"Over here away from eavesdroppers." The regimental commander's tired face was creased. "How are your old wounds holding up? Giving you any trouble?"

"No, sir. Not with the weather warming up the way it has."

"Glad to hear that. Mine have been giving me fits again. Frank, what I'm about to reveal I don't want repeated to anyone. Is that understood?"

"Of course."

"The army's going to retreat. It's got to go off unobserved under cover of this approaching storm."

"Retreat? With the Sixth Corps pushing toward us and thirty thousand fresh troops here to meet them?"

"The decision has been made at top level. We've no food, no ammunition. Full details from the brigade have been selected to cover the retreat, cover it until the main body has safely crossed the Rapidan and Rapahannock."

"Whew, that'll take some doing."

"It will. After a lengthy discussion, Meade, Griffin, Barnes and I have decided you're the one best qualified to command a rear guard force. Will you take the responsibility?"

"Me? Handle a full brigade detail? I've never handled more than a company."

"We're fully aware of that, however, your recent conduct and ability have impressed division headquarters and we feel justified in offering you the temporary post."

"Well, all I can say is, I'll do my best, Colonel. What are the instructions?"

"General Grifffin's supervising the movement personally. He'll give you your orders. Come along with me."

Within an hour the brigade was deployed at short intervals behind breast works; Captain Donaldson proceeded to caution the men regarding their duties and responsibilities.

"Our objective is that stretch of timber down there." He pointed. "Should you fail to reach the shelter of the trees on the first attempt, gather and reform in the hollow which lies about halfway down the slope. When you see the second wave leave the breastworks, spring forward and continue toward the objective."

McCool cupped his hands and shouted, "Don't you worry none, Cap'n. We'll carry them Rebs on our bayonets with the first rush. Frankford against the world!

Yeah!"

Vociferous support greeted the outburst.

The trace of a smile appeared on Donaldson's face. "I'll be banking on that. The signal for advance will be the dropping of a red flag in that battery over there, so keep a sharp lookout." He turned toward an Irish-born captain assigned to lead the right wing. "O'Neil, you all set?"

"Aye, Cap'n. The boys is devilish tired o' markin' time behind breastworks."

Donaldson turned to Lieutenant Batchelder in charge of the left wing. "Batch?"

"All set, Frank."

At the signal the flag was dropped, followed immediately by the sharp command, "Double quick. Charge."

It was repeated along the line. The Corn Exchange rushed headlong from its concealment and gallantly breasted a storm of bullets which met them as they dashed onto the open plain.

Encouraging shouts and cheers came from the rest of the brigade posted behind the breastworks, nerving the attacking soldiers to accomplish their purpose. Lieutenant Batchelder appeared to drag his men forward by the hair as he ran in front of them, slashing the air with his sword and bellowing loudly to keep his left in the advance. The center and right, not to be outdone, hastened to follow Batchelder's example and the whole line, without hesitation, swept into the blaze of musketry flashing from the timber, driving the enemy into the woods and overrunning its abandoned line. Overwhelmed by the enthusiasm of the successful venture, O' Neil and Batchelder urged their men forward in complete disregard of instructions until finally Batchelder, realizing the jeopardy of his men, called a halt.

Incensed at the restraint, O'Neil continued to shout in either anger or excitement at his company man, Tom Scout, whom he especially disliked. "Out, Scout. Bad luck to yez. Why do yez stand marking time? Go forward, every one of yez."

Cooler heads finally prevailing on the wild, controversial Irish captain, the point was effectually secured for the establishment of a line. As usual, with the best of men, there was lively competition for trees. Choice trees of large circumference were seized by groups of three or four men, the man in front being the only one who could use his rifle; the others were forced to seek other cover or take the risk of open exposure.

Having had it their own way for so long, the Confederates were now compelled to find protection and shoot as the opportunity offered.

Lieutenant Thomas returned with entrenching tools after reporting the successful occupation. The men immediately went to work constructing rifle pits for an extended stay. Shortly afterward, the enemy fell back and their fire slackened until an occasional slouch hat, bobbing up and down among the bushes, was all that could be seen of them.

Lieutenant Thomas, considered by his men as eminently brave and an excellent officer, regardless of his fondness for bodily comforts, secured the best advantages attainable for his personal satisfaction.

"What's it take to become a lieutenant besides a lot of heft?" McCool asked sourly as he surveyed the commodious pit he had just finished digging for the officer.

Tapping his head with a finger, Thomas winked, then quietly placed himself in the protection of the pit. He selected a Waverley magazine from among other literature abandoned by previous occupants and was soon absorbed in an entertaining story.

Mad over the fact that his impulsive desire to continue the advance had been restrained, Captain O'Neil decided to open an unauthorized communication with the enemy. From rifle pits and behind trees, the advance force watched with bated breath as he conducted a truce with some degree of diplomatic skill. He had intimated by signs that he desired to hold a parley and his invitation was accepted by a Confederate officer who met him at a log halfway between the lines. The two officers seated themselves and proceeded with deliberation to discuss the purpose of their mission. O'Neil cautiously refrained from revealing his name or command.

Luke Jobson watched, muttering and growling, "That crazy Irishman. If there's somethin' big in the wind, that fool's liable to tip it off."

"I don't think 'Old Teddy' would be quite that stupid."

"You don't think so, Mulcahy? Maltese cross on his cap tells Johnny Reb we're Fifth Corps. The number Hundred 'n Eighteen on his infantry badge identifies our regiment, he don't have to say nothin'."

"You're right. Once that Reb knows we're Fifth Corps, he'll know we're a fresh outfit. And what's a picket from a fresh corps get pushed up front for? Attack."

"Or to cover a retreat."

O'Neil and the Confederate stood up, nodded agreement, shook hands and departed for their respective lines.

"Mind if I inquire what the hell that was all about?" Batchelder asked as O'Neil sauntered back into the lines.

"Not at all, Lieutenant. Me and the Johnny was just havin' a wee bit of a talk. We both agreed that under the circumstances it's useless exposure and a waste of ammunition to have any exchange of picket firing. A cease fire begins as of now. Timely notice is to be given if either side's ordered to open again, or if either should be relieved. That's all. A restful night to ye."

Dumbfounded, Batchelder removed his kepi and scratched his head.

With a welcome respite from picket firing, the men went about the business of making themselves comfortable as the dark sky grew more threatening and the sound of a wind rose in the swaying treetops. The quiet afforded them an opportunity to ascertain their losses.

The happy fact established itself that while quite a number from the regiment had been wounded in the advance across the plain, and several had been hit on the line, all of whom refused to leave their post, no comradeships had been severed by death. While the men were congratulating themselves on that extraordinary stroke of good fortune, two mounted soldiers approached from the direction of the main Union line.

Tibben was standing guard. He quickly raised his rifle and challenged in a squeaky voice, "Halt. Give name, regiment and mission."

A stocky, well-proportioned sergeant reared back in his saddle, pointed at him and started to laugh.

"Will ya look who's guarding Olympus, Bill? Isaac Tibben's kid brother, Joe."

The sergeant bent over his saddle horn, pressing his face close to the frail sentry. "Hey, Joey, if we give you a lollipop, will you go home to your mother like a nice little boy?"

"I said give name, regiment and mission."

Bill Horrocks smiled, amused at the youngest son of his father's mill foreman. "Lieutenant William Horrocks, Hundred and Fourteenth Pennsylvania Volunteers. On duty to recover the body of Major Chandler, somewhere in this vicinity."

"Sergeant Nobel McClintocks same regiment, same purpose."

"That's better."

Tibben placed his rifle at port arms and grinned foolishly. "Gosh, I haven't seen you fellas since the day the war broke out. The same day you hauled old Jim Ryen up the borough hall steps so he could make a speech. Remember?"

Horrocks's face fell. "Old Jim's dead, Joey. Got word last week. Folks say he died of a broken heart because the nation his generation fought to create is now at each other's throats."

"Gee. Home won't seem the same without him."

"No, and like Jim Ryen, the past which we cherish is also gone, however, the boys from home seem to have come through the fighting in good shape. Now, can we pass?"

"Sure thing. Ride straight ahead. You'll bump into the other fellas. They're all down there."

"Thanks, Joey. Take care of yourself. We'll see you later."

The two horsemen moved off toward the picket line and a reunion with other old acquaintances. To give themselves more time in which to gather news of home, Paddy and the other Frankford volunteers scrambled from their rifle pits and sallied forth into the woods where they helped search for Major Chandler's body.

The number of unburied dead indicated that the vicinity had been the scene of serious fighting. Confederate dead predominated, their scanty clothing and poor equipment in marked contrast with the more substantial appointments of the Union soldiers. The men noticed a peculiarity which they could not account for, a strange difference in the positions of the Union bodies contrasted with the Confederates. The former were on their sides or their faces with knees drawn up. The latter were flat on their backs, legs spread out and hands clenched.

"That is the weirdest sight I've ever seen," Luke Jobson murmured. "Looks as if each army ordered its men to die in a certain position."

Lieutenant Horrocks glanced around apprehensively at the lightning flashes and shook his head. "I'm afraid it's no use continuing the search. We've gone over this ground three times. We've used up more than the hour Colonel Collis gave us. We'd better turn back."

Sergeant McClintock wheeled his horse and started off at a slow trot. "Suits me. I've had a strange feeling some Johnny's had me in his sights the whole damn time we've been out here."

Pausing for a few last words, Horrocks put the spurs to his horse and rode off. The weary Frankford group trudged silently back to position, the men occasionally stopping to pick up blankets scattered about the field until each had appropriated between fifteen and twenty. They used them to make their shelters more comfortable, bedding themselves down on soft couches as the temperature began to drop. At last the storm broke with a fury. Thunder became deafening as the rain poured from the black skies, bucketing down in slanting walls and rapidly filling the pits waist deep with water, soaking everything and everyone and turning the dirt into a miry muck.

In the process of bailing out his swamped quarters, Paddy was suddenly caught in the yellow glare of a dripping lantern. Standing over him in the raging downpour stood a Rebel soldier. Reflexes fine-tuned, he reached for his musket.

"Ain't no call to use that, Yank," the man said, his wet, bony face breaking into a heavy-lipped grin. "Just come ovah sociable like to warn you'll we'uns is being replaced up front by Mississippi boys. Better tell yore cap'n so he'll know the truce is off. Night, Yank."

Paddy, shivering to the bone, nervously watched the Southerner slip away into the night. Recovering from shock, he darted from his hole to locate Captain O'Neil.

Apparently anxious to make their presence felt, the relief detail from Mississippi began firing on the rain-drenched Union line.

"What kind o' divilish Protestant trick is this?" Cassidy spluttered from his water-logged dugout. "Thought we had a truce going."

"It's off," Paddy gasped as he raced by. "Re- placement column just moved in."

"The hell ye say. A plague on their dirty souls. Ain't no fittin' weather or time o' night to be tormentin' a soldier with picket firin'."

Paddy continued his search for Captain O'Neil, the quaint, erratic Irishman who loved to condemn the American Army when he could not understand their policies. "That's not the way we did it in Injee when I served with Her Majesty's Thirty-ninth foot under Lord Clive," he would say.

O' Neil had conspicuously pitched a shelter tent in full view of the enemy. Plentifully supplied with blankets and well-protected from the storm, he was enjoying his comforts and reading a newspaper. The resumption of firing did not seem to bother him, as he proceeded to light his den and adjust a candle so he could continue reading.

As Paddy approached his tent, he could see the officer's form plainly through the canvas where he lay reading, heedless of the bullets falling about him.

"Captain O'Neil, sir."

"Yes, what is it? Can't ye see I'm busy?"

"Reb replacements, sir. They're not going to honor the truce."

"Ye think I'm deaf? It's as plain as the nose on yer face. Now git."

Taking a piece of newspaper, he plugged a bullet hole through which rain was dripping. "Damn this water," he growled.

Thoroughly vexed, Paddy bellied his way back to position where, well into the night, the enemy continued to harass the Federal force. The tactic generally practiced was to creep close to the Union line, rise suddenly, flash a lantern, fire a shot and disappear.

Adding to the nerve-racking situation was the rain, which by now had covered the open field between the pickets and the main Federal line, casting reflections and convincing an observer that the objects, real or imaginary, were moving across the line. Close to midnight one of those objects assumed sufficient reality to prompt a challenge from Captain Donaldson, who had come forward to take charge of the picket detail.

The reply of "Friend" in a familiar voice erased his doubts and Major Herring entered the outer works.

"Good job, Captain. Griffin's told me to spell you and assume command."

"The retreat? Has it. . . ?"

"Coming off splendidly. The artillery's safe across the river and so is most of the army. Colonel Hays and the Eighteenth Massachusetts have volunteered to help us withdraw."

McCool, lending an ear to the conversation, turned to Tibben. "Cripes. Did you hear that, Joe? There's nothing between us and the Rapidan but one regiment. We've been covering a retreat "

"Oh, Molly. Let's get up'n git."

At three in the morning the withdrawal began. The Corn Exchange moved stealthily back over the plain without arousing the enemy's suspicions.

Surprised at daybreak to find the Union line deserted, a large Confederate force immediately set out in hot pursuit, their skirmishers covering twice the length of front as manned by the small rear guard of Philadelphia and Massachusetts men.

Rain poured from a blackened sky swirling with angry clouds. Torrents of water beat down on abandoned caissons, battery wagons mired to the axle and other impedimenta thrown off by Hooker's retreating army. Famished and exhausted, fighting every step of the way, the rear guard continued to fall back doggedly toward the Rapidan. They finally reached a stand of timber overlooking the United States Ford. From the border of the tangled wilderness to the turbulent river the land was cleared and sloped gradually to the ford. On the opposite bank a line of Federal artillery was drawn up in a battery.

Obedient to command, the small covering force made a dash for the river and quickly assembled on center under the protection of shepherding guns. The enemy charged at their heels, eager to intercept the retiring foe. The artillery went into action, exploding with a deafening roar. The jarring discharges swept the advancing Confederate lines and drove them back as the Federal rear guards scurried over rain-swept pontoon bridges to safety. The pontoons were then quickly hauled in by the rest of the brigade and loaded onto wagons. Minus seventeen thousand dead and missing comrades, the Union force began its retreat from Chancellorsville over roads knee-deep with leg-sucking mud. Ghostly apparitions, abandoned wagons and artillery caissons were mired axle deep in the tenacious clay. With shoulders sagging, eyes downcast, heads soaked and bowed against the driving rain, the dejected army slogged its way back to Falmouth.

CHAPTER 13

The gloomy rains of early May passed and balmy days of mellow springtime descended upon the rolling Virginia countryside. Bolstered by genial weather, the innate resiliency of youth helped the men's low spirits to rise from deep despair. The heaven-sent gift of forgive-and-forget restored to Hooker some semblance of respected authority. In a half-hearted way, the sad but wiser army was ready to sally forth under his command once again. As to just when and where this expected movement would be made became a principle subject for camp conjecture.

Weary from a day's extensive drilling, his blond Nordic features dripping with perspiration, Luke Jobson entered a dingy cabin and flung himself on a bunk. "Who says we're going to attack? I'll wager Lee's thinking about marching around our flank and we're only watching to see that he shan't," he said with exasperation.

Kimball tossed aside a sweat-stained shoe. "I don't think so. If cousin Robert uncovered his front at Fredericksburg, what would be stopping us from moving right down to Richmond?"

"Washington, that's what," Hallowell snorted in reply.

Kimball turned toward his former business partner who was removing chinks from between cabin logs in an attempt to freshen the atmosphere with a cross draft of air. "Why do you say that, Jake?"

"Because Washington is the tail that wags the dog. To throw our politicians and War Department into nervous conniptions all the Rebs have to do is take one step toward the Capitol. Immediately all plans of operation are thrown to the wind. Washington has to be defended at all costs is the cry. Hell, the South would gladly exchange pawns. Our capturing Richmond wouldn't mean a tinker's dam to them. The loss of Washington would end the war."

Sergeant Cassidy lifted his head from a tub of water and wiped his face with a soiled towel. "Sure'n it beats me why the Capitol ain't been moved to New York or Boston long ago," he said. "Like ye say, Jake, the whole strategy o' this bloody army's been mouthed by them tub thumpers up Potomac Creek. Protect Washington?

Faith an' the miserable town ain't good for nothin', besides bein' a hundred miles deep in Reb sympathizin' territory."

McCool, laboring to pick his uniform clean of crawling insect life, paused to hold one aloft. "That fella out West's got the right idea. Poop on capturing cities, destroy the enemy in the field wherever you find him, that's the ticket." He squashed a louse between his fingers. "Where you going, Mulcahy?"

"Out to watch the sunset. You fellas come up with an answer to this war let me know."

He seated himself on a rustic bench outside the cabin and leaned back, his eyes fixed on purplish orange streaks sinking low on the western horizon. His attention was suddenly captured by the sight of a small slender woman making her way up the company street. He stared and gasped open-mouthed. With curls resembling twisted wood shavings and a probing needle nose and tattered shawl, he knew instantly who it was. "Crazy Bet," he said under his breath.

Captain Donaldson appeared at the head of the street and Paddy saw the middle-aged woman hurry in his direction. He watched intently as the two shook hands and smiled greetings. She handed the captain a letter, but retained what looked like another in her hand as she conversed in low tones. Paddy started to rise from the bench when he heard Donaldson call in a clear voice. "Private Mulcahy. Come join us. Here's an old friend of ours and she has something for you."

Paddy joined the pair. "Evening, Miss Van Lew. Good seeing you again."

"And it is a pleasure to see you again under more favorable circumstances," she replied. She extended a hand in which was held a stained, wrinkled envelope. "This letter is for you. It was smuggled through the lines over a month ago." Her smile was more like that of a cupid-bow than a shrewd espionage agent.

Paddy reached quickly for the envelope. His eyes flew to the handwriting and he felt his heart pound. The letter was from Becky, no mistake about that. He recognized the handwriting.

"Ma'am. Cap'n. Would you excuse me? I'd like to...."

Miss Van Lew touched his arm. "You go right ahead. Frank and I wouldn't want to deprive you of a single precious minute with your letter."

Paddy tipped his forage cap and headed for a rise of ground that overlooked the Rappahannock where he could sit, read, and reread with undisturbed enjoyment.

Captain Donaldson turned to Miss Van Lew. "Would you care to meet our new colonel before you leave? We'd like to hear what's taking place in Richmond these days."

"I have a few minutes, yes. But I can only stay a short time. I've already given my report to General Hooker and must start south again as soon as it is dark."

Under the inquisitive gaze of the soldiers milling about in the twilight, the two walked arm in arm across the camp. Reaching regimental headquarters, Miss Van Lew walked boldly inside. Standing a pace behind her, Captain Donaldson nodded to the men present. "Gentlemen, may I present Miss Van Lew of Richmond."

The officers snapped to attention at the mention of the notorious name.

"Bet, this is Colonel Gwyn, Major Herring, Captain Crocker and Lieutenant Batchelder."

The woman studied Lieutenant Batchelder. "I've seen you before. Weren't you at...?"

"Yes. I'm an alumnus of Libby. I was in the Seventy-first with Frank."

"Thought so. I never forget a face. Can't afford to in my business you know."

Colonel Gwyn's Celtic charm filled the room. "We are greatly honored by your presence, madam. Won't you sit down?"

"Only for a minute, thank you, Colonel. Frank tells me you have just recently assumed command of the regiment."

"Yes, madam, that is correct. Colonel Prevost was forced to retire from service because of ill health. I shall find it difficult to emanate his scholarly, soldierly traits."

Crazy Bet stared directly into the colonel's eyes for a moment. "You will do well, sir. I see fire and determination in your face tempered by good judgment."

Batchelder suppressed a smile, his thoughts going back to Gwyn's behavior at the whiskey uprising following Shepherdstown.

"You are most kind," Gwyn demurred, "but tell us, what is taking place on the other side of the fence these days?"

The woman withdrew a hat pin from her bonnet and placed both on the table in front of her. "Sir, the South has mounted her soul on the stallion of Pride out of Conceit. She is riding for a fall over an unfamiliar, hazardous course. All indications point to an invasion of the North."

Major Herring gave a low whistle. "So that's the ticket, eh?"

"Yes, Major, that's the ticket. The battles of Fredericksburg and Chancellorsville have raised their confidence enough to cause the subordinate officers and soldiers to believe that, as opposed to the Army of the Potomac, they are equal to any demands made on them."

The grim-faced officers sat down on camp stools.

"Their belief in the superiority of the Southerner to the Northerner as a fighter is no longer, as it was at the beginning of the war, a mere provincial conceit, it is now supported by a continuous string of successes in the field. They point to the fact that before each of the last two great battles the North was reorganized under new generals each presumably abler than his predecessor and having the confidence of Lincoln and the War Department. In spite of that the results have been crowning victories for the South."

Gwyn's face turned an angry white. "Our defeats have not been owing to lack of fighting qualities on the part of our soldiers, rather to defective leadership."

"I agree with you, Colonel. I've heard that at Chancellorsville both qualities have been called into question. Precisely just what did go wrong?"

"You're better acquainted with those matters, Major. You tell her," Gwyn responded.

"Well, madam, in none of the previous battles between our two armies has a disparity of numbers been so great. Hooker had taken a fine initiative, the troops were eager for battle and the plans of operation were superb to the point that we caught Lee completely flat-footed and off guard."

Miss Van Lew sat transfixed, studying the major's face and manners carefully.

"With only an inferior force in position to attack the overwhelming numbers of our army pouring around their flank, the Confederacy seemed doomed."

"Yes, I seem to recall Hooker's boast that the Army of Northern Virginia was the legitimate property of the Army of the Potomac," she replied tartly.

Gwyn's face fell as if he had just swallowed brine.

Major Herring placed both palms on the table. "The boast seemed justified at the time. Then, at first contact with the enemy, advantages we had gained were thrown away by a timid, defensive attitude." He paused to pour some wine from a decanter and took a drink. "Lee's bold offensive in the face of Hooker's reluctance, the shameful rout of our Eleventh Corps Germans, and the subsequent retreat of our entire army, thirty thousand of whom did not see engagement, are enough to establish belief in the South that both in combat and generalship, they are superior."

Colonel Gwyn paused to light a cigar. "False confidence can be dangerous," he said in a wreath of smoke. "If Lee has decided to invade the North because of past performances he could be digging his own grave."

Miss Van Lew took a sip of wine that had been offered to her. "Lee is a brilliant officer," she said, "who knows that to remain on the defensive will eventually force him back to Richmond. Mainly for that reason he has decided to carry the field of operation from Virginia to Northern soil where victory might give him possession of Baltimore or Washington, perhaps lead to a recognition of the Confederacy by foreign powers and quite possibly end the war quickly."

"He couldn't have picked a better time."

"Why do you say that, Captain Crocker?"

"Because, madam, since Chancellorsville, a discharge of fifty-eight two-year regiments has cut twenty-five thousand veteran troops from our army. They have gone home."

Jaws squared he cast a challenging glance at Colonel Gwyn. "What chance is there of getting good replacements? None. The recent conscription act has sent men stampeding in panic. For three hundred dollars the rich can buy their way out or hire a substitute. Ten days after the act was put into effect there were fourteen thousand claims for exemption in New York City alone. Those who are still aliens are swamping their consulates, clamoring for certificates proving that they are foreigners and not subject to the draft. Men who have lived a long time in this country and prospered are now refusing to help."

The woman's face was grave. "Yes, and unfortunately, Captain, that information is well-known to the Southern commanders."

Batchelder fingered his watch fob. "No wonder they're so cocksure about invading the North."

Gwyn leveled his eyes. "There's more to it than that if we're going to be honest. They have a much better organized army than ours and they know it. Their corps arrangement is a model of efficiency under the direction of veteran officers with proven ability. Their cavalry is under one command and operates as a mobile effective weapon. Our horsemen are employed as playthings assigned to headquarters for escort duty, guards and orderlies. Mere errand boys."

Nettled by these well-known facts, Major Herring rose and circled his chair. "Don't overlook the artillery. Putting his under Pendleton was the soundest move Lee has made. The excellent reputation our artillery gained in Mexico has gone for naught. After Mexico, three-fourths of the authorized batteries were dismounted by the War Department. Our artillery is still a disorganized command facing hostility from the War Department. Two years at war and for battery draft the artillery still depends on refuse horses after the ambulance and quartermaster trains have been supplied."

Gwyn drummed the table with his fingers. "Yes, and how about that idiotic order published just last year by the War Department, saying. 'Field officers of artillery are an unnecessary expense and their muster into service henceforth forbidden.' Look at the able artillerists who have transferred to the infantry so they can increase their rank... Hays, Gibbon, Getty, Ayres, DeRussy, even our own division commander, Charley Griffin, headed the famous West Point Light Battery before changing over."

Miss Van Lew reached for her bonnet. "I'm sorry I must take leave of you, gentlemen. It is dark and I must slip back into Richmond before morning." She rose. "Frank, would you be good enough to escort me to my barouche?"

"Certainly, Bet. My pleasure."

Colonel Gwyn stood up and stepped forward. "One thing more before you leave, madam. The rumors we hear about Jackson. Are they true?"

"Yes, Colonel. Stonewall Jackson is dead. I viewed his body lying in state at Richmond."

"Killed accidentally by his own men, we hear. What a tragedy. He was a brilliant tactician, an honorable foe. The Confederates have lost heavily in their victory at Chancellorsville."

A lamp, swinging in the breeze, cast its pale light on the front porch of the headquarters. Major Herring stared after the silhouette of Miss Van Lew as she disappeared into the night.

"A remarkable woman. Truly remarkable."

Gwyn breathed deeply of the night air. "Gentlemen, let's retire inside and have a 'Here's how.' What say, Crocker? Can you put together a 'Hooker's Retreat' for us?"

"Now that is a foolish question, Colonel. Watch me."

As if compounding an intricate prescription, Crocker started measuring out contents from various liquor bottles, mixing the spirits carefully in a pewter mug. When finished he sipped the product, smiled through his thick beard and expressed satisfaction as he passed the cups.

Gwyn smacked his lips. "Mmm, very good, Captain. Never tasted better. Wish you would give me the secret..."

Conversation was broken off abruptly by the loud clatter of hoofbeats which halted outside the cabin. Heavy footsteps echoed on the plank porch and a dispatch courier hastily entered the room.

"Colonel Gwyn. Orders, sir. The army's moving."

"Thank you, Sergeant."

The courier's hand flew to the peak of his kepi and in a second he was gone.

Gwyn studied the orders with a grave face. "Major, have all company commanders assembled here in fifteen minutes. The woman gave us the correct information all right, Lee's heading for the valley."

"An invasion of the North?"

"Unless we can stop him, yes. We move at six tomorrow morning."

Breaking camp in the early light of June first, the Corn Exchange, in company with the Fifth Corps, began moving down a dusty road leading north, the martial sounds of drums, bugles and creaking wagon wheels echoing on the still air. With no outward signs of any immediate urgency, the march moved along leisurely. Troops long confined to dreary huts in their winter quarters, except for a brief, disastrous sojourn into the wilderness, proceeded to enjoy the beauties and verdure of lower Farquier County with a deeper conception of the surroundings than the actual scenery justified. The productive soil, uncultivated and abandoned, was abundant with golden field daisies, grasses, weeds and wild flowers. In peacetime, corn, wheat and oats covered the acres during the fruitful season.

Occasionally a lone cow could be seen browsing by a mansion house. Flocks and herds had disappeared and a vast amount of pasture lay fallow. The vigorous men had left, and only matrons and defiant maidens remained to watch jealously the little truck gardens, the single cow, the depleted smokehouse, the scant granary and attenuating fowl, meager representatives of their life-sustaining assets. Venomous and uncompromising as those women were, they could not resist the temptation to barter a part of their scanty store for the currency close at hand. A flourishing trade sprang up along the way.

If there was a pressing need for haste or action at that time it was not manifest to the rank and file of the Fifth Corps who, after short marches, were placed in bivouac for long periods. After two weeks of aimless shuttling back and forth in Farquier County matters assumed a definite course and the column pushed forward hurriedly toward the sound of heavy cannonading coming from the direction of the Bull Run Mountains. Dressed in the lush green of early summer foliage, the distant range stood as a historic reminder of the fierce struggles fought at its base, to which they lent their name.

Sweltering hot weather settled over the countryside in a sticky wave, and men began putting wet leaves inside their caps for insulation. Light boughs were cut to cover their heads for additional comfort. Winter's pallor vanished as faces reddened and bronzed. The imminent prospect of battle diverted attention from the burning sun, the dry, parched throats and the choking dust.

At six in the morning on June seventeenth the column crossed the plains of Manassas and passed by the Henry house, famed as the place where a year ago Union regulars held off the Confederates until darkness permitted withdrawal of Pope's disordered battalions. In both Bull Run battles the house had been the focal point of contest. Torn by shot and shell it was still apparently occupied. A citizen, sullen and uncommunicative, stood in a doorway as the troops filed by.

Covering the battlefield were leather accouterments, shoes, canteens, skins of dead animals, skeletons of soldiers and all sorts of abandoned military property. Those men in the column who had not taken part in either battle stared curiously at the shocking debris and startling scenes before them.

Off to one side the exposed remains of an officer from the First Michigan was discovered by several men of his regiment. Recognized, the dead officer's remains were given decent burial and the grave properly marked for identification.

Nearby, rain uncovered the body of a cavalryman who had been buried booted and spurred with belt and saber. His uniform and accouterments were in an excellent state of preservation, but when the men tried to lift his body by the belt, flesh slipped from bones and the skeleton fell in a confused mass of bones and clothing. A deeper grave was dug and sufficient earth thrown over it to construct a mound, and with that as a mark of recognition, it was left as another of the unnumbered and forever unknown dead. A great many unburied Confederates lay about, bodies recognized by the insignia on their uniforms as having been in the Eleventh North Carolina and Eighteenth Georgia regiments.

A grave marked as that of Colonel Fletcher Webster had received better attention. Son of the distinguished Daniel Webster, he was killed leading his regiment at the second battle of Bull Run and his final resting place, identified by a suitable head and foot board, had flowers on the mound blooming in season.

Overcome by a morbid sense of curiosity not to be denied, McCool and Tibben stole from the ranks and started ferreting souvenirs. Their activities, however, were soon detected by the watchful eye of Sergeant Cassidy.

"Git back into line ye grubby scavengers. Git back or I'll be stavin' yer heads in."

McCool blew up his cheeks and after exchanging glances and a few whispered words, both culprits began singing as they fell back into the ranks:

"Oh, I wish you were in the land of cotton
I smell you, and you smell rotten;
Go away, go away, go away, take a bath."

Guffaws of delight exploded from the rest of the men for the first time in weeks. The song was picked up quickly and carried by others with innovative ideas.

"Oh, we wish that Cassidy was in de land ob cotton,
We smell him and he smells rotten;
Go away, far away, go away, soak your head."

Happy at the moral support, the two roguish faces peeked at Cassidy from behind large skunk cabbage leaves that hung fan-shaped from their caps.

His face apoplectic, Cassidy turned and yelled, "McCool! Tibben! Fall out!"

Investigating the outburst, Captain Donaldson drew abreast of his angered subaltern. "Go easy on ' em, Andy. We' ve all been going sour. Don't choke them off just when they're beginning to laugh again."

"By all that's holy, sir, should I be after playin' end man to their minstrel show?"

"Andy, I'd even play the part myself if I knew it would help."

"I believe ye would at that, Cap'n. All right ye two sass boxes, back in line."

Someone waved.a cap and shouted, "Who's all right?"

A rousing response came from the section. "The Sarg is all right. Bully for Cassidy. Hip, hip, hooray!"

Beaming, his ego restored, Cassidy threw back his shoulders, nodded, and stalked on stolidly.

Two more days of touch-and-go marching and the tired, foot-sore column arrived hot and dusty at Aldie, a post village of Loudon County lying quiet and picturesque in a gap of the Bull Run Mountains. Beyond, towering above a lesser range, the distant Blue Ridge Mountains loomed majestically in the west. Beyond them was the valley of the Shenandoah, Lee's avenue for invasion.

Near the hamlet of Aldie a swift-flowing stream coursed northward carrying the waters of mountain and valley to the Potomac. Rejoicing at such an inspirational sight the perspiring, sunburned soldiers quickly shed their foul uniforms and jumped naked into the refreshingly cool water. They began to frolic in the manner of boys just released from school.

Having cleansed himself to his complete satisfaction and washing three weeks dirt from his uniform, Donaldson climbed the banks of the stream and spread his clothes out to dry. Lighting a pipe, he had settled back in the grass to enjoy the pleasant scene just as Colonel Gwyn rode up.

"Who authorized this company's departure from the regimental column?" he demanded.

"I did, sir. If I'd turned them down on this request they would have been ready to kill."

"That's what they are here for. Get them the hell out of that water."

"Yes, sir, if that's the way you want it."

With a sudden look of remorse, the colonel exclaimed, "What's the matter with me, Donaldson? What's the matter with all of us?" He gripped his saddle horn with both hands. "Let them stay a while longer. The dirty cusses need a good bath." He paused. "What kind of state would you say your men are in?"

"They are in a very bad state, Colonel. The State of Virginia."

Dust flew from Gwyn's pants as he laughed and slapped his thigh. "The State of Virginia. Wait till I tell that one at headquarters." He gave another hearty laugh. "When your men have finished, march them over to the west end of town where you will find the rest of the regiment in camp."

Refreshed and rejuvenated, the men of Company H marched gaily through Aldie. Around them was evidence of recent cavalry fighting, suggesting this was the point from which they had heard the sounds of artillery two days earlier. Questions and answers shouted back and forth between soldiers lounging about town and those in the marching company established the fact that a severe cavalry engagement had recently taken place at Aldie. Mounted Federal troops had pressed for the gaps in the Blue Ridge, trying to observe the Shenandoah Valley where a bulk of the Rebel infantry was believed to be. Jeb Stuart's horsemen had vigorously tried to prevent such observation. Lying on litters of straw near the roadside and in the yards of houses were wounded men with gaping saber cuts. Dead horses, swarming with bottle flies, were scattered among the lost and abandoned arms and trappings.

Captain Donaldson, who was marching at the head of H Company, suddenly raised an arm and shouted an order. "Uncover!"

Caught unaware, the startling command to show respect for a burial party sent men piling on each other's heels as they struggled to remove their caps.

Bits of fragmentary information filtered back from the head of the column.

Tibben spoke in a muffled voice. "It's Lieutenant Colonel Gleason of the Twenty-fifty New York. He's 'gone up.'"

"Aye? Wha' happened to the mon?"

"I'll find out." Tibben tapped the shoulder of Jobson standing in front and exchanged a few words, then turned to Gilmour. "Died from sunstroke. He's going to be buried in the village churchyard with suitable military honors."

"Aye. And when one o' us drops off, the only honors we get is dust in our faces."

The latecomers rejoined the rest of the regiment in bivouac and found themselves caught up in a celebration. The entire roster was gathered around a canvas-topped ordnance wagon parked in the middle of camp. Men were shouting and throwing muskets on a heap.

"Hey, what's going on?" McCool called to a corporal nearby. George Wade of E Company held up an oily new rifle. "Springfields. Ain't they beauts?"

Gilmour crowded closer. "Hoot, mon, 'bout time we got decent firearms. These damn English Enfields are worse 'n nothin' ."

Bob Dyer ran a fond finger over his wooden stock and long barrel. "Don't know," he replied, "seems like getting rid of an old friend."

Sentiment disappeared as the men rushed madly for the wagon and tossed away archaic muskets in exchange for new breech loaders.

With the onset of dark, cook fires sprang into sight, orange flames silhouetting darkened tents. An aroma of boiling coffee and salt pork lingered on the air. The weary troops, lounging around on blanket rolls, munched hardtack and examined and discussed the merits of their prized new weapons. A few talked of home, of what the immediate future held, and other matters.

Kimball's lengthy face was etched with concern as he said, "Frankly, I'm worried about Mulcahy. He hasn't said two words since we left Falmouth, and that's been over three weeks ago."

"He's sure been acting strange," Jobson muttered.

"Don't think he's going off his nut, do you?" McCool's eyes were caught in the dancing firelight. He spoke low. "Maybe he's figuring on deserting or something. He did drop out once...."

"Shut up, Willie." Hallowell's countenance was stern. "Mulcahy thinks deep, no matter how free and easy he may seem on the outside. If something's troubling him, he'll work it out his own way. Our job is to be on hand if and when he asks for help."

Tibben poked at the embers. "Paddy ain't gonna desert."

"Nobody says he is, you understand?" Hallowell turned toward the Quaker, who was busy whittling on a stick. "Walton, you and Mulcahy are close friends. He said anything to you?"

"No. Like thee said, when the time comes he'll let us in on it."

The sound of footsteps, accompanied by the rustling of a skirt, caused the men to turn around. Startled, they saw a gray-haired Negress step into the flickering light of the campfire. Dressed in a plaid petticoat and snuff-colored linsey-woolsy tunic, she carried two covered baskets slung on both arms. She removed a corncob pipe from her mouth.

"Evenin', sojer boys," she said.

"Evenin', Aunty. What can we do for you?" Kimball inquired.

She broke into a wide smile, exposing an extraordinary set of pearly white teeth. "Ain't what you can do fer me, sojer, it's what I'se gwine do fo' you."

"We're not buyin' any, thank you, Aunty."

"Buyin'? Why land sakes, what I has I'se gwine give away free."

There were apprehensive expressions.

"Now ah ask ye boys, how long's it been since yore mammys up north baked sweet cakes fo' you? A year? Two years?"

"It's been a while," Jobson managed to reply.

"That's what ah mean, sojer boy. That's why I say to muself this afternoon, Miranda, heah's dese nice white Northern boys come down heah to fight and git kilt in V'gini fo' you. Least y' can do is bake some cone cakes fo' 'em.'"

"You have cakes for us?"

"Sho' do, chile." Removing checkered cloths that covered the baskets, she passed each basket around the campfire so the surprised men could help themselves.

"Hey, these are good." Tibben took several bites. "Where did you get the sugar and stuff to make them, Aunty? Thought things were pretty well used up around here."

"The Lord doth provide, sojer boy. Whar thar's a will thar's a way."

"Aren't you afraid of being caught?" Bob Dyer asked between bites. "If your master finds you've been feeding and consorting with Yankee soldiers, won't he beat you?"

"Lawsy me, no. A field niggah mebbee get whipped. Not a house servant, we's too valuable. 'Sides...." Her face took on a mystic expression, her voice a hollow ring. "Yore gwine win two great battles soon and set us free."

"Two? Lord, Aunty, we'd settle for just one. Where'd you get that information?" Jobson inquired.

Her eyes flashed and she glanced from side to side as if in a voodoo trance. "It's written in de scriptures."

Jobson chuckled. "Too bad more of our generals don't read the Bible. Mind telling us where this can be found? We'll pass it on to headquarters."

"It's written by de prophet Daniel, 'leventh chapter."

Kimball rose slowly and tossed two logs on the dying fire. "Daniel, eh? Well, that's one I've missed."

The deep voice of the Negress resonated. "You shall be led into victory by Darius Mede."

"Darius Mede? We have no commander by that name." McCool scratched his forehead. "There's old 'Four Eyes,' George Gordon Meade, but he ain't running things, Hooker is."

"You shall be led into victory by Mede," came the esoteric reply.

Hallowell swung his head around. "Quaker, you carry a Bible. How about turning to the eleventh chapter of Daniel? Let's see what Aunty's referring to."

The Quaker reached inside his tunic and took out a small pocket Bible. He began leafing through it as he moved from the shadows closer to the light.

"Find it?"

"Yes, here it is."

"Read what it says."

"Daniel, eleventh chapter, first verse. 'Also I in the first year of Darius the Mede, even I, stood to confirm and to strengthen him.'"

McCool's mouth fell open. "That don't tell us nothin'."

"It might if Meade should suddenly become head of the army. It would be his first year as such. Maybe we could confirm and strengthen him to a victory."

"Doesn't say it like she says."

"Read v'ses 'leven to fifteen," the woman said in a monotone.

The Quaker ran his finger down the page. "'And the king of the south shall be moved with choler, and shall come forth and fight with him, even with the king of the north, and he shall set forth a great multitude, but the multitude shall be given into his hand.

"'And when he hath taken away the multitude, his heart shall be lifted up; and he shall cast down many ten thousands, but he shall not be strengthened by it.

"'For the king of the north shall return, and shall set forth a multitude greater than the former, and shall certainly come after certain years with a great army and with much riches.

"'And in those times many shall stand up against the king of the south. The robbers of thy people shall exalt themselves to establish the vision, but they shall fall.

"'So the king of the north shall come, and cast up a mount, and take the most fenced cities; and the arms of the south shall not withstand, neither his chosen people, neither shall there be any strength to withstand.'"

Kimball listened intently. "Victory at a fenced city could mean Grant takes the Confederate stronghold at Vicksburg. But where's the other victory? She said we'd have two."

"Here in the east, I hope," Hallowell responded. "Probably some place where there's a mount or hill like the last passage mentioned."

Tibben bit into a cake. "Sounds like mumbo jumbo to me."

"It does?" the Quaker replied. "Listen to the next passage and remember that we are a volunteer army. 'But he that cometh against him shall do according to his own will, and none shall stand before him, and he shall stand in the glorious land, which by his hand shall be consumed.'"

The slave spoke low. "Now read de fo'tieth verse."

He let his finger run down the page. "'And at the time of the end shall the king of the south push at him, and the king of the north shall come against him like a whirlwind, with chariots, and with horsemen, and with many ships, and he shall enter into the countries, and shall overflow and pass over.'"

Leaving her baskets behind, the slave had slipped away into the darkness.

In silence, the soldiers sat and listened to the sounds of battle coming from the direction of Middleburg.

Throughout the next day the 118th remained encamped at Aldie. On June twenty-first the march was resumed as they moved west toward Middleburg and passed through the rubbled town at eight in the morning. They were then deployed to the right of a turnpike that wound its way over the valley floor toward nearby foothills.

Open rolling countryside, green and beautiful, stretched out on every side of the battle line. Infantry resting on their arms watched intently as a gathering host of cavalry formed at the rear.

Seeking information, McCool strolled toward a horseman and proffered a cigar. "What's going on, yella leg? Anybody know?"

Raising the cigar to his nose, the cavalryman sniffed. "Stuart's up in those hills blocking Ashby's Gap. We're gonna drive him out."

"Just like that?"

"Just like that, dough foot."

Nearby, a chance meeting took place between Captain Donaldson and his older brother and Captain Ulrich Dahlgren.

"I've told you, Joe, nothing's going to happen," Captain Donaldson said. "Think how Father would feel if he knew you weren't carrying his watch into battle."

"He'll feel twice as bad when he doesn't get it back. I told you I had a presentiment last night and I shall get my 'furlough' today." His lean face looked haggard. "It was a whispering of the infinite beyond me to the infinite within me and my spirit heard it. Presentiments are not mere speculations as to chance, they are perception. Another argument for immortality. I say today I am 'going up.' I just know it."

"You sound just like Batchelder. To hear him, he's been going to get his 'furlough' in every battle we've been in. So far, he's never even been scratched."

Stroking his goatee, Ulrich Dahlgren stared down at the ground. "Frank's right. You're taking this thing too seriously, Joe. Kick it off before..."

The brassy notes of "Boots and Saddle" sounded across the meadows and the woodlands, echoing and re-echoing with spine tingling clarity across the rolling Virginia countryside. Breaking off conversation, tense-faced troopers raced for their mounts.

Crouching behind a wall of heaped-up field stones, infantry support watched the preparations with excitement. The prospect of seeing a grand scale cavalry charge for the first time sent nervous perspiration flowing from armpits, the secretion soaking into already reeking kersey uniforms.

Standing beside five thousand horses marshaled in battle line were five thousand riders, armed, booted, spurred and ready to mount. The bugles sounded "Mount" and instantly five thousand blue-clad troopers sprang into their saddles. Cavalry leaders wearing bright yellow chevrons and trappings moved to the front of their respective squadrons. Fluttering pennants and streaming guidons, ten to each regiment, marked the left of the companies. Schooled horses, awaiting the bugle notes to sound the charge, chafed at restraining curb and martingale bits, their nostrils dilated, their flanks swelling in response to their impatient riders.

Tibben's voice quivered. "Glory be. Would ya look over yonder, Willie?"

McCool shaded his eyes against the slanting rays of the hot sun and peered at the opposite slope on the plain, where five thousand plumed Confederate horsemen cantered out of the woods and formed. "Yowee! Glad I ain't got no horse. I'm happy enough right here."

The roar of fever-pitched voices drowned his words. The sharp notes of Federal bugles sounded the charge, calling forth a whooping and hollering of "Forward!" from saber-swinging troopers who dashed off at a gallop, their spurs planted deep in the flanks of nervous horseflesh. Down the lines and through columns in quick succession rang the echoing command, "Forward! Forward!"

Flying horses thundered across the trembling fields, hooves filling the air with clouds of dust and whizzing pebbles. Iron-rimmed hooves beat with remorseless tread, crushing stones to powder and crashing through the flesh and bones of any hapless rider who chanced to fall.

Echoing from the distant slope came the snarling bugle retorts of the enemy as five thousand Confederate cavalrymen spurred their mounts forward to meet the challenge. Five thousand sabers leaped from scabbards and flashed in the sun as the plain quivered beneath the furious, pounding tread of ten thousand horses.

Two gigantic tidal waves roared recklessly toward each other, the great bodies of mounted troops drawing closer, increasing their mad pace by the moment until they met head-on with a resounding crash.

Like storm-lashed water, the swirling lines of men and horseflesh boiled up in a tempest-tossed sea as horses were thrown end over end by the sudden, violent collision, crushing riders beneath.

Squadrons of men standing upright and stiff-legged in their stirrups cut each other to the ground with sparkling saber strokes. Furious riders slashed their way with sweeping blades, plunging headlong through opposing ranks, steel striking against steel, razor-sharp metal gashing faces, breaking arms, decapitating and splitting heads in the wild scene of war.

Crouching and watching from a distance, Captain Donaldson hissed through clenched teeth. "Break 'em up, Joe. Break 'em up."

Anxious men surrounded him, straining to hear the first yells that would signal victory for one side or the other, whether the screeching Rebel "Ki Yi" or the deep-throated Union "Hurrah."

Slowly, one by one, the enemy appeared to be unwinding himself from the writhing mass and finding safety in flight. Then, as a cracking egg finally breaks and spills its contents, the remaining Confederate force turned and fled to the west.

"We broke 'em! We broke 'em!" Tibben's hand came down hard on McCool's back. "Ya'. Ya'. Go get 'em boys! Sic 'em!"

From the bloody plain came a resounding Union "Hurrah!" as Federal troopers reformed into squadrons and started in pursuit.

Regimental bands struck up the triumphant strains of *"John Brown's Body"* as singing infantry sprang forward to follow them on the field.

Kicking up a choking cloud of dust as they marched toward the rear came the battle's flotsam and jetsam, sturdy Confederate prisoners passing the happy column of Philadelphians. For men having just suffered severe reverses, they seemed a rather communicative set and strangely enough, loud in their praise of the fighting and riding exhibited by the Union cavalry.

"You uns'll soon be as good as we'uns," one shouted at Cassidy.

"Sure 'n 'tis true what ye say, Johnny. We're just beginnin' to git up steam." A toothy grin split Cassidy's face.

Bayonets burnished by the sun overhead, the regiment marched toward Upperville, a small town nestled at the base of the Blue Ridge Mountains, entrance to the Gap which the Federal troops were trying to clear.

The pleasant countryside was populated by spacious houses, marking the region as one of farming and industrious thrift. A prominent feature of the landscape viewed by the men as they crossed was the large number of stone fences intersecting each other in every direction and at all angles. The green fields were laid out in a picturesque patchwork with mossy rock walls as borders. The scent of wild onion and orchard grass filled the air.

To make the going less pleasant, a Confederate rear guard rose up at times from behind the stone fences to obstruct the Union advance with faltering rifle fire. The march became a succession of halts and advances, ploys and deployments, the purpose of the enemy to force changes from column to line and line back to column.

Late in the afternoon both opposing forces entered Upperville simultaneously and the touch-and-go contest became a vigorous fight in the gathering twilight. Pistol shot and saber stroke played a part as angered, swearing combatants jammed a choked roadway. From the cover of fences and dwellings, dismounted Southern cavalrymen blazed away at the charging Union columns, but the exultant Feds, not to be denied, continued pressing successfully through the village and into the gap, up the timbered defiles and toward the summit where the enemy prepared a rally at the hamlet of Paris. Waiting to receive the retreating force, like the protective arms of a father standing at the family threshold, was a large portion of Longstreet's Infantry Corps behind which Stuart's men took refuge.

After several probing stabs had established that the mountain gap was too strongly held to overcome with the troops at hand, the Federal force began retiring back toward Middleburg under cover of darkness.

Cool night breezes played on sunburned faces encrusted with dirt and dried perspiration. The fresh air brought pleasant relief from the day's heat and activity. The 118th bedded down for the night.

"Whatever Lee's up to on the other side of these mountains," Kimball said, yawning wearily, "he sure doesn't want anybody peeking over his shoulder to find out."

"Thought for a moment we had the Gap in our pocket," Hallowell said with a grunt, "until Longstreet's boys showed up. Wonder what Lee's up to?"

"You mean where?" Kimball replied.

The sound of cantering hoofbeats approached through darkness: a cavalry troop returning to Middleburg. The command of fifty horsemen sang with gay abandon.

"Around her neck she wore a yellow ribbon
She wore it in the springtime and in the month of May.
And if you ask her why, oh, why she wears it,
She wears it for her lover who's in the cavalry
Cavalry. ..Cavalry."

"Cocky bastards," Gilmour growled. "Why don't they shut the hell up and let us dough foots sleep in peace?"

Bob Dyer cast a passing glance at the body of horsemen. His face brightened. Riding with the Sixth and Eighth Pennsylvania Cavalry were familiar faces from Frankford.

He cupped his hands to his mouth. "Hey there, Shallcross! How about hitching a ride?"

The singing stopped abruptly as the troopers reigned in their mounts. John Sidebotham held up a lantern. "I'll be chiggered. It's the Corn Exchange boys from home!" he shouted.

Duffield sprang from the saddle and with reins in hand, rushed toward McCool and Tibben. He threw his arms about their shoulders. "How did you like our performance this afternoon?" he asked.

Fatigue gave way to jovial reunion as old friends began joshing and talking as one.

Captain Donaldson strolled beside the silent figure of Paddy, who had disengaged himself from the hometown revelry.

"What's troubling you, Mulcahy? You haven't been yourself since we left Falmouth. Something I can do to help?"

"Not unless you can get me to Leesburg."

"Leesburg? Why? Is something wrong between you and Becky'? Is that what was in the letter Bet smuggled through to you?"

"Something like that." His head fell. "Becky's going to have a baby."

"A baby!" Donaldson gazed at the stars. The march from Antietam-eight months ago, he thought. His eyes leveled as he said quietly, "You've been thinking about jumping, haven't you?"

"Yes, Frank, I've got to go to her. Got to make it right with her mother. You could cover for me, Leesburg's not far. I got to be there."

Donaldson slipped an arm around his companion's waist. "You'd never make it. That whole region's swarming with Mosby's guerrillas. You've heard what they do to our wagon trains and escorts? You wouldn't stand a chance."

"I'm not worried about my chances. Just Becky's. What will people say and do to her when they discover the child is born out of wedlock? And to a Yankee soldier. You or nobody else is going to stop me. If you won't help, soon's we get back to Aldie, I'm heading for Leesburg."

"I'll help, but promise you won't do anything until we return to Aldie. It's rumored at headquarters we'll be moving north from there, anyway. Will you promise?"

"Beggin' yer pardon, Cap'n," Cassidy interrupted from the darkness, "there's a trooper back in the line askin' fer ye."

"Send him forward, Andy. Probably my brother, Joe."

In a moment Ulrich Dahlgren appeared, his face drawn with grief as he swung himself from a blood-stained saddle. Eyes lowered, and without a word, he withdrew a round object from inside his tunic and held it out in the palm of a quivering hand.

Stunned at the sight, Donaldson stared, his lips trembling. "Father's watch. Joe...."

Dahlgren nodded sorrowfully. "He...he was so sure about it."

"Oh...Joe." The tears burst forth, washing tiny streaks of powder smudge over Donaldson's cheek bones. Mechanically, he reached out and took the battered metal case from Dahlgren's hand, his tanned fist closing tightly around it, the watch chain dangling loosely between his cold fingers. "Where...where's his body, I've got to see it."

Dahlgren's jawbone tensed. "It's best you don't. Direct hit with a twelve-pound case shot." He bowed his head. "That's all we found."

CHAPTER 14

The column of the Fifth Corps, turned north at Aldie on the twenty-sixth of June and headed toward Leesburg through a drizzling rain.

Marching to the fore as usual, eyes peeled for anything new or novel, McCool stopped and pointed. "Boys, will you look at that shack?"

On top of a prominent hill an imposing yellow brick mansion stood beneath towering trees. Dark green boxwood lined a winding gravel driveway, mushrooming in beautiful contrast against the umber walls.

"We've seen it before," Cassidy retorted. "Eight months ago to be exact. That there's President Monroe's old home."

"So I remember. Eight months is a long time."

"Sure'n they say it's been taken over by Mosby as a hideout and observation post to check our movements. See them attic windows? Johnnies up there more'n likely this very minute. Lookin' right smack into your eardrums."

"You don't think Mosby's guerrillas would try to pull anything against a whole corps do you?"

"Niver can tell. Heard it said he's a livin' breathin' hornet. Ain't askeered o' nothin' or nobody."

Captain Donaldson approached the tail end of the regiment and called Paddy to one side. His eyes still conveying grief, the officer removed his black felt campaign hat and shook water from the broad brim. "No luck. Father Corby's too far in advance to be of help. The Irishmen passed through Leesburg three hours ago."

Paddy stared down at his muddy shoe tops. "And we'll soon be there. Do you think that maybe Chaplain O'Neil? I mean would he mind....?"

"He'd be more than happy to, but he's...."

"I know, Protestant. Slated direct for hell, or so we've been taught. Chirp, Billy, the others, your brother. Nobody can tell me they're not in heaven. Not now. I don't believe it. A papal bull against the comet...."

"Easy, Paddy."

"Easy? I need forgiveness of sin. Our baby needs to be blessed. Why should one type of Christian be superior to another? A good father settles his children's troubles directly. He doesn't need anybody butting in for him with army rules and regulations. If he will, I want Chaplain O'Neil to read over us."

Donaldson replaced his hat. "One who goes against the dictates and decrees of his church is usually left troubled and unhappy, Paddy. But if that's the way you want it, I'll speak to O'Neil. He'll be there, I'm sure."

The Quaker walked alone in preoccupied silence, a gum blanket draped over his head and shoulders. Reaching down, he picked up pebbles and flicked them at passing mud puddles, he looked up as Paddy fell alongside.

"Why so dejected, friend? Last time we neared Leesburg thee acted like Sir Lancelot approaching fair Elaine."

Diamond drops of rain ran off Paddy's lips and face. "I was no Galahad."

"Oh?" His friend looked up questioningly. "Is there something wrong between thee and she?"

"Not exactly." Paddy stopped to toss a stone. "John, you ever feel upset, troubled? I guess I mean unhappy?"

"'Bout what? This rain? No, I like the rain. The war? Yes, I hate it."

"No, I mean losing your religion because you went to war against the decrees of your church."

The Quaker squared his chin and drew in his lower lip. "Nobody ever loses true religion, or has it taken from him. 'The Letter of the Law killeth, but the Spirit giveth life.' A plague on mortal men who set themselves up as God's attorneys. Faith and the Holy Spirit weren't meant to be dispensed by proxy." He stopped abruptly, his voice apologetic. "I'm sorry. I've shocked thee."

"No, you haven't. Go on."

"Well, if thee mean do I feel remorse for being read out of Friends Meeting for carrying this," he tapped his rifle, "the answer is yes, the faith of my fathers means much to me. They gained it by remaining steadfast through trials and even torture and death. Someday I hope to be reinstated, and maybe, if I dedicate myself, no son of mine will ever be faced with the choices I had to make. But why does thee ask?"

"Because I've got the same kind of problem. I planted seed before I built fences. Becky and I are going to have a baby."

"Now?"

"In about a month. I want O'Neil to marry us because he's our chaplain and he's handy. I know I shall be looked upon by my church as living in sin. Do you think it takes a priest to make a marriage holy?"

The Quaker shifted the weight of his wet field pack and wiped raindrops from his thick eyebrows.

"We all live under authority according to the Word, friend. No matter what, we are obliged to submit to that authority. Submission, there's the rub. Ever since Eve helped herself to the apple." He wrapped an arm around Paddy's shoulders and pressed firmly. "But who knows? Maybe some good will come out of this war. Maybe man will learn to love his brother, learn to live harmoniously and drop the manufactured dogmas of intolerance." He ran the tip of his tongue across his upper teeth. "We are all His children when you come right down to it. The good, bad and indifferent."

The march continued in silence. Late in the afternoon the quiet streets of Leesburg echoed to the tramp of weary feet. The rain had stopped and left behind an enchanting afterglow of dripping freshness to greet the eventide. The time had finally arrived. Fighting off embarrassment and the inquisitive stares of his comrades, Paddy removed himself from the column, Chaplain O'Neil beside him. Hesitant, his heart pounding, he turned onto a side street. Dread and uneasiness seized him, yet deep down inside there was an anxious, burning anticipation.

Directly ahead and partially hidden by a hedge, its brick walls cloistered in ivy, sat the Chenewith home, snug and serene. Both men paused on the sidewalk before the house. Paddy shifted awkwardly from one foot to the other, the palms of his hands wet with sweat. Those passing by pierced him with icy stares which added to his discomfort and alarm. *Would they dare harm Becky?*

Chaplain O'Neil removed his pipe and tapped the bowl on a hitching post. "Would you rather I waited here a moment?"

"If you would, sir. It might be better."

"All right, son. Call when you want me."

"Yes, sir."

Nervously running the back of his hand across dry lips, Paddy mounted the vine-latticed porch. Hesitating at the door for a moment, he raised the brass eagle knocker and sounded it.

The twilight radiated with the soft hues that follow warm summer showers. Lily of the valley in a moist flower bed scented the air with a delicate fragrance. From the foliage, small glistening gems of water dropped gently and the wet bark of shade trees filled the atmosphere with a woodsy sweetness. A bird warbled softly somewhere overhead.

The door opened and Paddy stood face to face with the girl he loved. Instantly Becky's arms were about his neck, drawing him close, her lips seeking his.

"I knew you'd come. I just knew you'd return," she cried, her pale face flushed.

Tears of joy welled in Paddy's eyes at the thought of being needed, wanted and loved. Responding to her affection, he kissed her again. Then he drew back, his voice husky. "Where's your mother? I must see her at once."

"I'm here, son," a voice replied from the spice-scented hallway.

"Ma'am, can you forgive me?"

Mrs. Chenewith eyed him with a level, searching gaze, then laid a soft motherly hand on his chevroned sleeve. "I can't say this didn't come as somewhat of a shock. We mothers are a proud lot, however, what is to be will be. You both have my blessing, and I'm certain the doctor will see it that way, too. That which God joins together let no man put asunder. Make your peace before His throne, my son. He's wiser and more understanding about these matters than I."

Stunned, Paddy looked deep into her soft eyes. "You called me 'son'," he stammered in a voice strained from fatigue. "May I call you, 'Mother'?"

Mrs. Chenewith placed a kiss on his forehead. "Yes, I would like that very much. Come, let's go into the parlor. Becky, bring some warm soup. Can't you see your husband's tired and hungry?"

Radiantly beautiful, Becky smiled. "I shan't forget my duties, Mother."

In a simple ceremony performed before the Chenewith hearth, Chaplain O' Neil united the Union soldier and the Southern girl in holy matrimony. In the far corner of the room, a grandfather clock struck the hour as if giving its approval.

An impromptu wedding supper by candlelight was laced by pleasant conversation devoid of war's alarms. Becky clasped Paddy's hand tightly.

"If prices don't come down soon, I declare I don't know what we'll do. Imagine, calico a hundred dollars a yard, shoes a hundred dollars a pair and flour a thousand dollars a barrel. Just the other day I heard Mayor Orr say things would get worse before they get better."

Chaplain O'Neil sat forward. "That's a mighty pretty dress you're wearing, ma'am."

"This?" Becky responded. "This is a four-year-old cotton I recently dyed brown. The directions were in last fall's *Southern Illustrated News.*"

"You'd never know it, it's very becoming. I wouldn't mind having the formula to send home to my wife. She would make good use of it I know."

"Why, I declare, I'll give it to you right now if you like." She picked up a pencil and paper from a highboy and proceeded to write and read aloud. "Take the bark of the root of common wild plum, boil in an iron or brass pot until the dye looks almost black. Strain, and add a small quantity of copperas dissolved in a small quantity of the dye...."

Paddy beamed, proud of his wife's domestic capabilities.

"Add the articles to be dyed. Boil an hour or so, wring out and dip in strong, cold lye. When dry, rinse in cold water. There," she exclaimed, handing the paper across the table, "a gift from me to Mrs. O'Neil."

"I can assure you my wife will want to write and express her thanks." Suddenly his expression and mood changed. "War is such a pitiful waste, a practice conceived by rascals and suckled by the greedy. I don't mean to pry or be ungracious, but has there been any talk of the South giving up this costly struggle?"

"Not a word," Mrs. Chenewith replied. "The complaining about high prices and shortages are glossed over by our politicians who heap abuse on the 'Damn Yankees' to relieve the grumbling. I should say, too, that while our Confederate forces continue to enjoy success in the field, the Southern people will continue to react in the same way as my husband's old, failing patients, those whose bodies he bolsters with stimulant drugs. Harsh reality returns when the stimulant is removed or loses its effect."

Reverend O'Neil arose from the table and looked at the bridegroom. "In that case I must be returning to the regiment to see to the needs of my other boys. Ladies, the pleasure of your company has been a most enjoyable and heartwarming experience for me. Now, may the grace of God, which passeth all understanding, pass between me and thee while we are absent one from the other."

Mrs. Chenewith held out a hand. "Do visit us again, Chaplain whenever you have the opportunity. You, too, have become a part of the family. I'd like my husband to meet you."

"Thank you, Mrs. Chenewith. I shall look forward to that time, a time of restored peace. Good night. Don't forget, Paddy," he called over his shoulder, "the regiment moves tomorrow morning early."

"Yes, sir." He put an arm around Becky's waist. "That may be," he murmured when the chaplian had left, "but they'll be marchin' without me."

"Paddy, you don't mean that."

"I do mean it. I won't leave you this time."

"Paddy, my dearest, you must not desert your flag. I' ll be in good hands. Mother has helped Father many times. Please, for my sake, do not desert."

"My mind's made up. I stay with you."

"And when our son is grown? How will you explain it to him?"

The word "son" sent a thrill racing through him. "A son? How can you be sure?"

"Don't evade the question, dear. How will you explain the dishonor of desertion to our son?"

"He'll understand. Besides, it'll only be temporary, just until he's born." He bit his lower lip. "I can't leave you now, don't you see that?"

"I think it's time you children retired for the night," Mrs. Chenewith interceded gently. "Paddy must be dreadfully tired. Perhaps you can discuss this further in the morning, when you' re refreshed."

"Yes, Mother, you're right. Come, dear, take my hand."

Her long, delicate fingers entwined his as Becky led him to the staircase. "You know," she whispered, "ever since you've been gone I've occupied the bed in which you recovered from your wound. It made me feel close to you in the dark." She blushed and kissed him lightly on the cheek.

Entering the familiar bedroom in which he had been a patient, the two paused for a warm embrace. Then, following his wife's cue, Paddy unfastened the buttons on his uniform, took off his cracked, worn shoes and placed them beneath an end table. From the corner of his eye he observed the satin softness of his wife's naked body as she deftly removed her dress and slip. The contours of her firm, taut breasts stood out in tantalizing relief.

"I declare, it's stuffy in here. You're accustomed to fresh air when you sleep. I'll raise the window," she said.

She moved gracefully toward a window, which she opened wide. Her lithe, slightly out-of-shape form was outlined by the filmy while curtains rustling in the semi-darkness. She stretched her arms wide, allowing a gentle breeze to play over her. "The night air's so refreshing. Don't you think so, Paddy?"

"All depends." There was a quiver in his voice. "I've known it to frost men's eyeballs."

She laughed. "My, that's a romantic thought." Moving toward a table, she stopped and snuffed out the candle flickering beside the bed.

His hands trembling with nervous anticipation, Paddy drew back the crisp, clean smelling sheets and climbed into bed. The downy comfort of a soft mattress, soothing to one used to sleeping on the hard ground, helped ease the high-strung tension coursing through his body. The relief of the tension was short-lived as Becky quickly placed herself beside him and put her arms about his waist. Their vibrant bodies aquifer, they pressed close to each other, seeking each other's lips in the darkness.

"Oh, Paddy, I love you so much."

"I love you, Becky, with all my heart." He breathed heavily. "I' ve never known happiness like this before in my whole life. Someone to hold and love me. Someone I can hold and love in return."

"I'll love and hold you forever, darling." With burning lips she kissed his neck. "Will they like me in Frankford, do you think?"

"Yes. Yes, they'll love you. I know that."

"I'm sure I'll be happy there. Your friends, the town, the people. It all sounds so wonderful when we talk about it."

"Becky?"

"Yes."

"Are you sure you won't mind? I mean bein' married to a common blacksmith? You're used to..."

"We'll be happy, darling. Besides, there's no such thing as a common anything, life is what you make it. I'll be as proud of your craftsmanship as you are."

"But our house..."

"Any house can be a cheerful home if the people in it are happy, sweetheart. Size and value don't make a home. We'll make a happy home, won't we?"

"Yes."

"Paddy?"

"Uh huh?"

"Hold me close."

He responded instantly, eagerly. Both of them trembled with excitement as he stroked the swelling mounds of her breast. Rotating his head, his searching lips moved to the warm cleft between her breasts, the sweet pleasant scent filling his nostrils.

"Becky?"

"Yes."

"May I...I mean is it all right to...."

Her arms flew about his neck and she kissed him feverishly. "Yes. Oh, yes, darling."

In the distance, from the direction of the Potomac, came the muffled sound of singing from around the bivouac campfires of the 118th. The low mournful words, wafted by a gentle summer night's breeze, could be faintly heard by the occupants of the darkened room. Lying close and breathing heavily, the two listened.

"We're tenting tonight on the old campground

Give us a song to cheer;

Our weary hearts, a song of home,

And friends we love so dear."

The next verse seemed to be carrying echoes from Balls Bluff:

"Many are the hearts that are weary tonight

Wishing for the war to cease,
Many are the hearts that are looking for the right
To see the dawn of peace
Tenting tonight, tenting tonight,
Tenting on the old campground."

Becky nestled her head on Paddy's shoulder. Her long soft hair against his
bare chest felt like silk. He kissed the shell of her ear. "When will our baby be
born?"

"Four...maybe five weeks."

She snuggled closer. "I'm so happy for us, I can hardly wait. A son. Imagine.
Yours and mine."

"S' pose it's a girl?"

"Will you be disappointed?"

"No, not exactly."

"Paddy?"

"Yes."

"I think it would be nice if we named him after your father, don't you?"

He nodded silently and gathered his wife in a tight embrace. Sounding as if it
were from another world, the singing, accompanied by a lone harmonica, continued
drifting into the room on the still night air.

"We are tired of war on the old campground,
Many are dead and gone.
Of the brave and true who've left their homes:
Others been wounded long.
We've been fighting tonight on the old campground
Many are lying near;
Some are dead and some are dying,
Many are in tears.
Tenting tonight, tenting tonight... "

The final chorus trailed off until there was only silence. Clinging ivy on the
brick walls of the house rustled slightly in the luminescent moonlight as a soft
wind played over them. Paddy rolled over on his back and clasped his hands
behind his head as he stared at the ceiling. Becky ran her fingers through his
tousled hair and caressed his forehead. "What's troubling you, darling?"

"Nothing. Just thinking."

"About your friends out there? You can't desert them, Paddy. That's what
you're thinking, isn't it?"

"Yes."

"I knew you wouldn't." She cupped his face in her hands, her soft breath on
his face as sweet as blossoms as she pressed her lips tightly to his.

CHAPTER 15

Lee's design was now manifest. Forcing his cavalry westward may have interrupted, but did not alter, his purpose. A skillfully planned Northern invasion was consummated and the historic Potomac ceased to be the border which controlled the strife. Confederate legions put the Potomac River behind them, and the unsuspecting farmers of Maryland and Pennsylvania were startled to see the advance of a mighty army. Loyal people all over the North stood aghast, anxiously awaiting the impending conflict.

The Union Army, with no knowledge of these anxieties, and with no fear of the consequences, tractable and obedient, remained assured of its strength, and confidant of its ability. Advance corps trudged along complacently to again measure swords with their adversary. This time not through the swamp, forest or wilderness and bog of the enemy's less favored clime, but through the open fields, over broad dales and down the gently rolling valleys of their native heath.

Long June days and brief summer nights made for short bivouacs. Early Saturday morning on June twenty-seventh, the Corn Exchange Regiment broke camp at Leesburg. While song birds and locusts chirped greetings to a warm day, the stretching columns of blue crossed the Potomac at Edwards Ferry and proceeded north toward Frederick, Maryland. Troops with wardrobes so scanty that the clothing not on their backs could easily have been disposed of in a pantaloon pocket. The dilapidated, tattered remnants of more prosperous days were, in some cases, tied to bayonets. Laundry flapped in the breeze as the army moved on—an army with banners not beautiful, but picturesque.

Toward noon, they forded the waist-deep waters of the Monocacy just below Frederick City. On the other side of the stream the regiment halted and gathered beside a remarkable spring where hot, thirsty soldiers availed themselves of the ice cold water gushing from a horizontal cleft in a rock about three feet from the ground, which broadened into a stream fully a foot wide rushing with such force that a tin kettle, not held firmly, was quickly dashed away.

Sergeant Cassidy wiped his lips with the back of his hand and gazed across the sparkling waters of the Monocacy.

Tibben took a step forward. "It's Mulcahy. Hey, where you been?"

"Yes, me wanderin' wild Irish rose," Cassidy said, as he pushed forward, "how comes ye always git waylaid in Leesburg? Got yerself a Southern colleen hid away there?"

"Better than that," Paddy said, grinning, "I married one last night."

"Ye did what? Ye've been tipplin' pot likker, that's what."

"Here comes the captain. Let's ask him." With fingers interlaced, he everted his outstretched hands and gave his knuckles a sharp crack. "Now I can sit around with you married jokers at night and talk shop," he said with a chuckle.

"Is he speakin' the Lord's truth, sir?"

"No truer word was ever spoken, Sergeant. Now, have the men move out." He turned to Paddy. "O'Neil tells me everything went well. He was deeply impressed by both Becky and her mother." He reached into his knapsack and drew out a pair of silver candlestick holders. "Here's a wedding gift for you and Becky."

"They're beautiful, Captain. Where'd you ever...?"

"Some old folks in need of money stopped me on the street in Leesburg. Your gift came by way of a transaction."

Paddy turned the silverware over in his hands. "We never had anything this fancy in our entire house. Thank you."

"You're welcome. Here's hoping they light your future home with happiness. Now pack them in your hope chest and let's get moving."

They reached Frederick by early evening. The sidewalks were crowded, as they were before Antietam, with excited townspeople and a great many others hanging from windows and shouting encouragement to the passing troops. Unlike the previous time, bawdy women now plied their wares and solicitations openly as well as secretively. Many of the men from the troops who entered the town earlier had succumbed to the temptation to "do the village" and, despite stringent orders to the contrary, eluded enforcement. Obviously taken in by too much Maryland whiskey, whole regiments of riotous soldiers made merry with the citizenry, eating at hotel tables and drinking at the bars in a gala Saturday-night revelry.

As the 118th pushed its way along the crowded thoroughfare, a swaying private called drunkenly from the sidewalk, "Hey, there go them Philadelphia boys what fought at Shepherdstown. How'sha 'bout a drink, soldiers?" Getting no response, he jeered. "Whatsha matter? Too damn highbrow? Church ain't till Sunday." Laughing coarsely, he tossed an empty bottle onto the street.

"Close up the ranks," Cassidy barked. "First man who steps out o' line gits the back o' me hand."

Several men looked pleadingly toward the officers for a countermand of orders, but none was given. Marching five miles beyond the uproar in Frederick, the regiment was finally halted and placed in bivouac close to General Meade's Fifth Corps headquarters.

"Damned old Four Eyes," Jobson grumbled as he spread a ground cloth. "The old buzzard don't know how to laugh, and he don't want nobody else laughin', gathering us under his wing like an old biddy."

McCool threw his pack down in disgust. "We strike civilization for the first time in eight months, and what do we get, field bivouac while the rest have a good time in town."

Shocking epithets and vulgar phrases were hurled at Meade as the disgruntled soldiers bedded down in the pollen-filled hayfields.

Close to four in the morning, Paddy was awakened suddenly from a sound sleep. "Wh...what? Who's that?"

"It's me," Donaldson whispered. "Get your clothes and report to regimental headquarters at once. Don't make a sound."

"Why? What's..."

"Don't ask questions. Get dressed."

It was still dark as Paddy approached headquarters.

Through the canvas walls of a Sibley tent, he could see silhouetted forms moving back and forth in front of lighted lanterns. Tethered horses, used to all sorts of noise and interruption, barely turned their heads as he was challenged by a sentry.

"Private Mulcahy, H Company. Hundred 'n Eighteenth Pennsylvania."

The sentry yawned. "Pass."

Inside, the tent was a beehive of activity. Commander Barnes carried on a rapid-fire conversation with Colonel Gwyn while Major Herring, in response to certain questions, periodically thrust a finger at locations on a map spread out before them. A tall, severe-looking officer, whom Paddy could not recall ever having seen before, sat hunched over a chair in front of the three, acting in the capacity of a judge regarding the matters under discussion.

Outside the tent, Paddy heard Duncan Gilmour answering the challenge of the sentry.

"Pass," came the reply, and Gilmour entered.

"Hoot mon, Paddy lad. What are we doin' here? What's this all aboot?"

"Don't know myself. Just been standing here trying to figure it out."

Colonel Gwyn lay aside a pipe he had been smoking.

"Privates Mulcahy and Gilmour?"

Both soldiers snapped to attention. "Yes, sir."

"Good. Come with me. Oh, before we leave, this is your new corps commander, General Sykes."

The general looked up from the map and nodded briefly.

"Now, suppose the three of us retire to Major Herring's tent where we can talk."

Joined by Captain Donaldson, Gwyn seated himself at a table, ordering the others to do likewise. He folded his hands. "You're no doubt wondering why you were brought here at this hour. I'll make it brief. You can ask questions later. Last night at eleven o'clock General Meade replaced General Hooker as head of the army. President's orders."

"Hoot mon. Ye dinna say."

"Yes. Now for the important matters at hand. The whereabouts of Lee's army has finally been uncovered. It's blanketing southern Pennsylvania, how much, we don't know. We have reason to believe from the Cumberland Valley east to the Susquehanna."

"Bloody Mary."

"No more interruptions, please. Just where their hub is, we haven't been able to determine, nor has Lee furnished us with any indication of his intentions. At the moment we're between him and Washington, that's all we know. From his present strategic position, he can readily swing east and go for Baltimore or Philadelphia. Or he can move northeast through Harrisburg to New York. There's no further need on my part to impress on you the seriousness of the situation, if Lee captures Philadelphia or New York we're all washed up. Meade has got to force Lee to pull in his horns and commit himself. The most important thing now is to get accurate reports on every movement he makes. We can't depend on telegraph because most of the wires are down. We've got to depend on scouts. The job will call for keen ingenuity, hard riding and bravery."

Paddy and Gilmour exchanged glances.

"We don't want any dull-witted plow horses scouting for us, the ones who only work well when there's a strong hand at the reins. We want men who can strike out on their own. Captain Donaldson has advised me that for special reasons you two are ably suited for the mission. Before I ask whether you'll volunteer, let me caution you on the danger involved. You will dress as 'Jesse Scouts.' That is, with Confederate uniforms worn over your own. You could be shot by either side. Time is at a premium. I must have your answer immediately."

"Aye, Colonel ye ha' got one, mon. Wha' say ye, Paddy?"

"You've got two men, Colonel."

"Excellent. Good luck to you both. Donaldson will outline your instructions."

"What a friend you turned out to be," Paddy groaned after Gwyn had departed. "One day you give a wedding present, the next, an assignment for death."

"And if I'd passed you over?"

"You'd never have heard the end of it."

Donaldson managed a smile. "Thought so. Now listen closely while I run over the details. Any questions, stop me. As Gwyn told you, it's believed Lee's army covers all of Southern Pennsylvania from the Cumberland to the Susquehanna. In the geographic center of this large area is a small town called Gettysburg. Eleven roads, several of them well macadamized, branch out from this village like spokes from a wheel. Each affords ready access to Chambersburg, Hagerstown, Frederick, Taneytown, Baltimore, Hanover, York, Harrisburg, Carlisle and Shippensburg. If Lee's scattered forces see trouble coming, they will more than likely head for that spot over the available roads."

"You want us to go up to this town of Gettysburg and look around, huh?"

"No. That job's being handled by others. You two will go east to a particular point which has Meade really worried, the Susquehanna River. If Lee should force march his men across it, he could then push right through Lancaster and down into Philadelphia. There's a bridge spanning the river, believed to be held by a small force of militia. Meade wants to know the exact state of affairs concerning that bridge. It must be held at all costs, or burned, to prevent the Confederates from crossing it."

"Has the telegraph been knocked out in that area?"

"Not entirely, but Confederate agents are hard at it. Which brings up another subject to which you must alert yourself. It's a known fact this particular section of our state is crawling with copperhead sentiment. So you must not allow yourselves to trust anybody, however, make careful note of the amount of disloyalty whenever you encounter it. We want to know just what to expect should our army be compelled to pass through that region.

"Now for your route. Here, take these maps. Proceeding from this point where you're now located just outside Frederick, you will head in a northeasterly direction, traveling cross-country. Stay to the east of Taneytown and Littlestown, pass through Hanover, and bear due north till you strike the York-Gettysburg road which runs east and west. Turn east toward York on that road, pass through York and proceed to Wrightsville on the river which lies twelve miles beyond."

"Aye, and how far would that be altogether, Cap'n?"

"It's approximately twenty-five miles from here to Hanover, about twenty miles from Hanover to York."

"Aye. With good horses we should make it in six or seven hours."

"York? That's where Schneider and his German friends are from. Suppose we bump into them? Our goose would be cooked."

"You'll each have a brace of Confederate cavalry pistols. Shoot the bastards if they see you and start trouble. They're deserters."

"But we'll be in Confederate uniforms."

"So much the better. If any questions are asked, say you recognized them as Northern spies." He focused his attention on the map. "Now then, when you reach the Susquehanna, if you find Confederates have taken the bridge or crossed it, Paddy, you're to work your way back toward this point." He pointed to a cross marked on the map. "That's Pipe Creek in Maryland, close to the Pennsylvania line. It's where Meade hopes Lee will turn to attack when he finds our army is closing in.

"Gilmour, we depend on you to relay the same information by telegraph, if at all possible. Make sure the enemy is moving on Philadelphia and not just flanking to take Harrisburg in the rear. When certain which course is being followed, ride like hell for Lancaster. You can telegraph the message from there to headquarters at Westminster. It'll be a hot race between you and Confederate agents either way."

"Aye, Cap'n. Ain't a livin' Johnny What'll outdistance me if such be the case."

"That's one of the reasons why you were chosen. Now if, when you reach the river, you find it still safely in our hands, you'll give these orders to the officer in command. He's to make a fight for it if attacked by a small force, or burn the bridge if attacked by a superior force. In either event, Gilmour, you're to cross the river to Columbia. It's directly across from Wrightsville. From there you can feed us telegraphic information keeping us advised of the river's security and also of any changes that might develop. Understand?"

"Aye, Cap'n. Use the wire from Columbia if everythin's under control. Run for Lancaster if not."

"Right."

Paddy frowned and his eyes narrowed. "Suppose we run into trouble along the way, need help or fresh horses. What about the people?"

"You'll have to take your chances. From here to Hanover, they're mostly Scotch-Irish and predominantly Union. Presbyterian people mainly, who prefer to work out their problems directly through the law rather than around or under it."

"Meaning what, Frank?"

"Meaning that you'll find colored farmhands and servants in most of the households throughout the area, where they enjoy trusted and long-term employment. But, at the same time, you'll find the general attitude to the slavery question pretty well set, in that socially the blood of the Negro is still offensive to the more aggressive races."

"Union, but with some reservations. Aye, Cap'n?"

"That's as close as we've been able to figure it. Now then, above Hanover and around York you'll find an entirely different situation. Those people, after nearly a century in this country, represent a different view of society and government and have caused considerable friction, if not antagonism, the Germans. They are staunch church people who've had little fellowship with the Negro race and express little interest in or sympathy with their problems. Moreover, because of their arrogant, obstinate German nature, they're uncooperative with anyone or any power that might lay temporary claim on their personal obligations for the common good. It's probably because of this that most of them have turned copperhead. Watch yourselves, they're not to be trusted either way."

Paddy drew his lips into a straight line. "A helluva note. Fighting in our own backyard and still not knowing who we can trust."

"There is one group, the Quakers, but here again, you will find a variance of sentiments. The Hicksite Quakers are more aggressive in their hostility toward slavery than the orthodox branch of the church, although both will shelter and defend a man for humanitarian reasons."

"Any in or around York?"

"Yes. Quite a settlement about ten miles northwest."

"How 'boot Lancaster, Cap'n?"

"If you run into difficulty there, head south into Drumore, Colerian and Little Britain townships, they're Scotch-Irish who, to wax poetic, closely typify the turbulent flow of the Octoraro and rugged hillsides of that region, one hundred percent Union. If Lee breaks for Philadelphia, Meade will move our army through that region, probably passing through Oxford. You can rejoin our forces at that point." He paused to check his watch. "It's getting late. We must wind up quickly. I've given you the purpose, the route and what you're expected to observe and accomplish. One thing remains."

"Aye'n what's that, Cap'n?"

"Your passport to mingle with the Rebs if it becomes necessary."

"What?" Paddy's mouth flew open, his eyes bulging.

"Yes. If by accident you should bump into Confederates advancing on York or the Susquehanna, fall in with them and seek out the commanding officer. You are to pass yourselves off as advance scouts for Stuart's cavalry."

"Play me a pi'brock, Cap'n. We know nothin' o' Stuart'n his activities. S'pose we're questioned?"

"Your defense will be your offense. Upon reporting to any Confederate commander you might find in the vicinity, you'll tell him that Meade has replaced Hooker and the entire Federal Army has crossed the Potomac. That information is so recent there's no possibility of the Johnnies in Pennsylvania having had news of it. It should alarm them enough that they'll overlook questioning you."

"Hoot mon. Why should we have to gi' away such vital information?"

"Because it will be to our advantage, and serve a double purpose. First, establish your position as one of respected and reliable authority. Second, forewarn them that Meade is closer than they realize. We want Lee to commit himself to a definite course, pull in his horns. With the knowledge that we are close on his heels, he will have to concentrate his scattered army somewhere, which is exactly what we want him to do."

Paddy studied his fingernails. "But supposing they should question us?"

"I was coming to that. You are volunteers for the Southern cause from Ireland and Scotland. You jumped the blockade runner *Dolphin* at Savannah and joined up with Stuart following the Antietam campaign." He paused, the trace of smile appearing on his face. "The enchanting glibness you both possess is another reason you were selected, and you are reasonably familiar with Stuart's recent activities to pull it off. There's one last bit of information. Because of its importance, I've saved it until last, so listen carefully. Yesterday our cavalrymen captured dispatches being carried from Stuart to his subordinate, General Beverly Robertson. Robertson is still guarding the mountain gaps at Ashby and Snickers, while Stuart, with the commands of Generals Hampton, Fitzhugh Lee and Chambliss, has ridden clear around the rear of our army. They are now directly east of us at Rockville, Maryland."

"Cripes. That means they're heading the same direction we'll be taking."

"Exactly. Now you can see the need for speed. There's one thing that'll slow them down, they've captured a wagon train of nearly two hundred wagons and are carrying them as a prize. In all probability you'll reach the Wrightsville bridge long before they do. Finally, remember, Stuart's operating under Longstreet's orders, not Lee's. His objective is to join with Ewell's division at the Susquehanna. Here's a list of Ewell's division and brigade commanders. Memorize them so you'll be familiar with them. If you're asked the number of men advancing with Stuart, that figure is roughly twenty-five hundred. The greater part of Stuart's cavalry, roughly three thousand, are under Robertson, posted on Lee's right flank and rear in the Shenandoah Valley."

"Boy, this's gonna be a cozy little game. Who's got who by the tail?"

"Aye, Laddy. Just hope it ain't ours what gets scrubbed on the battlin' board."

Donaldson glanced at his watch. "Well, that's all. Are there any more questions?"

"Yes. Supposing we get to the Susquehanna and Ewell doesn't show up, or Stuart, or anybody for that matter? How long do we hang around?"

"Gilmour will telegraph that information from Columbia, and you'll both remain posted at the river until things resolve themselves one way or the other; there's bound to be a head-on battle soon. Now, if there are no more questions, here are compasses, field glasses and maps. Over in that chest you'll find light-weight summer uniforms and sidearms. Get dressed and I'll ride out as far as the pickets with you."

"Wha' time o' the marnin' be it noo, Cap'n?"

"Ten after three. If you hurry, you can just make church in York." He grasped them both by the arms. "Good luck, and take care."

"Thanks, Captain. You do the same."

With a final exchange of handclasps, both Jesse Scouts sprang into their saddles and started north at a trot. Planting spurs, they raced over the plotted route across meadow and farm and through tiny villages, stopping at intervals along the way to requisition fresh horses, leaving irate farmers vigorously protesting with clenched fists as they sped on.

A scorching hot sun was approaching its zenith when they finally reached the York-Gettysburg road. Dismounting their lathered mounts, they flung their aching bodies on the warm grass of a high knoll. A groan escaped Paddy's lips. "Boy, I feel like I've been beat with a million sticks. Been two years since I did this much riding."

"Aye, laddy. Thought bein' wet nurse to supply wagons had me tough as nails. Right now I feel as unhinged as the joints o' a skeleton."

Off in the dusty distance and heading east was a steady stream of farmers and merchants driving cattle and wagons loaded with merchandise and personal property. Frantic inhabitants fleeing toward Lancaster and Chester counties to escape capture.

Gilmour shaded his eyes against the sun's bright rays. "Aye, there goes the flock, the dogs can't be far behind."

The sound of a horse approaching from behind caused them to spin around and reach for their pistols.

"Och, no chentlemen. You neet no guns mit me. I'm der friend. Zaw you pass der house avile ago, zo I chust come by to zay ve velcome you. Doctor Wolf's der name. Liff chust down der road a piece at York New Salem.

Both scouts eyed the bearded, bespectacled physician narrowly as he got off his horse. Short and stocky, he was dressed in a plain gray coat, his trousers supported by suspenders. A heavy beard rested like a huge bird's nest on his white buttonless shirt and on top of his head he wore a square-crowned, broad-brimmed black hat.

"Och, zo it iss mit stubborn fools." He pointed toward the fleeing refugees. "Vor a vun dollar fee yet, we could have provided dem mit zecurity against conviscation of der property und livestock." He stopped and shrugged his thick shoulders. "But zey vould not lizzen."

Paddy stared at him through slitted eyes. "What do you mean you could give them security?"

"Vy sure now, haven't you been told of our zecret society? Der Knights of der Golden Zircle? Zix weeks now mit der help of Convederate agents, ve've been organizing York und Adams Counties to aid der Zouth."

"Is that right. First we' ve heard of it. We're scouts for General Stuart. Been out of touch with things." Paddy's manner was casual. "You sign up many members?"

"Och, ya. Zeveral thousand. Mit zo many Peace Democrats around, it vas no trouble."

Feigning a sudden return of memory, Paddy nodded his head. "Peace Democrats. Now you mention it, I do recall hearing your name. Jeb Stuart said if we ran into trouble up here to seek out Doctor Wolf. Said you were the leader of a secret society in this area. Remember, Dunk? That was one of the last things the general said?"

Gilmour yawned. "Hoot, mon. My body's so tired from ridin' it's hard for me to remember even my own name at this point."

"Vell, goot day, chentlemen. Rest comfortably. I must go down unt extend my velcome to der rest of your army I zee chust now approaching over der road." Eyeing both with an odd expression, he remounted his horse and started down the slope at a walk.

"Aye, there goes a lot o' loyalty for ya. The pock-a-book kind."

"Don't think he's on to us, do you?"

"Nay, lad. Right noo he's too overcome by his own feelin' o' self-importance to be o' much danger. But we'd better be aboot our business instead o' sunnin' oursel'es like a couple o' cats. Best I ride quick to the bridge and warn the militia, telegraph a report over the wire at Columbia."

"What about me?"

"Do as the Cap 'n said. Ride down and fall in with the Rebs. Check out their commander and give your report, that is unless ye' d rather...."

"No."

"Good, lad. Noo make yer story good. Keep 'em off balance." A firm clasp of sweat-stained, dirty hands and the two separated each in different directions.

Inwardly wishing he could turn back, a strange new fear gripping him, Paddy galloped toward the advancing Rebel columns.

Unaccustomed to brash intrusion by the baggage of war, birds high in the treetops held their ground, scolding him with angry chirping as he dashed by. Above the pounding beat of his horse's feet, he could hear bugle blasts drifting across the hot, humid air; enemy calls from the clouds of dust rising on the York road. Reaching the level of the roadway, he wheeled right and cantered parallel to the marching columns. Except for the color of their uniforms and the fact that they generally seemed older, he felt as though he were looking at his own comrades on route march. The Rebel uniform was a mixed hodgepodge of homespun butternut, gray kersey and dirty blue shirts taken from Yankees. Missing buttons had long ago been replaced with hickory nut shells and hardened service-berries. Their ragged, waspy trousers were toggled with a nail or two, and sometimes twigs. Thick socks sagged untidily over worn, dusty brogans. Their grotesque appearance was accentuated by barefoot men, some mounted double on huge draft horses with mangy-looking manes and hairy fetlocks. Floppy gray hats, dusty and full of holes, seemed to be the final attempt to spoil the landscape. Battered old headpieces, pliant to their owners' whim, expressed their mood like a clown's cap in a circus. Some were pinned up in the front with a thorn, a sprig of balsam or cedar stuck in the thong for an aigrette. Hatbands, long since vanished, were replaced by groundhog thong woven in and out of knife slits.

Mustering courage and his best Irish brogue, Paddy called, "Ho, there. And where would I be findin' General Ewell, lads?"

"Yore in the wrong pea patch, trooper, ol' 'Peg Leg's' up no'th of us. Sashayin' 'round the Yank's capitol at Harrisburg."

"Yeah," another called, "this heah's Gordon's brigade of Georgians."

"Sure'n where kin I find the good general? I'm carryin' a message from Jeb Stuart."

"Up front, ridin' at the haid."

"Thanks." Putting spurs to his mount, Paddy rode forward, an odd feeling in the pit of his stomach.

Thirty-one years old, the hawk-eyed, lean Confederate general was riding alone, distinguished from his men by gold-braided galloons on his sleeves. He sat his horse with ease, a tangled beard covering his face.

"General Gordon, sir?"

"Yes. What is it, soldier?" His voice was taut, vibrant, youthful, his eyes piercing.

A wave of relief surged reassuringly through Paddy's weary frame. Gordon was a man in whose presence one felt instantly comfortable.

"General Stuart's compliments, sir. I was told I'd be findin' General Ewell here."

"I'm in command here. Any message you have from Stuart can be delivered to me. It's about time we got some information. What's he been up to?"

"He has ridden around the rear of the Yankee army, sir."

"Ridden around? You mean to say Stuart's east of the Union forces? Where?"

"At Rockville, Maryland, when I left him, sir. He's bringin' a captured wagon train in this direction."

"The crazy fool. What we need is information at this point, not captured wagon trains. Is his entire force with him?"

"No, sir. Only twenty-five hundred. The rest are under Robertson, protectin' Lee's rear in the Blue Ridge."

"That's a relief. At least Lee has some eyes and ears. What information have you?"

Paddy let his reins hang loosely in one hand. "Meade's taken over from Hooker as head of the Union Army, sir." He looked square into the eyes of the Southern commander.

Gordon slapped his saddle horn enthusiastically. "Good. By the time Meade gets organized, we'll be in Philadelphia." Gordon hesitated a moment. "I didn't catch your name, soldier."

"Mulcahy, sir. Private Paddy Mulcahy."

"Come from Ireland to help us did you?"

"Aye, sir. That I did, sir. Just about a year and a half ago."

"Fine. Glad to have you with us." Gordon stroked his beard with a sweaty buckskin gauntlet. "When did the change take place?"

"Yesterday, sir."

"Hmm. Stuart lost no time in sending us that choice bit of information. Perhaps I've done him an injustice."

"Beggin' yer pardon, sir, but there's more Stuart thought the commander oughta know."

"What is that?"

"The entire Union Army's crossed the Potomac, sir. They're well above Frederick and drivin' hard into Pennsylvania."

Gordon sprang up in his saddle. "Good Lord, boy, does Lee know of this?"

"I don't know, sir."

A worried frown creased the general's face. "We're spread out all over, this could be disastrous. Ride back with the column while I mull things over."

Close to noon, the six Georgia regiments entered the town of York while pealing church bells filled the sultry Sunday air. Skirting the village on the western fringe was a creek, the Codorous, a deep, clear stream where many of the soldiers refreshed themselves. Acting as one of them, Paddy removed his dusty boots and dangled his hot, swollen feet in the cooling current. Finally plunging his head and neck into the water, he felt revitalized. A Confederate kneeling next to him poured water from a canteen so that it trickled slowly down his back. "Thought we'uns was a headin' east," he drawled.

"Faith and we are," Paddy replied.

The man stared at the course which the stream was flowing. "Well, I'll be jiggered. First time I ever seen a branch of water flowin' from south to no'th. Look at it. I declare anybody knows water's s'posed to run t'otha way, from no'th to south." A smile spread over his rustic, suntanned face. "I swanny, I' d sure enough call this'un a good sign, water flowin' same way we'uns is travelin', south to no'th."

Paddy wiped his face and glanced at the oddity of nature which the Southerner, reared in the ways of the outdoors, had so astutely observed. He put his soiled socks and boots back on his feet and mounted his horse. Clucking the animal into a walk, he crossed a covered bridge which spanned the Codorous and proceeded leisurely into York, a town of eighty-six hundred people that closely approximated Frankford in size. Antiquated brick buildings of quaint colonial design lined both sides of a wide, unpaved street. Spires and cupolas rose in the background. During the dark days of the Revolution, with the British occupying Philadelphia, York had served as the nation's Capitol. Many of the present buildings had housed the Continental Congress, the Continental Treasury, the War Board and other government offices.

Reining his horse, he halted near the head of the long Confederate column, which came to rest in the spacious center square. The gray-clad invaders began lounging in the shade of two large market sheds like so many docile hound dogs after a tiring night's chase. The church bells continued ringing, although by now the sidewalks and side streets were packed with excited townspeople.

The sight of church-going men, women and children dressed in Sunday attire contrasted markedly with the enemy's legions. Troops were begrimed from head to foot with the impalpable gray powder which had risen in dense clouds from the macadamized pikes, settling in sheets on men, horses and wagons.

Women with gayly colored parasols stared apprehensively from rockaway carriages parked around the square. The driver of a barouche took one look, then flailed his horses and fled wildly down a side street, followed by a group of terror-stricken Negroes.

Paddy turned his head to more closely observe several young ladies who were waving handkerchiefs and red streamers at the enemy. In a sudden movement, they left their place on the sidewalk and surrounded a group of Confederate infantrymen.

"Could we have a button from each of your uniforms?" one of the ladies squealed.

"Please do," the others chorused.

At that moment a clergyman rushed to the scene and shouted, "If you have no self-respect, at least have some for the people who live here. Get back on the sidewalk."

Shamefacedly, the ladies dropped their heads and retreated, the Confederate soldiers smiling at them.

Paddy's attention was attracted by another development unfolding in the center of the square, the sight of which made him seethe with anger and inner torment. Sitting immobile in his saddle, he watched stone-faced as General Gordon strode toward a flagpole located between the sheds. He paused to glance up at the American flag fluttering slightly in the hot breeze. Signaling for one of his men to bring a Confederate standard, he lowered the Stars and Stripes with the help of a local citizen who rushed forward to lend a hand.

Unable to view the spectacle, Paddy dropped his eyes. In the background he could hear a gasp of dismay escape several loyal Unionists standing in the crowd. Raising his eyes slowly, he bit hard on his lower lip as the stars and bars of the Confederacy waved defiantly atop the flagpole.

Hats in hand, several distinguished-looking men left the crowd and approached the general. Employing utmost discretion, Paddy urged his horse forward to within earshot.

"I see no reason for this renewed anxiety on your part," Gordon was saying in measured tones. "It is as I told you gentlemen earlier in the day when you rode out to meet me on the Gettysburg road, in return for a peaceful surrender, I promise that life and property will be protected by my staff and myself."

"We place the utmost confidence in your word, General," the group leader replied solemnly. "However, Sam Small and Mr. Farquhar, here, wish you would take a moment to reassure our ladies. The women are greatly disturbed by the presence of your troops."

Gordon turned and surveyed his dirty, disheveled soldiers resting at ease around the square. He faced the committee once more, smiling. "My apologies, gentlemen," he said, chuckling "Had I realized, I might have remembered the time-honored wish of Burns that some power could, as he put it, 'the giftie gie us to see ourse'ls as ithers see us.'" Gordon mounted his horse. "I should have allayed your ladies' fears by my first effort, gentlemen. Permit me to do so now."

Advancing his mount to within a few feet of the nearest carriage, he removed his dusty campaign hat and with a gallant sweep of his arm, bowed low to several startled women. "Fair ladies," he said in a loud voice, "I wish to reassure you that the troops you see, though ill-clad and travel-stained, are good men and brave. Beneath their rough exteriors are hearts as loyal to women as ever beat in the breasts of honorable men. You must realize that their experiences, and the experiences of their mothers, wives and sisters at home, has taught them how painful is the sight of a hostile army in any town. Rest assured, ladies, we are operating under strict orders from our commander in chief, General Lee. Both private property and noncombatants are safe, the spirit of vengeance and rapine has no place in the bosoms of these dust-covered, knightly men."

A Confederate soldier, close enough to hear Gordon's last remark, dug his comrade in the ribs mirthfully. "I grannys. Did ye hear what the gineral jist called us, Dave? We'uns is knightly men."

"Wal, now, that war downright obligin' of him," the other replied jocularly as he flicked his rumpled hair in an affected manner.

General Gordon put on his hat on with a grand flourish, stood upright in his stirrups, and raised one arm. "To the town of York," he shouted so everyone could hear, "I pledge the head of any soldier under my command who destroys private property, disturbs the repose of a single home or insults a woman." With that, he spun his horse and cantered off to hold a consultation with his staff.

"Lookee heah, Dave. I reckon the gineral sure 'nough meant what he said 'bout us bein' knightly men," one Confederate simpered.

"That's for damn sure," the other replied with a throaty laugh. "I ain't fixin' to lose my haid over some no 'count Yankee belle." He proceeded to muss his hair in apish fashion.

Knowing Gordon was closeted in conversation with his lieutenants, Paddy decided to dismount. He tethered his horse at a hitching post close to a crowd of curious onlookers and squatted nearby. Clenching a piece of straw between his teeth, he listened attentively for any bit of information that might prove to be either valuable or interesting. Two farmers in particular caught his eye. One of them was pointing toward a mounted Confederate officer riding aimlessly around the square.

"By golly, Howard," one farmer ejaculated, "ain't that the smooth-talkin' Bible salesman fella? The one sellin' Bibles and askin' questions in our township for the past month?"

"You're right, Isaac. Wonder why he's dressed up in a Confederate uniform?"

"Hell, it's plain enough to see. He was no Bible salesman. He was spying for the Confederates."

"Well, I'll be...."

At that moment, Paddy was startled by a young Confederate officer who seemed to be in a terrible hurry to reach someone in the crowd. "Sorry," he called over his shoulder in an accent distinctively Northern.

Paddy saw two young men suddenly emerge from the crowd to meet the officer. One hung back with a grim expression on his face. The other grasped the officer enthusiastically by the hand. "George. George Latimer. By gosh, it's good to see you. Doesn't he look good, Bob?"

"In that uniform? No. I'd think he'd be ashamed to enter his home town like this."

"If you feel that way, why aren't you in a blue uniform?" the officer replied.

"You know I've been crippled in one leg ever since I took a spill from a horse five years ago."

"I'm sorry. I had forgotten."

The civilian who spoke initially put his hands on the shoulders of both in a peaceful overture. "Let's not carry on this way. We are old friends, remember? Besides, I think we owe George our respect because of the forthright stand he's taken. By choosing to wear the Confederate uniform, he's proven himself more of a man than the copperheads we see around us. Look at them." He pointed to various men in the crowd who were apparently in great favor of the happenings.

"Where does that leave you, Charley?" the officer inquired casually. "I see you are wearing neither blue nor gray."

"I am in the middle where the money is. Do you blame me?"

"Knowing you, no. You always were a great one to look out for yourself."

"Yes, I enjoy health and wealth, always have and always will."

"More power to you. May you live long and prosper." He stiffened suddenly. "Say, isn't that Cass Small and Mary Wilson sitting in the carriage over there?"

"It most certainly is, but if you're thinking of trying your hand, George boy, let me warn you, be careful. They're both true blue. Red, white, and blue, that is."

The officer grinned. "We shall see." He walked swiftly toward the carriage and doffed his hat. "Cassandra. Mary. This is indeed a pleasure. How long has it been since we've seen each other?"

"Not long enough, sorry to say," Mary Wilson replied. She turned her head away sharply.

"Oh, come now, Mary. Is that any way to greet an old beaux? Just because I chose to..."

The slim, attractive girl cut off his protest by abruptly screening herself behind a parasol.

The young lieutenant leaned on the carriage. "Well, this is a fine how do you do," he muttered. "Entirely different from what I'd expected, I must say."

"And just what did you expect?" Cassandra asked haughtily. "Should we have rolled out a red carpet for you and this rabble?"

"Now, Cass, don't be nasty."

"Nasty indeed. You listen to me, George Latimer. A line has been drawn through this town today, a dividing line that will exist for a long time. You mark my words."

"You don't mean that."

"I do mean it, the die is cast. From now on collaborators and copperheads will be thoroughly ostracized by those of us who have been loyal to the Union. They will not be welcome in our homes and their places of business will be blacklisted."

"You are taking all this too seriously, Cass. Every man has a right to choose his own course."

"I detest traitors."

Lieutenant Latimer grinned. "All right, you win. Let's change the subject. Tell me, where are Phil, Lat and Sam doing their soldiering? Are they serving with the Union Army here in the east or out in the west with that Grant fellow?"

"My brothers are not in the army," the girl replied uncomfortably. "Papa and Uncle Sam need them here at home to help operate the mills."

"Oh?" The officer's voice faltered and he reddened, but recovered quickly. "Well, if the North wins this war, it will be the power of her mills and factories that will pull it off."

"That's how Papa and Uncle Sam feel."

Latimer cleared his throat. "Yes, I noticed your uncle was on the committee which has undertaken to save the local mills from being sacked, quite successfully, too."

"The Smalls helped make the war," a surly voice shouted from the crowd close to the carriage. "Now they can pay for it."

Cassandra flushed angrily. Flicking open a silk fan, she fanned herself at a furious rate. "Those ignorant Dutchmen," she hissed between pursed lips. "They've been saying those kinds of things for two years until they've come to believe that they're true, they're a blight on the community."

Latimer mopped his brow and glanced at Mary Wilson's parasol, still pointed rudely in his face. He quickly turned his attention to Cassandra. "How are things with that delightful cousin of yours in Baltimore, Cass?" From the corner of his eye he saw the unfriendly parasol twitch.

"Which cousin?"

"You know better than that."

"Oh, you mean Cousin Mary?"

"Yes. My, but she was a lovely girl."

He saw Mary Wilson shift her parasol to the opposite shoulder and stare straight ahead. "Will she be coming for a visit soon, do you think?" he asked airily as he shot a mischievous glance at the girl ignoring him.

"Both cousin Mary and George were coming for a visit over the Fourth," Cassandra responded, looking irritated, "but we don't expect them now since everyone leaving Baltimore must take the oath of allegiance, which, of course, we know they wouldn't do." She cast a nettled glance at her companion. "Besides," she continued after a moment's pause, "we'd rather they didn't come for fear they would be slighted by our friends. I know some who would not call at the.house, knowing they were there. Though I must say, I find true Southerners more bearable than the copperheads and traitors I see here." She tossed her head contemptuously.

Deeply engrossed in all that was being said, Paddy failed to hear General Gordon's initial beckoning call. A man standing nearby tapped him on the back. "Hey, soldier, boss man wants you." He pointed toward the center of the square.

Gordon was standing in his stirrups, his hands cupped to his mouth. "You there. Scout," he shouted impatiently.

Unfettering his horse, Paddy mounted and trotted forward. "Yes, sir?"

"We're moving on. You'll ride beside me."

"Beggin' your pardon, sir, but I should be returnin' to General Stuart."

"Nonsense, soldier, you've done enough hard riding for one day. I've dispatched one of my own couriers with a message to Stuart. I'm urging Jeb to drop those captured wagons and hurry here as quickly as he can."

Paddy broke out in a cold sweat as Gordon turned to his adjutant. "Jenkins."

"Yes, General."

"Order Captain McLeod to remain here with five hundred men. No liquor. Post guards at every drinking house and bar and post mounted patrols on every hill which surrounds this town. Have the patrols keep a sharp lookout for General Early and the rest of the division. They should be here any time. Have Jubal take charge of York, if he thinks it's necessary."

"You mean to say you intend pushing deeper into enemy territory, knowing Meade is closing in on us?" The adjutant was alarmed. "We should be drawing our army together, not drifting apart."

"Jenkins, my orders are in no way restricted, except to direct me to cross the Susquehanna. If possible, I intend to do just that. Once across, I will mount the men, pass through Lancaster and head for Philadelphia. That will compel Meade to split his army or send all of it to the defense of that city."

"But, General..."

"There's nothing to worry about. This latest in a long line of Union generals will no doubt be as vacillating and timid as the rest. After all, this Meade is the fifth change of commanders that Lincoln has made in a year. We can serve Lee best by adding to the consternation of the neophyte. Bugler," he shouted. "Sound the advance!"

In response, the men shuffled off. The center square of York echoed with the sound of the bugles, the staccato beat of drums and the heavy tread of feet as Gordon's Georgians started east over Market Street toward the Susquehanna River.

Filled with trepidation regarding his future safety should Gordon's courier return from Stuart and expose him as a spy, Paddy rode silently alongside the Rebel chieftain, trying to decide what he should do. From a crowd of people standing beneath old elms which shaded the lawn of a Presbyterian church, a rosy-cheeked girl in her early teens suddenly made a break for the general's horse."

"Cheneral," she cried with a German accent. "I haff some flowers for you. They zmell zo zveet. Zmell them, pleaze."

Paddy turned his horse to avoid trampling the thick-waisted girl.

Gordon doffed his hat. "Thank you very much, young lady." Graciously, he leaned from his saddle to accept the bouquet. "I have a great fondness for flowers. These are exceptionally pretty. Thank you again."

As quickly as she had come, the girl darted into the crowd and was lost from sight.

Casting a sidelong glance in Paddy's direction, Gordon sniffed the flowers. "A most kind and hospitable gesture, don't you think? One which I'd hardly expected to find this far north." A look of curiosity spread over his face as he withdrew a folded note nestled in the flowers. "So. What's this? Have I a secret paramour in this fair village?" He opened the note and glanced over the contents. As he finished it, his dark eyes became piercing slits and he read it again, this time more carefully. His voice was low. "Scout, read this and tell me what you make of it." He handed the note to Paddy.

Paddy took it and studied the contents. A feeling of rage seized him. "Someone," he answered thickly, "has given you the defenses of the Wrightsville bridge, complete with the number of Yankee forces there and describing the best way to successfully attack their positions."

"As a scout, what's your opinion of this? Can we place confidence in it?"

"I really wouldn't like to say, sir. There is a lot of disloyal..." he caught his breath and hoped to God the general had not noticed the slip, "I mean, pro-Southern sympathy around here. There's an organization of Peace Democrats who call themselves the Knights of the Golden Circle, led by a Doctor Wolf. Our agents have been working with them for two months. This could be some of their work."

"Hmm. Jenkins, come here a moment."

His adjutant rode forward at a trot. "Yes, sir."

"Jenkins, we've just run into a stroke of good fortune . Someone's supplied us with a map of the Wrightsville bridge defenses. It's lightly held by militia numbering not more than two hundred."

"Can you put stock in it?"

"There's every reason to. Pass word to the regimental commanders to increase the pace, we should make the river in three hours. We'll attack immediately by the secret route pointed out for us."

"Yes, sir. I'll communicate the message immediately."

As the Confederate column began moving east at an accelerated rate, Paddy's fevered brain churned with possible excuses he could use that would enable him to escape. The blue uniform which he wore under the Confederate gray, besides being hot, began to feel more and more like a tight-fitting noose.

Finally an idea came to him. Carefully removing a knife from inside his pants pocket, he slipped the blade under the saddle, the cutting edge down. Rearing in reaction, his animal whinnied with pain, sagged at the middle and began to limp on both hind legs.

Gordon turned quickly to study Paddy's distraught mount. "You'd better stop and examine that horse. Looks to me like he's been stricken with kidney colic, probably too much hard riding in this hot weather."

Paddy feigned concern. "Yes, sir, I'm afraid that's just what's happened."

Dismounting, he led the horse to one side of the road, removed the saddle and began inspecting him. About fifteen yards away, on the other side of a rail fence which bordered the road, a farmer was busily hoeing his tomato patch. As near as Paddy could determine, the middle-aged man was ignoring the passing troops. A burst of hope rose within him. If he could just talk the man into allowing him to stable his stricken horse in a nearby barn until dark, it would give him an opportunity to slip away unobserved. With that plan in mind, he was ready to put it into execution when a Southern voice cut in abruptly over his shoulder.

"Y'all havin' trouble with yore hoss, Jackboot?"

Paddy turned and recognized one of the men of whom he had asked directions earlier in the day. "Don't know," he answered, looking dismayed. "Went down in his back and off in the hindquarters, both at the same time. Thought he might have a touch of kidney colic."

"Le'mme look at 'im, trooper. Me and Paw took care of all the horses down to home fer quite a piece. Hey, Paw, come heah a minute, will ya?"

Paddy saw a tall, rugged Confederate break ranks, a boy in his late teens following close at his heels.

"What's up, Jim? Got a sick'un?"

"'Pears to be, Paw. Thought we'uns might help out."

"Be obliged to. You be one of Jeb Stuart's Jackboots, hain't ye?" the father asked, turning in Paddy's direction.

"Aye'n I'm afraid this mornin's hard ride's just about done my gelding in." He studied the vitality that glowed on the Southerner's tanned, leathery face.

"Walk the critter away from me, trooper. Slowly now. Want to see how he carries hisself. Now, jog him back."

"Sure 'peers to be goin' sound enough now, don't he, Paw?"

"Ay, grannys, that he does, Jim. You examine them front legs. I wanta check the hindquarters."

Father and son ran deft fingers over muscles, ligaments and tendons, picked up legs one at a time and checked flexions and extensions of joints, then examined the hooves.

"'Pears sound as a dollar to me," the father drawled, stepping back.

"That a Confederate or Yankee dollah y'all referrin' to?" the eldest son chortled.

"Wa'll, I grant there's a mite difference in soundness between the two. Trooper, my guess is the critter picked up a stone in the foot. Threw him off a bit at the time. Reckon he'll be all right." He turned to one of his sons. "Whar's yore brother, Ludy, at?"

"Over by the fence, Paw."

Paddy saw that the teenage son was attempting to engage the farmer in conversation.

"Ah say, neighbor, ah done said howdy," the Southern boy repeated politely. "You'uns up north heah got anythin' what fer to kill cutworms with?"

The farmer glanced up from the hoeing and leveled a malevolent German look at the intruder, then continued with his work.

In a flash, the boy reached between the fence rails, plucked a green tomato from a vine and threw it at the man. The semi-ripened vegetable struck the German flush on the temple and exploded with a splash.

"Ludy, you gone crazy, boy?" his father shouted. "What fer y'all hit that man?"

The young soldier retrieved his rifle which he had leaned against a fence post and ambled back toward his kin, casting angry glances over his shoulder at the swearing farmer. Paddy's hopes sank. As long as he wore Confederate gray, any thought of help from that quarter could be written off.

"What fer you hit him?" the father asked sternly.

"When ah howdies, ah likes to be howdied back, Paw, not made a jack ass of."

"Just 'cause Yankees ain't got good manners ain't no call fer to hit them with tomatoes, Ludy. 'Sides, these folks are mostly fer us."

"They ain't fer nobody but themselves, fer as ah kin make out. Y'all see the look he give me, Paw? Nobody looks at me like that and stays healthy."

"Thanks for seein' to my horse," Paddy interceded hastily. "Guess I'll be ridin' back to the head of the line."

"Anytime, Jackboot. Anytime a' tall." Father and son waved a friendly salute and fell in with the marching column.

Consigned to his fate, whatever that might be, Paddy rode forward until he reached the side of General Gordon.

"How's your animal, Private Mulcahy?"

"All right now, sir. Picked up a sharp stone somewhere."

"Glad to hear it was nothing serious. Want you to ride close in case I've need of your services. Might study this map some." He handed over the wrinkled diagramed note. "Fix that ravine clear in your mind, that hidden, roundabout cut the map shows leading in behind their defenses."

"Yes, sir. Would you want me to scout ahead and see if it's something we can depend on?"

"Won't be necessary. If it's not there, we'll make a frontal assault. No doubt but what their militia's already been warned we're coming. Just hope they don't decide to fire the bridge."

Praying secretly that Gilmour had carried out his part of the mission, Paddy slumped in the saddle and continued to ride in silence.

The dusty columns continued to push along with great haste over the dirt road that made its way in a straight line down the center of the two mile wide valley. A fertile valley placed between two parallel ridges and beautifully planted with crops of golden wheat and sweet corn that seemed to grow to the doors of the great barns. Cool, inviting limestone farmhouses were dotted here and there beneath an umbrella of majestic trees."

Toward evening, just as creeping shadows started playing down the wooded slopes on one side of the valley, the Confederate advance crested a knoll from the top of which the Susquehanna could be seen in the distance.

Suggested in the note as the place to best examine the Federal position, Gordon halted on the gentle swell of ground and raised his field glasses. Moving the binoculars slowly back and forth, he scanned the terrain to verify the truth of the mysterious communication or detect its misrepresentation.

The town of Wrightsville and its defenses were as described. A thin blue line of militia was drawn up as indicated along an intervening knoll. Across the road old men and boys guarded the approach to the bridge. In the background, stretching across the river and still intact, lay one of the day's engineering marvels--the longest covered bridge in the world.

Gordon lowered his glasses for a moment to study the map then, raising the binoculars, he focused them once more, this time on the terrain far to the right. Exactly where the map foretold it would be was the entrance to a deep gorge, a hidden ravine that extended around the left flank of the defense line, a perfect pathway for attack coming from behind at river level.

Putting away his field glasses, the general let out a low whistle. "Not an inaccurate detail. We owe much to our unknown correspondent. Moving down by that gorge, we can take the enemy in flank and rear and force him to retreat or surrender. Jenkins, have the column head for that ravine and order them to keep as quiet as possible. No bugles, we don't want to flush our quarry before we're ready. I don't think they've spotted our dust."

Paddy's temple throbbed. Had something happened to Gilmour? If not, why was the militia still in an advanced, exposed position? Should he try to make a break for it and warn them? Suddenly, just for a fleeting moment, he caught a glimpse of a familiar form posted on horseback on a distant hill, then Gilmour vanished. Paddy heaved a sigh of relief.

Snaking their way silently down the timbered ravine, the Confederates moved hurriedly, hidden completely out of sight. Completing the circuitous march, the Southerners, in a high state of elation, fixed bayonets in preparation for an assault. Their spirits were sent crashing in a wild outburst of anger. "The bridge!"

"Look!"

"The bridge is on fire!"

"The damn blue-bellies are skeddadlin'!"

Paddy forced his horse out into the open for a better view. To his great delight and satisfaction, he saw huge volumes of flame and smoke pouring from the entire length of the covered bridge, timbers crackling and spitting fire as burned-out joists crashed into the water below with a boiling hiss.

Gordon leaned forward and whacked his saddle girth with a buckskin gauntlet. "Tarnation. We can't cross that hellfire. Damn their Yankee souls." He turned around. "Bugler, sound the charge. Jenkins, we'll enter the town and see what we can salvage."

With a mad rush, as if pushed from behind, the six Georgia regiments went racing along the tree-studded river road and poured into Wrightsville like a flood tide.

"Buckets! Get buckets!" the officers screamed wildly at the men. "Lay hands on every damn bucket 'n barrel you can find! We'll soak our way across!"

Deployed squads broke in all directions, feverishly searching among houses for any container that could be used to dampen the holocaust, but they found none.

The inhabitants stood by and watched with frozen expressions, shaking their heads when asked if fire-fighting equipment was available and obstructing the Rebels in every way possible. The wind from an oncoming storm lashed the fire into a fury. Playing no favorites, the sparks darted dangerously overhead until the air was filled with thousands of the deadly incendiaries riding on the thick smoke. Anguished cries rose above the din as townspeople scurried like ants, yelling, "The lumberyard's on fire."

"Dear God! My house!"

"Oh, my God, the whole town's catching fire!"

Secreted buckets and fire-fighting equipment suddenly appeared as inhabitants worked together to save their village. It began to rain hard. Late that night, with help provided from the heavens, the flames were finally extinguished and most of the town was saved. The weather cleared and a full moon shone over the Susquehanna.

Following a sparse meal of hominy grits, black-eyed peas and salt pork supplied by General Gordon's commissary, Paddy sought an isolated spot in which to spend the night. Covered from head to foot with soot and reeking of tar and wood smoke, he stretched his aching body on the ground. A blanketed saddle served as a comfortable headrest, supporting a prone position from which he could study the foe.

The soft, Southern drawl of the Rebels contrasted noticeably to the nasal twang of his Philadelphia comrades, but other than that, the sight and sounds of the bivouac were strikingly similar. Most of the invaders had bared their torsos to the hot night. Some were hairy and muscular, others lean with satin-smooth skin.

The sounds of lighthearted badinage, discussions of recent happenings and speculations on the morrow filled the air. There was a clinking of tin cooking utensils, the soft strum of a banjo, the reedy cry of a harmonica and the metallic snap of hammers striking locks as rifles underwent inspection.

Paddy surveyed the Rebels through half-closed eyes. "Cannon fodder," he thought to himself and fell into a sound sleep.

CHAPTER 16

When Paddy awoke the next morning the sun was already up and the heat was beating down unmercifully; one of those hot, sticky, breathless days when pallid cumulus clouds heap up mountain upon mountain, then flush and darken into presages of a coming storm.

Summoned by an orderly to report to General Gordon, he stopped to soak his head in a small stream, wiped his face with a sleeve and, leading his horse, continued toward a brick house located on the main street. As he entered, the orderly pointed to a door.

"The general's in theah. No call to knock. Go right on in."

"Thanks ."

Opening the door, Paddy stepped into a large dining room where General Gordon and a crowd of enlisted men in worn gray uniforms were eating around a plank-top table.

Gordon looked up. "There you are, Scout. Have you had breakfast?"

"No, sir."

Sitting next to the officer was a modest, cultured, middle-aged woman. She rose instantly. "Do sit down at my place," she said graciously. "Come, sit down, there's plenty for everyone."

Paddy eyed the aromatic bacon and tempting fried eggs stacked on large platters. "Thank you kindly, ma'am, but I can eat standing. You keep the chair."

"Just as you wish."

He moved forward and helped himself to the bountiful supply of food, then stepped back against a wall and began eating with plate in hand.

The woman reseated herself at Gordon's side. Brushing a napkin across his mouth, the general finished eating and turned in his chair.

"May I say, Mrs. Rewalt, you are truly blessed with an abundance of the nobler riches of brain and heart which are the essential glories of womanhood."

Self-possessed and calm, Mrs. Rewalt did not reply. Her gaze remained fixed on the enlisted men satisfying their hunger.

General Gordon pushed his empty plate to one side. "'Tis a shame this war was thrust upon us, bringing so many heartaches, especially to you, dear women. Both sections could have separated and lived peacefully without going to war." He paused inquiringly, but still received no reply from her. "Lincoln and the Northern politicians had to have it their way." Again he paused. "But all of us shall win eventually. Don't you agree, Mrs. Rewalt?"

Too brave to evade the question, too poised to be confused by it and firmly fixed in her convictions, she did not hesitate to speak. "General Gordon, I fully comprehend what you say and candidly tell you that I am a Union woman. I cannot afford to be misunderstood, nor have you misinterpret this simple courtesy. Last night you and your soldiers saved my home from burning, and I was unwilling that you should go away without receiving some token of my appreciation. I must tell you, however, that with my assent and approval, my husband serves the Union Army. My constant prayer to heaven is that our cause may triumph and the Union be saved."

A deep silence fell on the room as battle-hardened soldiers stopped eating, a look of profound respect and admiration showing on their faces.

General Gordon cleared his throat. "Mrs. Rewalt, you are a courageous and honorable woman." He turned to Paddy. "Have you finished, Scout?"

Paddy downed a last bite. "Yes, sir."

"Good. Prepare to ride. I've had no word from your commanding officer, so you might as well act for me. Return to York and report to General Early. Advise him that since we can no longer cross the Susquehanna, we'll be retiring shortly to rejoin the division."

"I understand, sir. I'll leave right away."

With a song in his heart, Paddy quickly made his way outdoors and in short time was riding alone back toward York. Bursting with joy and feeling free as a bird, he began whistling softly to himself. There was nothing to do now but ride leisurely cross country until he reached the safety of his own lines, but the temptation that comes with success laid its invisible hand upon him.

Gathering up the reins at a crossroads, he paused a minute. No. Come what may, he would continue straight ahead and try his luck a bit farther, out of curiosity.

Reentering York some time later, he stopped to make immediate inquiry of the whereabouts of General Early. The streets swarmed with the enemy. Following the directions given him by a couple of soldiers, he made his way toward a courthouse and dismounted. In the dim corridors of the building, a loud hubbub of excitement could be heard. Confederate officers of every rank were being hounded and harassed by an angry group of country folk, all of whom were waving Knights of the Golden Circle cards above their heads in demonstration.

"Thieves!" they clamored, totally outraged. "Ve vant our money back."

"Ja. Ve showed der ticket und made der signs, but it varn't no goot," a belligerent farmer screamed. He pushed a card in the face of a Confederate officer, who struck it out of his hand.

"I said we don't honor those damned things," the officer roared. "Y'all been suckered by a slick scheme. Y'all gonna give us whatever we want. Clear out of heah."

Paddy approached a guard. "Where can I find General Early?"

"Inside that room." He pointed.

"Thanks."

Paddy entered a spacious, official-looking chamber. He recoiled at the sight of General Early. The division commander, dressed in a new uniform and wearing a black slouch hat adorned with an ostrich feather, was seated at a desk surrounded by his staff, a fierce expression on his face, his brown pig eyes deeply recessed in orbits of puffy flesh.

A redneck if I ever saw one, Paddy mused.

The general addressed the citizen's committee harshly. "I want two thousand pairs of shoes, one thousand pairs of socks, one thousand hats, one hundred thousand dollars and three day's rations, no if s, ands, or buts. If you don't meet the requisition, I shall burn your car shops, wagon works and any other industry which I consider useful for war purposes." He paused as he spied Paddy shouldering his way forward. "Yes, what is it, trooper?" he snapped.

"Message from General Gordon, sir. The bridge at Wrightsville's been burned by the Yankees. There's no way of crossin' the Susquehanna."

"The river be damned. You return to Gordon and tell him to get back here as fast as he can. Those are orders! Tell him I've just received word from Lee. Orders are for all elements to retire west toward Cashtown in the South Mountains." He scowled. "For once the Federals are moving faster than we anticipated."

Paddy saluted and left the room, glad to escape the presence of a general with whom he felt no sense of security, such as he had experienced with General Gordon. Now, if he could make good his escape, the entire mission would be a complete success. Gordon's effectiveness had been destroyed as a threat to the east. One door had been slammed in the enemy's face, others were closing. Lee's army was being forced to concentrate.

Paddy, not wishing to tarry any longer, left the town and headed his mount south over the York-Baltimore Pike. He had traveled about a mile when the storm, which had been threatening all day, suddenly broke loose in a blinding torrent of rain. Thunder crashed and echoed in the valleys, lightning flashed overhead. Soaked to the skin and unable to see his way as well as being overcome by fatigue, Paddy chose another course. Urging his horse up a steep, wooded slope, he arrived on top of a wooded hill from which he had an unobstructed view of the countryside. Spying a thicket of Scotch pine which offered a degree of protection against the slashing rain, he bedded down, settling back in a rude hut of evergreen boughs to await the developments of the next day.

Morning came, attended by the sight of retiring troops and wagons moving slowly out of York and heading west. Behind, in that part of town where the car shops had been fired, orange flames and black smoke wafted to the sky in billowing columns.

Watching until the last invader disappeared from sight, Paddy saddled his horse, mounted and set out toward Pipe Creek, Maryland. As he neared the junction at Hanover, through a deep cut in the hills, he suddenly saw a canopy of dust rising in clouds--a telltale sign heralding the approach of cavalry troops in large numbers. Without a moment's hesitation, he turned aside and led his mount into the forest. Tearing strips of cloth from his uniform, he soaked them in water and inserted them deep into the animal's ears so that it would not hear the sounds and respond with answering neighs. Crouching beside his mount, he watched and waited.

A cavalry force, led by Jeb Stuart, passed slowly over the roadway below. His men were swathed in slings and bloody bandages, showing the effects of recent combat. In a pitched battle at Hanover with Federal troops under Kilpatrick, the Confederates had been beaten and driven off; they were now detouring east toward York, heading into a vacuum where their presence would not be felt should the main forces of Meade and Lee collide in the near future.

Finally, after an anxious two hours, the last of the Confederate horsemen passed and Paddy decided it was time to strike his true colors. He removed his outer garments, exposing the Union blue beneath, and galloped toward Hanover.

When he arrived, the narrow streets of the small town were still heavily barricaded with boxes, carriages, wagons, hay bales, ladders and barber poles, mute evidence of severe fighting. Lounging cavalrymen, who had been in the saddle day and night continuously for the past three weeks without change of clothing or opportunity to wash, looked even filthier than himself. Their mounts, reduced by short rations and exhaustion to bony racks, wandered aimlessly; several luckless troopers on foot carried saddles in hopes of procuring remounts.

Paddy located General Judson Kilpatrick in his headquarters at the Central Hotel. Seated before the general, he related what had taken place at York. Kilpatrick, a wiry little man with sandy, mutton-chop whiskers on a gargoyle face, listened intently, asking questions occasionally as he jotted notes. Lending an ear in the background were three other cavalry chieftains, Generals Gregg, Farnsworth and George Armstrong Custer, an extremely young man with long golden curls and dressed in a showy velvet uniform.

When Paddy had completed his report, Kilpatrick tapped his scabbard with gnarled fingers, his steel-gray eyes showing a touch of admiration as he viewed the young man before him. "Valuable information, that. I'd say you've done an extraordinarily fine job, soldier. But enough daring-do for three days. Since the Pipe Creek line's been temporarily set aside, headquarters is now at Taneytown. I'll pass this information along to Meade through one of my men. You'd best wait here, Fifth Corps should be coming through some time tomorrow. Meantime, I'll arrange for quarters here in the hotel. Get a good sleep."

That evening Paddy slept peacefully for the first time since his night at Becky's home in Leesburg. His tired brain tried to think back. When was it? It seemed a year ago, was it only four nights? Even more difficult for him to realize was the fact that he was married and soon to be a father.

Next morning and well into the afternoon of July first, he fidgeted and fussed, waiting for some sign of the Fifth Corps. During that time, the ominous sounds of battle kept rolling into Hanover from the direction of Gettysburg, an insignificant little village lying eighteen miles away.

By late afternoon Paddy's patience had finally worn thin, and at five o'clock, he started toward the sound of gunfire rumbling in the distance. A veil of pale moonlight bathed the darkened battleground as he rode onto the field. Above the night sounds of crickets, locusts and frogs croaking in the marshes, he could hear the rattle of sporadic musketry and see the flashes of muzzle fire.

A picket called nervously from the darkness. "Halt! Identify yourself."

Paddy drew up short. "Mulcahy. Hundred'n Eighteenth Pennsylvania. Fifth Corps."

The picket lowered his rifle. "Boy, are we glad to see you fellas. Where's the rest of your outfit?"

"Don't know. They were to come through Hanover today. Since they didn't show, I thought maybe they'd switched routes and were already here."

The picket's voice fell. "They ain't here. Only ones here is the First and Eleventh, what's left of them, that is."

Paddy frowned. "Things that bad again?"

"Worse," the picket spat. "You'll find what's left over on that ridge. Can't miss 'em, they're in a cemetery." He pointed to a moonlit elevation which lay a half mile to the west. "If I was a funny man, I'd say they was in proper company. Say, if you came in on the Hanover road, you're lucky you made it, soldier."

"How come?"

"The Johnnies got us covered on the east, that's how come. Matter of fact, seems like they got us covered on three sides. Our line's shaped like a fishhook. The shank runs straight along that ridge over there, the bent hook part and barb curlin' 'round the northern tip of our line at the cemetery, endin' up there on what they call Culp Hill. The Rebs is west, north and east, their mouths open, ready to gobble the whole thing."

"Yeah, well here's hoping they get hooked."

Setting spurs, Paddy rode off toward the outlined ridge. Surmounting the wooded slopes of elevated ground, his horse suddenly reared and pawed the air, startled at the sight of objects spread over the ground, ghostly objects reflecting moonglow and the glare from nearby campfires. Dismounting, Paddy let the alarmed animal sniff at what proved to be nothing more than tombstones uprooted by soldiers in their attempt to eliminate the danger of ricocheting bullets.

A sign in large letters tacked on a tree caused him to smile wryly: "A FIVE DOLLAR FINE WILL BE LEVIED ON ALL WHO DISCHARGE FIREARMS IN THIS CEMETERY."

He strolled toward a group of soldiers lying near a fire. "What outfit you boys with?" he inquired.

"Doubleday's Third Division, First Corps," came the terse reply.

"What regiment?"

"Hundred'n Fifty-first Pennsylvania, Biddle's first brigade."

Paddy's heart skipped a beat. "Biddle? Is the Hundred'n Twenty-first with you?"

"The Philadelphia boys? Yeah, they're down the ridge a piece. Hear that religious singing. That's them."

His horse refusing to stir in the macabre setting, Paddy tethered him to a tree and started to walk at a slow pace. His thoughts turned back to the day in Frankford when he and captain Donaldson had been thwarted in their attempt to corral some of Captain Ashworth's 150 recruits. The family farewell scene at St. Mark's Church came to mind.

Any thoughts he may have harbored in regard to a happy reunion with old friends quickly disappeared as he stumbled on the pitiful handful plaintively singing a hymn. They were dimly outlined by a solitary fire. Feeling weak inside, Paddy pulled up short for a second and listened. Their voices were muffled as they sang:

"A mighty fortress is our God,
A bulwark never failing;
Our helper he, amid the flood
Of mortal ills prevailing:
For still our ancient foe
Doth seek to work us woe;
His craft and power are great,
And armed with cruel hate,
On earth is not his equal..."

His back braced against the trunk of a nearby tree, Aaron Settle sat cradling the head of his older brother as he poured water from a canteen into John's pain-twisted mouth. Although accustomed to such scenes, Paddy watched through tear-dimmed eyes.

In the shadows he could discern Mr. Gillebrand and Mr. Hilton, both in their middle forties, passing among the younger men, patting them reassuringly and offering solace. John Schlafer, not yet sixteen, had often brought his father's horses to the Mulcahy smithy to be shod. Now he sat huddled and sobbing, with his head resting on a blood-splattered drum.

"Are thee looking for someone?" a stern voice inquired from behind.

Paddy spun around, a look of astonishment on his face. The officer before him was the baldish Quaker he had seen at the Red Lion Inn.

"Speak up, soldier. I am Colonel Chapman Biddle. Are thee looking for someone?"

"Yes, sir," Paddy managed to stammer. "Friends of mine from Frankford. There are two companies of them in your regiment."

"Lieutenant Garsed," the colonel called. "Would thee come here a moment."

Joshua Garsed lifted his head from his knees, stood up wearily and walked forward. "Yes, sir."

"Do thee know this lad? He says he's from Frankford."

The lieutenant's eyes lit up with recognition. "Yes sir. It's Mulcahy, the blacksmith's son. He's like fly specks, find him all over."

The colonel smiled. "Well, keep him out of mischief while he's here with us, Lieutenant. And you might also tell your men that Hancock's Second Corps has just arrived. It will make them sleep better."

"I'll do that, sir." Garsed clasped Paddy on both shoulders. "So, the Philadelphia Brigade's come to help us out, eh?"

"The...I haven't been with the Brigade for almost two years."

"That's right. I remember you and that Captain trying to lift some of our recruits for the Corn Exchange. I see the red Maltese Cross on your cap. Is the Fifth Corps here?"

Paddy shook his head. "No. I don't know where they are. Supposed to pick them up at Hanover this afternoon. When they didn't show, I came on alone."

"Bad. Bad. We need help. Hancock's Second and what's left of our Corps can't fight off the entire Southern Army."

Paddy looked surprised. "I thought the Eleventh Corps was here."

"You mean the Germans," Garsed snorted. "They're here, and that's about all."

"They didn't run again, did they?"

"Caved in like a sand hole. See that ridge farther west? That's called Seminary Ridge, there's a Lutheran college on it. On the other side the land's fairly level until it runs into the foothills of the South Mountains five miles beyond. We started to fight over there about eleven o'clock this morning, between the Hagerstown and Chambersburg pikes. The Johnnies came pouring out of the mountains, outnumbering us three to one, and still we bested them for five hours. At different times and at different points we succeeded in capturing parts of three enemy brigades, taking them in open field fighting where there were no breastworks, entrenchments or protection of any kind other than what the field afforded us."

"Who you got there, Lieutenant?" a voice broke in.

"It's Mulcahy."

Tom Stott held out a hand, which Paddy gripped firmly. "News walking, Mulcahy?"

"Not exactly. Might say I outrode the Fifth Corps. How's your brother?"

"Joe? He's all right. Over there singing with the rest." Stott flopped onto the warm ground. "You been telling Paddy how we Frankford and Philadelphia boys held off the Johnnies today?"

"No, I was getting around to telling him about the Eleventh Corps."

"Them bastards," Stott replied. "Did you hear the latest about Howard? When Hancock rode in this afternoon with specific orders from Meade to assume command of the battle, Howard says, 'I do not doubt your orders, Hancock, but you can give no orders while I am here.' So Hancock tells Howard to go fly a kite and takes over anyways."

"I remember Howard," Paddy said. "Had a run-in with Colonel Wistar just before Antietam. But what happened to Reynolds? Shouldn't he've been in command?"

"He was," Garsed replied sadly, "but he was killed about twelve o'clock. After that, Wadsworth, swinging the old Revolutionary war saber that was his father's, took over with Doubleday until Howard arrived."

Paddy tugged at an ear lobe. "What was Doubleday swinging, one of his new-fangled baseball bats?"

"Might as well have been. We were doing our darndest not to strike out today."

"Getting back to the Dutchmen," Paddy said, "what happened this time?"

Stott drew his knees up under his chin. "When they got here in the late afternoon, Howard pushed them a mile north of town so that while we were fighting facing west, they were in line at right angles to us, facing north. Ewell's men came in from Carlisle and York and hit them about four o' clock. At four-thirty, the Dutchmen were running full retreat through town. Over half of them were captured."

"Is that what unhinged your corps?"

"I'll say it did," Garsed snapped. "While we were holding off Johnnies in front of us, other Rebs began threatening our rear." He paused and rubbed at his eyes. "At four o'clock, after almost five hours of constant fighting against heavy odds, we were ordered to retire to a stronger position just in front of Seminary Ridge. We drew back to Seminary just about the time the Eleventh Corps gave way."

"What position did you fellows hold in the line?"

Stott leaned back on the grass. "Left flank. And by God, try hard as they did all afternoon, the Rebs couldn't turn us, they even overlapped us three-quarters of a mile." He jerked loose a handful of sod and pitched it angrily. "Then Meredith's Iron Brigade, them 'black hat' boys from the midwest, had the gall to say our part of the line was the first to go."

Paddy hitched at his belt. "Did it?"

"Cripes no, you know how it is holding a flank. First the Rebs tried to turn our exposed left, so we changed front to meet their attack head-on. When they drove at us from due west, we changed front again to meet them from that direction. Then a little after four, the Rebs spotted a big gap between us and Meredith's brigade so they drove at us on an angle from the northwest, trying to pry us loose from the Iron Brigade holding center in an oak grove. Naturally our right companies refused to pivot with the left to meet the attack squarely. It was that movement which Meredith's men mistook for a retreat. Why, hells bells, if we'd caved in on their flank like they claim, they'd never have made it back into town, the Johnnies would have come in from behind and swallowed them up. The fact we retired through town last, after they did, should have given fair notice we held on to the very end and covered their retreat. Alex Biddle's hopping mad over the lousy slur."

"Alex Biddle?"

"Our new regimental commander."

"I thought..."

"Chapman? No, he took over as brigade commander. Alex Biddle is Chapman's cousin. Boy, what a fighting family that is for a supposedly quiet set of Quakers. You should have seen Chapman Biddle when the brigade began to waiver several times. He grabbed the colors in his fist and rode straight out from the lines, shaking the flag in the Rebs' faces. How he escaped getting killed is beyond me."

"Just living up to their ancient name," Garsed replied. "The name Biddle comes from Biddulph, meaning 'wolf killers' of the Saxons, dates back to William the Conqueror. Their father, old Clement Biddle, was quartermaster general of the army during the Revolution and a close friend of Washington's. That's how come the Colonel's oldest brother got the name of George Washington Biddle."

A lull in the vespers was broken by the refrain of another hymn. Soldiers moved about in the shadows and spread blankets on the ground in preparation for the night. Their singing flowed across the moonlit battlefield.

"Abide with me, fast falls the even-tide;
The darkness deepens; Lord with me abide,
When other helpers fail, and comforts flee,
Help of the helpless, O abide with me."

Tom Stott picked himself off the ground and made his way back to rejoin his brother. His voice joined in with that of others.

"Swift to its close, ebbs out life's little day;
Earth joys grow dim, its glories pass away;
Change and decay in all around I see;
O Thou who changest not, abide with me."

Paddy tried to moisten his dry lips, but to no avail. He watched young Schlafer lift his head from the blood-stained drum and begin singing brokenly:

"I need Thy presence every passing hour;
What, but Thy grace can foil the tempter's power?
Who, like Thyself, my guide and stay can be?
Through cloud and sunshine, O abide with me."

"It's Danny Mullen he'll be missing," Garsed whispered in Paddy's ear. "They were inseparable."

"Danny?" Paddy's voice was a hollow echo.

"Yes. Went up in the first attack."

The wounded joined in weakly on the final verse. Raising his brother's head to shoulder level, Aaron Settle looked away as John made a feeble effort to sing:

"Hold Thou Thy cross before my closing eyes;
Shine through the gloom, and point me to the skies:
Heaven's morning breaks, and earth's vain shadows flee:
In life, in death, O Lord abide with me."

"You said Danny," Paddy murmured. "Who else from home? There's so few here."

Lieutenant Garsed spoke in a monotone. "Captains Ashworth and Ruth, Tom Simpson, Pete McNally, Rob Ray, Ed Tibben...."

"Squeak's bother? Oh dear Jesus."

"Ed may have been captured, least we're hoping so. Last we saw of him was in front of Seminary. Went plowing into the Rebs like he was going to stop them single-handed."

"How bad was it altogether?"

"Went in with seven officers and two hundred and fifty-six men. All that was left after Fredericksburg and Chancellorsville. Those who came out of it today are just what you see here, two officers and eighty-two men."

After a moment of silence, Garsed put an arm around Paddy. "Come on, share my blanket for tonight. No use looking for the Fifth before morning."

"Thank you, Lieutenant," Paddy said, accepting the offer. Before the war, the mere thought of a Garsed being willing to share his bed with the local blacksmith's son would have been unthinkable, and a Roman Catholic, at that.

Stretched out on a ground cloth, Paddy put his hands behind his head and gazed up at the heavens. The sky was a dark blue canvas through which the stars sparkled like gems filling a myriad of weathered holes that had developed over the course of years in the age-old tarpaulin. The blinking, luminous bodies gave him an eerie sensation that the host of celestial eyes peering through the tiny apertures were looking down at the peepshow drama spread out over that small segment of the earth. He wondered if the eyes which had beheld such events as the creation of man, the Great Flood, and the Holy Nativity were not in a sense mocking this futile, pompous vain exhibition of the self-indulgent importance which man gave to his fleeting three-score and ten years.

Change and decay in all around I see: Oh Thou who changest not, abide with me. The words from the hymn ran through his weary brain until finally sleep came. Surrounding campfires burned and crackled with a soft, ruddy glow-silent sentinels of the night.

* * * * * * *

Elsewhere on that first day of July, the Fifth Corps broke camp early in the morning at Union Mills, Maryland, and resumed its march in a northerly direction.

All day the trains crowded by the marching column of troops, four and five canvas-topped wagons traveling abreast, the drivers shouting and lashing their beasts for greater speed. The clatter and tumult of artillery pressing forward amidst clouds of dust and the rattle and noise of the caissons, gave rise to dire speculation.

Not a breath of air was stirring. Leaves on the trees were motionless. Prostrate in the corners of rail fences and under trees and bushes, groups of men with red faces panted and perspired. Men were dying from sunstroke and still the march was continued under the most stringent, exacting orders the army had ever received.

Under no circumstances was anyone permitted to leave the column for any reason. Disobedience meant instant death. Officers were instructed to march in the rear and enforce the order. The men grumbled at the unusual measure, which seemed unjustifiable to them.

The distasteful duty of rear guard fell to Captain Donaldson, his instructions being to vigorously enforce the order and execute its penalties. Any drivers of pack horses, cooks, servants or other noncombatants were to be seized and placed in the ranks and made to do duty the same as the soldiers.

"I have to give Sykes credit," Tibben said as he plodded along. "He sure means business."

McCool pushed loose locks of black hair back under his kepi visor. "Havin' him as our new corps commander ain't makin' me any too happy, don't like the way he does things. He's too regular-army tough."

"Yeah, guess you're right. Wish he was back leadin' reg'lars instead of us poor volunteers."

Up ahead, an Irish laggard from a New York Regiment was hauled to his feet by Sergeant Cassidy and sent reeling along the roadway. "Git on with ye, soldier. Git a move on. Ye know our orders."

"Faith," the straggler pleaded, "me feet are killin' me. I can't move anither step." Overcome by exhaustion from marching, he slumped once more beneath the shade of a tree.

"Get that man moving," Donaldson called sharply.

"Can't, Cap'n. Says his feet is plumb wore out."

"So are those belonging to the rest of the army. Corporal Hallowell ."

"Yes, sir?"

"Level your bayonet at that man's back. If he refuses to move, run him through."

Hallowell grimaced. "Come on, fella, try and move."

"Sure'n I'll not be movin' anither step till me feet feel right. Run me through if ye like."

"Captain, I can't do it," Hallowell protested.

Cocking his pistol, Donaldson slowly raised his arm and took aim.

"Having trouble?" a deep voice suddenly barked from behind.

Donaldson and his men turned to see General Sykes and a staff of regulars approaching.

"Yes, sir. I'm afraid I'll have to shoot this man."

Sykes glanced at the cocked pistol. "Leave the man to me, Captain. I'll get him moving."

With that, he struck the straggler several smart blows with a riding whip, ordering him to double quick. Without stirring a foot, and apparently not heeding the whip, the headstrong, good-natured fellow turned his head to one side, looked the general full in the face and in all sincerity said, "I say, Gineral, 'ave ye any tobacky about ye?"

It was too much for everybody. Roars of laughter followed, Sykes joined in heartily and rode away, remarking as he did so. "Captain, let that man go. I'll be responsible for him."

At one o'clock in the afternoon rousing cheers, demonstrative shouts and ringing enthusiasm greeted the good old Commonwealth of Pennsylvania as the men of the Fifth Corps, with colors unfurled and drums rolling, crossed over the Mason-Dixon line. Their weary feet took a firmer step as loosely united ranks closed up and countenances took on a determined look. In the surrounding fields were signs of heavy cavalry fighting. Fences were down and the bodies of dead horses were scattered about, many of them bearing the telltale brand CSA on their lifeless necks. Rumors were rife that the enemy was close by and a battle could be expected momentarily, information, none of it authentic, was eagerly seized and disseminated with frightful exaggeration.

The troops continued marching north through a section whose inhabitants were wholly unacquainted with the military. The area was thickly populated and highly cultivated, alternating between wood, meadow and field. The undulating region rolled in gently rising knolls, one scene of grandeur appearing as another faded from view. The grasses had been garnered and vast fields of golden grain were ripening. Oats and corn filled the succulent meadows and on the green sloping hillside, flocks and herds reveled in the pastures. The rich green and golden yellows were evidence of thrift, in striking contrast to the wasted fields, bared woodlands and fenceless farms of battle-scarred Virginia.

Here, the country store bartered its wares and the roadside inn supplied its guests. The miller had grist to grind, the blacksmith horses to shod, the wheelwright wagons to build. Peace, plenty, thrift and prosperity abounded in the region. Along the way, men, maidens, matrons and children gazed in awe as the columns hurried through their villages. Many of them gathered around the bivouacs, eager to hear the soldier's stories of war. This was their army, the one of which they had read but never seen—Northern boys hurrying home to protect their own gates, firesides and loved ones.

Hanover, a town of considerable size and flourishing business, was the intended destination for the day's march. Its railway depot, extensive warehouses, large stores and substantial dwellings were evidence of its enterprise, thrift and comfort. One of the oldest settlements in Southern Pennsylvania, it had long been a center for the gathering and distribution of prolific yields from the surrounding country. Its streets were the terminals of excellent turnpike roads leading to the neighboring towns. Its main railway outlet, with branches from Gettysburg and Littlestown, was by the Northern Central to Baltimore and Harrisburg, its own branch tapping that line at the Hanover junction.

On the outskirts of Hanover, the column halted at five o'clock in the afternoon with the conviction that it was for an all night rest. Astonished at the sudden visitation by such a mass of men, people from far and near gathered to get acquainted with their uninvited guests, or as one of them so aptly expressed it, for a more intimate association with the travel-stained, dusty, walking arsenals licensed to do murder at their chieftains' bidding.

They were deferential people, respectful of the rifle and bayonet, though at first cautious and hesitant. Being assured that the arms were not meant for them, they asked questions about their mechanism and became quite friendly. The most attractive feature was the fair ladies of the vicinity. Their tastes ran wholly to culinary affairs and they were delighted by the explanations and demonstrations of the primitive, original and uncouth ways in which soldiers prepared their limited diet. The most fascinating and agreeable among the 118th's officers took pains to convince the ladies of the excellent social, intellectual and moral standing of the officers and men of the regiment. One bedraggled soldier was pointed out as the son of Reverend Dr. Henry Boardman, Philadelphia's most distinguished Presbyterian Divine. It was suggested that if he was of such excellent stock, they could well imagine how much higher the better-appearing ranked on the social scale. The twitting pleasantry was apparently enjoyed in as much as the citizens seemed reluctant to leave. It was assumed they were agreeably entertained as well as instructed.

The belief that they were stopping for the night was not to be fulfilled. It had been a busy day at Gettysburg some eighteen miles away. General Reynolds had been killed, and the First and Eleventh Corps had been badly worsted by the enemy. The army was ordered there with the greatest speed that human endurance could tolerate. A great battle had opened, one which would determine the success or failure of the Rebel invasion. At nine o'clock, under a brilliant moon, the Fifth Corps headed toward Gettysburg. To keep the men awake, a panoply of regimental bands played in the streets of every town through which they passed.

The column came to a point of concentration and moved through the batteries drawn up on one side. A mounted staff officer approached Colonel Gwyn and handed him a note. With the aid of a lantern, Gwyn read the contents, "McClellan has been restored to command of the army and will have charge in the next day's battle."

Gwyn's voice boomed. "Herring! Pass this bit of news to the men at once! McClellan's just been restored to command!"

Major Herring rose in his stirrups as if speared. "Bully for old Abe! The boys will fight like hell now."

The magic name swept back through the tired ranks with electrifying effect. Such a long time had elapsed since McClellan's removal, it had ceased to be a subject of conversation and it was thought that the old-time enthusiasm for him had disappeared. The announcement of his return was startling, the results astonishing, as shouts, yells and cheers echoed and reechoed from battery to battalion and back again. McCool and Tibben hollered wildly, slapping nearby comrades between the shoulder blades and forcing caps off heads and onto the moonlit roadway. Shadowy woods and fields, lying still in the moonlight, came alive with the enthusiastic celebration.

Having marched thirty-seven miles since ten o'clock that morning, the weary column finally eased off in their demonstrations and slowly subsided into fatigued silence. At three-thirty in the morning, they were halted a few miles southeast of Gettysburg in a section of timber. In the darkness that remained before dawn, the soldiers managed to find rest along the roadside. There was little comprehension of the situation beyond the fact that a great battle was likely, but it was not viewed as any different from many other bloody contests through which they had already passed.

There was no realization of its portentous implications, nor was it remotely conceived that history would record it as the decisive battle of the war.

CHAPTER 17

T he morning of July Second, heralded by a fiery red curtain draped on the eastern horizon, promised another day of sweltering heat. At daylight, the Fifth Corps marched again. Emerging from the timber after the predawn halt, the First Division was deployed in a line of masses. The battalions were doubled on the center with the brigades arranged from right to left--Tilton's, Sweitzer's and Vincent's--in numerical order.

The divisions were arranged with Barnes on the right, Ayres in the center and Crawford on the left. The movement was conducted with precision. Distances were established with accuracy over ground especially adapted for such a ceremony involving so large a body of troops, the land being extremely level. When the deployment of the masses was completed, the mounted officers could view the entire corps. Except for the proximity of a battlefield, it appeared to be preparation for a grand review.

The alignment perfected, colors unfurled and pieces at a right shoulder, the masses advanced toward Gettysburg, preserving their alignments and distances with the effect and impressiveness attending a display occasion. Fences were removed and grass, grain, bush and weed crushed under the heavy tramping of the solid advance. Pennyroyal, prolific in the area, permeated the air with its fragrance.

A strange silence prevailed as the men moved out, interrupted only by an occasional caution to, "Recollect the guide" and, "Observe direction." A short distance ahead could be seen wooded crests and promontories standing out boldly on the landscape. The sylvan bases of Culps, Wolfs, McCallister's and Power's Hills blended together, forming a large, shadow-laced valley. Pouring into this defile at eight o'clock that morning, the Fifth Corps changed directions by the right flank, faced east, and accomplished their purpose to protect the barb of the Federal fishhook line.

"Sure doesn't seem to be any fighting going on around here," McCool quipped. "Hey, Cap'n, mind if Tibben and I fill our canteens back at that spring we just passed?"

"Go ahead, but no news walking. See that you're back here in ten minutes,"

Donaldson replied. His voice sounded tired.

Tibben shook his head. "Cap'n sure ain't been like his old self since that brother of his was killed at Middleburg. Notice that, Willie?"

McCool unslung a canteen and swung it absently to and fro in a clump of ferns which dotted the path through the woods.

"Dunno," he replied after a moment. "Seems the disappearance of Paddy and Gilmour have broken him up more than his brother's death. Can't figure it out, myself. Mulcahy and the Scotsman, two of the best."

"Ah, they'll turn up, Willie. Probably went off fishin' somewhere. They'll be back."

At a place called Spangler's Spring, the two waited their turn in line to fill their empty canteens and plunge their heads into the refreshing cold water. Rising to his feet, McCool wiped an unruly mop of wet hair from his eyes and started to screw the cap on his water container. He stopped abruptly and stared at the hillside.

"Speakin' of the devil," he blurted, "look at who's comin' down that slope."

Tibben, lying on his belly at the spring, raised his head from the pool and shook the water from his eyes. "Glory be, it's Paddy and Gilmour!" He sprang to his feet. "See, I told you they'd show up. Come on."

Both boys sprinted toward the two men.

"Where you fellas been the last four days?" McCool asked breathlessly. "Everybody thinks you deserted."

Gilmour's mutton-chop beard bristled. "Aye? Who says we skipped?"

"Well, nobody actually said so, but you can see in their faces that's what they're thinkin'. Where you been?"

"We took a little cross-country ride," Paddy retorted. "Just dropped off our report at Meade's headquarters."

McCool's eyes narrowed. "You're crazy. Meade ain't in charge anymore. We got word last night McClellan's back in the saddle. Whatcha got to say about that?"

Gilmour reached for Tibben's canteen, unscrewed the cap and took a long drink. He wiped his lips. "If ye dinna believe Meade's still in command, just walk over this hill and have a look fer yerself. Ye'll find him at field headquarters on the Taneytown Road."

"That's right, Willie. We just left 'Old Four Eyes' no more'n ten minutes ago. Matter of fact, he's got his son with him, came from Philadelphia soon as he heard his father'd been made commander in chief. I think you've been suckered by this McClellan blarney."

Tibben scratched his crotch. "You really think so?"

Paddy drew in his belt a notch. "I know so. Now where's the regiment? We're anxious to report in."

McCool shouldered his canteen. "Follow me. The boys are due east of the spring 'bout a quarter mile."

"Thank God you're back safely," Captain Donaldson called out as the two scouts approached the regimental line. He grasped each of them by the hand. "How did it go? We've been moving so fast the past four days word about you was impossible."

"Everything worked out fine." Paddy grinned. "Like to try it again sometime."

"What's this all about?" Tibben broke in. "You two act like you're heroes or something."

Curious, the other fellows shoved and crowded around them, anxious to hear what they had to say. Luke Jobson chewed on a piece of hardtack. "What did you fellas do? Sneak into Cousin Bobby's tent and slip him a hot foot?"

"I'd say from the look on their faces they stole something," Hallowell blurted.

Captain Donaldson, who had been fanning himself with his kepi, held up a hand for silence. "If you don't mind, I'd like to hear their story. They have just completed a hazardous bit of scouting against the enemy."

"Bully, boys," Cassidy exploded as he muscled his way forward. "Sure'n I was cussin' ye under me breath for goin' over the hill."

"Hey, Cap'n," McCool interrupted, "Paddy says we been had. McClellan ain't returned to command. That true?"

A ripple of muttering ran through the group. The captain's expression was grim, his tones clipped as he said, "Yes, Meade's still top man. Somebody got a bright idea last night, thought we'd all perk up and fight better if we were told Little Mac was back."

Jobson spit out the hardtack. "The whole thing was a hoax? Suckered again."

Donaldson replaced his cap. "Think what you will, I say we're better off. For the first time you've got a rock-ribbed commander running things. True, his personality's about as sweet as pickle brine, but I for one have had a belly full of the prima donnas we've been fighting under. In the four days since taking command, he's gathered the corps which Hooker scattered all over Hell's half-acre, marching us over thirty miles a day, and he's brought us together as a unit."

"The captain's right on that score," Dyer said. "We never moved like this before."

"Yes, and one thing more. It's been Meade's bulldog chase that's forced Lee to pull his army together for a stand-up fight. Three days ago the Rebs could have had Pennsylvania for the taking. Now, they'll have to fight for it."

He placed his arms around Gilmour and Paddy. "If you don't mind, I'd like a word with these two alone."

Paddy stopped to mop sweat from his brow. He turned his eyes upon Captain Donaldson. "A friend of yours arrived at headquarters while I was there."

"Who was that?" the officer inquired.

"Captain Dahlgren. His report caused quite a stir."

"Oh?"

"Did you know Lee has been expecting Beauregard's army from Tennessee? Supposed to join forces here in Pennsylvania any day now."

"Good God, no." Donaldson's gaze drifted off to the west. "That will give Lee one hell of an army."

Paddy plucked a ripe cherry from a tree and placed it in his mouth. "Nothing to worry about now. Dahlgren captured a Reb courier with dispatches to Lee from Jeff Davis. President Davis has canceled the support from Beauregard. Lee has no way of knowing this." Paddy spit out a seed. "Might upset his strategy."

Donaldson grimaced. "Turn about is fair play." There was an angry tenor in his voice. "If Lincoln hadn't canceled the planned support by McDowell's forty thousand, McClellan could have ended the war at Richmond in the spring of sixty-two."

The three continued the walk in silence and rejoined their regiment.

Throughout the morning hours the division was constantly maneuvered and changed from one position to another. Shortly after midday the Fifth Corps was ordered to cross Rock Creek, situated close to the Baltimore-Gettysburg Pike. Massed in the vicinity of an orchard, it remained in reserve within easy reach of the Twelfth Corps, now protecting the right wing.

Several hours of ease were interrupted occasionally by the deep thundering discharges of artillery and the intermittent sounds of bickering musketry fire going on behind them to the west. Reposing in the shade of fruit trees, the men listened to the ominous preparations which they knew to be indicative of an assault.

Those less apprehensive proceeded to strip off their dusty uniforms and plunge into the shallow waters of Rock Creek for a welcome bath. Others, overcome by lethargy, slapped at troublesome flies and took advantage of the interval to rest and catch up on sleep.

A little after four o' clock, toward the main Union line at the west, musketry noises increased with intensity until it sounded like the roar of a train rumbling through a tunnel. Guns began thundering in front of Cemetery Ridge, which terminated in a round-knobbed, timbered elevation at the southern extremity.

Conjecture was quickly dispelled by the clattering arrival of a mounted courier who came dashing along the division line shouting wildly for General Sykes. The General galloped forward, sitting his mount as rigidly as iron. Eyeing the courier, he said, "You seek me, Sergeant?"

"Yes, sir," replied the messenger, dirty rivulets of perspiration dripping from his flushed face. "Longstreet's crumbling the front and flanks of the Third Corps. General Sickles begs you to bring your Corps to his assistance immediately."

"You tell Dan Sickles that's impossible. The key of the battlefield is entrusted to my keeping. I cannot and will not jeopardize it by dividing my force or moving it as a unit."

Hallowell shoved his kepi forward so that the visor rested on the bridge of his nose. "Here we go again," he growled disgustedly. "Nothing 'round here but fruit flies and belly-achin' green apples. Yep, it's the key to the battlefield, not to be jeopardized. Hog slop."

Kimball ran a thumb along his gleaming rifle barrel. "Don't know, Jake. This Dan Sickles has a knack for getting himself into hot water, you know that. Maybe Sykes is right in refusing aid."

Jobson edged closer to his older comrades. "What did you mean by that about Sickles?" he asked, curiously.

"Goes back before the war," Kimball responded, "when Sickles was a congressman from New York."

"Tammany man," Hallowell cut in. "Yes, Tammany. A rakish individual.

Nursed hopes of becoming Democratic nominee for president in fifty-six. He had a good chance, too. Then he killed Phillip Key in cold blood and the dream went up in smoke."

"Phillip Key?"

"Son of Francis Scott Key. Real tomcat with the women in Washington, 'specially Mrs. Sickles. That is, until Sickles found out about it. Came out big in all the papers, even her sworn confession. But a politician doesn't get to be president by killing kin to the Star Spangled Banner."

Hallowell snorted. "Sickles had every right to shoot young Key. Done the same thing if I'd caught him lyin' with my wife."

"Yes, but remember Dan Sickle's no cut-cat himself, Jake."

Jobson's eyes bugged. "Mighty Moses, I never heard none o' that before."

"Just as well. You're still a boy." Hallowell permitted one of his rare smiles to part his shaggy beard. "I remember discussing the incident with our congressman at the time. Amusing to hear how the ladies of Washington forgave Dan Sickles, even before he was acquitted. It was his wife's blood they were after. Thing that really shocked Washington society was not the killing so much as Sickle's forgiveness of his wife after it was over. For that unpardonable error, the lordly matrons of our fair Capitol ruined him politically. Treated him as though he were a leper."

Between four and four-thirty in the afternoon one sweat-stained courier after another came to the Fifth Corps with fervid pleas from the beleaguered Sickles, begging for aid.

Cassidy picked up a stick and broke it over his knee. "Why don't the general send us over to lend a hand? We ain't doin' nothin' ."

"Can't understand it, either," Donaldson replied. "According to Sykes, Meade still insists the Rebs' main blow will fall here on the right flank when all indications point to the fact that the Rebs are concentrating their main effort on our left flank. If they get possession of that little Round Top to the southwest, it'll be hell to pay. Our entire line will be enfiladed. If they should turn our left flank, they'll be between us and Washington and we'll be surrounded."

Cassidy chomped heavily on a plug of tobacco. "Ye think Meade's equal to this occasion, Cap'n? After all, he's only been in command four days. Runnin' seven full army corps is a lot different than directin' just one."

"What else can you expect," George Dyer drawled. "Ain't he the fifth commander Lincoln's pawned off on us in a year's time? Hell, I ain't changed my underwear that often."

"Wait a minute, something's up," Donaldson said, looking anxiously to his left. "I think Sykes has changed his mind. We're going in."

"Too right, Cap'n. There's the long drum roll. All right ye buckos, fall in!" Cassidy shouted between chews. "Wake them what are sleepin'. Be lively about it, lads. Ye there, McCool, go easy rousin' the lieutenant, that's a bayonet he's sleepin' with."

"Attention! Load at will! Load!" The barked commands came in quick succession. The columns stood ready, awaiting the order to advance.

Paddy nudged the Quaker's shoulder and spoke in a low whisper. "Got a feeling this is going to be a big one. What do you think?"

"They're all big ones far as I'm concerned. Sooner it's over the better."

Aligned with the First Division, the Corn Exchange moved by the left flank and headed toward the sound of heavy fighting. They marched by way of a pebble country road covered with inches of powdered dust thick as miller's flour that quickly filled their boots and shoes to the tops. Sheltering woods bordered both sides of the winding roadway most of the distance. The battle ahead was raging.

The enemy's batteries were being served with unusual determination and vigor as evidenced by the persistent, continuous whistle and screech of shot and shell. Noise and confusion, bustle and excitement among rear echelons was unusually intensified. Canvas-covered ammunition wagons, resembling canvas-backed ducks, clustered together to escape the fusillade. They parked close in the protective shelter of the larger trees.

Ambulances, constantly imperiled and threatened by bursting bombs and ricocheting shots, jostled each other in the crowded roadway. Wild-eyed horses reared and lunged forward against leather hames in a frightened effort to drag their bloody cargo away from the hellish holocaust.

The sight of wounds and bandaged limbs increased in number as the division neared the scene of action. Soldiers writhed on blood-soaked stretchers and screamed in agony from the swaying ambulances. Others limped along in pain as they passed in the opposite direction seeking refuge. Demoralizing rumors of the disaster grew in proportion as malingerers magnified the enemy's onslaught.

Where the roadway passed the base of the steep rocky eminence which had been referred to as Little Round Top, the column was suddenly halted by a mounted signal corps officer who waved his arms and advanced hurriedly to General Sykes.

The Quaker grabbed Paddy by the arm. "Look. That soldier with the signal flags. Isn't he the one who waited on us in the drugstore at Holmesburg. Remember?"

"By God, it is. It's Sam Cartledge. Sam!" Paddy shouted above the din, "come over a minute."

Cartledge shouldered his way forward. "Mulcahy! You're the third outfit from home that's passed here since morning. How are you?"

"Could be better. You remember the Quaker?"

"Sure. Stopped in the store with you and Castor the day Sumter fell."

The two nodded recognition. Paddy glanced around.

"What's up, Sam?"

"The general wants some men to defend Sugar Loaf Mountain."

"Sugar Loaf...?"

"Little Round Top, we've been using it all day as a tower."

He gave his red and white signal flags a snapping flip. "That's General Warren talking with your commander. We've gotta have soldiers up there and quick. Johnnies are attacking the southern and western slopes."

Paddy studied the rocky prominence. "See what you mean. If the Rebs get up there they'll pound our whole line."

"Right. You should see the view from the top, overlooks everything for miles around. While sending messages, we could look over the whole battle like it was being fought in miniature, toylike." He cast a wary eye at General Warren who was still engaged in animated conversation with Sykes.

"Don't dare to even show our heads now. The Rebs have sharpshooters lodged among the rocks and boulders below us. They're in a little depression three hundred yards west of here. It's a regular den of devils."

"If the position is of such importance," the Quaker inquired, "why has it been left undefended?"

Cartledge looked around to see that no staff officers were listening. "The usual muddle-headed reason, noncompliance with orders by our generals. Geary's Second Brigade, the Twenty-ninth. Hundred and Ninth and Hundred and Eleventh Pennsylvania spent last night and part of the morning on Round Top, but were ordered to rejoin their Twelfth Corps over at Culp's Hill on the right. Sickles was supposed to relieve them."

"The Twenty-ninth?" Paddy leaned on his rifle. "That's a Philadelphia outfit. Mustered about twenty from home."

"Yes. Matter of fact, I have Joe Fuller's diary in my pocket. Must've dropped it when the Twenty-ninth packed up to leave." Keeping a weather eye on General Warren, he picked at his nose. "Remember Al Burgin? Was talking to him while the messages were flying between Geary and Sickles. From what we gathered, Sickles seemed to think the best place to defend Round Top was in front of it, not on top of it, although Meade strictly ordered him to form his corps in a straight line adjoining Hancock's Second corps over to your right on Cemetery Ridge." He pointed north. "Sickles was also ordered to relieve Geary here at the south end of our line on Round Top."

"But he didn't do it?"

"No. Instead, he took it on his own and pushed out to Emittsburg Road, 'bout a mile in front. His corps broke contact with Hancock's on the right and was placed far in advance of Round Top instead of on it. Guess maybe he thought his troops would be more effective out there on level ground. Terrain he was supposed to hold down there below us does seem pretty indefensible, but you can't prove it by me."

"How 'bout Geary?"

"Waited here until ten this morning. Then, following his own orders, moved over to Culp's Hill. What's happened is the Rebs have flanked Sickle's advanced position, overlapped him. They're coming at us from the woods down on the left."

"Can you tell who's making the attack?"

"Appears to be Hood's Texans from Longstreet's Corps."

"What time did the fighting start?"

"Little after four. Longstreet's Corps of roughly forty-five thousand..."

"Forty-five thousand?"

"Near as we can figure it. Sickle's got only ten thousand. First Reb strike was against a peach orchard on Emittsburg Road, held by the Hundred'n Fourteenth, case you're interested."

"Horrocks? McClintock...?"

"Yep. The whole jolly crew from home still holding on at last account. Oh, oh, gotta leg it back to the general. See we got our soldiers."

Paddy turned to see five regiments wheeling left from the head of the division, men shouting and stumbling, dragging artillery pieces behind them as they ascended the treacherous rocky slopes of the steep promontory.

"Vincent's brigade. Good fighters, Sam. They'll hold your signal station."

"Sure hope so. Stop in the store again next time you're in town." With a wave of his hand, Cartledge raced after Vincent's troops.

The 118th began moving down the western slope of high ground that connected the base of Round Top to the main Union line anchored on Cemetery Ridge. Advancing into a boulder-strewn swale of marsh and swamp, the regiment was suddenly confronted by a stampede of frightened cattle and pigs freed when their fences were destroyed. As the stampede passed, the pace increased, and the resounding thud of steady tramping blotted out all but a few of the epithets hurled against Sickle by the dazed soldiers, blue blouses flapping open, who came running from the woods.

The cause of the outcry revealed itself as the general appeared on a stretcher, partially upright and ignoring the excruciating pain of a completely severed leg. Smoking a cigar, he called out encouragement to the fresh troops as he passed. A movement by the 118th over another ridge and through dense woods continued until they reached the edge of a wide wheat field, a field which only two hours before had been a peaceful bed of waving grain. It was now a bloody couch of trampled straw where tattered battle flags fluttered to the fore as the Corn Exchange halted for realignment.

Paddy turned his head for a moment to watch puffs of smoke and fire rim Round Top's crest a half mile behind. Turning around he could see lightning flash from the advancing Southern muskets and felt the resulting concussion hot on his face. The familiar piercing Rebel yell dominated the uproar. Then, tumbling back as if someone had toppled the head block of a stack of dominoes, came more broken ranks of the Third Corps.

Colonel Gwyn brandished a flashing sword above his head and commanded, "Fix bayonets."

An officer from a retreating regiment stopped either to mock or admire the new troops quietly awaiting the force of the Confederate drive.

"By God!" he hollered to his men. "This is them Philadelphia boys what fought at Shepherdstown. Let's go back in with 'em."

His demoralized soldiers began holding up in small groups, half-heartedly retying their shoes. They tucked their pants legs inside their socks, tightened their belts, and unfastened the lids of their cartridge boxes as they slid ramrods down their rifle barrels to make sure the weapons were loaded. Then jerking their forage caps low on their foreheads, they realigned themselves behind their officer.

In front and center of the Corn Exchange Regiment, Colonel Gwyn let his sword drop. "Fire!"

In response to the order, a sheet of avenging flame leaped from the barrel of every rifle in the regiment and the plunging Confederate line halted in its tracks.

"Load at will and fire!" Donaldson shouted to his men.

At that moment a large contingent of men and boys with rolled litters under their arms approached from behind, an aura of stoicism surrounding them. The Quaker glanced in their direction and scratched the nape of his neck with a forefinger. He gave a partial salute with his hand.

Paddy placed a cap on his firing nipple. "Know 'em?" he asked out of the corner of his mouth.

"Yes, they're from Meeting, a Quaker medical group from home."

Paddy's rifle recoiled into his shoulder. He wiped gun powder from his lips. "They must be crazy. I wouldn't be caught dead out here without a gun."

"Forward! Charge!" came Gwyn's command.

Company commanders sliced the air with naked swords as they raced to the lead.

"Come on," Tibben squealed at McCool's ear.

"Let's get us some Confederate colors this trip."

The two started off at a run, rifles tightly gripped in their tanned fists. Enemy bullets were striking dry soil all around them, causing little spurts of dust to rise up as if big drops of rain were falling. Undaunted, the 118th continued its advance through the wheat field. Comrades of bivouac and route march moved solidly side by side, shoulder to shoulder behind flying flags, mica dust making their blue uniforms sparkle in the waning sunlight.

Bigelow's Massachusetts battery of twelve-pounders moved up on the right to take the Confederates in the flank. Drivers lashed their horses furiously and circled in clouds of dust which at times obscured them. They wheeled the heavy guns swiftly into a battery and unlimbered for action. With barrels depressed, the artillery opened up, shaving the surface of the ground; the resulting carnage was terrible to behold.

The Confederate dead, clad in butternut, a color running all the way from deep coffee brown to the whitish brown of ordinary dust, littered the field, Undersized men with sallow faces, mostly from the coastal district of South Carolina, were heaped together with those of Benning's Georgians, men with strong, bony features. Resolution and energy still lingered on the pallid cheeks, in the set of the teeth and in the gripping hands.

As Paddy slowed his pace to reload, he looked down and saw a Confederate soldier with a cartridge clamped between his thumb and finger, the end of the cartridge bitten off and the paper clenched between his teeth. A bullet had pierced his heart. Close by was a young lieutenant who had fallen while trying to rally his men, his hand still firmly grasping his sword. Determination was written on every line of his dead face.

Cassidy shoved Paddy roughly. "Git a move on, Mulkayhee. Stoke that rifle."

The farthest boundary of the wheat field having been gained, the exultant Federal troops pulled up short and shouted hurrahs at the backs of the enemy, who were fleeing into the woods. Their moment of elation quickly passed as crafty Southern reinforcements and artillery, concealed and silent behind a breast-high stone wall, retaliated with vengeance.

Gaping holes began opening up in the wavering blue lines who had been caught unaware. Loud, vehement swearing rent the air as the scales of fortune turned and the joy of victory was now in favor of the screaming Confederates.

Paddy watched a spherical iron ball of grape shot plow a deep groove in the skull of Private Sam Caldwell of D Company; his blouse cut clean from his shoulders. He never stirred from his position, but lay there face down in the trampled wheat, a dreadful spectacle. At that moment he heard the hiss of flying lead and the telltale *sluck* as it sank into flesh. He felt the Quaker's body slump to the ground, blood gushing from his gaping mouth and fluid oozing from an ugly rent in his chest.

Paddy closed his eyes momentarily to blot out the scene. He dropped to his knees and shouted, "Stretcher bearers. Stretcher bearers!" Using water from a canteen, he washed and picked the coagulating blood from the Quaker's mouth to prevent his choking. "Damn you!" he cried. "Stretcher bearers!"

With steady fingers he opened his friend's blood-soaked tunic to examine the wound. A small Bible fell from the torn pocket and opened at the fly leaf. Paddy glanced at the inscription. "We hope and pray that thee may be permitted by a kind Providence, after the war is over, to return. Mother."

Tears welled in Paddy's eyes. "For God's sake, stretcher bearers!" he yelled again.

Two corpsmen flopped on their bellies and rapidly unrolled a canvas litter.

"Hurry up, get him out of here!" Paddy shouted as he grabbed the pole handles at one end of the stretcher.

The men looked at one another as they eased the still form onto a stained transport. "It's Friend John," one said faintly.

"We'll never make it, friend," the other called to Paddy. "Our Southern brothers are pressing too closely."

That simple observation was recognized by others in the Quaker medical detail busily engaged in the vicinity, and a tremulous movement swept over the entire company like a breeze over ripened grain. How their power of communication circulated in silence was difficult to understand. Hearts were communicating though lips were sealed.

Taking rifles from the dead and wounded, the medical detail cut loose with a deadly volley aimed at kneecap level.

"Mither o' God!" Cassidy roared above the din. "They're holdin' the Rebs back! Rally on the flag buckroos!"

The amazing exhibition of raw fearlessness on the part of pacifist corpsmen gave courage to the retreating troops and an onrush of reinforcements renewed the Federal onslaught.

Standard bearers turned about face and rushed the shredded Stars and Stripes back across the bloody wheat field. Screaming troops followed close behind with the regimental colors to the fore. The wounded, with the red Maltese Cross of the Fifth Corps on their caps, tried to raise themselves from the field and cheered as their comrades drove by. Retaking the wheat field the Corn Exchange drove the

Confederates over the stone-wall barricade and this time pushed them deep into the forest.

"All right, men. Hold up," Colonel Gwyn ordered. "We're stuck out here like the nipple on a tit. No use gettin' bit off."

It was close to seven o'clock in the evening and the blistering sun was beginning to fade. The tired men sought protective shelter behind rocks and boulders which were scattered about in the wooded glen. Directly in front, the land fell off on a slope and was interspersed with more rocks and a few straggling trees. Beyond the open ground, and in full view, was the Rose house on another rise of ground near the Emittsburg Road. To the right, on the other side of a small lane, was an open space apparently unprotected and the source of concern. The arrival and posting of Bigelow's Ninth Massachusetts battery along the lane helped ease the tension.

Captain Donaldson lay face down on the cool leaf mold of the forest floor. Cassidy squatted beside him. "Did ye iver see the likes of it, Cap'n? Sure'n I thought them Quakers was taught to turn the other cheek. Why, they was right good shots."

Donaldson grunted.

The sergeant picked up a dried root and chewed on it. "Jist can't understand it. They was all spread out, yit they moved together. Faith, I heard no orders given by a single one of 'em."

Donaldson rolled over on his back and clasped his hands behind his head. "The Spirit moved them."

"Somethin' sure's·hell moved 'em. But how?"

The captain raised himself on one elbow. "Don't know how, but I saw it work once. At a Quaker meeting in Philadelphia. Some question or other was up for decision. There was discussion pro and con, then instead of a voice or hand vote, there was a moment of silence. Following the silence the 'feeling' of the meeting was announced by an overseer, and it was accepted without argument. Odd thing about it, I had a 'feeling' which side of the question would come out on top before it was announced."

"Aye? Ye'd niver git an Irishman to submit to a vote like that." Cassidy grinned through his gaping front teeth.

Donaldson checked the cartridges in his box. "You've got to give the Friends credit, they're a well-disciplined lot from whom we could learn a lot of lessons."

"Dunno, Cap'n. Sich order would be contrary to me nature," Cassidy demurred, as he rose and stretched his legs.

"Aye, that's true enough ye Killarney Celt," Captain Scott barked in his Scottish burr. "Be off with 'ee. I wish to confer with the bairn of Donald."

"Before you leave, Andy," Donaldson interjected, "in case of attack, caution the men to restrain themselves long enough to let our skirmishers retire safely."

"Right, Cap'n."

"That's a good mon ye've got there, Donaldson. Wish 'ee were my top sergeant." The bearded Scot eased himself to the ground. "Quite a dry run we just had back there, aye? Me tongue feels rough as the nap of an auld kilt."

Donaldson remained silent. "How's the wife and children? Heard from them lately?"

"Ye know full well I dinna come to discuss me wife and three bairn. Ah said the top o' me tongue was rough."

"Oh?"

"Hoot mon! Stop actin' like an Edinburgh Presbyterian. Ha' ye got a wee' dock a' doras?"

"Whiskey? You know I never touch the stuff in hot weather." Donaldson winked, to show he was teasing. "But, if it's a wee drop you want..."

"Deserter! Captain! Deserter!"

Donaldson bounded to his feet and sprinted toward the forward line and the commotion.

Cassidy was poised with rifle raised to fire into the back of a Union soldier fleeing down the slope toward the Confederate lines.

"Hold it, Andy! Not in the back."

"But he's tearin' off his chevrons and desertin' to the enemy, sir."

"Even the back's too good for him, Cap'n," someone shouted.

"Shoot the bastard or by God, I will," someone else cried.

Donaldson drew a pistol. "I'll kill the first man who fires. Now, who is it that's deserting?"

"Bill Wise, sir. If he spills the beans to the Johnnies about our position, they'll be on us in a flash."

"Kill him, Cap'n! Kill him!"

"No. He's just a boy. Let him go."

"Let him go? Why the dirty..."

"Shut up, Jobson."

They watched the deserter disappear into a patch of woods.

Tight-lipped, Donaldson spat on the ground. "Look for the lesson in it."

"Lesson? What lesson?" came the sneering reply.

"Who was his friend?" Donaldson roared angrily. "Nobody. You Frankford boys stick together like glue. So do the Irish, and the Scots. Because Wise spoke broken German you cast him out, and I'm as much to blame as the rest of you. I recruited Wise in Philadelphia almost two years ago against his parents' wishes. Then because he wasn't my type, I forgot all about him."

"He never asked no favors," Tibben ventured.

"No, he didn't, and for two years he fought every battle with us without faltering. Made every march without lagging, too. The mind's a delicate thing, don't forget that. Sometimes just the smallest shock can make it go haywire." Donaldson put his pistol away. "The lesson is, don't be so clannish, and don't hurt other people with unkindness."

The silence was broken by the increased activity of guns covering the open ground to the right. The roar, along with shrill cries for canister, indicated the artillery had discovered the enemy whose lines were still out of sight of the infantry, and they were determined to inflict punishment promptly. The barrage was ineffectual and the Confederate attack soon fell on the brigade's left. Musketry started rolling in a continuous roar. Volley after volley poured in heavily as the enemy approached on the right.

"Eat dirt until ordered to fire," Lieutenant Batchelder commanded.

The earth trembled, trees shook and the branches quivered. Beneath their leafy cover, the exhausted troops lay on the ground with cartridges spread before them ready to fire when the time came.

"Shell without cutting fuse!" Bigelow shouted at his cannoneers.

Federal skirmishers hurried back to the safety of their own lines as a column of the enemy, intent on enveloping the exposed right flank of the 118th, appeared through a haze of smoke, moving across the unguarded space without shouting, shrieking, cursing or yelling. They moved obliquely, loading and firing with deliberation as they advanced, begrimed and dirty, fellows in all sorts of garb, some without hats, others without coats, none apparently in the full dress of soldier's uniform. The 118th opened with vigorous fire and the entire brigade became hotly engaged.

A teamster who had been summarily relieved of headquarters packhorse duty by the rear guard just a few days previously displayed conspicuous gallantry. Blackened with powder, hatless, a few paces in advance, he shouted continually, "Give them hell, boys!" Twitted and jeered for his previous failures, the slurs changed to commendations at his new leadership. The line preserved its regularity. There was no attempt to seek cover among the rocks or timber. The men stood erect, stepping a pace to the rear to reload and returning promptly to the front to fire. The enveloping process continued with alarming rapidity. Colonel Gwyn noted the progress and saw that a change of front or a disorderly break could prevent capture or annihilation. Discipline, firmness and courage were evident.

Colonel Gwyn's order was repeated by Major Herring. "Change front to the rear on A Company. Battalion, about face. By Company right, half-wheel march." A well-oiled, veteran fighting machine, the 118th, under withering, pelting fire, executed the movement with as much precision and detail as if on parade.

Hard pressed, the line retired slowly, firing and reloading with each backward step, for three hundred yards, crossing a corner of the wheat field and making another stand in the timber behind a stone fence about two hundred feet from a gate opening into the lane of the Trostle house. Sorely pressed, and with his battery in imminent danger, Bigelow followed the movement, withdrawing his pieces by prolongs. Taking position at an angle at the Trostle house gate, slightly in front and to the right of the Corn Exchange, the brass twelve-pounders continued their damage.

Like quicksand slowly engulfing its victim, the undaunted Southerners pressed on with savage yells until finally they were on top of the artillery and swarming around its flanks. Cannoneers fought back furiously with ramrods and hand spikes until most of them lay killed or wounded. Eighty artillery horses, some killed outright, others severely maimed, contributed to the havoc by falling and crushing the living as well as the dead. Paddy saw one Roman-nosed gelding with a front leg torn off at the knee, running amuck with blood gushing from another wound near the jugular vein. With a sickening crunch, one of its hoofs came down hard on the head of a prostrated Confederate, exploding the man's skull and sending his brains squirting in a stringy mass.

The yard and grounds of the rustic farmhouse soon swarmed with skirmishers from Barkesdale's brigade. The Mississippians crowded every corner, tree and rock that offered protection, and from there they poured destructive and accurate fire. The line of battle, with the defiant Stars and Bars flying well to the front, developed distinctly until it soon covered the rear as well as the flank of the besieged Union forces.

"Withdraw by left flank Half-wheel left," Herring ordered.

A color bearer of the 21st Mississippi Regiment advanced through the gate of the Trostle house and halted in the dusty roadway. He stood gallantly and courageously waving his flag in the thick of the melee. Beside him, a Confederate skirmisher dropped on one knee, took deliberate aim at Captain Richard Davids of B Company and fired. The ball penetrated Davids' body and he staggered, falling into the arms of Smith at his side. With Smith's aid and that of others, there was an effort to reach the rear, but Davids fell after a few paces and died.

Passing to the left of the 118th's retiring line was a Georgia regiment moving fast with arms at "right shoulder" and colors flying. They were prisoners of war, guarded by a small squad of captors, and were being hurried to the rear to get them out of the fire of their own men. In the flurry of capture, they had not had time to lay down their arms. Unconsciously, they continued to carry them, although they were prisoners. It was fortunate for the small squad who had them in charge that they forgot to use them. Lieutenant Batchelder and Sam Lewis, along with other officers, emptied their revolvers at the enemy, then threw the useless pistols into the faces of the charging Confederates.

The entire battlefield became a pinwheel of fighting and circling as a result of the frequent changes of front Directions and requirements became so intermingled that regiments were attempting to unwind themselves. There were times when the regularity of the formation was lost, but the colors indicated vantage ground and the confidence of the ranks was high. The men kept their eyes peeled on the regimental and national standards.

The batteries of McGilvery, consisting of thirty or forty pieces of artillery, were hurried into position with their front at the Trostle house, the Corn Exchange on the right. Together with Hancock's other batteries, they opened on the advancing enemy, catching the Confederates in a deadly cross fire.

"Bully for General Hunt!" Gwyn shouted, elated. He clapped his hands. "By God if we'd had front line artillery support before, the war would've been over a long time ago."

Major Herring smiled thinly. "It's taking time, but we're learning. Too bad it's at the expense of our countrymen."

Suddenly, attention was drawn to the solid tramp of a determined tread. Concealed by battle smoke and the irregularities of the terrain, an approaching force was heard before they appeared. As they drew nearer, Meade's splendid Pennsylvania Reserves came into view, sweeping everything before them. General Crawford led, hat in hand, waving his blue-coated lines to victory. With fixed bayonets, a steady tread and excellent alignment, the Union troops shouted and cheered as if victory were already theirs. They pressed on in a memorable charge that finally restored much of the ground lost, and recovered many of the guns taken during the afternoon. Their rush was so sudden that many of the enemy who had succeeded in working around the right flank of the Fifth Corps were caught between the advance of the Pennsylvania Reserves and Barnes's retiring lines. Sensing entrapment, the stunned Confederate forces began a hasty retreat back to the safety of their own lines.

Shadows of the hot summer twilight started creeping into the rocky gorges and dells. Crushed fields carpeted with corpses, streams running red with blood and leafy forests echoing the cries of the abandoned wounded, all became still as darkness fell.

In response to Meade's orders, the Union battle lines were withdrawn from the plateau and consolidated on the timbered ridge connected to Cemetery and Little Round Top. Except for a breaching of the Federal defenses at Culp's Hill later that night, the second day's battle at Gettysburg came to a close.

Under command of General Longstreet, the entire right wing of Lee's Army charged fiercely time and again only to be repulsed at each crucial moment. When compelled by darkness to cease, they failed to carry the key to the whole battlefield. Numbering close to forty-five thousand soldiers, they represented the largest body of men advancing together on any part of the field at Gettysburg during the three-day battle.

Sickle breasted the Confederate onslaught with slightly less than twenty-four thousand men, of whom twelve thousand paid the toll in casualties.

Bending beneath the mixed burdens of grief and exhaustion, Paddy trudged silently as the 118th recrossed the ridge at the base of Round Top and went into bivouac for the night. He stacked his rifle and sought Captain Donaldson whom he found conversing with Captain Crocker. "Captain?"

"Yes, Paddy. What is it?"

"May I have a pass to visit the field hospital?" The officer drew out pencil and paper from his torn blouse and scrawled a few words. "Here. Tell Doc Thomas I'll be along shortly."

The fields to the rear and east of Round Top were clogged with troops from Sedgewick's Sixth Corps, the largest and strongest corps in the army. After a long night and day march of thirty-four miles from Maryland, they had arrived on the field shortly after four o'clock, too late to be of any help in the battle. Brushing aside questions relative to the afternoon's events, Paddy hastened by them until he located the field hospital.

A slight evening breeze rustled the leaves of the great oaks. Outlined by lantern light, appalling sights of human suffering were all around as he approached a spot where Dr. Thomas was busily engaged in removing a soldier's leg.

"Show blood or get the hell out of here," came the challenge of a short-tempered orderly.

"I'm lookin' for my..."

"I don't give a damn who you're looking for. Suppose everybody came nosing around here searching for his comrade."

"I've got a pass," Paddy retorted, his temper rising.

The orderly advanced menacingly. "I'll give you five seconds to get up and git, soldier."

Dr. Thomas tossed aside his bloody bone saw and turned to rinse his hands in a bucket of red-stained water.

"It's all right, Mike. Let him be." His sweaty eyelids sagged from fatigue. "So it's you, is it, Mulcahy?" he said wearily. "Who are you searching for?"

"The Quaker, sir."

The surgeon nodded toward an ambulance with its canvas sides rolled down. "You'll find him over there."

"Is...how is he?"

"Too early to tell. Bullet passed clear through his chest." He picked up a cutting edged, curved needle and threaded it. "We've got his hemorrhaging stopped, but he's mighty weak from loss of blood." He turned to the stump of human flesh lying before him and thrust the needle through a flap of skin. "Go over if you like, but don't stay more than a minute. Remember, he must not talk or move."

The surgeon bent his head and concentrated on his stitching job.

Paddy mounted a wooden step on the back of the ambulance and peered into the dark, fetid interior. On a bed of straw he saw the Quaker lying still and quiet, his face a ghostly white. Taking the pale, cold hands in his, Paddy gave them a gentle squeeze. "You're going to be all right, John. Do you hear? Doc Thomas says so."

The Quaker's lips trembled in an abortive effort to speak.

"No, don't try to talk. Everything's all right. We held 'em today. Tomorrow we'll take 'em. Meantime, you keep this blanket tucked under your chin and I'll be back again real soon." He placed the clammy hands beneath a warm wool covering, then slipped quietly away.

Somewhere a voice sang softly. "Rock of ages, cleft for me...."

Retreating across the grounds of the emergency field station, Paddy came on Captain Donaldson, who stood with his head bowed, talking with a group of Massachusetts men. At their feet, outlined in yellow lantern light, lay the body of a dead officer.

Paddy glanced down. "Who is it, Cap'n? Anybody we know?"

"Take a look," Donaldson murmured sadly. Paddy went down on one knee to better identify the face which lay in the flickering shadows.

"Colonel Revere! He was in Libby with us."

"Yes," one of the Massachusetts soldiers said sorrowfully. "Paul Revere. The end of another famous name. First it was Dan Webster's son at Bull Run, now the grandson of Paul Revere at Gettysburg."

"The dirty Rebs'll pay for this one," another growled. "Wait'll we tangle with 'em tomorrow."

Paddy regained his feet. "You going back to camp Cap'n?"

"No. You go ahead. I want to check our wounded and talk with Doc Thomas when he's got a minute."

Raising a hand in salute, Paddy strolled once more into the closeness of a warm, sticky, summer night. A residue of battle smoke, mixed with that of many campfires, formed a wispy haze across the face of a silvery moon. The woods from Round Top to Cemetery Hill rang with axe blows as weary veterans strengthened their positions with log breastworks.

Most of the men of the Corn Exchange were slumbering when Paddy returned. Only a small group sat about the dying fire listening to Sam Cartledge give a recount of the battle as seen from his position on Little Round Top. He stopped speaking as Paddy approached, advanced a few steps and laid a consoling hand on his friend's shoulder. "How's the Quaker?" he asked solemnly.

"Not good. The ball passed through his chest and lungs."

"He'll be all right, son," Hallowell said softly. "We all prayed for him tonight at vespers."

"Sure, he'll come through all right," Tibben squeaked. "Wait and see."

Knocking ashes from his pipe, Kimball stood up and stretched his arms. "I don't have the endurance you young pups are blessed with." He yawned. "Guess I'll turn in. You comin', Jake?"

Hallowell drew out a watch and looked at it. "Believe I will, it's nine-thirty." He turned to the soldiers sitting around the fire. "Keep it low," he cautioned. "Can't sleep when there's loud talking going on."

"What's the matter? 'Fraid you'll miss somethin'?" McCool twitted.

"I said, keep it low."

"Hey, did you hear 'bout Sickles getting court-martialed on the field?" Luke Jobson blurted as he moved over to make room for Paddy.

"Court-martialed? No! For what?"

"Sam here says 'Old Four Eyes' was hotter'n a boil because Sickles disobeyed orders moving his Third Corps in advance of the line which Meade designated."

"I knew he'd done that, but a court-martial? Is that true, Sam?"

"Yes. The heavy losses we took, plus the fact we almost lost Round Top because Sickles left it undefended, made Meade see red. The court-martial orders passed through our station about five o'clock."

"That's a new wrinkle for ye, ain't it, laddy?" Gilmour cut in. "Court-martial'n a commander in the field during the course of a battle." He shook his head dispassionately. "Somethin' new evera day."

Cartledge stretched his lean frame on the ground. "Yes, but the charges of dereliction of duty have been dropped since Meade's learned Sickles lost his leg in the fighting."

"So he lost the leg? Didn't think it looked too good when he went by us."

"Hey, Sam," McCool chimed in, "tell Paddy 'bout the distinction us Frankford boys held in today's fighting."

"You're like a dog begging for a pat between the ears," the signalman retorted. "You were there. So what?"

"So what we were where?" Paddy inquired.

"The two most advanced positions in today's fighting were held by Philadelphia regiments made up largely of fellas from home. Your outfit was posted close to the Rose house in advance of the wheat field, the Hundred'n Fourteenth at the peach orchard." A glint showed in his dark eyes. "Though I'll admit it was quite a thrill watching you both holding up the Reb's drive, had my field glasses on you most of the time."

"Yes, sir. You can say us McCools saved the day, Joe and Henry with the Hundred'n Fourteenth, yours truly, Willie, with the Hundred'n Eighteenth."

"Blow it out your flutter valve," George Dyer tossed back lightly. "I'm going to bed. God only knows what we might have to go through tomorrow."

A nodding of heads greeted this sobering statement as one by one the friends rose and stalked off to their blanket rolls. A soft rippling of distant bugle calls floated across the moonlit battlefield and echoed against Round Top's bouldered sides.

Tibben squatted by the trunk of a tree in response to a call of nature. "Ever think of something, Willie?" His expression was deadpan.

"Think of something? Like what?"

"Like for instance what I'm doin' now?"

"Odds bodkin," Jobson growled close by. "Button up, will you. We want to sleep."

"What are you driving at, Squeaky?" McCool replied.

Tibben grabbed some leaves and cleaned himself. "I was just thinking, there's almost ninety-thousand of us Feds camped in a line about two miles long. Right?"

"So?"

"So, say each one empties his bowels twice a day, figure the total each man puts out at around one pound per day. That means we're loadin' this ground with ninety-thousand pounds of poop every daylight hour we stay here."

"Jumpin' Jehoshaphat. Mebbe we oughta wake the regiment and tell the colonel. Why, with dung from the horses thrown in, we'll be knee deep in the stuff by morning."

The whistle of a shoe flying past his ear sent McCool ducking for cover. "You dizzy pipsqueaks," Hallowell bellowed. "One more peep out of you before morning and I'll personally take you apart piece by piece."

CHAPTER 18

The flame-tipped spears of early dawn ushered in the third day of July as they probed a purple horizon. Finishing breakfast in the breaking light of morning, the Corn Exchange was ordered to the summit of Little Round Top to relieve Vincent's brigade. Taking up their new position was almost like being given a seat in the grandstand. Settled back among mammoth rocks, they commanded a full view of the battlefield, the two contending armies presenting themselves in a wide sweep of grandeur covering a nine-square-mile area.

Immediately in front, four hundred yards down the steep slope and to the south, was a ridge of thick timber stretching approximately half-a-mile and concealing a weird geological formation of mountainous boulders and caves called the "Devil's Den." Under that protected cover, the Confederate snipers kept up a steady, deadly accurate fire at any who dared expose themselves on Round Top.

Plum Run, a small sluggish stream through which the men had waded the day before, coursed its way parallel to the ridge until it was lost from sight around the curve at Devil's Den. Not confined by any channel, its waters spread out, forming a swamp over bog land that grew rank with tall swamp grass.

Beyond Plum Run and Devil's Den and the timbered ridge lay the wheat field, and beyond that open country rolled off to the west in arable, cultivated acres until interrupted by the wooded rise of Seminary Ridge three miles away. It derived its name from a Lutheran Divinity school located on its summit, which ran nearly parallel with Cemetery Ridge.

The main body of Lee's forces was based on Seminary, Meade's on Cemetery; a shallow, two-mile-wide valley separated them. Bisecting the gentle valley was the Emittsburg road, a dusty ribbon running at a tangent between the opposing two lines, a broad turnpike leading south out of Gettysburg. Along its path, and elsewhere over the scene, fine, old-fashioned farmhouses with large substantial barns, stables and outbuildings dotted the undulating landscape.

It was the season of wheat harvest and the whole country teemed with abundant crops ripening to maturity. It was a field that contrasted thrifty, prosperous peace with the harsh, relentless war more than any other place the Potomac Army had fought.

A section of the regiment, with somewhat less of a view, was posted down in a narrow woodland defile where the southern base of Round Top merged with a corresponding rise of ground. Suddenly, a Confederate officer, without sword or belt, his coat thrown back with an air of independent ease, moving about leisurely and enjoying a cigar, inadvertently walked into their lines. The enemy being so close, the regimental skirmishers cautiously advanced a few paces, aware that the Southern officer had either passed through them unobserved or been permitted to do so with the conviction that his capture was certain.

Astonished to find himself surrounded, he accepted his fate and was promptly conducted to the rear. He turned out to be a staff officer who had no idea he was in the proximity of Union lines. A few moments before he had sought respite from the bustle and activity of headquarters by strolling off in a direction where he thought he would be alone. He was keenly sensitive to the reproach that followed the unfortunate way in which he had permitted himself to be taken.

Back on the western slope of Round Top, the Union soldiers looked down on the distressing sight of torn, mangled bodies on the bouldered side. One Confederate in a death grip had seized the sharp edge of a huge rock, but with feet held fast in the cleft of a rock above, he hung head down between the two. Pigs feeding on corpses in front of the Devil's Den magnified the surrounding horrors. Turkey buzzards, black angels of death in search of rotting flesh, flew overhead in diminishing circles.

One of the enemy, shot early in the engagement on the previous afternoon, had been placed on a stretcher to await removal. His people had been driven from their positions and he had lain all night in fearful agony, scarcely able to articulate because of thirst. Rescued by a squad under Sergeant Cassidy, he was grateful for the water which was tendered him, temporarily allaying his sufferings. He, with others, spoke of the terrible punishment their forces had received. They were by no means sure of ultimate success. Having been encouraged and assured that they would encounter only militia, they took consolation in the fact that their failure to make good was due to the experienced soldiery of the Potomac Army.

The balance of the morning was hushed, an anxious stillness prevailing. Save for the bickering of pickets, the two great armies remained in quiet repose or gathered in preparation for another strike. Chaplain O'Neil, taking advantage of the lull, found his way to the front to minister consolation to the dying and call to the attention of the living the uncertainties of human existence with a liberal distribution of tracts and periodicals. His flock was not as appreciative as he might have desired, nor were his methods as convincing as he would have liked. The battlefield seemed not to be the place for the encouragement of religious training or gospel teaching.

Tiring of the cramped inactivity as the morning wore on, Paddy left the shelter of a rock and snaked his way along until he reached his company commander.

"Cripes, it's hot out here," he said.

Donaldson took a swig of water from his canteen and wiped his lips. He cocked one eye. "What's on your mind?"

"Nothing exactly. Just thought...."

"Just thought what?" Donaldson permitted a half smile.

"Understand our old outfit is over there on Cemetery Ridge, 'bout a mile from here. Thought maybe I could drop in on them. Haven't been close enough to chat with the boys since Antietam."

"You just can't stay put, can you, Mulcahy? The mood Meade's got this army in, you'd be shot first thing if you were caught news walking."

"No harm in trying is there?"

Donaldson removed his cap and wiped perspiration from his forehead. He drew out a watch. "Almost time for morning dispatches to headquarters. I'll ask Gwyn to let you carry them. That will give you an opportunity to drop in on your comrades on the way back."

With a leather courier's pouch tucked safely inside his blouse, Paddy skidded, stumbled and grasped saplings for support as he descended the rear slope of Little Round Top. He headed toward Meade's headquarters on the Taneytown road. Without pausing, he passed regiments, brigades and divisions of soldiers, most of whom were shirtless as they prepared a noon meal. Others were napping or sitting around cleaning rifles and sharpening bayonets.

Reaching the Taneytown road, he had turned north toward his destination when suddenly he heard his name, and it brought him to an abrupt stop. In a field off to his right he spotted familiar faces-men and boys from Frankford who had joined the 114th.

"Hey, you ruddy duck," Henry McCool cried. "Where the hell you going?"

Joe McCool, the oldest of the clan, came bounding across the grass. "Where's the Corn Exchange? How's our little brother?"

"Willie's in good shape, Joe. Tormenting as ever. We're over on Round Top."

"Lose anybody we know in yesterday's fight?" Frank Holden inquired anxiously, as he pressed closer.

"No, we were lucky. How about you fellas?"

"Well, Sam Rogers won't ever swim in Frankford Creek again," Holden replied. "Neither will Nathan Kelsey, both killed. George Messenger's in bad shape. So is Bill Williams, Wells and Weeks."

Lieutenant Bill Horrocks shouldered his way to Paddy's side. "Hi there, Mulcahy. Returning the visit Noble and I paid you at Chancellorsville?"

"Not exactly, Lieutenant. Delivering field dispatches to headquarters. By the way, where is McClintock?"

The officer fumbled with a cuff button. "At death's door. Got it bad out at the peach orchard."

"Gee, I'm sorry...." Paddy's gaze fell on the form of a soldier standing on tiptoe in the rear of the group. Dumbstruck with disbelief at what he saw, he nudged Joe McCool. "Hey, is that a girl back there?"

A roar of laughter burst from the surrounding soldiers.

"Course it's a girl. That's Mary Tebe, our vivandiere. Hey, Mary, come here and meet a friend of ours."

Paddy shifted awkwardly as the uniformed girl advanced through a path which the men opened up for her. Her face was a hard, olive complected oval of high cheek bones and an indistinguishable chin. Black hair hung to her shoulders in long unkempt strings from beneath her forage cap.

"Mary, meet Paddy Mulcahy."

The girl stuck out a callused hand, her voice deep and husky. "Glad to make your acquaintance, Mulcahy. Any friend of the Zouaves is a friend of mine. See you're with the Corn Exchange. Good outfit."

"Thank you." He gave his belt buckle a nervous tug. "You don't actually go into battle, do you?"

"She did yesterday," Joe McCool replied. "That's why we defended the peach orchard so damned well. Couldn't let the Rebs take our Mary."

"Way she was wielding her rifle," a voice from the crowd observed laughingly, "no Reb in his right mind would have dared come near her."

"Well, I have to be moving," Paddy answered. "I'll tell Willie and the others I saw you. Keep your powder dry."

Meade's headquarters was an anthill of activity. Mounted couriers dashed on and off the grounds as orderlies darted here and there on missions of minor importance. Answering the challenge of a sentry, Paddy stated his purpose and passed through a gate in a picket fence that surrounded a small, whitewashed clapboard cottage. A trellis of wisteria vines shaded the doorway to the building. Through an open window buzzing with flies, he caught a glimpse of Meade's gaunt figure bending over maps and dispatches spread out before him on the table. The commander's son stood in a corner of the hot room. Staff officers fanned themselves with their hats as they conversed in a huddled group. Several times Meade straightened and snapped an order, the result of which caused additional scurrying.

Depositing his pouch with the proper authority, Paddy paused to refresh himself with a drink of water from a pump standing in the yard. Finished, he handed the tin cup to a waiting courier.

"How far is the Philadelphia Brigade from here?" he asked.

"Straight ahead about three hundred yards. You'll find them holding center of the line on Cemetery Ridge, right in front of a clump of trees."

"Thanks."

"Hey, soldier."

Paddy turned. "Yes?"

"If you ain't got business up there, I wouldn't go if I were you. Talk has it the Johnnies are gonna strike there any time."

"I'll take my chances. Thanks again."

He crossed an open field and made his way through maneuvering troops. Parked ambulances, caissons and cannons impeded his progress. He emerged at the same location where he had spent the night of July 1st with his handful of friends in Biddle's 121st regiment. The area was now bristling with artillery and soldiers.

A burning sun, shining directly overhead, blistered the exposed arms and necks of the lounging troops. Paddy squinted his eyes against the brilliant glare and searched for an identifying trefoil, the club of a playing card which his old comrades wore on their caps. He spotted them crouching behind a low stone wall which formed an angle fifty paces in advance of a clump of trees. He rushed forward and shouted their famous battle cry, "Clubs are Trump!"

Resentful faces turned on him. "Who the hell do you think you are?" a stranger growled.

"Yeah, beat it, sonny. We don't take up with jokesters," another said.

Paddy scowled. "I fought with this regiment at Balls Bluff back in sixty-one. Didn't see any of you Johnny-come- latelies there."

"Careful how you jest, boy," an older man warned. "Name of that battle rides in honor above all others on top of our flag."

"At ease," an authoritative voice boomed. "You're addressing a lad who was wounded and captured fighting rear guard at the Bluff."

"Sorry, Sergeant. How were we to know?"

Isaac Tibben grasped Paddy by the hand. "Glad to see you again, Mulcahy. Come on down the line and visit with the rest of the boys."

"That's what I came for." He shot a disdainful glance at his shame-faced critics, then pivoted and strolled off with Sergeant Tibben.

"How're things going, Paddy? Haven't seen you since Antietam."

"Good as could be expected, I guess. Heard anything about your brother?" He hesitated a moment. "The boys in the Hundred' n Twenty-first said they were afraid he'd been done in."

"Still hoping he was captured. How's my favorite younger brother in the Corn Exchange? Hasn't got himself shot again, has he?"

"No, although we sure went through it hot and heavy yesterday. I haven't told him about Ed. Figure when there's nothing definite, it's best to keep quiet. Where's Colonel Wistar? I'd like to see him."

The sergeant looked surprised. "He hasn't been with us since Antietam. Didn't you know? His last wounds ruined him for active service. Last I heard he had a 'soft snap' command down on the Peninsula."

Paddy's face dropped. "I hadn't heard. Who's taken over the regiment?"

"Colonel Richard Penn Smith, another Philadelphia blue blood but, like Wistar, a good officer. Webb's running the brigade, Gibbon the division. Well, here we are, Company D, what's left of it."

John Heap roused himself from a catnap and grinned broadly. "Where did you get the reinforcements, Sarg?"

"Picked him up down the line. Some of the new men were giving him a hard time."

Adam and Charley Hafer shifted their positions to clear a space. "Sit down, Mulcahy. Fill us in on what happened out in the wheat field yesterday. Got word you fellas were in the thick of things."

"Not much to tell about," Paddy replied laconically. "The usual run-of-the-mill fighting. What happened here? Where is everybody?"

Dave Smith, who had seen his twin brother killed at Balls Bluff, placed his hands on the ground. "Ask Mother Earth," he said.

Crosby Slocum replaced a loose rock on the wall. "Yep, getting mighty lonesome. Less than forty of us left. Didn't figure it would end this way when we marched out of town a hundred and fifty strong."

The men shook their heads.

"Tom Pilling and Lightfoot?" Paddy inquired. "Were they...."

"Wounded and discharged," Sam Clausen said.

"Lieutenant Hibbs?"

"Killed at Fredericksburg."

"Let's drop the morbid roll call, shall we," Lesher pleaded. "Bad enough dreaming about it at night."

"Amen to that," Gus Everts replied. "Tell us, Mulcahy, did you ever see that Southern girl again? The one who helped pull you through at Leesburg?"

A Cheshire grin spread over Paddy's face. "See her? I married her!"

"You what?" came an amazed chorus. "When?"

"Last month. The twenty-sixth of June."

"The twenty-sixth? Why that's only a week ago today."

"A week ago. By gosh, you're right. Seems like a year."

"Listen to the boy," Slocum said, "talking like an old married man already."

Adam Hafer opened his shirt and poured some water over his head to get relief from the heat. "I'll grant Mulcahy this much, he sure knows how to pick 'em. She was a real good-looker."

"But think of the in-law complications," Charley Hafer said seriously. "How did you pull it off, Paddy? The old man's in the Rebel army, isn't he?"

"Battling with in-laws he'd have anyway," the older Hafer cut in. "This way it makes them legal enemies."

"For one, I'd rather face a dozen hot-tongued in-laws than lie out here in this damned sun," Heap grumbled. "This is murder."

Tibben grinned. "Quit your belly-aching. This is July vacation time. Remember lying around in boats on the Delaware? Jumping in for a swim now and then, and fishing? Sleeping long as you wanted in the morning? Why, we're just being rested up for the big holiday tomorrow, a grand and glorious Fourth."

"Very funny, Sarg. Very funny. You're a real nickel rocket. All we need to end this war damn quick, right here and now, is to have some politician go out between the lines and give us a two-hour oration about our founding fathers. I'll wager within one hour after he began there wouldn't be a soldier within five miles."

"Somebody dig up a politician real quick," Lesher announced with a half-laugh.

Dave Smith snorted. "You're off your nut. One sniff of powder smoke and those fire-breathing breast-beaters would take off like a gun-shy dog."

His marital venture having been forgotten, Paddy took advantage of the change of topic to familiarize himself with his present surroundings. Joining and extending the left of the 71st Regiment along the stone wall was the 69th Regiment of Irishmen. The rest of the Philadelphia Brigade, the 72nd and 106th, was posted in the rear, near a clump of trees.

A mile and a half to the south, Little Round Top overlooked the entire area.

In front of the stone wall a grass field sloped in a gradual rolling decline toward the Emittsburg road about a half-mile away, then leveled off to a plain which lost itself in the wooded protection of Seminary Ridge, a mile-and-a-half farther west. In the distance, beyond the Confederate line on Seminary, the South Mountains rose majestically in a bluish-green haze.

A half mile north, to the right, lay the village of Gettysburg, its outskirts clinging to the tree-sheltered base of Cemetery Hill. Enemy troops and snipers, who had occupied the town since the first day of battle, sent sporadic fire into the Federal forces posted above them on the heights. Periodically, jets of red flame leaped from attic windows and doorways, Rebel sharpshooters executing their deadly business.

Paddy checked the position of the sun in the cloudless sky. "What time do you have, Isaac? I'd better be getting back to my outfit."

"One o'clock on the nose."

Just then the relatively quiet atmosphere was split by the booming explosion of an artillery piece somewhere within Rebel lines.

"Humph. Rebs must've heard your inquiry, Mulcahy."

"I'm not so sure. That sounded like a signal for something."

By way of answer, a deep, earth-moving rumble erupted from one end of Seminary Ridge to the other as flame and smoke belched from the Confederate artillery hidden in the thick foliage of trees.

The hot, humid air became instantly filled with screaming, bursting shells.

Immediately the cry went up. "Barrage! Everybody down! Eat dirt!"

Paddy flung himself face down, hugging the stone wall for cover.

"God a'mighty," Slocum blurted, breathing heavily. "Listen to them guns. Must be tons of 'em."

The bombardment increased in intensity as grape and spherical case shots tore into the huddled blue coats, exploding fragments ripping chunks of flesh.

Then it came, a strange new sound that struck terror into the hearts of the men who heard it. Whitworth bolts shrilled overhead like the cry of a banshee, striking repeatedly and with unerring accuracy.

"Good Lord!" Lesher whimpered. "What are they shooting?"

Tibben doubled up closer to the wall. "Must be those new English cannons we heard about. Whitworths they call 'em."

"Look, yonder!" Everts pointed. "Cushing's going to work."

Batterymen who had been lounging around a rail fence over to the right of the 71st were standing at their places. In the methodical fashion distinctive of their branch, they began executing maneuvers around their guns. Those serving the nearest cannon suddenly broke away to the right and left in the manner of hell-raisers scampering from the scene of devilment. There was a crashing report and dense white smoke leaped from the muzzle. Runners sprang forward and, laying hold of hand spikes and spokes, ran the gun back into position. Sponge staffs, used to swab out the smoking barrel, were thrust into a leather water bucket amid the hissing of steam.

On Seminary Ridge the multitude of Confederate batteries worked feverishly to silence the Federal artillery. Their shells slammed into the Union lines. Limbers and caissons exploded in the air. Wounded horses ran wild and those that stood their ground were blown to bits.

Paddy watched in horror as one gunner, blackened and bared to the waist, went about his job of ramming solid shot down the gun barrel, as unruffled as though he were loading groceries in a quiet country store. Suddenly his body completely disappeared in a showering debris of dirt, fence rails and smoke. Paddy waited with bated breath for the smoke to clear. On the ground where the gunner had stood there was nothing but a confused mass of quivering limbs. Paddy shut his eyes to blot out the scene.

Defective shells, exploding short of their mark, burst in midair and showered incendiary sparks over the hapless countryside between the contending lines. Stacked in the fields, hay ricks crackled and burned in brilliant orange flames. Volumes of smoke rolled up to the sky in conical spires from burning farm buildings. The entire length and breadth of the valley appeared to have been torched by a band of marauding Indians.

The heavy Confederate cannonading, unprecedented in the annals of warfare, continued unchecked without pause or interruption. Paddy covered his ears to muffle the sound of screeching shells that whistled and exploded overhead.

Tiny white puffs accompanied each discharge from the enemy's guns. The Confederate field pieces were clearly outlined by the sun. A thick pall of smoke soon blotted the ridge from sight. All that remained to be seen were flashes of flame, which pierced the opaque haze in the valley.

It was unnerving to know that the distant wooded hillside, now veiled in smoke and obscured by timber, concealed an army. Stilled to an awful pause, save for the battery men who, with untiring energy and ceaseless activity, worked exposed, every Union soldier lay motionless and silent. They flinched at the deadly whir and buzz of flying fragments coming from shells bursting overhead. The dominating roar and whistle of bolt and solid shot caused them to glance at each other with anxious eyes until the sound died away to the rear.

The artillery sustaining the Union line continued to work with rapid fire intensity. Gunners sent solid shot slamming back at their adversary with the fury of a maddened bowler recklessly delivering balls, careless of aim and heedless of results, anxious only to get the task done. This time they were greeted by no such jocular phrases as, "Shorten your fuses!" "Elevate your pieces!" or "Depress your guns!" catcalls which in the past had been irresistible.

The grueling contest continued unabated for two hours in the unbearably hot weather. Canteens were nearly emptied of water. Sunstroke and heat exhaustion were beginning to take a toll.

Suddenly, the serviceable Federal artillery was ordered to retire to the rear. Paddy watched the withdrawal with misgivings. The sweat band of his kepi cut into his dust-caked forehead. He removed the cap and rubbed his aching brow.

Bob Lesher jumped to his feet, "They're pulling the guns back!" he screamed. "The artillery's deserting us!" Shell-shocked, he started to run toward the rear.

"Get down!" Tibben shouted. He lunged at Lesher's ankles and held on tightly, pulling the terrified soldier to the ground. "Don't be a fool! It's safer here than back there. The Rebs are over-shooting their mark, as usual. Look for yourself."

Lending credence to Tibben's words, the missiles which had passed safely overhead were fracturing rocks, splintering timbers and shattering the loose material of the hastily dug entrenchments in the rear. Lesher trembled, covered his head and lay still.

Several minutes later the Confederate barrage slackened, then ceased as abruptly as it had begun. An ominous stillness settled over the battlefield. One by one, after the fashion of turtles peeking from their shells, the men of the Philadelphia Brigade raised their heads to look around. The artillery smoke lifted slowly and the wide sweep of land in front of them came into focus.

Caught in the full glare of afternoon sunlight, Seminary Ridge was bristling with activity. From the woods which crowned its crests there suddenly emerged two solid, unwavering lines of battle. In the first line were five thousand men of Pickett's division, in the second, five thousand troops under the command of Pettigrew. Paddy watched with fascination. There was no attempt to protect or conceal the column of attack. There was no over-hanging mist of breaking day, no uncertain shadows or lingering twilight, no sheltering knoll. In broad daylight, the Confederates were aiming to strike directly at the center of the Union line held by the Philadelphia Brigade.

"Thunderation!" Heap blurted, a touch of admiration in his voice. "They're coming straight at us."

Adam Hafer shaded his eyes to get a better view. "It's a damn insult, that's what it is. Does Lee think Meade's got little boys posted here?"

Crosby Slocum let out a chuckle. "Reminds me of what Pa used to say, 'Don't mind uninvited company visiting the house overnight. Don't mind them dunging in the corners. But when they wipe their ass on our lace curtains, they are carrying things too far!'"

Gus Everts spit on the ground. "Too right! Some people have to be taught manners. Notice the lay of the land? This is going to be Fredericksburg in reverse. Now we'll see how good the Johnnies are when it comes to charging up a hill and attacking troops posted on the crest behind a stone wall."

"Amen to that," Tibben responded grimly.

Lesher chewed nervously at his fingernails and shifted uneasily. "Look at how many there are," he said weakly. "Never saw or heard of half that number ever making a single charge before, anywheres."

Charley Hafer opened his shirt and fanned his chest. "You're right, must be close to fifteen thousand of them. Must be trying for a record of some kind."

The attacking Confederate force continued gathering strength. Huge columns, twenty-five hundred men under Trimble, moved in support on the left flank as the advancing enemy lines cleared the woods. Large bodies of troops followed in reserve. Distances were being preserved with accuracy by mounted officers occupying their proper stations within the ranks. Scores of Southern battle flags waved defiantly at the fore and behind them were row upon row of muskets held at right shoulder, burnished bayonets glistening like silver in the bright sunlight.

"Wonder if Lee knows what he's doing?" Sam Clausen inquired of no one in particular. "Those troops have nearly a mile of open ground to cover before they get to us."

"Sure 'nough looks to me like they know what they're doing," Dave Smith retorted dryly.

"Man o' day," Billy Brown murmured. "They got 'bottom' all right. Just look at 'em coming, would you? Like a big parade."

For the first time in their memory, the enemy was advancing without the familiar crescendo yell, or wild shriek. The muted Southern force continued to move forward with a steady, solemn tramp as though each man fully realized the gravity of the situation.

Spellbound, the veterans of the Philadelphia Brigade gazed at the magnificent sight with awe and approbation.

Union artillery, withdrawn in a crafty design to await full disclosure of the purpose behind the Confederate's previous bombardment, suddenly reappeared on the crest of Cemetery Ridge. Cannon muzzles, resembling the evil eyes of a squinting Cyclops, were trained on the unsuspecting foe.

Withholding fire, they waited patiently for the enemy troops to reach a rail fence which lined the Emmitsburg road. With an earth-shaking roar, they spewed forth a deadly vomit of death-dealing metal. Great gaps appeared in the advancing lines. Mangled bodies were draped along the entire length of the rail fence.

"Hot damn, that rattled their teeth," Stokes cried gleefully. "Who said the artillery deserted us? They were just playing possum."

"Atta boy, shake 'em up again!" Adam Hafer shouted to nearby battery men.

Plying their punishment without encouragement, shells from the Napoleon ten-pounders and Parrott twelve-pounders continued to open huge holes in the oncoming dust-colored ranks.

"Yo ho!" Everts squealed. "Fredericksburg in reverse."

A worried expression clouded Tibben's face. "By God, I don't believe the artillery's gonna be able to stop them. There's just too many of them."

He watched with firm lips as the formidable charging columns pressed ahead in a full sweep of restless energy.

Adam Hafer scowled and fixed his bayonet. "It's gonna be left up to us, boys," he muttered. He pulled his kepi down tight on his head.

Paddy glued his eyes on the rapidly advancing foes who were a scant quarter of a mile away. He opened a cap box, placed it where it would be accessible and slid a leather cartridge case to the front of his belt.

He turned toward Sergeant Tibben. "How many men does the brigade have on hand to meet this attack?"

Tibben took a bite of tobacco. "Roughly twelve hundred. We're mustering three hundred and ninety-three. The Sixty-ninth mustered three hundred and forty." He jerked a thumb over his shoulder. "Backing us up, the Seventy-second had four hundred and seventy-five at roll call."

"Where's the Hundred'n Sixth?"

"A hundred of them are back of us in reserve. Meade sent the rest over to the Baltimore Pike to protect Howard's Germans."

"Protect Howard's Dutchmen? From who?"

"From the rest of our army. We're ready to kill the useless bastards."

Gus Everts sighted his rifle. "Maybe you'd like to put in for furlough, Mulcahy. Starting as of now."

"I'd feel a damned sight better than being stuck out here," Paddy replied.

"Wish I was furloughed," Bill Brown cut in. "I'd be fishing nice and quiet like along the Pennypack."

Sergeant Tibben clapped him between the shoulder blades. "That is no fishing rod you have in your hand now. Get it up."

There followed an immediate clicking of locks as each man raised his rifle hammer. Paddy felt with his fingers to make certain he had placed a cap on the nipple. Muskets and rifles being thrust on the stone wall in an aiming position sent up a sharp clanking sound as metal gun-barrels rang on rock. Axles squeaked nearby as cannons were hand-rolled to the front. Officers began opening their pistol holsters.

In response to a command from Colonel Smith, the regimental trefoil flags were removed to a place of safety in the rear along with the brigade colors. They would serve as a rallying point in the event of a breakthrough.

Alone at the front to encourage and sustain her loyal sons there remained but a single red, white and blue ensign which had first waved in battle at Saratoga in 1777. With its lance sloped defiantly toward the enemy, the American flag stood out in all its glory.

Dave Smith suddenly jumped to his feet and pointed down the slope. "Look at who's leading the parade!" he bellowed. "The Eighth Virginia!"

The eye of every Balls Bluff survivor turned in the direction Smith was pointing. Moved by anger and painful recollections, they saw the flag of Colonel Hunton's 8th Virginia advancing. The whilom foe hunched forward with Garnett's brigade at the head of Pickett's division.

Sam Clausen flicked a thumb across his rifle sight and hissed between clenched teeth, "All right you sitting ducks, come get a taste of what you gave us."

Sergeant Tibben sprang to his feet and shouted at the nearby 69th Regiment, "That bunch belongs to us! Leave them to us! We have an old score to settle!"

Several of the Irishmen turned around and gave a thumbs up sign.

The Philadelphians burning for revenge raised their battle cry and hurled it down the slope.

"Clubs are Trump!"

"Here we are, Johnnies!"

"Clubs are Trump!"

Some lifted caps and swung them in the air as they pointed tauntingly to the club trefoil sewn on the crowns. At the same time a crack of rifle-fire sallied from the low barricade.

"Give 'em a full volley for Wistar," Heap shouted, as rammers pounded into gun barrels.

The faces of the advancing foe, grim and anxious, became clear and distinguishable.

Paddy crossed himself. "One for Chirp and Billy," he murmured under his breath. Then, gritting his teeth, lips curled almost in a snarl, he braced his rifle on the stone wall and quickly drew bead on a bearded color sergeant. Taking steady aim and slowly pulling the trigger, the stock of his rifle recoiled sharply, slamming back into his collarbone with a jarring impact. A rush of hot air flew back in his face as he watched his intended victim pitch face downward.

The tall commander of the 71st halted behind the Frankford Volunteers, who were firing vigorously. A resolute man of calm mien, he called out in a loud voice, "Let 'em come up closer before you fire, boys. Then aim low."

The avenging volleys slackened off. Time for death was drawing near, and the men began to feel its clammy hand. The grim reaper, that invisible specter, was drawing back his scythe for the first stroke. Except for the sound of heavy breathing, a tomblike silence prevailed as battle-wise veterans fussed with last minute details, however trivial.

Recent recruits squirmed and fidgeted like nervous colts being broken to the halter. Had they been aware of Lee's overall strategy they would have had double cause for alarm; at that moment, poised on a level plain three miles to the east and directly on the rear of the Union line, were four brigades of Stuart's cavalry and four batteries, the flower and strength of the Confederate Army, led by her most distinguished commanders. Maneuvering with the express purpose of striking the rear of the Federal Army, simultaneously and in cooperation with Pickett's grand attack on its center, Stuart's command was preparing to split the Northern forces in two. Arrayed against him, to forestall such an event, were Union horsemen under Generals Custer, Gregg and McIntosh.

Matters at the front and center of the Federal line came to a head. From Cemetery Ridge, devastating artillery and rifle fire poured in heavy concentration upon the Rebel flanks, compressing the long Confederate lines into a wedge shape, the point of which was aimed directly at the Philadelphia Brigade. All of a sudden the apex of the on-charging enemy vanished from sight.

"Hey, where did they go?" Slocum shouted with astonishment.

Puzzled, Paddy peered cautiously over the stone wall. Smoke and a cloud of dust kicked up by enemy heels covered the slope.

"It's like they've been swallowed up by the earth!" Lesher cried.

Other defenders of the Union's center strained their eyes to catch a glimpse of the lead columns who had disappeared so strangely. A rumbling sound, the heavy tread of their feet, was coming closer. Federal artillerymen stood like statues alongside cannons loaded with canister; chains, belt buckles, tin cans, jagged pieces of scrap iron, broken rifles and shot were all loaded in gun barrels waiting to explode at point-blank range.

"Ki yi eeee!" The Rebel yell burst from parched, wide-open mouths as thousands of screaming Confederates appeared to leap out of the ground from nowhere. Rushing from a deep depression which had temporarily obscured them, the Southerners charged the stone wall with the fury of a tidal wave.

The death rattle of Federal small-arms fire roared an answer with sulfurous fury. Cannons, leaping forward like maddened dogs on chains, discharged their loads of canister. Staggered by the storm of lead and scrap iron, the charging lines reeled and recovered with wild firing which increased to a crashing roll of musketry running down the whole length of their front.

Aiming with vengeful ferocity, the survivors of Balls Bluff directed their fire on the men of the 8th Virginia. An old score was soon settled. Colonel Hunton's regiment was decimated. Similarly caught in the fiery maelstrom before the stone wall, all forward elements of Pickett's division suddenly melted away.

Sorely pressed and badly outnumbered, the Philadelphians defending the Union center received help from an unexpected quarter. Fifty yards to the left of center, two of Stannard's Vermont regiments, never before tested in battle, moved quickly down the slope under cover of the trees. They were green troops whose sole experiences had been manning fortifications at Washington for nine months. They wheeled sharply to their right and opened a telling cross-fire on Pickett's and Pettigrew's exposed right flank.

Boxed in by the Vermonters' flanking fire on the right, and stung on the left by withering volleys from 1st Massachusetts sharpshooters located on top of the ridge, the supporting elements of Pickett's division regrouped themselves with Pettigrow's onrushing five thousand troops, and the Confederate phalanx again charged forward in a determined effort to breach the stone wall. With an irrepressible surge, they stormed over the rock and rail breastworks.

The men of the 69th and 71st locked in mortal hand-to-hand combat, hacking and jabbing desperately with upraised rifles in a desperate effort to beat off the screaming Rebels. Some, like flotsam before a flood tide, found themselves being carried along by the overpowering onslaught of sheer numbers. Hapless swimmers caught in a strong current, they struggled and thrashed in a swinging melee of fists, sidearms and rifle butts as they were slowly pressed up the slope. No commands were needed nor could they have been heard. With skilled soldier instincts, they disengaged themselves quickly to regroup in the rear of their sister regiment, the 72nd Pennsylvania, whose firepower now swept the field.

Virtually captive, Paddy, along with the others, held fast at the stone wall. He clubbed like a wild man with his rifle stock. The scorching July heat and choking dust were stifling. Sickening to the stomach was the acrid stench of sweat-soaked kersey and homespun uniforms. Perspiration from dripping armpits and genitals threw off a nauseating, musky spoor which clogged nostrils and made breathing difficult.

A Confederate general, waving a black slouch hat on the tip of his sword, struggled over the breastwork and shouted encouragement to his troops. As he glanced down at the white trefoils sewn on the caps of the embattled Union defenders, his roar could be heard above the din.

"Gawd A'mighty, this isn't militia, it's the Army of the Potomac!"

The sole of a heavy boot ground into one of Paddy's ears. With an angry twist of his prostrate form, he rolled over and reached for the offending foot among the many churning the dust around him. He grasped a black boot and, with a vigorous jerk, pulled a young lieutenant to the ground. He hurled himself on top of the officer. "You son of a bitch!" he raged. A rock clenched tight in his fist, he pounded his adversary's head. Blood squirted from the Rebel's ears. His body quivered and went limp.

Long, gray columns, raked by the pulverizing artillery fire, continued to crowd in toward the Union center, building up a strength that finally overwhelmed the small rectangle of littered ground still held by the 69th and 71st regiments. Halting on their side of the stone wall, the Rebel columns opened fire at the Federal artillery posted higher on the crest of the ridge. Some Confederates lay prone, others knelt, while those in the rear stood and fired over the heads of their comrades. Red Confederate battle flags and multicolored regimental standards of the enemy waved above the dust and roar of combat.

The three Federal batteries around the stone wall were now reduced to almost complete destruction. The ground around the guns was in shambles. Several cannons had been dismounted and caissons and limbers exploded into fragments. Most of the horses were killed and there were just enough men left to work the two remaining guns. Wounded severely in both thighs and a shoulder, Lieutenant Cushing stood by his remaining field pieces and shouted orders for the gunners to load with triple canister. It being impossible to remove the wounded, they lay where they fell amid smashed wheels, wood splinters and the mutilated remains of comrades and horseflesh.

One artillery man, cut dreadfully about the belly by a shell fragment, drew a revolver and placed the muzzle to his temple. With an expression of anguish, he pulled the trigger as a Confederate volley tore through the area and completely destroyed Cushing's Battery, putting it out of action. Cushing, and two soldiers who had been supporting him, slumped to the ground dead. The cannons became quiet.

Over on the left and slightly to the rear, Brown's Rhode Island battery, which had given strong support to the beleaguered Philadelphians down at the stone wall, likewise met with annihilation at that crucial moment. Corpses of Rhode Island cannoneers were draped like windblown debris around their positions. The 69th and 71st Pennsylvania regiments, trapped at the bloody angle, continued to fight without benefit of artillery support.

Confederates ran amuck in the wreckage of Cushing's battery.

Paddy raised himself on one elbow and caught a glimpse of the Southern general who had jumped the wall a few moments before. The Confederate commander rested a triumphant hand on a silent cannon and waved his sword high, his black hat down to the hilt. Paddy reached for a pistol still clenched in the hand of the lieutenant he had just knocked senseless. Leveling the sidearm, he cocked it, took aim and fired. One of the general's arms flew upward, the other grasped feebly at the cannon barrel as he slithered to the ground.

Paddy grabbed a fallen rifle and wildly stabbed with the bayonet to help stem the onrush of Archer's 1st and 7th Tennessee Regiments who, at the moment, were swarming over the stone wall. The Tennessee troops were tall, slack-jawed men, backwoodsmen with a touch of hardship etched in their long, bony faces.

They stormed over the thinning ranks of Philadelphians at the stone wall and swept toward the clump of trees on the crest.

From the rifles of the 72nd and 106th Pennsylvania regiments came jets of orange flame that flashed through the opaque haze of battle smoke and dust. Unwavering blue lines that would not move, they poured fire into the charging foe. The dead pitched forward where they stood at the feet of resolute comrades.

Behind another stone wall that ran perpendicular to the front and to the right of Cushing's battery were two companies of the 71st. Withdrawn from the angle earlier, they had been placed there by Colonel Penn Smith in an exhibition of foresight and military acumen. Fifty paces removed from the spot of initial enemy contact, these battle-tested troops found themselves in the enviable position of being placed squarely on the naked flank of the Confederates trying to knife through the Federal center. At a signal from Colonel Smith, they cut loose with an enfilading volley that swept the exhilarated Rebels from their feet. Reloading, the two flanking companies sprang forward for the kill in a simultaneous movement with the 72nd and 106th Regiments. Driving the enemy before them, they charged the "bloody angle" where Paddy and his comrades fought off Confederate reinforcements coming from that direction.

On the far side of the clump of trees, a combined movement by the 7th Michigan, 1st Minnesota, 19th Maine and the 15th and 20th Massachusetts Regiments sealed off the boxlike trap sprung on the Confederate spearhead. Union troops moved by impulse so that not a single body moved by the right Rank or changed front forward or executed any other organized tactical maneuver. General Hancock, Corps Commander of the Federal 2d Corps, was knocked off his horse by a bullet that went through his saddle, driving a ten-penny nail and bits of wood into his thigh. General Gibbon, the Division Commander, was down with a bullet through his shoulder; General Webb, Commander of the Philadelphia Brigade, was rendered useless by a severe wound.

Although there were officers of lesser rank in their midst yelling hoarsely and gesturing madly with swords, no one was obeying the commands. No formal tactical move was possible in the cramped, dusty confusion. No shouted command could be heard above the furor. The finale from start to finish was one uncontrollable brawl of screaming, cursing, close-quarter combat in steaming July heat as the contestants kicked, throttled, slashed and clubbed each other in and around a copse of redbud and oak trees. Union soldiers from nearby regiments rushed forward to join the fray, all regimental formations becoming tangled and lost, every man fighting on his own.

A supporting column of Confederates, charging up the slope, was caught in the oblique fire from McGilvery's cannon on the right and the Vermont regiments on the left. The Rebel lines faltered and broke before the withering cross-fire. Netted by the center of the Union line, the penetrating Confederate spearhead came to a halt.

Colonel Smith glanced at his watch. The fighting had lasted a little more than half an hour. The greatest massed infantry charge ever made by a single body of men in the history of warfare fell apart, the shattered remnants tumbling back toward Seminary Ridge. Rebels, trapped in the clump of trees, dropped their rifles and raised their hands in surrender. "Remember Fredericksburg!" gleeful Union soldiers taunted.

Mean-spirited soldiers from the New York Tammany Regiment grabbed a young Confederate lieutenant and began shoving him around. One of them snarled, "Where's General Pickett?"

The Southerner was visibly shaken. "What fer you want with General Pickett?" he stammered.

"To dump him in the East-River, that's what fer," came the reply.

To get relief from the scorching heat, the Confederate unbuttoned his tunic and nodded his head in the direction of the Confederate main line on Seminary Ridge. "General Pickett rode out with us as far as the Emittsburg Road," he said with a drawl. "Then he turned back and rode out of sight."

One of the New Yorkers spat on the ground. "That figures," he growled. "Damn yella belly." He kicked a loose stone at his feet.

At the stone wall, Sergeant Tibben organized a cordon of men to prevent the escape of trapped Rebel forces. "Don't let any of them boll weevils sneak out this way!" he shouted. He slashed the air with a captured sword.

Gus Everts planted both feet firmly amidst the dust-covered corpses lying crumpled on the ground and leveled his bayonet-tipped rifle. One of his eyeballs, prolapsed from a severe blow to the head, was bulging and oozing blood. Flies feasted on the coagulating agar.

"First one tries to go home to roost this way'll be a pierced pigeon," he cried.

Beaten and bewildered, the disheveled enemy who drifted down the slope in the vain hope of escape were caught up like minnows in a net by the victorious Philadelphia Brigade.

Sam Clausen removed his kepi, mopped his blood-stained forehead and stared at the surrounding carnage in silence.

"Snap out of it," Dave Smith said, giving him a rude shove. "What are you daydreaming about?"

"The words of Anne of Austria," Clausen murmured. "'God doesn't pay at the end of every week, my dear Cardinal, but he pays at last.'"

As far as the eye could see was the debris of discarded guns, knapsacks, severed human heads, arms, legs and other parts of bodies. Wounded and prostrate Southerners lay among the dead that littered the field. They held up handkerchiefs in token of surrender. Many cried for water, others for aid.

In the process of turning back stragglers, Paddy suddenly felt a gentle tug at his sleeve. Spinning around, he faced a gray-haired Negro standing with tears in his eyes. "Please," sobbed the colored body-servant, "please, Mistuh Yankee, 'low me to go up yondah."

"Up where?"

"Thar, sur." The old man pointed toward the clump of trees. "Young Marsa's up thar somewhar. Ah done been wid him ever since he whar nothin' more 'n a barefooted little cricket of a boy." He wrung his mahogany hands in supplication. "Please, Mistah Yankee, 'low me through. Mah boy needs me."

A fleeting, fond recollection of Uncle Peter Marks struck a responsive chord, and Paddy said, "Sure, Uncle, pass through." He unslung a canteen and pressed it into the servant's hands. "Here, take this with you. You may need it."

The darky's eyes shone with heartfelt gratitude, and his deep, resonant voice quaked with emotion, as he said, "God bless you, Marsa Yankee. God bless you, suh." He passed on up the slope.

The mopping-up operation continued with dispatch until the job was completed. At final accounting, the men of the Philadelphia brigade tallied one thousand prisoners, six battle-flags and a fourteen hundred arms turned in between them.

Crosby Slocum stood contemplating the spoils. He grinned broadly. "Sure feels great to win a big one, doesn't it fellas?"

John Heap lowered his eyes. "Does it?" His hesitant gaze drifted toward the spot where Charley Hafer lay weeping on the chest of his slain brother, Adam. John Barlow, his arm wrapped in a bloody sling, was helping John Stokes remove Billy Brown's broken body from its slumped position at the angle of the stone wall.

Brown, the ardent fisherman whose constant desire had always been to "be somewhere else fishing," had been granted his wish by the Apostles.

Stokes removed a black packet from Brown's ripped blouse and turned it over in his hands.

"What do you have?" Barlow asked.

"Brownie's diary. I'll send it home to his mother."

Tears running down his cheeks, Sergeant Tibben removed the personal effects from the body of Bob Lesher. A perennial worrier, Lesher lay sprawled face down, his worldly fears removed. A stream of blood flowed from his gaping mouth mingled in a common pool with that gushing from the severed jugular vein of a dead Confederate. Death had succeeded in uniting the common blood of man where politicians, press and pulpit had failed.

Sergeant Tibben suddenly stood erect and bolted toward a mortally wounded Confederate officer who had managed to raise himself up on one elbow.

"What's the Sarg up to?" Stokes exclaimed.

Barlow pointed with a bloodied hand. "Notice the strange way the Reb spread his fingers on his chest?"

"So?"

"It's the Freemason sign of distress."

Tibben bent low over the form. The two spoke in muted conversation.

Near the wreckage of Cushing's battery, Frankford volunteers, serving with the various regiments in the Philadelphia Brigade, grouped together to exchange notes and experiences.

John Heap removed a blood-stained shirt to get relief from the heat. He examined the assorted bric-a-brac that Timothy Carr of the 69th had gathered from the field. Souvenirs of all sorts were slung, draped, stuck and pinned on his slender body.

"Boy, what are you planning to do with all that stuff?" Heap inquired. "You figuring on opening a swap shop after the war?"

The freckled-face, red-haired Irishman grinned good naturedly. "If I live that long."

"What do you mean, if you live that long?" Gus Everts blurted. "The war is over. We've licked Cousin Bobby for real today. It's all over but the shouting."

"You don't see us being ordered forward to establish that fact, do you?" Sam Clausen cut in tersely. "Mark my words, there's plenty of fight left in old Johnny Reb. You wait and see."

"Sure'n if there's to be any more fightin'," Silas Daniels of the 69th injected sadly, "we'll be in a helluva fix. Faith, we've lost every field officer in the regiment this day, includin' Colonel O'Kane."

"Every single one?"

"That's right," Bill Austin broke in. "From the Colonel right down to the last lieutenant, every one of them killed."

A beehive buzz and hum coming from a crowd of soldiers gathered around one of Cushing's shattered cannons caught their attention. Carr arched his thin, red eyebrows. "Wonder what that's all about?"

Paddy gave his battered kepi a backward tilt. "Don't know. There's Al Dungan and John McDonald with Phil Henry from the Seventy-second. Let's go over and find out."

They changed directions and elbowed their way toward the hubbub. A solemn private, holding a watch, a pair of spurs and other trinkets, was standing over the body of a prostrate Confederate general. Hovering like so many droop-winged vultures, bloodied and begrimed men from the 71st were exchanging whispers.

Paddy stared down at the pale, still form and drew back as he recognized the general he had shot earlier in the engagement. He nudged Al Dungan, his voice seeming to echo from a long way off. "Who...who is he?"

Dungan massaged a badly swollen, bloody wrist, his scarred face an expressionless mask. "General Armistead," he said quietly.

"He just die?" Carr inquired, as he kneeled for a closer look.

"Yes." Dungan's voice remained flat. "Just a few seconds ago. From what we were able to gather, he and Hancock were close friends in an army camp in California before the war. His last words were, 'Tell Hancock I have done him and my country a great injustice, which I shall never cease to regret.'"

Dungan pointed toward the awestricken private who was holding Armistead's possessions. "Just before he passed away, the general gave Walter those mementos. Ordered Walter to pass them on to Hancock in token of their friendship."

Paddy's knees were rubbery, his hands clammy. He took Carr by an arm. "Come on, let's go."

"What's the matter?" Carr asked, a puzzled expression on his face. "You look like you've seen a ghost. Don't tell me you can't stomach death yet."

"I said come on, let's go."

Carr brushed gnats off his eyelashes. "Keep your shirt on, I'm coming."

The two moved off toward the crest of Cemetery Ridge. A valley of Tophet lay behind them, a landscape of death and destruction.

CHAPTER 19

Timothy Carr, bending beneath his heavy load of plunder, slumped to the ground under the shade of a gnarled apple tree.

"Whew! This booty gets heavier by the minute," he exclaimed. "Don't know if I can make it back to the wagons."

"Why don't you ditch it?"

"Hell, no. Someday this stuff'll be valuable." He put a canteen to his parched lips and took a deep gulp.

Paddy flung his weary body on a pile of dried orchard grass. "You're crazy with the heat. Damn!" He slapped a huge horsefly which had bitten him on the forehead. A trickle of blood flowed from the puncture. "Say, what time do you have by that watch you picked up?"

"Five o'clock."

"Good grief." Paddy sprang to his feet. "I've got to get back to the regiment."

Carr started gathering his mementos as the rear echelon troops, lounging nearby, studied his clanking baggage.

"Sure been good to mosey around with you again, Mulcahy. Don't forget to remember me to McCool and Tibben." The slender redhead cocked an ear. "Hey, do you hear that singing? Sounds German."

Paddy turned his head. "Seems to be coming from down in that hollow. German, all right. They've sure done nothing to be singing about."

"There's a crowd gathering," Carr pointed. "Let's go over and see what's up."

Paddy checked the position of the sinking sun. "Can't waste too much time. Let's be quick about it."

The two hastened to a spot where an angry crowd of Union troops were gathering on the crest of a knoll. In a swale below, the 11th Corps Germans were singing lustily to the accompaniment of accordions and mouth organs:

"I've come shust now to tells you how,

I goes mit regimentals,

To schlauch dem voes of liberty

Like dem old Continentals
Vot fights mit England long ago
To save der Yankee Eagle:
Und now I gets my soldier clothes;
I'm going to fight mit Sigel."

"Cowards!" a battle-grimed sergeant roared contemptuously from the knoll.

"Yeah, you pretzel benders, dry up!" bellowed another. "Go back where you came from."

Not in the least fazed by the insults, to which they were accustomed, the men sang another verse:

"When I comes from der Deutsche countree,
I vorks sometimes at baking.
Den I keeps a lager beer saloon...."

The fellows listening, rankled by the behavior of the German Corps in previous battles and remembering how they caved in during the first day of fighting at Gettysburg, began pitching stones and shouting in unison, "Flee mit Sigel, und run mit Howard. Flee mit Sigel, und run mit Howard."

"We'd better pull boot out of here before a mob fight starts," Paddy murmured. "I've done enough fighting for one day."

The carrot-topped Irishman stood his ground. "Not me. If there's gonna be a donnybrook, I want to be in on it." He began unloading his paraphernalia. "Those damned Dutchmen have crapped out in every battle we've been in. It's time they learned a lesson."

"Don't be a fool. You'll only get into..."

"Flee mit Sigel, und run mit Howard!" Carr screamed in concert with the gathering mob.

The Dutchmen stopped singing and began scurrying for cover to escape flying missiles.

"Look at the square-heads run," jeered a bearded New Jersey private. "They're even afraid of stones."

"Let's rush 'em," another hooted. "Clean 'em out once'n for all."

Whipped to a frenzy by the ringleaders, the mob started to rush down the slope in pursuit of the retreating Germans only to be met head on by a cordon of Philadelphians from the 106th Pennsylvania, who faced them with fixed bayonets. The arrival of General Howard, who had come on horseback to investigate the uproar, further intimidated the surly crowd and they quickly dispersed.

"Look at 'em," Paddy said scornfully as he watched the rioters disperse. "Pleased as punch with themselves and grinning like monkeys. If the shoe was on the other foot, they wouldn't be so all-fired happy."

"What do you mean?"

"You know what I mean. How'd you like it when the Irish were stoned on the streets of Philadelphia? You like seeing the signs in employment offices which read, 'No Irish need apply' ? The Kensington massacre in fifty-eight, you approve of that? Two churches burned to the ground and eight hundred Catholics killed by the Know Nothings."

Carr forced a sickly grin. "That was different."

"Different my eyeballs. Persecution, whether for differences of religion, origin, or both, is still persecution. Six of one, a half-dozen of the other."

"Yeah, but the Dutchmen been asking for it. Instead of making themselves, well, like one of the crowd, they band together as Germans, not Americans."

Paddy began walking faster. "So they didn't want to become one of the crowd, is it? Then how about the New York Irish Brigade that flies the Irish Harp on equal footing with our national emblem? And the Irish Molly McGuires, those dirty draft-dodgers causing all the trouble up in the coal regions? Thousands of troops we could have used today stationed upstate to keep the rebellious Irish under control. And didn't you choose to join an all-Irish regiment that prides itself on being Irish manned and led?"

Carr fumbled with his trinkets as he hurried to catch up.

"That was because we have something in common. Besides, we never ran from the Rebs like those square-heads."

"Forget about the Dutchmen running off all the time. Maybe if we'd been in their shoes we'd have run, too."

Carr looked puzzled. "What are you getting so het up about? You never used to talk like this at home."

"Because I've been doing a lot of thinking lately."

"Thinking? About what?"

Paddy slowed his pace. "About the same sort of thing the Eleventh Corps got itself involved in." He frowned. "They said it was the Union we were fighting to preserve. Now the politicians have turned it into a war to free the slaves. We will win. The colored people will be free." His voice dropped off. "Free for what?" He turned and looked at his companion. "You think they'll be allowed to become 'one of the crowd' as you put it? Or will they be made 'outsiders' in the community, like us Irish, an oppressed class forced to band together for self-preservation?"

Carr remained silent for a moment. "They 're a different color from us," he offered awkwardly. "Only been out of the jungles little more than a hundred years. Got a different way of living than us. I wouldn't want to live next to them."

"We do back home," Paddy retorted.

Both soldiers jumped back to avoid being run down by a clattering troop of passing cavalry.

Paddy dusted off his blouse. He stopped to tie a shoelace. "What troubles me," he said, standing, "is how a union of people can survive when separate groups band together because of religious, national or color lines. A nation can't live healthy that way."

"Sure it can. If the coloreds want to stick to themselves, let them. They should. Who's going to hate them for that?"

"Mugs like the ones you just saw throwing stones at the Germans."

Carr toyed with a souvenir cartridge box. "Maybe you have something." He shrugged. "Maybe the trouble's like Monday morning garbage, it lies on both sides of the street."

The sound of a cavalry fight coming from the southwest grow louder and more distinct. It diverted Paddy's attention momentarily. He spoke slowly. "Guess I've seen too much death to stomach intolerance on the part of anybody, no matter what side of the street it comes from." He held out a hand. "Well, here's where I turn off. Good luck to you and the rest of the boys." His face broke into a smile. "You Irish Micks."

Carr shifted his heavy load of souvenirs and, wearing a curious expression, stared at the back of his departing companion. "Take care of yourself, Paddy," he shouted.

The previous gruesome aspects and activity of the 5th Corps emergency field hospital were almost completely absolved. Most of the wounded had been carted off in ambulance trains to Westminster, Maryland, for further treatment. Only two classes of patients remained. Those with minor injuries awaiting return to the line were lolling beneath shade trees and talking quietly among themselves. Some smoked pipes, some dozed in the hot sun, a few were writing letters. Those soldiers with wounds severe enough to preclude moving them lay pale and still in tents draped with mosquito netting. From these canvas shelters, the sonorous death rales of the dying blended with buzzing field insects and chirping birds.

Paddy drew back a fine mesh curtain swarming with maggot-laying bluebottle flies and entered one of the tents. He knelt beside a motionless form on one of the cots.

"Remember, Mulcahy," Doctor Thomas cautioned, "one minute. That's all."

"Yes, sir."

Opening his eyes, the Quaker smiled wanly and made a weak effort to speak. Beads of perspiration stood out on his forehead.

Paddy placed a soft hand on his shoulder. "John, it's me. How are you feeling? Don't answer. I shouldn't have asked a question. The doc says you have real 'bottom.' Wouldn't be surprised a bit if you were up walking in a week. What do you think of that?"

The Quaker's eyes closed.

Paddy struggled for words. "We clobbered them good today. The Philadelphia Brigade stopped the Rebs dead in their tracks."

The Quaker's eyes opened. He gave a faint nod.

"There were thousands of them. Made us sweat blue bolts just to see them coming at us. Waiting and knowing that soon they would be piling over us. It was like waiting for a twenty-foot wave to crash over your head, that's the way it felt. Never want to see that many men charging at me again."

An orderly poked his head into the tent. "Time's up, soldier."

"Right." Paddy wiped his sun-cracked lips with the back of his hand, then let it fall to touch the pale fingers stretched before him.

In a feeble effort to wave, the Quaker raised one arm several inches, then let it flop.

* * * * * * *

The Fourth of July dawned, fresh and clean, commemorating an old freedom and recognizing the nation's birth in liberty.

Tibben and McCool, their caps loaded to overflowing with wild berries gathered from the woods, pranced through bivouac of the 118th. Comrades were showered with handfuls of ripened fruit.

"Everybody pack a lunch," they chortled. Imitating the sprightly dance of Bacchus, they began sprinkling more berries as they sing-songed, "We're gonna have a picnic, we're gonna have a picnic."

"Go shoot yourself in the foot," came a disgruntled cry. Hallowell raised his weary frame on one elbow. "Don't you two ever light? You're worse'n the seven-year itch."

"Today's the Fourth," they cried.

"Faith'n I'll say it's a holiday," Sergeant Cassidy rasped as he stomped into the area. "Griffith, Clark, Rayson and Roberts deserted, took off durin' the night."

Men packing blanket rolls and preparing breakfast dropped what they were doing and shuffled around their sergeant.

"I don't believe it," Jobson said, sounding confused. "I knew Griff and Roberts well, they were good soldiers. Been with the regiment ever since it was formed."

"Just the same, they've gone over the hill," Cassidy retorted. "The way this army's been talkin' and actin', you'd think the war was over."

"Gee, desertin' on the Fourth," Tibben piped. "That's like kickin' your mother."

"Yeah, but you have to admit it's a real temptation," Dyer said. "We're pretty close to home."

Joe Sackett nodded agreement. "Yep, I'd sure like to walk east."

Several of the men looked at him angrily.

"I mean just for a short visit," he added hastily.

"Faith' n if there be any jack man of ye here what's harborin' intentions o' jumpin'," Cassidy said menacingly, "speak up. I'd be likin' the special privilege o' knockin' him apart with me bare hands." Placing doubled fists on his hips, he scowled. "No, is it? Then let's put an end to this disgrace. Nineteen desertions from jist this one regiment in the past three days."

"Say, Sarg, what about them fellas over there?" McCool chattered. "They gonna fight on our side now?"

He pointed to a group of four Confederate deserters huddled in conversation with Colonel Gwyn and Major Herring.

"Don't know yet. Up to the colonel, what he thinks about it. For meself, I don't care for deserters, no matter what side they come from."

One of the Rebel turncoats overheard the remark and looked around uneasily.

From another direction, Lieutenant Batchelder approached in his inimitable, easygoing manner. "Get the squad together, Andy. See that the men have filled cartridge boxes. We're moving forward at ten o'clock."

The men grumbled. "Moving forward? On the Fourth? Oh, come off it, Lieutenant, what for?"

"Have to take the enemy's pulse, that's what for. Meade wants to see how strong the Johnnies are feeling today."

An hour later the brigade moved to feel out the enemy. Winding their way around massive rocks, the blue lines descended the steep western slope of Little Round Top and filed through the gorge at Round Top's base. Spread about were ghastly scenes of blood and carnage. The dead lay in disarray, some on their faces, others on their backs, still others twisted and knotted in grotesque shapes. The progress of the advance was impeded as the living attempted to step around the dead. Some bodies were kneeling behind rocks where they had dropped for shelter. Men in the columns instinctively flinched as they saw rifle barrels aimed in their direction, guns frozen in the grip of glassy-eyed corpses who had been killed in the act of firing.

A number of the enemy lay in a shallow trench. In agony they had torn at the grass and their mouths were filled with dirt. They had literally bitten the dust. Several had been killed in the act of biting a plug of tobacco. At one spot thirty-seven bodies lay side by side their uniforms in better shape than most. All had on new black slouch hats doubtlessly purchased from a neighborhood dealer. In front of the bodies lay a handsome officer his head resting on a stone his limbs straight his hands folded as if prepared for death. The men found a letter on him through which a ball had passed and penetrated his heart. The letter identified him as Captain William A. Dunklin of the 44th Alabama.

The 118th pushed to the edge of the woods that bordered the memorable wheat field. Fearing that the remaining grain might conceal enemy pickets a skirmish line under Lieutenant Batchelder was sent ahead of the rest. They were met with a volley of fire as large bodies of Confederates appeared on either flank and a general movement in front indicated a willingness on their part to start an engagement. His mission to feel out the enemy accomplished Colonel Tilton ordered buglers to sound the recall. The skirmishers fell back on the brigade already formed in a battle line among the sheltering trees.

Overhead the sun appeared as a ruddy infarct caught in a gathering bank of black storm clouds. Heavy rumbles of thunder rolled down from the South Mountains. Javelin bolts of lightning speared the earth with a crashing bang. It grew dark. The heavens opened and rain fell in torrents. Drenched, the Union forces huddled together in the rain-lashed woods. Cap visors were pulled down over eyes and collars drawn tightly about their necks. They jammed their bayonets into the ground to hold the rifles upright and prevent water from running down the barrels.

The meadows overflowed quickly and fences disappeared with the raging streams. The torrential downpour was so unusual that the men were awed and speculated in hushed voices as to what it meant. It seemed to some that the Creator was displaying his displeasure by washing the battlefield and its occupants from the face of the earth.

Under cover of the storm Confederate wagons ambulances and artillery carriages assembled by the hundreds beyond Seminary Ridge. On the road leading from Gettysburg to Cashtown, there was one confused mass of the wheeled impedimenta of war and retreating, slump-backed soldiers. Canvas offered no protection against the fury of the strange maelstrom. Wounded Confederates, lying on the naked boards of wagon bodies, were soaked through. Horses and mules, blinded and maddened by the wind and rain, became unmanageable. The deafening roar of the commingled sounds from heaven and earth made it impossible to communicate orders, and equally difficult to execute them.

Efforts on the part of the Federal forces to engage the foe were suspended because of the freakish savagery of the elements.

Duncan Gilmour tugged at his leather boots, removed them and dumped the water out.

"Aye," he growled. "To think I gi' up a comfortable wagon seat to come sloggin' aroon like a webfoot."

"That's life," Jobson retorted. "If it ain't dust, it's mud. If it ain't blisters, it's foot rot. Sometimes people don't know when they're well off."

Sergeant Cassidy sat on the ground like a hog in a wallow, appearing perfectly content in the muck and mire and obviously enjoying the refreshing respite from the intense heat. His matted red hair and beard became a wet, stringy mop, draping his head.

"Hey, Sarg," McCool called, rain splattering off his lips, "how's chances of lettin' us fellas duck into that barn?"

"Barn? What barn?"

At that moment a loud crash of thunder and lightning illuminated the semi-darkness of the woods and outlined a large wooden structure several hundred yards away.

"Over there. See it?"

"Ye'll stay put right here, McCool. A bath'll do ye good."

"Aw..." His words were drowned by another heavy peal of thunder.

From nowhere, a lean figure, tall and bony, approached Lieutenant Batchelder. Garbed in an oilcloth raincoat pulled tightly around his frame, he wore a brown slouch hat pulled well over his ears.

"Where's your commanding officer?'' he demanded.

"Over there. Want to speak to him?"

The visitor growled something.

Colonel Tilton, sir, man here would like to talk with you."

The heavy-set commander sloshed to where the stranger stood. "Yes, what is it?" he inquired tersely.

The rain-coated figure raised an angry finger and shook it at him. "General, I want you to move your troops further out."

"Move further out? Preposterous. Who are you, sir?"

"Name's Timber. You're trespassin' on my land. Them's my house and outbuildings. They'll be ruined when you and them Southerners start fightin'. Don't want no heavy shot and shell tearin' across my propity." A resentful murmur ran through the group standing around.

"Should be offerin' us shelter, not drivin' us out," a voice growled.

"Probably one of them dollar-happy Dutchmen what lives around here," muttered another.

Colonel Tilton glared at the man and thrust the tip of his wet nose in the intruder's face. "This army's taken a lot of civilian guff from what should be loyal supporters, but you take the cake, mister."

"Don't see why," the farmer said unflinchingly. "One place's good as another for fightin'."

Tilton reached out, took hold of the farmer's raincoat and, drawing him close, hissed, "Now you listen to me, mister. These boys don't put in any preference as to what spot they want to get killed or maimed in. 'Bout time you people at home learned to sacrifice along with them. My orders are to hold this ground and that's exactly what I intend to do."

The farmer squirmed loose. "But I've built everything here with my own hands. Surely you could..."

"You ever seen a nice-looking eighteen year-old boy blown to bits, mister?" Tilton bellowed above the storm.

The farmer drew back, his lips twisted. "Then you're not going to move and protect my property, eh?"

"You've got it exactly right. These boys are staying put."

"We will see about that. I know my rights. I'll go see General Meade. I got property rights."

"Go right ahead, sir. I'm sure he will rearrange the whole battlefield just to suit your wishes."

McCool, gripped by a diabolical urge, cupped wet hands to his mouth and shouted at the departing land owner. "Hey, Rube! Think the weather will affect the price of rhubarb?"

A ripple of laughter ran down the drenched column of veterans.

"That will be enough," Tilton ordered sternly. He turned to Captain Donaldson. "I don't foresee any fighting or movement so long as this weather continues, Captain. Post pickets at once, we'll bivouac here for the night."

"Yes, sir. Any fires?"

"No fires. Way things are soaked, the men couldn't keep one going with a clinker from hell." The commander turned and strode off in the downpour.

"Batch," Donaldson called, "who's up for picket duty?"

"Jobson. Kelly, Kimball, McCool and Mulcahy. And it's Ashbrook's turn to go out, not mine."

"All right. Go find yourself a puddle and turn in. I'll hunt up Joe."

In a short time the picket detail was snaking its way forward through the trampled, soggy wheat field. Twenty-year old Tom Kelly, with a blue-eyed Irish face of cameo handsomeness, a trap for the unwary masking his inner toughness, shouldered his way to Paddy's side.

"There's pigs in here eating on the dead, saw them earlier when our skirmish line went through. Don't be trigger happy if something moves sudden at your feet."

"Don't worry, Kelly, I've been around."

"Didn't mean it that way. Just thought you'd like to know."

"Sure, Kelly. Thanks."

Putting the wheat field behind them, the pickets entered another patch of woods and were posted near the advance position which they had held during the second day's battle.

Surveying the situation from his deep-socketed eyes, Lieutenant Ashbrook turned and said, "So far, so good, eh Mulcahy? It's my idea the Johnnies have pulled stakes for home. What do you think?"

"Seems that way. Sure is quiet out here."

"Well, just the same we'd better be on guard. Take a place up by that rock and keep your eye on that farmhouse below. If the Rebs left a rear guard, that's where they'll be. May try to fake an attack to throw us off balance. Keep a sharp lookout. See you later."

"Right."

Because of the raging storm, night settled in an hour earlier than usual. Paddy drew a water-logged blanket tight around his chilled body. The length of time he spent staring into the pitch black night became a subject for mental conjecture, a game by which to keep himself awake.

It was after midnight when out in front of him he heard a crackling sound that indicated stealthy movement. He raised his rifle and commanded, "Halt. Who goes there?"

The movement stopped abruptly, then started in a different direction. Whoever the intruder was, he seemed to be trying to encircle him.

"Halt, or I'll shoot."

"Shoot and be damned, Yank."

He saw a burst of flame not twenty paces away and felt the weight of lead pound into his left thigh, the force of which unbalanced him. Recovering, he drew a bead on the spot and shot in retaliation. There was a gurgling cry of anguish, then silence. The weight in his leg became a throb of hot, searing pain as the limb buckled weakly. Placing a hand in his pocket, he withdrew it with a sick feeling. It was sticky with blood.

"You all right?" Ashworth called anxiously from his post.

"Got shot in the leg. Think the bone's been hit."

"Can you hold out? If not, you'd better retire."

"I'll stick."

* * * * * * *

The morning sun of July fifth filtered into the sodden area of the 5th Corps field hospital with its warm rays. Dr. Thomas laid aside a bone curette and began scrubbing his hands.

An orderly commented impassively. "He's coming out of it, sir. Do you want him to have more chloroform?"

"No. That's all we can do now. Pack the wound with bisthmus, iodoform and petrolatum."

"Yes, sir. Think you'll have to cut it off?"

"Not unless sequestrum of the bone sets in."

Paddy's head swam like a drunk. Stabbing pains from his leg began breaking through the effects of the anesthetic as he twisted and turned, fighting for a comfortable position.

The regimental surgeon, noting his patient's revival, squatted by his side. "How do you feel?"

Through thick lips, Paddy tried to reply.

"Don't worry, Mulcahy, you'll be all right. We'll be moving you shortly. The Rebs have pulled out and the college buildings will make excellent recovery wards."

Paddy lapsed into semi-consciousness. When he came to he was in the clean white interior of the Gettysburg College's administration building. The commodious room was jammed to capacity with clean emergency cots lined up in facing rows. The hot, stifling atmosphere reeked with the odors of putrefying flesh, choking anesthetics and pungent packings of iodoform. Gray-gowned ladies of the Christian Commission walked softly among the men and administered aid.

A severely wounded soldier cried deliriously, "Please, somebody, turn my face toward the flag before I die. Please, somebody turn...."

Others in less pain discussed in low tones the latest turn of events, the lifting of the siege of Vicksburg after seven months meant that the Mississippi River had finally been cleared and the South split in two.

Outside an open window by his bed, Paddy could see Orson Osborne of Company F struggling valiantly with a hideous armful of amputated limbs which he was burying. As he passed by, a group of recent amputees, complacently engaged in a game of cards, accosted him.

"Hey, there, Billy, come here a minute. Want to see if I can find my leg in that pile you're carrying."

"Go to hell," Osborne retorted. "I got 'nough trouble without searching for your parts."

"That ain't no way to talk to a poor cripple," chided the soldier from First Michigan. "Recollect my leg can be easily distinguished from the others by a carbuncle on the little toe. It gave me a lot of trouble. I'd just like to see how the ugly parasite is thriving without me."

Osborne glanced at his ghastly cargo. "Look, fella, if you believe in the resurrection of the body as a good Christian should, you can wait till judgment to take a look at your missing leg."

"Good enough," the amputee agreed and returned to his card game.

The hospital blanket on which he lay caused Paddy to squirm incessantly in an effort to get comfortable. During one of his twisting gyrations, his gaze fell on the solemn face of Captain Donaldson as he appeared in the doorway of the hospital ward. Halting a moment to speak with a nurse, who pointed in Paddy's direction, he came down the narrow aisle. Paddy hunched his body into a sitting position and waved a greeting.

"This will teach you not to play with fireworks on the Fourth," Donaldson said as he tapped the bandaged limb. "How's it feel to get shot up on a national holiday?"

"It doesn't feel good to get shot up on any day. But, say," his expression clouded, "how come you and the boys aren't hi-tailing after the Rebs? Meade got the 'slows' like McClellan and the rest?"

"Yes, but not without reason." Donaldson sat gingerly on the side of the cot. "This bother your leg?"

"No."

He patted it gently. "To answer your question. Meade took eighty-thousand infantrymen into this battle, there's forty-two thousand of us left."

Paddy closed his eyes, calculating. He opened them and asked, "We take thirty-eight-thousand casualties?"

"Not quite. Battle casualties were twenty-three thousand, but another fifteen thousand have been jarred loose as deserters, skulkers, and the sick, real or imaginary."

"Good Lord, that many?"

"The First Corps has been reduced to the size of an ordinary division. Reynolds, the best we had, is dead. Second Corps is cut to ribbons, Hancock is severely wounded and put out of action, along with most of the division commanders. Third Corps is a depleted skeleton, Sickles is hors-de-combat with an amputated leg. The Eleventh Corps is worthless, and so is Howard. Twelfth Corps is a question mark under Slocum."

Paddy shifted positions. "So that leaves the Sixth under Sedgewick and our Fifth under Sykes in halfway decent shape."

"That's it. Hardly enough to encourage an offensive attack against the Rebs, who are still in pretty solid shape from all reports."

"Think they'll get back across the Potomac scot free?"

"Probably."

"Bloody hell!"

"Costly fight. Many of our finest combat units have been destroyed on this field. The Iron Brigade for one, the Fifth New Hampshire, Sully's First Minnesota, Second Massachusetts and the Sixteenth Maine. Another group will soon be among the missing, but I'll guarantee no tears will be shed over them."

"Who's that?"

"The Eleventh Corps, the Dutchmen. Because of their wild flight the first day, the astounding number of prisoners lost, and their inability to keep the Rebs out of the guns on Cemetery Hill the night of the second, they're being shipped out west lock, stock and barrel. Right now their reputation and morale's so low it's got to reach up to touch bottom."

"I can imagine. But speaking of the West, how 'bout that fella Grant? Hear he bagged over thirty-one thousand prisoners at Vicksburg. Two large victories for our side and both coming at the same time, and on the Fourth of July at that."

"Yes, looks like it could be the beginning of the end."

Paddy stiffened, his voice an esoteric murmur. "Time of the end. Darius Mede...."

"What's the matter? You all right? Here, better lie down."

"No, I'm clear. It's what the colored mammy told the boys at Aldie, from the Bible. The King of the South shall push at the King of the North, we'd be led by

Mede. From a mount we would crush them and take their fenced city. Don't you see?" His voice rose, "the mount meant Round Top, Vicksburg was the fenced city."

"Uh huh. Could be. But for me, I like something with teeth in it."

"Like...?"

"Like Meade gaining victory here at Gettysburg on the same day that Pemberton surrenders Vicksburg to Grant. Meade, Pemberton, two close neighborhood friends from Philadelphia, bosom companions, one takes command for the North, the other goes South."

"By gosh, that's right. Almost slipped my mind. Been a busy three days for us boys from the City of Brotherly Love."

A sharp, shooting pain twisted one side of Paddy's face into a grimace. "Say, would you mind rubbing my left ankle? Damned thing tingles. Hurts too much to bend and do it myself."

"Be glad to." Donaldson started kneading the afflicted area. A heavy growth of black sideburns accentuated his powerful nose, firm lips and dimpled chin.

"Tell me," Paddy asked, looking fatigued, "do you think the regiment'll be moving south any time soon?"

"Very soon, or I miss my guess. The Sixth Corps and the Twelfth have already got their orders. Our Corps will probably follow next."

"So it's gonna be 'Carry Me Back to Old Virginny.' How do the boys feel about it?"

"Hard to tell. For one thing, the demonstrative and enthusiastic attitude of this army is not what it used to be. The boys have been stood up too often, two years of hard campaigning has increased their experience and made them cautious. They are more chary with their cheers and shouts."

Donaldson gave Paddy's ankle a soft whack. "There, how's that feel?"

"Much better, thanks."

"After what happened this morning, I'd say the army prefers to await results and come to conclusions before indulging in an untimely celebration. Business sense is developing. Until the fruits of its victories are safely garnered, the men consider it wise to refrain from any open expression of appreciation."

"What happened this morning to make you say that?"

Closing an eye, Donaldson gave one ear a thoughtful tug. "A rather awkward and embarrassing incident for the colonel. When Gwyn finished publishing a congratulatory order announcing success at Gettysburg, you could have heard a pin drop. The boys just stood there with a 'so what' expression on their faces. Then, when his urgent appeals still failed to secure responsive cheers for the commander in chief, he impudently did his own hurrahing."

"Yow! I'll bet that left the boys cold. Glad I wasn't there. Gwyn blow up?"

"Like an overloaded boiler, his Irish temper exploded all over the lot."

"I'm damned glad I wasn't there."

Donaldson spoke slowly. "Don't misunderstand this silence on the part of your comrades. It came from no lack of regard for General Meade, or any want of appreciation of his abilities. The regiment just couldn't see the wisdom or occasion for a show of enthusiasm. They know a great burden's just been lifted right here from the neck of the nation, but they also see, more clearly than most people, that long days of bloody war still lie ahead before the South can be brought to submission."

He slapped Paddy's sound leg, stood up and stared out through a window. Bandaged soldiers were sprawled on the tree-shaded lawn and ambulances rumbled to and fro on the dusty roadway. "Well," he said, "guess it's goodbye for a while. Going to miss you, fella."

Paddy's lips puckered and trembled. "Not for long. I'll be rejoining you and the boys real soon."

Donaldson buckled on a sword belt and picked up his hat. "I hope so, but I have my doubts. I'm afraid we'll not see much of you once you get back to the peaceful quiet of Bucks County."

"Bucks County? What makes you think I'll be going there?"

"Didn't Doc Thomas tell you? You're ticketed for the Andalusia Army Hospital above Croyden on the Delaware."

"The devil you say. Didn't know they had a hospital in that area. Must have taken over Bristol College or the China Retreat mansion." His spirits rose. "Boy, that'll be great. How soon'll we be leaving?"

"Soon as the tracks are repaired between here and York. In a fit of rage, Stuart tore them up following his defeat by Gregg's Cavalry on the third."

"York? Last Sunday this time, I was just entering that town. Seems ages ago."

"Everything seems ages ago," Donaldson replied with a frown. He added playfully, "I forgot to tell you, Joe Tibben will be going along with you."

"Squeaky? Did he get wounded again?"

"Not this time." The sparkle of laughter, dormant since his brother's death, returned to the black pupils in his deep blue eyes. "He was clowning around as usual last night when he tripped in a bucket and broke an ankle. McCool claims he did it on purpose He calls him, 'Bucket-foot Joe for the furlough show. "'

"He's good company. It'll be nice having him along." Paddy's face became sober as he reached for the captain's arm. "One thing before you go. Will you do me a favor?"

"Course I will. What is it?"

"On that long walk south you'll, well, I imagine you'll be passing through Leesburg. Stop in and see Becky for me? Tell her I'm all right. Tell her I'll come to her as soon as I can walk."

Donaldson nodded.

"And Frank, ask her to write about the baby."

* * * * * * *

Throughout the next three days, a dull, heavy rain fell continuously, dreary days during which the healthy body of the Potomac Army packed up and departed, severing relations with their injured. They marched south in pursuit of Lee's retreating forces.

Gloomy weather cloaked the emergency field hospitals set up in churches and public buildings in and around Gettysburg, wet weather with a penetrating dampness that cast a spell of depression over those left behind. On Thursday the dripping curtain raised, the sun shone with a purpose and the pleasant warmth of summer again comforted the sick.

Late that morning, a shuttle service of ambulances began transporting bandaged cargo to a railroad depot where boxcars, bedded with straw for the injured, waited on a siding.

At the loading point, cases were sorted into three classifications. Those who could sit up were directed to cars with empty ammunition boxes to sit on. Men unable to hold themselves upright were laid side by side on their backs in another section. With the amputees there was a different arrangement. Discovering that men took up less room if they lay on their backs, leg cases were grouped accordingly. If a man had lost his right leg, he could lie on his left side. They fit together like spoons.

Assigned to a crowded car under the second classification, Paddy managed to secure a choice place near the door, where he settled back and waited with half-closed eyes. Three short blasts from the stack of the locomotive and the loaded hospital train grated and ground slowly out of Gettysburg. At a snail's pace, it proceeded to traverse the green countryside of Southern Pennsylvania.

Doors of the wooden cars were thrown wide open for cross ventilation, permitting those in favored positions to watch the scenery. Farmers could be seen hard at work in the fields, ruggedly independent rustics busy with their harvest appeared here and there as moving specks on the landscape. Straw hats pushed back on their heads, chins resting on scythe handles, they stopped to gaze with expressionless faces at the crawling train carrying the harvest of war.

It was three hours later when they finally rumbled into York, Pennsylvania, and a majority of the wounded were removed, distributed by carriage to tent hospitals erected on the Penn Common and the fairgrounds.

An orderly grumbled outside the open door near which Paddy braced himself.

"How come these Philadelphia boys gotta be chauffeured another hundred miles? They ain't so special. Why can't they get off here like the rest?"

"If they wanta have truck with more ridin' in this blisterin' heat just to be near home, let 'em," a voice replied. "Feel the same way if I was them."

"Sure, but you don't have to make the trip with 'em. I do. It stinks to high hell in them cars."

The other man laughed. "Ride with your head hangin' out."

Just then the face of Joe Tibben poked through the opening. "Anybody in here named Mulcahy?" he yelled.

Paddy turned his head. "Yeah, over here Bucket-foot. Come aboard."

"You got room?"

"Plenty."

"Good, only don't call me by that name."

"You mean Buck..."

"Forget it." Tibben made a wry face and pulled his small body over the door sill. He smelled of creosote.

A smile trickled from the corners of Paddy's mouth. "Heard you were in a tough fight."

"Ah, cut it off, will ya? I'll never live this down." He glanced at his splinted ankle. "Say, guess who I just seen peekin' through the crowd out there?"

Paddy clenched a piece of straw between his teeth.

"Who?"

"Them Dutchmen that deserted us after Shepherdstown. Think we oughta turn 'em in?"

A sharp pain tore through Paddy's leg. He rolled his head sideways. "What's the use? They're mugs and they'll always be mugs. Can't change a leopard's spots."

There was a sudden jolt followed by several lurches as emptied cars were uncoupled from the rest of the train. Invalid passengers, rolled over like dice by the jostling, moaned and groaned and righted themselves into position. An amputee gave his crutch a vicious pitch. "Son of a bitch. Don't the driver of this egg crate know he's got soft shells aboard?"

"Must be a new apprentice," someone growled.

"Yes, and still learnin'. A real herky jerky," the amputee replied.

Several more abortive starts and stops, one on top of the other, followed in quick succession until at last the abbreviated rolling stock moved slowly toward Philadelphia. Open fields and rolling hills came into view again, basking in sunlight while hardly a breath of air stirred. It was one of those oppressively close afternoons when humidity hangs low in the air, a steaming vapor rag. Little time passed before sweat paled heads began bobbing and bending beneath the soporific influences of the continuous cradling movement of the swaying cars and the monotonous clicking of the wheels. One by one the weary wounded fell off to sleep.

Waning twilight merged with the hot summer night. Iron wheels clacked incessantly on the rails. Darkened interiors became filled with the sound of snores and muffled groans. It was one of those times, either early or late, and difficult to determine which, when an invisible hand seems to rouse a body by inexorably shaking the subconscious, causing one to awaken before fully ready. Paddy's eyelids flickered, opened a crack, closed, and then opened again. The swaying car was dark and silent, the gray light of dawn sneaking its way through the door space opposite him. He took a deep breath and a wonderful woodsy freshness came riding in on a gentle breeze.

Wide awake, Tibben sat in the doorway, his legs dangling over the side.

Paddy raised himself up on one elbow. "Where are we, Joe?"

Tibben turned. "Just passing through Torresdale. Went through Frankford junction half an hour ago."

"Why didn't you wake me?"

"What, and get a broken nose in the bargain? I got enough trouble. Look, old man Landreth's seed nursery." He sniffed. "Hmm, sure smells good, huh?"

Paddy squirmed to get a better view, his eyes feasting on the familiar scene.

Tibben bubbled. "Sure beats anything I seen in Virginia. Boy, just look at that Delaware. Could go for a swim right now."

"Me too, only it's a case of the spirit being willing where the flesh is weak. Look out the other side, Joe. Can you see the Red Lion Inn?"

Tibben rose stiffly, hobbled to the opposite side of the boxcar and peered out. "Yep. Can just make it out through the trees. Still up there on the creek. Got some lights burning. Carriage just driving away." He paused. His voice was full of melancholy. "Remember how we used to play soldiers in Washington 's army? Stopping off at the Red Lion after the battle of Trenton? You always used to be Colonel McLane, the cavalry guerrilla chief."

Paddy closed his eyes. "I remember. War was just a game then. Now...." He was silent. "How did that old school poem go?

Kind Mater smiles again to me,
As bright as when we parted,
I seem again the frank, the free,
Stout-limbed. and simple-hearted."

He lay back with his head cupped in the palms of his hands and closed his eyes.

* * * * * * *

Bristol College, taken over by the government for hospital purposes, was a large rambling brick mansion pillared in front and veneered with white plaster, in many respects resembling the White House at the nation's Capitol. Early on that Friday morning of July tenth, the hospital began receiving the wounded from Gettysburg, a pleasant haven of refuge where broken bodies could mend or pass quietly on to the grave.

Removed from the rigors of war, an incentive for living returned as the men enjoyed the spacious landscaped lawns surrounding the structure, beset with beautiful old shade trees and rose gardens. There was an open air solarium for walking patients and, for those in wheel chairs, a peaceful retreat in which to sit with comrades, heads bent whiling time away over games of cribbage, checkers or whist. A place where on weekends the graveled paths swelled with visiting relatives arriving by rail and carriage from the city and surrounding villages to be with loved ones, bringing gifts of jelly and cake. Mothers, wives, sisters and sweethearts—Victorian ladies all-promenading beneath gay frilly parasols and lending the light touch of home and hearth.

The Delaware, flowing in close proximity, lapped contentedly at grass-carpeted banks, its sparkling waters offering a delightful source of splashing therapy for those able-bodied enough to swim. A dulcet interlude for the bedridden was the mid-afternoon passage of the *River Queen* as it churned a frothy wake between Trenton and Philadelphia. Sound, smoke and sight of the steamer became a crutch for flagging spirits, a kindly visit from an old friend, an anticipated ritual.

Every day the ponderous side-wheeler drew abreast of the army hospital and slipped by in midstream. To listening ears came the salute of three short toots blown from the steam whistle at the hand of Captain Hinkle, a token remembrance of those devilish little boys he once knew who often hitched rides aboard his vessel, men now lying invalid.

On the national scene a great change in the order of war procedures was taking place, the inception of which had originated months before in the Oval Office of the White House. The President had heard of Colonel Wistar's acts and observations on the extravagant, inefficient and corrupt weaknesses of the volunteer system and called him in for private consultation. On two separate occasions, Lincoln had given Wistar a considerable portion of his time for the discussion of the best means of correcting a difficulty which he kept hearing about regarding the inherent problems with the methods of army organization.

Wistar spoke forthrightly. "Mister President, in every respect the volunteer system is the worst, most wasteful method ever conceived. After firsthand observation in the field, I believe it is speaking within bounds to say that a large proportion of the officers obtained that way are morally or physically worthless and must be discarded at the cost of delay and expense in order to reach efficiency. The system of commissioning the promoters of enlistments in proportion to the number they obtain or in accordance with the votes of those under their command, is not only fatal to discipline, even with individuals otherwise qualified, but brings into responsible positions a lot of rascals whose inability has paralyzed the army."

From these and other consultations, the Draft Act finally emerged, the inauguration and enforcement of which was to be put into effect.

On Saturday, July 11, one day after the wounded from Gettysburg arrived at Andalusia, the net was lowered. Crippled veterans sat back to read newspaper accounts of the new innovation.

In New York City, seventy miles away, a blindfolded agent picked twelve hundred names out of a draft wheel. The names drawn were published and those men would soon be in uniform and serving their country. They would have to march until their legs buckled, camp outdoors in winter's cold and summer's heat, survive on scant rations of the worst sort, serve under generals the newspapers labeled ignorant and incompetent and all the while face the specter of death, maiming or becoming a prisoner-of-war. For all of this they would be paid twenty-seven cents a day. There was an escape clause. Any man having three hundred dollars could buy his freedom from the draft. "A rich man's war and a poor man's fight," ran the talk in five thousand saloons and as many homes.

Anarchy and insurrection were fanned by angry outbursts from newspapers and copperhead Democrats. The cry spewed forth, "The poor will become the fodder of a tyrannical and oppressive Republican government which daily violates the Constitution and fundamental law of the land."

Paddy read with disbelief that at a mass meeting of Democrats in Concord, New Hampshire, Franklin Pierce, former President of the United States and a close friend of Jefferson Davis, hurled contempt at the government in Washington and expressed sympathy with the government in Richmond. "What a load of bunk," he said aloud. "Accepting Pierce's arguments we should all desert and join the Rebel army!"

In another newspaper account, Governor Seymour of New York heaped coal on the fire and echoed Pierce's sentiments in a speech at the New York Academy of Music, claiming the country was on the verge of destruction because of government coercion, "...seizing our persons, infringing upon our rights, insulting our homes, and depriving us of those cherished principles for which our fathers fought."

Paddy let the newspaper articles fall to the floor. He swore under his breath and turned to Michael Keady from the 42nd New York, who lay in the next cot. "What do you make of all this, Keady?"

"There'll be hell to pay, Mulcahy." Keady's dark eyes were deep set and overhung by thick black eyebrows. The bandaged stump where his left arm had been appeared to twitch. "Just hope my brother, Patrick, can keep his painters union out of it."

"Out of what?"

"Riots, me bucko. Riots. These fancy-born politicians don't know the temperament of the two hundred thousand Irish immigrants in New York City. Most of them are shanty Irish, not lace curtain, and you know what that means. They are dirt poor and don't like the war, or the Republican Party.

"The Republican capitalists have been bringing in black contrabands to work at cheaper wages and break strikes. There's racial hatred, believe me." Keady shifted to a more comfortable position. "The shanty Irish believe the Republicans brought on the war, inflation, high taxes and now a draft that singles out poor men who are needed at home to feed the family. They take their marching orders from Boss Tweed and the Democrats."

"Meaning what?"

"They'll take these preachy words from the copperheads and transform them into something a peasant can understand, rise up and revolt!"

Paddy's voice was barely audible. "Good God. It can't be true."

Keady reached for the Journal of Commerce at the foot of his bed. "You wait and see. I live on the East side, Eleventh Ward. I know the way things work. We're family. Birds of a feather flock together." He paused to clear his throat. "I fear for the blacks when this thing blows."

The pain in Paddy's leg was unbearable. He rolled over and tried to sleep.

The dire predictions of Keady were brought to fulfillment in bold headlines that screamed out from the front pages of New York's *Herald, Times* and *Tribune* that were delivered to the hospital wards on Tuesday, July 14th, and each successive day. Anarchy and insurrection had taken New York City by the throat on Monday the 13th in the form of draft riots. In stunned disbelief, the veterans at Andalusia read the reports of murder, rape and arson. Drafted men, along with their relatives and friends, reinforced by thousands of sympathizers, had gathered on vacant lots with clubs, staves, cart rungs and pieces of iron. With axes they had chopped down telegraph poles and torn up car tracks. Central Park acted as an assembly point, where they organized and began patrolling the city, venting their wrath and vengeance on draft offices which they wrecked and burned.

By the second and third day, there came livid newspaper reports of a general uprising of the masses against a government supposedly discriminating in its conscription between the rich and the poor. Criminal gang elements numbering between fifty to seventy thousand swarmed out of their hovels for loot and the diabolical joy of seeing the hated Metropolitan Police defied and overrun.

On Paddy's right a young private lay stretched out on his cot. His blinded eyes were swathed in bandages moistened with hyposulphite soda. He extended a pale hand in Paddy's direction. "Would you read to me what's in the papers?" he asked in a feeble voice.

"Sure you want to hear it, Tim?"

"Yes."

"Well, the mob has taken power from the police and law enforcement. They're trying to seize the armories, guns and munitions supplies and also the US. Treasury vaults and the surplus funds of banks. The United States Provost Marshal was driven from his office at Forty-third Street and Third Avenue and the draft wheels were burned along with the entire building. All stores and banks are closed. Orderly citizens are being kept off the streets. Private homes are being torched and pillaged. The entire block on Third Avenue from Forty-sixth to Forty-seventh street has been destroyed by fire and a whole block on Broadway between Twenty-fourth and Twenty-fifth streets has been burned to the ground." He paused to turn a page. "A crowd of ten thousand smashed the doors and windows and sacked the home of Mayor Opdyke. At midnight the home of Postmaster Abraham Wakeman was stripped of furniture, oil was poured over everything and then set on fire. The mob have been burning hotels, drugstores, clothing stores, factories, saloons where they were refused free liquor, police stations, a Methodist church, a Protestant mission, and—Holy God—the Colored Orphan Asylum at Forty-third Street and Lexington Avenue."

Tim turned his head. "An orphan asylum?"

Paddy continued to read in measured tone. "At the orphan asylum, the colored children were led out a back door to safety except for one little child who had hidden under a bed. When discovered by the mob, she was pulled out and beaten to death." His eyes skipped down the page. "Negroes are being chased down the streets and the corpses of dozens hang by the neck from lampposts, their bodies horribly mutilated. The Negro population, fearing for their lives, are fleeing to New Jersey." Paddy cast the paper aside.

The young soldier placed a hand over his bandaged eyes. "Who do they say is responsible?" he asked in a murmur.

"From all reports, the Irish Catholics," Paddy replied.

There was a moment of silence. Tim spoke in a plaintive voice. "Is this really a 'Rich Man's War,' as they say?"

Paddy stared at the ceiling. "That was my father's opinion. He figured slavery would eventually die a natural death."

Tempers in the ward were beginning to run high. A heavily bearded Pennsylvania mountain man from the Bucktail regiment was reading aloud from the *New York Times*. "The Invalid Corps, troops still crippled by battle wounds, faced a surly mob at Thirty-fifth Street and was greeted by a shower of paving stone and brickbats. Ordered to open fire on the rioters, they killed six men and one woman. Infuriated, the thousands turned like mad dogs on the soldiers, charging them before they could reload. Having wrested their guns, they clubbed the soldiers with their own muskets until they turned and fled." The Bucktail exploded in a rage. "Christ Almighty, what's the matter with you New York Micks!" He flung a bedpan at Keady's cot. "This is fornicating Irish treason!" he shouted.

Keady sat upright. "Watch your mouth, sucker, or I'll come over and take your other leg off!"

A burly orderly bounded down the aisle, his eyes blazing and teeth bared. "There'll be no swearing in this ward. Got it!"

His presence was met with silence.

Keady struggled for composure. His amputated stump sent sparks flying through his body. He finally found his voice. "Listen to me, Bucktail, there are thousands of good Irishmen patrolling the streets to put down the riots. If you look on page three, you'll see that my brother, Patrick, is one of them."

"Yeah," another Irishman called out from along the row of cots. "If you want to point a finger, try the copperhead Democrats who stirred up this mess. Now that four hundred people have been killed or wounded, they're crying for law and order!"

Keady swung both legs over the side of his bed and stood erect. He looked about with dark cavernous eyes and spoke in a soft voice. "Have you read this notice that Archbishop Hughes has had placarded all over the city? I'll read it for you. 'To the men of New York, who are called rioters: Men, I'm not able to visit you, owing to rheumatism, but that is not a reason why you should not pay me a visit. Come to my residence tomorrow at two o'clock, at the northwest corner of Madison Avenue and Thirty-sixth Street. I will have a speech prepared for you.'" Keady lay aside the newspaper from which he had been reading. "I think we should stuff all this religious bigotry until we hear what the Archbishop has to say."

An abolitionist soldier in a far corner jumped to his feet and shook a fist. "Your fine archbishop has made no secret of his Southern sympathy. He's openly come out against emancipating the black slaves!" Keady shrugged weary shoulders and lay down on his cot.

Paddy turned his head in Keady's direction. "Michael, does trash breed poverty, or does poverty breed trash?"

"Which came first, the chicken or the egg?" came an angry reply.

"The chicken. It was created."

A half smile crossed Keady's face. "Well, then, there you have it."

The Saturday morning newspaper delivered to Andalusia gave front page treatment to the Roman Catholic meeting which had been held on Friday. The entire ward read in silence that at the appointed time a crowd of nearly five thousand greeted Archbishop Hughes as he made an appearance on the balcony, clothed in purple robes and other insignia of office, surrounded by priests and influential citizens of the Roman Catholic Church. Responding to the loud applause, he spoke in a fatherly voice, explaining that a man had the right to defend his house for just cause. "I have been hurt by the reports of rioting. You cannot imagine that I could hear those things without being grievously pained. Is there not some way you can stop such proceedings and support the laws, none of which has been enacted against you as Irishmen and Catholics? You have suffered enough already. Would it not be better for you to retire quietly? Not give up your principles or convictions, but to keep out of the crowd where immortal souls are launched into eternity and, at all events, get into no trouble till you are at home? Would it not be better? There is one thing in which I would ask your advice. When the so-called riots are over, and the blame justly laid on Irish Catholics, I wish you to tell me in what country I could claim to be born?"

"Ireland," came the lusty reply.

"Yes, but what shall I say if those stories be true? Ireland, that never committed an act of cruelty until she was oppressed, Ireland, that has been the mother of heroes and poets, but never the mother of cowards. I thank you for your kindness, and I hope nothing will occur till you return home; if by chance you meet a police officer or military man on your way home, just look at him; do not throw anything or say anything."

Admonition from the Roman Catholic Archbishop and the arrival of ten thousand picked infantry, cavalry and artillery from the Army of the Potomac quickly put an end to the riots. The hard-bitten troops pulled from the front lines made it obvious they would tolerate no nonsense from Irish Catholics opposed to the war.

A postscript to the riots appeared several weeks later in the *New York Tribune* and it caught Paddy's eye. The report stated that Secretary of War Benjamin, of the Confederate Government, had summoned Lieutenant Capston and a Roman Catholic priest during the riots and sent both to Ireland to agitate against Irish workingmen emigrating to America, the emissaries advising the Irish that they would be promised jobs as railroad builders, but the real object of the Lincoln government was to lure them into the army.

Confederate-made posters were circulated among Irish priests with the headlines: "Persecution of Catholics in America!" "The Tabernacle Overthrown!" "The Blessed Host Scattered on the Ground!" "Benediction Veil Made a Horse Cover Of!" and "All the Sacred Vessels Carried Off!"

Paddy studied the report further. "The Confederate emissary, Father John Bannon, distributed an address to the Catholic Clergy and People of Ireland, as a six column newspaper sheet, alleging that Catholic churches had been burned by Union soldiers and Catholics ruthlessly shot down in the streets of Northern cities."

When he finished reading the newspaper account, he passed it over to Keady to read.

"The damn Rebs don't overlook a bet, do they?" Keady said when he handed the article back to Paddy. "I wonder how the *Tribune* got hold of this information?" Paddy gave a bemused chuckle. "I know a woman in Richmond who could have obtained it for them."

CHAPTER 20

Days rolled into weeks and weeks slipped into months at Andalusia. July gave way to sultry August and with September came Indian Summer. An ugly phlegmon developed in Paddy's thigh which refused to heal. The attending escharotic packings kept him in constant pain.

Few of his friends or acquaintances remained, many were discharged, others recuperated and returned to active duty. Tibben was assigned to the Invalid Corps because of an anchylosis in his fractured tarsal joint. In Frankford, Aunt Virginia and Uncle Peter Marks had gone to their reward in Heaven, passing away quietly within two weeks of each other.

There had been no word from Becky, no word from Captain Donaldson, nor from any of his comrades. Fretting, Paddy began to brood. His whole world had become meaningless.

War in the East had come to a standstill. Gettysburg had taken too much out of both armies. The eyes of the Nation turned toward war in the West.

In mid-October, the wound in his leg finally began to heal and he received permission to take his first long walk with the aid of a cane. Bundled in a warm greatcoat to ward off the autumn chill, he limped north over the river road, hoping to reach the estuary where the placid Neshaminy emptied into the broad Delaware.

The air was like wine and smelled of apples. Frost was bringing out the fall colors along the river, splashing leaves with her paintbrush and robing the hills in beauty. The wooded slopes on the Jersey shore appeared in the thin golden sunlight as a fine Persian carpet with sharp colors blended to a softness. It was good just to be alone in his beloved valley. He felt vitality surge through his body, an intoxicating feeling that increased with every inhalation of cool air and every faltering step he took along the familiar pathway.

To his awakening senses came the palpable feeling that the Creator, attended by Mother Nature, was present in the serenity of his peaceful surroundings. It reminded him of the Garden of Eden before Man's rebellion, and God's simple command, "Tend the garden and care for the animals." The profound spiritual aspect gave him pause and filled his heart with silent praise.

He paused in front of the China Retreat mansion, walked over to a bordering fence and leaned his elbows on a top rail that creaked beneath his weight. He followed the antics of the falling red and gold leaves as they played over the lush green grass and graveled driveway. Beyond, crowding close to the river, was the great mansion, marble steps leading to a semicircular portico supported by mammoth pillars, startling white columns that appeared as smiling parted incisors greeting an old acquaintance.

Moved by a sudden gust of wind, the bells that hung under the eaves of the house began tinkling merrily, reminding Paddy that on certain days that pleasing sound could be heard clear over on the Jersey shore. He remembered, too, a hot day several years ago before the war when he stopped in at that same manor for a drink of water and had been served graciously by the owner, an easy-mannered Southerner named Wade Hampton, a name now famous among the South's cavalry chieftains.

He was so deeply engrossed that he did not hear the carriage approaching on the road.

"Afta'noon," drawled a deep bass voice. "Ain't contemplatin' no mischief on the place, is you, sojur?"

Paddy removed both elbows from the fence, turned and looked into the expressionless face of a middle-aged Negro liveryman who had stopped the carriage at the driveway entrance.

"Mischief did you say? Not unless you call just thinking of how I'd like to own it mischief. You work for Wade Hampton?"

"Massa Hampton? No. Massa Hampton done sold dis prop'ty to Massa Gabriel Manigault of Cha'leston. I take care ob de prop'ty for Massa Manigault."

"Doesn't your master find it a little embarrassing living in the North in times like these?"

"Deed not, 'cause he still lives in Cha'leston. Way I sees it, he figgers mebbe thar won't be nuffin' much left ob de South when you Yankee boys get through wif it. Now if he calc'lates correctly, this place'll make a mahty nice spot to hab in de hand."

"I'd say Mr. Manigault leaves no stones unturned, except maybe one. How's he know you won't try to make a break for freedom while you're up here?"

"Freedom? North white folks always spoutin' 'bout freedom for us colored folks. Freedom fo what? To scratch and starve like po white trash?" He flicked at a leaf with his whip. "Y'all say you like to own yonder house. Me, I say I like to live in yonder house. Couldn't do it no other way, ceptin' I tie myself to a massa. Eat good, work easy like, don't have no worry 'bout nuffin.'" He shook a foot in Paddy's direction. "Don't see no chains, do ye, sojur?"

"No, I see no chains," Paddy demurred.

The man's expression softened and became searching. "You one ob dem from de hospital?"

"Yes."

"Be obliged to show ye through de house if yo like." He slid over to make room on the carriage seat. "Even fix yo a hot toddy from Massa's best rum."

"Mighty kind of you. I accept your offer, or should I say, Mister Manigault's."

The Negro chuckled. "Either way's all right. We's partners." With a strong grasp, he helped Paddy up onto the seat. "Shot in de leg was yo, sojur?"

"Yes. Took a long time healing, but it's all right now. Little stiff, that's all."

The driver clucked gently to the horses and the carriage rolled down the gravel driveway beneath a high arch of elm trees. A satisfied smile settled at the corners of his mouth.

"Yep, sojur. Nothin' lak sittin' on top ob a fancy carriage behind a team ob fine horses to make cuh'lud folk feel lak a million dollars. Just lak sittin' on top ob de world."

It was late that afternoon, with the sun sinking behind the western hills, when Paddy finally returned to the hospital in a happier frame of mind than when he started. Despite a slight ache in his leg, an overall feeling of well-being possessed him. His cheeks were a healthy pink. As the chief surgeon approached from a side hallway, he asked, "How'd it go, Mulcahy?"

"Fine, sir. The leg feels good as new."

"Glad to hear it. I'll want to have a look at it first thing in the morning. By the way, there's a letter for you in the office. Came while you were out."

"Letter?" The word fairly flew from his mouth. He scurried across the hall, one leg dragging slightly.

"Murphy," he called to the attendant, "you got a letter for me?"

"Yep, got one somewhere. Here you are." Revolving it in his hands, examining it, he smiled and said, "A real fat one. Somebody must've wrote you a book. It's from Virginia."

"Virginia? Give it here."

With a quick finger he tore open one end of the envelope, withdrew the stationery as his eyes raced over the first page, then stopped. His hands went limp and he looked for a place to sit down as he began reading it again, this time more slowly. The handwriting was Captain Donaldson's.

Beverly Ford, Virginia
October 4, 1863

Dear Paddy—old comrade,
Can you forgive an old friend and fellow campaigner for taking so long answering what I know must be uppermost in your mind?
It hurts to write what I must regarding your wife; I have postponed it until now with the hope that I might glean encouraging news of Becky's whereabouts through Miss Van Lew in Richmond. I trust by now you are well enough so that what I relate will not cause you anguish that will interfere with your recovery.
In response to your request, I paid a visit to the Chenewith home at Leesburg on the 22nd of July. I was shocked to find the house completely deserted and evidence of vandalism. Upon inquiring, I was able to learn that Becky bore you a fine little girl on the Fourth of July. Your wife is an upright, decent young woman,

Paddy; she attempted to conceal nothing from her inquisitive neighbors. In repayment for her proud, honest candor, both she and her mother and the baby were driven from the town several days before I arrived without a hand raised to help them. Though I begged, bribed and threatened, I could find no one who would tell me where they might have gone.

I contacted Miss Van Lew with the hope that she might uncover information about your family. I'm sorry to report that she could not. The only information Bet could give me was that Dr. Chenewith had been killed in the line of duty in Gettysburg.

How can I tell you to be of good cheer and not despair when we are all in the depths of despair. These are sad days for the army, and the coming winter is going to be a tough one.

Most of the new material sent us since the Gettysburg campaign are worthless as fighting men, tempted by the extravagant sums paid for substitutes and the large bounties offered by district organizations to complete their quotas and thus avoid the draft. Large numbers from the worst classes are entering the service. Those substitutes, bounty jumpers and conscripts are replacing the brave comrades who fell in battle or whose terms have expired. Many have enlisted under fictitious names and it's not uncommon at roll call to see them look in their hats to find their assumed names. I dread to think of the horrors this element will perpetrate on the homes and families of our Southern brothers if given the opportunity.

Last month Captain O'Neil and Adjutant Hand returned from Philadelphia with 109 recruits and substitutes (the allotted quota was 159). With that number, O'Neil and Hand started from the city; fifty eluded them and disappeared en route. That is a common occurrence; scarcely any detachments are reaching the front without large numbers deserting.

Many of the substitutes presume to have been captains and lieutenants; one man assigned to my company actually claimed to be a former brigade commander!

They presumptuously address each other by their titles and cannot be suppressed unless severely disciplined. Lem Crocker has helped set many of them straight.

The month of August was hot, breeding swarms of pesky insects that caused frequent malarial disorders in the lowlands along the Rappahannock. To counteract the unhealthy surroundings, we were issued quinine steeped in liberal amounts of whiskey. Despite the medication, many of us were stricken with flashes of hot and cold sweating, continual aches and pains and severe diarrhea. Piles are sending more men home than enemy bullets. Many are the trouser seats stained with blood and hemorrhoid ointment. Marching has truly become a pain in the ass.

An incident of unprecedented severity, which occurred at the end of August, bears repeating in detail. It has caused a sickness in the hearts of patriotic men far greater than any malarial illness.

On the 13th of August, five deserters were caught while attempting to recross the Potomac. Assigned to our regiment, they never joined us and were unknown to us. Charged with a crime calling for capital punishment if convicted, they were sent to the regiment as a forum where they could receive a judicial hearing. conviction, followed by any of the punishments usually inflicted for desertion, would have connected them with the regiment as prisoners awaiting trial, or as criminals awaiting approval and execution. They were thrown into our presence, where they were strangers. They had neither friends, memories or associations; they came as prisoners for the stern administration of military justice, and they could expect little sympathy.

Desertions and bounty-jumping have increased with such alarming frequency that the death penalty has become necessary. As you know, except for desertion to the enemy, capital punishment has rarely been inflicted. Determined to eradicate the shameful practice of bounty-jumping, the War Department has ordered all court-martials to issue the death penalty on conviction.

The court which tried the five offenders was presided over by Colonel Joseph Hayes, 18th Massachusetts Volunteers, and convened pursuant to General Order No. 35, of August 15, 1863, at Headquarters, 2nd Brigade, 1st Division, 5th Corps.

The number of men arraigned and the possible severity of the sentence attracted the attention of the whole army. It may have been the first of this class of case and was given unusual publicity by the army; the prisoners were found guilty and sentenced to be shot. For your information, I have enclosed a copy of the general order.

Paddy put the letter aside and picked up an official document. His gaze ran rapidly over it.

Headquarters
Army of the Potomac
August 23, 1863
General Orders No. 84
These men evidently belonged to the class trading on the necessities of the country and embraced enlistment with a view to desertion for the purpose of gain. It is hoped the punishment awarded their crimes will have the effect of deterring others. The commanding general will unhesitatingly punish all such cases with the severest penalties of the law.

This order is being published for every company in the army at the first retreat parole after receipt.

By order of General Meade.

Laying the notice aside, Paddy began reading again from the letter:

The order, affixing the time of execution as Wednesday, the 26th of August, between the hours of twelve and four p.m., reached the regiment on the 24th and was handed to the prisoners by Major Herring in the presence of the chaplain, through the aid of an interpreter.

Difficulty in securing the services of a priest and rabbi, who made special trips from their Northern homes, caused a postponement until Saturday the 29th between the same hours. The day following the announcement of their sentence, the condemned addressed a communication to General Meade requesting a merciful reconsideration of the punishment imposed. It was a composition in the handwriting of one of them:

Beverly Ford, Virginia

August 25, 1863

Major General Meade

General: We, the prisoners, implore your mercy in our behalf for the extension of our sentences so that we may have time to make preparation to meet our God. At the present, we are unprepared to die. Our time is short. Two of us are Roman Catholics and we have no priest; two are Protestants and one is a Jew who has no rabbi to assist in preparing him. We ask mercy on behalf of our children, and we also desire that you change our sentence to hard labor instead of death, as we feel we have been wrongfully sentenced. Being foreigners, we were mis-informed by other soldiers who promised us we would come to no harm.

Your obedient servants,

Charles Walter

Gion Reanese

Emil Lai

Gion Folaney

George Kuhn

The death penalty already having been announced, the guard was strengthened and the condemned men watched closely. An exhaustive search was made for everything that might be employed to commit suicide. Lem Crocker was placed in charge of the guard and Lieutenant Lewis, Bayne and Thomas were assigned duty with him; four men inside and four outside the place of confinement were constantly on duty. Lewis conducted the search. He took a pocketbook from the Hebrew, who pleaded earnestly for its return. Yielding to his entreaties, Lewis was about to return it without examination when Major Herring, who supervised the operation, promptly directed him not to do so until he had carefully examined the contents. Concealed in the folds was a lancet. The Jew had not observed the examination and when the pocketbook was handed back to him his countenance lightened as he nervously clutched it and began searching it. Discovering the lancet gone, his countenance fell, and he handed it back to Lewis, remarking through an interpreter that he had no further use for it.

From the publication of the order until the day of execution, not a soldier was permitted to leave the regimental camp limits, nor were visitors allowed to enter. All military exercises and camp duties were performed in a strangely quiet atmosphere. An order was issued forbidding noise or levity, but that was needless; the awfulness and solemnity of the coming event struck every heart.

It may seem strange that men who could shoot at the enemy in battle should feel so serious about the fate of the five deserters; it is one thing when they are heated and inflamed in face to face conflict. It is a different thing to see men deliberately put to death.

The morning was busy with preparations. Twenty men, including your friends Gilmour and McCool, under Sergeant Cassidy, were detailed to bear the coffins, and ten pioneers with spades and hatchets, under Sergeant Moselander, were charged with filling the graves and closing the coffins. Captain Crocker commanded a guard of thirty men.

Father S. L. Eagan, a Catholic priest, arrived from Baltimore the afternoon before and with Chaplain O'Neil spent the night administering religious consolation to the prisoners whose faith they represented. The Jewish Rabbi, Dr. Zould, did not arrive until shortly before noon the day of the execution.

The prisoners, clothed in blue trousers and white flannel shirts, accompanied by the clergymen, the escort guard and detail, were marched to a house in the vicinity of the 2nd Brigade's headquarters to report to captain Orne, the divisional provost marshal, and there await formation of the corps.

We assembled slowly. The 1st and 2nd Divisions were in position occupying two sides of the square when at three o'clock, without awaiting the arrival of the 3rd Division, which subsequently hurried into place, the solemn procession entered the enclosure. The band struck up the death march, followed by Captain Orne and the provost marshal, with fifty men of his guard—ten to each prisoner—as executioner. Then came the condemned men accompanied by their ministers. At a suggestion from Major Herring, the one representing the most ancient of religious creeds was assigned to the right. The prisoners were manacled. Four of them bore themselves manfully, moving steadily and stepping firmly. One moved with a weak, tottering gait, dragging himself along with difficulty; he required support to maintain his footing. Crocker, with his escort of thirty men, closed the rear.

The procession moved slowly, the guards, with reversed arms, keeping step to the mournful notes of the funeral march. The awful silence was broken only by the doleful music; whispered words of consolation from the men of God and the deliberate martial tread of the soldiers.

With slow, impressive pace the procession moved around three fronts of the square, halting at the open end and facing outward looking up the slope; five coffins were placed at the foot of each. The provost guard, subdivided into detachments of ten with loaded pieces, faced the prisoners thirty paces away.

The provost marshal read the orders directing the execution. The minister, priest and rabbi engaged in earnest, fervent prayer.

General Griffin, annoyed from the beginning with the unnecessary delays, anxiously noted the time and saw they had fifteen minutes left. In a loud voice he broke the silence, calling to Captain Orne, "Shoot these men. After ten minutes it will be murder. Shoot them at once."

The thousands of us assembled there will never face a more solemn moment until death overtakes us.

With a few parting words of hope and consolation, the clergy stood aside. Lieutenant Wilson quickly bandaged the eyes of the prisoners. The suspense lasted for only a moment. "Attention! Guard! Shoulder arms! Forward! Guide right! March!" Every tread fell heavy on the stilled hearts of our motionless corps. With an appropriate pause and stern deliberations, the commands were given six paces from the prisoners. "Halt! Ready! Aim! Fire!" Simultaneously, fifty muskets flashed. Military justice was satirized and the law avenged.

Four bodies fell with a solid thud, the fifth remained erect. "Inspection arms!"
Captain Orne ordered hurriedly and every ramrod rang on the breech. No soldier
had failed his duty; every musket had been discharged. With pistol in hand, it was
the provost marshal's disagreeable duty to dispatch the culprit if the musketry
failed. At the coffin, Surgeon Thomas pronounced life extinct and the body was
laid on the ground with the others.

The masses changed direction by left flank and to the tune of "The Girl I Left
Behind Me" (a poor selection, most of us thought), the corps was broken into
open columns and marched by the bodies to check the executioners' job. We were
soon back in camp.

Well, there you have it, Paddy, the whole sorry situation. I wish I could write
of more pleasant matters, but such is not the case under the present circumstances.
I presume we will be taking to the field soon and it may be some time before I am
able to write you again. It is my hope that this letter finds you well on the road to
recovery and that in some way Becky will finally contact you.

Your devoted friend and comrade,
Frank A. Donaldson, Captain
118th Pennsylvania Volunteers

Paddy slowly replaced the thick sheaf of stationery in the soiled envelope.
Close by, an orderly was lighting an oil lamp in the semi-dark hallway.

"Bad news, Mulcahy?"

"What makes you think so?" His voice was dull, flat.

"Take a look in that mirror. You're white as a sheet and shaking. Want me to
help you upstairs?"

"No, thanks. The chief surgeon still here?"

"In his office. Want me to fetch him?"

"I can make it." Using his cane as a lever, he stood up and moved off slowly
down the hall. Before a partially closed door, he halted, paused, then knocked
twice sharply.

"Come in," invited a tired voice. Paddy entered. The surgeon looked up from
medical charts spread out before him on the desk.

Dim light from a student lamp accentuated the deeply creased lines and circles
of care on his face. "Yes, Mulcahy? Thought our appointment was for tomorrow
morning."

"I've got to talk to you now, sir."

"Leg giving you trouble? Let's have a look."

"It's not my leg, sir. How soon can I get back on active duty?"

"Active duty?" The surgeon tilted back in his swivel chair and surveyed his
patient closely. "You're eligible for discharge. Service with the Invalid Corps if
you desire, but active duty...?" He shook his head. "No."

"Sir, I've got to get back in the field. There's something important I've got to
attend to."

"I'm sure we all have a stake in that matter, Mulcahy." He let a warm smile
of solicitude crinkle the tightly-stretched skin at the corners of his eyes. "But let's

leave that up to those who are sound of limb. Winter's coming on, and although you may have had a successful walk this afternoon, your leg will not hold up under the rigors of winter campaigning. If you should develop osteomyelitis there would be no recourse but amputation. You wouldn't want to lose your limb because of some foolishness, would you?"

"If it means finding my wife and child, yes. I've got to get to Leesburg. Some bastard's gonna tell me where they drove my family."

"Family!" The colonel sat bolt upright. "I didn't know you had a wife and child in the South, Mulcahy." He stroked his chin, thinking. "Suppose you tell me the circumstances. Perhaps I can be of help. Sit down and give me the details."

In a pained and faltering voice, Paddy reviewed the chain of events leading up to his marriage and the subsequent happenings. When he finished, he slumped back into his seat, completely exhausted.

The surgeon rose from his chair, struck a match to his pipe and circled the desk. After exhaling a few wreaths of smoke, he said, "I understand your desire to get to Leesburg and take up the trail while it's still fresh, but my advice about your leg still stands. Furthermore, may I point out to you the area you wish to invade is swarming with Mosby's guerrillas. For a lone Yankee to go poking his nose around there would be courting certain death. Even our heavily protected wagon trains and cavalry detachments aren't safe in that region." The surgeon eased his pacing and sat down on the edge of his desk. "Why don't you let me take this up with the Christian Commission. Maybe they can help locate your wife and child."

"Christian Commission? They can't do anything. They're behind the lines."

"Let's give their relief organization a try, for my sake."

"For your sake?"

"Yes." A forlorn expression crossed his countenance. "You see, we surgeons never hear about anything except our mistakes and shortcomings. In a case such as yours, I'm proud of my handiwork as an artist, in a vain way, maybe. I'd hate to see the fruits of my labor destroyed carelessly. Will you give me a month to help locate your family?"

"Must I stay here all that time?"

"Certainly not. If your wound shows no signs of erythema at tomorrow's examination, you may be discharged immediately. Of course I'll want you to return for a weekly checkup."

"You have my word on it, Colonel. I'll give you a month."

Paddy eased himself out of his chair and walked stiffly toward the door. He turned. "Sir, I...."

"Yes?"

"Thanks."

The next day was Sunday, a glorious fall morning. With medical discharge papers tucked safely in his tunic, Paddy hurried toward a carriage that had been put at his disposal for the trip to Frankford. He seated himself, and the open barouche was soon rolling along in a gentle, swaying rhythm toward Bristol Pike. He turned his head from side to side to study the sublimity of the surrounding countryside, simple ways and scenes which had captured his heart and imagination as a young boy.

Baronial mansions, gabled and porticoed, stood by carriage sheds that smelled of leather harness. Octagonal summerhouses graced the front lawns, browning and windblown with fallen leaves and awaiting winter's first mantle of white. Earthy farms, rustic in beauty, were perfumed by seed, feed and fertilizer, barn doors sagging open on strap hinges. Stored hay bulged from thrifty lofts. In the fields, crackling corn shocks with bending tassels hung over field-ripened pumpkins all caught up in an entwining net of Japanese Lantern vines. Alongside the road were baskets of Winesap apples placed to draw saliva from the wayfarer. Silent horse and buggies stood in communion before the plainness of the Friend's Meeting House at Torresdale.

The four-wheeled carriage clattered across the stone bridge that spanned Pennypack Creek and climbed the hill into Holmesburg.

The uniformed driver, his bearded face resembling that of a sheep dog, slowed the horses to a walk and turned to speak for the first time.

"Stop here ten minutes to give the team a rest. Want to refresh yourself, now's the time."

Paddy stretched. "Good. This gimpy leg's getting cramped. I'll get out and loosen it up a bit."

Alighting from the carriage, he started walking in the direction of Doc Arthur's drug store, the subdued sunlight of late fall playing lightly over his form and figure. The small country village was wrapped in Sunday stillness, mossy old limestone houses a mellow blend with the rambling wrought-iron fences and trees nearly bare limbed.

The Presbyterian Church had just let out, and the chattering congregation milled by. Suddenly a shout of recognition greeted him. "Hey, Mulcahy. You old sonovagun."

He pivoted to see three soldiers making a break toward him. Bursting with joy, he moved to embrace the lead one. "Sam, what a surprise. What are you doing home?"

"Might ask the same of you. Oh, you remember Tris Boileau and Bill Solly, don't you?"

"Sure. Think I got you out of bed one night at Antietam."

"You sure did," Boileau replied. "It was raining pitchforks."

"What are you doing here?" Sam Cartledge asked again, eyeing Paddy up and down. "And with a cane?"

"I got hit at Gettysburg. On the Fourth. Been up at Andalusia ever since. Just got discharged."

"For good?"

"Not if I can help it. Gonna rest up a month then head back to the regiment. How come you're home?"

"Our colonel pulled strings and got us a thirty-day furlough," Solly replied, his cherubic face aglow.

"A furlough? Thought they were for the birds. How'd you swing it?"

"After the trimming we Holmesburg Grays took at Fredericksburg, hardly enough of us left to stage a good street fight, we were placed near Washington and attached to the new Twenty-second Corps. Been stationed in Washington ever since. Furloughs are easy to come by so long's you're not in the field."

"Course if you're a signal corps hero like Cartledge," Boileau cut in, a simpering smile crossing his countenance, "all you have to do is snap your fingers for a furlough. Get Sam to tell you how he helped save Little Round Top at Gettysburg."

"Don't have to. I was in on it. Saw him there."

"Oh, no, a witness. Now we'll never hear the end of it."

Broad-shouldered Cartledge grinned. "See? Told you you'd have proof one of these days."

"Soldier, we're pulling out," the carriage driver called from a distance.

"Guess this is it for a while," Paddy said, shaking hands. "Can't keep my hack waiting. So long."

"So long, Mulcahy. Take care of the leg."

The pale October sun was sinking low when the carriage at last rumbled into the outskirts of Frankford, the air filled with the spicy goodness of frosted gardens, wood smoke from chimneys and burning leaves. Paddy inhaled deeply of the tangy scents.

"Home," he murmured to himself. "Home."

His soliloquy was rudely jolted by the appearance of something that fell beneath his searching gaze. The gentle beauty, the quiet reserve of staid old Main Street had been defaced by street car tracks, ugly iron scars running parallel as far north as the Seven Stars Tavern. In his absence somebody had ruined the face of his town.

"Let me off over there at the blacksmith shop," he called to the driver.

"As you say," came the listless reply. "Got everything?"

"Yes. Thanks for the nice, quiet ride."

"Think nothin' of it. Been a heap site better'n drivin' a lot of yappin' women around all day. Can't stand talkin' while I'm drivin', interferes with the music from me horses' feet."

Withdrawing inside his shell, the dour carriage man turned his team around and headed toward Bristol Pike.

Paddy stood alone before the barred doors of the smithy and surveyed the recently laid dummy-car tracks with a mixed feeling of contempt and displeasure. Improved transportation meant growth, and growth meant eventual destruction of the old Kings Highway as a quaint thoroughfare. A row of brick store fronts were already being constructed down the street. Alarmed, he visualized that with time a crowded commercial avenue would displace the quiet beauty still holding sway. Property values along Main Street would skyrocket, but what good was increased wealth if the old picturesque order of things was destroyed and one could no longer find pleasure in one's environment?

Disturbed by his thoughts, he limped across the street to take up lodging at the Jolly Post and await developments.

In the days that followed, long days in which time hung heavy on his hands, he accepted many invitations to dinner from old friends and comrades who were discharged because of disabilities. Table talk at these get-togethers invariably revolved around the war and politics and the reminiscences of mutual experiences.

There were other places, other invitations, which he felt his duty to accept, where there was crepe and sorrow behind drawn shades in grieving households.

Bereaved parents of the Castors, the Batts and the Williamses had haggard circles under their eyes from tears shed over the bright-eyed boys who would never come home again. In darkened and undisturbed rooms, fishing poles stood in a remote corner, a lock of hair under glass on a dresser, empty beds with boys' things still around to fan and torment memories.

At the end of these painful meetings, Paddy would take his leave with a consoling nod, a handclasp and silence.

During the long periods of restless waiting which he could call his own, he alternated between taking long walks in the country and posting himself in Jim Ryen's chair on the porch of the Jolly Post. Cap in hand, youngsters clustered around him and pestered him for stories of combat and campaigns until he began to feel like the reincarnation of the Revolutionary War soldier whose place he had taken. In moments of solitude, he reflected with a degree of sadness upon the passing of the patriarchs whose presence had given meaning to his life. In the past year, death had come as a windstorm carrying away Colonel Burns, Peter Craig, Aunt Virginia, Uncle Peter and Jim Ryen. The unyielding cycle of life was relentlessly transferring the yoke of community responsibility and public esteem to younger shoulders. The thought of growing old made him flinch.

October slipped away and November came, with a rush of cold wind and dry snow presaging a severe winter. Sleighs of all description appeared on Frankford's byways, some hauling coal and cordwood for village hearths. The tinkling sleigh bells and the crunching of sled runners over packed snow filled the air with musical sounds. Young boys, once eager to hear stories of war, temporarily suspended their military interests and expanded their boundless energy in games of shinny on ice-covered ponds and creeks.

Paddy's leg continued to improve with brisk walks in the invigorating cold. On the day before Thanksgiving, he made his last visit to the Andalusia hospital for a final examination. In two brief sentences, the surgeon sent his hopes soaring.

"Sound as a dollar. No reason why you can't return to your regiment." The doctor's next pronouncement sent everything crashing. "All efforts by the Christian Commission to learn the whereabouts of your wife and child have ended in failure, Paddy. I'm sorry."

Stunned and speechless, he managed to murmur his thanks and told the doctor good-bye. The discouraging words turned over and over in his troubled mind as his sleigh glided swiftly back to Frankford.

Alighting in front of the Jolly Post, he stood detached and alone on the snow-crusted ground and stared blankly at his father's smithy, bleak now and deteriorating. Through a frosted window of the inn, Mary Coates, an expansiveness in her nature matching the plumpness of her body, watched the soldier in the street with the mysterious power of a woman's intuition. Disappearing. she reappeared on the snow-swept porch, a shawl drawn tightly around her large shoulders. "Paddy Mulcahy," she called, "you come right in here out of the cold this instant. Standing out there inviting lung fever, of all things. You march yourself straight in here and let me fix you something warm to eat."

Removing his kepi and running a hand through his matted hair, he slowly turned and mounted the steps. Mary stretched out her hand and took him by the arm, ushering him into the hostelry's warm, cheery confines. "You just sit right down there, young man," she said, pointing to a table. "I'll have some pepper pot and hot coffee ready in no time at all."

Removing a coat puddled with melting deposits of powdered snow, Paddy dropped himself into a vacant chair and cupped his head in his wet hands.

In a few minutes Mary returned with a pot of aromatic coffee and a steaming bowl of soup indigenous to the region of Philadelphia.

"There," she exclaimed, placing the food before him. "See if that doesn't make the world look brighter."

He raised his head without replying. The woman sat down beside him. "I've seen your expression on the faces of men-folk before. It means one thing. You're going away, aren't you?"

"Yes."

"When?"

"First thing tomorrow."

"On Thanksgiving Day? A day set aside by the President to praise Almighty God? I won't hear of it. Jacob and I have looked forward to having you eat with our family tomorrow. Gracious sakes, how do you expect the youngsters will feel when they find out their 'Uncle' Paddy's forsaken them on Tom Turkey day, of all times?"

"Thanksgiving. What have I got to be thankful for?"

"Why, that you're alive and well," she answered.

"Sorry, Mary, my mind's made up. I have a family to find."

She studied him with fixed hazel eyes. "So that's the problem, is it? The people who were conducting the search have failed."

Paddy sipped at the coffee. "Yes, they have failed," he murmured. "Got the final word this afternoon."

There was a period of silence in which Mary Coates pushed back her chair and stood up from the table. "Well," she said, trying to find her voice, "one thing's certain. Your wife and daughter couldn't have just flown from the earth. They must be somewhere." She placed a hand on his shoulder. "When you're ready to pack, let me know. I'll help you."

Thanksgiving dawned clear and crisp. Paddy descended the long flight of steps to the dining room where he found a busy atmosphere swimming with tantalizing odors, the spicy scents of stuffing, pumpkin pies and other choice morsels prepared in the kitchen for the day's festivities. Flexing her fingers as she wiped them on a dough-blotched apron, Mary advanced to greet him.

"Good morning, Paddy. I have breakfast all ready for you. Put your bag down by the fireplace and come over to the table. By the way, that young Beeson boy who keeps pestering you to get him in the army is out in the kitchen. Says he heard you're leaving today, and wants to go with you. He's all packed. Can you imagine?"

"News sure travels fast. How'd he know I was going today?"

"Probably heard the menfolk discussing it over their ale last night." She tossed her head, mirth sparkling in her laughing eyes. "He reminds me of another young scamp I once knew around here, used to eavesdrop on adult conversations all the time."

Paddy struck an innocent expression and smiled. "Oh? Who was that?"

"You. That's who. Now come and eat."

Doing as he was told, he sat down before a large stack of griddle cakes drowned in maple syrup and butter. He surveyed the special breakfast with mouth-watering delight and reached for it with one hand while pushing a bowl of cornmeal mush away with the other.

"No you don't," she scolded with an owlish look. "You eat that, too. It's good for you."

He flicked his eyes wide. "Tell it to the Marines. A few more days and that kind of glue will be a steady diet again. I'm not making friends with it this morning."

"Of course. Enjoy the hotcakes. Want me to send the Beeson boy in?"

"Sure. There's no harm in that."

"All right, but don't you promise him anything. Do you hear? He may say he's eighteen, but I know he's only fifteen, if he's a day." Giving her well-padded hips a rolling flounce, she left for the kitchen.

Bursting from the kitchen came the would-be volunteer. Short and wiry as a pin, young and lean, a hungry face peppered with freckles, he had the inquisitive look of a squirrel as he pressed close, his eyes dancing with eagerness as he spoke. "Hear you're leavin' for the front again," he said with a rush of words. "Take me with you, willya, huh?"

Paddy bolted down a mouthful of food and pointed to a chair. "Sit down, Joey."

"You bet. You gonna take me with you? I'm all packed."

"Your mother and father give consent?"

"Aw, you know how folks are. They'll get used to the idea once I'm in."

"Folks never get used to the idea, once you're in. War is dirty business. I've told you fellas that more than once. I just can't take you with me. Besides, I haven't got the authority."

Beeson's squirrel-toothed face fell. "How 'bout as a drummer boy? You need drummers?"

"Look, Joe, with the kind of men coming into the army these days and the kind of trouble they're causing, you're better off staying just as far away from them as you possibly can. In sixty-one it might have been all right, but things have changed. It's become rotten lousy."

"That's why I want to volunteer. Prove there's still some who're willin' to fight for their country without bein' drafted or gettin' paid bounty for it."

"Very patriotic, but let me tell you what our surgeon said about this thing called patriotism. He's diagnosed several nice cases of it and says it's peculiar to this hemisphere. He says it first breaks out in the mouth and spreads from there to the heart causing the heart to swell. He says it goes on raging till it reaches the pocket when it suddenly disappears, leaving the patient very constitutional and conservative."

"That ain't the way you really feel, is it?"

Paddy's dark-lashed eyes became deadly serious. He put down his knife and fork and pushed his plate aside. "How old are you Joe, honestly."

"Why. ..I'm...fifteen."

"Fifteen. Only four years younger than me, but in war, four years can mean an awful lot. The answer is still no."

Defeated, his head bowed, Beeson fingered he tablecloth. "Can I go to the station with ya? I could carry your haversack." "Well, I'm just about ready to pull out. You can tag along if you like. Glad for the company."

Amid the scraping of chairs being pushed back came a concerted movement from several directions as Jacob Coates, his wife and children gathered close. Several wee tots, all seeking attention, tugged at Paddy's greatcoat as he slipped into it. Slowly he buttoned it to the left side from which hung a long cape from the shoulder; a cape that could be unbuttoned to cover the head like a hood, forming a mask for the face with a slit for the eyes in winter time.

"Can I hab your cane for keeps, Unca Paddy?" squealed a small boy, his toothless, moon-shaped face radiant.

Paddy bent down to give him a hug. "Promised it to you, didn't I, Little Jake?"

"Thure."

"Then it's all yours."

A noticeable huskiness developed in the throats of both the innkeeper and his wife as it came their turn to say goodbye to their boarder who, over the years, had been like one of the family. Tears streamed down Mary's cheeks as she handed him a boxed lunch of turkey sandwiches. "You be sure to give our love to the rest of the boys when you see them," she said, and began crying audibly. "Oh, may kind Providence end this terrible war soon and bring you all safely home again." She gathered him in an embrace, smothering a moist kiss upon his temple.

Becoming impatient and a little embarrassed, Beeson pulled his wool cap over his head and drew the ear-flaps tight about his face. "I got all your stuff, Paddy. The dummy car'll be along any minute now. We better be gettin'."

"Coming, Joey."

Led by Jacob Coates, walking with head bent as he conversed in low tones with his departing guest, the group left the room and made their way outside where the icy air nipped at their pale cheeks, turning them red. Moving on out into the street, the two passengers stood and waited for the horse-drawn dummy that came rattling along from the direction of the Seven Stars Tavern, the creaking yellow car swaying to and fro over the tracks. Beeson entered first. Paddy mounted the car steps where he paused to turn and wave farewell to the family grouped on the porch of the Jolly Post and to take a last look around at all that was dear to him. The car gave a lurch and began rolling.

From the silence which hung over the village came the soft sound of chimes ringing in the tower of St. Mark's, bells calling the Episcopal congregation to worship. Further on, through the open doors of the First Presbyterian Church, resonant sounds of organ music flowed out. The sight of a uniformed soldier linked arm-in-arm with a hoop-skirted girl, both of whom were just entering the church, caused Paddy to turn and crane his neck. "Say, Joey, isn't that Henry Mackie?"

"Uh-huh. Lot of fellas from the Hundred'n Fourteenth just got home on leave, came in late last night. Henry's gettin' married."

"Oh? Who's the girl?"

"One of the Corson girls. Hey, let's sit nearer the stove. I'm cold."

Being the only ones riding in the car at the present, both rose, moved toward the rear and took a seat close to a pot-bellied stove, the iron plates of which glowed red with heat.

Paddy settled himself and propped both legs on a seat in front. Conscious of something behind him, he turned and looked out of the rear window. There, sitting huddled and exposed on the rear platform, he spotted "Santy" Fry. A familiar man about town, the Negro, now graying, had for a long time gone by the nickname of "Santy" because of a limp similar to that of Santa Anna, the celebrated Mexican Revolutionist. Another characteristic was that he always held a thumb in his mouth while walking the streets. Those two traits had always been a source of amusement to the children of the village and given Santy an individuality which attracted the attention of strangers.

Years before he had been known as the boy preacher. Without an opportunity for education and without training, the humble youth had superior capabilities of eloquence. His talents were not of the imitative character which merely quoted passages from the Bible, but were logical and analytical, a rare gift.

Rapping sharply on the window, Paddy beckoned him to come inside. The Negro's face lit up, a happy smile of recognition on his face, but the toothy smile quickly faded, dispelled by a frown and a shake of his head.

"What's ailin' him? Does he want to freeze to death? Why don't he come inside?"

"Ain't 'lowed to," Beeson murmured. "It ain't safe. Last summer some of them foreigners what's been movin' into Kensington tossed old Reverend Baker off this car'n killed him. Colored folks all gotta ride on the platform."

"What? I've known Santy since I was a child. Colored or not, he's riding in here with me where it's warm. Any fish-town sonovabitch that begs to differ can stand up to me."

Paddy threw open the rear door. "Santy, get the hell in here before you blow away."

"Cain't Marsa Paddy. It's agin the law."

"The law, my ass. People don't even put their dogs out in this kind of weather.

Get in here."

The Negro shuffled forward, thumb in mouth. "Good to see you agin, Marsa Paddy. I' se much obliged. Us colo' ed folks gwine need considerate folks like you to help us when this heah wah is ovah."

Beeson moved to make room on the seat. "Hi, Santy. Goin' into the city?"

"Yassuh, Joey. Mistuh Fred'rick Douglas, de abolitionist, gwine to be preachin' dis heah Thanksgivin' day. Sees lak out brothers 'n sisters what's been escaped over de underground railroad thinks dey now be in Hebbin'. Hab a jubilee idee dis be pa'adise. Mistuh douglas tells 'em freedom 'quires 'sponsibility and edjication."

Paddy arched his eyebrows. "How do they take to that kind of talk?"

"Don't lak it mostly. Don't 'peal to 'em. Dey want de freedom but not de 'sponsibility. Ain't used to it. Mistuh Douglas be tryin' to set dem straight."

"Where do you hold these meetings?"

"Down to Miss Lucretia's house. Lucretia Mott, de Quakuh lady. A mahty gene'ous women. She find work for our people."

Entering Kensington, the car in which they were riding came to a sudden stop to take on four new passengers.

Beeson glanced up quickly and nudged Paddy in the ribs. "Oh, oh, this could spell trouble. They're some of that foreign gang. Eyetalians, real handy with knives. Look, they've seen us."

Slowly unfastening his belt, Paddy withdrew it, wrapping it around his fist so that the heavy army buckle fit like a brass knuckle. "All right, just let them try and start something."

"You can't take on all four of 'em," Beeson whispered uneasily.

Santy Fry started to stand up. "Ah'll move on back to de platform, Marsa Paddy. Don't wanna cause you no trouble on mah account."

"You sit still. If I have my guess, those alley growlers not only don't want to be in a uniform, they don't even want to get near one. How 'bout the conductor, old man Stearn, whose side's he on?"

"Ouahs, mostly. Been mahty obligin', 'ceptin' when white folks regista complaints."

Making overtures of aggression, the four men glared at the Negro passenger and conversed rapidly among themselves in a foreign tongue. Pointing toward Paddy, one of the group made a lunge, but the other three quickly restrained him, shaking their heads.

Paddy drew the belt buckle tighter about his fist and stared back at them.

Beeson's voice cracked as he bent low to examine a shoelace. "Ain't you scared?"

"Scared? Joey, you don't know what the word means."

Fully aroused, the four men in front began remonstrating wildly with the wizened conductor who, for all intents and purposes, and obviously bolstered by Paddy's presence, greeted their protests by turning a deaf ear. After arguing to no avail, the four seated themselves and confined their activity to loud, unsavory comments in broken English.

Beeson heaved a sigh of relief. "Whew, you bluffed 'em."

Paddy uncoiled his fist. "I wasn't bluffing. If left unchecked, pricks like them could poison our country."

"I don't know that I'd have the nerve to step in," Beeson whispered.

"You damned well better find the nerve, Joey."

At Third and Arch streets, Santy Fry said goodbye to his two friends and left the car to proceed, unmolested.

Through a window, Beeson followed Santy's gimp-legged progress until the Negro passed from view. "What's to come of all this, Paddy? How do the soldiers feel about it?"

"Don't know, Joey. I'd say feelings are all mixed up. Hard to tell what we're really fighting for anymore. Most of us thought it was to preserve the Union." He snapped his belt buckle back into place. "But from the way things have been going up North here, the way I see it, there isn't much of a Union left."

"Second and Market. End of the line. All out." Jacob Stearn hung up the change box and walked slowly toward the rear. "You, there, Mulcahy and Beeson," he called. "Hold on a minute."

Giving his handlebar mustache a twirl with one hand, he pushed his conductor's cap to the back of his head with the other. "Want to tell you boys something. Few years back when you scallywags, meaning you in particular, Mulcahy, were tying goats to my car tracks for the sport of it down by Whitehall, I swore you'd never amount to any good. Well, I was wrong. Old Reverend Baker was riding my car the night he was thrown from it and killed. Know now that if some of you Frankford boys had been riding along, it never would've happened. That was a good thing you did, standing up for Santy."

Paddy's face remained expressionless, his inner thoughts running deep with searching questions.

The conductor placed a hand on his arm. "You were at the Bluff and Shepherdstown, weren't you?"

"That's right."

Jacob Stearn nodded, water-blue eyes peering beneath scraggly eyebrows. "Remember seeing your name in the paper. When you see the rest of those scamps who used to plague me, tell them old man Stearn forgives every blessed trick they ever pulled, will you do that?"

"Word from home's always welcome news in the field Mister Stearn, good or bad. I'll see they get your message."

A cap-lifting wind, blowing in raw off the Delaware, whistled about Paddy's ears as he alighted from the dummy. He drew his kepi down tight on his head and raised the collar of his greatcoat. Except for an occasional carriage, Market Street was deserted.

Beeson, shivering in his flimsy shoddy, wrapped spindly arms about his waist to accelerate the circulation. "Think we can catch another car up to the station?"

"Doubt it. Looks like everybody is either in church or at home feasting on turkey, car operators included. Might as well start walking."

Both fell into step and, striding at a brisk pace toward the railroad depot, relapsed into silence. Wispy vapors of frosted breath puffed from their mouths at every exhalation.

Where Tenth Street crossed Market, they were forced to pause momentarily at the curb while a closed rockaway carriage drawn by a bay gelding made a turn into Market Street.

Prompted by the sight of a uniform, the partially obscured driver pulled up on the reins and halted the carriage.

"May I give thee a lift someplace?" he called in a voice strangely sibilant through the isinglass window.

"If you're of a mind to," Paddy replied. "We're heading for the railway station."

"Fine. Climb in." There was a teasing ring in his voice. "Can't let any of Sergeant Cassidy's men wander around in the cold."

Paddy's head came up with a jerk as he sought a better view of the driver's face. "Well, I'll be...Quaker!"

He clasped his former comrade by the shoulders "Should've recognized you by that well-ventilated voice. It's great to see you again. How's the lung?"

"Coming along nicely. How's thy leg?"

"Good as new."

"You two know each other?" Beeson cut in.

"I'll say we do. Joe, meet John Walton. He and I have seen a lot together."

The Quaker extended a hand. "Glad to make thy acquaintance, Joe. Don't tell me Paddy's dragging a young fellow such as thee off to the lists."

"Dragging, hell," Paddy retorted. "He's been sticking to me like glue. Made him promise he'd go straight home once he's seen me off."

The Quaker studied Beeson's intense, freckled countenance. "Do thee think he'll comply?"

"He'd better. I don't want any child's blood on my hands, he's only fifteen."

The Quaker set the horse in motion. "Thee listen to Mulcahy, Joe. This war's no game to be played by young boys." He turned to Paddy. "If thee are thinking of taking the train to Washington, thee will have quite a wait. The next one is not scheduled to leave for three hours."

"That long?" Paddy was vexed. "Oh well, what's a few hours more or less. I can wait. Say, we're not taking you out of your way, are we?"

"Not in the least. I was on my way to Meeting. I'll still have plenty of time."

Bracing his elbows against his knees, Paddy hunched forward in his seat. "They've forgiven you?"

"Not exactly. I'll have to be passed on by Yearly Meeting next spring. Chances look pretty good though, a liberalization of the old dogmas seems to be taking place. It's even rumored the Yearly Meeting's going to abolish the dogma dealing with marrying outside the faith." His inadvertent slip of the tongue caused him to turn around and try to smooth it over, but Paddy was leaning back conversing with Beeson.

Paddy hunched forward again. "Where is your Meeting House, John?"

"South Twelfth Street, just off Market. Why?"

"Joe and I were just thinking. Since it's Thanksgiving we sorta thought...well, we'd like to go with you. Better than hanging around a station for three hours doing nothing."

"Thee would be most welcome."

"Sure would be interestin' to me," Beeson concurred.

"Good, I'll turn the buggy around." Swinging the carriage in a wide arc, he headed in the opposite direction.

Paddy settled back in his seat. "What are you doing for a living? Anything?"

"Yes. Started with Jay Cooke and Company about a month ago, selling government bonds."

Paddy emitted a low whistle. "You' ve really gone 'big time.' Understand the Jay Cooke Company's been financing the war for the government."

"Which is true," the Quaker replied with an amused smile, "but hardly enough to qualify me as 'big time' with the minor position I hold. I'm merely a small cog in a great big wheel. Matter of fact, though, the company itself has realized very little financial gain out of its wartime venture." He looked serious. "The one reason I wanted to go to work for them was because of their patriotic approach in handling the war's finances." He gave the reins a light snap. "It might surprise thee as it did me to know that the company takes only one quarter of one percent as gross commission on the sale of all bond issues."

Paddy grunted. "Humph. Didn't know we had any patriotic businessmen left. A fella wouldn't mind fighting for his country if he knew everybody back home was that decent and honest."

"They're a decent company. The North'll never know how much they owe to Jay Cooke."

Paddy glanced out of a window. "How much money a day do they take in for the war?"

"About a million and a half dollars."

"Wow!" Beeson blurted. "Didn' t think there was that much money in the whole world."

"Yes, thee would wonder where it all comes from. Especially when thee realizes how poor the people are. Never knew until I started working for the company that the per capita share of the entire wealth of the country is only fourteen dollars."

"I've been gypped," Paddy said, grimacing as he turned his empty pockets inside out.

"Thee are not the only one. It's enough to make a veteran turn sick to see people getting paid off in postage stamps the way they are, street car tickets being used for currency, and old Spanish coins which we call 'fips' used. The issue of fractional currency has relieved the situation somewhat, now that shin plasters are available, but the thing that's going to hurt the little fellow, and be even rougher on the soldier, is the new inflationary Legal Tender Act. What is it, they say, the rich get richer...."

At Twelfth and Market the horse wheeled to the right and trotted onto the quiet church grounds as if it knew the way by heart. The rockaway came to a halt in front of a long, low-lying carriage shed. The Quaker knotted the reins. "If thee will hand me that blanket behind thee, I'll cover the horse."

"We'll blanket him for you. Joe, grab a blanket."

"Sure thing, Paddy." Beeson's voice became a whisper. "Hey, you have money you can loan me for collection? All I got's enough carfare to get me back home."

Kneeling beside a wheel, examining it, the Quaker overheard the remark and looked up. "Thee need no money, Joe. We do not make our offerings in public."

"You don't? How come? Thought all churches took up collections."

"C'mon, cover that horse with a blanket," Paddy barked.

"Yeah, Paddy. Right away."

The blanketed bay snorted frosty vapor from his nostrils as the three young men strolled toward a plain brick building that was inviting in its simplicity. They entered through a wide-silled doorway. In keeping with the exterior, the interior of the Friend's Meeting House was devoid of ornamentation, as plain as the William Penn style hats of black felt worn by the male members of the congregation.

Following the lead of their host, the two visitors entered a pew and took seats on a spine-stiffening hard plank bench, at the same time noting with some degree of curiosity that the women were seated together on one side of the aisle, and the men on the opposite side.

Feeling edgy in the silence, Paddy twisted uncomfortably, his meandering gaze finally falling on a solitary figure standing guard at the rear of the building. An old gentleman held a long pole in his hand, with what appeared to be a feather affixed to one end.

Turning around, Paddy cupped a hand over his mouth. "The one in the back. What's he represent?"

Laughter glistened in the Quaker's eyes. "With that feather pole he tickles the noses of those who fall asleep."

The stillness of quiet meditation continued as each member of the Meeting pursued his responsibility of conferring with God directly, without aid of clergyman or programmed service. Being unfamiliar with the procedure that silence was not an end in itself, but an opportunity to utilize, Beeson stared idly out of a window and watched the bare limbs of the trees as they bent beneath the rushing wind.

Whether real or imaginary, Paddy felt the bearded elders sitting on elevated facing benches were boring holes through his military uniform.

"Who are they?" he whispered.

The Quaker roused himself from his thoughts. "The committee of oversight."

"Boy, they really check you front and back. Isn't anyone allowed to talk?"

"If the Spirit moves them."

A stillness in the plain room had prevailed for nearly a half hour when an elder rose slowly to his feet. He spoke in a soft, measured voice. "Oh, Lord, grant that we may profit from this painful lesson of Civil War in so much that we, thy children, may purge from our daily business and community life, as well as our national and international life, all deceitful practices and lustful grab of power, position and profit that have brought this war of brother upon brother. May God strengthen us in our religious conscience and firm conviction that killing is a moral evil to the end that by our pacifist example and refusal to bear arms, others may eventually see the wisdom of the commandment 'thou shalt not kill' and come to understand that differences can and must be settled peaceably by Christian fellowship, not by blood-letting and wars."

The gentleman reseated himself and the deep hush of silent meeting once more filled the room. Across the aisle, a woman with bowed head murmured softly, "God is Love."

Paddy had reached for his watch to make out the time of day when a slight movement on the part of the Quaker took his attention. Slowly, the veteran gained his feet and coughing spasmodically. began speaking. "The Witness of the Society of Friends for peace is far-reaching in scope, and positive in nature. It depends on our conception of God and of His relationship to man. Christ taught the Fatherhood of God and the Brotherhood of Man. war is open denial of this Fatherhood and Brotherhood. Followers of Christ cannot take part in destroying other men in whom God has implanted His nature and who are potentially temples of His Holy Spirit. To carry out such a profession consistently is a life attainment and should be the aim of every Christian. It is a solemn thing to stand for one's nation as advocates of inviolable peace. Our testimony loses its power in proportion to the want of consistency in our lives. Youth is impetuous. I have learned that through experience on the battlefield."

Paddy's gaze was riveted to the hardwood floor as his friend continued. "War by its very nature is a contradiction of the message, the spirit, the work, the life and the death of Jesus. Christianity calls for a radical transformation, for the creation of a new person who loves his neighbor as himself, and for the building of a new social order. Our peace testimony must include the whole of life. Seeds of strife must be eradicated in every aspect of our daily lives."

The Quaker bowed his head and, emitting a soft cough, sat down. Beeson sat rigid. He studied his scuffed shoes and tugged at a loose sock. Following the pattern of the congregation, Paddy sat transfixed in quiet meditation.

The bleak gray overcast outside had lifted and slanted rays of sunlight began streaming through the splayed windows of the Meeting House. A golden cascade of finely powdered beams fell upon the worshipers. A bell in the tower of Independence Hall tolled the hour of noon in stern, measured tones in response to which the elders facing the congregation shook hands with each other to signal the end of Meeting.

Paddy slipped into his greatcoat and had moved to assist the Quaker when he felt the slight touch of a hand on his arm. He turned and looked into the face of a woman. She smiled. "It was good to have thee visit with us this morning, dear friend. Do come again whenever thy spirit should so move thee." She turned and departed through the doorway.

"Friend John," a voice broke in, "would thee introduce me to thy two fine-looking companions?"

"Why certainly, Friend Wanamaker. May I present my former comrade-in-arms, Padrieg Mulcahy. And Joe Beeson, his friend."

"It's a pleasure to make thy acquaintance, gentlemen." With genuine warmth, he gripped the hand of each. "We are always delighted to have friends meet with us." He fixed his eyes on the Quaker. "That was a fine message thee shared with us this morning, John. I shall carry thy thoughts home with me. Christian beliefs molded and fortified by true experience are of much sterner stuff than the overused platitudes drummed into us by untested elders." Wanamaker paused to thrust his hands into wool gloves. "Pity of the matter is that each succeeding generation must test for itself, by trial and error, the fundamental truisms that are worth heeding, if not rational obedience.

"Well, good day to thee, gentlemen. Our door is always open. Come visit with us again."

"Thank you, sir," Paddy replied.

The raw wind had subsided considerably and the November air was warmer due to the effects of the sun.

"Just throw the horse blanket in the back of the carriage," the Quaker called as he unknotted the reins. "I'll fold it when I get home."

"Right you are." Paddy hoisted himself onto the seat. "That's a fine gelding you have. Wouldn't mind owning that fellow myself."

"Dad had him shipped in from Kentucky just before the war. Gave him to me as a present the day I was discharged."

"A gift to the prodigal son, eh?" Paddy chuckled.

"Yes, I guess that was about it. Say, why don't thee and Joe come have Thanksgiving dinner with us? We'd love to have thee. Thee could catch the night train to Washington."

"That's mighty nice of you, John, but I'm afraid if I stick around you much longer, I'll be turning in my uniform. You make sense when you talk, and I'm in too deep now to pull out. I've got to rejoin the regiment. When I come back I'll have dinner with you."

"That's a bargain. How about thee, Joe? Care to join me?"

"No thanks, sir. I've sorta changed my mind. Think I'll catch the dummy back to Frankford. There's one leavin' in about ten minutes."

"Well, now, I call that most selfish on the part of both of thee. However, if those be thy wishes, I shall deposit each of thee at thy points of departure."

At Second and Market streets, Beeson skipped from the carriage, waved a farewell salute and darted for a streetcar just ready to leave.

"Your words must have sunk in," Paddy said, grinning. "I would have sworn that squirt was going to stow away on the train and turn up in Washington with me."

"Anything I might have said to deter him from enlisting will soon be forgotten. He's young, he'll find things out for himself sooner or later." The Quaker snapped the reins and set his team off at a gentle trot. "I warrant the very next time thy young friend hears the stirring sounds of drums and bugles and sees the Old Flag and uniforms, he'll quickly forget the words he heard spoken this morning."

"Guess you're right. What was the remark Wanamaker made, 'We all have to learn things the hard way.'"

Reaching into a coat pocket, the Quaker took out a cough elixir which he swallowed to ease a coughing spell. "That is life," he replied in a husky voice.

With a gloved hand he wiped frosty vapor from an isinglass window shield.

Upon reaching Broad Street, he turned left toward the railroad station.

Paddy gazed at the passing traffic. "How's support for the war holding up in the city?" he asked.

"Falling off. Philadelphia has always had close ties with the South. Mainly it's the copperhead Democrats who are the stirrers."

The carriage came to a halt in front of the grimy Prime Street Station. Carts and conveyances of all sort bustled to and fro. The Quaker looped the reins and stepped into the street. He pulled his Quaker-brimmed hat tightly onto his head and drew a scarf about his neck. He extended his hand. "Goodbye, old friend. I almost feel as if I should be returning to the regiment with thee."

Paddy glanced at the jostling crowd of bounty levies who were waiting for the three o'clock train for Washington. A majority were cavorting in drunken revelry, smoking cigars, slapping one another, swearing and shouting.

"No, you don't belong in the army, John. It's filling up with scum. Look at them. Your kind can best lead us to a better world when they've all been killed off." Devilment danced in his eyes. "Like they say, 'The meek shall inherit the earth.'" He took his comrade by the arm and gave it a firm press. "Now the Lord knows I must go south, to find my family."

"In that quest I wish thee success, dear friend. May God go with thee "

CHAPTER 21

Paddy approached the midsection of the standing train, mounted the iron steps of a shabby coach and buffeted his way down an aisle filled to capacity with a shouldering crowd of soldiers returning to the front, all pushing and shoving. The atmosphere of the packed car was fouled by the sickening sweet odor of exhaled sour whiskey. A miasma of cheap cigar smoke hung in a dense cloud.

Gasping for air, Paddy hurried into the next car, where, much to his relief, conditions were somewhat improved and less crowded. The train lurched forward and he thrust himself into a seat encrusted with soot and cinder dust. Unfolding a *Philadelphia Inquirer* which he had bought on the run, he glanced briefly at the headlines then placed the paper over his face and reclined in his seat. Comforting landmarks of the city slid by the window, hazily slipping from sight like an oft-repeated dream, and soon the train was rolling south over the rich fertile countryside of Delaware County.

Through the clamor and hubbub around him, Paddy caught the fleeting mention of a familiar name being discussed behind him. Removing the paper from his face, he sat upright and listened.

"...and if it weren't for Wistar, matters on the Peninsula would be one helluva sight worse than they are. Since he's taken over and started to clean up, the district resembles a base for military operations instead of what it used to be, a hodgepodge slabtown of filth, corruption and inefficiency."

"But can he be trusted?" a husky voice cut in. "He's been accused of disloyalty both in the press and in open public forum."

The remark made Paddy flush. He turned around sharply and faced the two soldiers sitting behind him. "You two speaking of Isaac Wistar?" he growled.

"One and the same," the younger replied. "You know 'Old Cockspur?'"

"Well enough, I think. Used to be his orderly." His eyes narrowing, he said, "What's this loose talk about him being disloyal?"

"Ain't you read the papers lately?" the other replied in a raspy voice. "He's become quite a hot potato."

Something in Paddy's movements caused the youngest soldier to hastily intercede. "Don't get us wrong, mister. We're all for the general. The Ninety-ninth New York, that's our outfit, never had it so good until he took over. The charges of disloyalty ain't our doin', they come from political sources. Anyways, us boys don't put much stock in 'em, do we Hank?"

"Not too much. The general's an all right good egg."

Paddy eased back in his seat. "What charges of disloyalty are you referring to? I haven't..."

"Look, you say you were Wistar's orderly," the husky-voiced corporal broke in. "Then why not go see him? He can explain things better'n us."

"What? Wistar's on this train?"

"Yep. Him and his missus is forward in the next car, first compartment on your right."

Like a shot, Paddy left both soldiers staring after him. Seized by the excitement that comes with expectancy, he momentarily paused before the closed door, then raised a hand and knocked lightly.

"Yes, who is it?"

Paddy gathered himself. "Private Mulcahy, sir."

Instantly the door flew open wide and the tall form of General Wistar stood framed in the doorway.

"You Irish sprite! You're a sight for sore eyes. Come in, don't stand there. Come in." He snapped a strong arm about the shoulders of his former aide and gave them a tight squeeze. "Don't believe you've ever had the pleasure of meeting my wife. Sarah, this is Paddy Mulcahy."

Turning self-consciously, Paddy faced a delicately featured woman of gentle composure, with infinite charm and beauty glowing in an appealing face as she stretched out her hand. He blushed at the warm touch, and was pleased by its firmness and the greeting.

"So you are Paddy," she said in a soft, musical voice. "It is indeed a pleasure to make your acquaintance." Brushing aside a stray brown curl from her forehead, she smiled teasingly. "There have been occasions when I've been jealous of you, Paddy. The way Isaac refers to your capabilities at times makes me absolutely envious."

"Sit down, Mulcahy. Sit down. Tell us of your fortunes since last we met. How have things been going with you?"

"All right, I guess." He moved a hatbox to one side and sat down, poker stiff. His discerning eye noticed the colonel's robust health. He appeared even younger and more vigorous than on the fateful day of their meeting two years before.

Wistar's countenance became searching. "You say, 'All right, you guess.' I detect something here. Suppose you elucidate for me and leave out no details."

Paddy murmured, "Yes, sir." Haltingly and apprehensively, his eyes flicking every so often in the direction of Sarah, he proceeded to unreel the chain of happenings that had befallen him over the past year. From time to time Wistar interrupted with a specific question or two, for clarification on particular points, then settled back cross-legged and silent, stroking his thick goatee.

When he had finished, Mrs. Wistar quickly reached out a patronizing hand and laid it on his knee, staring deep into his face. "You dear, good boy. It would make me proud to have a son as fine as you. Now I know why my husband speaks of you so often with such a genuine feeling of pride." She turned to her husband. "Dear, isn't there something you could do to help locate Paddy's wife and child? After all, you do have many influential friends in the Confederacy. And there is that courier who befriended you on the field at Antietam, the one who now controls the area around Leesburg."

"Mosby?"

"Yes. Could not he be of help?"

"That's all my enemies would need, catch me in correspondence with the enemy. Especially with Mosby, the notorious guerrilla chief. Besides, I wouldn't consider it ethical. I owe him one debt already. Pass me a cigar from the box, please, Sarah."

Paddy shifted positions while the general lit a cigar and exhaled a series of smoke rings.

"You say your wife has a younger brother?"

"Yes, sir."

"And you think he may be attending the Virginia Military Institute? Is that right?"

"The family had been discussing it, yes."

Wistar tugged at an ear lobe in a way that Paddy had often seen him do when planning strategy.

"Hmm. Perhaps...I say perhaps, Humphrey could be of some help, he's an instructor there. Of course, I'd be risking my neck."

"That will be something new for you," his wife said smiling coquettishly.

"Don't do anything on my account that will get you in trouble, sir," Paddy protested.

Wistar guffawed. "Trouble? Trouble and I sleep together."

"Isaac!"

Wistar grinned boyishly. "Sorry, my dear. Didn't mean it the way it sounded."

Sarah tweaked his cheek. "Well, I should hope not."

Feeling coltish, the general ringed her nose with a circle of cigar smoke. "Now see here, Mulcahy," he continued in a more serious vein. "Why don't you let me put you in for detached service. Come to the Peninsula for the winter with me and be my right hand again. We can work together on your problem. There'll be no more activity in the field until spring. Winter camp life is dull and boring."

"Yes, sir, but..."

"There will be nothing dull or boring where my husband is concerned, Paddy. I can guarantee you that much. Why don't you come?"

"Could I think it over and write you?"

"Yes, of course," Wistar replied. "The offer will stand. Sarah, pass Paddy a sandwich. He looks hungry. Care for a drink?"

"No thanks, sir. The sandwich will be plenty."

The general eyed him again curiously. "Come now, Mulcahy, here's something else on your mind. What is it? Don't hold back secrets from your old commander."

Paddy gulped a bite of sandwich. "It's nothing, sir."

"Nothing? What is nothing?"

"It's just that I happened to overhear some men in the next car garbling something about you being disloyal."

Clearing her throat, Sarah picked up a ball of knitting yarn and a brace of needles to which she directed her attention.

"I suppose you would like to hear all about it?" Wistar inquired.

"Not particularly, sir. I have no doubts in my mind."

"Well, perhaps you should hear about it, anyway. What I have to say may prove a helpful lesson someday if you should ever be placed in a post of public trust. My recent experiences have been an example of how honest and sometimes independent forthright action can get you in trouble with that jackal clique of politico-military patriots running things."

He poured a drink of Scotch from a decanter, leaned back in his seat and crossed his legs. His piercing countenance contained something of the cold November wind whipping outside the window.

"Last summer when I was ordered to assume command of the military district of Eastern Virginia, it was hard to know where to commence on the Aegean stables. The entire command and theater was an unholy mess. The first step was to have a large area of abandoned fields, a few miles to the rear, surveyed and laid out in two- and four-acre lots with streets and buildings in line, and all able-bodied Negroes set to work building log cabins of prescribed dimensions. I directed the provost marshal to sell oystering permits to the people and from these funds, seeds and implements were purchased and Slabtown, as it was dubbed, was soon in condition to hold the refugees in the district.

"The local troops were reorganized and employed, with a portion of the contrabands in policing and clearing up the fort and the town. Otherwise they were kept constantly at drill. Rogues, under the name of Sutlers, were engaged in a profitable trade across the lines in all sorts of contraband. I had the provost guard quickly put a halt to their trade and the scoundrels were driven from the district. So much clearing away of rubbish on my part could not go on long without raising enemies and resistance."

There was a moment of silence in the compartment, broken only by the active click of Sarah's knitting needles. Wistar stood up and stretched. "All the scamps collected in that snug harbor," he continued, "both military and civil, with wise discretion and enlightened regard for their own skins, confined their charges and imputations to the troublesome theme of my loyalty. It is an axiom with the rascals of today that any coolness or deficiency on the partisan Republican profession constitutes a formidable kind of disloyalty. In their minds the truly loyal man is he who asks the fewest embarrassing questions, and their ideal patriot would be something like the late lamented Colonel Yell of Arkansas, president of the Yellville Bank, of whom his sorrowing eulogist declared, 'Our deceased friend though unable to account satisfactorily for the funds of that institution, showed by his remarks on the busting of same that his heart beat warmly for his native land.'"

Sarah Wistar interrupted. "Oh, bless me, I've dropped my ball of yarn. Isaac, would you retrieve it for me, please?"

"Certainly, my dear." With a low sweep of his crippled arm he reached down and handed a brightly colored ball of wool to his wife. He sat down and continued speaking. "The incident which you probably heard the soldiers discussing was a serious affair that occurred just recently. The district of Eastern Virginia had of course been nearly denuded of white males of suitable age for the Confederate Army. Nevertheless, there remained a considerable population, including several hundred lunatics in the state asylum at Williamsburg, among whom it was necessary to maintain order and, during the supervision of their resources, to preserve from absolute want. Such duties involved questions of municipal government and general policy as well as the expenditure of government property for purposes authorized only by implication, or not at all, and where it was not difficult to fall into legal and other errors. Whether such an error was committed by me or by the President of the United States, in the following case, you may judge for yourself."

Paddy's lips puckered as if drawn by a purse string. "Whew! That's swimming in deep water, sir."

"Granted, but the spring shower that's been whipped into a hurricane is this. A lady whose husband and sons were absent in the Confederate Army, her pecuniary resources cut off, applied to the commanding officer at Williamsburg for leave to cross the lines into the Confederacy, taking her family and household effects and a Negro child six years old. The application came down endorsed, 'Approved, except as respects the Negro child.' Not wishing to decide the Negro question myself, I forwarded it to department headquarters with the additional endorsement, 'Approved including the Negro, since such a child if left behind and separated from its natural protectors, would require dry nursing, for which I possess no soldiers properly fitted.

"The application was disapproved at headquarters and there the official part of the matter ended, but the Negro question being what it is and attended by political excitement, some reporter at Fortress Monroe got hold of the correspondence and I was soon in receipt from friends at home of copies of a certain hyper-loyal Eastern newspaper which, after printing my endorsements with the liberal addition of capitals, italics, and exclamation points, devoted a column or two to violent abuse of me as a traitor, a slave-hunter, kidnapper, and inhuman tyrant who abused the power entrusted to him to hunt down, catch and return loyal, patriotic Negroes to their cruel, blood-thirsty, disloyal owners.

"I threw the newspaper in the fire, but when General Butler arrived at Fortress Monroe to succeed Foster in command of the department, he forwarded me a copy with an unofficial letter stating his pain at seeing the publication and said that if I had a reply he would see it received proper publicity."

Wistar clamped his teeth into the cigar butt. "This proposition from a superior officer came nearer to upsetting me than the libel itself, and I wrote an indignant reply to the effect that while holding myself at all times ready to meet charges or explanations required by official superiors, I owed no duty to lying and irresponsible penny-a-liners forced by their trade to invent such lies as might bring them the most pennies, and scorned to notice or reply to them except by cutting off the rascals ears if I should ever get hold of him.

"Butler, who knew me well, explained that I had misunderstood him, that he wanted no explanation but was only anxious on my account to give opportunity for public denial. Knowing his love of applause and notoriety, I believed as much as I chose of that explanation, but nevertheless accepted the apology and after giving some reasons which will readily occur to a humane person, added the following strictly legal one. Namely, the President had by proclamation announced the abolition of slavery throughout the State of Virginia expressly excepting the territory held therein by military forces. To send the Negro child from our military lines, where slavery had been recognized by the highest civil and military authority, to a point outside those lines where, having been abolished, it no longer had a legal existence, was in effect sending the child from slave territory to free territory; that is, from slavery to freedom, unless it was the opinion of those disloyal persons who scoffed at the President's proclamation that it was equivalent to the Pope's fulmination against the comet. That ended the discussion, though Butler afterward told me in conversation that should my argument become public, he feared that prejudiced persons might regard my law as stronger than my loyalty."

Biting his cigar, he spread-eagled his arms on the back of the seat. "There you have it, Padrieg, the whole chain of events upon which my unscrupulous opponents galvanized their vilifications to wreak a character assassination upon the head of one who dared challenge the powers that be."

Paddy moistened dry lips and scratched the side of his head, a look of perplexity written on his face. "Sir, I'll have to thumb a dictionary to unscramble those last words. Remember, I'm no Philadelphia lawyer. But if anyone kicked my reputation around like that I'd sure want to lop more'n their damned ears off." Immediately conscious that he had used army talk in the presence of a woman, he quickly turned to amend his impropriety.

"Sorry, ma'am, it was a slip of the tongue. Must be hard on you, having your husband slandered in public like that, I mean."

Smiling, the general's wife looked up from her knitting. "Why, that's a mighty considerate question you ask, Paddy. I don't recall anyone giving me a chance to express myself before."

Wistar cleared his throat, but his wife paid no attention.

"Shall I answer as a woman, or as the devoted wife, Paddy?"

"Why...as...as both, ma' am."

"I shall speak then, as both. I think it's high time that men, grown men, stop playing games like little boys. From the time they're born till the time they die, little boys and grown men give we women many moments of pleasure and delight, but when they go around hurting each other they cause us sadness and anguish."

"Good God, Sarah," thundered Wistar. "You don't call preservation of the Union and settlement of the Negro problem a game, do you?"

"The expedient way in which you men play at it, yes, it strikes me that way."

"Then don't overlook the fact," Wistar spluttered, "that a lot of good...a lot of meddlesome women have triggered and contributed to the present confusion with their rabid, idiotic writings and activities."

Paddy stood up, flustered. "I...I guess I'd better go sir. I've...."

"No you don't Mulcahy. You perpetrated this outburst of domestic forensics, so just sit here and listen." Amusement crept into his dark, flashing eyes. "After all, you'll be having times like this on your own hands some day, so fortify yourself."

Sarah stretched out her hand. "Yes, please sit down. I've had my day in court. There's nothing more to say on the subject. Won't you have another sandwich?"

"Yes, ma'am, believe I will," he mumbled, relieved. "Thank you."

The closed compartment was gradually becoming dark as the early shades of the late November evening drew across the window; the sun had long since retired behind the horizon. Wistar rose stiffly and moved to light several oil lamps that soon dispelled the darkness with a ruddy glow. Paddy sank back into the soft, upholstered seat, a strange feeling of warmth and contentment encompassing him, and in a few minutes he had dozed off into a sound, peaceful slumber.

It was some time later when he was awakened by a gentle shake of the shoulder and heard a woman's voice speaking in his ear. "Come, Paddy, we're in Baltimore. Time to change trains."

"Ugh...uh...Baltimore? Already?"

"Yes. Did you have a nice nap? You've been asleep for nearly two hours."

"I have? I'm terribly sorry, I..."

The general was placing traveling bags out in the aisle. "Don't apologize. At your age you need plenty of rest. We made the run from Philadelphia in four hours. That's traveling twenty-four miles an hour. Those iron horses are getting faster every day. At the same rate we should make the trip from Baltimore to Washington in two hours."

For some reason, the mere mention of the nation's Capitol sent a thrill racing down Paddy's spine. He picked up the general's bags. "I'll carry them, sir."

"Thank you." Allowing Paddy to pass, Wistar stepped to one side. "All right, my dear, after you."

His wife gathered up her hat boxes and knitting bag and started for the compartment door.

Outside, the dim lights of Baltimore station cut through the cold, bleak darkness with the eerie glow of yellow jaundice. Paddy was the first to notice that pandemonium reigned at the depot platform, where a riotous crowd of soldiers and civilians were wildly enjoying themselves, shouting and waving newspapers aloft.

Sarah drew her fur collar tightly about her neck. "What do you make of all this, Isaac?"

A shivering newsboy broke through, calling loudly, "Wuxtrie! Wuxtrie! Read all about it. Grant captures Confederate Army in Tennessee. Wuxtrie! Read all about it. Battle above the clouds. Bragg in retreat."

"Here, boy," Wistar called. "Three papers, please." He hurriedly opened one and began reading the headlines aloud. "Grant shatters Bragg's Western Army at battle of Lookout Mountain and Missionary Ridge. Confederates suffer twenty-thousand casualties." Folding the paper, he gave the palm of his hand a vigorous slap. "Bully! We need those victories of Grant's like a desert needs rain. Come along, both of you, we can read the details once we're aboard the train to Washington."

The short trip across town through Baltimore was made quickly; the darkened city with its avowed Southern sympathy remained strangely quiet.

Comfortably lodged once more in the confines of the general's private compartment, Paddy broke open one of the papers and began reading.

"Well," Wistar said, "I see where two castoffs from our Army of the Potomac are redeeming themselves in the West."

"To whom are you referring, dear?"

"Burnside and Hooker. From the account here, they've conducted themselves as fighting generals for a change. The change of scenery must have done them some good."

A matter of more personal interest came to Paddy's attention and he read rapidly.

In the battle above the clouds the first regiment to storm the heights of Lookout Mountain was the Twenty-eighth Pennsylvania of General Geary's Second division, Twelfth Corps. Their fierce struggle continued all day around the rock-strewn flanks of Lookout as the battle line surged forward; the clouds were lurid with fires. In the morning, when the mists had swept away, the host of soldiery in and around Chattanooga saw the Stars and Stripes waving from the cliffs.

A feeling of pride overwhelmed him. There were a lot he knew from home in the Twenty-eighth: Willie McCool's brother, Owen, Chirp Castor's cousins, Lewis and Frank, the four Vandergrift boys, Henry Horrocks, Ferdinand Stearn and several others. A vision of their faces appeared before his eyes.

"You look pleased as punch about something. What is it?" Mrs. Wistar inquired, leaning over.

"Huh? Oh, I was just thinking of some friends of mine in the Twenty-eighth. They're mentioned here in the paper."

The general lowered his tabloid. "The Twenty-eighth, did you say?"

"Yes, sir."

"Hmm. That's the regiment of fifteen companies John Geary organized, uniformed and equipped at his own expense back in June of sixty-one." Wistar's eyes narrowed. "Tell me something, Mulcahy. Do you know, or did you hear anything of the Twenty-eighth being on Round Top that decisive morning of the second day at Gettysburg? Heard a rumor they were there in brigade and that Sickles failed to relieve them as ordered when they were moved over to Culp's Hill. That's the reason why so vital a position was left unmanned for a while."

"That's correct, sir. I know through a friend of mine who was up there as signal man."

Inhaling between his teeth with cupped tongue, Wistar made an insect noise. "I'd like to see that famous Round Top someday. Understand it was the key to the entire battlefield."

"Geary? Geary?" his wife repeated, as if searching for something. "Dear, wasn't it he who recently saw his eighteen-year old son killed at the battle of Wauhatchie? Somewhere I recall reading an account of the incident. I think in the *Inquirer* about two weeks ago."

"Yes, I knew the boy well. A captain. Commanded Knapp's Battery with skill and determination."

Sarah Wistar clasped her slim waist. "What a dreadful thing, to see your own flesh and blood torn to bits before your eyes."

A lull developed and conversation fell off, flickering back to life every so often in small talk and relapsing again until terminated finally by a conductor's service call that the train was pulling into Washington. Wistar stood up and stretched his arms and legs.

"Rearrange your disheveled plumage, Sarah, we are approaching the righteous seat of Republican purity and patriotism."

"Isaac, please. Have you no respect for Paddy's feelings?"

"Unless he's undergone a change of heart, my dear, I don't believe he holds truck with the mixed-up radicals any more than I do. Am I right, Mulcahy?"

Paddy slipped one arm into a coat sleeve and lowered his gaze. "To tell the truth, sir, I don't know exactly what I feel."

A boisterous crowd milling about the terminal platform gave vent to its enthusiasm over the recent victory news. Shouldering his knapsack, Paddy followed the Wistars onto the crowded, windblown station platform that was covered with running bits of paper. He recoiled against the night air and dug at the corner of one eye in an effort to dislodge an aggravating cinder.

The nation's Capitol could be seen in the misty haze of darkness. Its dome not yet completed, it appeared a decapitated colossus. Great black clouds drifting overhead were blotched with pale patches of phosphorescent moonlight.

At curbside, Wistar hailed a hansom cab. "My wife and I have been invited to spend the night with my good friend, Senator McDougal of California. What plans have you, Mulcahy?"

Paddy looked up. "Figured on spending the night at Soldier's Retreat. Tomorrow I'll catch the morning boat for Alexandria, then take the cars to Brandy Station."

Towering above him, the general wrapped an arm around the shoulders of his former orderly. "Will you write if you change your mind about spending time with me on the Peninsula?"

"Yes, sir. I really appreciate the offer."

Having entered the cab, Sarah reached and clasped Paddy by the hand. He felt the weight of gold coins being pressed against the palm of his hand. "I want you to purchase something for your wife with this," she said. "Meeting you has been a special privilege. I do hope we'll see more of you soon."

"Thank you. I'll have Becky write to you." Turning, he said, "Goodbye, sir."

"Goodbye, Mulcahy. And good hunting."

CHAPTER 22

Brandy Station, Virginia, in ante-bellum days one of those drowsy little country crossroads at peace with the world, a whistle stop on the Orange & Alexandria railroad, had become a used, battle-scarred wreck. Now it was a Southern rail terminal held by Federal forces in Virginia, a collection and distribution depot for war baggage and hardware.

The Potomac Army, camped on a level plain, was spread out in all directions as far as the eye could see. Hundreds of regimental bivouacs dotted the landscape with pointed Sibleys and row upon row of squat pup tents that formed company streets, stacked rifles ready for instant service.

Enemy-held territory lay to the south beyond a range of heavily timbered hills that bordered the Rappahannock.

In the sparsely settled village, ravished by frequent cavalry engagements, there was an antiquated general merchandise store, a dilapidated old grist mill and a scattering of two-and-a-half story buildings, the jaded brick walls pockmarked with bullet holes and all of the windows either smashed or removed. Chunks of bark on bare trees had been blown away by small arms fire.

Sheds constructed of rough-hewn boards, warped and weathered, lined the deeply rutted dirt road that ran through the middle of town. Next to a rail siding a decaying plank platform still served as the vantage point for loading and unloading. Mountainous stacks of crated and uncrated war materials were piled high on either side of the tracks: ammunition crates, boxes of rations, cannon balls, artillery pieces, spare wheels, pungently creosoted and tarred railroad ties. all the necessary implements with which to deal death and destruction.

Paddy glanced at the cold gray overcast and flung his knapsack to the ground. He jumped from a car that was packed to overflowing with returning veterans and a sprinkling of clean-shaven levies, many of them soap-polished to the point of brilliance.

Immediately, the sounds and smell and sweat- stained activities of army life in the field acted as a cathartic and purged his mind of the recent placid domestic life associated with home and travel. Short-tempered teamsters were swearing at awkward draftees, whose bungling antics obstructed the loading process. A squad of toughened veterans, with mangy beards and threadbare, filthy uniforms, stopped to hurl taunts at the well-dressed newcomers.

Leering, a scarred eyelid drooping half shut, one grizzled old corporal called gruffly, "'Ave a taste o' Virginny clay, boys." He reached down and picked up a handful of horse dung and flung it at them, splattering it across the starched shirt front of a startled young private standing nearby. "Don't be brushin' it off, sonny," he shouted. "That's part o' regulation uniform in this ass hole of creation."

His companions laughed boisterously. Accustomed to that kind of horseplay and ignoring it, Paddy dodged from the path of a wildly careening artillery hitch dashing by, an empty caisson jouncing behind, and continued his way in search of the provost marshal's office. A short distance away he came upon a cupola-topped brick building, formerly a borough hall; over the doorway hung the sign he was looking for. In front, congregated about a mud-spattered buckboard that stood at rest in the roadway, stood a crowd of angry soldiers knotted together.

Inquisitive, he pushed his way forward and stretched his neck to get a closer look at the cause of the uproar. In the wagon, lying pale and still on a bed of straw, he saw the body of a teenage corporal, his clean, boyish features twisted by the rigors of death. Paddy turned to a sergeant next to him. "What's all the ruckus about?"

"Another butcherin' job by Mosby's guerrillas," came the snarling response. "A good-lookin' kid like him wasn't hurtin' nobody, hope the colonel hangs the lot of 'em."

"Hangs who?"

"Local people he's arrested as hostages for this atrocity. Colonel's got 'em inside now. He don't do somethin', we will."

Paddy shifted his knapsack to the opposite shoulder and, breaking away from the crowd, made his way toward the front door of the building.

"Where you think you're goin'?" challenged a sentry, his rifle coming down in toll-gate fashion.

"Arrange for transportation to my regiment in the field. Just been discharged from the hospital."

"Veteran, eh? What regiment?"

"Hundred'n Eighteenth Pennsylvania."

The sentry returned his rifle to its station. "A Corn Exchanger, eh? You got a real smart outfit. Where'd you get 'tumbled over' ?"

"Gettysburg."

"Okay, fella. Go and wait in the hall. But don't bother the colonel just yet, he's busy."

Paddy seated himself on an empty bench that faced the open door of the provost's office where he was able to see and hear what transpired.

Dressed in frock coats and holding beaver hats clutched tightly in their hands, a group of Southern citizens stood before a graying Union officer seated behind a desk, a benign sort of man who resembled a middle-aged schoolmaster more than he did a provost marshal. His voice was firm and even.

"I will not sacrifice any more of my men to protect your homes and families, and that is final. The depredation of your guerrillas have become so frequent and outrageous that I'm withdrawing the guards. You gentlemen will remain under arrest, your families may shift for themselves. In the meantime, until these wanton, barbarous attacks cease..."

The oldest gentlemen in the group stepped a pace forward. "Believe me, suh," he said haltingly, "when I say we..." he nodded in the direction of his friends, "are just as provoked ovah his mattuh as you are."

Placing a brown beaver hat on the officer's desk, he reached into a pocket and withdrew a folded paper. "By your leave, suh, would you listen to a petition we've drawn up among ourselves?"

The officer stared, curious. "Yes, you may proceed."

Adjusting pince-nez glasses to the bridge of his finely chiseled nose, the Southern squire began reading:

Cedar Run, Virginia
December 2, 1863
General Robert E. Lee
Commander, Army of North Virginia

We, the undersigned citizens of the county of Fauquier, living along the line of the Orange & Alexandria railroad, find it impossible to remain longer at our homes unless something can be done immediately to prevent the murdering of Union soldiers after surrendering as prisoners of war to the Southern Confederacy. The citizens are held responsible and we earnestly beg that General Lee will protect us by preventing a repetition of such horrible deeds. The occasion which prompts this appeal, and the last act for which we are held responsible, is the robbing, stripping, and brutal murder of a young soldier who was cutting wood near his camp. Eight citizens were arrested to suffer for the guilty act, but were finally released on condition we acquaint you with the facts and find if such vices are permitted by the commander in chief of the Southern Army.

The officers of the United States Army, while fully cognizant of our Southern sentiments, have always kindly protected us with safeguards when necessary, besides often showing us kindnesses and favors which we had no right to expect from enemies. Under the circumstances, it is sad that our own soldiers should cause them to withdraw that protection, and leave us to destruction and our country to desolation.

This is not the first instance in which the deeds of your scouts have been visited on us. We cannot believe the commander in chief of the Southern Army, of whom even his enemies speak with high respect, is cognizant of this injustice which falls so heavily on our innocent and unoffending families.

Yours respectfully,
(signed) S. G. Catlett
W. S. Edmond
A. S. McLearon
E. D. D. Taylor (A wounded and discharged soldier of the Confederate Army)

John W. Nichols
Captain James McLearon (A soldier of 1812)

Glasses removed, the Southern spokesman handed the paper to the provost marshal for inspection. "It is ouah intention, suh, to forward this petition to General Lee to advise him of the situation hereabouts. Ouah conditional release from arrest, as inferred and so stated in the petition, is dependent solely on your option as an officer in the United States Army and as a No'thern gentleman, suh."

The provost marshal's face became a careful study, as he eyed each man standing before him. "Will you, sir," he said, addressing the elder spokesman of the group, "read this petition to the men who are gathered outside?"

"I would deem it my duty and privilege, I feel honor bound to do so, suh."

The Union officer turned to his adjutant. "Release these men from arrest, Major. See to it that they're safely escorted to their homes."

Murmurs of "Thank you, kindly" came from the group.

"And, Major, countermand that order removing all guards from homestead areas in the vicinity with a substitute order to redouble the guard."

"Yes, sir."

As soon as the provost's office had been cleared of principals, Paddy rose from the bench, crossed the hall, and entered the domain of law and order. A bearded sergeant stopped him just inside the doorway.

"State your purpose, soldier."

"I need directions and transportation to rejoin my regiment, the Hundred'n Eighteenth Pennsylvania Volunteers. Third Brigade, First Division, Fifth Corps."

"Your name and rank?"

"Paddy Mulcahy, Private."

"Let's see your papers and identification."

Fishing in a breast pocket for his hospital discharge papers and proper identification form, he handed them over to the non-commissioned officer who, satisfied with their authenticity, moved behind a desk to consult a wall map.

"Hundred'n Eighteenth's camped on the George S. Patton property, a short distance from Culpepper. Wagon train's leaving for that area in an hour. You armed?"

"No, sir."

He hastily scribbled on a requisition blank. "Here, get yourself a rifle across the street at the quartermasters. Our trains all travel with heavy escort, but that doesn't seem to stop Mosby's men. Better look sharp all the way."

"Where are the wagons forming?"

"South end of town, two blocks down."

It was toward evening when the heavily laden supply wagons rumbled into the deserted village of Culpepper without incident. A detachment of men on provost duty hastened forward to help with the unloading. To test his leg, Paddy leaped to the ground, at the same time noticing that the brick and frame dwellings of the quaint country seat were boarded up and apparently tenantless. Of the fifteen hundred population not a single resident could be seen on the roads, and of the twenty stores none seemed to be doing business. Two hotels, the Piedmont and Virginia, still pretended to accommodate travelers. He studied other scattered landmarks that consisted of four churches, a large institute for girls, an academy for boys and several other buildings. Set amidst an impressive stand of trees in the heart of the village was an imposing public building, columned in front, that marked Culpepper as a shire town.

Paddy carried his rifle wearily at port arm and started walking slowly away, heading toward an encampment that fringed the horizon. After a fifteen minute hike, his tired feet burning inside sweaty socks, he entered the outer cordon of the Third Brigade area. Close by stood a sobering spectacle, the George S. Patton residence, one of those innocent victims in the pathway of war, that had been reduced to charred ruins. The ancestral home of the Twenty-second Virginia's Infantry Colonel was a bleak heap of ruin. Paddy stared at the destruction in disgust.

The Patton house had once been a fine old-time Virginia mansion. Its wide hallways, commodious chambers, grand old porches and picturesque avenues were evidence of ancient thrift and indicative of old time hospitality. Abandoned property, however, was an incentive to pillage. Deserted dwellings prompted vandalism. Hasty inferences might be drawn of a burning, personal hatred of their occupants and the demon of destruction roused by a spirit of resentment that prompted the best of men to deeds of plunder.

The Patton house had not been exempt from that kind of ruin attendant on all such derelict property. Its fine porches were destroyed, doors, windows and floors carried away. Everything movable found its way to the flames or was temporarily utilized in the quarters of neighboring troops. A large old-fashioned brass knocker bearing the ancestral arms and the honored aristocratic name of its founder had been torn from its place on the front door. The venerable ornament was being used to adorn a temporary door which a crude Northern mechanic had constructed for the entrance to his canvas quarters for no other purpose than to find a place for the accommodation of the insignia of the Patton aristocracy. Brass heads from ancient bedposts, lambrequins, andirons, fenders, stoves, spittoons, pitchers and basins were all put to use, or used for ornamentation, as the taste or inclination of the despoiler happened to dictate.

Despair mixed with a feeling of shame and associated with guilt, Paddy turned and walked slowly away from the scene while overhead a circling crow cawed in the sky and a startled rat scurried for its hole. A mean drizzle came out of leaden clouds and the bleak November wind groaned mournfully in the bare branches of dripping wet trees.

Located on a gentle swell of ground rising some several hundred yards beyond the Patton house, the ensign of the Corn Exchange Regiment sagged limply along a length of grease-stained staff. The colors appeared dimly blue and gold in the soggy haze of smoke and shadows.

Paddy halted in his approach for a brief moment, surveying the surroundings with a rush of memories. A camp once sprawling white with tents full to capacity, the regimental bivouac was now measurably reduced. The noticeable diminution of its former size and strength was a distressful sight to his searching gaze. He started walking.

The H Company street was deserted save for one individual. At the far end, McCool, wearing galluses of broad stripe over a red flannel undershirt, was standing with legs straddled. He was busy exercising with a fifteen-pound cylindrical case shot, thrusting the weights outward from his body, then upward, then down, and repeating the process, his Simian countenance distorted by the effort. At the sight of Paddy, he let the weights fall with a crashing whang as he boomed, "Lordy luva duck, look who's back."

Like corks popping, inquisitive heads showed at tent fronts. The name Mulcahy was barked from all directions. In a split second, the company street was flooded with swarming comrades back-slapping and chorusing rapid-fire questions.

Hallowell, deep lines on his face, showed his age. He grasped Paddy by one hand and began pumping it as though it were a handle. "How's my wife and family, Mulcahy? Bess wrote you were at the house to..."

Kimball, showing gray at the temples, spun Paddy by the other hand. "Forget about Jake, Mulcahy. Tell me first about my family. The children..."

Unshaven stubble on his face, Bob Dyer pressed himself to the fore ahead of others, his sharp, pointed nose acting as a forerunner. "You see my mother and dad before you..."

A rough thrust by Jobson put Dyer forcibly aside. "To hell with personalities. How's the old town, Mulcahy? Still look the same?"

"Whoa, hold on. Let me get my breath, will ya?" Wearing a smile, he turned to look around. "Tell me where I can dump my gear and I'll feed you all the news."

Vandergrift, still nursing a stiff arm from the Gettysburg encounter, stepped forward. "Want to come in with me? I've been bunkin' solo."

"Fine by me, Van. Just don't kick the blankets off at night."

"Don't worry, at night these long shanks of mine curl up and play dead."

"Good. Keep 'em that way."

Following the lengthy strides of his new tent-mate, he crossed the area with the others crowding close at his heels and in short time was established in his canvas quarters as comfortable as could be expected under field conditions. Sitting cross-legged, like a potentate holding court, he began answering questions.

Outside, darkness fell in a curtain of black before everyone had been fully satisfied in their thirst for news of loved ones and home. Campfires burned brightly in the company street as men prepared supper, their voices low, and flaming logs pitted their strength against a whipping cold wind.

Wearied by the long session with his comrades, Paddy returned to his tent. Rolling over on his back, he gazed into space. "Say, Van, where's the cap'n and Cassidy? Haven't seen hide nor hair of 'em since I got here."

"Went looking for turtles early this afternoon. Guess they're not having much luck or they'd have been back by this time."

Paddy raised up on one elbow. "Why the sudden interest in turtles?"

"Nourishment. Turtle soup's about all that's keeping the captain on his feet."

"That bad? Tell me exactly, how are they? I mean both Frank and Andy."

"The captain's not good, not well at all. Looks like a dog coming down with distemper. Cassidy? He gets rougher and meaner by the day, and no wonder with the kind of replacements they've been feeding us. They're enough to drive any man insane."

"Why? What's the matter? What do they do?"

"Do? Just wait till morning. Then keep your eyes and ears wide open. You'll see. Now how about dousing the glim. I'm ready for sleep."

"Same here." He reached out and gave the candlewick a quick scissors-pinch that plunged the tent into darkness and sent a thready white veil of tallow smoke curling upward, trailing off until it evaporated. Managing a yawn, he stretched himself. "Say, almost forgot to ask, had any late word from your brothers in the Twenty-eighth?"

There was a slight stirring in the blankets beside him. "Not since they took off on that Tennessee campaign."

"Oh. Guess you saw where they were first to storm Lookout Mountain."

"So I've heard." A bearish grunt and Vandergrift pulled the frayed covers over his head leaving a cockscomb of matted black hair protruding.

Daydreaming for a while, Paddy let his gaze focus on the shadowy canvas shelter above, then, burying himself in the blankets, fell into a sound sleep.

The gray light of dawn was just beginning to show its pearly face, dripping with hoarfrost, when Paddy became conscious of someone trying to rouse him. He felt a repeated, gentle shaking of one leg. Shivering and chilled to the bone he sat upright, a sudden cry escaping his lips.

"Frank! Wondered when...say, how've you been?"

Captain Donaldson, hunching at the front of the tent, appeared gaunt. Dark circles under his eyes spread black patches from cheekbone to cheekbone. The eyes once a lively blue were recessed in bony sockets dull and starey. His voice had a deep-throated rasp. "Heard you were in camp when I got back last night, Mulcahy. Too late to come see you so I made it this morning. Must say you look great."

"Feel great. But you? Cripes you look like death warmed over. Heard you weren't feeling too well." Throwing his covers off, he scrutinized his friend as he crawled cautiously forward so as not to disturb the sleeping form beside him. "You must've dropped twenty pounds."

"Just about."

"Then why don't you go home and rest up? Take it easy for awhile."

"Rest? After nearly three years, I've forgotten how to rest."

"Don't bet on it. You'd be surprised..."

The crass notes of a bugle sounded reveille throughout the camp.

Donaldson regained his feet slowly. "Look, I'll see you after formation. Have something important that might be of interest to you."

"It's in your face. It's about Becky. Come on, tell me now."

"Haven't time. See you after formation."

Paddy stepped outside to dress.

Sergeant Cassidy was standing with arms akimbo, his voice sounding across the area. "Top o' the marnin' to ye, Private Mulkayhee. And would ye be after findin' our accommodations equal to yer own in Frankford?"

"I would indeed, you donnygaul hard nose."

Cassidy advanced with hand outstretched. "Sure'n it's good to have ye back. Good indeed. Are ye sound of wind and limb now, to be sure?"

"Never felt better."

"Then it's glad tidings ye're bringin'. We could be after usin' more o' the likes o' them from the 'old line.'"

Just then a sudden disturbance arose in the form of a wild demonstration taking place in the neighboring bivouac of K Company. A young soldier, only half clad and with his juvenile face twisted in diabolical merriment, ran along a line of tents. He was swinging a skunk, which he carried by the tail. Passing the open fronts of each canvas and employing a short circling movement, he swung the writhing, helpless creature into each aperture, whooping with glee as he did so.

Cassidy pursed his lips and glared as he spat on the frozen ground. "Arrr. 'Tis them divilish little fairies o' Company K actin' up again. I'd be after seein' they was all shipped home to their mither's breasts where they belong."

Paddy looked amused. "Fairies? Is that what you call them?"

"'Tis a moniker we all gave 'em."

"Why?"

"Because they haven't grown up yet," Vandergrift snorted as he came up from behind. He fixed his attention on a belt buckle and snapped it shut then stood with arms folded across his chest and watched the proceedings with disgust.

"There's not one of them who's over eighteen," he said. "Look close. See how they are all light-weight and small. Their little forms, quick ways and smooth faces, along with those damned constant smiles, just naturally classifies them with the fairies you read about as a child."

"Bejabbers, the names by which they address each other wouldn't be securin' recognition fer themselves in the fairy world 'Gun Boat' Connelly, 'Forager' Smith, 'Killer' Kessler...." Cassidy threw up his arms in utter despair. "And saints preserve me if there's one of 'em what's been in the army more 'n two months. Tell Mulkayhee 'bout their first experience on picket. I've got to rout out me own brand o' troublemakers."

"What happened, Van? What went off?"

"Well, first they got lost, but somehow or other they managed to get back to the regimental lines. On the way they gathered together a large number of abandoned muskets and secured a lot of ammunition. When they got back they posted themselves behind our breastworks for resistance when the onslaught which they felt was close at hand should come. They didn't have long to wait. Resting their pieces on the works, and having an oversupply of ordnance, they managed to fire from each shoulder at the same time. One of their crew kept giving the command, 'Fire by battery,' and they all blazed away at once."

Paddy laughed out loud. "Must have been something to see."

"It was. But how effective their double-barreled gunnery operated will never be known. They did earn something by it in the form of another name tag, besides being known as the 'Fairies of Company K,' they have since picked up the title of the 'Jack ass Battery' of the Hundred'n Eighteenth."

Lieutenant Batchelder's high-pitched voice pierced the morning mist. "Fall in. Line up. Cassidy, drive out those beats."

"Right away, sir."

Paddy grasped his rifle and hurried into formation. Upon completion of company roll call, Captain Donaldson stepped forward to address the line, his manner of communication a mere echo of its former strength. "Morning detail. The following men will report to Private Mulcahy for picket duty. Jobson, Hallowell, Kimball, Brogan..."

"Well, what do you know," came a grating voice from the rear. "First day he's back and I get a chance to go out with the famous Mulcahy. Le' me have a look at this big hero you bummers talk so much about."

Paddy spun around, surprised. Knitting his eyebrows in annoyance, his searching gaze picked out the one who had done the talking, a stranger to him, a recent conscript. He was a behemoth of a man close to middle-age who had a hard-looking pockmarked face. His powerful head closely resembled a cannon ball set on his massive shoulders.

Donaldson scowled. "As you were, Brogan."

"And who says so? Just because this Mulcahy character's a flunky o' yours don't give you no call to send him out in charge o' picket first day he's back, get us all lost or killed, mebbee."

Two levies who were standing on either side of Brogan started grinning, their lips curled in an ugly twist.

Donaldson's command crackled. "McCool. Replace Brogan on picket. Brogan, report to me right after formation."

"Now ain't that nice? Ain't never had an invitation give me by a Philadelphia bluestocking before."

The two men on either side laughed coarsely.

"S'pose you want to drill me in the great name o' Donaldson, seein' how I worked in your old man's lumberyard. High and mighty mucky-mucks. You and your snot-nosed name ain't nothin' but crap in my book."

Stung, his nostrils blowing wide, fists doubled, Donaldson uncoiled and made a lunge for the hulking form only to have Cassidy at the last moment fly in between, his brawny arms pinioning his commanding officer.

"Don't be soilin' yer hands, sir. Le' me..."

"Outa my way, Cassidy."

"Not on yer life, sir. I've handled these wharf rats all me life. I'll cut 'im down to size in me own fashion."

Donaldson drew back, breathing hard. His words came with a ring. "No. Never had any brawling among our company before. Won't start now."

Slowly he withdrew a pistol from its holster and pointed it at the insubordinate's belly. "Brogan," his voice was a menacing purr, "you're going to take a nice little ride."

"Ride? What kind o' ride?"

"You're going to be first in this regiment to take the caisson cure. Sergeant, organize those named for picket duty into guard detail. We'll walk Mr. Brogan over to the artillery park."

"No you don't. You won't get away with this." He turned to the men on either side for a show of support as the guard detail closed in with leveled bayonets.

"You yellow-livered rats!" he shouted. "Ain' t nobody gonna stand up for me?"

There was dead silence.

"You sonovabitch, Donaldson. I'll get you for this. First time in battle, I'll stick a knife in your back."

Paddy stepped forward to within spitting distance of Brogan's distorted face. His voice had a hard edge to it. "Better think twice about that. I'll be a file closer right behind you with a sharpened bayonet."

A silent hike to the artillery park began, the guards harboring a sadistic eagerness to witness the new innovation prescribed for their prisoner. Brutal punishment had always been on tap, but hitherto not amounted to more than the army's backhanded way of cuffing the ne'er-do-wells and misfits who found their way into the ranks. In recent months harshness had become necessary because of the significant number of soldiers requiring that kind of treatment. A new mood had taken hold of the army, a mood that was destroying the old spirit. Veterans drew closer together, aliens in the army which they had created. The regulars had always been accustomed to hard cases and knew how to handle them. The volunteer regiments were now following suit, caste lines hardening and discipline enforced by brutality.

It was only natural that the artillerymen should lead the way. Volunteer batteries had always shown more army flavor than infantry regiments because General McClellan had taken pains to brigade one regular battery with every three batteries of volunteers, and the force of example was strong. It was not unusual to see park gunners pounding their recruits into shape on any sprawling artillery park.

Arriving at just such a place, Sergeant Cassidy held up a chevroned arm and signaled a halt. A barrel-chested, bull-doggish battery commander dressed in an oversized greatcoat approached the small detail.

McCool whispered in Paddy's ear. "Man, ain't he just about the closest thing to a grizzly bear you ever seen?"

The cannoneer had a cleft upper lip and when he spoke his lip seemed to roll up on every word. "You men have a bad one in need of military discipline and courtesy instruction?"

Expressionless, Donaldson stepped a pace forward and saluted. He proceeded to give a brief summation of the circumstances.

"A real tough 'alley growler, ' eh?" The artillery major strode to where Brogan stood. "I'm surprised at you, a man your age. Should have learned decency and refinement a long time ago. Perhaps it's not too late to teach you. What'll it be, Captain? Wheel or rack."

"Wheel."

"Good choice. Wheel it'll be."

Raising his voice, he called to two gunners working over their pieces. "Smitty! Baker! Over here with that caisson. On the double!"

McCool, eyes sparkling with anticipation, rested the stock of his rifle on the frozen ground and was leaning on it heavily his chin propped on the barrel, when the horse-drawn caisson rumbled into position. "Sure wish the cap'n had selected the rack, they say it's the worst."

Paddy raised his eyebrows. "What's the rack?"

"That wooden box what lays across the tail end of a battery wagon, the heavy rack used to carry forage. Sticks out a couple of feet from the rear wheels. They take a fella and make him stand with his feet in the rungs of the wheels, his chest pressin' tight against the rack, then they tie his wrists to the upper rim of the wheels, feet tied to the lower rim. That leaves him hanging with all his weight pressing against the sharp wooden edge of the rack. They always gag the feller first. From what I heard, ain't even the toughest customer can stand it without screamin'. Mostly they pass out after a few minutes."

Standing alongside, Jobson wiped the back of his hand across a light stubble of beard. "And from what I've heard, it leaves most of 'em permanently disabled. They say an artilleryman'll beg to be shot rather than racked."

Heavily muscled cannoneers dismounted from the caisson and approached their commander. "Where's the patient, Major?"

"That's him." He pointed. "He gets the wheel. You know what to do."

Brogan resisted as the gunners dragged him forcibly by the arms to the rear of the wagon. Mounted at the rear of the caisson was a spare wheel tilted at a slight angle from vertical so that it missed the ground by a couple of feet.

"All right, tough guy. Up on the lower rim of the wheel."

Employing arm locks, both battery-men hoisted their kicking, thrashing victim into place and, working as an experienced team, spread-eagled him on the face of the wheel, lashing his wrists and ankles firmly to the iron rim. They gave the wheel a quarter turn so that the insubordinate was suspended by a wrist and an ankle.

"You want we should put a stick in his mouth to gag him, Major?"

"No, Smitty, he's noted for his big mouth. We'll let him exercise it a while. Take him twice around the park at a gallop, then leave him on the wheel a couple of hours to cool off."

Jobson turned his head away. "Holy hell, I don't know whether I want to watch this or not."

At the crack of the whip, the artillery hitch sprang forward and took off at a mad gallop. Brogan, strapped to the spare wheel of the bouncing caisson, screamed in agony and begged for mercy as he writhed and struggled to free himself.

Fascinated, McCool leered at the passing demonstration. Others in the guard detail moistened their lips as they watched. Hawk-eyed artillerymen around the park dropped their chores and stood with arms folded. They stared at the punishment in callused silence.

Eyes cast down, Donaldson raised his hands to blow warm breath on them.

"Sergeant!"

"Yes, Cap'n?"

"Take the detail out to the picket line. I realize it's not your turn, but in a way, Brogan was right. Mulcahy doesn't know this region too well. Some mix-up could arise."

"Sure'n 'tis the walk I'll be enjoyin', sir." With a touch of sympathy, he added, "Shall we be after startin' right away, sir?"

"I think it best."

"All right ye lollygoggers, shoulder arms. Show's over. Forward, march."

The sky, gray as gunmetal, was piled with drifting banks of white clouds, mammoth snow-balling drifts under the cover of which birds were flying south for warmer climates, sailing and diving as they battled against strong headwinds.

Paddy cast a backward glance as the picket detail trudged north over a deserted country road. He noticed that long before the prescribed time, Donaldson halted the rampaging caisson and cut Brogan loose. The captain appeared to struggle beneath the heavy weight as he placed the unconscious form on the ground and began administering aid.

Hallowell grasped Paddy by the shoulder. "Say, how come the cap'n sent you out on duty first day you're back? Thought you and he were thick."

"We are. That's the reason he sent me out. On the way to the artillery park he told me Kelly just reported a friendly Southern picket in front of our position who might be of some help to me. The Johnny Reb's from Leesburg. Knows my wife. Will talk to me, but nobody else."

Hallowell's aging and usually dour mien softened. "I'd nearly forgotten. Here's hoping for you, but be careful. This fella might be a rejected suitor."

A smile crossed Paddy's face. "I don't think so."

Following a mile or so hike and at a place where the road forked, Cassidy signaled for a halt. He wore a puzzled frown as he scanned the barren scrub land.

"Well, now ain't that a fine kittle o' fish. Kimball, ain't this the spot where Cap'n Donegan's left flank's s'posed to be?"

"Best I can remember, it is. 'Left on south fork of the road. Right flank to rest on the river.' Those were the orders."

McCool's moon face popped out of nowhere. "Think something might o' gone wrong, Sarg?"

"Dunno. Say, where'd he come from?" A haggard worn specimen of a man suddenly appeared standing in the nearby brush. Jobson stepped forward for a closer look. "Must've been stooped over looking for roots and herbs."

The bent figure advanced toward the road, his wrinkled gray countenance expressing contempt for the entire Union Army.

Cassidy called to him. "Top o' the marnin' to ye, mister. Who be ye? Seen any Federal pickets hereabouts?"

"Not a damn one, suh. Not a damn one."

The men traded amused glances. Cassidy nodded toward the right fork of the road. "Tell me, old man, where's that branch go?"

"Don't go no place. Stays put right where it is."

Hallowell glowered. "Beware, old man, beware. There are Massachusetts men behind us. An answer such as that to them may bring down the vengeance of New England upon your hoary head."

The men laughed. Cassidy became impatient. "Enough o' this tomfoolery, ye blatherskites. Mulkayhee and Jobson, ye come with me. We'll hike down this road a stretch'n see where that divil Donegan and Kelly have put their picket line. Corporal Hallowell, ye'll take charge here and post the men accordingly."

With his two subordinates, Cassidy strolled off in the direction of the Rappahannock.

At a patch of woods a half mile distant from the fork in the road, the small search party finally came upon the divisional picket line under command of Captain Donegan, B Company.

"What's held you up, Sergeant?" the officer inquired, his lower jaw thrust out. "You were due here an hour ago. Where's the rest of the relief?"

Cassidy jerked a thumb over his shoulder. "Back there at the fork, sir, where I thought they should be."

"Never mind what you thought. They should be here. I found a wide gap between my right and the river, moved the whole picket line over and closed it."

Cassidy gulped. "Beggin' yer pardon, sir, but I take it the Second Division's pickets have been brought in?"

"Second Division?"

"Yes, sir. They been after holdin' an outer line anchored at the river, 'bout half mile in advance o' the interior line ye've set up."

"Nobody told me anything about them being out there. If they're still out in front, so be it, we'll have formed a double cordon, double protection."

During an interlude of silence, Cassidy bit off a chew of tobacco and stood waiting, fully expecting an immediate order to notify the misplaced pickets of their precarious situation. Instead, the round little officer, breezy and complacent, consulted a battered timepiece, gazed momentarily up at the overcast and started to walk away.

Paddy began seething. It was painfully evident that Donegan was apparently satisfied his error would not be detected and did not believe it worthwhile to disturb his posts-soldiers already comfortably fixed for three-day's work.

Cassidy changed expressions as he sensed the same thing. He squirted a thin stream of tobacco juice through the gap between his two front teeth. "gotta lot o' raw recruits out here with ye, ain't ya, Cap'n? Anyone comin' in from that outer picket line's liable to get himself plugged. Greenies might even wing an inspectin' general officer or two."

"Nonsense, Sergeant, they're alert soldiers. You go bring up those men you left on the road and then report back to me."

Cassidy's face turned red and he grimaced as he saluted and took leave, mumbling to himself. Waiting for dispensation to be made of their services, Jobson and Mulcahy leaned shoulder to shoulder against the trunk of a tree, both staring holes through the bum-bailiff Donegan, who finally spoke.

"You two split up. Jobson, you come with me. Mulcahy, report to Lieutenant

Kelly."

"Yes, sir. And how shall I find him?"

"Follow this road one mile through the woods. You'll probably find our newly commissioned lieutenant at leisure in the parlor of a vacant mansion hard by our right center." He giggled effeminately through pudgy jowls. "You'll find quaintly posted office hours on his door. See that you observe them closely."

"Thank you. May I go now, sir?"

"You're dismissed. Password for the day is 'River Bottom. Oh, one thing more," he winked slyly, "let's not breathe a word of this outer picket line that's supposed to lie in front of us. Understand?"

Paddy's arched eyebrows and compressed lips registered his disgust. He saluted, shouldered his rifle, and started off through the woods. Prompt use of the password got him safely through several posts manned by trigger-tense sentries of recent enlistment when all of a sudden his eye caught sight of something which made him draw up short and dodge for cover. Directly ahead a ticklish situation was developing, just as Cassidy had predicted. An incident that could end up on either a tragic or a humorous note.

A Union general, returning from his tour of inspection of the outer defense perimeter, had just been confronted by a sentinel of the interior and improperly posted cordon.

The uneasy picket stood with musket cocked, ready to meet any emergency. Jittery, and unaware that friendly forces were in front of him, he cried out, "Halt! Who goes there!"

"General Sykes," was the unruffled reply. "Put down that musket."

Paddy strained to get a better look at the mounted officer, whose craggy face was partially obscured by a flop-brimmed hat.

"I don't give a blue fart who you are," came the picket's retort. "Dismount! Every one of you! Be lively about it!"

The general threw wide his overcoat and pointed to his shoulder straps. "Now do you know me?"

"No. Get down off that horse and be damned quick about it or I'll put a ball through you."

Complying, as he could see no other way out of the dilemma, the general and his staff dismounted. Sykes, his anger on the rise, walked cautiously forward. "What the blue blazes do you mean by this? Do you fail to recognize a corps commander who's been among you almost daily for months?"

At that moment someone shouted from the nearby woods. "Hello, Billy. What kinda looking fellow you got? Has he got black whiskers?"

"Yes."

"Balls o' fire, you've got Mosby. Hold the son of a bitch, and call for the guard."

Panic-stricken, his musket leveled unsteadily at the general's forehead, the young picket shrilled, "Corporal o' the guard, corporal o' the guard!"

In a split second the guard came bounding into the clearing, his eyes darting in all directions. "What's up with you, Billy? Who's that? Phwee! General Sykes, sir!"

Visibly shaken, the picket's musket fell from his hands. "Di...did you say general?"

"Yes, you blundering idiot." He turned his perspiring face to the irate corps commander. "Beggin' your pardon, sir. These men are levies, first time out. You may pass, sir."

"Pass, my ass. Who and where is your immediate superior?"

"Lieutenant Kelly, sir. You'll find him billeted in a house over on the right 'bout three hundred yards."

"Take me to him at once."

"Yes, sir."

Not wishing to become too closely involved with the affair, Paddy followed at a safe distance. *Poor unsuspecting Tom Kelly*, he thought to himself.

Up ahead, choked in a dense entanglement of timber and tall weeds, was the place where Kelly had chosen to set up shop in a derelict frame plantation house rotting at the seams and sagging. Reaching its borders, Sykes and his retinue stormed up the warped steps, boots thumping across the naked porch planks. Nailed boldly on a closed door, staring him rudely in the face, was a large, crudely hand-lettered sign announcing Kelly's hours of business. Pausing in his stride to stare icily at the sign, the general burst inside.

Kelly was reclining leisurely in a camp chair constructed from an old discarded barrel and reading an out-dated gazette, his back to the door.

"Lieutenant!" Sykes bellowed. "What in the name of God are you running here?"

Like a shot, Kelly leaped from his seat and spun around. At the sight of the looming general, his mouth flew open. A cigar held tightly between his teeth plunked to the floor.

"Did you hear me, Lieutenant? What in the hell are you and this picket line doing?"

Wholly innocent that he was heroically maintaining an improperly posted line, Kelly had no notion that the general's interrogation was intended to stand him up. In a vain attempt to display his proficiency, he saluted and quickly replied, "To arrest all persons outside the lines, to be watchful during the day, and extremely vigilant at night, to keep a sharp lookout for Mosby and other guerrillas, and treat all persons outside the lines as enemies, sir."

Sykes stood speechless. The staff behind him doubled over with suppressed laughter. Getting his astonishment under control, the general was too disgusted for further comment except to say, "Great Heavens! What infernal stupidity!" Barging from the room, he mounted and rode off rapidly, an amused train following him.

When everyone had left, Paddy stepped into the doorway and leaned one shoulder against the sagging jam. "How do you like having bars now, Mister Kelly?"

"Mulcahy! Where'd you come from?" Kelly rubbed one hand along the side of his clean-shaven face now tinted pink and white, and exclaimed, "What the devil was that all about? Do you know?"

"So happens I might. You were done in." He explained what had happened.

Kelly's inner toughness belied his shy handsome features as he turned red. "That dirty Donegan, putting me in the bucket like that. And him staying a safe distance away. I'll be clobbered when the major gets wind of this."

"Aw, no you won't. Herring will laugh it off."

"Herring? He went home last week on disability. When did you get back?"

"Last night."

"Oh, and nobody's told you?"

"Told me 'bout what? Been too busy answering questions to ask any."

"'Bout the big shake-up. Henry O'Neil's the new major. Been running the regiment while Gwyn's home on sick leave."

"Not quaint Cap'n 'enry of A Company?"

Filled with repugnance, Paddy had fleeting visions of O'Neil's careless behavior the last night at Chancellorsville.

"The very same."

"Cripes. Why'd they ever pick him over Donaldson and Crocker?"

"His long service experience in the British Indian Army, or so they say." Kelly's thin lips contracted into a puckered knot. "But if you want the truth, I'd say it was politics and religion. You should've seen his first review of the regiment, he constituted himself both commandant and reviewing officer. What a mess. A circus. Mounted, he came on the field with trousers almost completely hidden by seven-league boots and with his sword at its favorite position, right shoulder shift. All prior ceremonies, the presentation of arms, opening of ranks, stirring music, the personal observation of front and rear rank, those were omitted entirely."

"What's he doing, instituting a new procedure?"

"Call it procedure if you like. All he did was bust in from nowhere, dash madly to the right of the regiment, pull up short and begin running off commands with such rapidity the words were scarcely distinguishable. He concluded with the command of execution in his typically high voice. It was probably better that he did. for that alone indicated the movement. The directions were of his making."

"Don't tell me. I already know how he hates to adhere to tactics."

"Well, fortunately for him, familiarity with his methods and a general knowledge of what he proposed to accomplish got the regiment out of staggering difficulties.'' Kelly mimicked O' Neil's manner, "'Break into open columns o' companies right in front, the 'livering sergeants'll be responsible for the distance march!' That was his opening command. Then, seeing the column properly in motion, he leaves his post as commandant and hurries off to take his place as reviewing officer. Crocker happened to be the leading captain. Passing in creditable shape, he was conducting the column to its place preparatory to formation of the line for the concluding 'present' when, either tired of the whole operation or believing that it had really ended, O'Neil suddenly broke up the review with the startling, unheard-of command, 'Halt! Dispense and be damned! Every man to his quarters at once.'"

Paddy sucked in his cheeks and stooped to pick up a moldy chunk of plaster, rolling it between his fingers. "Can see where things are going to be bloody awful till Gwyn gets back. Maybe I should've taken that medical." He let his gaze drift around the dank, barren room. Fallen plaster littered the bare flooring. Uncovered lathwork appeared as dried bones powdered white, and all around were spilled fragments of shattered glass from broken windows.

Kelly knelt to retrieve his partially smoked cigar. "You're not the only one who feels that way. Everyone's talking of going home. That's how I came by these." He lightly tapped the gold stripes affixed to each shoulder. "Jimmy Green gave 'em up last week. Took sail for home, and you can't blame the boys. Those who aren't eaten up with the constant sickness are just plain fought out, discouraged and tired. Heard Doc Thomas saying the other day that sickness and disease have taken twice the toll of Confederate bullets."

Paddy tried to untangle a cobweb wrapped around his left ear.

"How do the boys expect to win the war by returning home at this stage of the game? The deadbeats coming into the army sure as hell aren't capable of whipping the Johnnies."

Kelly put a match to his cigar. "Dunno. I'd say the Johnnies are probably experiencing about the same kind of trouble we are. Though I'll say this much, it's going to be mighty damned hard for anybody to crush their spirit. Having lived by the plow with horse and rifle seems to make them indomitable, willing to accept privation. Besides, they're mostly Celt and Anglo-Saxon like us, real stubborn."

He sat down, leaned back in the barrel chair with his legs stretched out and let a puff of smoke wreath his head. "So help me if I don't feel kindly toward the Rebs I've met. A warmhearted, happy bunch, a bit impetuous, like myself."

"They're a tough, mean lot of fighters in battle," Paddy replied. The deep azure suddenly came alive in his eyes. "Say, that picket you told Donaldson about, the one from Leesburg. Where's he posted?"

Kelly's expression clouded. "That picket from your wife's hometown. He's up the line a ways."

"Don't give a damn if he's in hell's half-acre, I'll find him."

"Take it easy, Paddy. There might be a chance you can contact him tonight, but I wouldn't bank on it. I talked to him, but he would not tell me much. Said he wanted to talk to you."

"If he knows Becky and her family, he may have some idea where she and her mother went. I have to talk with him."

Kelly stood up and placed his hands on Paddy's shoulders. "I'll see that you go on picket tonight and I'll personally point out the spot for you. But you'll be on your own from there."

Paddy fingered his leather cartridge box. "That suits me fine."

Later that evening, after the men had bivouacked and the evening meal was over, Lieutenant Kelly accompanied the pickets to their stations. After the rest had been stationed, he led Paddy some distance away to a grove of trees.

"The fellow was sitting on a log across that small field, Mulcahy. You be careful," Kelly said over his shoulder as he walked away.

In the gathering darkness Paddy strained his eyes, watching closely until he finally saw movement behind the log. He moved to the outer rim of the trees so he could be seen.

In a few minutes he heard a low whistle and he responded with an answering whistle. After a couple of exchanges, he moved along a row of bushes and the gray form across the way came out slowly to meet him.

When they could see each other fairly clearly, the young man called, "Hallo."

Paddy responded and they met by a clump of tall bushes. Paddy held out his hand. "I'm Mulcahy. Paddy Mulcahy."

"Glad to meet you, Mulcahy. Name's Tom Linton. Understand you're Becky Chenewith's husband."

"That's correct. Anything you can tell me about where she might be? I heard the people of Leesburg ran her out after the baby came, 'cause she married a Northerner. Any idea where she and her mother might have gone? Her brother was attending school at VMI, the last I heard. Did you know him? He was younger."

"I went to school with Becky. Knew her well, Yank. Wonderful girl, fine family. I didn't know her brother, but I might be able to contact him for you. I know Becky had relatives in the Shenandoah Valley, but I don't know where. Tell you what I'll do, though. My mother still lives in Leesburg and she's not as bitter as some of our people. I'll have her ask around and see if she can find out where Becky went. She can send word to her and let her know how to contact you. I think that would be the best way."

Paddy hurriedly took out a pencil and paper and wrote in the dark. When he finished he handed it to the shivering picket. "Tom, have her get in touch with me through Miss Van Lew. Here's her Richmond address." The two eyed each other for a moment and shook hands. "You don't know how grateful I am for this help," Paddy blurted. "I'd almost despaired of ever finding my wife again. Thank you."

"Think nothing of it, Yank. I'm sure you'd do the same for me." Each shouldered his rifle and headed toward his respective picket line.

Paddy was so excited he had no trouble staying awake that night. Hope was again alive, and he spent the night dreaming about his future, something he had not done for a long time.

The next day he sat in Lieutenant Kelly's office and related his experience from the night before. Suddenly there were heavy footsteps on the wooden porch and a corporal of the guard came crashing into the room.

Kelly looked up with annoyance. "Yes, what is it, Toy?"

"Better roust yourself, Lieutenant. The whole regiment just came up. Looks as if there's a general movement of some kind."

"General movement? I haven't heard of any movement. Major O'Neil along?"

"I'll say he is. Gilded up like a striped-ass circus monkey."

Kelly shrugged his shoulders. "Well, let's go out and face the old gallo glass."

The first public appearance of O'Neil in the garb of his new rank was attracting considerable attention. Gaudy beyond the wildest stretch of imagination, he stood bedecked in a bright new uniform, a design apparently his own that strangely contrasted with the rough, well-worn garments and insignia of his brother officers.

His cap was embellished on the top and around the brim with rows of braided gold tinsel and set at a jaunty, almost rakish angle as he peeked out from under.

An imperial mustache spliced the middle of his face and drooped warlike. Fitted tight about his small frame was a double-breasted blue jacket mounted with gorgeous straps at the shoulders, sleeves braided to the elbows. Broad gold stripes adorned both trouser legs mostly covered by an enormous length of boots that extended almost to his hips. A bright scabbard with a fine Damascus blade and shining spurs completed the outfit.

Junior officers gathered around in a close circle, marveling at such magnificence. An evil glint shone in Captain Crocker's eyes. His voice was deep and throaty as he remarked, "I'd say you've violently abused the bill of dress, Henry. Arraying yourself in such a get-up, you'll make an exceptional target for the Rebs."

Fashioning a grin, Donaldson fingered the expensive raiment. "And quite a mark for his own men in the bargain."

O'Neil drew himself to full height. "Out with 'ee, ye jealous bodies. Yer eyes are green. This is the way we used to dress in Injee. And a beautiful sight it was to see the 'callants"—his own term for British officers-—"paraded on occasions of state." Striking an attitude of pomp and circumstance, he gave one leg a slap with his swagger stick. "I disremember exactly when it was, but when the governor general made a Mason o' the Rajee, the lieutenant general in command was kivered with medals and medallions and his sash and plumes and the foot and the horse and the artillery was in full regimentals. Och, what a sight." He turned his head to see if everyone was listening.

"The Rajee came down with his camels and his aliphants and his whole ratinew and there was bowing and scraping and damn humbugging over the owld divil until our regiment was reached and then at command they let out o' them such a screech that it made the aliphants cock their trunks and trumpet like the divil and made the camels and the whole ratinew fooster fumble and tremble at Her Majesty's foot. Och! There was a divil of a time."

In lordly manner he gazed around, content that he had dismissed all adverse comments and seemingly conscious that his happy illustration had conquered the prejudices of his American associates.

"That was India," snorted Crocker. "This is the miserable state of Virginia and the Army of the Potomac. Don't you think it's time we were about our business?"

"Aye, it is that. Collect the pickets. And mind ye, this is an important 'chuty.' The enemy may be on us at any moment. We'll be far out in this country and with no troops to the left o' us. It behooves you gentlemen to look sharp therefore and not be marking time."

His head suddenly swivelled as he cast a fierce glare directly at Kelly. "Kelly, ye'll just be after keepin' on the line and not be prancin' about pickin' dry places. Ye'll mind and look sharp, Kelly."

"Yes, sir."

Captains were quickly assigned their positions in line. "Now how'n the hell'd he know I was standing way back here?" Kelly asked, dumbfounded.

Paddy shifted to Kelly's side. "Dunno. Eyes must be fastened on the same screw wheel his brain spins on."

Within a short space of time the regimental column was fully organized and on the march to the Rapidan. They crossed that turbulent river at Culpepper Mine Ford and a lonesome, dreary tramp followed. Save where the route led along the Stevensburg Plank Road, the march was along narrow roadways through dense forests so thick with underbrush that men could not see beyond a few yards from the roadside.

Back in working harness, Paddy gave ear to the familiar sounds and complaints that were the common experience of the route march, but this time there was a song in his heart that equaled hope.

Jobson growled beneath the weight of his knapsack. "What's the purpose of this damned foray? Weather's getting colder'n a dead witch's tit. We should be going into winter camp."

Kimball lifted his eyes. "Maybe the major wants to show off his new uniform to 'Cousin Bobby' before he hibernates."

McCool altered the position of his rifle. "No. Haven't you fellas heard? This here's just the major's way of putting Paddy's legs back into shape. Ain't that so, Mulcahy?"

"You go to hell. Pounding this hard ground's popping shin splints on both my legs."

"Aw, didn't mean it that way. Give me your pack. It'll make the going lighter till you get used to things again."

"All right, you asked for it." He removed his haversack and passed it over to McCool, who shouldered the extra burden with a spacious grin.

At a lonely desolate place called Wilderness Tavern, progress became measurably slower through dense thick underbrush and timber until the road over which they were traveling intersected with the Fredericksburg and Orange Plank Road, a locale that brought back bitter memories of Chancellorsville. The head of the regiment, upon reaching the intersection, turned abruptly right onto the Plank Road, the flankers conforming their movement to the new direction. Those marching in the column's van had advanced a mile or so beyond the intersection when they where suddenly greeted by a loud commotion that came from the rear. Though not in view, from the tail of the regiment came violent, urgent commands: "Halt!" "Front!" "Steady there!" "Load at will! " "Load!"

Off to the right and rear a single cannon boomed, followed instantly by sporadic musketry. Then it was quiet again.

Coat collars turned up to ward off the raw wind, Donaldson, his eyes narrowing darkly, rose in the saddle and watched as Crocker rode forward at a gallop to within earshot.

"Frank! Get your men to the rear on the double! Mosby's men've made off with an ammunition train right out from under Donegan's nose!"

In response to their captain's command, the men of H Company made an immediate about-face and started dog trotting toward the scene of ambush. A sight of topsy-turvy chaos met their eyes. Furious, frenzied teamsters worked among the over-turned wagons and dead mules. Recruits, high strung and perspiring feverishly, stood with rifles held at ready. They peered anxiously at woods fast becoming shrouded in the gathering dusk.

At one spot Gilmour stumbled on a former associate. His voice rose above the din of confusion. "Ho, there, MacGregor. Wha' in the name o' Saint Andrew happened?"

"Aye, Gilmour. We been done in, tha's what." Dirty and disheveled, pants sagging on loose suspenders, the wagoner spat.

McCool, scrutinizing the situation, pressed in close for information. "How'n hell did they steal a wagon train right from under your nose?"

"Sonny, them monkeys got tricks they ain't even pulled yet. We was movin' along parallel with the troops like always, nice and easy. Lead wagon'd reached the Plank Road, where it should've turned off right, when two o' Mosby's men, hidin' in the brush, jumped from cover. They was up on the wagon 'longside Burnett afore he could bat an eyelash. With cocked pistols probin' his belly, Burnett was o' no mind to argue. Just drove straight on ahead as ordered. None o' us in the wagons behind seen what happened. We tailed right on after him down the wrong path."

"Hoot mon. Did ye no' have proper instructions where to turn?"

"Nary a one, been travelin' blind secret." Squirting through the hole in his beard came a stream of tobacco juice. "Played follow the leader like ducks. No doubt be miles away noo if had no' been for your brigade inspector."

"Bankson?"

"Aye. He seen us windin' off over those hills like truant schoolboys, so he come after us. Seein' the jig was about up, that they might lose their prize, the rest o' the guerrillas waitin' in the woods began jumping us."

"Must've been that musketry we heard."

"Aye, and if yer mules be dead, who's to pull the wagons out o' here?"

"Figger that's what yer brigade inspector's turnin' over right now."

Nearby, Bankson, as brigade inspector, had at that moment concluded his deductive reasoning. As was evident, there were no animals to take the wagons back. Delay in procuring others to replace them and detaching troops to protect the wagons in the interval was not deemed warranted, as the enemy was believed to be close by in considerable strength. His decision came in a stentorian command. "Fire the wagons!"

Immediately the cry was raised and passed on by the drivers of twenty transports scattered immobilized along the road steeped in eerie darkness. The teamster by Gilmour's side lofted a fiery torch, getting ready to give it a toss.

"You lads better back out o' here. In a second this road'll be the biggest fireworks show you ever seen."

McCool's shadowy pupils opened wide. "Hot diggety damn. Let's search out the major. Wanta see how he takes to this. Bet it makes him blow his ruddy cork."

With a multitude of canvas fired by the torch, the blackened roadway rapidly became transformed into a rip-roaring inferno of red-orange flames shooting skyward. Small arms ammunition exploded in a continuous convulsive rattle. Above the sound of the holocaust was heard a bellowing roar of anguish from O'Neil. "Where's that old woman, Donegan? Why the divil'd he let the wagon train be captured?"

Looking grim behind a bearded mask, Crocker quickly interceded. "Henry, you can't attach the blame to Donegan. The entire line was more or less directly involved in this blunder."

Aroused, O'Neil struck out with his swagger stick. It was evident to the men surrounding him that he thought he had been personally charged with delinquency. In a fit of rage, he turned on Crocker, whom he thought had condemned his management.

"On me, is it? To the divil with ye. Do ye think I was botherin' 'bout a lot o' bushwhackers?" His temper abating somewhat, he drifted off to his chronic animosity toward Kelly. "And when did ye see Kelly last? Och, that Kelly's an owld Divil. Tell him I want him. I want to keep me eye on him."

With apparent conviction that whatever blame might fall, it must be on Donegan and Kelly and not himself, O' Neil dismissed the subject completely.

Some distance removed, Paddy stood absorbed in an incident taking shape before him. His attention was focused on a trooper dressed in a tightly buttoned greatcoat. He was observing the main column of Federal troops with intense interest and appeared to be making mental notes. Something about the man's demeanor caused him to recall his own unnatural behavior while scouting Gordon's army at York.

Lieutenant Colonel Sherwin of the 22nd Massachusetts, his suspicions likewise aroused by the curious manner of the horseman, spurred his mount forward and halted alongside the stranger. "Your name and rank, please?"

"Sergeant Wilcox, sir." The reply was scarcely audible.

"What are you doing here, Wilcox?"

"Scouting for General Kilpatrick, sir. Saw the fire, so I rode over to investigate."

Colonel Sherwin cocked a dubious eye. "You say you're scouting for Kilpatrick? Let's see. Open your coat."

Like a cornered animal, his head and eyes flicking one way and then the other seeking an avenue of escape, the horseman hesitated. Obviously a Rebel spy, the young Southerner's predicament caused Paddy to shiver as he anticipated the impending tragedy. He pulled his kepi down tight on his head and turned his face away to blot out the inevitable that he knew must follow. His reluctance to expose his uniform as ordered confirmed the suspicions of Colonel Sherwin. Drawing a revolver with one hand, he used the other to rip open the front of the cavalryman's coat. Beneath was the uniform of the enemy. Further parley becoming unnecessary, the revolver recoiled, spitting fire, smoke and destruction. The body of the clean-faced Confederate slumped on the saddle horn, slipped then fell to the road.

Paddy closed his eyes at the sight. Troops in the main column, once again in motion, slowed their steps to view the corpse with impersonal glances as they marched by. To Paddy the tragic circumstance was evident. The scout had probably been instructed to count the numbers moving to the Union left. Unable to secure a satisfactory point of observation from a distance, and deeming the duty of sufficient importance to warrant the risk, he had taken his life in his hands and ventured once too often within the Union lines.

With relative quiet restored, the night march was resumed. Flames from the burning wagons formed a fiery red aurora on the eastern horizon as the column moved westward.

Alert and cautious, acting as flankers and being careful to preserve the requisite distance from the main body, the Corn Exchange marched on through the black pit of darkness, the time of night becoming a matter of conjecture.

How long they had been traveling no one seemed to know when suddenly the entire regiment found itself plunged into the bed of an unfinished railroad cut that ran parallel to the road they were following. The excavation was six feet in depth in many places, with banks high enough to practically cut off all opportunity for observation. What purpose flankers could serve in such a place was beyond the ken of those who were the eyes and ears of the army.

When the situation had continued long enough to satisfy those in the rear that the path had not been taken to avoid obstacles and obstructions, several of the officers pushed forward to find the major.

Crocker and Donaldson, taking long strides, hurried past the darkly silhouetted slow-moving column. O'Neil scowled at their approach.

"Why aren't ye back with yer men?"

"Henry, the men and officers feel you're pursuing an unusual course by taking the regiment this route."

"Ye tell the men and officers for me, Lem Crocker, that O'Neil's runnin' this regiment. It's the enemy's business to find us, not us find him."

Donaldson spoke with a weary voice "Listen, Henry, it's our duty as flankers to protect the main column on the road. We can't see anything from this railway cut. We should move to higher ground on our left where we can observe things."

"I know what our duty is. We're performing it as I see fit'n proper."

"How long's it been since you've communicated with the main body?" Crocker demanded.

"Two hours ago. Right after we left the burning wagons. Och, that divil, Donegan."

"Two hours? Good Lord. Are you aware the First and Fifth Corps were to withdraw from Plank Road to Robertson's Tavern, taking a turnpike route some miles north of here?"

O ' Neil stared blankly. "First I heard of it. No one told me of any change in orders."

In the foreboding darkness, a look of horror passed between the two captains, it being evident to both that O'Neil had permitted himself to wander, notwithstanding the fact that the main column had changed directions.

Crocker spoke harshly. "I think we'd best halt the men here and send Lieutenant Thomas to contact the column."

Tight-lipped, O'Neil said, "All right. As we used to say in Injee, when in doubt, cast a look about."

An order to halt was passed down the line and brought the troops flopping exhausted to the cold ground as overhead wintry blasts whistled through the groaning branches of huge trees. Men huddled close together in their heavy coats and tried to catch a few winks while Thomas went in search of the column.

Moving quickly as possible in the tangled wilderness, Thomas traveled a mile or more in the direction he supposed was right, but his search was ineffectual. Seeing nothing of the main body, and hearing nothing to indicate their whereabouts, he returned to report his failure.

O'Neil looked grave for the first time. Clearing his throat, he said, "Report back to yer companies. I'm going to face the regiment left and move them as a skirmish line to that knoll over there."

Nodding agreement, Donaldson, Crocker and Thomas started back to their respective commands.

The men of H Company, at the return of their leader, roused themselves from catnaps and gathered round.

"What's it to be, sir?" Cassidy inquired huskily.

"Form a skirmish line, Andy. Face it left. We're to occupy a knoll 'boul half a mile from here."

Jobson's Nordic countenance twisted. "Don't tell us cap'n, let us guess. Fancy pants has gone and got us lost, ain't he?"

"You asking or telling me? All right, Andy, get the men moving."

Holding position on the knoll was not a comfortable task. With the long winter night ahead of them, the men of the Corn Exchange found themselves exposed and without support in enemy territory with no communication with their own troops or even any knowledge of where they were. The prospect of a hard fight or wholesale capture come morning was not conducive to the slumber to which their weary march entitled them. Most commanders so situated would have utilized the darkness to extricate themselves before dawn, instead, O'Neil was determined to rest and take his chances for withdrawal in daylight, his better judgment affected by the comfortable quarters at hand.

To the left of the skirmish line was a cozy old house locked, bolted and barred, which had apparently been recently abandoned.

McCool and Vandergrift confirmed that fact with a closer look. Employing their bayonets, they pried open a shutter and Vandergrift, raised on the shoulders of a couple of strong men, hoisted the sash and jumped into the total darkness inside. A loud crash followed by a scraping sound left those on the outside wondering what was happening. Vandergrift felt his way to the front door, which he managed to unbolt. With the aid of a candle, he discovered the obstruction that had impeded his progress. An old fashioned spinning wheel just beneath the window sill lay smashed where he had jumped on it.

Strings of dried fruit hung suspended from the kitchen ceiling. The floor of the loft was covered with walnuts, chestnuts, shellbarks and hickory nuts; the beds were neat and clean and well-covered with quilts on which lay inviting blue and white counterpanes. Embers still flickered and glowed in the stone fireplace. Fed with fresh logs and stirred by expert hands, they soon burst into a cheerful blaze.

The house had indeed been recently vacated. On the sideboard was a freshly cleaned chicken, picked and ready for the fire. A table was set with sliced bread, the cups filled with coffee, which meant the departed family had evidently been ready to sit down to their evening meal when the troops arrived. They doubtlessly mistook them for the advance of the army and abruptly vacated the place.

Influenced by his better judgment, O'Neil promptly availed himself of the accommodations for the purposes of a regimental headquarters. He and a few of his favorites feasted on the meal, all except the fowl, which had disappeared, a dainty morsel to be cooked and disposed of later while the major slumbered. The men drank the coffee and ate the bread without any concern that it might be poisoned.

After taking his fill, O'Neil, with no thought of the gravity of the situation and with no apparent anxiety, left directions for the line to remain as it was and for no one to awaken him unless there was some sort of emergency. Sighing wearily, he rolled himself, booted and spurred, into the best bed and slept until dawn.

Relieving each other occasionally from duties on the line, the officers quickly took advantage of the accommodations, enjoying the fire and partaking of the food. The situation seemed too perilous to them to warrant repose, so they spent the night cracking jokes and eating what food they could find before the roaring fire. Occasionally they discussed the gravity of their situation as their commanding officer snored lustily, totally oblivious of his responsibilities.

The night passed, followed by a dark, gloomy morning with threatening, low-hanging clouds promising an imminent deluge.

It was not yet daylight when a good-sized pig came wandering through H Company's bivouac. He was instantly sat upon by Bob Dyer who held his feet as Jobson clamped his hands around the animal's snout to prevent any protests. McCool endeavored to cut the animal's throat with a jackknife dulled by long use on salted pork. Suddenly Captain Donaldson approached, and the trio remembered that the Scriptures forbade eating pork. Rising quickly to their feet, they began kicking the animal to signify they loathed pork and the hog ran off into the wilderness.

Not far from the edge of a piece of timber and along a ridge of high ground, daylight broke and revealed the enemy's cavalry deployed on a skirmish line. Each side began watching the other intently, neither seemingly disposed to press investigations beyond what could be gleaned from observation. By some good grace, the thin line of Federal infantry evidently deceived the enemy into thinking that it had strong, available support behind, as it should have had.

The Federal boys remained anxiously watchful, figuring that a move by the enemy, although met, would empty a few saddles, but must eventually result in rout and capture. Not fearing the dash so much as they did the discovery of their situation on both flanks, it was becoming evident from O'Neil's actions that he was willing to fight to the bitter end if the enemy made the first move.

Crocker approached O'Neil with a worried frown. "Henry, what do you propose to do?"

"Observe the divils till further orders."

It seemed the major was neither to be cajoled, tricked or persuaded into doing anything, and there the line remained, wary and impatient, until around noon when, evidently concluding that something must be attempted to relieve the situation, O' Neil gave the order to retire, shaking a fist at the enemy as he did so and calling them a set of "dirty blackguards."

Rain began falling heavily and the retiring operation had scarcely commenced before O' Neil came dashing from the house and excitedly commanded a sudden halt. He had discovered that someone had purloined a counterpane and, not stopping to inquire who, but guided by his suspicions, he settled promptly on Kelly.

"Bring it back, Kelly. Put it where ye got it. Do ye want them to think us a set o' thieves and divils? Put it back at once."

It so happened that he was not mistaken. Kelly had taken the coverlet, prompted either by the weather or the rosy prospect of adorning his winter quarters with unusual splendor.

"But, Major, it's not wantonness. It's not even thievery. I'm not marauding or pilfering; I really need the thing."

The major would not be appeased. "Put it back, Kelly, do ye mind? Put it back, sir." Aside, he said, "Och, that Kelly is a divil. Wouldn't be surprised if he had a flat-iron in each pocket, the thief o' the world."

The major did not remain long enough to see Kelly carry out his directions, instead, he started the line in one direction just as Kelly went off in the other. By the time Kelly had deposited his bundle and was ready to return, he was forced to hustle so that he might not be left alone in uncomfortably close proximity to the enemy, who was by now alerted to the withdrawal.

The storm and the good luck usually attending an Irishman's blunders ultimately removed the difficulties that surrounded O'Neil and, stumbling onto the right road by three o'clock, the major found himself and his regiment safely in the limits of brigade lines near Robertson's Tavern.

Festering a long time below the surface, a sore boil now came to a head. The experiences of the past twenty-four hours and the gravity of the crisis on the eve of impending battle turned the men's thoughts to serious comprehension of the situation and a desire to seek consultation to know how to meet the difficulties. With one accord, the captains gathered about the bivouac fire for advice and counsel, their debate resolving on a single solution. O'Neil must be replaced. Respected for his courage and admired for his daring, any lingering hope that he might be helped through a crisis had wholly disappeared after the previous night's experiences.

Recognizing the official peril in which they placed their commissions by making such suggestions, the company commanders nevertheless decided to face up to their responsibilities and assume the attendant risk by boldly presenting the case for consideration to the brigade commander.

At their solicitation, Colonel Tilton, who had been partially advised of the difficulties, consented to hear their grievances at their bivouac fire. That nothing might be said or done in Major O'Neil's absence, he rode to the consultation and in encouraging, kindly tones, inquired of the cause of the disturbance. Crocker acted as spokesman, taking up the story and telling it fully and fairly. He covered the recent occurrences and emphasized his commander's unstinting courage, energy and endurance, but at the same time pointed out that with all those admirable traits, there was a definite ineptitude for intelligent direction that essentially made O'Neil unfit for the responsibilities his office demanded.

Speaking for his fellows, he urged that a field officer from the brigade be assigned temporary command of the regiment until one of the major's superiors returned.

Standing impassively, hands thrust deep into his pockets, jackboots stretched their full length on the ground before the fire, O'Neil listened silently to what was being said.

"Well, gentlemen," Colonel Tilton replied, after listening patiently and attentively, "I recognize your difficulties, but I cannot refrain from reminding you that it is very delicate and dangerous ground on which you tread. No doubt you were aware of that when you brought it this far. I'm satisfied the only motive that prompts your action is the maintenance of the excellent reputation your regiment has consistently borne. On the eve of an impending battle, the situation is particularly critical. I am therefore disposed not to view the matter in the strict military sense which it deserves. I recognize the efficiency and excellence of the Hundred and Eighteenth. For that reason I'm willing to lend my authority to relieve you from embarrassment. Who do you have in mind as a choice for commanding officer?''

The unanimous response was Lieutenant Colonel Throop of the First Michigan.

Slapping his hands together to warm them, Colonel Tilton nodded stiffly and withdrew. He returned a short while later accompanied by Lieutenant Colonel Throop.

An able officer, tall, trim and dignified man, Colonel Throop showed signs of reluctance to leave his present command. He was induced to do so only in obedience to positive orders that he recognized were given to meet the need of the hour. He attached one condition to his acceptance, and that was an understanding that the assignment be by unanimous acquiescence on the part of the entire staff of the 118th. When presented by the brigade commander, Colonel Throop's first inquiry was to that effect.

To the hearty affirmative response of the rest, Major O' Neil meekly added, "Certainly, sir, certainly. I don't care under whom I serve, just so he gives me an opportunity to fight. Certainly I will serve under you, and with pleasure, sir."

Relieved from that anxiety, a satisfactory solution was reached and it acted as an exhilarating stimulant for the troops, who planned to do some celebrating. Colonel Throop declined to participate, retiring instead to his own bivouac. Deft hands were soon busy with the "Joe Hooker' formula, concocting the stimulating ingredients. Limited supplies forbade free indulgence and by midnight it was quiet, everything forgotten in restful slumber.

Next morning, in the stillness of the ice-crystaled landscape, McCool stretched his aching muscles and wiped matter from his sweeping black eyelashes. He rolled to one side and asked, "Jobson, you awake?"

"Don't know yet," came the sleepy reply. "Wait'll I see. Yep, I'm awake."

"Good. Let's hustle around and see if we can find something in the line of grub. What say?"

"I'd say from what I've seen of this wilderness, not even a buzzard could live off this land. Let's stay put in the blanket-roll where it's warm."

"Seek and ye shall find, Luke. Seek and ye shall find."

Aware of his comrade's persuasive ways, Jobson threw off his blanket and reluctantly raised himself on an elbow. "All right. If it'll keep you happy, let's go."

The rest of the camp continued sleeping soundly as the two foragers wandered in search of anything that might be edible. After searching for a while, McCool suddenly drew up short and pointed at a spot in front between the Union and Confederate lines. He whispered, "Do your eyes detect a persimmon tree yonder?"

Jobson's sleepy gaze scanned the area and lighted on a tree loaded with frosted fruit. "I'll say so. Wonder how it's escaped? Think we should undress it?"

"Definitely. But definitely."

Sneaking along under the shelter of some bushes, both men quietly and stealthily approached the tree. Scrutinizing carefully from the base of the tree, they were assured that the Confederate pickets were still a distance away.

"You pitch and I'll catch, Willie."

"Right."

Silent as a cat, McCool climbed into the branches and began shaking down quantities of the delicious fruit, which his companion on the ground hastily stowed in a haversack. At one point an overly vigorous rattle of the branches caused Jobson to glance up with alarm. "Careful, Willie, you're making too much noise."

"What's the matter? Ain't you ever waved a red flag under a bull's nose before?"

Just then a single report rang out. The single zip flew past the occupant of the tree. McCool dropped to the ground in a flash. "Good God, the Rebs have spotted us. Grab the sack. Let's pull boot."

Not wasting any time, the two scampered off into the brush, and none too soon. A follow-up volley crackled through the air, sending twigs and persimmons scattering down on their prostrated figures.

When the firing ceased, McCool raised himself on his hands and knees and peered through the brush, ready to give the alarm in case of further danger.

Jobson tugged at him. "C'mon, Willie. Let's git."

"The hell, you say. Let's gather the persimmons them Johnnies so thoughtfully shot down for us."

"You crazy? We'll get caught. If not by the Rebs, at least by Cassidy. Or aren't you aware it's a serious breach of discipline to go beyond the lines without orders? We can be court-martialed for desertion.

By way of answer, McCool screwed up his face in a fiendish imitation of Cassidy addressing the company. "A soldier without discipline is like a musket without a barrel, a pail without a bottom, a fish without fins." He let out a laugh. "Hells bells, don't you think I know we're in a fix? But we've hardly secured enough fruit for our own consumption."

"What do you mean, our own consumption?"

"Like you say, there's bound to be an inquiry as to what caused the firing. Under those circumstances, how can we return until we've obtained enough fruit for our dear officers?''

"You think you can bribe your way out of this?"

"We can try. Scrape up some more of those persimmons."

Reaching the lines safely, both boys headed straight for their camp and found the place deserted. Jobson scratched his head. "Funny. Wonder where everybody went? They were all asleep when we left."

McCool swept an arm toward a mass of bleary-eyed men emerging from a nearby gully. "Here they come. Must've scattered for shelter when the bullets cut through here."

Jobson wiped a dry mouth and groaned as Sergeant Cassidy advanced, his shoulders bent forward, his teeth bared. With Cassidy was Deville, a new recruit in K Company, who up until recently had been an adjutant in a French regiment. The Frenchman shook his head and muttered, "Ow queekly you make one ven you are broke all to pieces. If ze regiment she was French, one week would not zem together bring again."

Cassidy passed over a reply. He fixed a piercing glare on the two sheepish-looking soldiers standing before him. Not a word was exchanged as McCool silently offered a handful of the fruit to his superior. His nostrils dilated in anger, Cassidy fingered the fruit, looked quizzically at the donors then took a bite.

Shifting his weight from one foot to the other, McCool endeavored to read his sergeant's thoughts. They seemed to change as he took another bite. These fellows have been outside the lines again. They give me no end o' trouble. I'll give the persimmons back and make an example o 'these two birds. Might as well eat one or two to see how they taste. By George, they're good. A handful o ' them won 't be missed. Thoughtful o ' the lads to share them. Generous to give me so many. Poor boys. Don't often get a chance to get anythin ' like this. Oh, pshaw, I 'll eat the persimmons 'n let the lads go this time. But the very next act o' disobedience must be punished."

Brushing a sleeve across his puckered lips, Cassidy growled, "Next time ye buckos go grubbin' for somethin' to eat, don't be kickin' up such a damn ruckus while yer about it. Ye understand?"

Keeping a straight face, McCool nodded. "Yes, sir." Aside to Jobson, as Cassidy departed, he said, "See? Ain't discipline a wonderful thing, Luke?"

By nine o'clock the entire brigade was again on the march, advancing slowly cross country until they reached the eastern edge of a valley through which flowed a stream that eventually would lend its name to the campaign—Mine Run.

They could see the enemy was already strongly entrenched on an imposing ridge fifteen hundred yards away. Not satisfied with their impregnable position, the Confederates were working hard at their fortifications, employing dirt, timber, ax, and spade. Sage veterans in the advancing Union force surveyed the terrain with wary eyes. Open ground, soft and marshy, lay across Mine Run at the base of the fortified ridge. It was no place to fight.

Almost a year to the day since Fredericksburg, the Potomac Army was facing its wily foe lodged behind formidable entrenchments. Convinced that the task was hopeless, they nevertheless went into bivouac with the high resolve to do their best.

As night approached, the temperature dropped to below freezing, so bitterly cold that the pickets were relieved every thirty minutes.

Bent over maps in the glare of oil lamps, the general staff worked throughout the night perfecting a combination assault that could be put into operation at dawn. The troops stripped early for action. Knapsacks were arranged in the shape of a horseshoe on the frozen ground, packs piled high one on top of the other and left in charge of Captain O'Neil. Heedless of the freezing weather, some of the men discarded their greatcoats. No fires were permitted. Without means of keeping warm, the soldiers huddled together and waited for the morning sun.

Apprehensive recruits and conscripts occupied themselves by writing their names and addresses on small slips of paper which they pinned to their coats, some going so far as to include, "Mustered out at Mine Run this day of December." The more timorous among them started to sing mournfully *"Just Before the Battle, Mother."*

The biting wind subsided with the coming of a gray dawn. Colonel Throop, thrashing his arms to keep warm, assembled the shivering officers of the Corn Exchange in front of the center division and explained the work cut out for them.

"Gentlemen, our orders are to be ready for the sound of two signal guns from Warren's position on the left. We will move forward and charge the enemy there." He pointed to a line of Confederate entrenchments. "You see those works? We either sleep tonight on the other side of them, or on the slopes leading up to them. A word of caution, our pickets tell us that during the night the enemy damned the Run toward its mouth and the banks are flooded knee deep. The Confederate line which we are to assault rests on a summit with water extending to its base. Are there any questions?"

The company commanders shook their heads, each confident of Colonel Throop's abilities. With long faces they returned to their posts knowing exactly what was expected of them.

The moment before battle is one of those times when the hearts of the bravest stand still. Looking up at the heights with lines of slashed breastworks on the slopes, strong works on the crest and a flooded creek between, the poised troops felt a sense of futility.

Colonel Throop positioned himself at the head of the 118th Regiment. Mounted and with sword in hand, he waited for the sound of the guns that would signal the attack. A courier, riding astride a black gelding, came dashing up. Soldiers praying for a last-minute reprieve crowded in close enough to hear the tidings.

The courier saluted. "Colonel Throop?"

"Yes, Lieutenant."

"General Warren's compliments, sir. The assault's been called off."

At the announcement, rifles and caps were thrown into the air with wild abandon, men shouting and cheering, the first genuine outburst of enthusiasm since Gettysburg.

Colonel Throop fixed his attention on the courier. "You bring welcome news, Lieutenant. Tell me, who's responsible for this last-minute change of plans?"

"General Warren, sir."

"Aye," Gilmour roared in approval. "Smartest thing the man's done since he occupied Little Round Top at Gettysburg."

Colonel Throop moved closer to the courier. "Has General Meade concurred in this?"

"I'm not sure, sir. All I know is General Warren's declined to attack without being directly ordered to do so by General Meade. He thinks it foolhardy to even consider taking that ridge. The loss of life would in no way compensate for a success, even if gained."

"Sound and judicious judgment," Throop replied. "Let's hope Meade concurs. To attack the Rebel position under these conditions would make Pickett's charge look like a cake-walk."

With a sigh of relief, the men of the 118th spent the balance of the day resting on beds of pine needles, and tried to keep warm. Rising above the banter were loud praises for General Warren who had been recently placed in command of the Fifth Corps. Toward evening the unmistakable signs of a general withdrawal began. The artillery was secretly removed from position and batteries of logs substituted as decoys. Orders were passed down to increase the volume of fires by piling the wood high so that the flames would show through the night and well on toward morning. With these ruses perfected to fool the enemy into believing the Potomac Army still faced them, the Union forces began pulling out on a retrograde movement to Beverly Ford.

CHAPTER 23

The third winter of the war began auspiciously at Beverly Ford, Virginia. Advantages of the situation selected for the permanent encampment had been tested through the seasons and if the privilege of choosing their own abode had been awarded the men of the 118th Pennsylvania Regiment, they would have looked no further. The upper side of the Rappahannock in the vicinity of Beverly Ford was convenient and accessible to the depots of issue and supply, within easy reach of desirable neighbors, was far enough from the front to be away from the annoyances of disturbing reconnaissance and not close enough to the rear so as to be within range of the ubiquitous raider, Mosby.

Almost to a man, the soldiers unloaded thrilling, embellished stories of field and fight on the susceptible and inexperienced friends at home. The approaching days of inactivity gave ample promise of the opportunity to do this when, in keeping with the season, leaves and furloughs would again be liberally dispensed.

Winter camp differed little from their quarters of the previous winter at Falmouth, although the log cabins were better mortised, the spaces tightly chinked, and larger fireplaces made a cheerier blaze with their tall chimneys insuring a better draft. The men were experienced and knew how to apply and appreciate the furnishings they had acquired. They had not forgotten their homes, but as the quarters were the only homes they had known intimately for three years, or expected to know for a while, they fitted them with the comforts and conveniences of home. Those graced with green thumbs went to work landscaping the area around the cabins with double rows of cedar tree plantings. Games and sports became the order of the day; hunting, cock fights, footraces, bag races and blanket tossing. On surrounding fields, enthusiastic crowds flocked to view a new game called football whenever the game was played.

New subterfuges were frequently attempted by the wily. One of a rather happy conception was predestined to fail. The men's quarters and everything in the vicinity were to be in darkness at taps, and the officer of the day saw that the lights were extinguished at that hour. By an oversight, someone charged with the responsibility used the word candles instead of lights. Promptly, the perceptive troops caught onto an opportunity for evasion. There was a plethora of pork fat on hand that came in tin cans like the canned goods sold by the Sutlers. The ingenious filled the cans with pork fat and inserted strips of flannel for a wick, creating a homemade device that gave adequate light for games of pinochle and seven-up. The order had said candles out——not lights out. The order had been complied with.

Christmas holidays came and passed and, except for a fortunate few, most of the men of the 118th remained confined to winter quarters. Gilmour, in long underwear, lay sprawled on his bunk. The Scot's weather-beaten face was etched by the glow of a roaring fire burning comfortably in the fireplace.

"Aye," he grumbled, "tis bad enough that we ha' got to hole up like bears for the winter, but to be forced into bed every night at nine-thirty like wee bairn is a bit much." Exasperated, he rolled over on his side.

Paddy whittled a piece of wood, fashioning it into the shape of a doll. "That's army policy," he replied. "Keep us in the dark. Or didn't you know?"

"Well, I still maintain we should fight a winter campaign instead of lying around idle," Hallowell grumbled. "The Rebs are worn out, so now's the time to strike them. I'll wager Cousin Bobby can't muster twenty thousand men in the field right now."

Kimball raised his tired eyes from a piece of patchwork on which he was working. "Don't be silly. Those twenty thousand Rebs, or whatever number they might be, could run rings around us on their home ground in this kind of weather. Our big military can't even run a fair-weather campaign smoothly, let alone a winter one. Somewhere they'd have us bogged down in a snowdrift before you could say scat."

Jobson poked halfheartedly at the burning logs in the fireplace. "Kim's right. Ain't nobody yet learned how to fight an army in the field during the winter."

"Grant's been doing it out West," Hallowell retorted. "This Valley Forge routine just isn't suited to my restless energies. If we don't give the winter campaign a try, mark my words, there won't be a body left in this man's army by spring."

A sudden flurry of driven snowflakes and a rush of cold air swept into the cabin's warm confines.

Gilmour sat bolt upright. "Hoot mon. Shut the damn door, McCool. Ye want us all to catch our death o' lung fever?"

The heavy plank door slammed shut behind him as McCool removed a snow-crusted greatcape and hung it on a wall peg.

Jobson turned away from the fire, eagerness written on his face. "Willie, any word yet on the outcome of the world's championship fight at Wadhurst, England?"

His eyebrows knit tightly, Gilmour studied McCool's downcast expression. "By the sword o' Saint Andrew, you bet he's had word. Aye'n tell us laddy, Heenan got whipped, dinna he?"

Glumly, McCool nodded.

"Aye, and wha' di' I tell ye? I tole ye King was the better mon. And that's two month's pay ye'll be owin' me, laddy. The rest o' ye can likewise be payin' up on the drumhead."

Hallowell shot McCool a reproving glance. "You told us it was in the bag for Heenan. What round did your Irishman take his nose-dive?"

Dejected, McCool sat down. "The twenty-fifth," he murmured.

"Twenty-fifth?" Gilmour jumped to the floor. "Aye, they must've fed yer Irishman potato whiskey to keep him on his feet that long against the likes o' King."

Head bowed as if bent beneath the weight of a great burden, McCool heaved a sigh and a tear started down one wind-burned cheek.

The poker in Jobson's hand came down hard on the stone hearth. "Get off his back. Why rub it in? You'll get paid off."

Lowering his gaze, Kimball examined his needlework closely. "I'd be careful with my sympathies, Luke. Those could be crocodile tears leading to another of his pranks."

McCool stiffened. "A joke, is it? You call losing Donaldson and Crocker a joke?" He flung himself face down on his bunk and buried his head in a pillow.

Jobson crossed the room in three strides and gently rolled him over. "What's this about losing the Cap'n, Willie?"

"He's leaving tomorrow. For good. He and Crocker. They're resigning."

The rumor had been around for several weeks, but the reality of it was shocking. Every throat tightened and a hush fell on the occupants of the musty room.

Paddy put his knife aside and stared vacantly into the fire. Hallowell, standing next to him, leaned forward, his blanched, raw-boned hands braced firmly against the side rail of a top bunk. He spoke through pursed lips. "They've been the heart and soul of this regiment since the beginning. They go and there won't be a three-year man in the whole outfit who will sign on again."

"Ha. Name one that was plannin' to anyways," Gilmour retorted. "This just clinches it."

Early next morning Companies H and K were drawn up in ranks. It was deathly silent, a pathetic muster of blue-coated men standing ankle deep on a carpet of fresh snow. Despair showed in their downcast faces. From the chimney barrels atop the squat cabins, nut-scented wood smoke curled upward into the frosty gray overcast.

A few painful moments of waiting, and the final moment arrived. Sergeant Cassidy commanded, "Company. Attention. Present arms."

Instantly, a metallic clicking and snapping ran the length of the rigid lines, the breath of teary-faced veterans coming in misty jets. Everything was still as first Crocker and then Donaldson stepped forward to say a brief farewell in uneasy words choked with emotion. Subalterns and comrades, close since the earliest campaigns, strained to catch every syllable. Bearded men grown older, boys still pink-cheeked, hardened fighters whose tensile strength had been forged to resiliency in the crucible of war-all struggled for self-control as the beloved captains concluded their final remarks and it was a over.

Paddy wept, his heart sick with a hollow feeling of aloneness, the feeling that men have sometimes alone in a crowd. Tearfully, he took the hand of his longtime friend and pressed it tightly. "Thanks for everything, Captain. Think you'll ever be back?"

"Might if I can get myself healthy again. There's still a big job ahead." Finding it hard to speak, he lowered his head. "Best of luck in everything, Mulcahy. Take care of yourself. I hope you locate your wife and baby soon."

"Thanks, Captain. At least there's some hope now."

The departure of Donaldson and Crocker, along with others of like caliber, began eating away like an insidious disease at the morale of those remaining behind in the army. During the days that followed, incidents of desertion skyrocketed alarmingly and punishment of the captured became a commonplace sight.

With the word "deserter' emblazoned in paint across their backs, the criminals were forced to stand under guard on a barrel four hours a day for ten days until final sentence was delivered, the sentence depending on individual records. The few who begged for compassion and a second chance were restored to duty with loss of pay and bounty.

In keeping with the situation, Hallowell's tongue and forefinger continued to wag incessantly. "And I tell you again..."

Kimball cut him off. "That there won 't be a jack man left in the army come spring without a winter campaign."

Vandergrift looked up from a platter of beans. "Why don't you stuff your mouth with loblolly, Jake. Quit your infernal jawing."

"Aye, shut' up'n eat," growled Gilmour."We're sick o' hearin' aboot yer grand strategy. Tell it to the Marines."

Jobson pushed an empty tin to the center of the rough-hewn dining table and leaned back in his chair. "Are you fellows going to the big dance tomorrow night?"

"Dance?" Hallowell exclaimed."You mean with those young corn-fed shoats the Christian Association brought in? Not me."

"You crotchety old goat," Kimball chided. "You're just peeved because none of them gave you a tumble last time."

Jobson picked at his teeth with a fork. "How old are you now, anyways, Jake? Fifty?"

"Fif...why you young whippersnapper. I'll have you know I'll be forty-two next month. Now, take my friend Kimball here, there's a man of fifty, if he's a day."

"Don't make matters worse'n they are, Jake." With the back of his hand, he wiped food residue from his beard and cleared his throat. "You know as well as I we're both the same age."

"You dirty old men should of been sent home on pension years ago," Jobson said with a grin.

"Aye, 'n speakin' o' age, wonder what's keepin' them boon laddies so late? Mulcahy 'n McCool. Rehearsals niver lasted this long before."

Jobson gave his chair a backward kick and started to clear the table. "I'll keep their shingles warm by the fire." He chuckled. "Can't wait until Saturday night to see McCool play his part of Juliet. Juliet McCool. Man oh, man, won't his mother be proud?"

Hallowell grunted as he stood up and retired to his bunk. "The part that'll roll old Shakespeare over in his grave'll be when Cassidy comes on stage as Romeo. Can you picture it? Casting a red-bearded Irish alley growler as Romeo? Such gross miscarriage of casting."

At that moment they heard Willie McCool chattering as he came bursting into the cabin. He waved a recent edition of the *Philadelphia Inquirer* in one hand. "Hey, you blokes, feast your eyes on this. There's been a bit of action for a change."

Hallowell reached from his bunk bed, snatched the uplifted paper and began reading the headlines aloud. "Surprise dash into Richmond foiled by traitor. Union Forces under General Isaac Wistar turned back from complete success at the gates of Richmond because of treachery." He stopped and looked toward the door. "Wistar? He's your old commander from the Seventy-first, right, Mulcahy?"

Paddy closed the cabin door and removed his coat. "That's right. The only general in this army that's got both brains and backbone. Read the report that Butler sent to Halleck."

Hallowell's eyes slid down the page. "You mean this?" He held up the paper.

Headquarters 18th Army Corp
Fort Monroe, Virginia
February 12, 1864
General:

I have the honor to forward to you, with commendation, the report (dated February 9th) of Brigadier General Wistar, of his brilliantly and ably-executed movement on Richmond, which failed only from one of those fortuitous circumstances against which no foresight can provide, and no execution can overcome.

By the corruption and faithlessness of a sentinel, who is now being tried, a man condemned to death and reprieved by the President was allowed to escape within enemy lines and gave them information that enabled them to meet our advance. That fact is acknowledged in two Richmond papers, the Examiner, and the Sentinel, published the day after the attack, and is fully confirmed by the testimony before the court-martial which is trying the man who permitted the escape. I beg leave to call attention to the suggestion of General Wistar in his report that the effect of the raid will be to hereafter keep at least as many Confederate troops around Richmond for its defense from any future movement of the Army of the Potomac as we have in its neighborhood.

I have the honor to be your obedient servant.
Benjamin F. Butler
Major General Commanding
Major General Halleck
Commanding the Army

Jobson whistled. "Holy cow! How far did Wistar get?"

Paddy replied with a contemplative look in his eyes. "Feinted the Reb defenders completely out of position all the way to Bottom Bridge. He could've had Richmond lock, stock and barrel, except for some bastard named Boyle."

Gilmour spat at a cuspidor. "Aye, the traitor?"

"The traitor. After Lincoln pardoned him for one crime, Boyle beat it to the Reb lines and tipped them off. Another hour and it would have been too late. One measly hour."

Hallowell sprang from his bunk. "There, you see? What have I been telling you? A concentrated winter campaign could crush the Rebs. Right now. They haven't got the men to defend their lines."

"And what kind of straits do you think our army's in that we could accomplish it?" Vandergrift replied. His elongated, stooped frame made him appear a bird of prey.

"You talk like McClellan," snapped Hallowell, his wrinkles stretched taut. "Scared to move against Lee unless odds are two to one in our favor. I say we can whip him and his boys with what volunteers we have left from sixty-one."

Paddy made a move toward his supper. "Tell you what I'm going to do, in case anyone's interested. I'm putting in for detached service on the Peninsula. Under Wistar."

"Aye, laddy? And are ye sure ye dinna want to fly to the moon while y're aboot it?"

"Go ahead and have fun. You'll see. I've already been invited."

"Listen. Here's something else that's funnier," Jobson cut in, laughing as he pointed to a piece in the newspaper. "It says here that a captain recently complained to Lincoln that the Irish gave his company a lot of trouble. 'Sir, our enemies, the Rebels, make the same complaint,' Lincoln replied."

Howls of laughter shook the dingy cabin.

Paddy separated himself from the horseplay and ate some of the raw oysters that were set out on the table in an iron-stone bowl. Then he made his way to a far corner and sat down at a crude desk fashioned out of a cracker barrel. He took a pen with a scratchy point, ink and paper and began writing. Inside a week, the exchange of correspondence brought what he so eagerly sought— permission from Wistar for a period of detached service on the Peninsula. He bid his friends farewell and after a comfortable two-day journey found himself in the district below Richmond under the immediate command of his former Colonel.

A bitter, raw wind, whipped to intensity, blew in from the choppy York River at West Point, Virginia. A wind so fierce that it forced Paddy to pause and catch his breath. Before him was a closed gate in a wooden picket fence in need of paint. The enclosure surrounded the barren grounds upon which was located the red brick headquarters of General Wistar.

A sentry, frozen to the bone, approached the gate, "State your business soldier, 'n be damn quick about it."

"Private Mulcahy. Hundred'n Eighteenth Pennsylvania. Detached service by General Wistar's order."

"The Commander's house guest, eh?" He lowered his rifle and, placing it against the fence, began beating his gloved hands against his bright red cheeks. "Say, ain't I seen you somewhere's afore? Sure. You're the young fella who sat in front of me'n my partner on the train from Philadelphia, back in November.

Should've told us you'n the General was thick. Pass through. Commander's expectin' you."

A log fire crackled merrily on the hearth in Wistar's private study. The General was seated alone at his desk with his back to the doorway. Paddy knocked lightly. Wistar spun around in his swivel chair, jumped up and advanced with arms outstretched. His embrace caught Paddy's shoulders in a vise grip.

"Good to see you, Mulcahy. Glad you could come, good to have you around again. Here, take off your coat and hang it over there." He pointed to a rack standing in a corner.

"Good to be here, sir. How's Missus Wistar these days?"

"Just fine. Inquires about you in every letter."

"Oh? She's not here?"

"No. She returned home to Philadelphia right after the Christmas holidays. Army headquarters are no fitting residence for a lady. And how are things in your sector?"

"Not very good, sir. Not good at all."

"Hmm. So I've heard."

Wistar returned to his desk while Paddy seated himself in a ladder-backed chair. There was a dryness in Paddy's voice. "Have you had any word from your friend at the Virginia Military Institute? The one you said might put me in touch with my wife's brother?"

Wistar shuffled some documents on his desk and moved a paperweight. "Three years of war closes the door on many things, Mulcahy, foremost among them being friendships. I received no answer from that inquiry, but through another contact I did learn that Becky's brother left school after his father's death. They didn' t know where he went nor if he was in touch with his mother and Becky. I'm sorry that I have nothing more for you."

"Oh...I guess I was hoping too hard. I had a strange experience just before I came here." Paddy proceeded to tell Wistar about his encounter with the Southern picket. "I was really expecting to hear something from Becky through that contact, but so far, nothing. For a while I was encouraged, but I'm feeling sorta discouraged again. There has to be some way to find her. I'll be glad when this war is over and I can look in earnest."

"I understand how you feel. Don't give up hope, something will come through. You're persistent enough." He smiled.

A loud knock on the study door startled both of them.

"Yes, Marx, what is it?" Wistar asked sharply.

"Colonel Jamieson of the Fifth New Hampshire to see you, sir."

"Send him in."

Paddy detected a change and strain in the General's voice, a sudden transformation on his face.

"Shall I leave, sir?"

"No. Stay where you are." He turned to confront an officer entering the room. An officer whose tight-lipped countenance was blue from the weather, his mustache bristles crisp.

"You should be with your regiment, Colonel. You are no doubt aware the execution will take place in exactly one half hour?"

"Precisely what I've come to see you about, General. My entire regiment is mutinous. If you force me to execute the three prisoners in front of them, there's no telling what may happen. I refuse to accept the responsibility."

Wistar stiffened. "I anticipated that, Jamieson, and have taken steps to relieve you of the responsibility, as you put it. Your regiment will be drawn up in the designated line, as planned, a few paces from the spot occupied by the prisoners. Your firing party will be closely watched by a picked detail of the provost guard. On one flank of your regiment, at right angles with it, I'm posting two reliable regiments of my brigade, one deployed in line of battle with a section of artillery at its center, the other in two columns, each doubled at the center in rear of the respective wings."

"But General..."

"By your leave, Colonel. A few squadrons of cavalry will be drawn up at the edge of the woods a quarter of a mile distant. A field battery harnessed and mounted is placed in position in the nearest bastion of the fort and another harnessed and standing ready on the road inside the nearest gate. As far as your men are concerned, Colonel, it will not require an experienced military eye to perceive that in case of any mutinous demonstration, they can be mowed down by an enfilading fire of the regiment and guns on their flank. If they choose to break, they can be annihilated by the charge of the two infantry columns and every straggler cut down or captured by the cavalry in the rear. Now, does that relieve your mind of all responsibility in case of a forward incident?"

"But General Wistar, as I asked at the court- martial, why must these men be shot in public, in front of their own comrades?"

Wistar's dark, piercing eyes blazed. "I gave you the answer to that at the court-martial. One reason for firmness in this matter is the prevailing feeling existing among the newly-drafted reinforcements that prisoners cannot be publicly executed without insubordination and perhaps mutiny. Such doubts render it imperative that the entire command should know by public test whether the officers' authority is or is not stronger than the mutinous conscripts and drafted men's. Good day, Colonel."

Paddy watched as the abashed regimental commander withdrew from the room. He began to shift uneasily under Wistar's level gaze.

"Your eyes are brimful of questions, Mulcahy. Why don't you ask them?"

"It's not my place, sir."

"Then I'll answer them at random for you." He eased himself into a chair as though it were a great effort and spread the palms of his hands on his bony knees.

"Colonel Jamieson is a good soldier but, like many of our volunteer officers, he lacks the courage or will to enforce discipline. The Fifth New Hampshire is an old and good regiment, one of long service, as you well know. Having been reduced by various casualties to barely one hundred fifty men, the regiment has just been refilled with six hundred drafted men, all of whom are foreigners, most of whom can't even speak the language. Picked up in New York, they were drugged, kidnaped and then purchased by the quota agents of New Hampshire. Their muster papers were made out for them. Heavily ironed and confined in boxcars, they were shipped here like cattle to be provisionally brigaded the next day. During the night, eighty of them deserted and tried to reach the enemy. The first three picked up by our patrols were court-martialed and sentenced to death." He paused to rub at his eyes again. "I can't help but sympathize with the poor wretches. Nevertheless, their chains have been forged by experienced hands and are without flaw. They have come here with regular forms complete, as duly enlisted sworn and mustered soldiers of the army. I am bound by every consideration of oath and duty to treat them as such until discharged, regardless of their individual misfortunes."

"If they are foreigners, it serves them right, sir. People shouldn't enter a burning building unless they intend to help put out the fire. I' ve seen their behavior. We' ve been getting the same kind of replacements. They're a class that will have to learn the duties of citizenship the hard way."

Wistar continued stroking an ear lobe. "You have an earthy way of stating your position, Mulcahy, but as a lawyer, I must take an opposing point of view." With one hand he reached out and held up a sheet of stationery. "I have just finished writing a letter to Major General Dix, commanding at New York, in which I have set forth the violence and fraud by which immigrants and other friendless persons are being pressed into service against their will. The outrages committed in New York are worse than the acts of the old British naval press gangs."

"Sir, no one asked them to come to our 'fire.' They came anyway."

"There, you are ill-advised. Inducement has been made through the new Homestead Act. Nonetheless, an infamous outrage has been committed, not only on the poor ignorant victims, but on commanding officers constrained to such painful measures as I face shortly. It angers me that these measures should be rendered necessary by the base acts of those quota-hunting villains in northern cities who, if justice could have been done, would have first felt the halter."

A half smile crossed Paddy's face. "Aren't you afraid you'll get another 'wooling' from the War Department? I mean, supposing this letter finds its way into the newspapers like the others."

"I'm accustomed to hot water. The sooner our War Department corrects this outrageous injustice, the quicker I'll cool off." Stretching his long legs, he regained his feet. "If yours was the choice to make over again, Mulcahy, would you take the counsel of your father and steer clear of this war, or would you join with the old Seventy-first as before?"

"Same decision I made three years ago, sir. To follow you."

"Thank you for that." His gaze focused on the floor, hands clasped behind his back, Wistar slowly circled his desk. "One more question. By now you should have attained the rank of lieutenant. Yet you've never accepted a commission. Why?"

"As I said once before, sir, I'm a follower, not a leader. I like my independence. I'd never make a good officer.''

Wistar's gaze drifted. "Mulcahy, Sarah and I have prayed often and hard for a son. One who'd be somewhat like…"

His words were cut off by the distant low drumming sound of the Death March. Hearkening to the dirge, both men looked somberly out the window as Marx entered the study.

"Your mount is saddled and ready, sir."

Wistar turned, his shoulders sagging beneath an invisible burden. "Will you join me, Mulcahy?"

"No, thank you, sir. If it's all the same to you, I'll remain here and billet down."

"As you please. Marx, show Mulcahy to his quarters." Wistar took a deep breath, then strode through the doorway and out into the gray bleakness of the late February afternoon.

Marx, a rugged, strapping breed of man in his mid-twenties who could be as gentle as a kitten or as dangerous as a bear, whichever the circumstances called for, spoke in a polite, pleasant, but firm manner. "If you'll gather your things, Mulcahy, I'll show you upstairs." He started for the hallway. "You from the city?"

Paddy slung a haversack over one shoulder. "Not exactly. A small town on the outskirts called Frankford. Where's your home?"

"Salem. South Jersey."

"Salem. Good duck hunting down that way. Visited there a couple of times with my father. Seems a hundred years ago."

"Everything seems an eternity ago. War's like that. Time and events lose themselves, become dwarfed. I can't even remember how it was to live in peace. Here's your room."

Paddy gave his possessions a pitch onto the spindle bed and sat down in a chair. "How do you like working for the General?"

"Wouldn't trade it for the world. You might say, it's a liberal education. Care for a stag?"

"Yes. I'll try one. Thanks."

Putting a match to one cigar, Marx handed another to his ward and then stretched his muscular form lengthwise on the bed. "The General tell you he expects to be reassigned to command the Second Division, Eighteenth Corps?"

"No. We haven't had too much time to talk. When is the change to take place?"

"Sometime soon. It's a new army to be called the Army of the James and it is being organized under Ben Butler. Being fitted for the field right now."

Paddy bit into the cigar stub. "Butler. We've heard he's quite a rogue. 'Butcher Butler, the Beast of New Orleans,' I think the Rebs call him."

"You boys in the Army of the Potomac are better informed than I thought. He's an eel, all right, quite the pompous one. He and the New England cranks infesting this peninsula in the guise of missionaries are cut from the same bolt of cloth."

"Missionaries? What kind of trouble you been having with them?"

"Plenty. They've all got some slick scheme to fleece the Negroes. The orderly condition of this district, or I should say, the prosperity of much of the large Negro population, has attracted quite an army of unmitigated scamps, mostly from New England. I wouldn't trust any of them further than I could throw the shore batteries at Fort Fisher. The last so-called missionary the General threw out of the district was charged with tying nineteen Negroes up to trees for refusing to let him remarry them for a fee of twenty-five cents a pair." Marx paused to pass an ashtray to Paddy.

"At the dinner table shortly after the trial, I remember a stiff comment by the General that gave us all quite a laugh. He said, 'Though the price did not seem unreasonable for a good article of connubial felicity backed by a solid New England guarantee, it was only fair to the Negroes to ascertain what sort of title they were getting'. When the reverend rogue was brought to book, it appeared he had convinced the poor darkies that the principal thing required to make them equal to the whites was to be remarried by him for a cash consideration."

"What a rotten kettle of fish. Damned shame Lincoln ever let politics and military considerations change his position on gradual emancipation." Paddy exhaled a wreath of smoke. "Way things stand now, the poor colored people will be exploited more'n they ever were under slavery, and by the same ones who set themselves up as their saviors."

"The old story, Mulcahy. Beware of Greeks bearing gifts. You might like to hear what finally happened to our thrifty moralist. Just one month after the General found him guilty and sent him packing, he came back into the district with an appointment from Washington as Superintendent of Negro Affairs, with the authority to disport himself among the Negroes and their savings at will."

"Bloody hell! What are we coming to? Is this just an isolated case?"

"For the good of the country, I wish to heaven it were. Unfortunately, such is not the case, at least not around here."

"Marx! Hey, Marx! Where the hell are you?" cried an excited voice from downstairs.

Marx disengaged himself from the bed. "That's Chamberlain from communications. Must have something important. He never whistles on syllables like that unless he's worked up over something. Be right down, Champy."

"Mind if I come along?"

"Yours is the velvet carpet here. Come on."

Both men bounded down the bannistered staircase.

"How soon will the General be back?" whistled the plump Sergeant through a missing front tooth.

A crack of rattling musket fire echoed in the distance.

"Any time now. What's got you?"

"Plenty. Kilpatrick and four thousand cavalry will try to break into Richmond tonight. Have orders to free the prisoners at Libby and Belle Isle. We have been alerted to stand by ready to help any who might come out this way."

Marx grimaced. "Wonder if any of them will make it? Quite a stint if they do, but it sounds crazy to me."

That evening and well into Sunday night of February twenty-eighth, Wistar and his aides speculated on the chances of success for the bold adventure fostered by President Lincoln's desire to have his Amnesty Proclamation circulated within Confederate lines.

Elsewhere, army machinery was moving to cover up the daring raid and its element of surprise. Sedgewick's Sixth Corps began a determined demonstration toward Madison Courthouse on the Rappahannock. The flamboyant young Brigadier General, George Armstrong Custer, with his gaudy uniform and anointed curls, took his cavalry division off on a dash toward Charlottesville, and the dangled bait was taken.

The Army of Northern Virginia moved hurriedly to protect its left flank, to meet what it thought was an attack from that quarter, while Kilpatrick, like a thief sneaking through the back door in the dead of night, crossed the Rapidan at Elys Ford and struck hard for Richmond. Federal troops, posted on the peninsula east of Richmond, impatiently waited for some hint of success or failure all through the next day, Monday, February twenty-ninth. There was none. Tuesday came and went and still no word of the raiders. During the night it began raining and the rain turned into sleet and snow. A premonition of disaster gripped those who waited.

Fists clenched, Marx paced the hallway at headquarters. "I tell you, Mulcahy, somebody had a crazy romantic dream from the very start. Who with any brains could possibly think peace can be brought about at this stage of the game by planting amnesty pamphlets in the Confederate capital? And if they were fuzzy-headed enough to believe such a thing, why not have our agents spread the literature instead of sacrificing four thousand sorely-needed troopers? The whole affair is a departure from reality, the stuff bloodless bookish wars are based on, a festival of glory. Just pile it with the other boners pulled by our armchair generals in Washington."

Chamberlain, a waddling ball of lard, came bursting into the headquarters building, his round fat countenance wringing with despair, his mouth hanging open. "They're comin' in, but something's wrong. Tell by their faces, it's terrible."

Paddy, following after Wistar and Marx, rushed to the doorway. Out in the wintry darkness they viewed a pitiful sight. Thousands of mud-spattered troopers soaked through and pelted by the driving sleet, swayed exhausted in their saddles. Men bent double as they gripped the saddle horns with both hands to keep from sliding off their mounts.

Their weapons and uniforms were frozen stiff. Icy saddle leather creaked beneath the weight of riders and clanking accouterments. Their mounts sagged, miserable beasts that slogged mechanically through the deep mud.

Silvered with a frozen sleet, the branches of bare trees tinkled when moved by the wind, a mournful sound scarcely heard above the heavier sounds of rattling sabers and clanging metal canteens.

Kilpatrick road alone and sullen at the head of the disheveled troopers. He reined in his charger and dismounted before the headquarters' gate. His gargoyle face appeared eerie, muttonchop whiskers frozen stiff. He stood there, dazed.

Wistar rushed forward to take him by the arm. "Come in where it's warm, Judson. I'll have the commissary boil coffee for your men. Marx!"

"Yes, sir."

"Get over to the cook shack right away. I want every trooper warmed up before he leaves here. Mulcahy, see that every horse gets a half bale of hay, no grain, or the poor beasts will founder. Marx!"

The orderly stopped in his headlong rush toward the commissary.

"One thing more, replenish each trooper's whiskey and quinine ration from our stores. Now then, Judson, we'll go in and have some brandy. We've been anxious about your welfare."

"Thank you, General. Can't begin to tell you how much my men and I appreciate this kind of reception. We've been in the saddle for most of four days, without sleep for almost three."

"Go into my study and lie down. I'll fix the brandy." Kilpatrick flung his small frame on an overstuffed sofa, his muddy jackboots trailing on the floor. "Suppose you are wondering what happened to the raid?" he said with great effort.

Wistar poured a glassful of brandy from a decanter and handed it across to the prostrated figure. "In a way, yes, but you don't have to talk about it now. Here, drink this."

Kilpatrick took the glass and drank deeply. "Ah, that's enough to loosen a man's tongue. Can't drink too much of it, though, or I'll fall asleep. The heat from the fire feels good. Too bad I have to ride the men on down the peninsula to Williamsburg. Could curl up right here and sleep for a month."

"Williamsburg? In this weather? Why not stay at West Point until the weather clears?"

"Orders. Say, this brandy's certainly good."

"Then have another."

"I will, thanks." Taking a second glass, Kilpatrick gave his boot a sharp, impatient slap. "I'd give my spurs to know if Dahlgren's safe. His situation worries me. You haven't seen or heard from him, have you?"

"Dahlgren? No. Thought he was out of the war. Heard he lost a leg in a skirmish right after Gettysburg."

"He did. But it takes more than a missing leg to slow that boy. How he ever found out about the raid in the first place is beyond me. The whole thing was supposed to be a deep, dark secret. At the time plans were being drawn up, he was away at sea, convalescing on his father's flagship at the siege of Charleston. Two weeks ago he showed up in Washington. Came to me with a wooden leg, a Colonel's commission from Abe Lincoln and a strong desire to join the expedition. If you're acquainted with his charm and persuasive techniques, you'll know how hard it was for me to refuse him."

"Yes. And besides, he is the son of Admiral Dahlgren."

"That fact had nothing to do with my decision. You know damn well he's the best cavalry officer we've got in the army. If it wasn't for the fact he's only twenty-one, he'd be pushing me right out of a job."

Wistar smiled amiably. "Yes, I understand his capture of a courier bearing a dispatch from Jeff Davis to Lee just before Gettysburg enabled Meade to plan his defensive strategy more intelligently."

"That's correct. If Dahlgren hadn't captured that vital bit of information, we would never have known Jeff Davis had scotched the movement of Beauregard's army to the support of Lee's northern invasion at the last minute. Matters might have turned out a lot different. As it was, Lee never found out until too late." Kilpatrick upended his glass and drained it.

"It tears my heart out to see him now," he said, "a strapping, good-looking youth with crutches strapped to his saddlebags."

"You say you've had no word from him? Did he become separated from you during the raid?"

"No. No, he didn't." Kilpatrick rose to a sitting position and cupped his hands around the empty glass. "How's chances for a refill?"

"Very good. Here, help yourself." He passed the brandy decanter.

The wiry cavalry commander refilled his glass, took a shallow sip and began speaking slowly and deliberately. "When our forces got as far as Spottsylvania, that was about noon on Monday, I decided to cut Dahlgren loose with five hundred men and let him move in a southwesterly direction so that he could ride on Richmond from the south while I struck the city from the north. Our attack was to be synchronized. As soon as Dahlgren heard the sound of my guns, he was to strike across the James and head for Belle Isle and Libby, free the prisoners and head north with them. By Tuesday morning my column had driven down the Brook turnpike to within five miles of the heart of Richmond. We were at the inner defense line of the Confederacy. I brought six field guns into position for the final assault, and the men began the attack. After about an hour, with no indication that Dahlgren and the liberated prisoners were driving to join me, I sent up rocket signals in desperation. Still there was nothing. As the day wore on, I became convinced that something had gone amiss. At three in the afternoon, I decided to abandon the attempt to enter the city and fell back several miles to camp at Atlees Station. About eight o'clock, Captain Mitchel, with three hundred of Dahlgren's men, came galloping into camp."

Wistar bent forward, his lips compressed. "Don't tell me your expedition want afoul because of treachery?"

"That's exactly what happened, only this time it wasn't one of our men, but a Negro, the ones who stand to gain the most out of this foul war."

"I sometimes wonder."

Kilpatrick placed his glass on a table. "Mitchel told me Dahlgren heard my guns all right, but he was in no position to cross the James to fulfill his mission. Here is the dastardly bit, a supposedly loyal and trustworthy Negro guide purposely steered Dahlgren's force to an unfordable spot on the river. Ulrich immediately went north along the James in search of a shallow ford where he might effect a crossing. The attempt was futile and his command split up. If anything happens to that boy...."

"What about the Negro guide?"

"He made a vain effort to escape, but the men caught him and hung him on the spot."

The wiry cavalry commander rose to his feet and wiped his lips. "Thank you for the drinks. Now I must be leaving. Keep a sharp lookout for Dahlgren. He and his men will probably try to break out in this direction, God willing."

"I shall alert the pickets to that fact, Judson. I'll also send out patrols to render whatever assistance they can. There's still one question."

"What is that?"

"Why the President ever agreed to such a disabling experiment with the flower of our cavalry, a foolhardy attempt to have his Amnesty Proclamation distributed in Richmond, where the word 'pardon' is scorned."

"The distribution of the pamphlets you refer to was a subsidiary factor, an expedient concession to the President. Militarily, our chief concern was to free the fifteen thousand prisoners held in Libby and Belle Isle. Concern for their welfare was raised in the War Department a month ago when a ciphered message from Miss Van Lew disclosed a Confederate plan to move the prisoners to Andersonville, Georgia, in the near future. We have every reason to believe such a move will result in wholesale deaths from exposure and starvation. The sole purpose of the raid from the army's standpoint was to thwart that plan. Now I really must be going."

"I'll see you to your horse."

In response to a hand signal, Kilpatrick's mounted bugler sounded the "Boots and Saddles" call and from every direction troopers scurried for their mounts, looking like bedraggled barn cats racing for the milk pail.

The General swung himself into a deep McClellan saddle, fitted his feet in the stirrups and raised the collar of his greatcoat as protection against the driving sleet. Looking down, his steel gray eyes fell on Paddy standing beside Wistar. He leaned forward, his hands propped on the saddle horn.

"You, there," he called, "haven't we met somewhere before?"

Paddy stammered under the startled gaze of those around him. "Yes, sir. At Hanover, Pennsylvania, sir."

"By God, I recognize you now. The young fellow who scouted York so cleverly. You've got a good man there, Wistar. Better hold onto him. I could use his type."

"What's this, Mulcahy? What have you been holding back from me?"

Paddy grinned sheepishly. "I'll tell you about it at supper, sir."

"You're well informed. You will." His voice tinged with pride, he turned for a parting salute to the horsemen.

The lapse of several days brought a welcome change, a break in the weather which turned balmy, making the men dream of an early spring. Wistar pushed his chair away from the dinner table and struck a match to his briar pipe.

"Open the windows, Marx. Let some of that warm fresh air clean out the mustiness."

"If it's spring air you want, spring air you shall have, sir. For me, I hold no craving for it."

"Why is that?"

"Spring air can mean but one thing, the renewal of full scale war."

"Bosh. Campaigning in the field again will do you good, you're putting on weight."

Sergeant Chamberlain's pudgy face presented itself at the doorway. "May I come in, sir? I have a copy of the *Richmond Examiner*. One of our pickets just brought it in. Thought you might want to read this one."

"Bring it in, by all means. Something of interest?"

The communications sergeant bit his lower lip. "I wouldn't call it that, sir."

"Oh?" Quickly taking the news sheet, Wistar scanned the bold headlines, then let the paper slip from his hands as if it were deadly. His voice was low and grating. "Gentlemen, Colonel Dahlgren is dead."

Paddy stared, unbelieving, as he murmured, "When, sir?"

"Four days ago."

Turning slowly, Marx looked through the window. "So he didn't make it. The fortune of war."

Wistar snapped. "It is not the fortune of war to be thus accused. Listen to this. 'On his body were found orders to his command, which were to enter the city, set it on fire in as many places as possible, liberate the prisoners...'" his voice rose to an angry crescendo as he thrust a finger at the print, "... 'capture and kill the President and his cabinet and commit every possible horror on the Capitol.'" He slammed his fist on the tabletop. "I know the orders Dahlgren carried. Committing horrors on Richmond and killing Jeff Davis were not among them."

Marx spoke over his shoulder. "Reb leaders must be trying to incite their people into greater fury and desire for war. You know how newspaper stories twist and magnify things."

"Twist and magnify? Why, this is a vicious lie. It also goes on to say that three Confederate generals, supposedly men of honor, have publicly attested to reading a memo taken from Dahlgren's pocket, an address to his troops stating, 'Jeff Davis and his cabinet must be killed on the spot.'"

"What generals were they?" Paddy asked, his hands thrust deep in his pants pockets.

"Bragg, Fitzhugh Lee and a General Gorgas."

A shock ran up Paddy's spine. "Did you say Gorgas, sir? Josiah Gorgas?"

"Yes. chief of Confederate ordnance. Know him?"

"I know of him, and the curse of Cromwell upon him. He's no man of honor. He was Captain Gorgas, in command of the arsenal at Frankford before the war. Worked with the Secretary of War to clean out our arsenal. Then took off for the South with Floyd. Turned traitor on his own people and state."

"I recall the incident, now that you mention it," Wistar replied.

Deeply interested, Marx picked up the newspaper and let his eyes travel across the finer print. He let out a roar. "Cripes, will you listen to this! 'The wicked Yankee design was to turn loose thousands of ruffian prisoners badly brutalized by acquaintance with every horror of war, who have been confined on an island for a year, away from any means of indulging their sensual appetites, and inviting this pandemonium to work on unarmed citizens, the women and children of Richmond. The South must realize that we are barbarians in the eyes of our enemy and that a war of extermination, indiscriminate slaughter and plunder is now their program."' He dropped the paper. "What foul rot. Wonder if the rank and file will believe that sort of garbage?"

At that moment a loud hubbub of excitement arose amid the scuffling of horses' hooves at the hitching post beneath the dining room window.

"Marx, see what all that damned commotion's about."

Before the order could be fulfilled, an officer of the pickets appeared in the doorway. "Begging your pardon for barging in like this, General. My patrol just picked up a lad who claims to be one of Dahlgren's men. Thought you might want to question him. Could be a Reb spy."

"Bring him to me immediately."

"Yes, sir."

The officer hurried into the hallway and returned with a stripling youth in his early teens. His pale, beardless face drawn with fatigue, dark circles encompassed his soft brown eyes and his black curly hair was matted and tangled beneath his frozen kepi.

Wistar addressed him curtly. "Captain Finney tells me you're one of the cutthroat barbarians who rode with Colonel Dahlgren. Is that true?"

"Beg your pardon, sir?"

Wistar stroked at his nose. "You deny that you are a cutthroat barbarian?"

The trooper stiffened. "If you're referring to those trumped up charges in the Richmond papers..."

"Oh? How did you find time to read what appeared in the Richmond papers?"

"Miss Van Lew, the one the Rebs call Crazy Bet, showed them to me while I was hiding in her house."

Wistar's tone softened. "Have a chair, son. What's your name?"

"Private Henry Yohn, sir."

"Your regiment?"

"Hundred'n Sixty-first Pennsylvania, sir. Sixteenth Cavalry."

Curious, Paddy moved to the edge of his seat. "The Hundred'n Sixty-first? That's a Philadelphia regiment. You from the city?"

"No, Berks County."

"Do you know Johnny Duffield?"

"Yes, rides with the Frankford Company, he and his brother, Joe."

"And who's their closest friend?"

"Harry Harrison."

Paddy turned to the General. "This fella's no Reb spy, sir. A Reb couldn't possibly..."

"I'll take the word of a former scout on that, it takes a thief to catch a thief." Wistar frowned. "We've just been reading in the *Richmond Examiner* that Bragg, Fitzhugh Lee and Gorgas made statements to the press that they'd actually seen penciled notes in Dahlgren's notebook to the effect that Jeff Davis and his cabinet were to be killed on the spot, that Colonel Dahlgren so ordered his troops."

Tears, long held back, flooded the young man's eyes. "That's not true. Our orders came direct from General Kilpatrick. Free the prisoners at Libby and Belle Isle, distribute pamphlets and get out of Richmond on the double. Whoever tampered with the Colonel's notebook was deliberately trying to stir up trouble. The dirty butchers who mutilated the Colonel's body are the ones who should be strung up."

Wistar gasped. "How's that?"

The trooper struggled for composure. "It was pitch dark when we were ambushed. The Colonel got 'tumbled' on the first volley. I scrambled and hid beneath a heavy growth of myrtle vines that lined a gully, close enough so I could see what went on. When the Rebs found the Colonel's body, they ripped off his wooden leg and swung it in the air like it was a flag or something. Then one of them cut off his ring finger for a souvenir and stuck it in his pocket, ring, finger and all."

"Good Lord. And then what happened?"

Yohn's hands gripped the armrests of his chair. "They took his body to Richmond, put it in a boxcar at the York River Railway Station, least that's what Mister Lohmann told me. He's the one who picked me up and steered me to Miss Van Lew's. They work together. Later, the Reb government had the Colonel's body buried at eleven o'clock at night, like the papers said, so no one would know where to find it."

Marx doubled his massive fists. "If I were the Admiral, I'd bombard every Reb town on the seacoast. Blast 'em to hell for such sacrilege."

"Easy, Joe. Tell me, soldier, does this man, Lohmann, know where the Confederates buried young Dahlgren?"

"There's nothing goes on in Richmond that Lohmann and Miss Van Lew don't know about, General, least, that's my opinion. They found the Colonel's body and moved it to safety in a metal coffin. Took it to a nursery belonging to a Mister Rowleys. Lohmann and a Martin Lipscomb, he's another one of her agents. Managed to smuggle the coffin out of Richmond beneath a wagonload of young peach trees. Got through the Reb pickets in good order." He paused to cast a wary glance at the others. "When Miss Van Lew slipped me out of Richmond, she told me to get word to the Admiral quickly as possible that his son's body now rests at peace on the farm of a German named Orrick at Laurel Station."

Silence filled the room. "I will see to it personally," Wistar replied after some length. "Furthermore, I order everyone here to forget what you've just heard regarding the whereabouts of Colonel Dahlgren's body."

Tears bred of exhaustion and unbridled emotion began flowing again as the cavalryman reached inside his tunic, withdrew an oilskin packet and handed it to General Wistar. "If you'll pass this along, too, sir, I'll be much relieved. All of the Colonel's hair that could be spared was cut off." He nodded toward the oilskin. "It's in there. It's to be sent to his father."

Paddy felt a lump rise in his throat and let his gaze fall to the floor.

During the days that followed, a storm of controversy rose and spread like wildfire in the wake of the Dahlgren affair. A maddening fury swept the people of both the North and South. Photographic copies of the penciled remarks found in

Dahlgren's notebook were sent by General Lee to General Meade, together with an angry letter demanding to know whether those alleged designs and instructions to Dahlgren were authorized by the United States Government, or by his superior officer, or were approved by them.

Kilpatrick's reply to Lee was quickly published. "Nowhere," he stated emphatically, "do the photographic records contain the endorsement referred to as having been placed by me on Colonel Dahlgren's written instructions. Colonel Dahlgren received no orders from me to pillage, burn or kill, nor were any such instructions given me by my superiors."

Admiral Dahlgren, grieving aboard his flagship at sea, hurried home from the siege of Charleston to examine the controversial papers purported to have been found on his son's body. Subjecting the document to a close, careful study, he openly branded it as false. The signature could not possibly have been his son's. It was not even his name. The Colonel's name, Dahlgren, had been misspelled "Dalhgren" by whoever created the forgery. Further, it was pointed out by the Admiral, and supported by evidence, that his son always signed himself Ulrich Dahlgren, never with the single initial "U," as was on the papers.

Finally, Lieutenant Barley, Dahlgren's signal officer, having made good an escape from Richmond, was called to appear before an investigating committee and his testimony became widely disseminated. "In the capacity of signal officer, I was the only staff officer with him on that expedition. I had charge of all material for destroying bridges, blowing up locks, aqueducts and so forth. I knew all his plans, what he intended doing, and how he intended doing it, and I know I never received any such instructions as those papers contain. I also heard the orders of the command. Men cannot carry out orders they do not know about. The Colonel's instructions were, if we were successful in entering the city, to "take no life except in combat, to keep all prisoners safely guarded, but to treat them with respect. Liberate all Union prisoners, destroy public buildings and government stores, and leave the city by way of the peninsula."

Breeders of hate and dissension in the propaganda mills of both North and South thrived on the incident. The conflict was hardening into a pattern for total war, something no one had bargained for in the beginning. With that new denominator finding its way into the military equation, there came a front-page announcement to further stir emotions. On March tenth, a General-in-Chief of all the armies was created and appointed by President Lincoln so that from now on the various far-flung armies of the Union, instead of working at cross purposes with each other, would operate as a team. General U. S. Grant, given three stars, more rank than any American soldier had worn since George Washington and Winfield Scott, was planted firmly in the saddle, with full control over all military operations. Other changes followed swiftly. The Army of the Potomac was immediately reorganized into three consolidated corps instead of five.

Remnants of the 1st Corps, decimated on the first day of Gettysburg, were transferred to the 5th Corps. Two divisions of Sickles' 3d Corps, still bearing scars of the second day's fight at Gettysburg, were incorporated with the 2nd Corps but were permitted to retain their distinctive flag and badge. The remaining division of the 3rd Corps was transferred to the 6th Corps, but directed to abandon its flag and badge and assume that of the Greek Cross. Thus, the famous, old-line 1st and 3rd Corps passed out of existence. General Hancock retained command of the 2nd Corps, General Warren the 5th, and "Uncle John" Sedgewick, the 6th.

Extensive changes also took place on the peninsula and the Army of the James. Wistar, relieved from command of the district by a general order, was getting ready to resume command of the 2nd Division in the 18th Army Corps.

Paddy, seized by a hungry yearning to rejoin friends and comrades encamped at Beverly Ford, prepared to leave on an afternoon packet. He slowly buckled the straps of his knapsack and cast one last glance around his room to make sure that he had not forgotten anything.

Joe Marx appeared in the doorway. "You about ready?"

"Guess so."

"Good. Your boat leaves in a half hour. I'll see you to the wharf."

The two descended the creaking staircase.

"We'll have to wait here in the hall a minute. The general has visitors."

"Visitors? Who?"

"Butler, Stedman and Smith."

"Whew, that's an imposing array of heavy military. Come to see me off, did they?"

"Not from the sound of things. Listen."

Wistar's angry voice could be clearly heard. "Why did you wait so long to divulge this scheme of yours affecting myself and others? The preparations must have required at least a month. In that length of time, I could have put in for transfer to the Army of the Potomac. I can see your desire to get Weitzel back under your command, since he was a former favorite of yours in New Orleans, but to give him command of my division?"

"But, Isaac," remonstrated General Butler in his silky voice, "the only command suitable for Weitzel's superior rank is your division. I'm doing the best I can under the circumstances by giving you the third division, which is stronger in numbers."

"Yes, composed of Negroes dressed up like soldiers and euphemistically styled 'Colored Troops. ' Of course it's the strongest division in the corps. It's never suffered any casualties, and I've had the dubious assistance of one of its brigades in action, where they suddenly ran away before the charge of two small Confederate regiments, nearly causing my personal capture. No, I share the opinion of most that, while good at marching and just now an interesting and popular government pet, the colored troops are no good at tying into battle."

"That will be your job. Turn them into good troops."

"I refuse to accept the command. You've craftily readjusted your little scheme to meet all obstacles so that Weitzel, who has hitherto distinguished himself for political and civil rather than military achievements, can take over my division. I shall not stand in his way, but I will not lead a colored division by way of forfeit. I will seek reassignment elsewhere."

There was a long pause.

"Will you listen to me, Isaac?" spoke a cool, steady voice.

Marx nudged Paddy's arm. "That's General 'Baldy' Smith, the one who saved the Western army at Chattanooga."

"It's clearly too late for remonstrance here. On the other hand, all the other armies are freshly reorganized and in motion. It would require considerable time to get yourself assigned to the Potomac, or any other army, and should you venture to leave the Army of the James now, while it is in contact with the enemy, you might have to sulk in Washington for a month or two during the most active part of the coming campaign, before the casualties of war will make room for your reassignment. You're a man of action, Isaac. You'd fret with inactivity and wither on the vine if forced to sit on the sidelines."

"Our cagey Butler here has doubtlessly foreseen the fact that I do not entertain such a contingency for one single moment. What course of action do you suggest I take?"

"Take over the responsibilities of your old brigade until matters can be straightened out. We need you in the field."

"And let one of the best divisions in the service fall unearned to a follower of Butler's fortunes, a man of my own rank who antedates me slightly? His best known recommendation is his obedient usefulness to Butler in the persecution and, as many have charged, plunder of non-combatant citizens and property owners in New Orleans."

"Now see here!" Butler shouted, "I'll entertain no such talk from a subordinate! I can have you cashiered out of the service for those uncalled-for remarks. I have friends."

"You don't have any friends. You're a skillful, wily politician, at odds with almost every military man of repute in the army."

Butler's artificial glass eye glared from its socket. His face blanched beneath the mane of long black hair pulled back into a duck tail on the nape of his neck. He appeared as jowly and fleshy-eyed as an alligator-menacing and dangerous. Without further ado, he reached for his hat, stormed out of the room and lunged through the front doorway.

Colonel Stedman continued pleading with Wistar in friendly sympathy. "Do as 'Baldy' suggests, Isaac. Take your brigade back at least for a while."

"If I do that, I'll be pushing you down the ladder to regimental command. The brigade is rightfully yours."

"I know, but we think of the country's welfare above everything else. It was I who first suggested that you retake command of the brigade. Butler can't last long, not with Grant and Lincoln taking a firmer hold on affairs. As you say, Butler is as helpless as a child on the field of battle and as visionary as an opium-eater in council. They will find him out."

"One thing you seem to forget is that Butler controls a powerful voting block and there's a presidential election coming in nine months. No, Lincoln won't dispose of Butler until after the election. You can bank on that."

"But nine months? Is that so long a time to nurse wounded pride compared to what our brave boys have been sacrificing for over three years?"

Neither said anything for a few seconds.

"Stedman, you're a good, gallant officer. Wish to God there were more like you. If you can step down to regimental command so unselfishly, what better can I do than put aside personal feelings and accept self-imposed demotion to brigade commander? It shall be done."

The three top-level commanders entered the hallway and shook hands.

General Smith was felicitous. "You won't regret your action, Isaac. Butler's injustices will catch up with him shortly. Mark my words. Good day."

Paddy eyed Colonel Stedman closely as he said a few final words to Wistar. Paddy admired the man's make-up and demeanor. Slipping his hands into heavy gauntlets, he nodded curtly to both enlisted men and strode from the building.

Wistar eyed Paddy from across the hallway. "See you're all packed and ready to leave the sinking ship. Good riddance, I was plagued with serious trouble the day you arrived and I'm plagued with serious trouble the day you leave." He smiled broadly and crossed the hall to rumple Paddy's hair. "Hate to see you go, Mulcahy. Heaven only knows when we'll meet again."

"By all that's holy, sir, let's hope that won't be our next place of meeting."

"Outside of heaven and earth there remains but one other possibility. Maybe that hot spot would be more suitable for the likes of us, eh?"

"That remains to be seen, sir."

"Let me know if you hear from your wife. Sarah and I are as interested as if you were our son. I have a feeling that everything is going to turn out rosy for you. Keep up your spirits."

"I will never give up hope, sir."

CHAPTER 24

ffairs at Beverly Ford had undergone considerable change during
Paddy's absence. The place had become an unsavory hog wallow
compared to the well-kept quarters Paddy had stayed in on the peninsula
under Wistar's jurisdiction.

He surveyed the surroundings thoughtfully, brow furrowed, arms folded across
his chest. It was difficult to determine whether the unsavory environment was the
result of carelessness or had resulted from it. There was something else he felt,
something he could not put his finger on—-an unruly demeanor that made the
atmosphere tense. Knotted groups of slothful, lounging enlisted men conversed in
low overtones, idleness showing itself in their unkempt appearance, and intoxication
was rampant.

"Hey, there," Lieutenant Kelly called from his cabin. "You going to pass me
without so much as a hello? How was the vacation?"

"Good trip, Tommy. Just what the doctor ordered."

"Glad to hear it. Got time to drop in a minute?"

"How 'bout you coming over to my quarters?"

"All right. Like to hear about the outside world for a change. How do things
look?"

"Helluva sight better'n they do here. What goes on, anyway?"

"Nothing much to write home about, except yesterday we had a visit from the
new General-in-Chief Grant."

"Oh? What do you make of him?"

"Ever seen a little bearded bulldog smoking a cigar? That's him. Guess
time'll tell how he stacks up as a general here in the east." Taking out a chain with
a whistle attached, he whirled the chain around his index finger. "Yessir, only
time will tell. We've been exposed to McClellan, the debonair, pompous Pope,
Burnside the cocky, Rosey Joe Hooker and dyspeptic Meade. Don't know about
this fellow, Grant. He's such a little one, but he looks like he means business."

In the distance, a low-lying sun, alive with the promise of springtime, dissipated
its elongated rays on a Western horizon steeped in deep purple.

At their comrade's approach, the Frankford volunteers swarmed out of doors, a clamoring of happy faces rushing forward to greet Paddy.

"How was the boat ride?"

"Any word of your wife?"

"Just had a personal visit from Grant. Say, you really missed something."

"Aye, and a pretty little speech from Meade," Gilmour cut in.

Kelly reached out and took Paddy by the shoulder. "Look, you have plenty to talk over with your bunkmates. We'll chew the fat later."

"Don't rush off, Kelly," said Jobson. "You're one officer we like. Even if you are the thief of the world in the eyes of O'Neil."

Kelly delivered a playful punch to Jobson's midsection. "Go blow your nose. I'll see you all later."

Paddy tossed his haversack to the ground. "Dunk, Kelly says this Grant looks like he means business. What do you think?"

"Generals are all the same to me, lad. Just got different faces, so ye can tell 'em apart."

Jobson picked at his nose. "He's completely annihilated two Confederate armies at Donelson and Vicksburg. At Chattanooga, he drove a third Reb army into headlong retreat from what was supposed to be an impregnable stronghold. That's good enough for me."

Hallowell grunted. "The West is a side show. Any general can win a reputation out there without amounting to much. Take Pope. A big hero out West. At second Bull Run, a complete flop. This Grant'll find out quick enough he's up against the Reb's first team when he locks horns with Cousin Bobby Lee."

"What Jake means," Dyer broke in with a grin, "is that we'll soon know whether his first name's pronounced 'Ulysses' or 'Useless.'"

"Aye. Verra funny," said Gilmour. "The thing we should all be worryin' aboot is whether he can stay sober long enough to fight a battle. I hear he's quite a drinkin' mon."

"Why is it you heavy drinkers always point to another man as being a drunkard?" retorted Kimball. "Is it to take the glare off yourselves?"

Gilmour's gnarled fists doubled. "If ye weren't such an auld mon, I'd clop ye one for that."

Kimball smiled. "Forget it. You heard what Lincoln said on the subject. If whiskey gave Grant victories, he was going to order barrels of it for the other generals."

Paddy found a stool and sat down. "They say he's made more mistakes than anybody, but he never makes the same mistake twice. That's something in his favor, we're not used to that."

Strangely silent until now, McCool took a knife from his side pocket and started working the dirt from under his fingernails. His eyes had a faraway look. "Got a letter from my brother out West. He claims Grant's a lonely man who'd rather be teaching mathematics in a small school somewhere. Said the general impressed him as one who'd like to get away from the war and live quietly. A man who needs lots of love and warm understanding, from a woman, for instance. Had a hard time all his life, that's what Owen thought. Maybe it's because of those things he drinks too much."

"By the sword o' Saint Andrew, our bonny jester has taken to philosophy. Hoot mon." Gilmour spit on the ground.

"Lay off," Hallowell said with a scowl.

"Aye'n I' ll speak as I please. Right noo I'm reminded of the lines, 'And so the jester doffed his cap and bells and knelt upon the floor. They could not see the bitter smile behind the painted grin he wore....'"

"I said lay off the youngster," Hallowell replied. "That was the last letter he'll ever get from his brother. Owen was killed shortly after he wrote it."

Gilmour's face fell. "I dynna noo. Why dynna ye..."

"'Course you didn't know. None of you knew. I'm the only one he can confide in."

The palms of Paddy's hands became moist. "What's come over you fellas? We're all friends, or have you forgotten? What's eating on you, anyways?"

McCool began working diligently at his fingernails.

"Might as well face it," Vandergrift answered dryly, "we've had it. It's time to go home. Finally, after three long years."

"Go home? What are you driving at?"

Helverson spooned peaches from a can. "Like Gilmour mentioned a while ago," he said between bites. "Yesterday we were treated to a pretty little speech by Meade why we veterans should re-enlist for another three years. All regiments re-enlisting can go home on a thirty-day furlough and can keep their old regimental numbers and flags. Also, those re-enlisting will be cut in on the bounty money that's floating around. With state and Federal bounties lumped together, we would get about seven hundred dollars. Only nobody's buying, not a man jack in the whole regiment. None of us take stock in government promises anymore."

"Aye, Paddy. Helverson's right," Gilmour said with a bite. "That seven hundred dollars ain't temptin' none of us. Since the legal tender act started floodin' the country wi' cheap greenbacks, a dollar bill ain't worth the paper it's printed on. That seven hundred dollars's got the actual purchasin' power of aboot two hundred dollars, and we're still drawin' pay at the old rate, eight dollars a month, same as when we started three years ago."

"Which means," Jobson broke in, "that what we could buy for eight dollars three years ago we now have to shell out twenty-eight dollars to get. Where we saved a month to buy something, we now gotta save three'n half months to buy the same thing."

"Aye. The depreciated value o' money has already caused a loss o' two hundred'n fifty million dollars in buyin' power to us bonny soldiers, who've been doin ' the bleedin' ' n fightin' for the past three years. I say it's high time we return home to make money. Let them who've been gettin' rich 'n fat do the fightin' for a while." He shot a glance at Hallowell. "And despite what's been said aboot the comin' o' Grant, if Abe Lincoln thinks he can spruce our spirits by presentin' us wi' a new general, like a mon gi'in' his wife a bonny new spring bonnet. he's daft. This Grant'll turn out same as last year's model."

Paddy cast his eyes to the ground and spoke in a murmur. "How do the others from home feel about this? You talk with them?"

"Aye. The feelin's mutual among us."

"All right, if that's the way things stand, let's put it to a vote. We volunteered as a body, let's decide if we go home as a body."

His eyes beading, Kimball tugged thoughtfully at his graying beard. "That's fair enough. After all, we've got to live with each other a long time once we do get home." He pointed a finger at Hoffman. "Lew, you go fetch the others. Bring them here. We'll light up the cabin."

"Will do, but what about Hank Colebaugh and Burke? They just enlisted six months ago. They have three years coming regardless."

"They're Frankford. They get a chance to speak their piece. Get going."

Hoffman returned shortly with the other Frankford volunteers. In muddied boots and faded uniforms, they took up places in the cabin, some standing, some sitting.

Christian Burke, a recent recruit from Tacony, coughed spasmodically as he crossed the room. Tall, frail and sickly, he paused to shake Paddy's hand and extend a word of greeting.

His square forehead fringed with tight black ringlets, Vandergrift sat on the floor, knees drawn up, a forage cap with a broken visor pushed well back on the crown of his head. His expression was that of a hardened campaigner, with the quiet tolerance of authority, but not especially respectful, he looked around inquiringly. "Who's monitoring this coffee klatch?"

"No one in particular," Hallowell replied, stepping to the center. "We all know why we're here. Anybody's free to speak."

"Okay, I'm not reenlisting for two reasons. First, I don't want to hog all the glory and I have no desire to monopolize the patriotism. I'm quite willing to give others a chance. Second, I've served my three years, duty to my country has been performed. My next duty's at home starting a family. That's it."

Picking at a hole in the sole of one boot, Jobson glanced around, then cleared his throat.

"What's on your mind, Luke? Speak up," Hallowell said.

"All right. I came into this war to preserve the Union. To be honest about it, also to see new places. After three years I've seen enough, some of it is too damn familiar. There's nothing new to see."

Joe Sackett flipped a jackknife end over end so that the blade stuck in the floor. His scarred cheek twisted into a smirk. "Like the old sayin', Jake, familiarity breeds contempt."

"Drop the comedy. What about preserving the Union, Luke? You giving up on that, too?"

"Since you're pressing for an answer, no. But if we're going to save the Union, I say the best place to do it is at home, not in the army."

"How do you figure?"

"Because back in sixty-one, the best and brightest spirits in this country volunteered for service. Month after month and year after year since then, the native stock of this country's been killed off. It's time those of us who are left returned home and stand against the beggars who've been taking over in our absence, them foreigners who've come to dance on our coffins."

Gilmour slapped his thigh. "Hoot mon! I'll stand by the lad on that. I'm a Scotch immigrant. Aye. Twenty years standin'. But the type o' foreigner driftin' noo on our shores is a different breed. Comin' fer wha' they can get out o' America, wi' no thought o' puttin' anythin' in." He fixed a leathery eye on those about him. "Only last week I received the disturbin' news that those wi' strange soundin' names be already biddin' and fightin' among themselves over the freight trades I left behind when I come to drive fer me country." His fist came down in anger. "I'm goin' home to save me business. Let them foreigners come 'n do the fightin' for awhile."

"Bully! Bully!" The supportive cheer rattled the cabin's timbers and shook the metal accouterments hanging on the walls.

Bob Dyer's sharp voice sounded above the din. "Gilmour's right. We all go home and let the damned foreigners fight for the country instead of milking it."

Fired by passion, cheeks flushed, Ashton of B Company sprang to his feet. "And we get rid of Lincoln's Homestead Act! That's what's attracting the foreigners, thousands each week. One hundred sixty acres for free. All over Europe they must be wondering what kind of strange country we have where land is given away. I say we don't have to open our western territories that bad."

John Yost, also of B Company, stood with anvil-blocked shoulders next to Ashton. His face flushed as he spoke. "Let's not forget the rich dandies who've been buying their way out of the fighting by hiring substitutes or paying three hundred dollars. They are the real culprits in my book. Give my right arm to see them forced into one of the new regiments where they'd have to mix with thieves, pimps, bloated libertines, vagabonds and all the other riff- raff the army's been sending lately."

Lew Hoffman tapped the ashes from the bowl of his pipe. "I'd like to see those dandies get fleeced, but good. Have you seen the apes in the new regiment camped next to us? Pass their time practicing picking pockets and springing locks. What a motley crew, that's all they do all day."

His long legs leading the way, Vandergrift slid his powerful frame from a lower bunk and stood erect. His deep voice had a testy sound to it. "It's fairly well agreed they use a man here same as they do a bird at a turkey match, fire at it all day and if they don't kill it, raffle it off in the evening. Since we haven't been killed in three years, they want us three more years. Let's put it to a vote. Everybody has been heard from."

A loud crack filled the room as McCool's fist slammed hard against a pine bunk post. His half-closed eyes were spilling tears. "No, not everybody. Not everybody's been heard from. Where's Tibben's consent? Joe Byram, anybody heard his voice? You," he flew across the room and glared into Bob Dyer's face, "you got a proxy from your brother's grave at Fredericksburg to vote for him?" Crying hard now, he turned on Paddy. "You brought us all in. How come you don't speak? You letting Batt and Castor's memory go for nothing? They'll really love you for that."

A garbled rush of words poured from him as, sobbing and choking, he shook a fist in the astounded face of Gilmour. "Go ahead and stare. See the bitter smile behind my painted grin? See it? Can you?" One arm swung in a wide circle. "You're worse, the pack of you, than any foreigner you' ve slandered here. Who do you think's been feeding us? Making our clothes? Sending us guns and bullets? Those who've come over here for freedom. They're fighting, same as us. You're worse, all right. Why? I'll tell you why. Because you're quitters! Mother murtherin' quitters! Quitting on our flag and country when it needs us most. And when you go home," his shoulders heaved, "be sure to strip the Shepherdstown pennant off our flag. You ain't no longer worthy of the honor of flying it! Other regiments still point proudly at us and shout, 'There go them fellas what fought at Shepherdstown.'"

Quaking with emotion and openly weeping, he brushed a threadbare sleeve across his streaked face.

"Self-interest! Self-preservation! I'm fighting for something better than that. Go ahead, take a last good look at yourselves, if you can. The regiment that thumbed its nose and stood ground to Hill's whole Rebel corps. Now you're turning tail and running. Well, go on home if that's what you want. All of you. Go and be damned! I'm reenlisting. Alone."

Outside, drawn by the noise and excitement, others of the 118th Regiment stood around listening. Hardy men stared at the scene through the open door and windows while a cool spring breeze played lightly on their peering faces. They watched intently as Hallowell placed an arm about McCool and led him to a lower bunk.

Slowly Hallowell turned to those who sat stunned and silent. Like a fierce, shaggy-haired prophet, he spoke in a rasping voice. "Thank God for one man among us. Now, I'm going to have my say. I've kept still too long. One thing you've forgotten. There is a commonplace but important truth, the aggregate character of a people of any nation depends on the personal character of its individual citizens. Lincoln put it better than any words of mine when he said, 'It is for us the living rather to be here dedicated to the unfinished work....'"

A sigh escaped from Bob Dyer as he dropped his head to his chest.

"The stability of popular government depends far more on the personal character of its people than it does on any constitution that it adopts, or any statute it enacts." Hallowell's voice rose. "What would those safeguards be worth if the people did not sustain and enforce them with character?"

Several standing outside broke into a fit of nervous coughing.

"The Constitution would be broken and the law defied. Plots and anarchy would destroy both, and the government would crumble. If we quit now and go home, our country will be endangered by that much. You know as well as I that forces of evil and destruction stalk the streets of every city and town in the North, seeking opportunity to wipe out all that our comrades died for. This great country, with its universal suffrage, its divergent, conflicting interests, its huge land mass and large population from every class and clime, is more dependent on the character of its people than other countries." His voice fell. "We've all been reared in the same town where a good family name is revered. Shall we sustain that heritage and continue fighting? Or do we vote to call it a day? All right, Vandergrift. How about you?"

Lips taut and drained of blood, Vandergrift hesitated a moment as he rubbed the healed wound on his arm and thoughtfully said, "Re-enlist."

"Kimball?"

"Jake, you know I couldn't reopen the store without you. I'll stay if you do."

"Yost?"

"I got tumbled at Shepherdstown, that battle pennant ain't gonna be disgraced by any action on my part. I'll stick."

"Woodfield?"

"Stick and fight it out."

"Gilmour?"

Every eye focused on the gnarled Scot as he hesitated and mopped his shaggy brow. "I stand to lose too much. I'm returnin' home to save me business."

"Jobson?"

Head bowed, eyes fixed on the floor, Jobson murmured, "What was it somebody said? A good name's rather to be chosen than great riches, and loving favor rather than silver and gold. I vote to reenlist."

"Sackett?"

"Stick."

"Dyer?"

"Re-enlist."

"Mulcahy?"

Paddy shot a sideways glance across the room at Gilmour. "For the want of a nail, a shoe was lost. Dunk will have to get someone else to do his shoeing. My forge stays closed. I stay."

"Hoffman?"

"Hope to have a son someday. When I tell him I was wounded at Fredericksburg, don't want to admit I gave up and quit when the going got rough. I'll reenlist."

"Helverson?"

"I'll ride along."

"Ayers?"

"Re-enlist."

"Ashton?"

"I'll rally 'round the flag once again."

"It is done then. Everyone's been heard from except Woodhead who's been sent home on disability. Colebaugh and Burke still have an unexpired term of two'n half years. Tomorrow we make known our decision at headquarters."

By morning the patriotic fervor of the Frankford volunteers had spread throughout the entire regiment. Rejuvenated veterans, goaded into action, flocked to affix their signatures to reenlistment papers that tied up their lives for another three years.

Elsewhere in the Potomac Army, which was girding its loins for renewed battle, the re-enlistment of veterans fell short of the mark. A solid nucleus of only 28,767 veterans chose to stay and fight under stranger, Grant. By the end of April a perceptible change in the army way of doing things began to take place and the soldiers felt it. There was a tightening up and straightening out, a firm hand inexorably cracking the whip. Every moment of the day became one of inspection, dress inspection, general inspection, and dress parade. The loud, stringent bark of drill sergeants echoed across the parade grounds where new levies were being pounded into shape. At nightfall the strong fell into bed exhausted without waiting for taps.

Orders went to all corps and division commanders to make radical cuts in the number of men who were on the rolls as on "special," "extra," or "daily" duty and attention was called to the discrepancies between the numbers reported "present for duty" and those listed as "present for duty equipped." In brigades and divisions, the Inspector General became a busy man and where equipment had been lacking, it suddenly materialized. Long trains of freight cars clanked into Brandy Station daily to unload food and forage, uniforms and blankets, shelter tents and munitions. Wherever veteran troops assembled, it was with a genuine sense of satisfaction when they talked of working harder than ever before. Subtly, but unmistakably, an air of competence and preparation manifested itself.

Coming in for its share of attention, the cavalry was being hammered into a hard-fisted arm of the service with new businesslike weapons, seven-shot Spencer magazine carbines.

Pleasanton and Kilpatrick were sent packing, and riding herd on the troopers was a wiry, sawed-off, bandy-legged, tough little man named Phil Sheridan. His bullet-shaped head and hard eyes were a common sight as he made the rounds of the camps at a pounding gallop astride a black over-size stallion. His uniform constantly mud-splattered, in one fist he flourished a flat-crowned black hat which on him seemed to be at least two sizes too small for his head.

The artillery arm began feeling the whiplash, a demand for increased efficiency and execution. Gunners went through endless maneuvers as they wheeled back and forth in the dust and mud to become letter-perfect in such intricacies as changing front to right on the first section. Field pieces banged away at targets from early morn till late at night. Batteries galloped up to a line, halted, unlimbered and completely disassembled their pieces until wheels, guns, gun carriages and limber chests lay separate on the ground. Then at a sharp command, they reassembled the whole works and galloped off again.

Veteran artillerymen grumbled among themselves that such drill was of no practical use, but it was monotonously repeated over and over until the crew could perform the whole maneuver in less than one minute.

The heavy hand of Grant proved to be long and far-reaching. To the delight of seasoned infantrymen, the new General-in-Chief reached back to Washington to pull idle troops from their safe quarters and put them to work in the field. Since the outbreak of the war, ponderous regiments mustering eighteen hundred men, had led a soft life with permanent barracks, regular well-cooked meals and a clean bed every night. The only casualties had come from barroom brawls, or venereal diseases picked up in the social life of Washington fleshpots.

To the unconcealed joy of troops in the field, these regiments were being dragged from their cozy nests and , marched down to the Rapidan and forced to pitch their tents in the mud just like everybody else.

Cynical and battle-hardened campaigners began looking at Grant's silent figure with awe, admiration and respect for his power. Veterans realized that only a man with prodigious strength could override the White House and the War Department's unyielding insistence that forty-thousand men be kept around Washington for defense purposes. Now, at last, it seemed the country's strength was being fully used.

April passed and the signs of activity leading to renewed warfare increased. On the twenty-eighth of April, a sure sign presented itself. Field hospitals were abandoned and the sick ordered to the rear. All able-bodied men were issued six day's rations and twenty rounds of ammunition. One more day elapsed, and the smudge of billowing smoke and flame was all that remained of the winter quarters of the Army of the Potomac. Under Grant, the army began to march, 127,471 strong.

The long blue columns snaked their way down to the fords of the Rapidan and crossed the sweet-scented river on swaying pontoon bridges. The weather was warmed pleasantly by the balmy breath of spring. All of nature seemed bright and fresh.

Despite the felicitous atmosphere, there was a veiled threat in the air, a weird encroaching power, the kind that draws men close together on a dark night. The overwhelming number of fresh levies caught the feeling and quailed at the thought of facing death for the first time.

Self-anointed tough guys and "alley growlers" succumbed to a sense of dread, which they found almost impossible to shake off. Even battle-scarred veterans moved uneasily, casting wary eyes at the enveloping, tangled wilderness into which they were advancing. They knew that every step forward was being carefully observed by a wily old fox and his gray-clad legions.

In the lead, marching two abreast, was the 118th, who soon found themselves swallowed up in the cavernous mouth of a dense, trackless forest. The piercing cry of the whippoorwill rang through the pines and the screech of owls echoed from the treetops. The gloomy woodland stretched far away, apparently endless. Clearings were so few and so concentrated that they scarcely broke the monotony of trees, chaparral and undergrowth.

Dark cedar-stained streams that had never seen the sun twisted reptile-like along their water courses that wandered aimlessly, turning on themselves and soaking the black ground into bush-covered swamps overhung by trailing, entangling monkey vines. It was a poor place for armies to fight, but Grant marched the entire Army of the Potomac straight into it. The goal of the new commander evidently was not the oft-tried, ill-fated one to capture Richmond, but to fight the army of North Virginia where it could be found, attack it as quickly as possible, and keep attacking until one side or the other was the victor.

Well-pleased by what they believed to be true, the old, tested regiments moved with zeal and resolution into strong lines of battle. The snapping of boughs and branches, the tramping of cracking underbrush broke the silence of the noiseless forest, indicating that an army was in motion.

On the fifth day of May the inevitable clash occurred when the two warring hosts under Grant and Lee confronted each other. It was a contest unparalleled for absolute slaughter. Throughout the course of four days and nights, the beleaguered Northern army slugged it out toe to toe with the Rebel forces until Grant backed off to survey this new adversary who maneuvered an army so staunchly and with such skill and determination.

The battle was costly, claiming the lives of Generals Wadsworth and the beloved "Uncle John" Sedgewick. A pall of gloom settled over the Federal Army. Tried and true campaigners who had been through war under an assortment of commanders now took stock of the eighteen thousand casualties. They wagged their heads and mourned the loss.

Halted temporarily by the side of a road that had previously been raked by heavy shelling, the dispirited men of the 118th assumed all manner of reposes-heads thrown back, lips blackened, vacant stares. Paddy rested against the trunk of a tree completely denuded of bark. Vandergrift stretched out on the ground, stirred next to him then rolled over on his side, his attention focused on the main fork in the road.

"Which branch do you think we take? Left or right?"

"Left. Haven't we always?"

"Don't you think this Grant's any different from the rest?"

"No different. He'll retreat. We'll go high-tailing it back to Washington."

Face in the dust, head resting on a crooked arm, Jobson raised up slightly, his voice coming in a muffled croak. "Ladybug, ladybug, fly away home. Your house is on fire and your children will burn. Washington, here we come." Suddenly he stopped. "Hey, what's all that commotion about?"

Hearing the sound, Paddy shaded his eyes and glanced in the direction from which it was coming.

"What do you make of it, Mulcahy?"

"Gang of pioneers with axes. By all that's holy, that's Grant with them."

It was a galvanizing new experience. The soldiers sprang to attention as the General approached. A relatively short individual, unshaven, a cigar stuck in one corner of his mouth, his quiet aplomb seemed to fill the discouraged men with fresh inspiration. He presented a commonplace appearance in his slouch hat and unbuttoned frock coat that hung loosely from his heavy shoulders, a coat covered with dust and devoid of any insignia. His whole being bespoke a bond of kinship with the men. Bulldog tenacity was written on his fixed expression as he jerked his head and indicated to the axe-men what he wanted done. The men started felling timber from the right hand fork in the road.

Open-mouthed, not believing what they saw, the Corn Exchange veterans stood gaping. To all intents and purposes, it did seem that the army was finally taking the road south. There would be no retreat.

As if to relieve the questioning glances, Grant turned on the troops standing nearest him. "At ease, boys. There'll be no retreat. We're going to fight it out on this line if it takes all summer."

His voice was soft and mild. He pivoted sharply and walked off. A wild, spontaneous outburst of cheering rose at his back.

"Hey, boys, at last, we got us a general!"

"Three rousing cheers for 'United States' Grant!"

"Hip, hip, hurrah! Hip, hip, hurrah! Hip, hip...."

At Paddy's elbow, a pioneer leaned heavily on his axe handle, a look of satisfaction on his face as he stared after Grant's disappearing figure.

"Just like you heard, ain't he? I was there first time he laid eyes on Meade's colored headquarters flag, the one 'Four Eyes' keeps unfurled with the golden eagle in a silver wreath as the emblem. This Grant takes one amazed look at it and pops out with, 'What's this? Is imperial Caesar anywhere near?'"

Paddy smiled, one eye peeled on Cassidy, who was standing, arms akimbo in the narrow roadway, a whistle plugged in his mouth. He blasted loudly.

"All right ye buckos, ye heard what the man said. Fall in."

The men fell into ranks and began moving forward behind axe-swinging pioneers clearing the way. A mile or so and the path through the wilderness opened onto a traversable road.

A stone lodged in one shoe, Helverson plodded ahead with a gimp. "Anybody know where we're going?"

"Heard Kelly mention a place called Spottsylvania Courthouse."

"You did, Willie? How far is it? He say?"

"Fifteen, maybe twenty miles. Puts us between Lee and Richmond, smack across his right flank." He sprang nimbly into the crouched position of a prizefighter, arms extended, fists doubled and body slowly circling. "We slide off to our left like this. See? Get a good clean shot at Cousin Bobby's jaw, and...."

"Uh huh. Let's hope it works."

Tedious miles unraveled underfoot while the warm shadows of evening lengthened into night. The forced march became an eerie one as blue-coated columns, except for the clanking of canteens and accouterments, made their way in silence, boxed in on both sides by dense, wild growths of impenetrable timber and swampland, dark environs where fate could still stalk and plague the Army of the Potomac.

It was toward eleven o'clock when suddenly the pace slowed noticeably, and finally they were standing still. The men stepped out of rank, craning their necks and peering into the blackness, but could see nothing.

Dyer relaxed with his chin resting on the muzzle of his upright rifle. "What do you figure, Lew?"

Hoffman 's reply indicated that he needed sleep. "Don't know. Find out soon enough, I guess. Here comes Cap'n Ashbrook."

The stern, broad-shouldered replacement for Captain Donaldson wore an angry, perturbed look. His nose, broken earlier in the war, ran zig-zag down his face from forehead to upper lip.

McCool pressed forward. "What's up, Cap?"

Ashbrook spoke through a stuffed nose. "Third Pennsylvania cavalry and a regiment of recruits having a hard go at it. One helluva fist fight. Spilling over into the forest and got the whole road blocked. Over two thousand of them having a bloody riot."

"A riot? Let's put a stop to it."

"You stay put. All of you. Ain't a damned thing we can do. Others have been trying."

"Don't they know time's awasting? What brought it on?"

"Third ain't read the Bible That part that says 'Thou shalt not covet.' They've been gunning for this bunch of recruits since they first saw them riding fresh new horses."

Paddy spoke with anger. "But why now? Why at such a critical moment?"

"First real chance they' ve had. Way I got it, they were passing this recruit column in the dark. None of the Keystoners said anything particular until both columns were stretched out side by side abreast of each other. Then by common impulse the Third jumped the rookies, knocking them off their horses. Took to the empty saddles and started off with what they'd been after."

"Took off? Then how come the riot?"

"Quicker than the Third thought possible, the dazed rookies got their senses back. Counterattacked to recapture their stolen mounts."

"I'll be go-to-hell."

"Well, there isn't anything we can do but let them fight it out." He called to Sergeant Cassidy.

"Yes, Cap'n?"

"Order the men to get what rest they can till this thing's over. I'll let you know when the way's been cleared."

"Right ye are, sir."

Mumbling to themselves, the grim-lipped infantrymen started moving to the sides of the road, eyelids drooping as they flopped to the ground, disgruntled men curling up in the forest for a nap while up ahead in the dark, Yankee cavalry fought Yankee cavalry.

The fight ended an hour later with the Pennsylvanians getting away on their new horses while the severely-chastised rookies sullenly mounted the sway-backed nags to which they had fallen heir. Irreparable damage had been done. Lee had caught wind of Grant's maneuver, and taking full advantage of the costly delay brought about by the brawling Union troopers, quickly marched his army into Spottsylvania Courthouse ahead of the attackers. A howl of anger and dismay rose up from the Federal rank and file when they reached Spottsylvania and found the Confederates already there.

Ten days of bloody hand-to-hand fighting failed to dislodge the entrenched Rebel army and eighteen thousand Union casualties paid the price for the delay in getting to Spottsylvania first. At the same time, wholly unmindful of the heavy casualties for which their willful brawling was responsible, the blase' devil-may-care cavalry under Sheridan rode off in a daring dash to Richmond. In a skirmish at Yellow Tavern, they killed Jeb Stuart, the intrepid Rebel cavalry chieftain who for some time had been a thorn in the flesh of the North.

The Plumed Knight of the Confederacy had been stricken from the chessboard.

Union infantry, fighting in dense woods and behind log breastworks at Spottsylvania, were confronted with a stalemate, unable to make a dent in the enemy defenses. Grant studied the situation and decided to prowl again. In another effort to outflank the Confederate Army, he side-slipped his forces to the left once more, the Army cutting and clawing its way through a tangled mass of trees and vines that bordered the dark banks of the North and South Anna rivers.

Confronted again by Lee's main line which lay just beyond Tototpotomoy swamp, the Army of the Potomac emerged at last from the seemingly endless tract of wilderness, the men blinking like bats blinded by unaccustomed sunlight. Ragged, footsore and dirty, the soldiers of the 118th went into camp on the broad barren plain at a place called Bethesda Church. The blazing sun beat down unmercifully on the dusty fields, the heat stifling in the absence of trees and shade. The distant but unmistakable roar of battle could be heard in the southeast.

Stripped to the waist in the face of the summer's heat, the Philadelphians busied themselves about their field bivouac. Paddy, pant legs rolled to the knees, sat soaking a pair of swollen feet in pickle brine to toughen them.

Jobson, squatting nearby, worked over a meal of salt pork and hardtack while McCool, a bundle of restless energy, paced back and forth, his ears trained in the direction from which the sounds of battle were coming.

Jobson spoke without looking up. "See anything, Willie?"

"No, but I hear tell that our boys can see the spires of Richmond. We're that close."

"So was McClellan in sixty-two." Jobson fell silent for a moment and stirred absently at the salt pork crackling in the frying pan. "Our corps in advance must be getting pretty close to the old battlefield at Gaine's Mill, only this time we're the ones who'll be trying to force the Chickahominy." He tasted a portion of pork, "One thing's for sure, this is it. No further flanking marches are possible. Richmond's dead in front.

McCool nodded. "You're right. Wonder how it's going?" His gaze drifted off. "This standing by just waiting for victory or defeat edges me."

Paddy stood on his feet in the tub of brine. "Victory or defeat," he said, "the words lose me, they've become obsolete. There is no such thing anymore. This whole war has changed. It isn't war anymore, it's plain murder. Fight and kill, fight and kill, twenty-four hours a day, every day. No let up. Day and night, kill, kill, kill, right around the clock. The army with one live soldier left will be the one to claim victory." He stepped out of the tub. "The past few weeks, haven't you had the hopeless feeling of being trapped? Like being strapped to a sled that's racing downhill. No way to get off, no way to slow down. Just sit tight, hold your breath, and keep riding to the bottom."

McCool, expressive blue eyes showing infinite concern, slowly drew the back of a dusty hand across his mouth. "You been thinking too much lately. Don't think about things."

"Don't think, you say. Don't think about a daughter I've never seen who will soon be a year old. A wife whose face and form I've nearly forgotten. I keep wondering if it really happened. Don't think? That's how come we're in this stinkin', lousy war, nobody bothered to stop and think."

Jobson, mute and feigning preoccupancy, took a sampling of pork cracklings from the skillet, then rose suddenly to his feet and dusted off a trouser leg, his narrow gaze pinpointed on an approaching ordnance hitch. "Here comes an ammo wagon from the front. Maybe we can get some news on how things are going. Let's amble over to the dump and help him load. We can eat on the way."

The driver of the wagon, an animated figure in his late teens, swung his lathered team in a wide arc and brought them to a halt before a pile of cylindrical case shot. A mouse in stature, tasseled black hair blown all over his head, shirt opened wide at the collar, he sprang to the ground, his diminutive body moving in quick little jerks as if pulled by hidden strings. "Load 'er to the brim, boys. We're sure gonna need plenty."

McCool rested one hand on a singletree. "Things good or bad, mister?"

"Not good, I can tell you." The young teamster stopped to wipe perspiration that was streaming down his face. "We're fightin' at a place called Cold Harbor. Man, somebody must've been smokin' the opium pipe. Cold Harbor? It's hotter'n the hinges of hell. The Second, Sixth, and Eighteenth Corps are bein ' chewed to pieces."

Paddy stepped forward. "Did I hear you say the Eighteenth Corps is in on it? They're part of the Army of the James. How come?"

"'Baldy' Smith force-marched 'em up from the peninsula. Got here yesterday in time to help out Sheridan. How's the loading?"

An ordnance sergeant turned his head and called over his shoulder. "Got you just about packed, Shorty. Sure glad I ain't the one hauling this live stuff back over that field. Reb artillery will be lying for you now they know you're loaded."

"Ain't worrying me none. I can outrun their blasts. Always overshooting their marks anyways. Besides, there's something special I gotta take care of."

"What's that?"

"Squad of skulkers. 'Bout six of 'em, half mile from here. Must've run from the fight. Out in the open they think they're safe. Boiling coffee and having a good old time while the others do the dying. I'll show 'em."

"What do you plan to do?"

"You got field glasses? Watch."

The wagon loaded, he sprang nimbly on to the driver's seat and with a crack of the whip sent the team galloping off.

Paddy shaded his vision with one hand and stared after the wagon as it traveled back across the level, open plain. Curiosity had the best of him. "Wonder what he 's up to? You've got glasses, Lieutenant, can you tell?"

Kelly, binoculars pressed tightly against his cheekbones, thumbed the focusing screw. "Yes. There, I've got him. Real clear. He's put the team to a walk."

"See the coffee boilers he mentioned?"

"Yes. He's just drawn even with them. Now he's stopped."

"Stopped? Say, you don't think...?" A deafening roar drowned his words.

Not a mile away, a concealed Rebel battery had been patiently waiting for their prey and sprang into action, concentrating their fire on the loaded ammunition wagon which was now a sitting duck.

Kelly gasped. "He's laughing. That damn fool. The kid's laughin' like a hyena."

The first shell screeched harmlessly by, and the driver, with a whoop of fiendish glee, turned around to look at the startled band of skulkers. Wildly thrashing the reins, he put the team into a racing gallop and went tearing away to safety. Where the wagon had stood, the shells began striking with ferocity. Several of the bursts landed directly among the coffee boilers, jarring explosions which sent severed arms, heads, legs and bits of torn uniforms in all directions amidst clouds of dust and smoke.

Those watching from the rear stood stunned, eyes bulging with disbelief. Kelly was the first to capture his voice.

"The little bastard. And he seemed such a nice fellow."

Paddy's lips were tightly compressed, the corners of his mouth drawn down. "Bastard indeed. Can you blame him?"

"Blame him? Man, they're all dead. I tell you he was laughing hard. Nobody's safe anymore."

Walking away, Jobson thrust both hands deep into his pant pockets. "Good riddance, I say. C'mon, let's finish supper. Let somebody else scrape up the pieces."

It was later that same evening when Colonel Herring ordered the three hundred and fifty men remaining in the ranks of the Corn Exchange into formation. Recently elevated to command the regiment in place of Colonel Gwyn, Herring's broad, scholarly face was deeply creased with tired lines. A worried frown lent a serious note to the assemblage standing at ease in the lengthening shadows. Of solid intellectual character, a power felt by all who stood in his presence, level-headed under stress, he began speaking.

"Men, I'll be brief, and try not to be alarming. At present there exists a two-mile gap between our Corps and the Eighteenth holding right flank before the works at Cold Harbor. At daybreak we will move forward to fill that gap. I feel it my duty to tell you we'll be running into something entirely new, a new concept of fighting that has recently been whelped by the Southern dogs of war. Word comes that our generals are wholly confused by this unexpected change of field tactics on the part of Lee.

"The enemy has dug an intricate maze of trenches, zigzagging, well-fortified enfilading positions, that take full advantage of the existing terrain, no two positions running in a straight line. I must caution you. This new trench warfare, together with newer and faster-firing rifles, has increased their fire power and efficiency fourfold. One properly entrenched defender is equal to four attackers.

"Pay heed. We will no longer be faced with important points to take or defend as in previous battles. No more capturing this or that strong point. Charging in solidly massed ranks is proving to be disastrous. My advice for tomorrow is to break up, in squads preferably, and move toward the Rebel trenches in short rushes, lie down between volleys to protect yourselves as you fight.

"One final word. I am told the time of the actual advance this afternoon was not over eight minutes. In that brief period, ten thousand of our men fell, more casualties than in any other like period of time. You are going to hear it said that our generals, without bothering to test the strength or position of the enemy, foolishly and wantonly sacrificed troops in one grand assault after another. Such a proposition, sad to say, is fairly correct. So far, this has proven to be the worst-planned battle that we' ve ever engaged in. There has been no concerted plan. Meade, who up till now worked out the plan for every move since we crossed the Rapidan, has become sullen and angry, incensed because the papers are full of *Grant's* army, and he says he's tired of it. At this crucial juncture he has determined to let Grant plan his own battles. As a result, the three attacking corps today were allowed to go in divergently separated so that they presented six exposed flanks instead of two, and those exposed flanks were pounded to pieces.

"Tomorrow we are going to fight by our boot straps because it is our duty. Tomorrow I want no repetition of today's mistakes. You will move forward in short rushes, fight on your bellies as much as possible and above all, no exposed flanks. Major O'Neil will take command of the first battalion. I'll command the second. I want no straying. We strike straight forward, regardless of diversionary points that might seem tempting. Cohesion can bring us success. Remember that. Cohesion of effort will be our key to success."

After a brief moment of silence, broken by a terse command of dismissal, the men exchanged sober glances and broke up into small groups. Vandergrift spit out a wad of tobacco. "Jesus Christ! Grant's throwing us into a bloody meatgrinder."

June 4th dawned clear and sunny, the cool freshness of early morning breezes greeting the apprehensive troops. They remained quiet until the crass notes of the bugles split the stillness. Hitching nervously at their belts, they began moving forward to attack. Not a word was spoken as the distance was covered, each man envisioning the tortuous trenches ahead.

Mouth dry as cotton despite a ball of grass on which he chomped, Paddy began counting the distance to himself. "Seventy yards...sixty...fifty...."

Like a thunder crash and a sudden bolt of lightning, the skies parted as the enemies' shot and shell plunged into the advancing line with devastating effects. Destructive frontal fire cut down great swaths of men who seemed to melt away, others wilted into slumped positions. Acting quickly on the common sense advice given by Colonel Herring, the men of the 118th fell prone. Letting loose with their own volley, then reloading and springing to their feet, they charged forward in short rushes, re-peating the process. Their principal objective was within a few yard's reach when O'Neil began brandishing his sword in the air, circling it wildly, his ire directed at the cross-fire pouring in from an enemy trench to the right and parallel to the line of attack. His shrill voice carried above the roar of battle as he screamed for a change of front by the first battalion.

Cassidy spun him around by the arm. "Major, remember our orders! Cohesion!"

"Out with yez and be damned! Bad luck to yez! Wipe out that nest o' bastards!"

On pivot, the battalion swung around instantly and went charging off at an oblique angle to the right, both flanks naked and exposed. For a split second Paddy shut his eyes as he saw Cassidy go down, bleeding at the throat. When he opened his eyes, dust-coated Confederates were pressing in from both sides and running the entire length of the front. Trapped forward elements of the battalion threw down their arms and raised their hands in surrender. Seeing the utter hopelessness of the situation, and swearing at O'Neil's recklessness, those who were able turned and fled back to the main body.

Herring clenched his teeth, the blood vessels standing out hard at his temples. "Fall back! Fall back and entrench."

Executing the command, firing grimly as they retired, the surviving remnants of the Corn Exchange began a painful withdrawal of seventy-five yards, bullets snapping around them as they feverishly scraped shallow rifle pits in the dust. With some degree of protection, they dug deeper and connected their trenches as the hot sun boiled overhead.

Sweat coursing down his mud-streaked face, his uniform a shapeless bag of dust, Paddy sat with his knees drawn up, his back propped against the freshly-dug parapet. Eyes half closed, he gazed up at the sky and sighed.

"How many men did O'Neil cost us? Had any word?"

Vandergrift angrily pitched down the digging tool in his hand. "Six killed, five wounded, eighty-six captured, including Jobson. A fine day's work."

"Any word on Cassidy?"

"Be all right. Just lost part of his fat neck, the meathead."

"How long you figure we'll stay dug in like this?"

"How long can two cats spit at each other over a fence? Thing's got me wondering is how long a body can live in these open graves. We sleep standing up? Where and how do we cook? How do we..."

Crawling up on all fours, Captain Ashbrook said, "You plug-uglies want eighteen hours off?"

"Do we want...?" Paddy arched his brows. "What's the catch? What do we have to do?"

"Help dig a feeder trench at the rear, eighteen hours free duty behind the lines for those who volunteer."

"Van?"

"Sounds good to me. Anything to get out of here."

"You've got your horses, Captain. When do we start?"

"Right now. Others have already started. Follow me."

The linking trench was completed by late afternoon. As a respite from the day's heat, a refreshing breeze rode in on the wings of evening. With aching shoulders, those who had accomplished the back-breaking task went in search of food and rest in the rear echelon parks of heavy-wheeled ordnance. The hospital area, under white canvas, was crowded to capacity with tormented bodies.

In an open field, a ceremony was taking place. The squad of weary trenchers stopped to observe.

Drawn up in review, a small body of men stood at attention, their regimental flag unfurled and hanging limp in the stillness. A regimental band was posted in front. With a roll of drums, the crash of cymbals and a blare from the instruments, the sounds of the national anthem rolled skyward.

A trencher beside Paddy spoke low. "'Nother outfit going home. Lucky bastards. Man, look at the battle pennants on that flag, will ya. Say, you cryin', mister?"

Tears coursed freely through the powdered dust on Paddy's cheeks as he stared straight ahead. Before him were the skeleton remains of the 71st Pennsylvania Regiment, now a shadow of its former greatness.

A kaleidoscope of memories flashed before his eyes—Chirp and Billy, Colonel Wistar, Senator Baker, Balls Bluff, Becky, Libby Prison.

Backbone of the Second Corps, they had saved McClellan on the peninsula, had single-handedly covered Pope's retreat at Bull Run, had beaten back Pickett's charge at Gettysburg, and ferociously held the bloody angle at Spottsylvania. Cold Harbor was their final blow.

The crescendo notes of the Star Spangled Banner faded away and the 71st began casing their shot-torn battle flags for the last time.

One hundred nineteen men remained of the two thousand two hundred Philadelphians who fought from first to last under her banner. Shaking off the spell in which he had been caught, Paddy wiped the grime from his face and started walking slowly toward his former comrades. Many faces were missing, but their presence could still be felt. Of the one hundred forty-seven Frankford volunteers in whose company he had enlisted three years ago, only five were there to give him a warm embrace; Charley Hafer, Bill Bromley, Henry Rhile, Tom Haig and Isaac Tibben. The absence of the others represented a change that was taking place. The army reflected the makeup of the nation, and the nation was changing. As with the army, it contained new people and the magical light that had come down from the past was beginning to cast unfamiliar shadows.

Paddy was gripped by depression. Old unities were fading away. Unities of blood, race, language, shared ideals and common memories and experiences, everything which he deemed essential to America. He heaved a sigh. If he could only find Becky to help him cope.

For the next eight days, a stalemate existed along the five-mile front covered by the two contending armies. To bolster tottering confidence on the home front, northern newspapers worked overtime, trying to combat the cries to stop that came pouring in from mothers and fathers alarmed at the way "Butcher" Grant was sending their sons into the slaughterhouse. False and exaggerated newspaper reports so angered those engaged in the actual fighting that reporters were tarred and feathered and driven from the camps.

On the dusty battlefield, a bedeviling weapon arrived to harass the thousands of men encamped there. Like poisonous toads, the belching, snub-nosed mortars operated around the clock with a dull *boom, boom* as they tossed their deadly erecta into the trenches with devastating effects.

Among the Union commanders, there quickly evolved a complete breakdown at the bewildering strangeness of this new kind of warfare. They hesitated and then refused to give orders for their men to attack. Still holding sway in the clique-ridden army, other Union generals, by their antics and eccentricities, continued to overshadow the noble efforts of the individual soldier. Meade's foul temper and lack of tact had stripped him of all friends.

Below Richmond, General Butler, retained in command because of political ties with the President and the party in power, bungled an opportunity to end the war. With Lee's forces tied down at Cold Harbor, Butler's Army of the James was in an enviable position to sweep in on Richmond from the south. The Confederate capitol, undefended in that sector, could have been taken with little or no opposition. He could have taken Petersburg without so much as firing a shot. Acting with his usual indecisiveness, he contented himself with wandering around the Virginia countryside, starting for Petersburg, turning back, lunging ineffectively toward Richmond, and wound up letting a small Confederate force trap his Army of the James in the formless peninsula of Bermuda Hundred.

Discussing these and other sore points, the men in Paddy's squad sat closely huddled together in a dark, bomb-proof shelter on the night of June 12th. Outside, mortar shells burst overhead with monotonous regularity. With each explosion, sandy loam sifted in streams through the cracks in the log shelter protecting them from above.

Helverson nursed a rifle held upright, pinched tightly between his knees.

"Willie, how did you do it?" he asked. "How did you ever talk us into re-enlisting three more years for something like this? God, it stinks in here."

McCool smiled thinly. "Sometimes I wonder. Sure isn't what I expected. Didn't know we'd run into anything like this." He coughed. "The character's gone out of this war. So have the old slogans. This has become a down and out street brawl."

"You can say that again. Only it's a helluva...look alive, here comes Ashbrook." A silhouetted, humpbacked form appeared at the entranceway.

"What's up, Cap'n?" Dyer inquired.

"You men get your things together. We're pulling out."

"Pulling out? Where we going?" McCool cut in.

"You mean after digging and slaving over these gopher holes we have to give them up? What's the big idea?" Vandergrift growled.

"Save your wind for a long walk. Since we're getting nowhere here, Grant's decided to sneak out of the house. Most of the army's already on the move. The Rebs can keep their bloody trenches. Soon they're going to find Lee's dug himself a grave."

"So where does that leave us?" snapped Hoffman.

McCool made a move to stand up. "Where we sneaking off to? What's the plan?"

Ashbrook cleared his nose. "Grant's moving us to the left again. Vanguard's already across the Chickahominy. We'll move east around Richmond, cross the James, and come in on Petersburg. At Petersburg we'll be south of Richmond and square in the rear of the Reb positions still holding here at Cold Harbor. Lee will have to come out in the open for a fight."

Using the mannerism copied from Colonel Wistar, Paddy tugged at an ear lobe, his lips compressed in a fine line. "Sounds very nice, but will it work? We're toe-to-toe with the Johnnies along a five-mile front. What makes Grant think he can get away with a disappearing act? Pulling an army of ninety thousand right from under Lee's nose without him getting wind of it..."

"I say Grant's been hitting the bottle again," Hallowell said, scowling as he rose to his feet. "Imagine, the entire army chancing a hazardous march directly away from the enemy with our rear exposed and gambling that we won't be missed. Good God! We are also faced with a fifty-mile cross-country hike and a tidal river to cross that's a half mile wide and deep enough to be patrolled by Confederate gunboats."

"I'll take my chances with gunboats on the James," Kimball interjected grimly. "What makes me jumpy is the chance Lee will find out what's taking place and move to break it up. If he catches us in the act of marching down to the James with our backs to him, it will be taps for all of us."

Ashbrook spoke tartly. "If you dough faces are finished figuring out why this gamble won't work, would you mind doing as ordered. Get your things and get moving. And muffle everything that will make a sound."

Across the pitch dark sweep of the battlefield, streams of Union soldiers were crawling stealthily toward the rear on hands and knees. The slightest cough became a tell-tale roar. The accidental dislodgment of earth and pebbles sounded like a landslide as anxious men turned to glance over their shoulders at the dreadful silence in the enemy lines.

All through the night the Army of the Potomac continued to slip away from Cold Harbor.

CHAPTER 25

By dawn of June 13th not a single soldier from the Army of the Potomac was left at Cold Harbor. Confederate skirmishers, feelers who crept forward with caution under cover of the swirling early morning mist, were completely astounded to find silent rifle pits and empty trenches where the day before eighty-six thousand Yankees had been in the line of battle.

In column with Warren's Fifth Corps, the Corn Exchange crossed the Chickahominy at daybreak on the 13th, marching over the tidal river by means of Long Bridge, fifteen miles below Cold Harbor. Jones Bridge, five miles further down, had been reserved for Wright's and Burnside's Corps, and still four miles below that, at the head of navigation, was Windsor Shades where the great trains moving from White House Landing on the Pamunkey found their way over.

The marches assumed a businesslike aspect; long, exhaustive marches, from twenty-five to thirty-five to, in some instances, forty-five miles in length. They halted for rest but not bivouac. At seven in the morning, the Corn Exchange made its longest halt at White Oak Swamp, where the men rested all day awaiting Crawford's call for aid if he should need help with the rear guard. There was nothing to do, and at eight in the evening the division was off again to make up the distance which the rest of the army had gained.

At nine o'clock on the morning of the fourteenth, a lengthy stop was made at Charles City Courthouse for breakfast. The 2nd Corps was the only one ahead, and at one o'clock they were abreast of the 6th and 5th Corps on the bank, gazing with admiration at the broad sweep of the majestic James River.

Lands bordering the stream, sensibly not affected by McClellan's rough usage in the '62 campaign, were fruitful and abundant. The magnificent James River was famous for its wealth, its bounteous products, its learned and patriotic aristocracy, from the days when Gosnold, Newport and Smith wrenched ownership from the savages. It lay bright and picturesque, a landscape unrivaled for beauty.

The great river bore a mighty fleet. There were craft of all descriptions; vessels of burden, steamers for passage, transports and luggers, ferryboats, schooners, sloops, and the high wooden walls of river boats that carried gay, happy crowds on summer journeys up the Sound, the Hudson, the Delaware and the Chesapeake, each of them now subordinated to the urgent needs of the occasion. Dominating all those, with their black, gloomy hulls and frowning guns, silent, reliable and impressive, were the ships of the American Navy. Chief among them was the Rebel ram *Atlanta*, unchanged in shape or name, a recent trophy won in a valiant fight in distant Southern waters.

A long pontoon bridge of 100 boats stretched from shore to shore. Old Fort Powhattan was revived, reconstructed, and improved, with its sloping parapet, and barbette guns, bristling and formidable on the other side. The 2d Corps, its columns attenuated by distance, slowly wound its way over the bridge. Trains and artillery were arriving and parking, and boats and transports were ferrying to and fro to cross the soldiers as fast as possible.

For form's sake, the river fronts needed looking after, and the men of H Company, under Ashbrook, were sent as a detail to picket along the banks. For them it was a short season of luxury. They were willing to fight it out on that line, even if it took all summer. Removed a short distance from where the pressure of numbers had exhausted the country's rich supply, there was no limit to the good things available. Shad were still running and were easily caught. Shad dinners shared divided attention between diet and duty. Milk, eggs and steaks, both pork and mutton, supplied wholesome suppers. With appetites satisfied, the tour of duty ended and the detail yielded reluctantly to their relief command. The Aaron Burr and Judah P. Benjamin plantations had supplied many of the good things the men had gone without for so long.

Grant gambled correctly. He was right in his fixed belief that the pounding of the last six weeks had taken the steam out of the Army of Northern Virginia so that it was no longer capable of responding to an offensive as it had in the past. By June 15th he finally scored his end run around Richmond and across the James River, a brilliant maneuver masterfully accomplished. After forty-three days of continuous fighting, the Northern army had out-flanked their adversary at the cost of over fifty-four thousand men.

Not since Antietam had the Potomac Army been placed in a more formidable and strategic position than it was now. The Federal Army sat squarely to the rear of its erstwhile foe, who still held to their trenches around Malvern Hill and Glendale, preparing themselves against an attack that was not going to happen.

At six o'clock on the morning of the 16th, the regiment embarked on a steamer at Wilcox's Landing, crossed the river and debarked at Wind Mill Point. The men lounged about, bathed, swam and sported in the river until half past one, when the division, the 118th leading, began a forced march which terminated at midnight within a few miles of Petersburg. The journey was enlivened at times by the sharp rattle of musketry in the distance and rumors that a division of colored troops had carried the outer works at Petersburg.

Of more immediate consequence was the first experience in that vicinity of water scarcity. The fatiguing march was accompanied by the usual grumbling when word spread along the column that the division would halt as soon as it reached water. Eventually it was found, fit, perhaps, for thirsty soldiers, but certainly nothing else. A green slime floated on the surface so that a skillful, sudden movement with the bottom of a tin cup opened the scum, permitting a hurried dip before it closed. So urgent was their thirst that the foul, slimy liquid was swallowed regardless of taste or consequence.

Come daylight, any attempt to wash in the swampy bayou was speedily abandoned. It hosted forbidding animalcule of tadpoles, zigzaggers and other squirming insects. The morning's coffee tasted terrible. Rather than fill their canteens, the troops moved on in hopes of finding something better. They soon discovered their mistake. Instead of finding something better, there was no water at all. In the section they were approaching there was no water anywhere. At every change of position the men dug first for cover and then for water.

In bivouac on an open field covered with dust, the Corn Exchange men stood by their arms, alert and wondering, every ear bent toward the sound of battle near Petersburg. Paddy and his comrades maintained guard around a well to keep off intruders. Helverson and Vandergrift had dug it to a depth of six feet and it was cribbed at the bottom with two barrels, one sunk on top of the other.

McCool helped himself to a cupful and pronounced it excellent. "Bully job, boys, bully job. When I build a house after this bloody war, you fellas can have the well-drilling contract."

Helverson replied with a low growl. "Stand to. Here come some mavericks."

They turned their heads and saw a small party of soldiers approaching from the front. Shoulders bent, rifles held wearily at trail arms, the effects of recent fighting showing on their faces, they moved toward the jealously guarded oasis.

"That fresh water you fellas got there?" one of them called. His voice seemed to come from far away, like an empty echo.

Vandergrift towered tall and menacing, blocking the way. "That's right, and we aim to keep it."

"Aw, come off it, Van." McCool stepped forward, his expression open, palms outstretched. "Sure you dug the well, but s'posin' we was them? You'd want a share, huh?"

"No more of your preaching, Willie. I say no dice."

Paddy stepped a pace forward. "Might be able to find out what's been taking place the past few days. You fellas from the Eighteenth Corps?"

"Yep."

"Willing to trade information for water?"

"Mister, we'll trade our lives for water."

"What say, Van? There's only four of them."

"All right, go ahead, drink."

The deserters pressed parched lips to cup brims. Water slopped over their bearded chins.

The spokesman for the group wiped his mouth. "Your outfit just pull in?"

"Last night. What's been going on up ahead?"

"Plenty, but it's all going wrong. 'Fraid what might've been the work of a summer afternoon will take us months to accomplish."

"Why's that? Thought we had an open field."

"Did, but that was two days ago. You fellas were still marching down from Cold Harbor and Lee was thirty-six miles away, not knowin' which end was up. On the fourteenth, three days ago, Grant sent us racing over here to take Petersburg while nobody was around."

Paddy interrupted. "You're the ten thousand under 'Baldy' Smith we heard tell about!"

"That's keerect, Eighteenth Corps, and with orders to attack Petersburg at daylight come the next day. Next day came sure enough, but our generals, the devil take 'em, spent the hull time dillydallyin'. It was seven in the evening before they got the attack underway." He took another deep swallow of water and swung one arm in a wide arc. "The whole town's encircled by infantry parapets and trenches, line of about two miles. Our attack was a breeze. Drove the Rebs real free and easy. Captured most all the redans in their outer works. Hell, there weren't nobody defending the place 'ceptin' a brigade of militia under General Wise and Dearing's cavalry. Odds eight to one in our favor and old 'Baldy' doesn't press the advantage. When he ordered halt for the night, we knew something was beginning to foul up. Imagine, sitting down for the night in front of works just waiting to be occupied."

"Any reason you know of?"

"The General had gotten word two of Hancock's divisions were coming within supporting distance, so he decided to wait for them and continue the attack in the morning. Say, any you fellas got tobacco?"

Kimball held out a cut plug. "Here, help yourself. Pass it around."

"Thanks, mister."

Impatient, Vandergrift's moody black eyes blazed. "Go on, what happened with Hancock?"

"Well, seems Hancock had no idea Petersburg was to be assaulted on the sixteenth. Spent most of that morning rationing his corps. Finally he was directed to a spot on the field that didn't even exist. Ain't that one fer the books? Something to do with faulty maps. Then Meade came on the field and balled matters up even more."

"You mean the rumble heads let another whole day slip by without doing anything?"

"Oh, there was some activity, but nothing like it should've been, no forceful direction, no concert, just willy-nilly hodgepodge."

"How 'bout Reb reinforcements? Any come in you know of?"

"Not until the day was over. Gathered up some prisoners just a little while ago. According to them, Beauregard's been in command. Either he's had more information, or he's got a better grasp of things than Lee. Last night he got hold of Hoke's division. Moved 'em here and into the trenches on the double. Now word has it Lee's finally seen the light and is starting to send more 'n more of his army down here as fast as their legs'll carry 'em. The Reb line was five miles long already this morning. Gettin' bigger'n stronger by the hour."

The other three men in the party made a move to leave. Vandergrift side-stepped to bar the way. "One more question. Just out of curiosity, what are you doing back here?"

"Last night, by mistake, we got mixed in with Potter's division, Ninth Corps. Found ourselves being ordered to make an assault with them, in silence and with the bayonet. Mister, we only been in this man's army three months. We ain't used to slaughtering in cold blood. Caught nearly a thousand Rebs asleep with their guns in their hands. What a God-awful nightmare, stabbing them to death right and left where they slept. Officers finally called a stop and we took the rest prisoner. Six-hundred of 'em." He turned to put an arm around a stripling youth still dazed and close to tears. "We're walking away from this war just as fast as we possibly can and you or nobody else better try'n stop us. You boys were smart, you'd leave too. Sure'n hell this army's gonna pay the fiddler for the three-day pussy footing around by our dumb-john generals. And the colored troops ain't gonna help your lot none, neither."

"We heard Hink's division of colored troops were fighting along with your corps," Vandergrift replied.

"Yes, and there's a division of 'em in Burnside's Ninth. Wish to God we didn't have 'em. Been like waving a red flag under a bull's nose. Them Southern boys have become wildcats now they're up against niggers. Well, thanks again for the water, and now we're leavin'."

Vandergrift pointed to the horizon. "You fellas better head over that way toward those woods. Might get picked up the way you're going. There's a provost detail camped behind us."

The deserters trudged off in silence.

The assaults for June 17th were confined almost entirely to the Ninth Corps, with Barlow, Gibbon and Birney's divisions supporting, and Crawford's division of the Fifth Corps thrown in as further support on the last attack. Sometime during the night, Beauregard, who had been managing affairs for the past two days, determined to withdraw to an interior and shorter line which his engineers had laid out for him. The new line was back a thousand yards, extending from the Appomattox first southeast and then south and intersecting the original line at the Jerusalem Plank road. The withdrawal was accomplished after midnight, and entrenchment began at once.

The blood and sweat soldiers of the Potomac Army were becoming increasingly furious. The rage of the enlisted men, who knew that they were going to be sacrificed on the morrow, rose to dangerous heights never before known in any army.

When June 18th arrived, the sands of time had run out on the situation. Seventy-two hours had elapsed from the time General Smith first came into possession of the key to final victory. Lee's main army was up and in position. It became the 118th's lot to fling themselves at the heavily reinforced, impregnable Rebel fortifications and die in vain to pay for the ineptness of their superiors.

Moving out amid the shadows of early morning, the sun not yet up, the Corn Exchange headed toward the front, toward the left of the Hare House. The moving columns passed over the site of previous fighting, the dead of both sides still unburied. In a breastwork which had been occupied by the enemy, the Confederates lay four deep. Nearby, a Federal burial party had started to work. Word came that the 1st Michigan sharpshooters had made their attack over that ground the day before. The new regiment of sharpshooters, skilled in the use of the rifle, were proficient, as was shown by the number of dead Confederates shot either in the forehead or face. Unable to withstand the Michiganders' overpowering onslaught, the Confederate defenders had held up their hands as if surrendering, waited until the men closed in on the breastworks, and then, with a treacherous yell, opened fire. At one spot, three brothers belonging to the sharpshooters were lying side by side. Together in life, they were not separated in death. There were few survivors on either side.

By mid-afternoon all corps were in position—-the 2nd, 5th and 4th—-and the assault began. Attacking consecutively, each corps hammered unmercifully at the Petersburg trenches, but to no avail. By late evening it was over; the Southern trenches could not be overrun.

Generals Grant and Meade, satisfied that they had done everything they could, finally ordered the assaults to cease and the troops placed under cover. With spade and axe, the disgruntled Potomac Army started about the business of throwing up fortifications and bomb-proof shelters which would serve as their homes throughout the coming months. In Petersburg, belfry clocks, striking the hours, sounded like voices mocking from a distance, tolling the message that months more of futile war would be the result of poor Union leadership at the corps and division level.

The siege of Petersburg was underway. Forts and subterranean dug-outs took the place of canvas-covered camps. Under the supervision of the engineers, the 118th Regiment began the construction of Fort Sedgewick, a place quickly dubbed Fort Hell. The log earthworks assumed a character for strength and endurance heretofore unknown, and the Corn Exchange Regiment, along with the rest of the army, realized they had settled down to the tedious work of investment. A new experience was waiting for them. The sortie, the bombproof, the mine, the counter-mine, the covered way, were matters for serious contemplation. They would have to learn to use them as they had learned the use and purpose of the advance, the charge, the assault, the repulse, and other perils of deadly foray in open fields.

The days that followed were monotonous. An oppressively hot sun beat down unmercifully upon the trenches laid out in the yellow dust of Virginia. In front of the 5th Corps there was a gentleman's truce that was in marked contrast to the affairs in front of the 9th Corps, where Rebel bitterness toward the division of colored troops called for no terms or conditions which would induce the cessation of hostilities. The black flag of "no quarter" was flown on both sides.

Late in September, Paddy stood with his back braced against the rough-cut timber that formed an abatis of Fort Hell. Arms folded across his chest, he studied the clouds that scudded overhead. Distracted, he let his gaze fall on Robert Parks of D Company, a Scotsman who could imitate the sound of a rifle ball to perfection. He was one of the group standing behind the entrenchments. They watched an officer approach who had persistently condemned dodging by the troops. The temptation was irresistible and Parks plied his imitations so rapidly that apparently the whole line had opened fire. The effect on the officer was instantaneous. Dodging handsomely, he sought cover, much to the amusement of Parks and his companions.

Smiling, Paddy let his attention drift back to the clouded skies. He turned toward Hallowell. "Looks like it's going to be a cold winter, Jake."

"Yes, and I doubt if my lumbago'll let me see another winter through." He raised one leg and gave the bowl of his pipe a light tap on the sole of a dusty boot. "'Specially if we remain cooped up in these pneumonia pits."

"Well, as long as Grant is content to let Sherman and Sheridan wind things up for us, guess this is where we'll stay. What a way to..."

"Hey," McCool called from a log-lined dugout, "any of you seen my pet racing cooties? Had them in a jar right here on the stoop."

Vandergrift squirted a stream of tobacco juice between his teeth. "They've been emancipated," he spat.

"Up yours with a meat hook," McCool snapped. "Where are my cooties? I have to work them into shape for the derby tomorrow. The division championship's at stake."

Hoffman, lounging in long underwear, lay stretched out on his bunk. He started to sing in a gay manner.

"Tramp, tramp the bugs are marching,
Cheer up comrades I have four,
And between my fingernails,
I will pinch their little tails,
Till they promise not to bite us anymore."

At that moment all heads diverted their attention toward what promised to be an interesting experiment unfolding further down the line. They knew it was essential that the recently issued amnesty proclamation should reach those invited to accept its immunities. Consequently orders had come down that front line troops find some means to deliver it to the enemy. Knowing that if their mission were known, the enemy would refuse the paper, everyone had resorted to subterfuge in making deliveries. It was an order, and no matter how distasteful, it must be obeyed.

Placed in command of a picked detail chosen earlier that morning, Captain Walters of C Company, feeling that if he entrusted it to his men, they would either be slovenly or avoid the task entirely, resolved to look after the matter himself. He took off his uniform and robed himself in the garb of an enlisted man. Intimating by cabalistic signs the soldiers used between themselves that he desired to exchange newspapers, he loaded himself with an armful of the daily journals containing the proclamation and started for enemy lines. The fellows in the trenches followed his progress, murmuring their own personal comments as he slowly made his way across the shell-pocked, litter-strewn no-man's-land that separated the Union trenches from the Confederate.

Helverson growled through his beard, "That bastard. He'll wreck the whole exchange setup. What's he doing, scratching for promotion?"

A moment of strained silence followed as the Captain disappeared from view.

Within Confederate lines, he received a single copy of the *Richmond Despatch* in exchange for all the papers he carried. Not stopping to parley or complain of the inequality, he hastened back, convinced that if he were detected he would be detained. Safely inside Fort Hell, he had scarcely resumed his proper garb when a volley of bitter denunciation followed him. The reason for his generosity having been discovered, a rain of musket balls whistled overhead, striking the works and rattling the timbers.

Everything quieted down as suddenly as it had erupted and a lone Southern voice called, "Yanks, don't fire! The hull thing's a mistake."

Exercising extreme caution, Paddy raised his head above a parapet of sand bags. On the Rebel battlements, a solitary Confederate stood, fully exposed.

"Can you make out who it is, Mulcahy?"

"It's Lumpkin, their spokesman. Hey, Florida, what's the big idea?"

"Sorry, Billy. Got some new uns heah. No'th Ca'lina boys. Ain't been prope'ly edjicated in gentlemanly conduct. Won't happen agin."

"Well, see that it don't. Remember, we're your friends until fired on."

On both sides, the heads of other soldiers popped up.

"You've made yourself a bargain, Johnny. Thanks."

In a short while, matters between the opposing lines settled back to normal. Idle troops filled with an intense boredom resumed their loafing status, apathetic men doing what little they could to pass away the time. With the onset of nightfall, flickering rays of pale light from burning oil lamps illuminated the dugouts, rank with body odor, coal oil, stale food and moist clay. In a stolid, mechanical way hunchbacked figures, jaded and grimy, went about the work of preparing an evening meal.

Outside, dampness crept along the dark trenches, clammy wet fingers that felt their way into every crack and crevice, swirling into nooks and crannies. Strange, eerie shadows played mysterious games over the outlines of parapets and embrasures lying still and ghost-like. Somewhere out in the black of night, sounding above the clink and rattle of mess kits, a group of pickets sang a different type of song from that of days gone by. The refrain, which they had picked up from the colored troops, was mournful and sad, typifying the mood of the men:

"I know moon-rise,
I know star-rise;
Lay dis body down.

I walk in de moonlight.
I walk in de starlight;
Lay dis body down.

I'll walk in de graveyard
I'll walk troo de graveyard;
To lay dis body down.

I go to de judgment

In de evening of de day,
When I lay dis body down."

At the entrance to a dugout occupied by the Frankford men, Sergeant Cassidy stood framed in the passageway, gnarled hands resting on the support beams, a grizzled Sampson at the pillars. His voice came weakly, a shadow of its former strength.

"Evenin' buckos. Got a handout for an old soldier returnin' to the wars?"

"Sarg!" McCool shot out of his bunk. "Go to war, Miss Agnes, if you ain't just the sight for sore eyes!" he shouted.

"The same to you, Willie lad. And I see we still have Mulkayhee among us. How be ye, Mulcahy?"

"Passing good, Andy, passing good. You look fine. How do you feel?"

"Take a while to git me sea legs back. Little wobbly yet." His gaze fell on Hallowell and Kimball. "You two still here? Thought you'd be off restin' in an old folks home by this time."

"Well, it's not that we aren't ready, Sergeant. Good to have you back," the older man replied.

"Arrr. In a way it's good to be back. Vandergrift, Woodfield." He nodded toward each. "Dyer, how's yer head?"

"Still in place, Sarg."

"Sackett, Helverson, Hoffman, ye lads seem pretty well intact."

"We've been lucky." Hoffman paused. "How are things at home?"

"Not worth discussin'."

"Come on. What kind of an answer is that?"

"Just like I said, ye're better off bein' cooped up away from it all. Ain't nobody gonna offer me a seat?"

Several camp chairs were pushed forward simultaneously.

"That's better. Thank 'ee, lads." With slow deliberation, he eased his hulking form into one of the chairs that had been fashioned from a wheelbarrow. The other men remained standing, looking on silently. Cassidy studied their level gaze. "All talk's centerin' on the coomin' election," he said in slow, measured tones. "Abe's fightin' fer his political life. Fer the average bloke to be after blamin' himself fer his failures ain't easy, fer a group or nation, it's impossible. The run o' the mill bucko must place the blame on a leader and sure 'n tis a great man must bear the burden o' his country's foolishness or ignorance. And that's just what they're doin', they're tearin' Abe Lincoln apart, piece by piece. Ever'thin' he stands fer's goin' up on the auction block. The Republicans've gone to the extreme o' droppin' their political name. They got Lincoln and Johnson runnin' on a Union ticket, not..."

"Johnson? Who's Johnson?"

"Andy Johnson. Union Democrat they dug up in Tennessee. Lincoln's dumped Hamlin. Figgers his new runnin' mate'll help bring in Democrat's votes from the border states. He'll be after needin' 'em. His own party's split bad. Greeley's taken off on another o' his dizzy swings. Claims Lincoln's already beaten and can't be re-elected. Him and other radical Republicans got together and held a convention o' their own. This radical Republican faction's come up with General Fremont as a candidate. And the crusty old mountain goat's been wastin' no time spoutin' his criticism o' the commander-in-chief. Been chargin' that Lincoln's violated the Constitution. Been unable to find a winnin' general, overlookin' the strikin' fact he himself was one o' them generals, and accusin' the President fer failin' to bring the war to an end."

His elongated face closely resembling a dried out cucumber, Joe Sackett jutted his dimpled chin forward. "How they expect one man to bring this whole war to an end before it's fought out? They must be pretty dumb."

"When voters are all fired up over somthin', they don't stop to think or reason, lad. Faith'n it's gotten so bad poor old Abe can't even depend on his own cabinet. Them right hand sooth-sayers o' gloom and doom been seethin' more 'n ever with their petty jealousies and their intrigues, cabals and presidential aspirations. It be the talk o' every hospital ward in Washington. Word's out the President's thoroughly despaired o' bein' re-elected."

Paddy moved to put a light to another oil lamp. He looked back over his shoulder. "Who are the Democrats running? Any word yet?"

There was a moment of silence on the part of Cassidy. When he spoke, it was harsh. "It's here in the marnin' paper. I brought it down on the boat with me. Hold tight to yer hats. The Democrats nominated McClellan."

"McClellan! You mean Little Mac?" The match which Paddy held lighted in his hand fell to the dirt floor. "He didn't accept, did he?"

"He did that. Took it hook, line and sinker, and from such an odd assortment o' bed fellows as ye'll ever run across. Reports say Chicago was filled with the traitors."

"Traitors? Who says we Democrats are traitors just because we hold to different views?" Vandergrift drew to full height, head nearly touching the beamed rafters. "We're as patriotic as any. Only difference is we've been opposed to the forcible abolition of slavery and the reduction of states' rights. Don't anybody here refer to us as traitors."

Cassidy's thinning red hair started to color at the roots. "Easy, me hearty. A few such honest folk indeed there may've been at Chicago, but they were joined and manipulated by strong elements o' the copperheads, the Sons o' Liberty and a sneakin' band o' Confederate agents bent on stirrin' up trouble. Read it fer yerself, it's all spelled out fer ye here in the paper."

"Let me see it." Vandergrift made a grab for the folded newspaper.

McCool's expression became quizzical, the black visor of his cap slanted down over one eye, partially hiding it. "Why do you say Little Mac's been taken in by traitors, Sarg?"

"Because in the first order o' business, the Democrats adopted a peace plank brought forward by that noisy crank Vallandigham. Campaign promise it is, appealin' to all o' them who been after tirin' o' the war, or them who never believed in it in the first place."

"Vallandigham?" Dyer looked up sharply. "You mean that Ohio congressman who was tried and convicted for spreading treason in sixty-three? The fella Abe Lincoln banished to the Confederacy?"

"One and the same. Tis an evil, unhappy man he is, without a country. Faith'n it seems he didn't like livin' in the South, neither. Fled to Canada and from there smuggled himself back into the country under a false beard when the Democrats convened in Chicago. Accordin' to the paper, he spoke to the convention about 'four years of failure to restore the Union by the "experiment of war" and was after callin' fer an immediate cease fire in order that peace might be restored."

"How come he wasn't taken into custody and arrested?"

"Would o' made a martyr out o' him. Lincoln and the government must've figgered it best to turn their heads and look the other way."

"And he got away with it?" Paddy asked, incredulous.

"He did indeed. Worse, after listenin' to the traitor's view, the Democrats cheered when he finished and voted to adopt his plank. Now, with his peace plank, they're preparin' to play it safe both ways by havin' a general fer their standard bearer. The endurin' hero o' the enlisted man'll be after carryin' the Democrat's fight to the President." He set his lips in a thin hard line. "Faith'n he'll not be gettin' my vote. Fer me, McClellan's nothin' but a handsome little toy trumpet left over from our first Christmas. Ain't fit to scrape the boots o' a man the likes o' Abe Lincoln."

Helverson cleared his throat. "I don't know about that, Sarg. We sure had a better and stronger army in sixty-two when McClellan was in charge than we got now under Grant."

"That we did, me buckroos. And if Grant had a been in command in sixty-two, we'd o' had victory instead o' two years more o' dragged-out fightin'."

Off to one side, Kimball seated himself on an overturned barrel and grasped both knees in his liver-spotted hands. "Yes, and I'll wager if Little Mac had the run of things these past six months, he'd have ended the war in the wilderness by handing victory to the Confederacy. Like as not, he'll do the same if he gets elected."

Paddy loosened a button at his collar. "Can I butt in with a question? What is in this peace plank? How do they propose to have peace? I'd like to know before I make up my mind."

"Sure'n 'tis the same old Mulkayhee. Still a stickler fer the facts. Well, lad, if ye'll take a look there at the paper, ye'll see that the armies would be ordered to cease hostilities and go home. Second, the Southern states would be asked to join a convention to restore the Union. How's it appeal to ye?"

"Disband the army? Convention? Why, that puts us right back where we started four years ago."

"A fine deduction, lad. While cryin' fer peace, they evade mentioning the issue o' slavery, which still lies nestled at the root o' the hull shootin' match. Just to be after gettin' the feel o' runnin' the government again, they're willin' to turn back the clock four years and start all over. They got nothin' to say as to how they'd be settlin' the slavery issue. They've blinded their eyes to the South's fierce doctrine o' faith that each state is sovereign in its own right and can be after secedin' at will whenever they chose.

"Treat yourselves to a good look at their campaign slogan, 'Peace, Union, Victory.' Sich buncombe. Way they got it set up, puttin' them three together be like tryin' to breed fleas with elephants. The hull thing's ass backwards. Should read 'Victory, Union, Peace.' What McClellan and the Democrats be offerin' us is a sock with a great big hole in the heel."

Hoffman gave a low whistle. "Sounds to me as if Mac's moving to sell us boys out."

"Who says Mac's engaged in a sell-out?" The clear ring of an old affection sounded in Vandergrift's voice as he glanced up sharply from the newspaper. "Read his acceptance speech here in the paper. He says the complete opposite from the way some of you been interpreting the peace pledge. Says it's a mandate to carry the war through to victory. Insists that to settle for anything less than triumph of the Union cause would be to betray the heroic soldiers he's led in battle."

From a prone position on his bunk, hands clasped behind his head, Hallowell snorted. "McClellan has always been evasive and straddling. How do we know he's really kicked over the Democrat's platform or is merely handing out sucker bait?"

"Sucker bait? What do you call what we've been getting from Abe Lincoln the past four years?" Vandergrift cut in with a harsh voice. "As for selling out, McClellan had the opportunity when the army was all for setting him up as a dictator, but he turned it down cold. I say Little Mac's the better man."

His attention riveted on the log armrest of his chair, Dyer probed at the loose bark with a fingernail. "Well, as of this moment," he murmured, "I'll have to go along with what Van says. Look at the way Lincoln broke his word to our corps commander just recently. If he'd really been out for our welfare, he would have kept his promise to Warren about replacing used-up major generals with the fighting brigadiers he knows we can trust and follow."

Face smudged with charcoal, Helverson busied himself before the wood stove with an expression of deep study. "Right. I heard that not more 'n an hour after Lincoln agreed to muster out all major generals not serving at the front, Halleck came to him with a full list of those whose services could be dispensed with."

"Yes, and what happened?" Vandergrift's fist came down hard on a plank table-top. "In that one hour that meant so much to better leadership, the word got out what the President was up to and every Republican politician and his brother jumped into the act. Those strong men our distinguished heroes keep at the Capitol to maintain their shadowy hold on military life. The political hacks got to the President but quick, dominated the situation as usual, and all the good Warren had done was speedily wrecked. Because of the oncoming election, Lincoln went back on his word, sustained the politicians, and we remain stuck with the same misfit major generals who've been gumming the works from the beginning."

"Bein' President's like bein' sergeant, me excited bucko. Ye can't be after pleasin' everybody. Ye gotta put first things first, and right now Lincoln's gotta get himself re-elected," Cassidy replied.

"Why?"

"Because he's the only man in the field what knows how to hold this country together, if sich a thing remains possible. Behind every unpopular move he's made there's been a compellin' good reason, which the lesser breeds couldn't find courage enough to step up and face. When it's become necessary, he's been able to run over all obstructions to keep the country in tow. He kept England and France from join' the South in sixty-two. If the Congress'd been allowed to debate the Emancipation Proclamation, they'd still be talkin' and we'd a been licked long ago. The man's a pathfinder, out in front pointin' the way fer them as is slow to follow."

Cassidy rose to his feet. "One thing more. Take this promotion o' brigadiers ye been discussin'. Supposin', against the advice o' his political advisers, he'd gone ahead with the removals and lost the election as a result. Is there a man jack among ye what thinks if that happened we'd have use fer any generals at all, good or bad? Not on yer life. There wouldn't be a war left fer 'em to fight. Course if that's what ye lads want at this stage of the game, go ahead'n vote fer yer little toy trumpet."

Wearing his perpetual prophetic scowl, Hallowell raised up and swung both legs over the side of his bunk. "You are all overlooking one important fact," he said. "The South is in real trouble. Their philosophy of secession is beginning to show its inherent weakness. Their papers are full of it. The western half of North Carolina, in an attempt to drop out of the war, has virtually seceded from the eastern half of the state.

"With her lands trampled and overrun by Sherman, Georgia refuses to send any more troops and munitions to Lee in Virginia. South Carolina, in deadly fear that Sherman will turn on her next, refuses not only to send further aid to Lee, but has turned her back on her neighboring state of Georgia, hoarding her resources to stave off Sherman's march when it finally arrives in South Carolina."

He glared around with hands on his hips. "There you have examples of so-called states' rights, sovereignty in full-blown operation. The same loose-jointed way our country was run in its earlier days under the Articles of Confederation. An unworkable piece of governmental machinery, a prime example of what Daniel Webster meant when he charged that a Union so constituted is nothing but a 'rope of sand.'"

He paused and ran a hand through his thick beard. "From the very beginning, Lincoln's been the bellwether, the only one in authority who's kept his mind fastened on this all-important principle. He's stood firmly for one thing, preservation of the Union. Strong Federal Union, indissoluble, indispensable, now and forever, and in that, I stand with him to the end."

A deep silence had filled the underground dugout when suddenly from outside came the thundering roar of artillery opening up in battery. Bursting star shells illuminated the darkened battlefield and phosphorescent streaks of light shot in all directions. Seeming entirely out of place with the immediate situation, a squad of soldiers, linked arm in arm, came swinging wildly down the trench line and singing at the top of their voices. Behind them were others shouting and waving their caps in the air, whooping and hollering with glee.

McCool sprang to the passage post and thrust his head outside. "Hey, what's up? The war over?"

"Atlanta's ours and fairly won, soldier. News just came in. Sherman's in Atlanta!"

McCool turned and tumbled back into the room. "You hear that? You fellas hear that? Sherman's got Atlanta. This'll put starch in the backs of the voters. Three cheers for good old Abe!"

Throughout the night the celebration raged and continued, then, like the moving hand on a clock of doom, the next few days revealed further glad tidings, word that set the hearts of Northern loyalists aflame with greater zeal. Farragut's fleet rang up an impressive victory at Mobile Bay and Sheridan soundly defeated Early at Winchester in the Shenandoah Valley. A new feeling swept through the old Potomac Army-an exciting, swelling conviction that a mighty tide was flowing at last.

* * * * * * *

To further the investment of Lee's beleaguered army, Grant decided that the Confederate's southern supply line running up from North Carolina, the Weldon Railroad, would have to be cut, thus drawing the net tighter. The Fifth Corps, the 118th Regiment to the fore, were pulled from their trenches and marched south into the field in columns of attack. In a series of pitched battles at Yellow Tavern and Reams Station, fought through fields of standing corn, over broad meadows and through vine-covered potato fields, the railroad was successfully wrested from Southern hands. Federal infantry parapets sprang up along the new line.

The country between the Plank Road and the railroad was mostly a wooded waste, but along the railroad and beyond it there was a sprinkling of well-kept farms. The autumn air had become bracing, clouds scudded across the sky and the days were growing shorter. It was the height of the preserving season and the forager, ever mindful of his opportunities regardless of the dangers and consequences involved, accepted the risks. McCool made his usual venture. The nearest house to Yellow Tavern, occupied by a Mrs. Lewis, had been pretty well stripped. With adroit skill, he managed to secure the good will of the only inhabitant of the dwelling, who bitterly complained that the Yankees had robbed her of everything, but she was willing to disclose the contents of her neighbor's larder.

"There," she said, pointing to house a little way off, "you will find a plentiful store of grape jelly, put up by Missus Perkins and ready for market."

McCool, not disposed to lose an opportunity for the want of a vessel to transport it, proposed to borrow a bucket. This was cheerfully conceded and he was off on his new investigation. He found the house deserted, family, Negroes, everyone had gone. The flight had been recent, as all the doors were open and the table was set for dinner, but others had preceded him and from the second story window, bedding, clothings, furniture and an eight-day clock were being tossed out onto the ground; nor had the grape jelly escaped observation. In a small outbuilding, a soldier stood over a vessel, ladling it out freely. The large label, "This is poison! Look out!" did not deter a lavish requisition of the toothsome article, and pots, kettles, mugs, pans—everything about the house, including McCool's bucket-were filled to overflowing. An Irishman, wild with delight at such a refreshing haul, appeared on the scene. He kicked over a beehive and was off with a comb of honey. The bees, angered at the intrusion, made a desperate onslaught. The spoilsmen ceased their spoilage, the avalanche of household goods from the second story window stopped, the loaded vessels were overturned and there was a mad rush to escape the wicked stings of the angry bees. McCool, though, stood fast, and with an old shirt gathered from the wreck of wearing apparel, fought them off manfully.

The sound of hoofbeats approaching caused him to pause and turn around. To his utter dismay and alarm, he saw a provost-marshal and a large cadre of guards approaching on horseback. As they neared the homestead gate, the bees suddenly turned their attention to them. With the luck of the Irish, the guard turned and fled. McCool heaved a sigh of relief. Now sole owner of the jelly bucket, he carried it off, not forgetting to reward the lonely female with a liberal portion for her patriotism.

On the eighth of November the country marched to the polls. Within the Corn Exchange Regiment, 137 votes were cast for Lincoln, 13 for McClellan.

Laden down with newspapers several days later, Sergeant Cassidy distributed them among his men. "Here ye are, buckos!" he barked. "Lincoln's been re-elected. Carried every state but New Jersey, Delaware and Kentucky."

Hoffman scanned the headlines and pitched his cap in the air. "Good show!" he shouted. "Abe carried the army vote with seventy-eight percent!"

Subsequent events followed closely. To the joy of many in the army, the President began relieving misfits from command. Ben Butler was quietly shelved. Burnside and Hancock, who owed their jobs to politics, were similarly discharged and the deserving promotions of able men were forthcoming.

News of a more disquieting nature became the subject of conversation. In the South, a mighty furor had risen over the way her non-combatant's soil was being trampled by a ruthless foe. In retaliation, and with a spirit of vengeance, those in charge of Federal prisoners had initiated inhuman and devastating programs.

Captured Yankees were being herded into naked fields that served as prison camps. Lack of shelter, overcrowded conditions, stagnant pools filled with human excreta that served as drinking water and a meager supply of food no better than offal caused the men to die like flies in the summer heat and winter cold. It was reported that in ten months alone, over fifteen thousand had died in Andersonville as a result of cruel and callous treatment.

It was in late January when the close-knit band of Frankford volunteers in the 118th viewed an army bulletin that bore grim tidings. Of the eighty-six comrades captured at Cold Harbor, sixty-eight had died at Andersonville Prison in Georgia. Midway down the list of grave registrations, one name stood out from the rest: Jobson, Luke. Grave number 12007. Cause of death: Starvation. McCool's eyes filled with tears.

Helverson thrust a stubby finger at a photograph showing the physical state of survivors. The others stared in disbelief at the pictures, which seemed like caricatures.

"Are those men?" Kimball asked in a hollow voice.

Hallowell adjusted his spectacles for a closer look at the livid, brown, ash-streaked, monkey-like dwarfs. "Good God," he muttered. "They're more like dwindled mummified corpses."

Tears flooded Vandergrift's hate-filled eyes. "The Rebel bastards," he growled. "Gleefully they brought this war on themselves. I say it's time we make them suffer for this." He jabbed at the photograph with a bony finger and pierced it. "Civilian and soldier alike. No mercy," he shouted, extending a clenched fist. "All agreed, lay on a hand."

"Not civilians," Paddy protested.

"They're the biggest sons of bitches of all. You layin' on a hand?"

Paddy's dirt-encrusted hand moved forward to join with the others.

Elsewhere, with the breathless attention of a nation focused on it and other parts of the world looking on, Sherman's army completed its remarkable march from Atlanta to the sea and came into full possession of Savannah and Charleston.

Around Petersburg, the fighting men in the Potomac Army prayed for an early spring as they shivered and burrowed deeper in their trenches to keep from freezing in the coldest winter in several years.

All the while, Grant kept them probing and jabbing at Lee's defenses while seeking for a soft spot, drawing the cordon ever tighter. The series of winter battles that resulted—Peeble's Farm, Pegram's Farm, Hatcher's Run, Dabney's Mill—were fought through pine woods that were bare and cold, at tiny out-of-the-way crossroads and over frosted farmlands, through all kinds of weather, snow and sleet predominating.

Commonplace in name and sounding insignificant, the attrition and death encountered at those places was as permanent and sure as that which had occurred on the more historic and earlier fields of greater renown. A dwindling list of names on regimental rosters attested to that fact. In the 118th, Captain Scott of A Company, the jovial, respected, hard-drinking Scot, last of the original ten captains, was left to die on the frozen field at Pegram's Farm. From the same engagement Colonel Herring was sent home, his right leg amputated, and now the regiment was run by those who had come up through the ranks.

In addition to the serious loss of trained and experienced personnel, another dangerous situation and glaring weakness was developing, which centered around the fact that replacements were far below par. Of the four thousand seven hundred men in Griffin's Division to which the 118th Pennsylvania was attached, over one thousand were ignorant of the manual and over two thousand had never fired a rifle. Toward the end of March, the perennial harbinger of renewed large-scale military operations burst upon the scene.

CHAPTER 26

The spring of 1865 erupted in all its glory. Woodlands were sprinkled with dogwood blossoms, and the soft, resinous odor of Virginia pine filled the air. Along the roads, violets sheltered their shy little heads beneath lush green grass and bush honeysuckle. Orchards had started to flower beneath an umbrella of multicolored pastel blossoms and song birds returned to the treetops.

It was a time of decision, a feeling that the time of the end was near at hand and the soldiers of both sides could sense that meaning. Aiming for a final knockout blow, the Army of the Potomac slowly prepared to strike.

If they could cut the Southside Railroad, which ran west from Petersburg to Lynchburg, Lee's last principal supply line would be severed and he would be forced to pull out of the trenches at Petersburg.

On the 31st day of March, in the face of a driving rain, the Fifth Corps moved out from camp to join with Sheridan's men, who stood poised and ready at Dinwiddie Courthouse. The 118th moved to the fore. Four years of bloody war had exacted a staggering toll from her ranks. Of the 1,800 men from Philadelphia who had served under the now famed banner of the Corn Exchange, only 93 remained to take their place in line.

Adjusting the shoulder straps of his knapsack with hands whipped raw by the wind and cold, Paddy stopped to shake out a rain-soaked kepi and survey the sea of mud that covered the area around Hatcher's Run. "God a'mighty, what Grant needs in this campaign is gunboats, not foot soldiers. Look at this soup, would you. Like wading through a barnyard knee deep in you know what."

Raindrops dripped from his lips along with scorn as Bob Dyer said, "I'll say. Grant should change his name to Noah if he figures us to go very far in this goop."

"Well, there is one thing. This time he's taking no chances with any fumbling, mixed-up antics on the part of subordinates. Word's been passed down he's taken our entire corps from the overall command of Meade and handed it to Sheridan. They say he's promised to do the same thing with the second if Sheridan finds he needs them."

"Yes, and I'll wager our doughty little cavalry chieftain's really chomping at the bit. It'll be interesting to see how this Fightin' Phil conducts himself, we've had so many..."

From a position at the tail end of the marching column, Cassidy bellowed in his fog-horn voice. "Mulkayhee! A greenie back here what says he wants to see ye. Says he's from yer hometown."

"Tell him to swim upstream. I'm not risking drowning by back watering in this torrent."

Brushing rainwater from the sweep of his eyelashes, Paddy turned around, curious, as a short, slightly-built uniformed figure came slogging up in the mud and downpour and pulled abreast with a huge grin on his freckled face.

Beneath an oversize forage cap mouse-like ears stood straight out from the side of his head. His voice was shrill. "Hi, Paddy! Hi, fellas!"

Paddy fought to control himself, "I'll be go to hell if it isn't Missus Beeson's little boy, Joey. Now I know they're scraping the bottom of the barrel. What are..."

"Children, they're sending us," Vandergrift scowled, disdain written across his face. "Next it will be old women. And look, fancy leggings and all. You afraid of snakes, Joey?"

"Don't mind Grumpy, Joey." Paddy thrust his hand through a slit in his poncho. "It's good to see you. Tell us, what are you doing in these parts?"

"Signed on with the Hundred'n Eighty-seventh Pennsylvania last September. We'll be fighting alongside you fellas this campaign. We're in the first brigade, first division."

"You'll be doing what?" blurted Hallowell. "Why only yesterday I was chasing you out of the store for filching fishhooks and sinkers off the counter."

Kimball smiled insipidly. "That was four years ago, Jake. Beeson's a young man now. You heard what he said, he's going to help out with the fighting. And will you look at what he's toting?"

"A Spencer!" Dyer whistled at the sight of the new repeating rifle. He made a quick step forward with hands outstretched. "Say, Joe, you sure you know how to use that thing? Here, let me see it, will you?"

Like a boy with the only new bike in the neighborhood, Beeson beamed proudly as he unslung the coveted weapon.

"Sure. Here, you can look it over."

The others crowded in close, their eyes bulging with keen interest and envy. With a kind of affection, Dyer ran his fingers over the closed breech, then toyed with the lever which formed the trigger guard. Carefully, he examined and studied the magazine with a tube in the stock that spring-fed the cartridges in the breech mechanism.

Beeson pressed his face in close. "Don't let no water get in it."

"What'll you take for it? Name your price."

Beeson reached out quickly. "It ain't for sale. Give it back."

"Say, the boy's got the spark of a real fighter," Lew Hoffman chortled. His expression turned serious. "How come my brother didn't come with you? Mother wrote and said you and he had enlisted together."

"He stayed back in line with Bill Haddick. Says it's your duty to look him up, not t'other way around."

"Why that fresh young pup."

Shouldering his Spencer, Beeson cast an appraising glance at the moving column. "See you still have a full company. Been lucky, or are most of them replacements?"

"Company?" roared Vandergrift. "Boy, you're looking at what's left of an entire regiment."

Abashed, Beeson's face turned crimson, but before he could rectify his mistake, he was interrupted by a loud commotion arising from the head of the column. Recently promoted to captain, Kelly's voice rose in a shrill cry.

"Deploy in skirmish formation! Rebels in the woods ahead! Deploy on the double!"

Paddy spoke rapidly. "Better dog it back to your regiment, Joey. With Sheridan riding herd, news walking days are over. Anyone not found in his proper place these days is liable to get himself shot, and not by the enemy."

"Well, so long, fellows. Don't forget, we'll be right behind you. Frankford against the world!"

"A comfortable thought. Now git." Paddy pulled the visor of his cap well down over his eyes to protect them against the driving rain and raced forward with the body of the 118th.

Throughout the balance of that day and well into a dark, stormy night, the Fifth Corps rocked back and forth in deadly combat with the Confederate forces holding Hatcher's Run. Finally, at ten-fifteen in the evening, action was broken off by orders from Sheridan to concentrate all Union lines immediately on Five Forks. Tired and badly in need of rest after the severe engagement, the Federal troops instantly availed themselves of the break while preparations for disengagement were being formulated by General Warren. The Fifth Corps lay down on the muddy forest floor to catch what sleep they could.

Fatigued to the limit of endurance, the soldiers slept soundly so that when time came for the non-commissioned officers to arouse each one individually, the task was difficult. Because of their close proximity to the enemy, they could not use drums or bugles and every order had to be communicated personally from the commanding officer to the subordinate. On a dark, starless night, in a gloomy forest, the search for the commanding officers and soldiers was not easy.

April first broke fresh and clear, and by noon the bone-chilled men of Warren's Fifth Corps, their wet uniforms sticking fast to their bodies, completed the march from Hatcher's Run to the Dinwiddie Courthouse. By two o'clock in the afternoon the columns were in motion and moving through timber; they came out within a mile of Five Forks in open country above Moodys.

At four o' clock, the order for a general advance was handed down by Sheridan and the entire Fifth Corps again moved forward, this time in line of battle across a rough, wooded terrain that was difficult to negotiate because of the deep ravines cutting across the area.

Overhead, the sun shone brightly with the warmth and splendor of springtime. Troops with the red Maltese cross on their caps stepped forward. Heading in a northerly direction, the left division in the first line was commanded by General Ayres, a hard-bitten survivor of the army's original officers. The right division in the front line operated under the guidance of General Crawford. Griffin's division and the 118th followed behind, forming the second line.

Sunlight glinted off thousands of bright muskets and rifles. Unsheathed flags snapped in the breeze with the gaiety and pageantry of war, and in an inspirational move, Sheridan ordered regimental bands to march to the fore where they were directed to play and continue playing. The veterans smiled favorably, remembering and hearkening again to the stirring sounds of martial music which restored an old-time flavor that had been missing since Antietam. Brigade fronts were taut with parade-ground precision and everybody keeping step. In a way, it seemed to those who participated that the war was ready to end on the same note that it had started—-full of pomp and glory.

The immediate objective of the advance was Pickett's division entrenched at Five Forks, an unheard-of little country crossroads buried deep in the pine woods.

The day before, Sheridan had spotted an open gap between Pickett's command and the main body of Lee's army, who were still holding to their trenches around Petersburg. Hoping to drive Warren's Fifth Corps as a wedge into that gap, Sheridan proposed they swing left and come down heavily on Pickett's uncovered flank. He would attack and defeat the Army of Northern Virginia piece by piece.

The crucial moment was at hand and everything was in readiness for the final execution of an excellent plan when all of a sudden a series of unfortunate miscalculations, to which the character of the wooded terrain contributed, endangered the ultimate success of the maneuver.

Crawford's right hand division, in the first line of the advancing Fifth Corps, hit the White Oak Road to the east of where it expected Pickett's line to be. Unmindful of that fact, Crawford's men continued to forge north while the battle commenced somewhere to the west, out of sight and reach.

Ayres' Division, on the left in the first line, had accidentally brushed against Pickett's left flank a short time before and was no longer in the line of march. Being thus appraised of Pickett's whereabouts, they spun about in a ninety-degree turn and became heavily engaged in fighting the superior Confederate forces at Five Forks.

Completely in the dark as to what was taking place, Griffin's division, which formed the second line, tailed blithely after Crawford's into the vacuum. The 118th Regiment was fretting and apprehensive. Kimball's usual taciturn countenance appeared uneasy.

"By God I don't like the looks of things. Sounds as if there's fighting over that way." He jerked a thumb over his left shoulder.

Cassidy halted to cock a weather ear at the sound of gunfire rolling in from the west. "Believe yer right, we're marchin' away from the battle."

McCool wailed. "Oh no! I thought those days were over."

"Don't fool yourself," Vandergrift snarled. "So long as we have overaged generals, we're gonna have trouble. They're worse 'n middle-aged husbands resting on the laurels of their youth. When they do get the urge, it's usually to chase around places where they shouldn't. Hey, Captain, how about informing our brigade commander the fighting's over that way?"

Kelly approached the length of columns at a dead run. "Pipe down. Bartlett's ahead of you. Just sent orders back to O'Neil. We're changing directions. Company by the left, wheel."

Heaving a sigh of relief, the Corn Exchange, together with the entire Third Brigade under Bartlett, faced and broke away from their errant division and charged toward the sound of battle.

Preparing for action, Dyer swung a cartridge box toward the front of his belt as he ran forward panting. "Joe Bartlett'll sure catch hell for this from Griffen if things don't pan out."

Vandergrift's long legs covered the ground in long matching strides. "So what good is a brigade commander if he can't exercise his better judgment? Damn, I wish I had one of them Spencers. Bam, bam, bam, just like shooting ducks."

"Yeah, and what's the army do? Gives 'em to youngsters not yet dry behind the ears. Don't that..."

"Look alive!" Cassidy boomed in a grating voice. "Rebs comin' in on the right flank. Take cover. Load'n fire at will!"

McCool snickered. "Hey, Sarg, which one's Will?"

Kneeling, a ritual regularly performed to keep their charmed circle intact, the Frankford volunteers thrust out their hands, clasping those of comrades one on top of the other.

Paddy was the first to rise. "There they are." He pointed toward Confederates in the line of battle. With heads depressed and backs bent, some of them made a rush across the field and headed for a rise of ground. The large enemy force, which had caught Bartlett's isolated brigade completely unaware, now came charging down upon it from the cover of the nearby woods. A deafening roar of small arms fire rose from the narrow aisle of open space in the pine and scrub oak forest.

"My God, we've been set up like tenpins!" Paddy shouted. He aimed and fired deliberately.

Dyer slammed a charge into the barrel of his rifle and quickly withdrew the ramrod. "Told you we should have stayed with the division." He took aim and fired. "This your idea of exercising good judgment?" he snapped at Vandergrift.

"So we got caught with out pants down. Boy, if I just had one of those Spencers," Vandergrift replied.

The overwhelming Confederate force, running at full tilt, came driving forward without wavering. Stung by the Federal fire, they halted at the woods and then came on again with a rush. Those in the beleaguered Union column started breathing hard.

Joe Sackett wiped the sweat from his high cheekbones. "They're going to roll us up like a carpet!" he exploded.

Kelly brandished his sword. "Don't anyone break. We're committed."

The situation seemed hopeless when suddenly at the crucial moment a rallying cheer greeted the ears of the trapped brigade. Another Union brigade appeared from out of nowhere and with the force of sledgehammers, pounded the Confederate's left and rear.

Due to one of those quick, uncertain twists of fate on which history revolves, it was the gray-coated troops who now found themselves in a precarious situation. Caught in a vise, they were being cut from three sides. The trapper becoming the trapped. The pressure became too great. Those who were able broke into a run for Pickett's main line, located a short distance to the west.

The two Union brigades quickly fused themselves and followed in hot pursuit.

"Who do we owe our thanks to?" Vandergrift shouted as he raced forward.

Paddy shot an over-the-shoulder glance at the flags fluttering to the fore of the succoring brigade. "Chamberlain must have decided to pull his brigade out of the division line shortly after he saw us leave."

"The man has my eternal gratitude."

The pursuit slowed to a walk. Paddy halted beside the body of a dead man and knelt to pick up a fresh load of cartridges from an opened belt box. Lew Hoffman, breathing heavily, dropped on one knee alongside. "Man, listen to their firepower, will you. Must all be carrying Spencers. Sure can play pretty music on those repeaters."

Two soldiers from Chamberlain's brigade, both wearing happy grins, approached the kneeling figures from the rear. With a light jab of a bayonet tip, the taller of the two touched Hoffman in the seat of the pants. Spinal column arching sharply, his head thrown back, Hoffman sprang to his feet and spun around.

"You clumsy sonova....Bruzz!" The brothers fell into each other's arms.

"You little pip-squeak. So you finally decided to look me up, after all." He gave his younger brother a vigorous whack across the shoulder blades. "And boy, you couldn't have picked a better time."

Beeson stood off to one side with a waifish grin and fondly stroked his Spencer. He ran his tongue up and down inside his cheek. "Like I told you, we're fightin' alongside."

"Joe, boy, never will I doubt you. You're all right," Paddy exclaimed.

"Look, this isn't the time or place for reunions," Lew Hoffman cut in. "Let's leg it, I want Pickett for my own." He turned to his brother and Beeson. "Let me give you two a word of advice, no prisoners. Since Weldon, the Rebs have been playing dirty pool. They'll make as if to surrender, but soon as they have your guard down, they'll murder you. No prisoners."

"Got you, big brother."

The two recruits, glowering fiercely, raised their repeating rifles and charged forward with the body of the 118th. All along Pickett's breastworks on the White Oak Road, dismounted Yankee cavalrymen were attacking. With their tight-fitting uniforms, natty jackets and short carbines, they looked as if they had been especially designed for crawling through knotholes. Swallow-tailed pennants fluttered above them, crossed swords of black sewn on a field of white.

The brigades of Bartlett and Chamberlain rushed forward to help the dismounted troopers and Ayres' division press the attack.

The fight waxed hot and heavy as into the thickest part of it rode Sheridan at top speed, his mounted color-bearer close behind him. Men gasped at the General's daring. He brought his horse to a rearing halt in front of Chamberlain, who was directing the attack with one arm in a bloody sling.

"By God, that's what I want to see! Generals at the front!" cried Sheridan. "Where's Warren and the rest of the Fifth Corps?"

Chamberlain gestured toward the north and tried above the roar of battle to explain what had happened.

Sheridan's tightly-pinched features and drooping handlebar mustache wrinkled with wrath as the errant march was described to him. Instantly, and with unbridled anger, he dispatched a cavalryman to look for Warren and the missing infantry; then, spurring his horse to a gallop, he proceeded to cover the entire field, rallying his men wherever they faltered. The Federal skirmish line, which had met severe firing at one point, had wavered and seemed ready to fall back. Sheridan raised his curved sword and shouted madly. "Come on, go at 'em!"

His fiery voice steadied them. "They're getting ready to run now, and if you don't got on them, in five minutes they'll get away from you."

An infantryman at his side was struck in the throat and fell, the blood flowing from his jugular vein.

"You're not hurt a bit," Sheridan thundered. "Pick up your gun, man, and move!"

The soldier looked at Sheridan plaintively, then obediently took his musket, got to his feet, and staggered forward, only to drop dead after a dozen steps.

Sheridan swung his head around as General Chamberlain approached him from the side.

"I beg you, sir," beseeched the brigade commander, "don't expose yourself out here on the front line. The men will press the attack. Have no fear of that." Sheridan gave no reply. He tossed his head in a devil-may-care attitude and dashed off to a sector where the firing was even hotter.

Finally the line was formed as he wanted it. Deep in a boggy woodland, with heavy smoke clouding out the last rays of sunlight, Sheridan gazed down on the shifting mass of soldiers. With a look of satisfaction, he turned in his saddle and called in a loud commanding voice for his battle flag. The color-bearers, struggling to keep their high- strung horses under control, cantered forward. Sheridan grabbed for the battle pennant and, lofting it high above his head, trotted along the front.

Kimball gripped his rifle. "Here we go."

Hallowell snorted. "Yep, and that banty rooster Sheridan's gonna get his damn fool head blowed off if he ain't more careful. Look at that damn fool idiot."

The Union line surged forward after their commander and scrambled to the top of the Rebel works. Sheridan had already leaped his horse over the breast-works and the infantry followed in a riot of screaming, jubilant men. The Rebel flank broke, and the men of the Fifth Corps were not forestalled in the venture this time. Grimly determined, they fought their way down the length and breadth of Pickett's battle line.

By this time, General Warren had managed to swing Crawford's wayward division around to the Rebel rear, where they were rounding up the fugitives from Pickett's broken line and cutting off retreat in that direction.

Under personal supervision of the now exultant Sheridan, the men of Bartlett's brigade went about the pleasant business of herding Confederate prisoners together and stacking the captured arms into huge piles.

Tired veterans and fresh levies, happy and excited, surveyed the long line of ambulances and the wagon train loading the supplies which the brigade had seized from Pickett's division on the Ford Road. General Warren's chief of staff rode up to the joyful scene to give Sheridan a glowing report of the situation as it existed in Warren's sector.

In rapid phrases, the emissary recounted his superior's recent achievements. Sheridan cut him off with an abrupt, angry flourish.

"By God, sir, you tell General Warren he wasn't in this goddamn fight!" roared the cavalry chieftain.

Soldiers close enough to overhear looked aghast. To a man, they knew that Warren's Fifth Corps had been late getting to Dinwiddie and had been late getting into position at Five Forks, two-thirds going astray and Warren with them, but regardless of that, no one in the Army of the Potomac had ever spoken that way about a distinguished corps commander. Some of the men still remembered Warren as the savior of Little Round Top at Gettysburg.

Warren's chief-of-staff was dumbfounded and protested vigorously. "But, sir, the General has been doing his level best under the circumstances."

Sheridan was clearly implacable. A black scowl crossed his face and his eyes flashed. "By God, sir, I repeat. Tell Warren that he wasn't in this goddamn fight."

"I dislike to deliver such a message verbally," stammered the emissary. "May I have it in writing, sir?"

"Take it down. Tell him, by God, he was not at the front."

The chief-of-staff hastily scribbled the message on a piece of paper and rode quickly away, completely stunned.

Sheridan turned to General Griffin, a regular army man and the ranking division commander in the Fifth Corps. "Charley, you'll take over command of the Fifth Corps, immediately."

The rough and tumble division commander touched the peak of his cap in a stiff salute. "Yes, sir."

Sheridan withdrew a pencil and paper from his tunic and wrote down a few chosen words.

"Courier, find Warren and deliver this written message relieving him of his command. He's to report to General Grant at headquarters at once. Do you understand?"

Beeson moistened his dry lips and whispered, "This fella sure plays rough, don't he?"

Vandergrift shot a sullen, resentful glance at Sheridan. "Yeah, plenty rough, but he's gone too far this time. Warren's been a pretty good general. Wasn't his fault the corps got mixed up on the march."

"Thought you said you were against slow-moving generals," Dyer retorted.

"That was grouse talk. Warren's all right."

Rising above the conflict of loyalties to commanders, one unavoidable and distinct fact remained plainly evident. Pickett's force had been wiped out. Thousands of Confederate prisoners were on their way back to the Provost Marshal's stockade and there were so many captured muskets that arm loads of them were being used to corduroy the soggy roads.

For the first time in their history, the troops of the Potomac Army watched a determined, bold leader overcome the obstacles thrown at him and with clever maneuvering bordering on brilliance, bring them through to triumph over their adversary. Heavy-handed though his manner might have been, Sheridan accomplished his purpose.

The cavalry chieftain was still not satisfied. Now was the time to complete the annihilation of the entire Confederate Army. All possible routes of escape must be cut off. One of them was the Southside Railroad, which Lee had to protect if his army was to survive. From the clearing at Five Forks where Sheridan had just broken Warren, there was a road leading directly to the railroad. While Sheridan sat brooding in his saddle, an officer of rank came riding up triumphantly to report that his command was at the Rebel rear and they had captured five guns.

Sheridan's head flew up. "I don't care a damn for their guns or you either, sir. What I want is that Southside Railway!"

Seated on the ground within earshot, Hallowell squirted the sassafras juice he was chewing on.

"Before this day's over he'll be wanting us to fetch him the moon. The man ain't human."

"He sure as hell don't satisfy easy," growled Cassidy.

The sun was slowly disappearing over the treetops and the clearing in the pines was dim in smoke-hazed twilight when Sheridan called Griffin. Ayers and Chamberlain to his side.

"Get together all the men you can," he commanded, "and drive on while you can still see."

As the subordinates dashed off to fulfill his orders, Sheridan stood to his five-feet-four inches in the stirrups and waved his battered flat hat at the men lounging about the clearing. Shouting in his shrill voice, he said, "I want you men to understand we have a record to make before the sun goes down that will make hell tremble!"

He pointed his hat toward the north, the direction in which the railroad lay. "I want you there!" he cried.

The men scurried into ranks as though Satan himself had given the order. The columns were preparing to move when a slight figure rode up to Sheridan and began speaking in quiet, but emotional tones.

"It's General Warren," Dyer murmured.

Joe Sackett raised a hand to shade his vision. "Yes, and look at the poor bastard. He's still clutching the written order that'll knock his career into a cocked hat."

"Reconsider, hell!" Sheridan roared in the man's face. "I don't reconsider my decisions! Obey the goddamn order!"

Hard-crusted veterans, who had often prayed for this sort of treatment of fumbling commanders, cringed as they watched.

Warren's chin fell to his chest as he wheeled his horse and rode off, a broken man. Sheridan went on with the business of organizing a force that could break through to the railroad, but, as it soon turned out, no more could be done that night.

Darkness arrived and blanketed the treacherous forest, making further movement impossible. The exhausted cavalry and infantry were ordered to bivouac on the spot. Fires were permitted in view of the fact that no Confederate forces remained in that sector. The tiny band of Frankford Volunteers disposed of a simple meal consisting of the usual fat back pork, hardtack and coffee, then laid out their blanket rolls.

Sitting cross-legged on the ground, Jake Hallowell extracted a burning faggot from the campfire, lit his pipe and with a sour expression and addressed his comrades reclining nearby.

"I tell you that little bow-legged popinjay over-stepped his bounds, the way he handled Warren. Crawford's the one who caused all the trouble today, yet Sheridan lets Crawford off scot free. It just downright galls me to see one man broken for the mistake of another. Yesiree, I tell you, this fella Sheridan's cruel and unjust."

"Well, one thing's for certain," Paddy broke in softly. "Those tough Western generals sure don't play according to Eastern rules. Maybe that's why they managed to clean up the Rebs so effectively in the West while we played ring-around-the-rosy here in the East."

Helverson stretched himself on a blanket and yawned. "From the results Sheridan's been producing, I'd say that if his 'cruel and unjust' conduct had been present in this army from the beginning, we'd have been home making a living the past two years instead of draggin' our asses all over Virginia."

The snapping of dry boughs cracking beneath the weight of approaching boots caused the small group to turn their heads. Into the zone of light cast by their fire stepped a short, wiry figure—the devil himself—Sheridan.

In an instant each man was on his feet and standing rigidly at attention.

"At ease, men. As you were. Please be seated."

McCool's expression registered wholesale alarm as to whether he should take the General at his word. Sheridan squatted on the ground as the goggle-eyed soldiers followed suit.

"Did you men have enough to eat tonight?"

"Oh yes, sir," Vandergrift replied.

The trace of a smile crossed Sheridan's leathery countenance. "Come now. You can be frank with me. That was a foolish question on my part. No fighting man is ever satisfied with the commissary in the field."

He picked up a stick and probed the ground with it.

"You're part of the Hundred and Eighteenth Pennsylvania, aren't you?"

They nodded their heads.

"You men performed well today, as I understand it is always your custom to do. Anything on your minds you'd like to take up with me?"

Glances were exchanged and several of the men cleared their throats. Exhaling a puff of smoke, Kimball cupped the pipe which he held in his hand. "Well, since you've asked, sir, we all felt deeply attached to General Warren. But, since you've given us leadership such as we've never had before, I reckon we can overlook what happened this evening."

Sheridan's expression remained impassive. "Thank you for that, soldier. I'll do my level best by you and this corps. Now, I must go find General Griffin."

"He's right over there by the next campfire, sir," McCool blurted. "I got a lantern if you'd like to borrow it."

Sheridan smiled from under his black drooping mustache. "No thanks, son. I can find my way."

Too stunned to speak, the flabbergasted Frankford volunteers watched in silence as Phil Sheridan stalked off toward Griffin's campfire.

Huddled with his division and brigade commanders, Griffin, as new head of the Fifth Corps, was talking things over when Sheridan approached unexpectedly. In quite a different mood now that the fury of battle was past, Sheridan interrupted their conversation. "Please excuse me, gentlemen. I'd just like to say that if I've been unduly harsh and demanding with any of you this day, I want to say that I'm sorry. I hope you'll forgive me, as I have no intention of hurting anybody. You know how it is, we had to carry this, and I was fretting all day until it was done. I want to say that every one of you did a splendid job."

His genuine apology caught the corps commanders totally unprepared, the same way it had the enlisted men. A few garbled words of dutiful reassurance were offered by several generals, who gaped as Sheridan strode away into the darkness.

That night, experienced soldiers, who had always been able to sleep through stress, found themselves waking at mysterious intervals with a feeling of excitement. There was an intangible, unseen promise of something good in the air.

Throughout the night, heavy guns boomed around Petersburg and Richmond, the fulminating flashes of red-orange gunfire running close together, piercing the heavens like an aurora. The ground on which the men slept shook and trembled from the concussions.

Peering over the top of a threadbare blanket, McCool looked out at the sheets of light illuminating the sky.

"Grant and the boys sure ain't sleeping over there tonight. Just look at that barrage, will you."

Paddy reached out a hand. "Yes, and you'd better get some sleep. We just may wind up this whole war tomorrow."

Clouds were riding fast on a driving wind in the starless sky and a lonely crescent moon shone against a field of black.

At four o'clock the next afternoon, while the men in the Corn Exchange were gleefully burning a captured train of cars on the Southside Railroad, a staff officer dashed past them. He waved his hat and shouted, "Boys, Petersburg and Richmond have fallen! Lee's in full retreat toward Lynchburg!"

The men were incredulous, unable to comprehend or believe what they heard.

"Tell it to the Marines," McCool called over one shoulder as he heaved an empty crate onto the crackling fire. Hot flames licked his face.

"Put it in a canteen!" Dyer hollered. As it turned out, the officer had anticipated events, Petersburg was not abandoned until three o'clock on the morning of the third, and the surrender of Richmond followed a few hours later.

The deadly race had begun. Lee retreated hastily to the north of the Appomattox River. Somewhere above the river, he picked up the fragments of shattered commands from Richmond, Petersburg and Five Forks. With everybody assembled, he could move west, then south and tie up with Joe Johnston's army in North Carolina. But a large segment of the Army of the Potomac was almost as far west as he, and a good deal farther south. Properly handled, the Fifth Corps should be able to head him off because it had a shorter distance to travel and Sheridan was in the saddle.

The Richmond & Danville Railroad loomed as the important target. The main trunk line slanted down from Virginia into Joe Johnston's territory in North Carolina and bisected the Southside Railroad halfway between Petersburg and Lynchburg. Lee's quickest route put him on the Richmond & Danville at Amelia Courthouse, sixteen miles northeast of the point where the two railroads intersected.

Sheridan, anticipating such a move, applied the crop and spur to his eager troops and, by sunset on the fourth of April, he had them in a line of battle across the Danville Railroad at Jetersville—-a station just a few miles southwest of the Amelia Courthouse. Lee was checkmated in that direction. Now he would have to await darkness and the opportunity to find a new route.

The spirits of the Union soldiers ran high. Even dog trotting after the cavalry no longer seemed a bad assignment. No one was entirely clear as to just what was happening, but the rank and file were certain of one thing—-the Johnnies were on the run at last. Like a house of sticks, the Confederate Army was falling apart piece by piece and every Federal soldier considered it his pleasant duty to pick up the pieces. Prisoners were being rounded up by the thousands. Out in front rode the fantastic outriders of victory—-Sheridan's Jesse scouts.

In some instances they dressed as Confederate officers or couriers. Other times they wore faded jeans and rode decrepit horses or mules with makeshift bridles and saddles, pretending to be displaced farmers or roving horse doctors. In either guise they visited Rebel picket posts, rode blithely through cavalry cordons, ambled alongside Lee's wagon trains and paused to chat in Confederate camps. Most of them got back alive and kept Sheridan informed about the enemy's position and where they were going next.

Lee's army was at the Amelia Courthouse, only six miles away from the spot where the Fifth Corps blocked the escape route. The hard-pressed Confederates had used up all their rations and to their utter dismay found that the courthouse was a barren cupboard. The ogre of hunger and starvation haunted the steadfast soldiers remaining in Lee's butternut legions. Surveying the Yankee line carefully, the crafty, white-haired Southern chieftain concluded sadly that his army was not strong enough to fight its way through. One move remained. The Confederate army would have to go west cross-country and strike the western part of the Southside Railroad somewhere in the vicinity of Lynchburg. If they moved fast enough and were lucky, there was an outside chance that they might still slip around the Federal flank and get south.

At Jetersville, Meade arrived on the scene in an ambulance and, though sick with nervous indigestion and strain, made preparations to take over the direction of field operations.

The old wrench of conflict in command found its way again into the machinery of military operations. Sheridan, whose driving instinct was to attack before anybody got sixty minutes older, feared that Meade would be content to wait for Lee to start the fight. Without a moment's loss, he hurriedly dispatched a note describing the situation and suggesting that Lee's army could be captured, urging Grant to come and take charge. The dispatch was given to a scout dressed as a Confederate colonel who took the note, concealed it in a wad of leaf tobacco, put the tobacco in his mouth and galloped cross-country to find Grant twelve miles away. Late that night Grant reached Sheridan's tent.

During the day, Meade did not sit down to wait for the fight to be brought to him as Sheridan had feared. 'Old Four Eyes,' sick as he appeared to be, was itching for a scrap. With unexpected vigor, he sent the Fifth Corps racing into the Amelia Courthouse, only to find that Lee had left. The slippery Confederate commander had put his tired, half-starved troops on the road for a night march and was striking farther west for the town of Farmville. As soon as the flight was discovered, Meade ordered immediate pursuit, but the order was modified by Grant, who wanted only part of the infantry to follow Lee's rear and press him to stand and fight.

The rest of the infantry was ordered to follow the cavalry and get west as fast as possible, always keeping south of the Confederates. The idea was to win the footrace; if Grant could plant infantry across Lee's path just once more, it would all be over.

The plight of the retreating Confederate Army was that it now found itself encased on three sides as it slid westward; Meade, pushing from behind, the Fifth Corps boxing from beneath, and the cavalry poling the front.

On the sixth of April, at Little Sailors Creek, the Sixth Corps under Meade crashed headlong into the Confederate rear guard and inflicted eight thousand casualties, cutting off a large segment of the fleeing Southern Army and capturing Generals Ewell and Kershaw along with many other notables.

Late in the evening on April seventh, the Philadelphia Corn Exchange passed through Farmville. The streets of the tiny Virginia hamlet were lined with bright bonfires and glowing torches that seemed to herald victory. As they trudged quickly on between the fires, the tired veterans suddenly spotted the figure of an unassuming little general sitting on the porch of a homey country hotel. U. S. Grant was puffing idly on a cigar and appeared to be smiling at his troops with an inward satisfaction and admiration. Erupting like spontaneous combustion, the Philadelphians raised their blue caps, waved them jubilantly and shouted accolades for the man who was at last leading them to a victory they had only dreamed of. Grant acknowledged the outbreak of enthusiasm with a poker face and a gentle nod of his shaggy head. The regiment moved on.

The country through which the army was moving had seen nothing of war. It was a fertile, productive region and the well-stocked larders of thrifty plantations paid handsome tribute to the exorbitant demands of the hungry soldiers.

Lee again crossed the tattered remnants of his army to the north side of the Appomattox River and set fire to the bridges in an attempt to cover his tracks and slow down his pursuers.

The Second Corps, pressing close at his heels, pounced on the burning bridge timbers, beat out the flames with their coats and once more lunged after the quarry.

On the morning of April eighth, the Fifth Corps plunged into the foremost position, replacing the Second Corps, and after a hard, grueling march of twenty-nine miles went into bivouac two miles from a place called Appomattox Courthouse. Dog tired and supperless, the weary infantrymen fell out of line, dropped to the ground and were instantly sound asleep.

At four o'clock in the morning they were aroused by the electrifying news that Sheridan had succeeded in putting his cavalry squarely in front of the Rebel Army. Lee was trapped! At Appomattox Station, a mile or so from the courthouse, General Custer took the Confederates by complete surprise, seizing several freight trains loaded with food. With that accomplished, he took the main body of his troops on past the station and seized a big pack wagon and artillery train. Back at Appomattox Station, former railroad men among the Yankee troopers flung themselves from their saddles and sprinted for the locomotives. From a distance, a drowsy-eyed infantryman could hear whistles blowing and bells clanging as the cavalrymen bumped the trains back and forth in aimless celebration.

McCool shinnied part way up a tree to afford himself a better view. Looking down on those standing below, he said, "Go to war Miss Agnes! Listen to 'em. Must've captured food. Let's leg it. Hey, Sarg, what say? We get fed now?"

Vandergrift crawled out from his bedroll. "What about that, Sarg? I don't care a damn bit if it's Confederate grub. I'm so hungry I could eat a dead mule."

"In proper time, me buckoes. Right now ye'll all be after fallin' in and be damned quick about it. This ain't no time to be thinkin' o' feedin' yer faces. Fall in."

He turned to the officer standing beside him. "Captain Kelly, sir, would ye be wishin' to tell the men what's to be expected of them this day, sir?"

Kelly stepped a pace forward in the grey light of early dawn. Knee deep around him the ground mist slowly rose from the woodland floor. The only man in the entire regiment who had not been home at one time or another throughout the four years of war, he was one of those unfortunates from the city slums who had found a home in the army. Gone now was his cameo handsomeness and instead was a mature hardened countenance with furrowed lines. He addressed the company in low, measured tones.

"Men, our cavalry is due west of here, across the main road to Lynchburg. Sheridan wants us to get there on the double before Lee can brush them out of the way." He stopped, seized by a fit of coughing. "Now, which would you men rather do, eat or fight and end it all today?"

"My stomach's just about grown shut," McCool moaned. "Wouldn't be no place for food to go even if it had the chance. Let's fight, sir."

Others concurred reluctantly. In the background a bugle sounded, followed instantly by the long roll of drums.

Kelly's commands rang out across the clearing. "Com-pany. Atten-shun. Right, Shoul-der arms! By the le-ft, face! For-ward march."

In perfect step, following the lead of their young captain, the nineteen surviving members of H Company moved out from their bivouac to join with their seventy comrades-in-arms, all that remained of the 118th Pennsylvania.

The once mighty regiment marched quickly toward its honored place at the head of the brigade, swinging into position past the larger Pennsylvania regiments with only seven month's service to their credit. Numbering almost one thousand men in each regiment, drawn up rank on rank in bulging columns, the 155th, 190th, 191st and 198th Pennsylvania regiments seemed at that moment reminiscent of the war's first days of glory.

Standing by in the 198th regiment, the youngest and by far the largest of the Philadelphia regiments, Joe Beeson dipped his rifle in deferential salute as his friends in the Corn Exchange marched past, heads erect, shoulders back and eyes forward.

It was the ninth of April. Birds were astir overhead in the balmy, spring-scented air. A soft breeze blew, and the countryside bent beneath a lace curtain of blossoms. Mother Nature surveyed her flower show with a special kind of satisfaction—-it was Palm Sunday. A Palm Sunday atmosphere seemed to permeate the whole region of rolling Virginia countryside with a reverent quiet broken only by the trilling of song birds on the wing, their songs sounding like tiny bells against a blue sky. Sunlight bathed the green meadows and rolling hills in golden beauty.

Along the route of march the abrasive sounds of an army on the move could be heard. With slanting rays of sunlight pouring down upon them, the men of the Corn Exchange moved into a skirmish line near a delightful country lane on the crest of a high hill. Below them at some distance, lying peacefully at rest, was the quaint courthouse village of Appomattox. The tiny, tree-cloistered village was set on a rise of ground beyond which the country dropped off to a wide, spacious valley, a valley crawling with gray-coated infantry, their wagons and artillery.

"Well, there they are," Vandergrift said, pointing. "All bottled up. The whole kit and caboodle, or what's left of them."

Dyer peered down the hillside. "Think there's many of them left in the village?"

Paddy shaded his vision with one hand. "Real hornet's nest or I miss my guess," he said after a moment's observation.

Lying prone, McCool sighted his rifle. "Wonder why Lee doesn't quit? More killing at this stage of the game is outright foolish."

A bugle blast sounded the charge. Mounted officers stiffened in their saddles, sabers raised as they gave the order to attack. The charmed circle formed themselves quickly with a clasp of hands. Vandergrift stood erect, towering above the others. He squared his shoulders. "Don't anyone get careless this trip, stick together," he rasped. Turning as one, they moved out in a body.

The assault against Appomattox Courthouse mounted and swelled with intensity as line after line of blue infantry, rifles tilted forward, crested the hill. The Union lines grew longer as rank upon rank came into view as if there was no end.

Sheridan, on the right flank, scowled, pounded his fist and pointed out to Chamberlain where his brigade should strike.

"Now smash them, I tell you, smash them!" he screamed.

The blue-coated avalanche rolled down the hill and in a short space of time the village was enveloped, its defenders retiring hastily into the valley to join their trapped compatriots.

Severely winded and suffering from heartburn brought on by hunger, the men of the Corn Exchange dropped to the ground near the weathered clapboard house belonging to a Mrs. Wright. The tufted spring grass in her yard felt warm and spongy. Paddy clutched at his ribs in a futile effort to squeeze out the agony in his chest.

"My God," he panted painfully, "if there's any more running to do, somebody's going to carry me."

"Like who, for instance?" gasped Hallowell. "I swear to God, I don't move another step until I get fed."

A sudden garbled warning exploded from Sackett. He raised his rifle and took level aim at a Confederate horseman dashing forward at a mad gait, heading directly for them.

"Hold it!" Paddy cried out. "Don't shoot! He's carrying a flag of truce! Look!"

All along the line the ragged, dirty veterans, the red clay of Virginia ground into their blue uniforms, blinked with shock and the dull realization that the supreme moment had arrived. Men grown old with mangy beards matting their leathery faces, and a few who still possessed round, smooth, boyish faces, watched and waited, hardly drawing a breath. A gentle breeze ruffled and curled the loose strands of their long hair, uncut and uncombed for weeks.

The Confederate officer reined in his horse and, with obvious distaste, approached the regimental position of the 118th Pennsylvania. "Where is your commanding officer, General Sheridan?" he asked harshly.

For a second there was complete silence, the stunned Philadelphians unable to say a word.

"You'll find the General over there, sir," Paddy said in a low monotone. He pointed to his right.

With a contemptuous toss of his head, lips curled in thin tight lines, the Confederate wheeled his horse and trotted off.

Helverson watched his departure and stammered, "Wh...what d...do you fellas think? This really the end?"

"I'd say we'd better keep our wits about us," Vandergrift retorted. "The Johnnies have pulled this surrender trick before. While our generals dally over a flag of truce, Lee could sneak his army off to Lynchburg. Don't forget, the top to this trap is still open."

Using his field glasses, Kelly scanned the surrounding hills and valley below. "They mean it this time," he said finally, almost with a touch of sadness. "Here, take a look."

One by one the men of H Company took turns peering through the binoculars. All doubts vanished and any hesitancy was stayed by what they saw. In the valley and on distant hilltops, the broken, shattered battalions of the hard-fought Army of Northern Virginia could be seen stacking their arms. More white flags, mere specks, were coming down through the Confederate lines.

Then it came. The command to cease fire was passed down to the troops by Sheridan, and almost immediately the Union lines were thrown into columns of divisions and speedily covered with a heavy cordon of sentinels. Orders were explicit. No one was permitted to pass beyond the sentinel line under any circumstances, and no guns were to be fired.

The men were still suffering from excessive hunger, but the triumphant feeling of the Palm Sunday peace swelled inside their breasts as the victorious Potomac Army laid their rifles to rest. Even nature seemed ready to respond with them in a great Hallelujah Chorus.

On April 12, 1861, the first gun of the war had sounded at Sumter. Now the last gun was laid down on that anniversary date four years later. Arrangements were made for the formal surrender and the signing of paroles.

The 1st Division, 5th Corps, by way of tribute to her faithful veterans, was given the honor of receiving the formal surrender. At nine o'clock on the morning of April twelfth, the troops of Bartlett's division drew themselves up in two lines, facing each other across the main thoroughfare in ranks extending beyond the village of Appomattox Courthouse. General Joshua Chamberlain, the heroic, scholarly brigadier from Maine, commanded the occasion, even though the division rightfully belonged to Bartlett, who had assumed command on General Ayres' promotion to corps commander.

Beneath a gray overcast, and in low voices, the Philadelphia Corn Exchange formed itself on the left of its brigade on the grounds surrounding the McLean house, close to a picket fence enclosing the rambling brick dwelling.

Every man appeared in his best attire, arms, accouterments and clothing showing little of the rough usage they had received.

While paroles were being prepared and signed within the house, those standing at rest on the outside fidgeted with expectancy, awaiting the appearance of the surrendering army.

Cassidy stood with arms akimbo and surveyed the company line.

"McCool, be after brushin' that hair out o' yer eyes. Ye'll be standin' inspection by some real soldiers any minute now."

"Aw, let up, Andy. The war's over."

"Don't Andy me. Not until ye see me in civilians."

"Better take it easy, Sarg," Dyer broke in with a chuckle. "Willie here just might end up being your boss some day. He's a live-wire go-getter, you know."

"In a pig's eye he will."

Hoffman, standing close by, was deeply engrossed in thought. The point of his chin rested on the muzzle of his rifle. He studied the porticoed, redbrick building that was bustling with activity.

"Life sure is funny," he said at last.

Sackett arched his stringy eyebrows. "Funny? Funny like what, for instance?"

Hoffman nodded in the direction of the McLean house. "That fellow, McLean, used to live at Manassas. Comes the first battle of the war at Bull Run, and his home gets shot up proper. So what's he do? Moves down here to this quiet spot and bam! Four years later the war ends up right in the middle of his parlor. Isn't that something?"

"I'll say. I heard about that yesterday. Guess it just goes to prove that nobody can hide from war once it gets rolling," Sackett replied.

Not far off, Woodfield stood with his back propped against a picket fence, his legs crossed and one arm draped over the palings. He called to Cassidy, "Sarg, all right to light up a toby?"

"Go ahead. Just be sure ye throw the damn thing away soon's the ceremony starts."

Woodfield disengaged his impaled arm and struck a match to the rolled leaf tobacco, then inhaled and exhaled a puff of smoke. He sniffed the air like an expectant rabbit. Contentment registered in the sound of his voice and showed on his face.

"Boys, I can smell home already."

The scar running the length of Dyer's face wrinkled into a wry smile. "What do you mean you smell home? I didn't know Frankford smelled."

"Like the smell of fresh ground coffee down at Castor's store on a Monday morning," Woodfield replied, "the smell of freshly tanned leather over at Hilles', the odor of pork roast and malt beer breezing through the doors of the Eagle Hotel on Saturday nights...."

McCool downed a swallow from his canteen and brushed the back of his hand across his lips. "Tom's right. And don't forget the smell of seeds and fertilizers and freshly painted garden tools over at Holden's hardware store." His face took on a drowsy expression. "Remember the leafy scent of maples budding along Main Street? Or the smell of warm spring rain spanking the surface of Frankford Creek?"

"Know the thing I've missed most while we've been away?" Snyder interjected. "The sounds of home."

"The sounds?" McCool asked.

"Yes, like the ringing of the church bells on a quiet Sunday morning, children laughing at play in the yards, the older folks chatting in the market, horses clomping the streets, the mailman's whistle down by the gate of a morning. Used to ride the mail route a lot with old Pop Shephard, got stamps for my collection that way."

Kimball spat on the battered visor of his kepi and rubbed the spit around with his fingers to bring about a polish. "Smells, bells," he said in a rare outburst of levity. "Thing I miss most is three square meals a day and a soft bed at night."

Hallowell moved in close and put an arm around Paddy's waist. "Speaking of mail, we haven't received any in over two months. Have you had any word from your Southern bride?"

"No, I haven't, Jake. I just pray that she and my daughter have made their way to Frankford. Mary Coates has the key to my house. Maybe there will be a light at the window when I get home."

A sharp command brought every man to attention.

Like the approach of a storm came the dull, heavy thud of the shuffling and tramping of thousands of feet across the creek bed of the Appomattox to the right.

Down the length and breadth of the blue-coated ranks, caps were quickly set in place, tunics smoothed down and belts straightened as every eye fixed itself straight ahead. The long awaited moment had finally come, but it was unbelievably grim. Each blue coat felt a throb in his tightening rib cage.

The vanguard of the surrendering gray columns was still hidden from sight. They marched up from the floor of the valley and forded the shallow waters of the Appomattox. As they headed up the steep, winding hill leading to McLean's house, they moved with the swinging route step that had taken their infantry so many miles. Some of the color-bearers kept their flags tightly bound to the staffs, but most were waving in the breeze, flapping in clusters as they had done on the field of battle.

Over the crest of the hill they came, men marching four abreast. In the fore was Evans' Brigade of Gordon's Corps. They trod heavily onto the surrender grounds. A deep hush fell over the proceedings. Not a whisper could be heard; not the sound of a trumpet, nor the roll of a drum. Motionless, the men in blue stood at attention. There was nothing but an awful stillness, as if they were witnessing the passing of the dead.

The men in gray had worn-out shoes that flopped in bits and pieces. Many of them had no shoes at all. Their uniforms of faded butternut were ragged and dirty, yet despite their pathetic attire, they bore themselves with proud mien as they moved toward the designated point to stack arms and surrendered their battle flags. They challenged the admiration of their conquerors.

Sitting astride his great war horse, General Chamberlain was suddenly moved to tears, a scholar, and without a doubt one of the knightliest soldiers in the Federal Army, he lifted his sword in command as a solitary bugle sounded the call to "shoulder." Instantly, with a mechanical snap of arms, the solemn Union troops executed the maneuver reserved solely as a mark of respect for dignitaries. There was a soft, ordered slapping of hands on wood and metal along the line as regiment by regiment in succession raised rifles simultaneously to position-arms reversed.

The vanquished foe appeared startled at the unexpected salute. Riding majestically at the head of his soldiers, General Gordon quickly caught the significance of the moment. In a breathtaking response, the Confederate chieftain wheeled his mount so that he faced General Chamberlain and the Union lines. He touched his steed with a spur so that the animal reared slightly, horse and rider performing in one motion. The animal's head swung down in a graceful bow and at the same time Gordon dropped the point of his sword to the toe of his boot in salutation. As further acknowledgment for Chamberlain's courtesy, he ordered the entire Confederate column to wheel so they faced the victors as they returned the salute.

Through it all, Paddy kept his gaze riveted on General Gordon's familiar face, the memory causing him to bite his lower lip.

One by one, Southern bayonets were affixed to muskets, arms stacked and cartridge boxes unslung and hung on the pointed stacks. Very slowly and with deep reluctance, the Rebel color bearers leaned their tattered and torn battle flags against the stacks, or laid them on the ground beneath the trees. The pent-up emotion of the proud sons of Dixie was almost too much to witness. Young and old, men with hard-chiseled features, seasoned campaigners who had survived four long years of strife, began rushing from the ranks, heedless of discipline, to bend over their flags and press them to their lips. Tears streamed from their emaciated faces as they sobbed mournfully. Some of the more emotional tore flags from the staffs and hid them in their bosoms.

McCool shook convulsively as he watched the painful proceedings, tears running down his cheeks as he garbled, "Oh my God, I feel like I've smashed something holy."

The muscles in Vandergrift's face became taut, hard lines. "What you see smashed is man's rebellion."

Hallowell whispered, "Outwardly, yes, but can man's rebellious nature ever be completely extinguished?"

The purple veins in Vandergrift's neck corded. "No. Those gimlet-eyed rednecks are going home to beat up on blacks. Mark my words. We should have finished them off."

Sergeant Cassidy, deeply moved and fighting hard for self-control, issued a terse command, "Silence in the ranks."

The solemn procession of defeated men continued into the day.

Shortly after the noon hour a brigadier general riding at the head of his brigade attracted Paddy's attention and the others in the 118th. He was a small, thin, priggish individual with a red face and shrill voice. He wore the Confederate colors with the exception of his coat, which was blue and covered with gold braid. Brusquely, he halted his brigade in front of the Philadelphians and shrieked orders to his men, placing them in a position to receive the Federal salute. When his soldiers failed to form up rapidly enough to suit him, he showered them with verbal abuse.

The Union men could see at once that he was not admired by his men, but it was evident they were used to his abuse. Now that his authority was broken, they would not stand for it. Several of the men turned to him angrily and one of them said, "Look at him. He's brave enough now, but he was never this near the Yankees before."

Thinking better of replying, the Rebel commander scowled and wheeled his mount to where General Chamberlain sat posted in front of his troops. Showing unmistakable signs of strain and fatigue, Chamberlain moved in the saddle to greet the brigadier and held out a gloved hand. The proffered handshake went unaccepted and unnoticed.

"Your men are tired, General. They've been put through a grinding ordeal," Chamberlain said. He withdrew his hand slowly. "I had sincerely hoped, sir, that goodwill and friendship could be restored between us today."

"You may forgive us, but we won't forgive you," snapped the Confederate commander. "There's rancor in our hearts which you little imagine. We hate you, sir."

Chamberlain's expression became as cold as the granite from his state of Maine. He eased his tall, angular frame back into the saddle and with a fixed gaze, surveyed the officer in silence. A hum of angry voices rose from the men in the ranks.

Noticing the icy stares, the Southern general appeared ill at ease. He commented on the bullet holes in Chamberlain's coat, asking in his high-pitched voice, "Where did you get those, sir?"

The question could not have been more unfortunate. Chamberlain squared his shoulders, knit his brow into a frown and replied, "Those were taken, sir, while driving your brigade up the Quaker Road on the twenty-ninth. I believe you had already departed the field."

"Oh, I suppose you think you did great things that day, but I stopped you until I realized I was fighting three divisions."

"I am a brigadier, sir. I had only three regiments."

"I know better," the Rebel snapped. "You go home and take those fellows with you and that will end the war."

"We are going, General, but first let us escort you."

At a signal, the mounted guard moved forward to conduct the Confederate general from the field.

Witnessing the whole affair, the men of the Corn Exchange were enraged. They began calling to the men standing in the gray-coated ranks.

"Hey, Johnnies, who was that?"

"That was General Henry A. Wise, suh," several of the Southern enlisted men responded. "Not much to look at, air he?"

For a moment the Philadelphians could hardly believe they had actually seen the imperious governor of Virginia turned on by his own men. Nor could they let the opportunity pass without firing a few well-chosen shots at the disgruntled Rebel. Feeling the kindred bond of sympathy which one common soldier feels for another despite the color of his uniform, McCool and others began peppering General Wise with derision, much to the delight and satisfaction of the Southern troops.

"Who hung John Brown, General Wise?"

"Hey, General, where'd you steal that circus coat?"

"Hang him to a sour apple tree!"

If there was a disgusted-looking man who rode from Appomattox that day, it was ex-Governor Wise of Virginia.

In a field near the McLean house, a group of sad, suffering men gathered around General Gordon, many of them weeping as they saw their old banners laid on stacked guns like trappings on the coffin of their dead hopes. The gaunt Georgian general tried as best he could to allay the fears and apprehensions of his followers. Sunk in the deep recesses of an impenetrable gloom, the Southern infantrymen talked about leaving the country and beginning life anew in some other land.

They knew that burned-out homes and fenceless farms would greet them on their return to a life of poverty and ashes.

"What are we to do? How are we to begin life again?" they asked one another. "Our confederate money has been rendered worthless, our banks and wealthy are broke. The assets which formerly gave us credit have been destroyed. Who will loan us money to rebuild without houses, animals and implements for cultivation as security? How safe will our families be with four million freed slaves running loose?" The most hopeful were dismayed and the stoutest hearts filled with dread.

Shades of twilight were falling in a smoky haze by the time the last act of surrender and parole was completed. Along the length of roadway churned and powdered into dust by the passing army, Confederate arms and baggage of war were stacked in heaps and piles, mute testimony to their one-time power.

Wearied by the long ordeal, the order at last came down dismissing the Federal troops from parade formation. Letting out a sigh of relief, the Corn Exchange broke ranks and stacked their rifles. Gathering in a small group, they hobnobbed with the conquered who still lingered about the McLean house.

Paddy, lips tightly compressed, hitched his belt and glanced over his shoulder. With a look of grim determination on his face, he started walking toward General Gordon who was counseling his men beneath a stand of oak trees.

"Through the rift in the clouds above us," Gordon was saying, "I can see the hand of Almighty God stretched out to help. He will guide us in the gloom and bless every effort to restore desolated homes with the sunshine and comforts of former years. It is time for me to bid each of you goodbye. I leave you with one last bit of advice. It is your duty as patriots to remain and work for the recuperation of our stricken section with the same courage, energy and devotion with which you fought this war."

Heads were bowed as if in meditation and it was perfectly still as Paddy advanced to within a few yards of the spot. He stopped and stood motionless, feeling alone and exposed. Drawing in a deep breath, he stepped forward.

"General Gordon, sir. May I speak with you a moment?"

Bleak Confederate faces stared at him, wondering at the intrusion.

"Yes, soldier, what is it?" Gordon asked, scanning Paddy's face and uniform with a penetrating gaze.

"I came for two reasons, sir. First, I would like to apologize for having deceived you...."

"Say! You're the young Irishman who pawned himself off as a scout from Stuart the day we entered York."

"Yes, sir. That's what I came to tell you. I'm sorry about that."

"Hang it, soldier, that was war. You were given a duty to perform and you did it, very cleverly, I might add." There was warmth in his voice. "You mentioned two reasons. What is the other?"

Paddy cast an uneasy glance at the Southern soldiers staring at him. "It's about my wife, sir. She was from Leesburg. We have a daughter. Because of me, she and her mother were forced to leave town when the baby was born."

"You say you are married?"

"Yes, sir."

"Very well, proceed."

Paddy cleared his throat. "I thought, sir, that since her father was a surgeon with your army, he was killed at Gettysburg, I thought maybe...well, I just thought maybe there would be some records you could steer me onto that would help me locate my family. My wife's father was Doctor Chenewith. Did you know him?"

"Son, I'm afraid all our records have been lost, burned or otherwise destroyed, but I did know Doctor Chenewith. A brave man. Died in the line of duty. Sorry to say, that is all the help I can give you."

A youthful Confederate, seated on the ground with his legs crossed and a ragged hat pushed back on his straw-colored hair, started playing a mouth organ. The reedy tune was low and mournful.

Gordon bared his head. "I promised my men that I would sing a final hymn with them before we depart. Will you join us?"

Lost in a daze of confusion, Paddy nodded his head. Standing among the Confederate soldiers, his mind strayed back to the early days of the war. There were misty images of each engagement, prison, his encounter with the Chenewiths and his marriage to Becky. It all seemed like a dream. He contemplated the future with a troubled mind.

Around him, their voices filled with sorrow, the Southern troops were singing.

"Rock of ages, cleft for me,
Let me hide myself in thee;
Let the water and the blood,
From thy riven side which flowed;
Be of sin the double cure,
Cleanse me from its guilt and power."

Union soldiers standing nearby moved in slowly, their low-pitched voices joining in chorus with those who only a few short days before had been mortal enemies. The shoulder of Northerner touched Southerner and a few locked arms in friendship for the final harmony. In husky, deep-throated unison, they concluded.

"Nothing in my hand I bring,
Simply to thy cross I cling;
Naked come to thee for dress,
Helpless look to thee for grace;
Fowl, I to the fountain fly,
Wash me Savior, or I die."

By one and by twos the paroled men in gray began to disperse down the dusty roads toward home. In a steady stream they walked off through the blossoming woods and disappeared over the hills.

One final chore fell upon the tired soldiers of the Corn Exchange Regiment before they could depart. Much work was left to do in gathering up the stores and munitions of war. In the woods where the Rebel Army had camped, ordnance was scattered upon the ground in every direction.

Under the supervision of Major Ashbrook, division ordnance officer, the grueling task of clean-up was initiated with swearing and muttered threats of insurrection. In an orgy of burning, the rolling landscape was soon covered with huge bonfires consuming all flammable material and munitions. Dangerous explosions rent the air.

By way of surprise, it was discovered that whole battalions, refusing to surrender and sign paroles, had stacked their arms and left for home.

McCool struggled under an armload of muskets which he threw upon a flatbed wagon. He wiped sweat from his brow and turned to Major Ashbrook. "How many do you figure sneaked off, sir?"

"Enough to have swelled Lee's army to over fifty thousand at the surrender," the officer replied.

Vandergrift dumped another load of arms on the wagon. He spoke angrily. "Major, we have no rations and many of the men have no tents. There is a big storm brewing. When do we pull out?"

"I would say in a day or two, Corporal." Ashbrook gazed at his bedraggled troops. "Like you, I feel more the vanquished than the victor." He turned on his heel and walked away.

The next day, rain began to pour down in torrents. Streams overflowed their banks and, to add to the misery, the weather turned bitterly cold. Twenty-four hours later, on April 15th, the 118th Regiment received the long awaited order to march to Washington by way of Richmond—through a sea of mud.

CHAPTER 27

Sansom Street Hall in the center of Philadelphia was bustling with activity on Friday night, June 9th. The staid old building echoed with revelry as the Corn Exchange Association staged a grand banquet for the men who had served in the 118th Regiment. The lean veterans had mustered out of service the day before at Camp Cadwallader, located between 20th and 22nd Streets off Ridge Road. Receiving pay for the first time in over four months, they were ready to return to civilian life. Clean, barbered, and sporting new uniforms, they no longer resembled the dirty, unkempt threadbare troops who had received the surrender at Appomattox. Illuminated by the glare of gas lamps and tapers, the veterans of the Corn Exchange Regiment milled about the spacious banquet hall. Gilded Federal eagle mirrors spaced around the walls of the room reflected uniformed images in soft silhouettes of blue and gold. The freshly polished hardwood floor was gleaming.

Paddy, shunning the lively conversation, stood to one side near the doorway. He felt slightly uncomfortable wearing his new officer's insignia. Glancing at the festoon of patriotic bunting and garlands of laurel leaves strung across the ceiling, suddenly his eyes lit up as a man in civilian clothes entered the room. Dressed in an exquisitely tailored brown and white striped outfit, he wore an ivory brocade cravat around his neck. He removed his Stetson hat and hung it on a coat rack.

Paddy strode forward and caught the surprised gentleman in a bear hug around the waist. Captain Donaldson spun around.

"Mulcahy! You old son of a gun!" he exclaimed, returning Paddy's embrace with a warm hug.

They stepped back to survey one another. Paddy noticed the diamond stick pin in Donaldson's cravat. Grinning, he said, "Well, you sure look like high society, Frank."

Donaldson's blue eyes twinkled. "That's what it takes to succeed in my business, old friend. Along with good service, of course."

Paddy teased him. "All one needs with horses is a firm hand and a gentle voice. That's my business," he said, laughing.

Donaldson fingered the gold braid on Paddy's shoulders. "What's this?"

he exclaimed, "lieutenant stripes? You finally decided to be a leader?"

Paddy blushed a deep red. "Colonel Gwyn forced them on me," he replied apologetically. "He had me promoted just before the Grand Review on Pennsylvania Avenue last month. Said we needed a lieutenant in the line and he figured I had earned them."

"You certainly have. That and more." Smiling at Paddy with an arcane expression, he took his arm and said, "Let's step over to the bar. I'm dry as a bone."

Affectionate hoots and calls greeted the former officer as he walked through the crowd.

"Hey, Lieutenant," McCool called, "Who's that dude with you? Ain't he a dandy."

"That'll be three hours on the saw buck for you, McCool," Donaldson shot back good-naturedly.

In a far corner of the room, Colonel Gwyn stood conversing with General Meade. Lt. Colonel Herring, with one leg missing, leaned heavily on crutches.

General Meade spoke, deep penetrating eyes peering over a beak nose. "Frankly, the ruthless, one-dimensional view of reconstruction by the radical Republicans alarms me."

"That's not the way those of us in the Union League see it," Gwyn retorted. His high forehead was flushed and his cheeks were red from drinking. He clutched a glass of Scotch tightly in one hand. "There can be no vacillation," he thundered. "The South must ratify the thirteenth amendment."

Sergeant Cassidy passed within earshot. He spoke between bared teeth. "Rich slave owners brought on this war, now they can bloody well pay for it."

Colonel Gwyn raised his glass, "I'll drink to that, Sergeant."

Herring, appearing pale and weak, hunched forward on his crutches. "Well I, for one, still hold for Lincoln's more moderate approach."

"The President is dead," Gwyn fired back. "They killed him one week after Appomattox. Or have you forgotten?"

The sweeping accusation caused Meade to stiffen and draw himself to full height. "If you gentlemen will excuse me," he said in a deep baritone, "I would like to greet a young neighbor of mine who has just arrived."

"Of course, General," Gwyn replied. "We'll be sitting down to dinner shortly."

Meade walked to where Donaldson and Paddy were filling glasses from a decanter.

Meade extended a rough-hewn hand. "Frank, I'm happy to see you could make the party. How is your insurance business developing?"

Donaldson dried his hand on a pant leg and clasped the general's hand firmly. "Going great guns, General. The Corn Exchange has helped greatly by steering business my way."

"That's good." Meade glanced around the room. "Will I be meeting our valiant one this evening?"

A silent signal from Donaldson's eyes gave warning as he cleared his throat and said, "General, I'd like you to meet a friend of mine, Lieutenant Mulcahy."

Electrified, Paddy snapped to attention and saluted. "Sir."

The sternness that personified Meade seemed to evaporate. "At ease, Lieutenant. No formalities this evening. I did want to take a moment to..."

Donaldson cleared his throat again. "General," he broke in, "you're being summoned to the head table."

"Blast. Well, duty calls. Perhaps after dinner we can get together." They exchanged handshakes again and Meade made his way to the head table.

In a prominent spot behind the speaker's podium stood the shot-torn battle flag of the 1118th, proudly displayed with a cluster of pennants representing the regiment's engagements from Shepherdstown to Appomattox. The foe had often trembled at the sight, but the flag now reposed in peace and dignity.

Donaldson took Paddy by the arm. "Let's find a seat, shall we?"

An opening prayer by Chaplain O'Neil was followed by a moment of silence in memory of those who had given the last full measure of devotion to their country. The remembrance of fallen comrades caused some eyes to water as the assembled remained standing for the National Anthem. Black waiters attired in red coats with shining brass buttons began delivering plates of food to the lines of tables.

Placing his nose close to the steaming roast beef, boiled potatoes and fresh carrots, Paddy remarked, "This sure beats camp life, eh, Frank?"

"Certainly does," Donaldson replied, sipping his bourbon. "Think you'll have any difficulty making the transition to civilian life?"

"None. After mastering the depths of boredom and the excitement of combat, false hopes and mismanaged affairs... I'll cope."

Donaldson tucked a napkin inside his cravat. "If you have any difficulty, you might consider joining our Loyal Legion."

"Loyal Legion?"

"An organization of veterans pledged to keep old memories alive. We also plan to prevent those who supported the South during the war from being elected to public of office."

"Politics? That's not my cup of tea."

"Well, never forget that it was Democrat bullets we were dodging." He twirled a sterling silver napkin ring around an index finger. "Have you any word of your wife and daughter?"

A cloud of dejection darkened Paddy's countenance. "No, not a word. I'm praying that, with the war over, she was able to make her way to Frankford."

The former officer tongued the inside of his upper lip. "Here's to that," he said tersely. "I hear Frankford is having a parade and review of returning soldiers tomorrow at noon."

"Yes. We're supposed to board the Pennsy at Eleventh and Market Streets tomorrow morning at ten. Formation takes place at Frankford Junction. We'll march into town."

"Sounds exciting. I'll try to be there." Donaldson put down his knife and fork. "The Colonel's about to introduce General Meade. I hope they keep the speeches short."

General Meade stood tall, gaunt and erect at the podium. He kept his words simple and direct, heaping praise and admiration on the record of the Corn Exchange Regiment. He was greeted by a standing ovation at the end of his speech.

Colonel Gwyn rose to close the ceremony, his Irish sentimentality showing through the tears in his eyes.

"Soldiers, comrades and friends," he began. "The curtain has fallen and the footlights are out. The audience has gone home. The gaudy tinsel before the footlights will be exchanged for civilian life. Historians will now decide how well we have acted our parts." Choking, as he tried to hold back the tears, he bid them a fond farewell.

The next morning, June 10th, soldiers representing eighteen different regiments bustled aboard the train to Frankford. It was a perfect day of blue skies and soft breezes. The new Pennsylvania Railroad passenger cars were clean and comfortable, a sharp contrast to the boxcars the men were used to.

In twenty minutes they arrived at Frankford Junction, where the men tumbled from the cars. They spread their arms and inhaled the sweet fragrance of spring air.

"Home," someone cried. "Hot damn, home!"

Colonel Ashworth of the 121st Regiment approached the parade marshals.

"Gentlemen," he inquired, "what are the orders of the day? I'm the ranking officer here, but your wishes are my command."

Ben Solly grasped him by the hand. "James, good to have you back. We've organized the parade and festivities, but we'll leave the military details to you."

Ashworth, appearing considerably older than when he left three years previously, removed his hat and fanned his face. "Because of the disparity of numbers, I would suggest we parade in company front, eight abreast, irrespective of regimental designation." He paused. "I suggest the cavalrymen bring up the rear. The infantrymen have waded through enough slop to last a lifetime."

Howls of laughter greeted this observation.

Ben Solly gave his suspenders a hitch. "Organize the men as you see fit, Colonel. We'll start in fifteen minutes, or as soon as the band gets here."

Rifles were issued from a boxcar and the column of blue slowly organized itself. The honor guard moved to the front with the Stars and Stripes.

The sun was reaching its zenith when McCool, shading his eyes against the glare, suddenly spied a familiar face. "Bucketfoot!" he screamed.

Squeaky Tibben broke into a run as the two met and embraced.

McCool pulled away and demanded, "What in the bloody hell are you doing in a gray uniform?"

Tibben stiffened. "I'm a postman, you jack ass. Can't you tell the difference?"

They both doubled over laughing. At that moment Tibben caught sight of Paddy. He leaned over and started whispering something to McCool. McCool stared at Paddy, his mouth hanging open. Paddy noticed and thought to himself, *What the hell is that about?*

Tibben broke away from McCool and made his way back along the column, whispering to the men as he went. Necks craned in Paddy's direction.

The Decatur Fire Company band arrived with a flourish reminiscent of the halcyon days of 1861. They were nattily dressed in red and white turbans, short blue shell jackets with brass buttons, baggy red pantaloons and white gaiters as they took their position at the head of the parade. Two horse-drawn fire company ambulances, the canvas sides rolled up, fell in behind the band. Seated quietly inside were a host of young boys and girls.

"Who are they?" McCool called to a marshal.

The man turned and quietly replied, "Their fathers won't be parading today. They're war orphans."

McCool stared at the road.

With a resonant *ba-room ta ba-room* of the drums, a blare of brass and a clash of cymbals, the parade began moving. The troops, rifles held at right shoulder shift, joined in the familiar tune:

"When Johnny comes marching home again,
Hurrah, Hurrah!
We'll give him a hearty welcome then,
Hurrah, Hurrah!
The men will cheer, the boys will shout,
The ladies, they will all turn out,
And we'll all feel gay,
When Johnny comes marching home."

Young boys, dressed in summer shirts and jeans held up by suspenders, cavorted in the street ahead. The more dexterous rolled hoops with a paddle, the hatbands on their straw skimmers trailing in the breeze. For a better view, they finally shinnied up trees and lampposts, where they hung precariously by arms and legs.

The timbers of the covered bridge spanning Frankford Creek echoed with the tramp of marching feet as the troops entered town to the tune of "*Hail, Columbia.*"

Old Ned, the gardener, his arms full of fresh-cut lilacs from the Womrath estate, rushed into the street and pressed flowers into waiting hands. Soon every rifle sported a purple bloom from its barrel.

The buildings were covered with red, white and blue bunting swags and evergreen sprays. Women cheered and threw flowers. Men wept openly.

"So many marched away," one cried, "and so few have returned."

In front of the reviewing stand at Borough Hall, a crowd of dignitaries waited on the platform as the marching columns formed into ranks eight deep, thirty men to a line. Mounted cavalrymen brought up the rear.

By accident or design, Paddy was in the front ranks. Off to one side, Santy Fry's A.M.E. Church choir was singing "*The Battle Hymn of the Republic*" with heartfelt joy:

"Mine eyes have seen the glory
of the coming of the Lord......."

Perspiring, Paddy raised his kepi and mopped his brow as he studied the faces on the front row of the reviewing stand. Congressman Wright was flanked by the mayor. Who was that officer? Paddy gasped. It was General Wistar. Beside him sat Mrs. Wistar, dressed in a flowered Duplex hoop skirt and shading herself with a parasol. Next to her was Captain Donaldson in full uniform.

"What's going on here?" Paddy mused.

The mayor's speech got underway as Paddy focused on Mrs. Wistar. She seemed to be having difficulty with her hoop skirt as she pushed it back every few minutes. The elevation of the platform made it impossible to identify anyone standing behind the front row of dignitaries.

The mayor finished and Congressman Wright made a short address. Paddy strained to hear. He heard a child's voice crying, "Nad, Nad," as Mrs. Wistar gave her skirt another push.

General Wistar was the final speaker. He rose to his feet, walked down the steps, and took a position in the street. In one hand he carried an impressive-looking, highly-polished mahogany box. He paused to clear his throat.

"Ladies and gentlemen, men of Frankford..." he began.

Paddy's eyes locked onto Captain Donaldson's and he noticed a mysterious glint. This time the Captain winked, and once more Paddy heard a child cry, "Nad. Nad."

His attention suddenly riveted itself on General Wistar, whose voice rang out with parade ground precision. "Lieutenant Padrieg Mulcahy. Front and center."

Paddy broke into a cold sweat. Feeling naked and exposed he stepped forward at an uncomfortable pace, faced his commanding officer, halted and gave a stiff-armed salute.

The general began reading from an official looking document, his voice strong and level. "For exceptional bravery and devotion to duty while scouting the enemy during the Rebel invasion of Pennsylvania in eighteen sixty-three, I am authorized by the Congress of the United States to present you with the Medal of Honor."

He opened the mahogany box and took out a gold medal emblazoned with Columbia's head affixed to a purple ribbon.

"While it would be my great pleasure to award this medal, there is someone here today from whom I know you would rather receive it."

He turned to Captain Donaldson, who stood up and moved aside as Mrs. Wistar lowered her parasol. A white-gloved hand appeared on Captain Donaldson's arm and Becky stepped forward in breath-taking beauty. Golden sunlight sparkled from her hair that hung full length to her bare shoulders. She dabbed her eyes with a lace handkerchief.

Paddy broke with a gasp and bounded up the wooden steps. Tears of joy streamed down his crimsoned cheeks as he lunged at his wife and gathered her into his arms. They clung together in warm embrace.

"Darling!" he cried.

He felt a tug at his trouser leg. "Nad. Nad," came a small voice.

Paddy turned and looked down into the azure eyes of his daughter. Gently, he lifted her up in both arms and gave her a tender kiss.

From the street below, a spontaneous cheer arose from the blue-coated ranks of veterans. A cheer reserved solely for victory and affection.

"Hip, hip, hurrah! Hip, hip, hurrah! Hip, hip, hurrah!"

Sources of Information and Reference Works

I. Printed Works

Abbott, John S. C. *The History of the Civil War in America.* Springfield, Massachusetts: Gurdon Bill, 1912.

Baltz, John D. Senator E. D. *Baker's Defense at Ball 's Bluff.* [Author was formerly a private, Co. H. 71st Pennsylvania Volunteers]. Lancaster, Pennsylvania: Inquirer Printing Company, 1888.

Banes, Charles H. *History of Philadelphia Brigade.* Philadelphia: n.p., 1876.

Bates, Samuel P. *History of the Pennsylvania Volunteers.* Harrisburg, Pa.: Authority of Pennsylvania State Legislature, 1869.

Battles and Leaders of the Civil War-IV Volumes. New York: The Century Company, 1888.

Beyer, William Gilmore. *On Hazardous Service.* New York: Harper and Brothers, 1912.

Blackman, George C., M.C., and Chas. S. Tripler, A.M., M.D. *War Surgery.* [handbook for the military surgeon]. N.P.: Robert Clarke & Co., 1862.

Blumenthal, Walter Hart. *Women Camp Followers of the American Revolution.* Philadelphia: Geo. S. McManus Co., 1952.

Buche, Franklin, M.D., and George Wood, M.D. *The Dispensatory of the U.S. of America.* Philadelphia: Grigg and Elliot, 1834.

Catton, Bruce. *Glory Road.* Garden City, New York: Doubleday,1952.

—*Mr. Lincoln'sArmy.* Garden City, New York: Doubleday, 1952.

—*A Stillness at Appomattox.* Garden City, New York: Doubleday, 1953.

"Ceremonies at the Dedication of the Monuments Erected by the Commonwealth of Pennsylvania." *Pennsylvania at Gettysburg.* Vol. 1. Harrisburg, Pennsylvania: n.p., 1893.

Civil War Through the Camera, The. 10 Vols. Springfield, Massachusetts: Patriot Publishing Co., 1912.

Coffin, Charles Carleton. *The Boys of '61.* Boston: Estes and Lauriat, 1886.

Commager, Henry Steele. *Blue and Gray.* New York: Bobs Merrill Co., 1950.

Confederate Scrap Book. Richmond, Virginia: J. L. Hill Printing Company, 1893.

Congressional Committee on the Army of the Potomac. *The Tribune War Tracts No. 1.* New York: Tribune Association, 1863.

Dahlgren, Rear Admiral. *Memoir of Ulrich Dahlgren.* [Author was father of Ulrich Dahlgren]. Philadelphia: J. B. Lippincott,1872.

Duganne, A. J. H. *The Fighting Quakers—-with letters from the brothers to their mother.* [written by the authority of the Bureau of Military Records]. New York: J. P. Robens, 1866.

Faith and Practice of the Religious Society of Friends of Philadelphia and Vicinity. Philadelphia: Friends Book Store, 1926.

Freeman, Douglas Southall. *Lee's Lieutenants.* New York: Charles Scribners Sons, 1942.

Gordon, John B., General. *Reminiscences of the Civil War*. New York: Charles Scribner's Sons, 1905.

Grant, U. S. New *Personal Memoirs of U. S. Grant. Vols. 1 & 2* York: Charles L. Webster Co., 1885.

Harris, Wm. C., Lt. *Prison Life in the Tobacco Warehouse at Richmond by a Ball's Bluff Prisoner*. [Lt. Harris was a member of Col. Baker's Calif. Regiment]. Philadelphia: George W. Childs, 1862.

Headly, J. R. *History of the Civil War*. Vol. 1. Boston: Hurlbut Williams Co., 1863.

Hensel, W. V. *The Christiana Riot and the Treason Trials of 1851*. Lancaster, Pennsylvania: The New Era Printing Co., 1911.

Hotchkin, S. F., Rev., M. A. *The Bristol Pike*. Philadelphia: George W. Jacobs, 1893.

Jacobs. *The Rebel Invasion of Maryland and Pennsylvania*. [Author was professor at Penn. College, Gettysburg]. Philadelphia: J. B. Lippincott, 1864. Kephart, Horace. *Our Southern Highlanders*. New York: Outing Publishing Co., 1913.

Kirwan. *Letters to the Hon. Roger B. Taney, Romanism at Home*. New York: Harper & Brothers, 1852.

McClellan, George B. *Manual of Bayonet Exercise*. [Prepared for the use of the U.S. Army]. Philadelphia: Order of the War Department/J. B. Lippincott, 1852.

McCurdy, Charles. Gettysburg-*A Memoir of a Ten- Year-Old Boy Living in Gettysburg During the Battle*. Pittsburgh: Reed and Witting Co., 1929.

McDermott, Anthony W., Adjutant. *History of the 69th Regiment Pennsylvania Volunteers*. Philadelphia: D. J. Gallagher Company, 1889.

Meade, George. *Did General Meade Desire to Retreat at the Battle of Gettysburg?* Philadelphia: Porter and Coates, 1883.

Miers, Earl Schenck. *Gettysburg*. New Brunswick, N.J.: Richard A. Brown, Rutgers UP, 1948.

Murphy, Thomas, Reverend. *One Hundred Years of the Presbyterian Church of Frankford*. Philadelphia: Published by the Church, 1872.

Myers, Ephraim E., Lt. Co. K 45th Reg. Pa. Vol. Inf. *A True Story of a Civil War Veteran*. York Pennsylvania: n.p., 1910.

Narrative of Privations and Sufferings of U.S. Officers and Soldiers While Prisoners of War in the hands of the Rebel Authorities. Boston: at the office of "Lettell's Living Age," 1864.

Philadelphia Brigade Association. *Reply of the Philadelphia Brigade Association to the Foolish and Absurd Narrative of Lt. Frank A. Haskell*. Philadelphia: Bower's Pnnting, 1910.

Pringle, Cyrus. *The Record of a Quaker Conscience*. [Diary]. New York: The Macmillan Co., 1918.

Raucher, Frank. *Music on the March 1886-'65 With the Army of the Potomac-114th Reg't Collis Zouaves*. Philadelphia: Press of Wm. F. Fell & Co., 1892.

Reilly, John E., Captain. *Reunion of the Survivors of the Philadelphia Brigade and Picketts Division of Confederate Soldiers.* Philadelphia: D. J. Gallagher Company, 1889.

Sandburg, Carl. *Abraham Lincoln-The War Years.* 4 vols. New York: Harcourt, Brace & Company, n.d.

Scrugham, Mary, Ph.D. *The Peaceable Americans of 1860-1861*; A Study in Public Opinion. New York: Longman's Green & Company, 1921.

Sigaud, Louis A. *Belle Boyd-Confederate Spy.* Richmond, Virginia: The Dietz P, 1944.

Still, William. *Under Ground Railroad.* Harford: Betts & Co.,1886.

Survivors Association. *History of the 118th Pennsylvania   Volunteers Corn Exchange Regiment.* J. Philadelphia: J. L. Smith Map Publishers, 1905.

—*History of the 121st Regiment Pennsylvania Volunteers.* Philadelphia: Burke & McFetrdge Co., 1893.

Taylor, Frank H. *Philadelphia in the Civil War.* published by the city of Philadelphia, 1913.

U.S. *Infantry Tactics for the Instruction, Exercise, and Maneuvers of the United States Infantry.* [By the authority of the Secretary of War, May 1, 1861] . Philadelphia: J. B. Lippincott 1863.

Wilkeson, Frank. *Recollections of a Private Soldier in the Army of the Potomac.* New York: G. P. Putman's Sons, 1893.

Williams, T. Harry. *Lincoln and his Generals.* New York: Knopf, 1952.

Wistar, Isaac Jones. *Autobiography of Isaac Jones Wistar 1827-1905.* Philadelphia: Wistar Institute of Anatomy and Biology, 1937.

Woodward, W. E. *Years of Madness.* New York: G. P. Putnams and Sons. 1951

II. Miscellaneous papers and records

Allen, R. C., Dr. "The Colored Population of Frankford." Paper read before the Historical Society of Frankford. Vol. 1.

—"Maj. George L. Ritman." Paper read before the Historical Society of Frankford. Vol. 1.

—"No. I Col. James Ashworth." Paper read before the Historical Society of Frankford. Vol. 1.

Castor Family. "Inscriptions of the Headstones in the Presbyterian Churchyard." Paper read before the Historical Society of Frankford. Vol. 2.

Creighton, Thomas. "No.5 Boyhood Impressions of Frankford During the Civil War." Paper read before the Historical Society of Frankford. Vol. 2.

"No. 5 Frankford Soldiers who Enlisted in the Civil War." Paper read before the Historical Society of Frankford. Vol. 1.

Price, James, D. D. "No. 7 Recollection of Frankford 1855-1873." Paper read before the Historical Society of Frankford. Vol. 1.

Small, Cassandra. *Letters of '63.* [Written in York, Pennsylvania, durng the occupation of that town by Confederate Troops in the summer of 1863]. Detroit: Stair-Jordan-Baker. Inc., n.d.

Detroit: Stair-Jordan-Baker. Inc., n.d.

Wright, Eleanor E. "The Jolly Post." Paper read before the Historical Society of Frankford. Vol. 2.

Wright, Mary. "No.3 Hon. Richardson L. Wright." Paper read before the Historical Society of Frankford. Vol. 2.

III. A grateful acknowledgment is made to the following individuals and institutions for their kind reception and inspirational assistance

Batchelder, William, Lieutenant. Personal diary and letters. Courtesy of Robert and Etta Tressler.

Beeson, "Uncle" Joe. Former private in the 198th Pennsylvania Regiment. [A gallant little man who in later life carried the famed banner "Frankford Against the World" at all of Frankford's public functions. A gentle soul who always found time to answer the probing questions put to him by we boys of the town].

Cartledge, Samuel, Private. Personal diary and letters. Courtesy of Inez Cartledge Thorp.

Donaldson, Frank, Captain. Personal diary and letters. Courtesy of West Blaine, Museum of the Loyal Legion.

First Presbyterian Church of Frankford. [Records].

Haverford College. [Information regarding Isaac Wistar].

Historical Society of Frankford.

Historical Society of York, Pennsylvania.

Johnson, George. Post Historian of the G.A.R., Ashworth and Kearny-Cocker Posts of Frankford. Records and personal communications that proved invaluable.

Martin Memorial Library of York Pennsylvania.

Miller, J. Jerome, Private. Personal diary and letters. Courtesy of George Hay Kain, Jr.

Museum of the Military Order of the Loyal Legion. 1807 Pine Street, Philadelphia, Pennsylvania.

Pennsylvania Historical Society of Philadelphia.

St. Mark's Episcopal Church of Frankford. [Records].

Shallcross, Omar. [To the venerable curator of the Frankford Historical Society, I extend my heartfelt gratitude for the pleasant hours he so graciously afforded me amongst the old relics, pictures, and records of that society].

Yohn, Henry I. Past commander of George E. Meade

Post 1, (G.A.R.), Philadelphia. [At the age of fourteen, in the year 1862, he had the distinction of being the youngest cavalryman then in the ranks of the regular army. His vivid stories and accounts were the inspirational wellspring of this work].

To capture the mood and original setting, much of this writing was done on the actual spot and at the precise time and season that they happened: Ball's Bluff, Sharpsburg (Antietam), Fredericksburg, Chancellorsville,

Gettysburg, Petersburg (Fort Hell) Appomattox.

And above all, a personal word of gratitude to my assistant, Caroline Bowman, whose long hours of typing, editing and preparation made this book possible.

Many thanks to my son Cameron Thorp for the splendid book cover he designed.

About The Author

Dr. Don Thorp grew up in a Quaker family in Frankford, Philadelphia. At the age of ten, Don frequented the Grand Army of the Republic, Kearny Cocker Post in Frankford. He associated with aged veterans and listened to their stories. At the age of twelve, he was given primitive materials and other information to read. From this beginning, he has devoted a lifetime of study and writing about the Civil War and the Frankford soldiers who served in the Union Army.

Dr. Thorp attended Penn State and graduated from the University of Pennsylvania Veterinary School. He has been in practice fifty-four years and resides in Delray Beach, Florida. Don is an Eagle Scout, member of the Sigma Phi Epsilon fraternity, Past President Delray Beach Rotary Club, former chairman of the Palm Beach County School Board, father of seven children, and grandfather of nine.